LADY LAZARUS

LADY LAZARUS

ANDREW FOSTER ALTSCHUL

HARCOURT, INC.

Orlando   Austin   New York   San Diego   London

Requests for permission to make copies of any part of the work should be
submitted online at www.harcourt.com/contact or mailed to the following address:
Permissions Department, Houghton Mifflin Harcourt Publishing Company,
6277 Sea Harbor Drive, Orlando, Florida 32887-6777.

www.HarcourtBooks.com

Permissions acknowledgments appear on page 563 and
constitute a continuation of the copyright page.

An index of attributions for allusions and references
in this book begins on page 556.

Library of Congress Cataloging-in-Publication Data
Altschul, Andrew Foster.
Lady Lazarus/Andrew Foster Altschul.—1st ed.
p.   cm.
I. Celebrities—Fiction.   2. Popular culture—Fiction.   I. Title.
PS3601.L858L33   2008
813'.6—dc22   2007028550
ISBN 978-0-15-101484-2

Text set in Dante MT
Designed by April Ward

Printed in the United States of America
First edition
A C E G I K J H F D B

For Ida and Arthur
For Manny and Ruth

A poet makes himself a visionary through a long, immense, and systematic derangement of the senses. All forms of love, of suffering, of madness; he searches himself, he exhausts within himself all poisons and preserves their quintessences. . . . So what if he is destroyed in this ecstatic flight through things unheard of, unnameable?

—*Arthur Rimbaud*

If you're so special, why aren't you dead?

—*The Breeders*

LADY LAZARUS

1. EARLY INFLUENCES

ON CHRISTMAS MORNING OF 199_, Calliope Bird Morath, age seven, slid quietly out of bed, took her father's yellow, rhinestone-rimmed sunglasses from the dresser, and, perching them on the crown of her head in the manner of the famous photo of him from the cover of *Time,* crept through the hallway and down the stairs, flipping on the giant-screen TV and depositing herself next to the Christmas tree. The enormous tree was still lit—neither her mother nor her mother's current spiritual adviser had turned it off the night before—and against the weakening, liquid darkness outside it burned magically with thousands of ornaments, crates-worth of blinkers and Santas, glowing guitars and mini-microphones, gingerbread men and reindeer, snowflakes and Silly String and psychedelic tinsel, some of which had been brought in by the boxload from the garage of the Rancho Santa Fe mansion, but much of which, as always, had been sent by devoted fans.

Despite this surfeit of light and color, however, there was no star atop the tree. Such had been the case for three years, since the infamous "Funeral Interview," during which her mother, resplendent in Donna Karan black, had offered Barbara Walters that memorable trio of anapests: "There shall be no more stars in my sky."

Given the Calliope with whom readers are undoubtedly acquainted, it will be difficult to imagine the taciturn creature who sat before the television that morning—but indeed, this scion of one of America's most storied families had not uttered a word since the day of her father's death. Despite her mother's frantic ministrations, despite house calls from neurologists, psychiatrists, mediums, and exorcists, the child remained mute.

She ate what was placed before her, she read whatever was at hand, but she expressed no will or opinion. She came when called, she displayed no signs of cognitive or sensory deficit, she simply had shrunk into the small shell of herself, as though refusing to touch the world around her, afraid she might break it. The widow had privately begun to despair, this second bereavement unbearable, as though the family had been targeted by jealous gods, laid waste for partaking, however briefly, of their fire. Twice abandoned, she wandered the halls of the mansion like a tourist in a cathedral, wondering at the huge and terrifying silence.

The magnificent tree which stood before the living room's picture windows was an anomaly, a last remaining concession to fame and adoration. After the funeral, Penelope Morath, née Klein, aka Penny Power, had withdrawn utterly from the public eye, shutting all the curtains of the twelve-bedroom Tudor on Azalea Path, removing Calliope from the La Jolla Krishnamurti School where she'd spent many a happy day since her second birthday, and employing a phalanx of tutors and cooks, music teachers and gardeners, nursemaids and accountants to keep the house running and her silent daughter occupied. For months the cul-de-sac was lined with despondent fans, who pushed against the police tape, wept openly and prayed, pleading for just one glimpse of Penelope or Calliope, one instant of connection to help them in their grief. Penelope forbade it. Calliope was not to go near the doors or windows, nor to so much as peek between the slats of a venetian blind. The tabloids were offering $100,000 for a photo of the widow, a cool quarter million for a shot of the demi-orphan.

"You'll understand one day," Penelope told her silent daughter, then four, as workers hung heavy darkroom curtains in her bedroom. "They don't leave you anything for yourself. Their hunger is so terrible, you have to give them everything."

She scrunched the mute child's face between her hands, eyes hot with devotion. "We're not going to let them do to you what they did to your father." Penelope had seen firsthand the depredations of celebrity, seen her husband's star come blazing to ground. In her grief, she would all but abandon her own tumultuous career, cupping motherly hands around the small ember of her only child's life.

"We don't owe those cocksuckers a thing," she said. "Our bill is paid."

But when that first Christmas had come, Penelope could not bear to break the family tradition. In the six years since she'd met Brandt Morath in the back room of the Casbah, San Diego's legendary punk-rock club, they had always celebrated lavishly, driving the pickup truck under cover of night out to the forests near Julian, cutting the biggest spruce they could manage, buying whole inventories of ornaments and ordering others custom-made from as far away as New Zealand. Even at the height of Brandt's fame, and the depths of his depressions and addictions, the family had awoken before dawn each Christmas and gathered at the tree to open their gifts. This day, he had not minded the fans and photographers who'd crept through the bushes, peering in at the famous family in their pajamas*; this one day each year, Penelope determined, she would continue to live according to his example.

On this Christmas morning, Calliope's eighth, she had awakened before her mother, whose descent was delayed by the aftereffects of the ayahuasca she and her adviser, an Inca shaman, had ingested the night before. Calliope sat before the silent, flickering light of the huge television, trying to ignore both the mountain of gifts she desperately wanted to open and the blurred movements of the small crowd gathering in the cul-de-sac. The front lawn, shaded by an enormous jacaranda, was an untidy shrine of flowers and candles and dew-smeared pastel sketches, photographs of Brandt Morath and his band, burning sage, and a battered, bashed-in guitar amplifier; but the throngs had shrunk considerably since those first months, dwindling to a few drive-by tourists each day, small packs of high schoolers in Terrible Children T-shirts who sat on the curb and smoked pot, blaring Brandt's music to the neighborhood. (Since the well-publicized incident a year earlier, in which a clearly intoxicated Penelope shocked these teenagers by strolling out to the front lawn, asking if anyone would sell her a joint, and French-kissing a sixteen-year-old girl, the family had had no contact with the trespassers.) There had been a slight upsurge in recent months, due to the strange, tragic deaths of the thirty-nine Heaven's Gate cult members in a house just around the corner, and the proximity of

---

*Cf., for example, *SLAM* magazine, December 29, 199_, the cover of which offers Brandt, Penelope, and Baby Calliope in reindeer antlers, waving.

the two houses endowed the otherwise-patrician neighborhood with the bizarre energy of an anti-carnival, which Calliope would later immortalize in the poem "Sunday on Suicide Row."*

Given Calliope's legendary impetuousness, her much-reported self- (and other-) destructive tendencies, it should come as no great surprise that she soon found herself unable to resist the lure of the gifts beneath the Christmas tree. But however disorganized and rash her life was later to become, it should be noted that on this morning she set about opening her gifts in the most careful of manners, taking the long pearl-handled letter opener from its accustomed place on the mantel† and slicing ever so gently through the wrapping paper, folding it neatly and setting it aside in piles organized by color.

The gifts, no doubt, were lavish. Brandt had made no secret of his intention to "spoil the fuck out of Calliope," and though he had burned through spectacular sums of money in the months before his death, the royalties from Terrible Children recordings and merchandise were flowing more vigorously than ever, like a debris-choked stream that had needed only the removal of some obstruction to become a mighty, roaring river. There is no way to be sure exactly what she was given that morning, nor how many gifts she actually opened. She gave many different accounts over the years, citing gifts as varied as a guitar once owned by Robert Johnson, a training bra, an eighteenth-century quarto edition of *Hamlet*, one of her father's ribs encased in Lucite (Penelope has never denied this claim), master tapes from Elvis Presley's Sun Studio sessions, and a lump of coal. The one item consistently mentioned is the leather-bound edition of William Blake's *Songs of Innocence and Experience* which became her prized possession and which is now housed in the Morath Collection at the Harry Ransom Center for the Humanities, University of Texas.

She started with the smaller gifts, keeping one eye out for her mother,

---

Paris Review, Winter 200_.

†Scholars disagree as to whether this was the same letter opener which a kneeling Brandt had once offered, handle-first, to Penelope, begging her to end his suffering, an incident detailed in the Rancho Santa Fe Police Blotter, October 6, 199_, as well as in *People, Billboard, Guitar World,* and *The Christian Science Monitor.* All agree, however, that it *was* the same letter opener used in the Terrible Children video for "Take My Life, Please!" which reënacted that incident.

who still had failed to materialize. Probably she would have gone through the entire pile in due time, had she not been distracted by something on the television, a chance bit of early morning programming which may well be responsible for irreversibly changing the course of American letters. In the context of all that was to come, one might easily overlook what happened that morning, write it off as merely one of many spectacles in a life destined, from the first, to be spectacular. The author would remind readers of the obvious, then: that this was long before Calliope Bird Morath was to become the most famous poet in America, perhaps the most famous poet in American history, beloved to deconstructionists and culture theorists and fifteen-year-old girls alike, long before she would take the literary world by storm with her first and only book, long before the infamous interview with Charlie Rose and the *Saturday Night Live* debacle, her heartbreaking disappearance and the terrifying advent of the Muse—and long before the shocking, and still-unexplained, Graveyard Riot.

That she was only a seven-year-old girl, unremarkable except for the splotchy birthmark on the side of her neck, her pale red hair, and the deep dimple in her chin that would one day bewitch the masses, captured on the covers of *Jane, SPIN, Tiger Beat, Poets & Writers,* and so many others, inspiring untold numbers of feverish, third-rate love poems—all of this goes without saying. It is brought up here only to highlight the singular way in which this moment served as both confluence and catalyst, gathering all the strands of genetics and poetics, of nature and nurture and her own formidable will, and propelling her thenceforth into the life that awaited her, the life of a true monstrosity, of Calliope Bird Morath, Death Artist.

The program on the television was a documentary history of the Vietnam War. As she painstakingly piled wrapping paper and squeezed tape into a sticky ball, Calliope watched soundless scenes of stock footage: helicopters whooshing over rice paddies, straw huts buckling under a deluge of napalm, young soldiers in foxholes, faces smeared with camouflage and the unmistakable mix of terror and exhilaration. One immediately wonders what possible interest such a program could hold for a young child. In an early interview with poet Donald Hall, Calliope suggested that she had "always been fascinated with combat, that place where the architecture of death becomes most apparent, where it is distorted into an artificial binary: you or me."* Such a fascination seems a bit precocious, however, even for a child who had seen the things Calliope had seen. A former employee of the Morath household recalls that the child had, at the time, been reading the complete works of World War I poet Wilfred Owen; a more convincing explanation, then, is that her "fascination" was merely that of having been provided images to go with the words.

She went on opening her gifts, perhaps thumbing through the gold-edged pages of the Blake volume, or quietly strumming Robert Johnson's guitar, in her mind hearing one of Terrible Children's hit songs, her father's forlorn and vulnerable voice as real to her now as it had been in her infancy. There were no sounds from upstairs, only the quiet buzz of the Christmas tree, the tiny ticking of the lights flashing on and off, the merest drift of music from the cul-de-sac. It was nearly dawn.

It would have been then that Antonio "Skip" Cárdenas, then an ambitious intern for the L.A. Weekly, having crawled on his belly through the shrubbery, arrived outside the living-room window and took out his camera. "She was sitting cross-legged at the base of the tree," he recalls, "all the presents around her. She looked just like any other kid. It was hard to believe this was the one—'sprung from the skull,' like everyone said. Just a cute kid."

Calliope would have had no inkling she was being observed. For three years she had not set foot beyond the property, had had no contact with humans other than her mother and the staff. She would not have understood the lengths to which desperate people go to get close to their desires, the terrible lengths to which emptiness and grief can drive us. She could not have understood rapaciousness.

What we know is this: At some point, Calliope looked up from the gifts in her lap and the scene on the TV had changed. Soldiers and refugees had been replaced by a long line of people, a slow procession through the streets of Saigon. It was not a parade—there were no spectators yet as the file of robed men and women, all with shaved heads, made their way into

*London Times Literary Supplement, November 13, 200_.

a busy intersection, a crowded car crawling behind them. The people milling about on the sidewalks, wheeling past on bicycles and scooters, the vendors in the covered market and the one uniformed policeman directing traffic, all glanced up with expressions of only slight curiosity, even annoyance. It was wartime, after all, and they all had, as Auden famously put it, "somewhere to get to."

Calliope immediately recognized the marchers as Buddhist monks and nuns. Even at age seven, she had more than a passing familiarity with Buddhist monks—after her father's hurried funeral, they had filled the house for weeks, gliding about in whispers of saffron, burning incense, strewing flower petals, lining the hallways and balustrades with their prostrate, chanting forms, standing watch outside her mother's door—although in the confusion Calliope had come to believe they were called "Bootish" monks, so named, she assumed, for the dark, leathery smoothness of their polished heads. It is also conceivable that she would, even then, have been aware of the well-traveled rumor which placed her father's remains in a sealed room in the Mount Baldy Zen Center outside Los Angeles, though it would be some years before she would begin her quest to recover them. Perhaps it was this recognition that caused her to put down the Blake she'd been browsing and turn her attention to what was unfolding on the television.

When the procession arrived at the middle of the intersection, the line of monks divided, turned in opposite directions, and moved out toward the street corners, doubling back until the perimeter was filled, a crowd of robed figures three and four deep against the curb. As the last of the marchers entered the intersection, the car was permitted to pass inside the circle, where it came to a halt. Several monks got out, all but one moving to the rear, where they opened the trunk and took out several large jerry cans; the last monk moved solemnly to the middle of the intersection and sat with legs folded in the lotus position. Behind him, the monks and nuns had begun to chant. Calliope watched their lips moving in unison, though she still had not turned on the TV's sound. Bystanders had gathered outside the circle, craning their necks, and the police officer struggled to break through the line of monks who stood shoulder to shoulder and refused to let him pass.

"Bootish," she said aloud, her small voice ringing up into the rafters, the balcony at the top of the stairs. Her hands were folded, her face without expression. "Bootish flutish rootish brutish."

She may even have surprised herself, her voice unheard since the morning of the suicide. Certainly she surprised Skip Cárdenas, who moved closer to the window when he saw the child rise to her feet. As the crowd in the Saigon intersection deepened, their attention fixing on the seated monk, Calliope's litany continued.

"Sootish, crudish, lutish. Prudish."

The seated monk's lips moved slowly and in his left hand he gently manipulated a string of prayer beads. The monks surrounding the intersection, shoulders high, continued their silent chant; the nuns clasped their hands and held them beneath their chins, tears streaking their cheeks. None looked away.

"Nudish," she said, her voice louder, steadier. "Trudish! Foodish! Judish!"

The monks standing by the car consulted in brief whispers and then approached the seated monk. One by one they emptied the contents of the jerry cans over his head, soaking his robes, spreading a dark pool over the pavement. As Calliope looked closer, she recognized something in the monk's serene, distant expression—and in that moment something kindled inside her, a small flame that would never be extinguished, that in time would grow to an inferno. The police officer fought valiantly to break the circle, angrily shoving his way between two monks, his face contorted with urgency. As the other monks stepped away, the seated monk's expression did not change, his left hand fidgeting rhythmically with the beads, with his right hand he produced a small box from beneath his robe, took a breath, and lit a match.

The television screen exploded with soundless light, flaring more brightly than the Christmas tree, more brightly than the light crawling over the horizon, reflecting in the windowpanes and in the wide, almost ecstatic eyes of the young girl as the monk's body was swallowed by flame.

"Burning! Burning!" Calliope shouted, her voice shrill enough that Skip Cárdenas heard it through the glass, distraught enough to break through the ayahuasca haze and awaken Penelope and the Inca shaman.

"Turning! Yearning! Learning!" she shouted, and the black-and-white image on the screen danced and roiled, liquid flame and dark smoke filling the picture to every corner.

"For a minute I couldn't even look," Cárdenas recalls. "It was just this intense light. I could see it through my eyelids. But then I could see her again, standing in the middle of the room wearing her father's sunglasses, this wild look on her face. I thought all that light was coming from *her*, like she was *glowing*, getting brighter and brighter each second."

As Calliope's form was emerging from the glare, on the television the flames took shape again, organizing around the monk's body, the onlookers just dim shadows in the background.

"Fire!" said the young poet. *"Fire!"* and this was when Penelope and the shaman sprang from the bed and sprinted down the upstairs hallway, she in a satin robe with a fur collar that billowed open behind her, he wearing only a necklace of human teeth, both emerging at the top of the stairs to stare down from the balcony in terror.

"Wire! Dire! Gyre! Pyre!" cried the child, raising her arms above her head like some tiny otherworldly priestess, pixels of light dazzling from the rhinestone sunglasses. The monk's form now visible amid the flames, which leapt up and up from his lap, over his chest and shoulders, caressing the top of his head with preternatural fingertips. Calliope could see his hands folded, palms turned upward in a posture of deep meditation, such that the flames seemed to be pouring upward from those hands, to be *produced*, in some way, by those hands—as if the fire that was overwhelming him, that was consuming his life, were in some way the product of his own body, the expression of his desire grown uncontrollable, doubling back upon itself, devouring itself.

"Fire! Sire! Liar!" Calliope shouted, her words clearly audible now to Skip Cárdenas, to Penelope and her spiritual adviser, frozen on the balcony, watching the girl in the grip of the strange, awful fever, the lights of the Christmas tree dull next to that other light—and though both Cárdenas and Penelope insist this was not the case, we simply must assume that Calliope, in her rapture, stepped close enough to the tree that her nightgown touched some overheated ornament or worn length of wire, because to believe the version that her mother has told for the last fourteen years is to subscribe to a kind of mythology that this author hopes studiously to avoid. For in the next second it appeared to the three bystanders that the fire on the television, that ghostly, silent articulation of the monk's soul, had somehow leapt from the screen and ignited the air around Calliope—the child who had for so long been a shadow, a walking absence, continued to shout her first and most inspired poem—*Sire! Liar!*—over what was suddenly a roar of sound, while the monk's body slowly darkened, shrinking slowly to a charred coal at the core of a fountain of flame, and the crowd wept and chanted and prayed, the policeman only now managing to force his way past the monks, only now when there was nothing left to accomplish, standing dumbly a few meters from the vicious heat of the body, staring dumbly, and then absently, automatically taking a cigarette from his breast pocket which he dangled from his lips without lighting, while outside the mansion the photographer fumbled with his camera, setting his f-stop, having no idea how quickly this photo would be seen on front pages and nightly newscasts worldwide—blazing child behind glass, her mother and the shaman nearly naked and clearly visible, clearly awestruck in the upper left-hand corner—and in that last instant before the shaman would shake off paralysis and leap from the balcony, cover the child's body with his own naked form only to discover that the flames they had all seen had burnt not one hair on her head, not one inch of her precious flesh, the three spectators stood as if in a dream, mesmerized by the apparition before them, while Calliope Bird Morath raged brighter and brighter, burning with the glory of her furious apotheosis.*

---

*Although no footage of the November 196_ self-immolation of Thich Quang Duc has ever surfaced, the corroborating details given by Calliope, Penelope, and Skip Cárdenas all but confirm its existence. This author devoted considerable effort to locating the source tape but found only photos and a brief account by the late David Halberstam. According to legend, the venerable monk's heart did not burn.

2. DAWN'S HIGHWAY

IF YOU REALLY WANT TO HEAR about my lousy childhood and all that David Copperfield crap, you're much better off looking through back issues of *People* magazine, whose damned reporters and photographers have fit me like a glove, like a shoe!, since the day I caught fire. What's that you say? Since long before that? Well, I don't remember much before that morning, my bohemian friend, so let's just go by your version.

In fact, why don't you tell it, why not take over the entire account? With your magnifying glass and your thick *Roget's,* your tarot deck and your Audubon guide, it will probably make more sense to you, anyway.

Was there a single incident in my childhood unreported, unlionized, unscrutinized, and unhyperbolized? My mother had magazines brought in by the cartload, we'd sit on the floor of her bedroom and clip stories with toenail scissors, paste them on posterboard, she'd read aloud to me and I'd hear every detail of our hermetic lives transmogrified by language—language so strained it would burst, language that turned against us with sharp claws and tried to gouge extra meaning from a thrown-away toothbrush (ROCK STAR'S DAUGHTER FORSAKES HYGIENE!), a canceled piano lesson (MORATH SCION SAYS GOOD-BYE TO MUSIC!), a shirtless gardener on a hot day (PENELOPE UP TO HER OLD TRICKS!), the stone of our closed world bleeding for them in thick, imaginary rivulets.

After my father's funeral, she shut us in, the house on Azalea closing on us like lips on a lozenge. I was kept away from windows and doors. I did not handle a telephone until my teens. She begged me not to speak to strangers, to be careful with what I said, even to the cooks, the tutors—terrible things could happen, she said, terrible damage be done. Of course she was right—who knew that better than I? I spoke to no one. I had dreams you would not wish to hear. I moved through a miasma of murmurs, the house humming around me, I said nothing for years and years.

Reborn on Christmas: ill-starred from the start, destined to be interpreted, to be analyzed and mythologized without my consent or awareness. What else could I be but what I am? What was there to keep for myself, to hold back from a ravenous world? I spoke in rhyme and in meter, I let my rhythm do the talking, sentences doubling on themselves, homing to me like carrier pigeons. I knew this way I was safe, this way they would never find me: Poetry, thank heavens, is only about itself.

When I left that house for Mountaintop Arts Academy, and later in Irvine, it only got worse, at the same time more personal and more disconnected from anything I recognized as "me," as Calliope. I knew then they were building something, a Frankenstein doll or I don't know what, a dangerous girl with a come-hither look and a love of the bolts and the nuts. Who was I then? Was it for me to decide? In classrooms and coffeeshops, markets and airports, even my beloved Zen Center—I watched my words float out of me and up, gathering like storm clouds that would soon spit their lightning, smiting friend and foe alike. Who'd be the only one left standing? Me.

I must be the only poet in history whose first submission—an immature sonnet I wrote at thirteen and feverishly sent off to the *Riverside County Review* and which, to this day, they insist they never received—was recited on MTV by Queen Latifah. After that it was registered mail only, certified to the hilt. The Arts Academy—how I loved that place, my pine-shadowed Helicon; O the troubles I visited upon them, undeserved!—had to post a guard in the mailroom. The pay phones on campus rang night and day, the high cackle followed me into the cafeteria, the recital halls, deep into the woods. Back home my therapist was besieged, my neighbors bribed, my swim coach offered a movie deal. Cell phones arrived in the mail, padded envelopes vibrating in my hands; I took them out to the creek, built a shrine on a stone, and let them ring and ring, a sound sculpture—how passersby must have wondered at such a thing!

They wanted everything, you see—and yet nothing could ever be enough. There was always something more they were waiting for, whiling away the time with the monster they had built, adding a new gear here, a button for an eye, a zipper that never closed. Waiting. It was hard for them, too. I don't deny it.

For a long time I thought it was my father they wanted—they were looking for him in me, as though I had swallowed him, kept him inside, his hiding place betrayed only by the swatch of blood on my neck. My friends—admittedly few—were afraid to mention his name; my lovers unsure which of us they'd taken to bed, which of us they wanted more. This was partly my mother's doing—all the years on Azalea she kept him alive in word and deed, kept the recording studio in working order, locked up like a museum, his guitars polished and tuned. I was forbidden to enter. She didn't have to tell me what she was thinking: Once was enough! She asked him for advice, spoke of him in the present tense—and he *was* present, I could feel him, and I was sure they could, too. So when they climbed up to my window or hid in the pool shed, when they posed as butlers, as substitute teachers, hungry agents, visiting poets, when they'd finally cornered their prey, ready to pounce with cameras and tape recorders, just waiting for me to open my mouth—there was always something sad on their faces, mixed with the zeros on the checks they'd been promised. They were underwhelmed, they didn't know what to feel. There was something they had not found, a priceless secret I had somehow managed to conceal.

And so they took their revenge. First the tabloids (CALLIOPE CARRYING BRANDT'S DNA CLONE!) and then the mainstream scandal sheets, *Entertainment Tonight* and *Rolling Stone* (FAMOUS DAUGHTER ABUSES FATHER'S LEGACY), finally the "serious" literary critics (CONFESSIONALISM WILL NOT GO GENTLE: SELF-REF/VERENCE IN CALLIOPE'S EARLY VERSE)—churning out story after story about this imaginary monster I'd never met, this mad poet-girl who'd risen from her father's ashes to blaze a path of narcissism and pain through the pristine skies of contemporary poetry.

Everywhere I went—there she was. Orange County was unspeakable—those poor poets who endured workshops in that fishbowl, my darling professor with all his laurels upstaged by a first-year brat with tangled red hair and a cleft in her chin. Terrible Children groupies wandering the halls, Ph.D. students trying out the latest theory with the cold gusto of undertakers and crooks—at long last they'd found her, something sexier than books!

The transformation was successful—a flash of light, a puff of smoke. It was a tale worthy of Ovid: I tried to be an artist, they turned me into a joke.

But you, my friend, you know this already. What need for a firsthand account? The record is there, in every supermarket checkout stand and bus stop—wipe the gum off your shoe when you walk on my face, please! The parallel world, the shadow economy of lonely Calliope, a place I've inhabited against my will. And wherever I've been since that day I first opened my mouth has been, somehow, less real than the world they've constructed, that rickety structure of twenty-six letters.

But I'm not supposed to talk about it—that's what everyone always said. My mother, my publicist, my four-year-old's conscience: *Keep quiet,* they told me. *Beware of loose lips!* Traitor, patricide, bird of prey—that's what they called me.

Must I continue? Are we done for today?

Sweet *amigo,* you'll learn soon enough: In the end it hardly matters what I say. The world is carrying on just fine without me: Saint Calliope, a strange and silent memory. My words, as ever, could only do harm. So let's just forget I said anything.

> I wish I'd never said a word.
> I wish you'd let me be "just Bird."

There. I wrote that for you. Just now. Happy?

✱

I am the ghost of a famous suicide. I am the subject who won't sit still. Yorick's psycho-sister, a bloodstain at my throat; daughter of Memory, enslaved to a sloppy riddle-note. Awoke at seven from Lethe's nearer side, left home at fourteen, my father sewn into my thigh and waiting to be born anew—O you!, act five, scene two.

✱

Once, if I remember well, my life was a feast where all hearts opened and all wine flowed.

Don't bother getting up: It's Rimbaud. His favorite.

And maybe he's right (Rimbaud, that is)—but I don't remember the feast or the wine, only the heart that my father opened, excised, clamped, and cauterized. Three years of hazy silence. Then Christmas. You know this. All I have are images, fragments I can't be sure are mine. You knew him—my father—better than I ever will.

Does that sound strange? Think of it this way:

There was a room, dark and damp and buzzing like a hive, faces moving together and apart. This room—not large, a bar to one side and walls covered with padded vinyl, the upholstery of old car seats stripped like animal hides and tacked up to absorb the noise, deadening the sound so the neighbors can sleep. A small stage, barely rising above the floor—two feet, maybe three—amplifiers stacked high on either side, woofers like giant eyes cataracted by waves of cigarette smoke, the drumkit. One spindly microphone stand at the center, pathetic and unmanned, patch cord snaking down to a nest of wires that slithers out of sight. The night moves on, the muttering crowd packed like crayons, energy gathering invisible—something will burst. They are late again.

This is the Casbah. I know it like the back of my hand. The shabby singularity from which his Big Bang exploded, spreading outward inexorably until it had restructured the universe, until his reality had conquered all others, until everything *was* Terrible Children. And then, well, you know what they say: To make a god of something, make it disappear.

This is where they met, long ago in imaginary time, when she was still the scandalous singer of Fuck Finn, Terrible Children a barely known garage band out of Ocean Beach that got stuck at the bottom of a five-act bill. You know the story: how she saw him tuning his guitar, how she followed him to the back room, pinned him against the pinball machine—such a slight, delicate man, big blue eyes begging her not to hurt him, devouring her at the same time, and she said, "You and me, baby—we're going to change the world," before pouring a black Russian over his head and then kissing him *bang, smash* on the mouth. He was so surprised and overwhelmed, his eyes stinging blind, he lunged, bit her cheek, drew blood, they stood there grinning and disheveled and aroused, the rest of the room drawing back, astonished—and that's where that photo comes from.

But back to *my* memory—isn't that why we're here? It was years later, the band's big homecoming, the raggedy finish line of their only World Tour. They'd flown in from Johannesburg that morning. Rumored for months, the show had been announced only forty-eight hours earlier—"Kids in the Kasbah," the hottest ticket in town. Fans lined up for blocks, mobbed the radio stations and the promoter's headquarters, attacked some poor high school student putting up posters in Chula Vista; inside, watching that empty stage, you could feel it outside, the mob pushing against the walls of the old club, threatening to implode it—max. occupancy 250, more than twice that many made it inside. They were standing two on a bar seat. They were sitting on the stacks. Bodies, friction, such punk-rock heaven, such heat!

Take another look around, my shy voyeur: There's Danny Grier behind the soundboard, snorting a line off a pocket mirror, screaming into a clunky old cell phone; there's Gary North, chatting up a girl half his age. The whiskey-sipping crowd, the old-school punks with the high mohawks, goth girls weeping mascara, industry lackeys in their L.A. suits, standing against the back wall with their PDAs, the camera crew in the corner protecting their gear, the grizzled bikers, ratty skaters, the outcast and the lost. The bartender walks from one end of the bar to the other, balancing a tower of glasses in either hand, arms waving money like handkerchiefs, the reek of smoke and stale beer. A toilet that's been blocked up for a year. Danny is still screaming—unbeknownst to us he's talking to Talia Z, the Kids' manager, who is at that moment pulled off at the side of the 94 freeway, administering CPR. The press got the story the next day: how she'd met him at the airport, driven straight to Jamul to buy heroin, how she'd sat with him in a veterinary-hospital parking lot while he injected himself, how he almost didn't make it back. The details are well known. So he's sprawled on the side of the road and Talia's riding him, pumping and breathing into him while five hundred fans are building toward a detonation of desire—and there, in the back room, next to the very pinball machine where they'd met years before, stands my mother.

"We created all this. Look around," she says, her voice nasal; she leans toward the camera, face grainy in black and white. "It was just energy before, no focus. We made this out of nothing. *Sui generis.*"

She sweeps her arm and the camera sweeps with her, ghoulish faces growing brighter and dimmer as the lights pass over them—I could name almost everyone in that shot, San Diego's punk-rock royalty holding smelly, tweaked-up court, celebrating themselves and all they'd accomplished, not quite believing what they'd wrought.

"We're bigger than God," my mother says. "Nothing will ever be the same."

By the time Talia got him to the club, it was two hours past onstage time and the crowd was ready to tear the place down. Billy and Connor and XXX were pissed off—jet-lagged, exhausted, they wanted to play the set and get home. They were sick of the antics, the unpredictability. (In Paris he'd been arrested for climbing out the hotel window, hanging by his fingertips above the Place Vendôme; in Cairo he'd gone into a trance in the middle of the show, stood motionless before the microphone for ten minutes, nothing but the sound of his breathing—when he finally came to, all he said was, "I need a cigarette," and walked offstage.) But when the side door opened and Talia brought him in—leaning cadaverously on her shoulders, his shoes abandoned at the side of the road—a bolt of electricity coursed through the crowd, the speakers began to feed back seemingly of their own accord, and, as if guided by an unseen hand, XXX started the drumbeat intro to "Terrorist Methodist"—all was forgiven, the magic of Terrible Children holding him up as he strapped on his guitar and stepped to the microphone, girls in front of the stage swooning, boys crushed by the tidal force of devotion.

"What time is it?" he muttered, haggard and unshaven, and though no one could tell if he was joking, if he was even technically conscious, they ripped into the first song. "It's good to be back in Chicago," he cried, and everyone stared for another second before he flashed a slow grin, the last tension blown from the room as five hundred fans and dozens of journalists, promoters and agents and A&R interns, three bandmates and one wife and one adoring, starstruck bird all gave themselves to him, never to be given back.

> Three foot two and eyes of blue—
> Daddy, Daddy, I see you
> Up on the stage with flying hair
> A line of spittle running where your mouth

has kissed me, tucked me in,
your hands so gentle—not the hands
that slashed the strings and burned the spoon,
the hand that played the final tune upon your daughter's

waiting skin—how can I let this moment in
when it's not mine, when even then
you were not ours, you belonged
to them?

Do you remember this now? Does it all begin to seem familiar, a distant recollection as of a dream or story heard in childhood? Can you feel the guitar carving into you, Connor's bass shaking you to bits? Would you know this song if you heard it on the radio, if you heard it in an ad for orange juice, if you heard it in an elevator? Sing along with me—you know the words!

Watch my father step to the mike—that cramped stage he'd trod a hundred times, and though his bandmates are only a few feet away my father looks so alone, as though he has walked to the edge of a gangplank, waves churning below. Five hundred sirens, the sadness pulled at his eyes; as he sang the first lines every mouth opened, five hundred chicks and one baby bird waiting to swallow his regurgitations.

I remember.

I remember their voices were louder than his. I remember the stink of sweat, the crush of knees, how I walked at the feet of giants and begged for a view. Separated from my mother, I felt no fear—everyone knew me, I could move through that crowd like a favorite puppy, a pat on the head, kind words spoken in goo-goo. I pushed on, ever closer, knowing that when he saw me the sadness would leave his face. It was my job, I thought, to take it away.

But I couldn't get close enough, a forest of legs tightening, bodies smashing into one another, bouncing away. The music swam to me as though I were at the bottom of the pool. His body trembled with the force of it. Lights flashing, a black-and-white crowd, and as that first song ended in a shatter of sound I found a passage, a narrow gap through which to approach him—the applause was endless, cacophonous, I was drenched in it.

When it died the room was almost still. They shouted his name. I remember Connor saw me first, he bent down—giant string bean—pointed his finger and waved, a space opened around me as though I were a pebble in a pond. Billy tuning his guitar, XXX rolling the drums. Waiting again, everyone wanting the next song. In their eyes was pure love, hot and tormented—the kind you feel only for someone who won't give you what you want.

My father's eyes closed, guitar hanging from his neck like something a condemned man would wear. His hair strung out like strands of kelp, his body swayed back and forth.

"Brandt," XXX hissed behind him. "Wake up, man. Get with it." No response. I saw a droplet of sweat glide down a lock of hair. "Brandt!" XXX said, then shook his head, exasperated, flung his drumsticks behind him, they thudded against the vinyl padding, clattered to the floor. "Fuck!" he said.

Soon the crowd took it up—"Brandt! Fuck! Brandt! Fuck!"—my father floating in his private space, Talia at the side of the stage hiding her face in her hands. Someone threw a glass of beer which splashed all over him as it passed, crashed into the bass drum. "Brandt! Fuck! Brandt!" I took another step. If I could just reach him, take his hand, I knew he'd wake up. Billy played the opening riff of "Fishing Pier Frenzy" but my father was far away, nearly lost.

I closed my eyes and thought, *Wake up, Daddy.* I squeezed my eyes until I saw colored spots. *Daddy, wake up,* I thought. *Please. For me?*

Then I said it out loud: "Daddy!"

And when I opened my eyes, so did he.

His body swaying, his blue eyes swept the crowd. No one dared breathe. Finally he found me, his gaze fell on my head like angel snow. He shuddered, let out a heavy sigh.

"Oh," he said.

Nothing else, just that one desolate "Oh" before he pitched forward, toppling toward me, guitar and all, his body stiff and wrecked, tiny bird beneath falling timber.

I waited for him, I wanted him, I knew he would never hurt me. When the hands came up to catch him, when he was stretched across those hands like a cloud on treetops, I felt robbed—to come so close again and not touch him, this father who had vanished for months, known to me only by the pushpins my mother stuck in the map. I stood wailing among kneecaps, while overhead my father-shadow drifted across the room, obscuring and revealing the hot stagelights, and the band kicked into their anthem, "Dirt-nap." I reached up my arms and waited for him to lift me out of there, a shipwrecked girl lost in a sea of my father—his music, his fans, his ex-hausted body.

What else do I remember? Only the strange sense of permanence I felt, lingering in the seaweed while my father was again taken from me—but waiting, still waiting for his rough voice to awaken and drown me.

✲

And yet, and yet . . . why does my mother tell me I was home in bed?

When I can remember every detail—the whiskers on his face, the smell of the bar, Connor's finger waggling at me across the room—when I can *hear* the music, hear my mother shouting to be heard—when I *know* I was there, my memory assures me of it—why, then, does she smile, ruffle my hair, and say, "You've got it all wrong, little Bird"?

The documentary, *The Kids Are Not Alright,* came out when I was nine or ten and quickly became known as the definitive chronicle of the mete-oric career of Terrible Children. It was Wally Weeks, the filmmaker, who interviewed my mother that night in the Casbah, a mere six weeks before the funeral. In the opening scene, my father is carried into the club by Talia, and the band plays half of the opener before he collapses into the crowd. The whole thing is beautifully shot in black and white, Weeks captures perfectly the surprise and ecstasy on the faces of the fans who caught him, the way they held on to him, how each tried to keep a piece of him for themselves.

I have watched the scene a thousand times. In slow motion and freeze-frame, in forward and reverse. I can tell you what each fan in the front row is wearing, what drink the bartender is mixing, which strings on my fa-ther's guitar are sharp and which are flat. But I cannot find myself.

"But I remember," I used to tell my mother, working myself into a teary, insistent fit. "I remember. Daddy looked at me. I was there! I was there!" My mother pursed her lips, folded her hands, and, ever the Buddhist, practiced detachment.

"Well," she said. "Maybe you were."

*

Dear Sir: Who are you? May I please see some ID?

Why do you need to know this? Why must I constantly tell and show this?

What business is it of yours?

Who ever asked you in, by what invitation, who took your ticket, who stood at the station and shouted, "All aboard!"—who knew what you wanted in that secret, silent place you call a heart?

Who called it art?

Surely now you're satisfied. You've heard the story of how I tried to get back, back, back to him, and how I failed—and then he died. Isn't that enough? Or is there something more you want? Please don't dicker, don't be coy, if I haven't quite fulfilled your voyeuristic need to see the blood, to see his body stretched in mortal desperation—let me guess: You're dying to know it all, to witness the transubstantiation?

Is that what you crave, the guts and gore? Or is there something even more exciting than death, less permanent—some well-heeled, verbal masturbation?

But no, you're not the gruesome type who slows at crashes, not the one who throws a penny, reads the obits, blows eyelashes—your tastes are more refined, more pure (though not devoid of prurient interests, you prefer them soft-boiled, scrambled, or poached, told by inference, by simile— a Peeping Tom? Never, not me!), happy to skip the bloodiest part—that's not your style, not what you were waiting for . . .

O mon semblable, hypocrite lecteur!

★

Here's something else I can't remember.

It was the bluest morning I've ever known. Blue I love you blue. Blue of the tide, blue lightning. A San Diego morning poured out of a bottle, our big new house quiet except for the rattle of the wind, the scrape of branches against windows. Jasmine had bloomed in the night and the scent lay heavy on the air—April Fool's Day, the world filled with the promise of endless beauty reserved for me, Calliope. My mother had promised we would go out to the desert to see the new cactus flowers, the yellows and purples I'd always loved, happy to shred my hands to pieces to pick them. We were to go that weekend, or the next, as soon as he was done making the new record. The morning before, or maybe the one before that, she had turned to me in the car, eyes raw and swollen as she drove me to school.

"After the album's done," she said when she pulled up at the curb. "We'll have him back then. You'll see."

"But the flowers will be gone soon," I said, small in the passenger seat. "You promised!" Down the street, a few reporters were watching us. They always waited in the same place. They didn't scare me anymore. I knew they wouldn't bother me—they'd been ordered to stay fifty yards away.

My mother was sniffling, touching her forehead to the steering wheel. "We'll go as soon as we can," she keened. "I'm sorry, Bird, I'm sorry!" I was used to these outbursts: Lately she'd been crying every day, floating through the house like a soap bubble, any hard surface or sharp word could make her pop. After the tour he'd gone away again for thirty days—"drying out" my mother said. I pictured him standing in the sunshine, seawater dripping from his clothes. My mother spent whole days in bed, reading the Bhaghavad Gita and drinking G&Ts; I'd sneak in the bedroom door to surprise her, she'd clutch my shoulders and stare, as if she didn't recognize me. He came home with a haircut and a nervous smile, smoking cigarette after cigarette with a force that made his fingers shake. Four days later, he was gone again.

"We just have to be patient," she told me. She hugged me until I thought my neck would break. She smelled of perfume and sleep, and something sour, singed around the edges. "We have to let Daddy finish what he's doing."

"What's he doing?" I said. She had told me before, but I liked to hear the words: *production, distortion, isolation, mastering.* I didn't know what any of it meant. I would imagine him standing at the prow of a ship, shielding his eyes from the sun, keeping watch for some magical island while Billy and Connor and XXX waited belowdecks for him to shout, in his thin, crackly voice, "Land ho!"

My mother's voice was husky and breaking. "I don't know what he's doing."

"Can I help?" I said. But that just made her squeeze me tighter, the motor still running, her body shivering against me.

"He's got to do this by himself." My mother blew her nose and started the car. Before I could get out, she gripped my arm and brought her face close to mine.

"He can do it," she said slowly, lips exaggerating every word. "He can do it because he loves us."

"I know," I chirped, and hopped out.

But what did I really know? In that big, silent house I knew there were rooms I couldn't enter, locked doors that held irresistible mysteries for a curious child. We'd been in that house only a few months. I missed our familiar, run-down apartment at the beach, the sound of the waves in my sleep, the rattling of recyclables in the alley behind my bedroom. I longed to explore this new palace, to make it my own. I waited for him to take me by the hand and lead me into the forbidden places, his kingdom. I knew I just had to be patient—to be a good little bird and not bother him. On the rare occasions that he came home, he and my mother disappeared into the bedroom and I could hear her crying, begging. He responded in mutters, if at all. After a while he'd fling the door open and shamble into the hallway to find me crouched on the carpet—he'd stare at me as if he wasn't sure who I was, glance around at the long hallway, down into the living room with its enormous television, the tall windows and the manicured lawn, the jacaranda, a film of confusion over his eyes. He couldn't recognize any of it. He'd turn back to me, and for one second that fog would lift, his eyes sparkled to see me, my mother watching cross-armed from the doorway as he knelt down to ruffle my hair.

"It's you," he said. I clutched at his big hand; I tried to pop it in my mouth. "It's you, Bird. You're the one." In tears I tried to climb his arm, to sit on his shoulders. But he pulled his hand gently away. My mother glaring, he heaved himself down the stairs and left the front door open.

Look: I know all about his problems. I've read the same things you have. I know about the thousand-dollar-a-day habit, the rehabs and the busts. I know about motel rooms near the airport, about weeklong parties and wrecked cars. I know who he was: Brandt Morath, the shy, misanthropic beach rat who saved rock and roll, who remade the world in his image, the face that sold a thousand clips to MTV and was recognized from Boston to Buenos Aires to Bangkok. He was the world and its image, the medium and the message, all rolled into one. But to me, he was even bigger: He was my daddy, and I missed him.

That morning—sit up higher, you know the one—I heard the front door open, two quiet clicks and his careful footsteps across the living room, down the stairs to the basement. I waited, holding my breath, for him to come to my room. I waited for my mother to wake up, for them to start fighting. But the house was quiet again, and I saw my chance.

Padding through the halls and down the stairs, thumb in my mouth, sleep tangled in my hair. I took a violet from the basket on the kitchen table—she always had violets—stood atop the basement stairs and wondered if he knew I was there, if he would come to get me, take me down into his lair. The door at the bottom was closed and I knew that what was behind it was a sacred place where I was never to go: the practice studio, a Bird-free zone.

Down one step, and then two, I held my breath and listened to a sound I'd never heard before—no giant's laugh, no lion's roar—a sniffle, a whimper, a long, deep sigh. At the bottom, I reached for the knob, hesitating, as though our lives would be changed by what I was about to do. Slowly, terrified, I opened the door.

He sat cross-legged in the middle of the dim room, his back to the doorway where I stood. His head bowed, shoulders hunched in the fur-lined jacket he'd taken to wearing in all weather. He was wearing the hunter's cap with the flappy ears, the same one he'd worn on the back cover of the first album. The ears jiggled as he wept, mumbling things to himself and wiping his nose on the back of his sleeve. The room smelled strongly of new paint and metal, the woody scent of the cork sheets that lined the walls. Every corner was stacked high with amplifiers and mixing boards and processors, much of it still in boxes, a semicircle of guitars arrayed around him like a tribunal before which he sat to be judged. From where I stood I could just see the edge of the notepad in his lap. He scribbled in spurts, the scratch of the pen across paper magnified under the low ceiling. I wanted to go to him, to touch his shoulder, have him wrap me in his arms. But I didn't have the nerve. I tried to whisper— *Daddy?*—but nothing emerged.

He finished what he was writing and stared at it—I could hear his breathing, slow and ragged, as though he were awed by what he saw on that page—before tossing the pad to the side. The dim room waited, dull gleams off chrome, six-keyed guitar heads watching. He picked up something from the floor next to him—I couldn't see it at first, something heavy and dark that fit in his hand. He took a deep breath and held it in his lap.

"Brandt?" My mother's voice came from a great distance, from the other side of the house, light and sleepy. "Is that you, baby?" He bowed his head into his hands and moaned. Still I waited. I tried to stand very still, so that when he turned around he would know I hadn't disturbed anything.

"Brandt?" she called again, closer now. My father wiped his nose once more, sat up straight, lifted his hand. Her footsteps were directly above us, but I hoped she wouldn't find us. As long as she didn't find us, it would be our secret, just the two of us holed up here, maybe the most intimate moment we'd ever had.

Between sobs he was talking to himself again, words that came out low and smeary. As the footsteps approached the top of the stairs I thought I heard one word come through clearly. I thought I heard him say, "Alive."

"Brandt!" she called from the top of the stairs, and my father's back stiffened.

"Daddy!" I cried—it had worked once before! I couldn't wait any longer to be seen. I couldn't wait to feel him. But I didn't realize how loud my voice would be in that acoustically engineered space, how sharply it would ring around us, how it would startle him.

What they tell me is he didn't feel a thing.

They tell me he was gone before his body hit the floor—and given where I was standing it was lucky I didn't go with him.

They say there was blood everywhere—on the guitars, the amplifiers, the ceiling. There were chips of bone embedded in the walls. My mother flew down the stairs, the shriek caught in her throat, and when she saw me standing stiffly at the bottom, clutching a crumpled violet, the first thing she thought was that I'd been shot, my nightgown dripping and a bright, bright spot of him splattered on the side of my neck. I didn't make a sound, just stared at the mess on the floor until the paramedics pushed me aside; Talia wrapped me in a blanket, shoved her fist into her mouth, and collapsed on the bottom stair; Billy threw me over his shoulder, took me to the kitchen where he punched the refrigerator until his hands split open and bled. But I would not stay away, crept again and again down the stairs. The police came and went, and then the lawyers; the label and the newscasters did their thing—but I was rooted to carpet, staring wordless at the spot where he'd lain, until finally Connor carried me upstairs, past my mother's room where she was prostrate under a doctor's care, staggered by Klonopin, Ambien, knocked out by Nembutal. He put me to bed and sat with me, kissed my head. I gripped his shirt and would not let him leave. I pulled him close and whispered in his ear.

"Alive," I said.

He smoothed my hair and blinked back tears. "It was only a dream, Bird," he said. "Just a nightmare." He sat on the floor and watched over me. When he thought I was asleep, he reached out a fingertip and touched the hot stain on my skin.

"*He's alive,*" I whispered. The last word he'd spoken was the last word I'd speak.

That's what they tell me. That's all I can tell you.

All these years I've tried to recall—my memory reaches weakly into a dark inkwell. And all it brings back is the sound of my voice, how it rang and rang, grew deafening, blotting out sight and time. The last thing I saw was my father—alive!—sitting before me, both of us breathing; the last thing I felt a terrible, swift wind moving through me, and a violent shiver as his tired, conquered soul slipped into mine.

3. MILESTONES, MILLSTONES, AND MAELSTROMS

WHAT MAKES A DEATH ARTIST? What combination of forces—arbitrary, un-coordinated—converges upon the mind of the child, what fearful synergy inspires the implacable drive, the terrible destiny that was Calliope's? Any examination begins with her father's grisly departure, the public's unend-ing fascination, the media's opportunism, the traumatized child's immer-sion in poetry. But if many of the recognizable elements of her character were already apparent on that Christmas morning, we must still take into account the aftermath, the years during which the child—now volubly awake, her rhymed couplets and ad-lib haiku and limericks chirping through the mansion—continued to live in that singular home: part fun-house, part necropolis. Nor should the influence of her mother, Penelope Morath, be overlooked or underestimated.

While no one doubts the sincerity of Penelope's distress during the years of her daughter's silence, it is equally true that Calliope's long fugue enabled the widow to defer certain agonizing questions. Now, with a fa-therless daughter very much aware, very much inquiring, Penelope was forced to make decisions. Drawing upon the iron will with which she had prosecuted her career, the same leonine protectiveness with which she had defended her husband's interests, she made it clear to the child that the topic of Brandt's death—its antecedents, its ambiguities, its aftermath—was *verboten*. She would not discuss that tragic morning; she dismissed with a scowl Calliope's questions about her own role in the event. Perhaps most significantly, she refused to reveal—to Calliope, as to the world—the whereabouts of her husband's remains.

"We will honor his *life*," Penelope told her daughter. "We'll remember his genius, his love. That's how we keep him alive. Not by pissing on some patch of grass or building some stupid monument.

"Impermanence, kiddo," she said, repeating what she had learned from the Buddhists. "Get used to it."

Some scholars see this refusal as indicative of Penelope's own inability to accept her husband's death; others point to the Inca shaman, rumored to be conducting séances in the mansion, alchemical experiments in a spare bedroom. Certainly the couple's regular use of ayahuasca—a powerful hallucinogen brewed from a South American vine and sometimes used to contact deceased ancestors—would have exerted some influence on her psychology during this period.*

"*Si se cree en su muerta, le mata,*" he told the widow. "She who believes in his death will kill him." That he also communicated this doctrine to the seven-year-old Calliope is suggested by the last lines of "Cruci-Fix Me," an early, uncollected poem: "Kneel before my open wounds / with love of life instill me / But never, my child, believe in me / for that belief will kill me."

Thus Calliope was never able to say that final farewell. She was forbidden to enter the recording studio in the mansion's basement, the site of her father's suicide. Whether due to the trauma she witnessed there or to Penelope's threats and admonitions, the child developed a paralyzing fear of the long stairway, trembling and breaking into whimpers at the sight of the basement door. By age nine, according to one neurologist, she had developed a number of obsessive-compulsive rituals, including an inability to walk past the basement stairs: She could move from living room to kitchen only on hands and knees, eyes shut, and only after whispering to herself the lyrics of an entire Terrible Children song. This fetishistic disavowal of the existence of the studio is what gives the opening line of "Sunday on Suicide Row" its authority: "My house has no basement."

In contrast to these severe prohibitions, Penelope energetically encouraged Calliope's study of poetry, working with her tutors to develop a regimen that included the production of one poem each day of her young life.

---

*There are no studies on the interactive effects of ayahuasca with Nembutal, Vicodin, or Neurontin, though the author imagines such effects not to be particularly conducive to rational thought.

"I had no doubt in my mind. The minute I heard her voice that morning I knew who she was," Penelope recalled, in a rare interview. "It was inside of her—the gift—it was a part of her. She was too young to understand, but I know how the world conspires against brilliance, to strangle it in the cradle. I was hard on her—but I wasn't going to let anything stand in her way, not even her self."*

Hard indeed. Penelope spent the next several years grooming her daughter's talent with a singleness of purpose more common to the parents of sports prodigies: pushing, cajoling, rewarding, punishing, warping the world around the child's talent until the child sees the world only in terms of that talent, her purpose in the world simply to perform. Calliope was granted respite from her studies only for her daily swim lesson— by age ten she could swim one hundred laps without tiring—and to help the housekeeper fold laundry, her favorite chore. In 199_ Penelope arranged—by way of endowing a substantial scholarship fund—for her daughter to work one-on-one, through the mail, with the faculty of Warren Wilson College, a low-residency (or, in this case, *no-residency*) graduate writing program based in Asheville, North Carolina. Calliope received no academic credit for her work, but the influence of poets Mahmoud al-Shakil and deirdre v. deirdre was, in the view of many scholars, essential to her early artistic development.

By the time Calliope was delivered to the secluded Mountaintop Arts Academy, a well-respected boarding school in the San Jacinto mountains, 120 miles from San Diego, Penelope had made it clear to her fourteen-year-old daughter, as well as to the staff of the mansion, to a handful of agents, editors, handlers, hairdressers, reviewers, designers, and financiers, to the executives at her husband's record label, and even, through intermediaries, to the Poet Laureate of the United States, that Calliope Bird Morath was destined for a life in poetry of such towering greatness as to eclipse even her father's colossal fame.

"She basically saw Calliope as an extension of Brandt," says one friend of the family. "Brandt had the talent to conquer the world, but not the

---

*Michael Azerrad, "The Fall of the House of Morath," *Vanity Fair,* October 200_. The interview was the basis for Azerrad's book *Make Me: The Story of Penny & Brandt.*

strength to rule it. Penny thought Calliope would be stronger, less vulnerable. She thought she could have it all."

Penelope's policy regarding the public's access to her daughter had clearly undergone a revision. Still, she knew Calliope must be prepared carefully for her inevitable renown, lest it overwhelm her young psyche as it had her father's. It was for this reason that none of the daily poems she wrote before age thirteen has ever been made public, despite exorbitant offers from several publishers.* For this reason also, the young poet had been brought to a psychotherapist, the respected Lacanian analyst Michaela Breve, thrice weekly since her tenth birthday.†

Insufficient though these efforts may have been, one can hardly blame Penelope for wishing to spare her daughter the psychic agony that had befallen Brandt. What parent does not wish for their child the twin blessings of success and happiness? What parent does not hope for the child to be recognized as exceptional while somehow avoiding the crushing self-doubt and loneliness the exceptional so often endure? Does not every parent strive to spare his child from pain? Is not every parent therefore destined to stand crestfallen and shattered when his selfless labor comes to naught?

Perhaps it was a premonition of the ultimate vanity of her efforts, and the anxiety of imminent separation, that inspired the episode on the eve of Calliope's departure for Mountaintop. Mother and daughter had spent the better part of the summer preparing—shopping together for new clothes (though after one incident at San Diego's Horton Plaza, this activity was confined to catalogs and Web sites), choosing furnishings and decorations for the woodland cottage Calliope was to share with two other youngsters, and, finally, directing the loading of two cargo vans to transport these belongings to her new home. Calliope took particular interest in this last activity, as she did in all things spatially related—former employees of the

---

*Most of these early writings have been collected and housed with Calliope's other papers at the Ransom Center, where they have been sealed until 2099. Two notebooks—one written in the months after Brandt's death and the other after Calliope's Christmas awakening—are missing. According to Penelope, one of these "disappeared" several years ago; the other, she destroyed.
†The author wishes to thank Dr. Breve for her generous time and for providing copies of papers and articles she wrote about Calliope, as well as video and audiotape from a number of their sessions.

Morath household still marvel at the efficiency and precision with which her abundant belongings were made to fit in the available space.

"The child was as orderly as the mama was messy," recalls Esperanza Medina Blumstein, who kept house at the mansion from 199_ until 200_. "We used to say 'Whose daughter is she, that is so clean? Not hers! Not his! Whose?' "

This, too, may point to the influence of the shaman, who continued to live in the mansion, sequestered in his laboratory, even after his relationship with Penelope ended. Though the notes he left are largely inscrutable, he seems to have perceived Calliope's combustion as an alchemical event, the first stage of a *"transmutación."* Calliope was thus the only one permitted to enter the laboratory, provided she stood perfectly still in a designated corner while the shaman carried out his delicate work, sweating over a small crucible in his ongoing attempts to change base metals into gold.* And it was only Calliope whom he bid farewell when he left the mansion days before her twelfth birthday, his macabre necklace serving as a parting gift.

"The fire is still burning. I feel it," he told her, showing her the backs of his hands, scarred pink and smooth from the Christmas blaze. "One day you will help me, as I helped you." Then, according to Blumstein, who was watching from a second-floor window, he laid the toothy talisman over the child's neck, kissed the top of her head, and walked away down Azalea Path, never to be heard from again.

Two years later, it would be Calliope's turn to say good-bye. It was a warm San Diego evening, the last of the sunset filtering through the jacaranda branches. The breeze carried the scent of the ocean and brought a small storm of purple buds fluttering down around them. As they stood together in the mansion's circular driveway, Penelope handed her daughter two small, wrapped boxes, gifts for Calliope's new roommates. Calliope wore blue jeans and her favorite, worn tennis shoes and a summery blouse with a collar high enough to hide most of the birthmark on her neck. Her hair was pulled back into a ponytail. Her mother, still quite fit at thirty-nine, wore a bikini top and an immodest leather skirt.

---

*Calliope provides an impressionistic description of this work in "Nigredo, or Burn Baby Burn!"

"Why should I give them anything?" Calliope asked. "What did they ever do for me?"

Penelope hooked her sunglasses through the cleavage of her bikini. "You'll want them on your side," she said. One of the staff slammed the door of the van and returned to the house. "Living with you's not going to be easy, you know."

She lit a cigarette and leaned against a wrought-iron lamppost while Calliope considered this. The young poet frowned and carefully peeled the wrapping paper from one of the gifts, revealing a copy of the unreleased Terrible Children CD box set. The cover art—subject of hot dispute between Penelope and the surviving band members, the arbitration and litigation of which would delay release for several years—was a photograph of a headstone bearing Brandt's name and an inscription from Baudelaire:

These vows, these perfumes, these infinite kisses
Will they be reborn from a depth we cannot sound?

"What if they don't like it?" Calliope asked her mother, who watched with raised eyebrows as her daughter meticulously rewrapped and retaped the gift. "What if they don't like Daddy's music?"

"I'm sending you to a school for gifted artists, not morons." Penelope crushed her cigarette on the driveway and strode back into the house.

According to Blumstein, the mood deteriorated quickly at the dinner table. Penelope, characteristically unable to cope with the stress of her daughter leaving home, took several Valium and poured herself a tall gin and tonic. Since Brandt's death, she and Calliope had grown close as sisters, held hostage together in the house on Azalea Path. Whatever indiscretions Penelope had previously indulged in the mansion, whatever bacchanalia she might be anticipating in the child-free era to come, life without her daughter must nevertheless have been difficult to imagine.

Calliope was unperturbed. She sat across from her mother, spooning mouthfuls of macaroni and cheese and leafing through her well-worn copy of Dante's *Inferno* in the original Italian. As the gin began to take hold, Penelope watched the side of her daughter's serene face, her young skin smooth and unblemished except for the birthmark, and found herself annoyed. Her daughter's silence always worried her: the sense of some hidden pressure building, the fear of that silence being broken.

"Aren't you excited?" she prodded Calliope. When there was no answer, she took the book from her daughter's hands and laid it on the table. "Aren't you scared, Bird?"

"Of what?" Calliope reached for the book; her mother took her wrist and held it.

"Everything's going to be different. A new bed, new teachers, kids your own age." Calliope shrugged. "Pretty soon you'll forget all about this." Penelope swept her arm to indicate the house around them. "You'll forget how good you had it here, with Mommy."

Calliope pulled her wrist away. *"Forse,"* she said, knowing that speaking Italian would infuriate her mother.

Penelope leaned back and finished her drink, handing it to one of the servants for a refill. She stared down the long table at the photo of Brandt on the wall—standing with Gary North, chairman of NorthStar Records, wearing a tuxedo, his normally unkempt hair immaculately groomed, grabbing his crotch with one hand while with the other accepting a gold record for the band's breakout single, "Dirtnap."

"You'll probably meet lots of boys up there," Penelope said, her voice low and jaded. Once the earsplitting shriek that powered Fuck Finn, years of seclusion, alcohol, and filtered cigarettes had smoothed her voice into near unusability. "I'm sure you'll find yourself a little boyfriend. Won't that be fun."

Calliope stared at her plate, blue eyes narrowed. According to Dr. Breve, Penelope had, on a number of occasions, arranged "play dates" with neighboring boys; all Calliope had ever said about these incidents was that they were "apocalyptic."

"Oh, you'll have lots of boyfriends, running around in the woods." Penelope leaned back in her chair and closed her eyes. "Some guitar-playing shit will probably get you into bed soon enough. Next thing you know, you'll be sleeping with the faculty."

Calliope looked up. "No I won't."

"I know how these places are. It's going to be one long fuck-fest, believe me. You'll have to beat the boys off with a stick."

She stared at her mother. "Maybe I don't like boys," she said quietly.

That got Penelope's attention. "Of course you like boys."

Calliope raised an eyebrow. "You don't."

They regarded each other for a moment and a thin smile came over Penelope's face, as though she were just now recognizing the girl sitting across from her, just now understanding how worthy her adversary. "Sometimes I do," she said.

Calliope smiled the same smile. The servants, familiar with the signs of a battle joined, began to leave the dining room.

"Mommy," Calliope said, in the sweet babytalk voice she sometimes used, "can I ask you something?"

"Anything, my chickadee."

Calliope batted her eyelashes, the picture of innocence. "What's a cunt?"

Penelope refused to be flustered. She leaned forward and folded her hands on the table. "A cunt, my darling girl, is something that brings joy to all the world."

"*Come interessando!*" Calliope said, reaching for the Dante, barely suppressing a giggle. "I guess the housekeepers must really like you, because they all say you are one."

Penelope stared for another moment at the spine of the *Inferno* which her daughter had interposed between their eyes, then rose, unsteadily but majestically, gin and tonic in hand, and went to the front door. The sky had grown dark, the lamps lining the driveway threw amber cones across the shadows. A murmur came from the street, where a number of passersby had noticed the vans parked in front of the house and stopped to investigate.

"You want to see a cunt?" Penelope shouted, though probably not addressing the people on the street, as was first reported. Half-stumbling down the front steps, she threw open the rear doors of the nearest van and began pulling her daughter's belongings out, flinging them onto the driveway, the lawn. Boxes of books and compact discs, stuffed animals and loose bedding and clothing on hangers, suitcases and jewelry boxes and paper bags piled with knickknacks—Penelope hurled them from the back of the van with surprising force, creating in the space behind her the kind of scatter pattern one associates with the crash of a light aircraft.

"I'll show you the biggest cunt you've ever seen!" she screamed as Calliope's stereo smashed to the ground, the windows of the mansion now dotted with the tired, unsurprised faces of the staff.

The passersby stood astonished as Penelope dragged ever-larger items out of the van, her curses amplified by the metal interior, heaving onto the hard pavement first a priceless Louis XIV nightstand and then the full-length jeweled mirror she and Brandt had bought for Calliope in Mexico City and, finally, piece by cumbersome piece, the four-poster bed in which her daughter had slept since graduating from the crib and which it had taken two servants the better part of the afternoon to disassemble and haul downstairs, all the pieces now clattering and clunking atop one another on the driveway, the embroidered silk canopy immediately catching on a gust of wind and fluttering up to tangle in the branches of the jacaranda.* She stood in the doorway of the van, one bikini strap fallen off her shoulder, and stared defiantly into the lamplight as though it were ten years earlier and she were onstage at a boisterous Fuck Finn concert.

"We want more!" someone shouted, a cry taken up by several voices.

"Sing something, Penny!"

Penelope listened for a moment, her chest heaving, mouth agape.

"Show us your tits!" someone said. Penelope grabbed the nearest object—a pyramidal brass paperweight—and flung it past the lights, striking a pedestrian on the jaw.†

"*Fuck you!!*" she shrieked, straining toward her antagonists, drool spilling from her lips and her voice approximating the power it had once known.

"Where's Calliope?" someone yelled.

"Bring out Calliope!" they said. "We want Calliope!"

But Calliope was still inside the mansion and, as previously noted,

---

*Marjorie Perloff points out that the canopy, which remained caught in the tree until the next morning, provides a perfectly reasonable image for the controversial lines in "Electra Returns to Azalea Path": "My bed became your ghost for all to see / Though mother, servants, nature condemn me" (Perloff, "The Fame of the Father," *GQ*, October 200_). In the author's view, this interpretation is far more credible than the vile suggestions made by Harminder Singh in his recent history of the family.

†Charges were later dropped.

Penelope had no intention of parading her before the public just yet. Whether it was therefore for the purpose of distracting the crowd or was merely, as she would later insist to the Division of Child Protection Services, a spontaneous outpouring of motherly emotion, exacerbated by the strain of her daughter's departure and an actionably overprescribed dose of diazepam, or whether some combination of both, it is pointless to speculate. Suffice it to say that the crowd, as well as the servants, were duly distracted when Penny Power gulped the rest of her drink and smashed the glass on the driveway, flung bikini top and leather skirt behind her, and threw herself facedown on the mansion's freshly watered lawn, clawing at the wet grass and kicking her feet into the soft, warm earth, screaming "My baby! My goddamned baby!" through a sea of tears and mucus, through fistfuls of soil which she crammed into her mouth, smeared into her hair, while flashbulbs flashed in the summer night and behind the mansion walls her daughter sat reading at the dinner table, under the eyes of her celebrated father, pretending not to hear the clamor outside, and savoring her own, slow descent into hell.

The present work traces its origins to the moment the author saw Ms. Morath on the cover of *SPIN* magazine.* The photograph by Sebastião Salgado was, in a way, Calliope's pop-culture coming-out, the feature story her first major-media interview, a cornerstone of the advance-publicity machine which was created, fine-tuned, and turbocharged for the release of her first volume of poetry. No reader will fail to bring to mind the image, in which the nineteen-year-old Calliope sits naked and splay-legged in a field of heather, her hair tousled, split-ended, and draped strategically over her breasts, her pudendum concealed by a gigantic black orchid in whose center could be made out the faintest image of her father. As has been noted elsewhere, the lighting of the shot is exquisite, the long grass reflecting a soft, early morning sunshine in such a way that the poet's form takes on a dreamy hyperreality—but what caught the author's eye, more

---

*May 200_.

than the skillful composition of the photo, and certainly more than its crude carnality, was the expression on Calliope's face: exhausted and stupefied, her thin lips dry and cracked, barely parted, her eyes suggesting the wariness of a cornered animal, hunted and tormented for sport, down to its last reserves of self-preservation.* It was an expression the author found arresting and tragic to behold on the face of one so young, one to whom, as all the world knew, so much had been given. The headline on the magazine's cover read: A SEASON IN HELL.

It had been fifteen years since Brandt Morath's suicide and the disintegration of Terrible Children, fifteen years in which the cultural revolution begun by the band had achieved a victory so complete as to have become invisible: No one remembered the world as it was, those who harkened back to a more innocent time were dismissed as nostalgists and kitschmongers, advocates of an aesthetic simplicity which, in this version, had never existed. In this brave new world, a photograph such as the one of Calliope on the cover of *SPIN*, though captivating, seemed almost commonplace in what we might call its "statement," in the particular codes it marshaled to convey what might once have been called, quaintly, its "meaning"; such that even if one were tempted to apply a traditional hermeneutics to the image—to point out its exaggerated references to sex and sexual violence; the invocation of the legend of Brandt Morath and the attendant rumors, never adequately debunked by the family, regarding his relationship with Calliope;† and the textual reference to Rimbaud which did triple duty by impressing those unfamiliar with Rimbaud by its melodrama, contextualizing Calliope in the pantheon of poetry, and alluding provocatively to the contents of Brandt's suicide note—one would eventually have to doubt the validity and significance of one's own analysis, based as it was in an antediluvian mode of thought. And even this critical dilemma seems to be anticipated and frustrated by the image itself, which deploys a bygone

---

*Salgado is renowned for his work with displaced peoples and victims of calamitous Third World conflicts, the influence of which is glaringly clear in the *SPIN* photos.

†"He was my first and only love," Calliope told David Fricke in the *SPIN* interview. "His death was my deflowering," leading astute readers to wonder whether the interview had preceded the photo, or vice versa.

pastoralism, a "harkening back," the ironic distance of which is entirely indeterminate.*

The author had been aware, had almost subconsciously kept track, of Brandt's daughter in the decade and a half since the suicide. But such awareness had entered his thoughts only on the occasions, grown somewhat less frequent, of some new tabloid story or legal skirmish, most of which had revolved around Penelope—the reconstitution of Fuck Finn, the recording of their third album, *Ulysses,* and subsequent tour; the later attempt at forming a "supergroup" comprised of Penelope, XXX, and members of Rocket From the Crypt, and produced by Butch Vig; the frequent rumors regarding her romantic liaisons with various musicians, actors, and political figures; her ongoing legal battles with Connor Feingold and Billy Martinez; and of course the arrest for public nudity and intoxication described previously. When Calliope was mentioned in the press it was most often as an aside in a story about her mother, though of course the Christmas fire had not been forgotten, nor MTV's endless airing of her sonnet, "I Shall Not Soon Forget the Day He Died," and the rumors that Penelope had threatened to pull her husband's videos from circulation if the network did not showcase the thirteen-year-old's magnum opus. Speculations about Calliope's own romantic affairs, most notably with Connor Feingold and wunderkind poet L. Moreno, had not yet seeped into the muddy mainstream of the Morath family epic. In short, there was the sense that Calliope Bird Morath would one day inevitably achieve exceptional celebrity, but that day had not yet arrived; whereas what the publicists were banking on was that her father's name and reputation could still serve as a powerful engine, a first-stage booster rocket which would blast her high enough for her own star-power to take over. The cover of *SPIN* represented the first tendrils of smoke on the launchpad, the shudder and countdown, all systems, as they say, *Go.*

The author was, of course, a fan of her father's music. Even had he not been assistant editor of *SLAM* in the early days of Terrible Children, even had he not been a frequent patron of the Casbah and other San Diego

*For further analysis of the image, see Jean Baudrillard's excellent article, *"Original Américain," L'Express,* May 26, 200_.

clubs, there was a certain moment after which he could hardly have ignored the tectonic shift epicentered in Ocean Beach, nor avoided the re-
sultant cultural tsunami. Some critics have suggested that it was Brandt's
suicide, and not the band's career, which served as a "tipping point"—i.e.,
that before 199_ Terrible Children were just another popular rock outfit,
that we have collectively edited our memories in light of the terrible
tragedy to make of that period a kind of punk-rock Camelot.* This author rejects such revisionism; his own memories of the 199_ "Kids in the
Kasbah" show, after the band's World Tour, are proof enough of what Gina
Arnold called "Kidsophrenia"—a global obsession so pronounced one
would literally have had to dwell in a cave in some Andean backwater to
have missed it.

Additionally, it might be surmised that for a young man such as the author who, though not lacking in intelligence and education, had not quite,
shall we say, found his way in the world, a young man—like many bright,
sensitive young persons—who couldn't help feeling at times as though he
had missed the proverbial boat, or lacked knowledge of certain arcane but
crucial social codes, and therefore walked through the world with the
slightly wounded though still endearingly curious look of a dog who has
not yet made the all-too-important connection between urinating on the
Persian rug and a hard swat on the nose; that for such a young man Brandt
Morath's revolution, a revolution of outsiders and misfits, would have
seemed heaven-sent. He had, and has to this day, all of Terrible Children's
albums—as well as two T-shirts, a concert poster, a keychain bottle opener,
a rare Japanese bootleg, and various other merchandise.

The author distinctly remembers the first time he met Brandt Morath,
on a summer morning in the late '80s. In those days, SLAM was a new and
largely unread publication circulated intermittently out of a two-room office in a condemned warehouse. The local music community was as yet the
only readership, and occasionally members of new bands stopped in at the
cramped office to introduce themselves, to deliver their demo tapes, or to
avail themselves of free coffee. The author can recall the exact date of the

---

*A signal example of such idiocy is provided by Mark Lipschitz in the September 200_ issue of
SLAM.

meeting—July 25, 198_—as it was his birthday, and he had come to work only to gather a few papers and deliver a hastily written review of the new Alison Moyet greatest-hits package; as he sat at the office's only desk, cluttered with cassette tapes, a dead computer, and amateurish promotional packets, the door smacked open and a young man lurched into the room effusing the foulest odor the author can recall having smelled. The man was roughly the author's age and had long hair dyed green and orange. He was unshaven and barefoot, wearing a shin-length swimsuit and a tattered, oil-streaked mechanic's shirt and his skin was blotched with peeling sunburn and open sores. The odor he exuded was a combination of sweat, cigarette smoke, urine, and the distinct, sharply citric smell of a sewage spill. The author, being a trained journalist, noted all of these details in the first second; in the next, the visitor stepped wobblingly forward and vomited spectacularly across the desk.

The stunned author rolled his chair back into the corner and watched as the man held to the edge of the desk, eyes fixed on a point in space, and vomited again, spitting the last phlegmy remnants onto the floor. Having apparently rid his body of discomfort, the visitor took a cleansing breath and beamed winningly before dropping into the office's only other chair.

"Bad tacos," he said.

The author could only stare, beginning to feel a bit queasy himself due to the admixture of odors in the poorly ventilated space.

"Okay if I smoke?" asked the intruder, taking a pack from a shirt pocket. He scanned the desk and picked up the only dry piece of paper— the author's unedited review—and looked it over, nodding and pursing his lips in great seriousness.

"Right on the money, man," he said. "Couldn't have said it better myself. I like the line about 'the poverty of our musical zeitgeist.'* I mean, how dare they subject us to this garbage, you know?

"But let me ask you something." He poked his cigarette at the air as though it were a professor's pointer, while the author struggled to crank open the only window, which promptly jammed, forcing him to suck fresh

---

*Andrew Altschul, "Snapshot of a Yaz-Been," SLAM, August 4, 198_.

air through a two-inch opening. The visitor waited until he had the author's attention, then said, "What are you going to do about it?"

The author looked up, too woozy to reply.

"They turn out truckloads of this crap, and even though everybody
knows it sucks you still hear it on the radio, and you see it written up in
your magazine. Why do you think that is?

"It's because nobody's making them stop," he said before the author
could respond. "You're playing their game reviewing this stuff. Even a bad
review acknowledges this shit *exists*, accepts the premise that this is fucking *music*, that it's fucking *art*. Meanwhile, there are people living under
fishing piers making great music. There's a whole revolution going on, a
new Golden Age happening right under your nose, while you slaves are
still listening to the radio, sucking on the corporate teat.

"You're gonna miss the whole thing," he said, and shook his head sadly,
extinguishing his cigarette in the puddle of desktop vomit. "Alison Fucking
Moyet. She's as rock and roll as a lizard fart."

Suffice it to say the author was not overly pleased at being referred to
as a slave and a corporate teat-sucker, nor by the implication that his life's
work was enabling a conspiracy of widespread artistic degradation. Additionally, he had recovered his senses sufficiently to survey the ruined desk,
the soaked cassette tapes, many of which he had planned to bring home for
review, and the suspicious splatter marks on his own shoes. He responded
querulously to the visitor's diatribe, explaining that while, no, the greatest-
hits package hardly represented a high-water mark in art history, that Alison Moyet had nonetheless made important contributions to the music
world, particularly on such early Yaz records as *Upstairs at Eric's*, and that
if her star had somewhat fallen—as all stars do!—that that in no way put
her outside of what intelligent listeners would think of as musical relevance. The author recalls the bizarre sensation of listening to his own spirited defense of a performer whom he found, quite honestly, to be devoid
of such relevance, while being grinned at mockingly by the garish, odor-
iferous figure before him, and wondering just what kind of person he had
become that his mouth, and presumably some portion of his brain, could
produce logically coherent statements that were nevertheless utter mis-
representations of his beliefs in the matter.

When the author had exhausted his own tirade, the unkempt visitor stood and reached again into his shirt pocket. "This is what you need." He tossed a cassette tape into the author's lap.

The author examined the unlabeled tape and inquired as to the visitor's name and the name of his band, where they lived, etc.

"When Dionysus wandered the forests," the visitor said in response, "men and women left their homes and families just to be near him. They had orgies in broad daylight. The women suckled bulls and goats and tore them apart with their bare hands. Anyone who got in their way was driven mad and threw themselves into the ocean. It was total chaos, man. It made the Beatles '64 look like a Tupperware party." The visitor opened the door—to the nauseated author's great relief—and said, "You think anyone asked him his fucking name?"

The author, wiping off his shoes with a used paper napkin, asked if the band was then called Dionysus. The visitor sighed and rolled his eyes, as though despite the author's egregious denseness he nevertheless had impressed the visitor as a kindred spirit. Then he departed, leaving the mess on the desk to waft in the crossdraft.

Attentive readers will note the many ways in which the Brandt Morath of this vignette differs from the public persona that evolved over the course of his career. That he sought out the attentions of an influential local writer, literally throwing his demo tape at him, that he engaged in an informed, if cantankerous, discussion of the state of the contemporary music industry, that he so unmistakably indicated his penchant for seeing himself in mythological terms, all of this works against the familiar portrayal of Brandt as a socially fearful, overgrown runaway who lived for years under a fishing pier before being dragged, kicking and screaming, into the klieg lights of global adoration.

Contrast this conversation, in which he evinces some solidarity with the music lovers who would be his fans, with a BBC interview only two years later, just after the release of the *Hanged Man* EP:

BBC Announcer: Tell us, Mr. Morath, why do you think English audiences have responded so well to your music?

Brandt: Isn't that your job?

BBC: Perhaps. But surely you must have your own theories?

Brandt: Not really.

BBC: I see.

Several seconds of dead air.

Brandt: People don't give a [expletive deleted] about my music.

BBC: Surely you're joking. The album's a smash! Your fans broke all the windows at Piccadilly Virgin Mega when they ran out of copies.

Brandt: People don't care about the music. The music's just a doorway. [*Sound of a cigarette lighter flicking.*] You know what people want? They want to be smacked around a little. They want to be teased, disappointed, mocked, manipulated. They want to be turned on and then rejected, they want to laugh and then find out the joke's on them. They want to be insulted. Abused.

Dead air. Announcer coughs.

BBC: And why would they want that?

Brandt: They need to feel small. You think I'm [expletive deleted] you? Don't look at me like that, you [expletive deleted]. They need to feel that someone is bigger than them, more powerful, worthy of their worship. People are hungry. They need to be fed.

Dead air.

BBC: Yes, well. Interesting thoughts. Very, er, Nietzsche, isn't it?

Brandt: What the [expletive deleted] is Nietzsche?

This is, of course, much closer to most people's image of Brandt Morath the misanthrope, the miserable soul for whom even great fame could not restore faith in the world—for whom, indeed, that very fame and worship could only confirm his terrible suspicions about the worthlessness of existence. This is the Brandt Morath whom Robert Christgau would compare to Keats in his widely read obituary: "Having written the songs, there was nothing left for him to do except die."*

A punk-rock Janus, or a casualty of precisely the need he diagnosed in

---

*"April Is the Cruelest Month," *Village Voice,* April 2, 199_ (Special Extra).

his fellow man? Was his peculiar wisdom inborn, its expression the engine of Terrible Children's great rage and great appeal? Or did his superlative fame and all its trappings and obligations lead him to such dark beliefs in a universal desire for victimhood, a Will, as it were, to Powerlessness?

The author once tried to engage his son in a thoughtful discussion of the topic. His son was barely fourteen at the time, but had already begun to exhibit the signs of a difficult adolescence—the truculence, the secretiveness and withdrawal, problems regarding school behavior and his alleged treatment of the neighbor's cat; the author was in the habit of finding any pretext for father-son interaction, hoping to stop this slide into pain and bile. He brought out the unmarked tape Brandt Morath had given him on that prehistoric afternoon and had autographed years later at the Casbah, thinking to impress his son with this demonstration of undiminished coolness. He turned the stereo up rather loud and watched his son carefully through "Kill the Surfers," "Feeblemind," "Bingo Slut," and an early, imperfect version of "Dirtnap," the quality of the tape atrocious and having worsened with time.

"What do you think?" he asked, when the tape ended. "Don't you find it amazing that someone so troubled was able to sublimate his emotions into art, that despite his misery he was able to make music the whole world adored, that he took lemons and, as they say, made lemonade?"

The author's son, inexplicably, was unmoved.

"Whatever," he said, and left the room.

Calliope's quest for her father's remains has been the subject of an astonishing range of misinterpretation and distortion. For lack of better insight, many theorists settle for a thin psychological explanation: Her own fame, according to this rationale, was so sudden and traumatizing, bearing such disturbing parallels to her father's—the rapid rise, a reputation based on a small body of work, the misunderstandings between Calliope and the press, the unrelenting pressure to give of herself to her fans as candidly and absolutely as she did in her poetry—that she became obsessed with her father's career as the paradigm of what not to do. Every detail of his life would have taken on Delphic importance to the confused young poet; his body became a symbol, a fetish. Her search, then, as transference and synecdoche, referring, in the end, only to herself.*

Others resort to the cliché of psychosexual drama: The daughter must culminate her rivalry with, and attempts at separation from, her mother by achieving a sexual victory over the mother, the body as trophy, an interpretation so trite as to require little attention here. Not surprisingly, many of these so-called Freudian critics are the same who insist—taking cues from such poems as "Electra Returns to Azalea Path," "310," et al.—that this sexual victory had *already* been achieved, before Brandt's death.[†]

Few have seen Calliope's quest as a literal one, i.e., as a need to find her way through the labyrinth of rumor, doubt, memory, and myth, to the Minotaur himself. Certainly there was no shortage of mysteries, no dearth of crackpot theories, tales of foul play, conspiracy, alien abduction and the like—all easily dismissed by the adult mind, but not so the bereft, adoring child. Here we might sympathize with Penelope's draconian measures,[‡] but the parental dike could hold back the waters only temporarily—once she entered the world, Calliope would have been left treading water in a raging flood. Her own statements to that effect have often been deemed irrelevant—a frustrating state of affairs bemoaned in the poem "Death of the Author." But interviews with classmates, confidantes, and Dr. Breve—not to mention Occam's razor—would seem to favor this simplest explanation: that her search began earlier than previously believed, and was catalyzed by a number of events during her last year at the Arts Academy.

The years Calliope spent at Mountaintop Arts were mostly happy ones, despite the trials and emotional upheavals of an ordinary teenager. She was a good student; her academic transcripts indicate that she received A's

---

*For the most convincing example of this, cf. Sandra M. Gilbert, *Ashes, Ashes, We All Fall Down* (Harvard University Press, 200_).
[†]Kristof Meersch's article, "Whither the Phallus: Genital Fixation in the Morath Canon" (*Revue Canadienne de Psychanalyse* 12: 200_), should suffice to demonstrate the inanity of this approach.
[‡]Esperanza Medina Blumstein recalls the following incident: "She was asking about the book, the Rimbaud from Señor Brandt's nightstand. Nobody have seen this since he dies. Señora Penny is looking for it for years, she think it was stolen. Some people think, you know, *he took it with him* . . . But when Calliope asks, Where is the book?, Señora is so angry she locks Calliope in the pool shed until she will say there is no such poem as 'A Season in Hell,' until she admits she makes this up just to be troublesome."

and B's in all of her classes, with the exception of Ceramics, which she failed year after year until finally the exasperated administration bent the rules and allowed her to fulfill the requirement by writing a sequence of poems about ceramics.* (This touched off a certain amount of resentment among the ceramists, and prompted her roommate, Rhoda Lubinski, to inquire as to whether she might fulfill her creative writing requirement by "throwing pots about poems.")

Her SAT scores were excellent and would likely have earned her admission to the undergraduate institution of her choice, a fact lamented repeatedly by Marshall Vaughn, the director of creative writing, during their discussions regarding Calliope's decision to go straight to graduate school.

By this time, Calliope's work had begun to appear in small literary journals, and in the fall of her senior year "Sunday on Suicide Row" was accepted by the *Paris Review.* It would be her most visible publication since "I Shall Not Soon Forget . . ." Word of the acceptance at *Paris,* and at the University of California, Irvine's prestigious MFA program, spread quickly through the tiny academy. Vaughn recalls the mood in his Honors Poetry seminar during her final semester:

"There was the sense of greatness among us. This is the students' sense, of course, of which I speak, not my own. The sense, if 'sense' is the proper word—delusion, perhaps? absurd, onanistic wish fulfillment, perhaps?—of a wondrous birth in process. The others shrank next to it. The girls, the young poetesses, were rendered mute, lost confidence in their own work. They flocked to her like handmaidens. If I, or anyone else, suggested a flaw in her poetry, they sprang furiously to her defense. The boys—well, you can imagine how she appeared to them: dangerous, even terrifying. I doubt there was one of them who didn't wake sweating in the night, trembling with fear and desire. This despite her obvious lack of what men of my generation might call 'physical charms.'

"I, of course, was not so impressed," Vaughn goes on. "I had the gravest reservations."

---

*Though none of the poems from the "Clay Sequence" was ever published, "Earthenware Head in the Oven" borrows lines and images from several of those earlier pieces.

In May of that year, only weeks before she was to give her Senior Reading, Vaughn wrote Calliope a long letter regarding what he viewed as potentially fatal limitations in her poetry and troubling ethics in her overall approach to art.

"I am overcome with misgivings for the progress of your verse—and, dare I say it, for your future as an emotional being in a world which, as you shall soon learn, is not as dedicated to your success as we at Mountaintop have endeavoured to be," he began, in a letter which scholars have variously praised for its disinterested kindness and condemned as an assault on a young poet's independence.

There are many worlds, Miss Morath, many subjects for a poem— the beauty of a flower, which clings to life through the long winter; the vulnerability in the eyes of a child [. . .] The death of a loved one—however tragic, however shocking—is, in the end, an inescapably personal affair [. . .] You witnessed a terrible spectacle, I don't deny it, and something no doubt to you a great deal more than spectacle; but I ask you to see that *as verse* it can be only that: spectacle. If you are ever to be more than a novelty, you must dive deep within yourself and find something other than your father to interest and challenge you as an artist [. . .] I say these things as one who considers himself a mentor, a kindly uncle perhaps, who dreams only of your fulfillment; one who stands willing to take you by the hand in whatever capacity is desired.

Calliope took it as something else, however, and Vaughn could not possibly have expected the swiftness and fury of her reaction. For three nights she stayed awake composing a response, brewing pot after pot of ginseng tea and blasting the Terrible Children CD box set (still unreleased) into the chilly alpine night. One can only imagine the shock the eighty-one-year-old Vaughn experienced when "For Marshall, Who Implores Me to Dive Deeper" was distributed to the workshop. Though many critics find it to be a penetrating rumination on the purpose of art and the translatability of experience, a provocative glimpse of Calliope's adult voice, the poem's verbal aggression and sexual suggestiveness horrified the older poet and scandalized the school's administration. It was only thanks to Penelope's intervention that Calliope was not expelled as a result. One strains to imagine her classmates' expressions as she read the last stanza aloud, the wheelchair-bound teacher's face draining of color:

> If you won't be fulfilled by verse alone
> Let my bloodstain represent that other wound,
> that opening—your fantasy of depth.
> Unless—
> unless you wish to take me by the hand,
> dive deeper and deeper, your legs grown strong again,
> our lithe young bodies mingling in the sand
> at the bottom, the sand, the bottom,
> deeper and deeper—O Uncle! O Uncle!—
> until our cries awake us:
> my bedroom, your bedroom,
> my fulfillment, yours.

Readers can certainly see how incidents such as this quickly gave rise to stories about Calliope's sexual voraciousness. Of course it was none other than Rhoda Lubinski who would first leak the story of the poet's weekends at Connor Feingold's Malibu home to the *OC Weekly*—though, as with everything that can be sourced to Ms. Lubinski, and the inestimable number of things that cannot, it is nearly impossible to determine whether this leakage is best understood as the vindictive act of a close friend nursing a simmering envy and her own artistic frustrations, or as a carefully wrought addition to the myth, an act of marketing brilliance of the highest order. (It is just this insolubility—or, as Ms. Lubinski famously terms it in her seminars, "Scambiguity"—which has made her the most highly paid publicist in the entertainment industry; at the same time, it rather complicates the enterprise of ascertaining the truth in such matters, as no statement by Ms. Lubinski in any context can be determined, beyond a doubt, to be unmotivated.)

Despite the many rumors, and the graphic imagery in much of her poetry, Calliope herself almost never discussed the details of her romantic résumé, responding to questions in a prickly manner which fans and critics, accustomed to the candor of her poems, often mistook for coyness.

Terry Gross was perhaps the first interviewer to learn better; in a 200_ interview on *Fresh Air*, Calliope set off an avalanche of speculation by making reference to a "mountaintop monk," whom she refused to identify by name.

"He is my equivalent," she declared, "my negative image, the proton to my Electra [*sic*]." Though by then an experienced interviewee, Calliope later claimed to have been surprised and offended by a question about her "normal teenage interest in the opposite sex." When Ms. Gross pressed her to talk about the relationship, or even to give the man's name, Calliope bristled, scolding her for her nosiness and inquiring as to the last time Gross, herself, had "gotten laid."

"If you can't understand that some things are unspeakable, that some things are *sacred*," she said icily, "then it's no wonder you spend your life behind a microphone—which, by the way, can you say, 'big fat phallic symbol'?"*

It appears Calliope first encountered this "mountaintop monk" during one of her long walks in the woods surrounding the academy. In winter months, in particular, she liked to set out before dawn, trudging through snow and frost and clearings carpeted with pine needles, collecting and focusing her thoughts in anticipation of the strenuous morning of poetry ahead. Her meanderings often ended at the river gorge, a half-mile stretch at which Inyo Creek burrows deeply into the igneous rock, creating a descending stairway of shallow canyons and waterfalls. The region's chronic droughts had caused the waters to recede over time, leaving in one spot a large, exposed shelf of gleaming white rock presided over by ponderosa pines, an area known at the academy as the Terrace, serving in summer as the students' prime suntanning and swimming locale, and year-round as the rendezvous of choice for nocturnal psilocybin research.

Sufficiently invigorated by her walk, Calliope sat on the Terrace and took notes for an hour or more, bundled in an army-surplus parka, warming herself from a thermos of hot tea. Winter days in the high sierra were brilliant and clear, the sun refracting sharply off the icy creek and the white

---

*When reporters first inquired at the Mountaintop Zen Center, the roshi stood in the entrance to the *zendo,* a dozen meditating students visible behind him, and assured them, "There is no one here."

rock. On this morning, Calliope found herself too restless to work, perhaps irritated by the glare, or distracted by the anxiety of awaiting a decision from Irvine. Ignoring the school's warnings about the instability of the ice, she set out to cross the creek. She glided across its surface, the weak ice groaning, the water beneath it rushing and careening down through the canyons as though speeding to a destiny which could only be found at lower altitude. When she had gained the opposite bank, she climbed the steep slope, grasping for exposed roots and stones, hauling herself gradually to a plateau from which she could see the bright gash of the river, the Arts Academy, and the town of Mountaintop and, beyond those, the whole of the San Jacinto range and the deserts laid out below. Perhaps she stopped a while to ponder her imminent departure from this peaceful, nurturing place, all the unknowns of her future and her past, before pushing farther into the woods than she had gone before.

She likely did not know that Inyo Creek serves as the property line between the Arts Academy and Mountaintop Zen Center. Eventually she entered a large clearing, a field sifted with snow and ringed by tall trees. The frozen ground crunched under her feet and a hawk circled above, sunlight stunning the scene. In the center of the clearing was a large object, and as she came closer it revealed itself to be a box of some kind, perhaps four feet tall and half that in width and depth, wrapped in shiny black building paper. The whole assembly was bound with string like a giant gift and sat a few inches off the ground on slats of wood, the snow at its base spattered a sickly brownish yellow. As she stood contemplating this mystery, she became aware of a strange sensation—not a sound, precisely, but the feeling of sound rumbling and tickling in her belly, the kind of imperceptibly low hum one might associate with electrical fields or geologic events. She wondered whether the box weren't some kind of transformer or node in the power grid, but there were no cables of any kind, nothing leading in or out. In the center of all that vivid sunlight, the box stood alone.

"Touch it," said a voice behind her, and Calliope spun to find a man grinning at her. With the sun haloing behind him, she had to shift her head to make out his features: bushy eyebrows and dark eyes, a nose as jagged and protuberant as his Adam's apple. He wore a heavy sweater and a knit watchman's cap from under which sprang unruly curls of dark hair. "They won't even notice you," he said. "They're just trying to survive."

Calliope shielded her eyes against the white light, then turned back to the puzzling box. The tickling sound rose in her throat like a flavor; she found herself simultaneously wanting to touch the strange object and afraid to do so, as though performing this small act would constitute the irreversible crossing of a threshold.

"Permit me to present a miniature state," said the young man. She could feel his humid breath on her ears, as he took her wrists and pressed her hands to the top of the box. "I'll tell of its fierce-hearted leaders, their pursuits and manners . . . ," he went on, quoting Virgil's fourth *Georgic* (or misquoting, rather), which Calliope had memorized years earlier, during her work with neoclassicist deirdre v. deirdre. As her palms flattened against the rough paper, the humming in her belly doubled in strength, the energy inside the box passing into her body—and, as though this energy contained its own knowledge, she understood.

"And their high passions?" she responded. She could feel but not see the man smile behind her. "What of their desperate encounters?"

"Hard to say," he whispered, his mouth at the nape of her neck. "It didn't go so well for Eurydice."

" 'The pleasure of sex, its annihilating sweetness?' " Calliope breathed, hands pressed to the beehive, the dazzling sky, the wide field and the trees beyond, growing dark.

"These mean nothing to them."

" 'They say that a spirit fills earth and sky and sea. That man and his fellow-creatures take from it the stuff of life.' "

He shuddered, held her more tightly. "There is no death, even when the body fails."

For several minutes they stood, his arms around her, hands flattened over hers, their eyes closed as they absorbed the low, stupefied purr of the wintering bees. Calliope would later write in her journal that she found it hard to breathe, that she had the sense she was "staring directly into the mouth of Hades, holding between my hands this death-in-life. Like Orpheus, so close to attaining his object, I dared not turn around."

Her account of the meeting becomes tantalizingly vague from this point, and as readers are aware (and as Terry Gross learned at some cost), she never spoke the young man's name in public. In a later interview with *Seventeen*'s Debi Dennison, Calliope claimed that the young man then took a tin from inside his sweater and produced a large marijuana cigarette, which he lit and offered to her.

> "You're that famous poet," he said, the tasty sizzle of the joint mixing with the humming of the bees, which was so loud that Calliope swatted the air near her ears. The sound of his voice was the powerful seduction she'd dreamed of her whole life; his animal masculinity radiated like hot gravity itself.
>
> "And who are you?" stammered Calliope.
>
> "Names are like boxes," he said, his eyes misting over, smoky breath mingling between them. He motioned with his eyebrows to the buzzing black beehive. "They keep everything locked inside. Is that really what you want?"
>
> "Heavens, no. Then I wouldn't get to see it," replied our heroine, giving as good as she got and ready to give more.*

The article, like so much of what has previously been written, is of limited value in understanding the true Calliope. From the overly romanticized, purple descriptions that follow—"heaving breast" and "savage embrace" and such—one can't avoid the conclusion that our clever young poet, coached by her brilliant publicist, was inventing from whole cloth just the kind of story that would interest readers of *Seventeen*.

"Did you know that male bees have the largest genitalia, proportional to their body size, of any animal on earth?" the stranger asks, at which point a sophisticated reader can do nothing other than close the wretched periodical and fling it as far as the confines of his office allow.

Thus, despite the Beekeeper's recent claims, the widely held myth that Calliope lost her virginity on an icy morning in the woods of San Jacinto, a colony of wintering bees muttering unintelligibly nearby, must be regarded as precisely that: a myth.

---

*"Stopping by Woods on a Snowy Morning," *Seventeen*, June 200_.

The literary world, however—if not the world of scandal sheets and pitiful voyeurs—was most certainly blessed that morning. As nearly all scholars agree, "The Bird and the Bees" is Calliope's first great poem, and to read its intricate cinquains—as well as the stanzas of the other three poems* in the cycle she entitled "HymenOpera" (a pun on *Hymenoptera,* the scientific classification for the order of honeybees)—is to hear the voice of the adult Calliope, the voice of a poet who had found her true and ultimate subject: herself.

Calliope and the Beekeeper continued to see each other throughout the winter and spring—her last in Mountaintop—meeting occasionally at the clearing or the Terrace, perhaps sharing an early morning cup of tea while discussing poetry or making the rounds of the hives scattered over the Zen Center's property. Readers should treat with skepticism Rhoda's claims that he was a frequent overnight guest at the cottage she shared with Calliope (their third roommate, a flautist from Denver named LaTonya Hammond, had sued the academy for a change of residence the previous year), and that she was often forced into "sexile"—the nocturnal projections of an adolescent rival, like the cynical exaggerations of a publicist, frankly are not credible.

By all accounts it was a happy period for Calliope. In May, however, as a glorious spring was arriving, the Beekeeper abruptly broke off contact. In a curt note, he explained that it was time to apply himself to his studies, to move to the next level of Zen devotion. He was soon to be ordained as a Buddhist monk, to take his place as the roshi's "dharma heir"—physical relationships could serve only as distraction, an unnecessary tie to the illusory world.

"I must preserve the essential parts of myself for this journey into emptiness," he wrote, "a journey I must make untainted by impure attachment." In preparation for ordination, he planned to embark upon a thirty-day fast, the first of many, the increasing severity of which would later wreak such havoc in Calliope's life. "I cannot eat," he informed her. "Nor can I be eaten."

According to Rhoda, Calliope's reaction was almost frighteningly

---

*Four, if one includes the disputed elegy "In Clover."

muted. Rather than an emotional outburst, the tears and moans and girl-ish embraces one would expect from such a first jilting, Calliope stood in the cottage's small living room and read the note several times, nodding silently, before tearing it to pieces, which she put in her mouth and swallowed. Then she picked up her pen and got back to work.

The storied relationship between Calliope and the Beekeeper has received much recent scrutiny, particularly in the wake of the disaster in Portland. What had not been pieced together until now, however, is the role he played in the uproar at Calliope's Senior Reading. Anticipation for the event had run high throughout the Mountaintop spring, among students, faculty, and administration alike, all eager to hear the rising star read her work. In tacit acknowledgment of Calliope's growing renown, the decision was taken to hold the event outdoors, on the main lawn of the campus, rather than in a recital room as was customary; even so, the hundred or so chairs arranged on the grass before the lectern indicate that the school was in no way expecting the hordes who began camping out at 7:00 A.M. for the noon reading, nor the minor traffic jam that snarled Mountaintop's main road and the entrance to the Academy throughout the morning. Music fans, students of poetry, Terrible Children hangers-on from all over Southern California made their way to Mountaintop; the press turned out from all corners, including one bewildered fellow from a newspaper in Fiji. Had she not had the foresight to charter a helicopter from Rancho Santa Fe to Mountaintop, the poet's mother might not have made the reading at all.

The account by Skip Cárdenas, the former *L.A. Weekly* photo intern who had recently been named entertainment editor, provides the crucial details so long overlooked by the self-proclaimed luminaries of Morath Studies:

"I got there around eight in the morning, and got one of the last chairs, all the way in the back. You can't imagine what I had to do to hold on to it! I hadn't seen her since that Christmas morning—some photos, maybe—but I wanted to see her in person, see what she'd become. I felt connected to her.

"All along there was this *feeling* in the crowd, this bottled-up energy. She was late for the reading—nobody knew where she was, everybody watching all the buildings. Finally, after twenty minutes, she comes out of a maintenance shed and walks up to the front wearing a long red dress, and something about the way she walked . . . You've got to understand, she's never been a typical beauty or anything—there's that birthmark, and that weird chin, something just not symmetrical about her face. But I've never seen anyone seduce a crowd like that—especially not an eighteen-year-old girl. I guess I should say 'woman'—because that's definitely what she was."

Calliope began the reading as she would begin all readings after: with a recitation of "I Shall Not Soon Forget the Day He Died," the sonnet she had written five years earlier, with which the majority of those present were undoubtedly familiar. It was to become her signature poem, and on this spring morning she read it flawlessly, her voice carrying over the crowd and into the forest as the reporters held recorders and boom mikes forward to capture the sound and Calliope's mother, flanked by bodyguards, beamed from her seat in the front row. By the third quatrain, many had been moved to tears, and just as many were flushed with that unique mixture of tenderness, envy, and lust that Calliope always inspired, a rising tension among those gathered which only grew more tumescent as the air rang with the sonnet's powerful final couplet:

> Eli, eli, lama sabacthani?
> Behold thy daughter, quench her thirst for thee.

As the last echoes dissolved into the trees, Calliope held the audience in a triumphant stare, the only sounds the twittering of birds, the uncomfortable squeaks of the folding chairs. She shifted her papers, preparing to read the next poem; it was a new piece, unknown to her workshop, announced by the poet in a voice of steely dignity:

"'Impure Attachment.'"

She looked out at the crowd, making eye contact with each person in the front row. Before she could utter the first line, a voice rose from the back of the lawn.

"There is no death!"

Calliope, whose lectern was facing into the sun, peered forward to look for the speaker, and several hundred faces, cassette recorders, boom mikes, and cameras swiveled madly, trying to locate the source.

"There is only birth and rebirth!" the voice called again as the murmurs rose in the crowd and the spectators stood, further obscuring Calliope's view. The poet moved to the side of the lectern, struggling to see between the moving bodies. A chain reaction had begun, the cryptic cry had touched a nerve in those present, some of whom responded with the enthusiasm of those long kept silent.

"It's true! Brandt's not dead," a female voice cried. "He's running guns in Africa!"

"It was all a big stunt—it's just publicity!" a young painter shouted.

Gasps and groans mingled with the outrageous claims as Calliope kept looking for the source of the interruption. Penelope sprang from her chair and scowled at the crowd.

"It's a cover-up, Calliope! You know he's alive!"

"He was trying to get a divorce! He was trying to get away from Penny!" came another voice, at which Penelope climbed over her chair, leaving her two bodyguards to scramble after her, the current of unrest quickly growing into a wave of some size and force, a wave which began to push bodies and recording equipment backward, chairs toppling, reporters struggling to protect their notes and their microphones as well as to find the individual who had provoked the disturbance.

"My cousin saw him last year in Vancouver!" someone said.

"He was only paralyzed! They've got him on life support in Paris!"

"No, man—it wasn't even his body! He's in Argentina with a new family!"

"She killed him!" cried one of the music teachers. "Penelope killed her husband!"

Reportage of the melee that followed focused on Penny Power: how she climbed over chairs and fallen bodies, swinging her arms and slashing her fingernails in every direction, makeup smeared over her face, her bodyguards caught in the impossible position of trying to protect her from the crowd while, more vitally, protecting the crowd from her; how the Mountaintop sheriff's deputies, all three of whom had been present not in a professional capacity but out of a desire to hear the reading, were forced to employ pepper spray to break up the fracas; Penelope's later claims that the uproar had been staged either by jealous classmates or, perhaps, by

members of a rival rock group in an attempt to cast a shadow on the upcoming release of the Fuck Finn retrospective; the flurry of lawsuits, in
both directions, which are largely unresolved to this day. And few, of
course, can forget the photograph the world saw the next morning: the
furious mother captured mid-leap, arms spread wide and mouth contorted
into a grimace as she is frozen above the terrified crowd.

But Skip Cárdenas kept his eye on the real story—and though he was
not able to rescue his camera from the many stampeding feet, a careful examination of his notes yields the identity of the interloper. Cárdenas recalls
watching Calliope move slowly through the crowd, past classmates, professors, and reporters, the din behind her growing as she doggedly made
her way to the back of the lawn in pursuit of a receding figure. Skip followed her into the trees, the hem of her dress fluttering as she caught up
to the departing figure and spun him by the shoulder, and though in the
next second a sheriff's deputy sprayed Mace into his eyes (and here the
notes become somewhat less legible) Skip's journalistic instincts were keen
enough to note every feature of Calliope's companion—his shaven head,
his hooked nose and large Adam's apple, the long black robes he had gathered in his flight—as well as the terrifying look on the poet's face as she
kissed him fiercely, a look Skip describes as that of "a woman who has seen
her lover rise from the dead."

4. HIDEOUS PAGES

ONCE, IF I REMEMBER WELL, *my life was a feast where all hearts opened and all wines flowed.*

Do I have to spell it out for you? Don't you read *Newsweek*?

O my anguished forebear—did he not have a fabulous and heroic youth? Did he not partake of the promised feasts, did he not see magnificent cities? Having gained the throne did he not pay with his life—his body torn to bits and boiled, all that trouble and toil only to wind up a cheap tourist's *prix fixe*?

"Once, if I remember well . . . ," he scrawled on a hellish morning, and in the sidebar one Ph.D. opined "Dementia!" and another, "Amnesia! Possibly due to traumatically or chemically induced cerebral lesion!"—because apparently no one bothered to source it, not one person on that highly respected editorial staff recognized the lines. Should he have left them footnotes, left an index to a suicide?

"Pagan blood returns—I want to be ugly as a mongol," he wrote—and the hacks cackled "Dissociative disorder! Signs of early stage schizophrenia, body dysmorphic delusions, as specified in DSM-IV!"—the whole shebang laid out tastefully on pages thirty-two and -three, graphic of a torn sheet of yellow notebook paper sprawling across the gutter, singe marks at the edges (for reasons unclear to me). A ghoulish picture of my father from an early show at CBGB: hair dyed black, white contact lenses, dark bags under his eyes, and fake blood streaked on his wrists. It was Halloween night and he dressed up as Death: a little fun, a little showbiz, a thrill for the kids.

But what did the caption say? *Brandt Morath.* Nothing more.

And O did they have a field day with the last line! They saw it as his parting shot, his coup de grâce, his kiss-off; never mind that it was written 120 years earlier. That didn't stop the critics and the theorists, the sociologists and the clothing designers from taking up his last rallying cry, it didn't stop the biographers from turning it into his anthem, his *memento mori,* didn't stop Larry King from splashing it across the marquee while he discussed the rising generation with Billy Graham and Sting.

"Life is a farce we all have to lead," my father wrote, a topic he knew something about. But how strangely it read in those slick pages, how different from the singsong refrain he trilled walking around the house in pajamas, or helping me dig a hole at the beach.

"Life is a farce / We all have to lead—" He'd raise his eyebrows and tilt his head clownlike, and a certain tousle-haired toddler would clap her hands and squeal at his funny, broken voice—chanting over and over, *Life is a farce,* a descending little melody, *we all have to lead,* while Mother sat and smoked in her beach chair, her eyes hidden behind sunglasses, her lips curled indulgently. It was a game, a way to catch a baby's attention, our own little "Row Your Boat"—not the slogan of disgust and defeat they turned it into, my sweet father's face forever after under the sign of revulsion, of surrender.

My dear worried mother, how she tried to protect me, to shield me from such things—as if I weren't a walking billboard, my father's will and testament tattooed across my trachea. Even later, when I'd woken, she brooked no argument, no discussion: We did not speak of it, we passed over it in silence.

"What's down those stairs?" I'd ask, while she stood at the stove frying my egg.

"What's that, Birdie?"

"There's a door," I said, with the vague sense that I'd asked it before. Standing in that hallway I felt cold, queasy; something was calling to me, something else telling me: *Run!*

"There's no door, honey."

The shaking would start in my little right toe, wash over my ankles and up to my knees. Soon I was leaning against the wall, my teeth starting to chatter, I found it hard to breathe.

"Are you okay, Birdie?" My mother would pull herself away from the stove and rush to my side, throw an arm around me and lead me upstairs to bed. "You're so sensitive, so imaginative," she said, smoothing my forehead, drying my tears. "I worry about you, Calliope. I worry what the world will do to you."

"What's down those stairs," I'd mutter, lying back on the pillows, my certainty starting to fade. *Was* there a door? Had I *really* seen it? But that would mean my mother was lying. It would mean she was nuts. "Is Daddy down there?"

"Shhh," she whispered, closing her eyes. She'd smile then, kiss me— nothing could touch us, nothing in our little world was amiss. *"Hush little baby, don't say a word,"* my mother sang—not the rasp from her records but the sweet mewl of a kitten, the close croon of a lover—*"Mama's gonna care for her beautiful Bird. And if that beautiful Bird don't weep, Daddy's gonna visit her while she sleeps . . ."* And what drowsiness came for me then, world shrinking around my mother's face, arms all around me—release.

There was no note, no body, no grave. That morning had never happened—my father vanished into the air, swallowed up by the world that wanted him so. Once a brave giant, he was now simply absent: abracadabra—*persona non presto.*

So I didn't know what they'd done to him until much later, until I found that old *Newsweek* buried in a drawer of letters and contracts. Nine years old, I sat on the floor of my mother's bedroom and stared at the pages, this facsimile of his words, my father's torment in ten-point type, laid bare for interpretation by strangers and experts who'd never read a poem in their lives, would-be prophets telling the new Gospel of Brandt: the story of a loser, an addict, a weakling. The desert he wandered was all in his mind, his Word was incoherent, his sacrifice meaningless.

But I'll tell you the truth, my insatiable friend: My father was a genius.

And if, in the end, he was brought low by his own bad blood, if there was something within him (or without him: some small replica, beggar of his breadcrumbs, heir to his X), some fatal gene waiting to be expressed, a ticking bomb awaiting the right moment to *tock* . . . well, let that not conceal what else he was, let's not confine him to past imperfect tense—let it not stop us from contemplating undazed the extent of his innocence.

"If I ever find the son of a bitch who gave it to them, I'll rip him a new asshole wide enough to drive a truck through."

I turned guiltily to find my mother standing in the doorway of her bedroom, frowning at me where I sat on the floor amid a scatter of her papers, the forbidden magazine in my lap.

She crossed her arms and leaned against the doorframe, eyes boring into my skull. My mouth hung open as I stared at my lap—my father's last words, twisted and filtered, coming to me across five years, a message in a bottle, a scratchy old LP. I tried to look up, to meet her gaze. But that was something I was never good at.

"What did you expect me to do?" she said. "Should I have made you a framed copy? Read it to you like a goddamned bedtime story?"

It was hard to breathe, all the air in the room flowing, as always, toward my mother. I had that hot, sharp feeling under my jawbone—but I knew crying would only make her turn away in disgust. For a moment, sitting on the floor with my father's splashy obituary, I could feel it again: the glass wall behind my eyes, the hard fist gripping my throat, the panicky paralysis that had kept me quiet for three years, throttled every word in its cradle.

"Don't think I didn't try to find out," my mother said. "I had the servants lined up on the driveway. I demanded their bank statements. Billy, Connor, Talia—no one would admit it. I used to think it was one of the goddamned monks—standing around with their saffron and their *Om mani padme hum*. But how do you accuse a Buddhist of selling your husband's suicide note? What was I supposed to do?"

I was starting to shiver, my lips in a pout. "Mommy," I wanted to say, but the invisible fist had closed tight. She stared at me, in one hand the ubiquitous G&T, faint rattle of ice trembling in a glass. I knew then what an effort she was making not to look at what I held in my lap. I clenched my teeth, but one tear leaked out; I wanted to crawl to her feet, beg her not to walk away, but I knew that would only make it worse. So I squeezed the shiny magazine, held it over my head, and shook it at her. Sobbing, I brandished his picture, his words—the words of a long-dead vagrant.

She could not help but look. Her eyes fell across the page and softened, glazing over. She stared at the ceiling and bit her lip, but it was no use. Her face squeezed on itself and she fell to her knees, the drink spilling onto the carpet.

"Oh, baby," she wept, throwing her arms around me. "I didn't know what to do. Can you understand?" Her voice rising and rising, she hugged me too hard, lay on the floor with her head in my lap, mascara smearing across the pages.

"I'm such a fuckup," she whimpered against my knee. "Please forgive me—I'm sorry your mother's such a fuckup." She gripped my waist, nose running over the magazine, my knees. "Tell me you forgive me," she bawled. "Tell me it's all right."

I knew what was expected of me. I stroked her henna-streaked hair—my own tears had dried up as soon as hers began—and whispered, "It's okay, Mommy." She curled up and sniffled, pushed her face into my thigh. "I forgive you," I said. I didn't mean it.

She fell still. After a moment she peeked open an eye. "Really?" The magazine crackled under her head, the silent expanse of the house held its breath.

I nodded.

"You love me, Bird?" Slowly she pushed herself up until she was sitting next to me, Alice Cooper streaks down her face, she gripped my shoulders, brought her face close to mine. "You still do?"

I nodded. I still loved her. That was true.

"Am I the best mommy in the world?" she whispered, playing a beloved game of ours. "Am I the best mommy in the whole wide world?" Sitting so close to me, she was all I could see. She was everything left.

So I played my part, gave the answer that was pro forma, that gave me such a thrill. "You're the best mommy I have."

She pursed her lips and nodded, the contract fulfilled. Then she took the magazine from my lap and threw it with a riffle back in the drawer, slammed the drawer shut, and stood over me.

"Good." She straightened her clothes and wiped her nose with the back of her hand. I felt better, warm and calm, as I always did after our confrontations—as though a great nausea had come over me and been expelled. "Then if I ever catch you looking at that again, I'll burn all your books," she said.

I accepted this without objection and watched her turn to the door. I called to her and she looked back with a flat grimace; with her black blouse and smeared face she looked like some kind of vampire.

"Who did it?" I asked.

"Who did what?" my mother said, her veil falling once again.

"Who sent the note to the magazine?"

For a moment I thought she wouldn't answer, that she'd pretend the whole conversation hadn't happened. She let out a breath. "It doesn't really matter, Bird."

"But don't you want to know? What about—"

"I said it doesn't matter!" Her voice rang through the house, seized my throat again. "Look," she said, "just don't pay attention to what you read. Don't think about it. Whoever sent it was in a pretty big hurry, you know? They only sent the juicy stuff."

"I don't understand," I pleaded.

My mother just sighed and disappeared down the hall, left me small and alone on the bedroom floor. A moment later, I heard her humming to herself, the chorus from "Kill the Surfers," and suddenly I knew: There was more.

✫

I should have been a Monk and not a Bird—
I'd tickle the ivories in five-spot clubs and play
my voiceless heart out, never say a word—

I wish I were a potter, not a bard—
I'd plunge my fancy elbow-deep in clay,
mute earth between my hands turning to shards—

How nice to be a you and not a me—
to live this distant life and never say
what's on my mind. At last, I might be free.

For once I was the daughter of a god.
He ruled my heart—until the silent day
I called to him, I broke the spell he'd laid

upon us all. Would that he had not heard
my childish whisper, picked up his guitar
and strummed another tortured melody!
O Father, my pretty one, my lightning rod:
Who conducts me now, to whom shall I pray?

✶

Before there was Terrible Children, Global Sensation, Purveyors of the
New Punk, Saviors of Our Souls, Billions and Billions Served (and it was
for them, of course, that the term "Titanium Album" was coined); before
there were world tours and limos, halls of fame and handshakes with pres-
idents, photo ops and front pages and Rancho Santa Fe mansions; before
there were five-star hotels and fifty-dollar tips and custom DeLoreans and
dealers on speed-dial; before Wal-Mart banned the *Hanged Man* EP and
John Lydon (aka Johnny Rotten) told Kurt Loder, "It's the most bloody
awful thing I've 'eard in fifteen years; makes me want to scratch meself—
if you only buy one record this summer, make sure it's that whatchamacal-
lit, those ugly fucks from San Diego . . ."—before any of that, there was
Terrible Children, four penniless, obnoxious, bedraggled kids from Ocean
Beach (*Ahem,* two slight qualifications: My father, as you know, grew up in-
land, in Santee, ran away to the beach at sixteen, crashing on friends'
couches and, when hospitality was lacking, under the fishing pier; XXX,
still living with his mother, was studying for an MBA) who practiced their
loud, screechy songs in alleys and carports and recently disoccupied apart-
ments; whose first concert—at the ramshackle Arizona Café: a broken
pool table, plugged toilet, three besotted septuagenarians in the audience,
and an Irish bartender named Joe—lasted exactly twelve minutes, the
length of time it took to play the two numbers they'd finished writing and
a ludicrous cover of "Like a Virgin" during which my father repeatedly
smacked himself in the skull with his guitar until he passed out; who hung
around outside the Casbah on weekends and pestered the members of
Rocket From the Crypt and Drive Like Jehu and Pigstick and Fuck Finn as
they exited after the show; who ate Jack In The Box and Dunkin' Donuts
throwaways and drank NyQuil under the fishing pier; who sent off their
demo tape to local indie labels, who promptly returned it as "unlistenable"
not because the music was so bad but because the shoddy dime-store cas-
settes spooled apart and ruined their tape decks; who, in short, were the
kind of no-good, clueless, abrasive, immature, dissolute, unwashed, un-
educated, unlikely, amoral diamonds in the rough that have started every

revolution from Nazareth to North Beach; and who just happened to be led by a skinny blond kid with beautiful blue eyes and a rubber-banded copy of Rimbaud in his pocket, who somehow understood, despite his own colossal sense of failure and even greater sense of the world's stupidity, that everything was going to change, to crumble under a musical tidal wave upon which he—unsteadily, faithlessly, but unflinchingly—would surf, and that this watery cataclysm was the only chance he had to rescue himself from the hell of obscurity and self-hatred and so resolved to ride, ride, ride it to its end because, when you think about it, what else did he have to do?

The big moment came: a long-awaited RATT reunion canceled at the last minute, the Casbah scrambling to fill a Saturday night bill (O Saint Stephen Pearcy, how could you know what your fickleness would wreak!, the widening gyre that started spinning that night, your big-hair-and-leather admirers crestfallen, their brief reign ending as Brandt Morath's magic turned the world 'round and 'round . . .)—and more out of a sense of absurdity, curiosity, Rocket's John Reis said to the promoter, "What about those idiots from OB?"

Are you getting the picture, my flannel-sporting chickadee? Do you draw your breath, mop your brow, sickened by this world's contingency?

She saw him standing there by the pinball machine. She knew he must have been twenty-two or -three. They kissed, he drew blood, and by the end of the night she'd foreseen it all—and next they were moving in together, and then they were with me.

Yeah, me.

That early period, before and after their Tijuana wedding, the first three years of my life, when Fuck Finn and the Kids played six shows a week, their tours expanding up through California to Portland and Seattle, out through Tempe and Durango and Telluride, playing fraternity parties and biker bars and backyard keggers, the billing eventually flipping to reflect the Kids' growing popularity; those years in a tenement on Abbott Street, living next door to runaways crammed eight or more into a studio, tweak dealers, post-traumatic vets, and zoned-out Rastafarians, during which, somehow, they managed to scrape together enough studio time to record a six-song EP—it's all been covered, well enough, by Gina Arnold in *Prelude to a Hanging.* My mother gave me the book for my tenth birth-day. I remember poring over its pages, rifling through it three, four, five times, gobbling up the stories about my parents but also mining its chap-ters ravenously for glimpses of myself, needing to fill in those childish blanks, place myself inside that context from which the rest of the world would never, ever separate me.

But there was so little. I, tiny, play a bit part. Arnold retells the story of my mother's long labor at the Alternative Birthing Center, surrounded by Tibetan midwives, how she'd had to call the police (untrue) to roust my fa-ther from under the fishing pier, where he still slept on occasion, how he'd held his new daughter in his arms and wept, sat against the wall and hunched over my shivering, mucus-soaked body and would not let the midwives take me (true); they had to clean me off as best they could, wrap the both of us in yak-wool blankets, and wait for him to nod off. Arnold tells how they took me on tour, still nursing, left me with groupies in the green room or sitting in the van with Talia Z, how the local punks would crowd around for a look at my blessed face, how Thurston Moore once dandled me on his knee.

But these weren't the things I needed, not the moments I was most desperate to see. I wanted to know what happened, how my father could leave us.

A sequel, Gina, a sequel! My birthright for the sequel!

Soon after, my mother brought me to Michaela. She'd caught me in her drawers again, poring over *Newsweek,* sifting through her lingerie. After that, she knew—I wanted the note, all of it, I would stop at nothing.

For weeks I lay taciturn on Michaela's ridiculous couch, arms crossed over my chest, wishing I could just go home. She scared me, that pinch-faced lady with the thick accent, who I knew was getting paid a lot of money whether I said anything or not. Mondays, Wednesdays, and Fri-days, I found hiding places in our house, I made myself scarce as the hour approached; Esperanza, my trusted one, had to lure me out.

"I'm not going to have one of those damaged children," my mother said, wrestling the steering wheel on the way to Del Mar. Her hair pulled back, no makeup, dressed in a jade sari and sandals (she was in her second

Buddhist phase)—she was still terrifyingly beautiful, my perfect Penelope, my long-grieving tyrant. "You'll sit there until you remember something."

"But she doesn't even say anything," I said.

"I don't care," my mother growled, taking her eyes off the road to fix me where I sat. "Talk about anything you want. Tell her what you ate for breakfast."

And so I did.

I listed for her what I'd eaten that morning, sitting on the terrace, staring out over the trees of Rancho Santa Fe, toward the ocean where I so seldom went anymore. I'd been reading Virginia Woolf, which made me feel very sad; despite the lovely, cool day, the very beginnings of salty California spring breezing over my skin, her words opened a bottomlessness in my soul, an ache that had little to do with Mrs. Ramsay's dinner plans and that stayed with me throughout the morning. I closed my eyes and tried to imagine myself back on the terrace instead of in this metallic witch's office.

Michaela cleared her throat. "Eggs and what?"

"What?" I asked her.

"Do you realize you said, 'eggs and beacon'?"

"No I didn't."

But in the silence that followed, I looked up at my reflection and felt the wind of a long-ago morning whispering through my hair, the weak heat of the sun on my face, and—yes—the touch of his grown-up hand; I remembered a lighthouse, jutting out of a rocky point, a great and spangled sea; I felt my mother holding my other hand as we walked along the promontory, waves cascading against the rocks, drawing back with a rumble, the buzzing behind my ears, sand flies and midges, when he looked down and said something the wind took it away before it was ever mine . . .

"What do you think of when you think of a beacon?" she asked. "What does that word mean to you?"

"Shhhh!" I said, remembering deviled eggs and jelly sandwiches wrapped in paper napkins, packed hastily into a basket, those rare days when they were both awake before dark, my father would stand on the walkway outside our apartment, smoking against the rusty railing, staring out at the ocean; he'd look down so seriously—as though I'd said something of great importance—and say, "Let's have a picnic."

By then he couldn't stand to be in public. Once the *Hanged Man* was out and first local and then national radio put "Dirtnap" into Regular, and then Heavy, and then finally Obsessive-Compulsive Rotation, my father left the apartment less and less. On the rare occasion we would walk into OB— to buy cigarettes or coffee, or to sit in the Arizona Café and have a beer with Joe—people would stop him constantly, ask him to sign their CDs, or their T-shirts, or their breasts. They mobbed around him in front of the tattoo parlor, jockeying knees pushing me away as they herded him against the wall—until finally he snatched his little girl off the concrete and hurried home to lock himself in the bedroom with his guitar for the rest of the day.

And the beach, that lovely and constant siren that had called to him, at sixteen, drawn him from his desert home; that magical place where, as he sang in "Kill the Surfers," "Going out with the tide / absolution is mine"?

Forget about it. Only under the fishing pier—O hangout of hungry hippies; O dirty redoubt of the paranoid, the spastic, the spaced; O gracious giver of greasy anonymity!—could my forsaken merman contemplate the ocean unmolested.

But this day he wanted a picnic. We drove to Cabrillo Monument, the tip of the peninsula just a few miles past Ocean Beach. In the parking lot, strolling retirees and Japanese tourists watched us with sneers and shakes of the head—Disgusting freaks!, they seemed to say, glancing at my parents' ripped clothes, their stringy hair, the innocent child they had no business raising. My parents loved getting these looks—they competed with each other for the most obnoxious response, whether sticking their tongues out, or scratching their groins, or squatting down and leaping around shrieking like a crazed monkey—my favorite, of course!

("Why was the 'crazed monkey' your favorite?" asks Michaela. "How did that make you feel?")

We walked to the end of the land—wild Pacific crashing just below, the chilly tingle of spray. *"At the top of my game, strike a bargain with shame . . . ,"* my father hummed under his breath, the chorus from "Feeblemind," the Kids' latest hit.

"See?" my mother said to no one in particular. "It's not so bad."

She spread a blanket and lay in the sun, scrunched the bottom half of her T-shirt under her bra, took off her jeans, and stretched her long legs. My father hoisted me on his shoulders and picked his way down to the waterline, to a small eddying pool where the water sat shivering and clear over pebbles and jagged slabs. Barefoot, he stood ankle-deep in the ocean, both of us shielding our eyes against the glare. "Ahoy there, Birdie, trim the mainsail and full speed ahead till mornin'," he said, and I said, "Aye aye, Daddy!" He shook me gently by the knees, rocked me like a mast in a storm. The sun and the air, my body pressed firmly to my father's, the rhythmic sound of the ocean lapping the rocks along the promontory—how to describe how I felt at that moment: so complete, integrated with the world around me, a world of which Calliope was an undifferentiated aspect. Past the horizon lay only a warm and joyous eternity. He'd be leaving for Japan soon, but I didn't care—I'd never be without him, any more than a wave could be without water.

"What's that, Daddy?"

He put me down on the sand and I held to his pants as we looked at a strange object bobbling against the rocks. It was a wooden doll—a purple-painted totem in the shape of a walrus, floating face up as though discarded by a passing ship or a child in some distant land. Sea-worn in places, one big tusk snapped off; we stood and stared at this gift the sea had offered up. And that's when I noticed our reflections: one, two, three—Daddy, walrus, Calliope, faces staring back from the clear pool, shuddering and dissolving and coming together again. Slowly it dawned on me—whoever had lost this ugly toy was someone I knew nothing about, who knew nothing about me. We were different, separate—even my father, whose body I had been all but attached to a moment ago, his face swam apart from mine, I looked from his reflection to my own, and the very act of having to move my eyes, of not being able to see *him* and *me* at the same time, of realizing that my mother was somewhere else entirely, that at that very moment I didn't know what she was doing, nor she I, that there was no guarantee even that she would still be there when we returned . . . As all these thoughts moved through my young mind this hideous purple *thing* was staring up at me, dispassionate, dipping in the water and leering half-tusked as though to say, "It's all over, Calliope, your beautiful idyll. From this moment, life will be episodic and solitary, your separateness will lock you into yourself—like a prisoner in a gulag gouging the walls with a spoon, you'll have only the dull utensil of language to try to scrape your way out."

"Goo goo g'joob," my father said. I looked up at him, and he must have seen the panic rising in my face. "What's up, Birdie? It's just a toy." He bent to pick it up and I started to cry—first a low sniffle and then, as he crouched and held it out to me, a shaky wail, growing louder against the gentle throbbing of the ocean.

"Don't be silly," he said, scooping my struggling form with his other arm and climbing back toward my mother. I screamed and pounded against his hip, his buttocks, but he just squeezed me tighter and sang, "I am the Eggman . . . I am the Eggman . . ."

My mother sat up at the sound of my screams, as my father deposited me on the blanket.

"Look what the Bird found." He handed the walrus to her.

"Throw it away! I don't like it!" I cried. She squinted at me and at the waterlogged wooden walrus.

"What's the matter, baby?" she said.

"Throw it away!" She cocked an eyebrow at my father, who shrugged and lay back on the blanket, flipping his sunglasses over his eyes.

"I am he as you are he as you are me as we are all together . . . ," he chanted, and though his singing could calm me out of most any tantrum, by now I was near hysteria, choking on my own sobs and pointing at the wooden walrus.

"Brandt, get rid of it. It's scaring her," Mother said. My cries were loud enough to attract the attention of an elderly couple, reading a nearby bulletin board describing Cabrillo's discovery of the West Coast.

"I'm crying . . . I'm cryyyying . . ." He propped himself up on an elbow. "Bullshit." He took the doll back. "It's just a doll. See, Bird? It's a toy." He tried to hand it to me, but I hid behind my mother and kept screaming. The old couple shook their heads, the woman muttered something to the man, who looked around for someone to notify.

"Dammit, Brandt. Just throw the fucking thing out. What are you trying to do?" Mother was watching the old couple out of the corner of her eye. She detested people looking at her as though she were a bad mother. Sensitized by the constant questions she got on tour—once, in Salt Lake City, a team of social workers knocked on the door of the motel and took pictures of a trash can overflowing with diapers, of spilled ashtrays, a suspiciously smeared mirror lying on the table—she tried to maintain in public an image of what she considered to be ideal motherhood. (Though *her* ideals were not the most conventional, like her habit, in my first year, of nursing me onstage, while Fuck Finn played their hit, "Suck Me Dry.")

By now I was purple in the face, my shrieks carrying across the promontory. The old man had begun to walk to the lighthouse, presumably in search of a park ranger, while his wife glared at us.

"Why do you have to be such an asshole?" Mother said. "Can't you see your daughter is upset? Is that stupid doll so important?"

My father looked at me as though I'd just run a knife through his innards. It was just a doll, after all, just a bauble he'd plucked from the ocean, thinking it would make his baby girl laugh. Now that baby girl had betrayed him.

"Fine," he barked, rolling to his knees, staring at the two of us and then at the handful of people now watching. "Fine!" he shouted, and raised the doll above his head and brought it smashing to the ground with a crunch. Gravel shot off in every direction, my mother shielded my face; the other half of the walrus's tooth snapped off, but otherwise the doll was undamaged. He held it in the air again, and again smashed it on the ground; a large grayish gouge appeared in the side of its head, and my father smacked it on the hard ground once more.

"I am the walrus!" he bellowed, hammering the doll on the gravel. "I am the walrus!" he shouted, a man in a khaki uniform striding our way, tiny stones and splinters of wood zipping through the air, "Goo goo g'joob!!" On the last word he hurled the splintered, accursed wreck with all his strength; it flew up and up and out against the shimmering backdrop, a dozen pairs of eyes following it into the sky as it arced across the white lighthouse and dropped down to oblivion.

When it had disappeared, everything was silent, but for the rhythm of the ocean and the distant whine of a speedboat. I buried my face in my mother's neck and she scooped me into her arms and rocked me, holding up a hand toward the park ranger, who came to a halt a few yards away. My father reached for his cigarettes. The old man and his wife stood glowering another moment and then wandered away; the other spectators shuffled at the bulletin board, pretending they hadn't been watching us in the first place.

My father smoked and my mother cooed, and they didn't look at each other.

"Give me the kit," he said quietly, a moment later. When she didn't respond, he said in a low hiss, "Give me the fucking kit, Penny."

I felt my mother stiffen, but she said nothing, reached into the picnic basket and took out a small black satchel, tossed it in his lap, and looked away. He stood and strode off toward a Porta-John, stopping to feign a menacing lurch in the direction of the unamused park ranger.

"Where's Daddy going?" I said, but she didn't answer.

The whole time he was gone, she sat staring at the ocean, at the white track traced by a speedboat. The sound of its engine approached and faded, the occasional burst of laughter or fragment of music. They came in for another pass, and caught sight of my mother, in her bikini bottom and scrunched-up T-shirt, her smooth legs and wind-strewn hair. A chorus of whistles carried over the rocks, one faint voice calling, "Hey, beautiful!" My mother's expression never so much as twitched.

My father reappeared, ambling across the open space with a dreamy smile. He reached down and lifted me high in his arms while my mother shook her head. From that great height, his face was broad and open, the source of all light; I was a dark and insignificant planet, staring into the sun. He brought me down again, settled me across his chest as he lay back on the blanket. Neither he nor my mother said a word, and I watched his eyes drift closed, felt his body rising and falling, opening and closing, my own breath taking his rhythm, as though the walrus had lied—we were not, would never be!, separated, as though the great peace he had found in the Porta-John were seeping into me through the touch of our skin.

Later—a moment? an hour?—this trance was broken by the drone of the speedboat, closer than before, the aggressive swoosh it made as it cut through the water, the bellows and hollers of good old boys having a good old time in the good old Pacific, of sunshine and beer and fast machines, the kind of people my father referred to as "plankton."

"For Christ's sake," I heard my mother mutter, sitting up to shield her eyes with her hand. My father did not move, but his eyes fluttered open and looked into mine.

The boat roared past again, kicking up a curtain of spray, wolf whistles and yee-haws, and then . . . and then . . .

"And then what?" said my therapist.

The music came through, a few lines of a song. We all recognized it at the same time, and I watched as my father's eyes rolled up in his head, the lids shutting gently:

> At the top of my game,
> Strike a bargain with shame—
> Give me someone to blame—
> What's my name? What's my name?

The boat sped past and the music washed over the peninsula, Billy's epileptic guitar solo fading in and out as the boat banked to sea. My father took a deep breath and lifted me off him. I sat on the blanket and watched him turn away, hug his knees to his chest—I wanted to put my arms around him, but they were too small; I wanted to kiss his face. But it was no use, I was just a little bird, there was nothing I could do.

When it was quiet again, he said, "I wish I'd never written that fucking song."

★

Breadcrumb by breadcrumb, this Bird pecked her way home—through the forests of forgetfulness, the footpaths of a mother's privacy, the halogen flashes of the famished hordes. Week by week I lay on the couch, dreaming of my father, that kelp-covered Goliath—from the near shore I pleaded, I put down my slingshot and opened my arms; weary and arthritic, covered in rime, the giant groaned and budged for me, his every movement rushing outward in ripples, a salty tsunami in my poor child's memory.

And yet nothing could satisfy me—each answer birthed a hundred questions, a barrage under which I buried my analyst. She sat sternly while I tossed and turned, the only sound the scribble of her pen. "But what does it *mean?*" I whined, and she slurped from her coffee cup. "Why did he do it?" I begged her to explain, but she turned on the lights and said, "I'm afraid our hour's up."

We kept up the sessions while I lived at Mountaintop—poor Rhoda, banished thrice weekly while I draped blankets over the windows and Michaela's voice drifted from the speakerphone. When I stepped outside an hour later, sucking on some new recollection, savoring it with my tongue, what would I hear but "Dirtnap" or "Acid Rain" blasting from a neighboring window, Cat Power's version of "Thorazine Days" from a passing car, another video tribute on TV at the sandwich shop in town. His image was my ether: I found him every time I fell out of bed. He was inescapable, unreachable, unburied and without peace—and I, a blood-stained Antigone, was stuck between two worlds, not at home with the living nor the dead.

"Everything you need is right *here,*" my beekeeper said, touching my forehead with a fingertip, leaning in close so his voice filled me. "Don't listen to the TV, the radio, don't listen to some psycho-mortician—there's nothing buried, nothing hidden."

"You don't understand," I moaned, clutching at his hand, pulling him over me like a blanket. Here, at least, was something I could hold on to. Sweaty nights in his spartan cell, stolen afternoons sprawled on the Terrace—his scrawny biceps, the press of his body, scratch of his two-day beard—here was something I could sink my teeth into! Here, at last, was something that was *mine.*

"I *do* understand." He stretched against me. I could feel the outline of each of his ribs. I could smell the musk under his arms. His black robe lay in a puddle—how the mere sight of it filled me with heat! "Desire is the root of suffering."

"Since when do you have a problem with desire?" I whispered.

"You act like it's a treasure hunt, like there's a buried nugget in there you've got to dig out." He dipped his hand in the creek and splashed freezing water across my flesh. He kissed my goose bumps, his hot tongue licked the moisture from my chest. "But you know what's down there?" He moved toward my navel. "Nothing."

I tried to explain it again—the fragments and sense memories, things I could never quite grasp. Even the moments that did come back to me, fished out by my therapist's lures—how often those mental pictures turned up in documentaries, home movies, things I thought I remembered him saying lifted from magazine articles, my flashbacks sourced to decade-old tabloids. Even my father's sweet face was indistinguishable, my memory corrupted by photos and posters, iron-on decals, cartoons.

"I can't trust myself, I don't know what's real," I said.

"That's because nothing is," he said, and bit the ticklish part of my thigh. He passed a hand over my belly, my breasts; the goose bumps vanished, as though they'd never existed. "Form is emptiness," he grinned, and got back to work.

O my summer lover, drawn to his fasts; O my black-robed boy and his black boxes of bees. With him next to me, I could drown it out for a time. When we shared a booth at the diner, or lay rolled in his scratchy blanket at the monastery, the nearness of this other body held my own together, kept me from flying into a thousand fragments, a thousand versions of myself. Those things I read in newspapers, or online—my mother could not protect me now, though she tried—all faded when he wriggled me out of my jeans, sank to a dull babble, the chitter of squirrels. So many years of restless travel, my mind darting everywhere; when I climbed astride him, when he was inside me, his hands clutching my rib cage, I was anchored, grounded: I knew what it meant to be here, now.

Soon enough, autumn came a-calling, the high sierra cooled, the evening breeze carried the first wisps of woodsmoke. I waited until the last minute before clearing out the cottage, packing a used Volvo with everything that would fit, sending the rest back to that San Diego museum of which my mother was both curator and sole patron.

"You've got too much stuff," said my beekeeper, as we stood next to the car. "You'll never find anything that way." He stood statue-still as I hugged him—a straw man, a bag of bones. As the day approached, he'd been drifting—I could see it in the back of his eyes, feel it in his clutches: the void calling him again, his pursuit of pure nothing. He was down to one bowl of rice gruel a day, meditating in the *zendo* most waking hours, planning another assault on the Everest of emptiness.

"If I don't find anything, I can always come back," I said, pressing my ear to his chest. "Someone's gotta cook you a good meal once in a while."

"Don't come back," he said.

I looked up, but he didn't smile; I started to argue, but he closed his eyes. The clatter of a woodpecker mixed with the mutter of the engine, the scent of pine with impatience and exhaust.

"There's nothing to come back to." He kissed the top of my head, turned, and walked into the afternoon sunshine.

*

How different the flat heat and poured concrete of Irvine, how different that arid trough into which a university had been dumped like so many LEGO blocks. How fast and shiny Orange County, how small and impersonal the trailer I'd rented at the edge of campus, the serious faces that rushed through parking lots, beetled across paths. The young theorists (though none quite as young as I) in their Doc Martens, their Che Guevara and Brandt Morath shirts; stereos in dorm windows blared mash-ups of *The Hanged Man* with *Fear of a Black Planet;* signs in the halls of the Humanities Building—THIS THURSDAY! DISSERTATION TALK: "IS COUNTERCULTURE POSSIBLE?: LYOTARD, MORATH, MÖBIUS, METANARRATIVE." Billboards on the freeway, or at Fashion Island Mall—the box set released at last, the lawsuits settled, she'd agreed to change the cover art: an image of my father in long white robes, offering with outstretched hand his beating, bloody heart.

The night before classes began, I sat on my tiny stoop. Two new beehives hummed reassuringly beneath a nearby tree—his parting gift, his big surprise. They'd been waiting for me, wrapped in shiny paper with a bow, two young queens in their small mailing cages, just waiting for hives to rule, and a card that said: *There is no one here.* Past the hives, lights patterned the desultory buildings; the rushing sound was not the nearby ocean, but traffic from the freeway. Gone was my cold babbling creek, gone the cozy cottage, the scent of pine. Later, lying awake, I strained to hear my bees outside, to concentrate on their monotonous sound, follow it like a compass needle back to Mountaintop; all I heard was cars looking for park-

ing spaces, the moan of a plane taking off, the hollow sound of his voice—
There's nothing to come back to—and the sinking fear that he might be right.

In the morning, a knock came at the trailer door, a flimsy rattle—Was
it him?—I knew no one else here. I'd been taking notes on a dream I'd
had: my fingers detached, one by one, from my hands, zipping through
the air like hornets, zeroing on my open mouth. I'd woken in a sweat, not
recognizing the walls of the trailer, nor the harsh light slicing through the
blinds.

"Calliope Morath?" said the woman on the stoop, her face haloed by
dry desert light, a voice so grim and monotone it gave me a shiver, put me
in mind of Dickinson's carriage man. "I'm here to take you to class."

I grabbed my notebook, twisted my dirty hair atop my head and stuck
in my fountain pen, pulled the wobbly trailer door shut, and stepped out
into shearing sun. "I wasn't expecting an escort," I said, shielding my eyes.

"It's hard to find your way around campus," said my companion, who
introduced herself as Taryn. "It's very disorienting." Her blond hair had
been yanked into a bun, her pretty green eyes hidden behind horn-rimmed
glasses, her body clamped into the kind of suit my mother used to wear
when she had to meet with the lawyers and label execs, or the snooping social workers of DCPS.

"It's classic interpellation," said Taryn. "The campus was designed to
deter public demonstration, keep the masses from organizing." We passed
through the courtyard of a tinted-glass titan of a library, the horizon filled
with crenellated behemoths, sun-soaked eucalyptus trees. Dry orange heat
crawled over me, prickling my skin. "Standard post-Paris fascism," she said,
not noticing the appreciative glances of a pair of boys in baseball caps.
"Soon you have no desire to be heard, since the system makes no allowance
to hear you."

"We'll just see about that," I said, and her mouth turned up imperceptibly.

"The repressed always returns," she nodded, raising ruthlessly plucked
brows.

"Who are you calling 'repressed'?"

We found our way to the ring road, joined the great circling student
body, two Daisy Millers on a Jamesian stroll. I could feel her studying me,

sizing me up; I closed my eyes, tried to put myself at the Terrace on a summer morning, tried to remember the soft Mountaintop sun.

"Do they send someone to accompany every new student?" I said when we arrived at the right building, the ugliest of the bunch—a neo-industrial cube, concrete stairs and olive-green fire doors. The roof scarcely visible, cornices blocked by glare.

"Actually"—she looked past my shoulder—"I want to use you."

"Use me?"

"For my dissertation."

"Is that a fact?"

"It's called 'The Ideological Apparatus of Death: Thresholds and Immanence in the Neo-Confessionalists' Couplets.'" She was warming up slightly, her voice breathier, the hint of a heartbeat somewhere inside that iron maiden.

"Couplets?"

"You know, couplets as the system's preferred verse, rhyme as presence, the collapse of logocentric opposition, lots of Marx and Hegel, and of course Althusser . . ."

"Oh *that*," I said.

"It's just in the prospectus stage."

As I opened the door I could feel her watching me from behind those silly glasses. On a whim, I turned back and kissed her cheek. I wanted to see her stoic expression falter, to see her eyes light up for a second—and they did.

"Thanks for the lift," I said to her astonishment.

She touched her cheek and stammered, "So, um, what do you do for fun?"

I took the pen from my bun, let my hair fall across my shoulders. "Nothing," I said, and gave the stunned girl my number.

The shade of the building was a relief, and I stood for a moment in the linoleum hallway, leaned against the cool, painted cinder blocks outside the classroom. From inside I heard mutters, a laugh and a shout swimming through closed doors. I repeated to myself my mother's stern dictum: "Be who you were born to be." Clutching my notebook, standing up straight, I made my entrance.

"Ah the prodigal daughter," boomed a voice, and for a moment I couldn't locate who'd said it. But then I recognized L. Moreno at the far end of the long table. He looked even younger than he did on his book jacket, his feminine face and unruly dark locks. He lounged insolently in a tweed jacket and bow tie, leaning his chair back on its legs. It was this arrogance, I knew, that lent him such mystique, made him so legendarily irresistible to older female poets and students alike.

"One hopes you've been composing something truly wonderful in your spare time," he said in his fluid Argentinean accent, his upper lip drawing back in an Elvis-like sneer. "Perhaps then we might dispense with the *garbage* I've been hearing so far today."

He aimed a baleful glance at a boy halfway around the table— feathered brown hair and a tidy beard, a collared shirt with the sleeves rolled up, and the expression of someone with a terrible fear of dogs confronted with a wild pack in an alley. I quickly took in the other faces— young and old, black and white. One middle-aged woman in a hijab, two surfer dudes in blue jeans, an odd fireplug of a man with a dyed-purple crew cut and shards of metal driven into his eyebrows and lower lip.

"One man's garbage is another girl's masterpiece," I offered, trying to smile at the boy with the beard, who leaned on the table and hid his face in his hands. The others watched me cautiously, an exotic specimen, no idea whether I was ally or adversary.

"We've been having a little get-to-know-you session, Calliope," said Moreno, "minus our quote-unquote *superstar,* of course—and I asked these quote-unquote *poets* to introduce themselves, and say something about why it is that they write, what purpose they hope their work might serve. Do you know what Dennis here said?"

"Now how would I know that, L?" Moreno mimicked my smile, his version seductive and acid-tinged, his eyes fluttering half-closed.

The poor kid placed his palms flat on the table. "I said it was like Blake said, that we have to cleanse the doors of perception so we can see things as they truly are." He lifted his eyes to mine. "I said poetry was like a broom made out of words."

"A broom!" Moreno chuckled, then leaned menacingly toward poor Dennis. "Have you ever seen a broom made of words?" He spread his arms, daring anyone at the table to answer. "I've never heard something so pretentious in my life," he cried, settling back in his chair. "Blake. Overrated, pseudo-mystical, lotos-eating drivel . . ."

"I love Blake," I said, pulling out the only empty chair. The others studied their cuticles, shot secret glances at Moreno—I'm sure I wasn't the only one thinking he might read his own recent volume, *In the Shadow of Achilles' Shield,* to discover true pretense.

"No ideas but in things!" he thundered, slapping the table with each word. "I must say, Calliope, I'm surprised to hear such a quote-unquote *accomplished* poet defending such an adolescent emission." He leaned his chair back, hands behind his head, long legs brashly spread. Across the table, Dennis stared at me, gratitude pooling on his lips. Behind him, through the room's tall windows, who did I see but Taryn, my brainy blond theorist, peeking in, a small group of students jostling for a view. The word was out, the Eagle had landed—now they'd gathered around this aerie, expecting a show.

"Perhaps," said Moreno, "being such an expert, you might grace us with *your* idea of our collective enterprise . . ."

I opened my notebook, uncapped my pen. *Asshole,* I wrote at the top of a page.

"Well?" said Moreno, and everyone held their breath. If they'd had popcorn, they'd have taken a big handful.

"Just taking some notes," I said. *But cute,* I wrote.

"If you're ready . . ." He glanced at his watch. The others leaned forward. Taryn pressed an ear to the glass. "Why do you write, Calliope? What is it you hope to convey? Please tell us, my quote-unquote *prodigy:* What does poetry mean to you?"

*

Sit tight, Captain Kirk, and I'll tell you a thing or two about our collective Enterprise:

The warp engines are shot, the phasers gone to pot—truth is, we are near our demise. Look around you, O Intergalactic Scourge—can you not see the gloom in your young crew's eyes?

Two thousand light-years from home—(yes it's true, we've come a long way)—and what have we found here but fallen cities, untended vegetation, decay; our monuments are covered with moss, my liege, but where is our rolling stone?

Back on our dear planet, old heroes groan and turn to dust—shall we cower beneath their armor for another century, Jim, or reach for their buckles and with their own swords deliver the final charity? Were they born heroes, or did poetry make them so—I think the latter, don't you? What's to stop us from beaming down, having a look around, trading the old for the new?

Blind Homer knew something about it, and Marlowe, and Sexton, and Yeats: One can sit in a basement room for life, discussing cadavers, semicolons, line breaks; or belly flop into the world, splash around, crash a few gates. "Live life to the hilt!" said dear Annie, an orphan if ever there was—and forget the garage, my dear professor, she turned more heads than your haberdashery: That woman knew how to create a buzz!

I'd rather be a laughingstock, a jester, a scapegoat, a fool—rather do my little turn on the catwalk, swell a scene or two—than to linger in these chambers of the blind, suspended animation, forfeiting the race; there are new legends to be designed, gods to make from swans, while you lean back and ogle the girls, so happily lost in space.

When Dylan read, the ladies swooned, the men reached for their drinks. For Yeats the world was tantamount, the poet in service of his bleeding nation; for Ginsberg, speaking out was all, to send the call to the best minds of his generation.

But what do we do, old prof, but bicker, backbite, piss each other off? Is this what Whitman had in mind, this esoteric thing we call poetry—is this why he bade us Sing? Who listens to you when you read your lines—are your Maenads crowding the door? Who can parse your obscurantist diction, your trochaic tetrameter, your Icelandic sestinas, even your ill-fated attempts at fiction? Do they weep and drool and beat their breasts? Do they beg you for more, more, more!?

This starship I would bring to Earth—it's time for a long drydock; a brand-new poetics is my highest Everest, a language that rolls and rocks.

Dusty old bookstores and library clubs—I'm not satisfied with these, are you? To poets belong the hysterical crowds, the mosh pits, the Lollapalloos—lay in a new course, dear Mr. Sulu!

Let's put the "lay" back in good old "wordplay," I like a little "per" with my "verse." Watch me climb to the wire, leap 'round without a net—feast your eyes, Charlie Chaplin man, this beauty doesn't need to rehearse! While you quibble and kvetch about whats, wheres, and whys, I'll soar through the air, risk absurdity and death, a trapeze made of couplets clamped between my thighs.

No coy mistress, you see, no hothouse flower, no plastic bird in a plastic tree—stand aside, Captain Kirk, you've been boarded! Stop worrying and love the mutiny!

And you, my fellow cosmonauts, the time has come to rise. Stand with me now and let's save poetry: Lock and load, click your heels—*Energize!*

*

I stopped for breath, leaning against the workshop table and straddling Moreno's chair. I could feel the other poets behind me, staring dumbly. Some shook their heads and huffed, others tried to hide their glee. Out the window, the theorists went wild, embraces and shouts and high fives; Taryn scribbled furiously in a notepad, two strands of her hair having come undone and drifted into her face.

Moreno smirked at me, closed his eyes.

"Why thank you, Calliope, that was quite an event, an unexpected workshop perk." He batted long eyelashes. "A lovely polemic—though to be frank, we prefer things a bit more academic. And your quote-unquote *meter* needs work.

"Still, though," he said, rocking forward, "it was clever, if more than a bit crass." He put his hands on the table to either side of my hips: "If you'd like to discuss this in more privacy, feel free to see me after class."

*

The rumors had begun virtually the day of his death, though for years I was blissfully unaware, tucked into my catatonic toddler's shell, my mother moving heaven and earth to keep the poison from my ears. The censored television shows, the backyard magazine pyres—even Wally Weeks threatened with the full legal weight of my mother's empire if he didn't remove the Tangiers segment from *The Kids Are Not Alright!* The simplest inquiry would provoke from her a torrent of venom, an hour of pitiful tears—I knew to stay silent, to float through her sphere like the mute wraith I'd once been.

But once I was out in the world, there was no way to avoid it: the casual question, the outlandish hypothesis. From strangers, the snickering aside, "Brandt Lives!" pins on backpacks and lapels. From friends, the knowing wink, the slow nod of the head, the inevitable, timid approach: "Come on, Bird, you can tell me: Is he really . . . ?"

While I was at Mountaintop, Antonio Cárdenas wrote a series of articles for the *Los Angeles Times,* a virtual compend of the rumors and mysteries, the lingering ambiguities. He meant to show how thin these stories were, to debunk the mythology; but seeing the whispers in stark black and white, column inches in a major paper set aside for their retelling, a special link on the newspaper's Web site, only solidified the issue in some people's minds. Chat rooms and Listservs and zines sprouted up; Leeza Gibbons was heard wondering aloud. At the annual Terrible Children convention, Talia Z was assaulted, cornered in a bathroom by threatening fans. There was no escaping the questioning looks, the interview requests, no way to know whom I should believe: my shaky memories or the persistence of the public's love and dreams.

On visits home, I'd beg my mother for answers, for explanations. I would have accepted the flimsiest denial. "Don't talk to me about such trash," she'd say, and reach for her drink. "Why can't anyone leave your father in peace? Even his daughter wants to tear away the shroud!"

"But what about the photos in *Weekly World News?*" I said. I knelt by her armchair, took the New Testament from her lap. (Her Christian phase lasted all of a month.) "What about the Seychelles, the credit cards, the offshore accounts?"

"Little Bird, life is confusing; what can I say? Why don't you write a poem? That'll help make things clear."

"Why don't you start by telling me where he's buried? Start by letting me see the note? Cruelty, thy name is Mother!" I said, curling into a ball on the Persian rug.

My mother reached down to pluck the Bible from my hands. "He loves you so much, Calliope," was all she said.

He was living in Morocco, sharing a mansion with William S. Burroughs, who'd once made a guest appearance at a Terrible Children concert (ostensibly to play the harmonica solo during "Shave Me, Shrieve Me," though in the event he only stood in his three-piece suit and bowler, facing the microphone zombielike, before climbing down to the crowd and walking back to the stadium exit).

He was selling guns in Rwanda, as Rimbaud had done a hundred years earlier. Or heroin, my father buying vast quantities from smugglers in Eritrea, transporting them by camel caravan to Tangiers, from whence he and Burroughs supplied much of Spain and Italy.

He was a Bedouin, leading a slow parade of believers across the Sahara, founding a religion based on rock music and intravenous ecstasy.

He was in Bolivia, fomenting a civil war, leading general strikes against the government.

He was in a VA hospital in Brownsville, Texas, where the FBI kept watch over his vegetable form.

Or Paris, a mime in the Jardin des Tuileries, or Punta del Este, remarried to Colombian pop star Shakira, whom he'd met at the South by Southwest music conference years earlier, when she was only fifteen.

I knew these stories couldn't be true (*But what if they* are . . . ?, a voice said)—but somehow that wasn't enough. With each outlandish sighting, it seemed there was more to my father than I'd known before; his story was larger than anyone had told me. Like the house on Azalea, there were unknown hallways, strange garrets, locked rooms—I was still a tiny, wandering child, lost within the walls of my own home.

The death certificate was always a point of contention—exhibit A for the hungry prosecution. No agency ever identified it as having issued from their office; the San Diego coroner, the AMA, the IRC: all mystified, the document under none of their auspices. Signed the first day of April, in the year 199_, by a Dr. Cornelius Roberts, whom no one has ever tracked down. Cause of death: cerebral hemorrhage, understatement at its most extreme ("Would you prefer it said 'Death by stupidity'?" my mother bawled,

"'Death by itchy trigger finger'? 'Death by terminal selfishness'? How much better would that seem?")—the decedent: "Brant" without a "d."

There was the missing copy of *A Season in Hell* that my mother insisted was there the night before. There was Danny Grier, the Kids' soundman, who went MIA the same day. (It turned out he was on the lam, fleeing an ex-girlfriend and court-ordered child support.) And then there were the records, the "death clues" his fans turned up—or imagined, or outright fabricated—over the years. On the inside sleeve of *The Fisher King,* their first full-length LP, all the Kids wearing military dress, my father shown barefoot, playing his guitar right-handedly (as everyone knows, he played it the other way, not because he was a lefty, but because that's how Jimi Hendrix played), the neck of the guitar pointing to a line of lyrics: "The time will come when I'm long forgotten / The end of my works and my days."

The inscrutable sounds on "Take My Life, Please!"—the so-called backward masking that various experts have analyzed, though no two seem to agree: When you play the chorus in reverse, a voice that is clearly my father's mumbles something which has most often been interpreted as "Don't shut the lid, baby—I can't see," though others insist he is saying, "See what you did, Penny—you killed me." When I turned sixteen, I had Connor take me to the best stereo store in Santa Monica to buy a $3,000 turntable; I raced back to Mountaintop and played the song backward again and again, ruining the stylus, my father's hoarse mutter filling the room like a phantom.

What *I* heard was: "You're just a kid, Birdie. You'll miss me."

None of this would have mattered—all in good fun, just more of the legend of B. Morath—had there been a grave I could visit, just the tiniest stone in the ground, or a polished urn on a mantel or in a niche, something to rub and make a wish. But on this, too, my mother was intractable, an immovable object in a designer sarong. I knelt at her bedside, I flooded her with e-mails, I appealed to her sense of duty—all to no avail.

"It don't matter, sweetie," said Esperanza, my favorite. I'd just offered her a thousand dollars for a snippet, an address, a clue. She sat in my rocker, and I on the floor, she combed and stroked my hair until it shone, as she had done every day until I left home. "Your daddy live inside you, *Pajarita*. He live inside all of us. You very lucky, you know? You want to see him, you turn on the TV!"

"That's not what I mean," I sobbed, and squirmed away. I knew it then—she'd outgunned me; my mother was no fool. She must have tripled my offer, quadrupled, or more. With her unlimited resources, she could control the truth. My reality was a product of her pen stroke; my truth fit on the memo line of a meaningless check.

I thought I had her when I received the tape from ABC News. I sped down from Irvine, barreled through the front door, surprised my mother on the living-room couch, strumming her bass guitar in the nude.

"Where is it?" I shouted, popping in the tape, the "Funeral Interview" that had been such a coup for Barbara Walters but which, before airing, had been suppressed. On-screen, my mother and Barbara Walters strolled a country path surrounded by green grass and headstones; in the distance was a group of Tibetan monks, their eerie murmurs droning like bees.

"Where's the graveyard? I want you to tell me right now," I cried, practically hyperventilating, chasing my mother from room to room until I had her cornered. "You liar!" I shouted, pushing her against a door. "Horrible mother! I hate you!"

She took a breath and straightened her hair. Even naked and panting, her self-control was terrifying, her dignity an accusation. I wanted to fall to my knees and beg forgiveness.

"Take another look, Bird," she said very softly. "Go on, watch it again."

I stared at the screen, the indistinct images of mourners passing by while she cried on Barbara's shoulder. "Recognize anyone?" my mother said. "Do you see Connor or Billy or XXX? Do you see Talia or Gary?" I shook my head. "Do you think I would profane your father's funeral that way? Bring the press—those bloodsuckers—to feed on his corpse?" she whispered furiously. "Is that what you think of your mother, Calliope?"

I watched and I watched, crestfallen, until I saw the same anonymous couple stroll by a second and a third time—it was doctored, a blue screen, a backdrop, a loop. "No, Mommy," I said, and she ejected the videocassette, pulled the tape hand over hand from its plastic case, my last great hope destroyed before my eyes.

I ran out to the backyard, past the pool shed, the cracked tennis court, out to where the rosebushes and brambles thickened in front of the high brick wall; in the farthest corner of the property was an old wood arbor, long since conquered by ivy and jasmine. When I sat beneath it, I could just make out the top windows of the house—no one would come look for me here. Beneath the vines and brambles I had gathered the few of his belongings I'd managed to secret away, stashed them in a metal box and hid them in the brush; as a child I'd spent hours out there, fallen asleep in the shade with his memories clutched to my chest—it was the only grave I had, you see, the only place I could let him rest. Despite the fortune his music had made, he was a man of very few possessions, and most of what he had my mother had hoarded or burned—the few keepsakes I'd managed to gather had turned up one by one, under couch cushions and in dusty corners, each sending me into an ecstasy of fresh grief, each seeming like something he'd sent especially for me: an old, wrinkled photo of him and Connor on Westminster Bridge, taken the day before the Reading Festival; four badly worn guitar picks; a pre-mastering copy of *Hanged Man* across which someone had scrawled *Shit* in felt-tip; a gold-plated Zippo engraved with his initials, a gift from Japan's Minister of Culture. And my prized possession, a clipping from the *Union-Tribune*, yellowed and fragile and crumbling, the interview he'd given the day after my birth—I'd had it laminated, preserved it like a work of art:

"Holding my daughter is like being born again," he said, and in the faded photo, he is smiling into my newborn face. "She makes me want to live."

Can you imagine, O dear one, my conscience, my twin? Fifteen long years of his image—in newspapers, movie screens, and books. And I, his only daughter, could not find his grave—I, his one fair copy, had no idea where to begin. Week after week strapped into the couch: Step right up to Michaela's Recovery Machine! Thousands of dollars per memory, come one, come all! Fifteen years of dredging the silt from his throat, waiting for a word—but I, too, would never get this colossus put together at all.

"I know a guy . . . ," said the purple-haired poet, the one with the shards in his lip. "He's a cyberdetective, a digital bloodhound, he reads lots of Philip K. Dick . . ."

"The body is nothing, it's his quote-unquote *spirit* you want," L. Moreno offered once, in bed. "We can go to Venice, I'll organize a séance—you can ask him yourself!"

"You know what you're asking, it's a pretty big job," said Skip Cárdenas, when I contacted him. "There's all sorts of problems—injunctions, sealed files—I've already gotten as far as I can."

And Connor, poor Connor—how I begged him, down on my knees in the Malibu sand. "Please help me!" I cried, but he just closed his eyes, shook his head. "Your mother!" he said, and threw up his hands.

With the box set just out, I couldn't walk through the grocery store, couldn't drive down Newport Boulevard without hearing his voice, seeing him towering over me in his white robes, offering me his red red heart. It was enough to drive a girl mad! My mailbox was crammed with envelopes containing blurry photographs, forged documents, news clippings, résumés . . . letters fashioned of words cut from magazines: "Dear Calliope, this is your dad . . ."

Only in the workshop was I safe—Moreno had thick curtains put up to thwart spectators. (After our rocky start, we'd reached a kind of détente.) For three hours each week I thought about nothing but poetry—I breathed it, slurped it, wallowed in up to my throat. Once those doors closed, the ten of us somber around the long table, I wasn't the daughter of a rockstar, not the strange, inflammatory child—just the struggling author of an Italian sonnet, or a long lyric in the voice of Jeanne d'Arc. Thank god for the workshop, I whispered at night: On paper, if nowhere else, there was only one me.

Until one Tuesday just before Christmas, when a loud knock came at the door. I stared at my notebook, a sour warmth beginning in my stomach. *"Occupado!"* L. Moreno called, then watched, outraged, as a man shoved his way into the room and clapped a tape deck onto the table. He was husky and bald, with a wide, pockmarked nose; he wore ripped jeans and a ridiculous flannel shirt unbuttoned halfway. He pulled out a long-eared hunter's hat, smooshed it on his shiny head, flashed me a demented smile, and pressed PLAY.

It was like a bad dream, a Beckett farce: My father's song "Fishing Pier

Frenzy" filled the room. We all stared, incredulous, as he played air guitar and started to sing:

> Your daddy split and no one's seen him now for fifteen years—
> His baby daughter all grown up is drowning in her tears . . .
> But he can't run, and he can't hide, we're gonna track him down—
> In London, Beijing, Amsterdam—oh yeah, he will be found!
> We specialize in wand'ring dads, in vagrants, deadbeats, jerks—
> And reuniting families is our favorite kind of work!
> So don't you cry, no don't you fret, my friend Calliope—
> 'Cause we're the RT Dunleavy Detective Agency.

When he finished, he stuck his card in my face: *RT Dunleavy*, it read. *Ruthless. Thorough. Discreet.*

It was the last straw. I picked up my notebook and ran—through the building, the campus, all the way to my trailer. Panting, head spinning, I got in the Volvo, sped out to the freeway in the nacreous December evening. The stupid song—everyone's least favorite, except my father—rang in my head, the absurdity of that dumpling-man danced before my eyes. What was I supposed to think, how could I live in this free-for-all? If my father was lost forever, why did so many people insist he could be found? Outside the car, traffic bunched and released, roads merged and cloverleafed. I blasted the radio, turned it off. Something was still alive, it seemed, whether word or flesh. They were looking for something—something had not been laid to rest.

Out into the desert, through Riverside and Banning, up into hills of scrub and pine. I had not yet admitted to myself where I was going. As the panic ebbed, I blinked into the shadows of the looming mountains, negative space swallowing my headlights. Behind me the grid of Los Angeles shimmered from the desert floor, each light clutching at me—*Come back, Calliope, give us more!*

"Be as clean as a knife slicing an apple," my lover once told me, one of the roshi's favorite sayings—but all of it clung to me, claimed me and named me. I had nothing to fight back with, no version I could confidently call my own. I had to know the answer, the referent of all these signs.

It was after ten o'clock when I rumbled and scratched up the dirt road to the Zen Center, swerving around potholes remembered by instinct, the gnarled, blackened oak that had been struck by lightning long ago and stood at a bend in the path like a wizened lookout. No one was awake, and as I tiptoed through the monastery, the only sound the breath of sleeping monks, I thought back to those blissful nights when I'd hike there from my cabin just to spend a few hours by his side; weekends we pitched a tent in the forest, nothing but granola and condoms in a backpack, on Monday morning we'd emerge from the woods like two pure souls from the be-ginning of time. Had it been only months? I'd missed him, his soothing voice, the touch of his hands. But I'd kept my promise.

We'd spoken only once—through the phone I could hear winter com-ing to Mountaintop, the thickness of hunger in his voice. "Please," I whis-pered, lying in my trailer and masturbating. "Let me come see you," I said. But he wouldn't budge. His fast was opening doors he'd never known of, he said; his deprivations revealing secrets he had yet to comprehend.

Now, with shaking hand I pushed open the door to his cell, the whole hot bolus of it rising in my throat: the detective, the rumors, my mother's infernal silence. He wouldn't turn me away, I was sure. He'd keep me from flying apart until these troubles dissolved, passed through me and soaked into the monastery's stones.

But his pallet was empty, amber candlelight guttering shadows on the wall. His thin blanket folded neatly, a musty smell as though no one had opened that door for days. Stifling panic, I raced through the house, peeked into the cafeteria, the kitchen, the office—no creature was stirring, no roshi, no monks. I flung the door open and ran into the night, up the steep path and into the woods, teeth chattering, feeling my way past boulders and brush and the woodpile they'd been gathering against the imminent first snow. If he was gone, I thought, if he'd left without telling me . . . Or worse, his fasting, what if . . . ?

At the end of the path, the open-air *zendo* stood silent in its clearing. He sat in the shadows beneath the pagoda, a penumbra of moonlight ad-hering to his silhouetted form. I waited, heart beating hotly, and watched my beekeeper meditate; he must have heard me crashing up the path, but he made no move. Savoring the liquor of relief, I looked up into the streaked stars, out across the hilltop and the world below, just a handful of tiny lights visible in that dark ocean—I thought of my childish daydreams: my father a ship's captain, standing on the prow, steering his vessel through uncharted seas.

"How's tricks, Birdie?" he said when I knelt behind him. His voice was weak, his body fragile. Even as I held him, kissed the side of his face, I could feel him shrinking further, like plastic held to heat.

"What are you doing, you fool?" I said. "Hasn't this gone far enough?" The thin air shaped itself around my voice, sharpened it like a stake piercing soil.

"I'm nothing," he answered, his lips just barely turning up. They were dry and cracked, shreds of flesh catching the moonlight. His head, when I held it to my body, felt too big for his neck. Instantly I understood why he'd refused to let me come: He didn't want me to see what he'd done to himself. He didn't want me to stop him.

"To noth," he said. "It's a verb: I noth, you noth, he noths. We are nothing. Get it?"

"Two poets in one family," I said. "What luck."

I ran my hands over his shoulders, down his arms, the bones like saplings, shivering in the night's cold.

"I closed the hives this morning." When he spoke, there was no resonance in his body; the words came from his lips and dissolved. "I took one frame of honey for myself and left them the rest. That should be enough to make it until spring."

I pressed my face to his. I took his chin in my hand. "For who to make it?" I stared into his dull eyes. "What are you saying?"

"Roshi says we have to let the outside world pass through us like the wind, that we have to let the ego evaporate, so the world has nothing to catch on. But that's misleading. There are other things, parts of ourselves we don't know about, waiting to rush into the vacuum—and then what?" I started crying again, tears hot against both our cheeks. "I don't know how to make myself any emptier," he said.

"I don't want to hear any more of this self-abnegation shit, do you understand? I don't want you to disappear. Please don't disappear." My beekeeper stared at a point in space. "I came here for help."

"Just sit," he said.

"I don't have time for—"

"Just sit," he said. "That's all I can tell you. That's Zen."

"I don't want Zen," I said, heat rising up my neck. "I don't want to starve myself or freeze to death. I'm tired of the stories, everyone telling me what happened, what it all meant. It's like I wasn't even there, like it all happened in another dimension, on the other side of a looking glass. I don't even know anymore which side I'm on!" A weak smile moved over his lips. "I need to know the truth."

He dragged a hand along the floor and offered me a small pebble. "Here's the truth."

"Spare me the fucking parables, will you?" I threw the pebble into the trees. I wanted to smack his poor face, to squeeze him until his ribs groaned and gave. "I need you to talk to me. I need you to help me."

"Nothing I say can lead you to the truth." His hand shook with a subtle palsy; when he blinked, I saw that his eyelashes had fallen out. "Words are empty, just random sounds, marks on the page. The truth is the space around them."

"Thanks, Derrida. Don't I get enough of this at Irvine?" I said. "Words are all I've got."

"They're just icing on the cake, Birdie, wrapping paper on an empty box. They're like the frets on a guitar—not the music. You used to know that."

"How about these words?" I lowered my voice: "*Get up and get in the fucking car.* I'm taking you to Sizzler."

But he sat unmoving, his body did not respond, even when I snuck a hand under his robe, ran my fingers across his withered thighs. The skin was cold and loose, like a turkey's wattle. "Don't tell me you're not hungry," I whispered. "Come on, tell your little Bird the truth . . ."

"They're little desire machines," he said, sitting stock-still while I probed his lifeless groin. Reaching my goal, I closed my fingers, squeezed ungently. He took my wrist and looked at me with moist eyes. "Desire perpetuates the cycle of life and death."

"So the answer is suicide?" I hissed. Then I shoved my hands under his arms and tried to haul that poor scarecrow to his feet. He didn't resist, made no attempt to push me away—I stumbled beneath his weight, fell backwards a few steps, and sat heavily at the edge of the *zendo*, wound up on my back, staring into shadows.

For the first time that day, I felt like laughing—the two of us out here in the dark, bandying philosophy and falling on our asses. But when I sat up, I heard something—a terrible sound, my beekeeper groaning softly.

"I'm so sorry," I said, and started to my feet. He was doubled over, his shoulders shaking—my rough tug must have been agony for his tortured body, must have felt like the tearing of muscle, meat from the bone. "Are you okay?"

But his voice stopped me in my tracks: hoarse and tight, pregnant with a sob. The moon edged out from behind a cloud and stunned the clearing. The pines surrounding the *zendo* stared at our tiny forms with quiet pity. "It's noise," he said. "How can anyone live with the noise?"

"Baby . . ." I wanted to go to him, but my legs wouldn't move. I stared at the back of his head, smooth and robin's-egg blue in the moonlight and a swift freeze iced my mind over. The woods were silent. I couldn't breathe.

"Not suicide," he whispered, rocking and nursing his bruised arm. "I'm trying to be alive."

Alive.

Dizzy, I leaned against a post, cold air swimming behind my eyes, pulse pounding at my bloodstain. I felt my legs turn liquid, saw spots swim through the dark. I was there and not there, the strange feeling that I'd wandered onto a movie set, interrupted some bizarre production. Gagging, I swooned in the shadows, I was the ghost in the machine, drifting bodilessly by.

When I opened my eyes, he'd turned around—my ascetic darling, so gaunt and pale, eyes wide as an infant's. "I have to go now," I said, my voice strange.

I went to him, knelt at his side, and kissed his dry lips. I stroked his hurt arm, inspected his ribs with my fingertips. Slowly, he crossed his legs in lotus.

"Then go," he said.

"I'll be back," I said, cupping his skull in my palm.

He closed his eyes, a weak smile. "That's how it works."

But in my mind I was already on the highway, barreling out of the mountains under mottled midnight, land pressed flat by the nose of my car. I knew now why I'd fled the workshop, I understood where I needed to go. As I walked down the path and back to my car, the hills seemed to hum with the Beekeeper's *Om*. The monastery was dark and still, the dirt road seemed straighter, less bumpy; the dead oak tree stood black as blood, one tortured limb pointing the way home.

*

Once, if I remember well, my life was a feast where all hearts opened and all wines flowed.

From a gas station in Anza, I called Rhoda, babbled frantically into the phone: "Detectives and mediums, crank phone calls, karaoke!" The night sky was cloudy, a promise of rain, wind thrusting violent over the sierra.

"What, baby? What are you saying?" said my old roommate, my co-conspirator, through the cotton of sleep. "Slow down, take a breath. Try to talk to me, C."

"Words," I gibbered, "the frets on the guitar—but I don't even have those, Rhoda."

"Don't have what? You're not making sense." I could hear her fumbling for her glasses, turning on a light. My car idled under luminous gray, nose pointing south.

"What if I find it," I said. "Please meet me there. I can't do it alone."

"Hang on," she said. "Let me check my planner . . . How about next Friday?"

"Just get there! Now!" I slammed down the receiver.

Words! I thought, as the mountains drifted back, pastures and vineyards, the faithful interstate coming up under my wheels. More words! I'd spent years rummaging through them, gobbling up song lyrics and liner notes, videotaped interviews and transcripts, mid-concert chitchat; I knew every syllable by heart, had memorized it more carefully than my own poetry. I'd sifted through my father's words like hot sand, waiting for something shiny and priceless to turn up—but in the end I'd come away empty, no buried booty, no exquisite corpse grinning beneath language's pall.

There was only one thing left to hear, one statement to isolate from the noise—I would hear it now, if I had to tear that house apart, pull up the carpets, peel the paint off the walls.

When I got to Azalea, Rhoda was waiting in the driveway, leaning against her Miata and staring at the dark house. Mother spending Christmas in Ibiza, the guest of a famous soccer player, the hero of Réal Madrid; the servants all gone, only the security cameras, cycloptic red pinpricks silently tracking as we mounted the front stairs.

"What, exactly, sweetheart, are we here to find?" Rhoda put an arm around my waist. Since the last time I'd seen her, she'd cut her hair, dyed it blond, frosted the fringes—at five feet one, she looked like some kind of pixie; as always, she vibrated with energy, the exultation of her vast ambition. With her parents' help she'd opened a business, a publicity firm in the Silverlake district—though when I'd asked her about her client list, she'd been coy, hinting at unheard-of marketing heights, glorious campaigns, supernovas waiting to be born.

"Let me in on the secret," she said now, eyes glimmering in the gaslight. "I'm your ace in the hole, your number-one asset. Who loves you, C?"

I fished for the keys, my hands shaking, pushed through the door, disarmed the security systems, fumbled for the lights. The foyer blazed alive, cold echoes of our sneakers on polished floors. I held tightly to Rhoda's hand as we climbed the staircase. My mother's bedroom was the place to start, that oft-desecrated shrine to my father, that inner sanctum in which, as a child, I was allowed only according to her whims.

"If you're not going to tell me, how can I help?" she asked. But I was already opening dresser drawers, rifling through the closet, flinging dresses and suits to the side. Rhoda threw herself across my mother's bed, propped an elbow beneath her chin, watching me with those lively eyes I remembered so well—how they used to follow me across our Mountaintop cottage, how I'd feel them on my back when I wrote at my desk, appraising my face with a jeweler's expertise.

"Well, then, I'm just going to *talk,*" she said, pursing her lips in a princessy pout, her hands dancing with each word she spoke. "I've been trying to get hold of you, but you never return my calls. I've got so many ideas, so many strategies. I'm putting together something unprecedented, C. Something that's just *to die for.*"

"Mmm-hmm," I said, barely listening, pulling out the desk drawers, tossing their contents into the air. I found the old *Newsweek,* which I threw on the bed; I found trinkets and love letters, court papers galore. Galleys from the forthcoming Azerrad book, whole pages red penciled, marginalia in my mother's firm hand: *Over my dead body!* and *Not if my lawyer has anything to say!* and *Michael, forget it!*

"It's a juggernaut," Rhoda said. "By the time I'm done, my client will be a household name, a legend, a star," she mooned. "We're talking front-page stories, after-school specials, press junkets, action figures, cosmetic lines, limos."

"That's great," I muttered, ducking under the bed, examining the box spring, the metal frame, a crispy wad of old Kleenex.

"My client's face will be known in every corner of the world. She'll be a firestorm, a tsunami—Mother Nature, you've met your match!"

I forced her off the bed and stripped the sheets, unzipped the pillows, flipped over the mattress. I took paintings and framed posters off the wall—each time, sure I'd broken the code: TERRIBLE CHILDREN LIVE!, ROSKILDE FESTIVAL, DENMARK, JULY 2, 199_—a triumphant headline booking they would never make. I smashed the frame and sifted through the shards. I swept through the bathroom, the linen closet, the wardrobe, Rhoda trailing behind me, chattering to the walls.

"All I need to start are a few attention-getters, to put my client on the front page—you know, titillating rumors, shocking photos, kiss-and-tells. A little scandal never hurt anyone's celebrity. I don't care what anyone says—tits and ass still sells."

By now we were moving through the spare bedrooms, her voice echoing off hardwood, brass, and molded cornices as I threw piles of moth-balled clothes and bric-a-brac out of the closets. Every scrap of paper, no matter how small, threw my heart into arrhythmia; every sealed box made me shake with anticipation.

"What we'll need first is a love interest—that's pretty well SOP. A few well-placed photos'll get the ball rolling, the interview requests will pile up, the tabloids. Then he cheats, or there's a pregnancy scare, an African baby . . . The sky's the limit."

I rolled up a long Persian runner, ransacked the hall closet. I poked around the guest bathroom, unrolling the toilet paper, sticking my fingers into ancient aspirin bottles. Under the sink I found an unlabeled bottle and opened it for a sniff; my eyes burned, my stomach heaved—I recognized the horrible stuff my mother and the shaman used to drink, the nasty swill he made in his lab, which he said helped them enter the spirit world: "to come in contact with our real selves."

"Anyone out there you can think of, C? That Henry Thoreau wannabe isn't quite going to cut it, you know." I capped the bottle and put it away, headed for my mother's office, the last door on the upstairs hall. I toppled the file cabinet, pawed hamsterlike through a mountain of paper, punched out the bottoms of the drawers; all the while Rhoda stood in the doorway, watching me like a prized pig.

"Who can it be? Who can it be?" she wondered aloud, but I waved her off, flipping quickly through a photo sleeve of my mother and the shaman, their eyes dilated like dark, shiny coins. "Someone a little bit dangerous, with some kind of an edge—ooh, maybe a lesbian, or a black!"

Beneath the desk was a small safe—I racked my brains for the combination, tried birthdays, anniversaries; holding my breath, I turned the dial to 04-01-9_, the date of my father's death . . . but the handle held fast.

"No, I've got it!" she cried. "I'll make some phone calls tomorrow. I'm sure he'll do it! Baby, what do you think of Ben Affleck?"

I was about to give up, when I thought of a song, one of Fuck Finn's first hits—a set of measurements, on the album cover a close-up of my mother's leather-bound chest: "36–26–36." *Click.*

"I think this is it," I whispered, clutching Rhoda's arm, my heart in fibrillation, my mouth dry as the Irvine trailer park. But I needn't have feared—the safe was empty, my hands groped greedily in the small metal space.

"I'll never find it," I cried, falling back on the hardwood floor. "She must have destroyed it."

Rhoda watched me with that shrewd eye. "Keep trying," she said, "whatever it is."

"It's pointless. I'll never know." I hugged my knees, rolled on my side, and sobbed. Rhoda stood over me, tapping her toe. The house was as silent as it had been that long-ago morning—only the occasional creak, the scratch of a tree branch, the whisper of central heating.

"This won't do." Rhoda clucked her tongue. "Not at all." She bent down and hauled me to my feet. "The Calliope I know doesn't quit or complain. She sticks to it till she gets what she needs. Now march!"

Down to the kitchen, where we pulled out every drawer—Rhoda was starting to have fun—utensils and cutlery, napkin rings and bottle openers and whisks and presses, silk tablecloths and candleholders, Scotch tape and spare pens and batteries and more went flying over the stainless steel counters, clattering on the terra-cotta. In the living room I ransacked the couches, the armchairs, pulled stuffing out of cushions, took every DVD from its case. I turned on the big-screen, flipped through a thousand channels—maybe there'd be another message, a satellite relay, a last will and testament on tape.

"But this is just the overture, just to get us on the map," Rhoda said, prattling on about her agency, her mystery client, her schemes for unprecedented fame. "That old saw about second acts is a lot of bullshit. Wait till you hear what comes next . . ."

I scoured the bookshelves, turning over picture frames and statuettes and knickknacks, a trail of rubble across the living-room floor. "But listen," said Rhoda. "Don't think I've forgotten what's important. It's all about the art. Poetry *über alles,* baby. The most important thing is that you finish the book."

"The book?" I said. Behind her, the living-room windows were losing their dark shimmer, a shy dawn outlining the pool shed and tennis courts. My ears rang with fatigue and caffeine. A book fell over on the shelf, started a small avalanche, a rustle and crash to the mess on the floor. "Rhoda?"

She stared into my eyes, then gave me a hard shake. "Okay!" she said. "I'm taking over! What's next? Where haven't we looked?"

I shook my head. "Unless she buried it in the yard, or plastered it into the wall . . ."

"What's in there?" Rhoda said, and I followed her gaze to a small hallway off the kitchen, a stairway leading down into shadow.

"Nothing," I said.

"There's something . . ." She raised an eyebrow.

"No. Nothing."

She pulled me behind her to the top of the stairs. "There's a door down there, C."

"Rhoda, I'm telling you—"

She smiled quizzically. "Well *I'm* going to find out," she said, and started down.

I lunged after her, nabbed the collar of her blouse, and yanked her back. "Calliope!"

"You can't," I stuttered, hardly knowing what came out of my mouth. "No one's allowed down there. Just Billy, just once a year to tune the guitars."

She stared as though I were a lunatic. "There's nothing to find," I said. "It can't be disturbed! He said his spirit can only return if it's untouched, if there's a vessel . . . a familiar place, beloved possessions, that kind of thing . . ."

"What? *Who* said . . ."

"That's what he told us . . . things transform, they have to be . . . purified." I felt giddy, suddenly ashamed: My tongue had again taken over, the words too strange.

"Baby, what are you talking about?"

"I can't go down there." I sat on the top step, head in hands. "She told me not to interrupt him."

I heard Rhoda groan. Then she took my wrists and gently pulled. I came down one step, and then two. I felt tiny again, naughty, my mouth dry as asphalt, ears starting to ring. Whimpering, I tried to pull away, but she held me fast.

"Hold on, C," she cooed. "Everything's going to be fine."

At the bottom, she twisted the knob and the door opened into darkness. My whole body was shaking. Sweat trickled between my shoulder blades. *Daddy!* She took the last step and I held my breath as she clicked on the light.

"Holy fuck!" she said.

It was all as it had been fifteen years before, as I'd seen it in memories and dreams, as I'd described it to Michaela, alluded to it in verse. Rhoda gaped at the mountains of equipment, the amps and effects racks, the nine-piece drumkit, the microphones and mini-stacks. The studio was alive with meters and indicators, blinking reds and greens and flashing whites. In the back corner, the English phone booth they'd used for vocals—its windows covered with carpet, the bright red door half-open. I could see him in there, headphones muffling his ears, slouched against the wall with a cigarette, silently watching the other three. (On disc 5 of the box set—"Outtakes and Fuckups"—you can hear his voice calling from far away, in the dead space between takes of "Make Me": *Let me out of here, guys—I feel like a fucking fetus in a jar . . .*) One guitar lay on the floor, attached to an antique tube amp by a cord—a Fender Telecaster once smashed to bits by Pete Townshend at Radio City Music Hall; meticulously rebuilt, this was the axe my father had wielded when the Kids recorded "Thorazine Days," the aficionados marveling at what my father dubbed the "Humpty Dumpty sound."

Behind it spread the wide arc of gleaming guitars—Rickenbackers and Gibsons, a twelve-string acoustic made custom in Prague, a handsome old dobro he'd bought in a Memphis pawnshop and spent months refurbishing. Every stand occupied, every pickguard polished, every string impeccably tuned—they stood in perfect silence, as they had for fifteen years, machine heads shining, a hundred living eyes observing us.

I had the panicky feeling of a child lost in a department store, except it was the opposite: I knew too precisely where I was. I averted my eyes from that spot on the floor where I'd last seen him. I covered my ears, but I could still hear the sound of my own childish voice.

"Okay, C." Rhoda stroked the back of my neck. "Just a quick look around—"

I shook my head, on the verge of throwing up. "I have to get out of here."

"Give me one second—"

"Now!" I said.

I leaned on her shoulder and we moved back toward the door. Lights swimming in my peripheral vision, I had to stop and close my eyes. I thought I was going to black out. I sank slowly to the floor. "Just a second . . . ," I whispered, my cheek pressed against prickly carpet, in the back of my mind the sickening understanding that I was lying virtually in the same spot. I stayed there, sucking air, until I heard Rhoda's voice, a sound as though she'd been punched in the gut.

"Oh, shit. Is that what I think it is?"

I followed her gaze to the back wall. Even in the dim light I could see the outline, the gruesome Rorschach that no amount of scrubbing, no coat of paint, could ever conceal. Thick in the middle, like an engorged crab, legs splayed and bent, streaks and dots struggling upward like the last bubbles of a drowning man's air.

In the center of that design, nailed to the wall like Luther's theses, was the note.

Two stiffened, discolored pages, curled like parchment, torn from an old yellow pad. Like stills from a nickelodeon, I saw him hunched over and scribbling, heard him whimpering and sniffling, a grunt as the pad flew from his hand.

Rhoda ran a hand through her hair. "Is it—"

"Don't touch it!" I screamed, and she jumped back.

It was here. After all this time. The one place she thought I'd never look. The scene wouldn't be the same without it, of course—this morbid tableau she'd maintained, this diorama of denial, this hidden grave.

"Once, if I remember well . . ."

From where I knelt, I could make out the first line—the sight of my father's chicken-scratch made me retch. But I forced myself to stand. My hands shaking, I grasped the pages and gently slid them off the thick nail. Rhoda said something, put a hand on my shoulder, but I couldn't hear her. Only my father's words—his voice breathing from the old paper— mattered now.

"Life is a farce we all have to lead!!" scrawled in huge letters across the bottom, the unlovely lines above matching what I'd already read, what I'd heard on the radio, on cable TV. But this was just the beginning—my long-ago hunch was right. Just flashy slogans for a scandal-hungry world. Behind them was something more, a message he'd left for his beloved bird. A warm drop splattered onto the top sheet and I rubbed my eyes, half-laughing, hands steady now. Rhoda kissed my cheek and slipped upstairs.

What would he tell me? Was it all written down? All the things I'd won-dered for so long—I was about to know. So nervous, so hopeful: as if I could turn over this one leaf and find him there—flesh and blood—waiting, so proud of his little girl who'd braved the basement stairs once more. Squinting through tears and fluorescence, struggling from elation to terror, I said a small prayer and pinched myself. I bit my tongue. I sat on an old amp and closed my eyes, whispered, "I'm sorry, Mother," and turned the page.

✮

Take two.

What is there to say except I love you? You, you, you—I look at your face and I'm terrified, you can't understand that, I see the future and the past and the present all together and I ~~want~~

No!!! Resolve!

De profundis, Domine! Remember me as a fool, not an ass. It was inevitable, some seed or kernel inside of me; you knew one day it would pop. Everyone's better off this way. I wish I could leave you more than just these hideous pages from my notebook of the damned. But they won't let me. There's no time.

O take me to the SEA!

I rebel against death—I mean life. It's an echo chamber, a house of mirrors, they keep showing you to yourself, thin and fat and tall and short. I can't anymore. Zero is the only honest number.

Wait for me, my girl. I'll return with limbs of iron, dark skin and furious eye, I'll rise from the wine-dark sea. When you need me, I'll be there, I promise. Wait for the signal: Mr. Bath and Rot, that's how you'll know me. Don't forget about

Here she comes

5. THE HARD KERNEL OF THE REAL

THOUGH THERE WOULD BE—and, according to more sensation-prone scholars, already had been—other men, other women, in Calliope's life, none would affect her so deeply and lastingly as the Beekeeper.* It does not take an Austrian physician to note that the young poet had first learned about impermanence, that most Buddhist of concepts, at the hands of men. Given her father's awful departure, the subsequent abandonment of the Inca shaman, and the disavowal of her Mountaintop mentor, Marshall Vaughn, it's no stretch to say that *disappearance* was the leitmotif of her relations with the opposite sex. She was shaped by the knowledge that the recipient of one's love, the repository of one's trust, one's dreams, might in the next moment simply vanish. How, in such circumstances, not to understand disappearance as an act of aggression, a repudiation of that freely given love? How to resist the temptation to reinterpret that disappearance as temporary or fraudulent, how to stave off the fantasy of return?

Who was the man who came to be known as the Beekeeper? Scholars have been frustrated by this question, in no small part because of the strenuous efforts of Lubinski Management, Snow Lion Press, and the Mountaintop Zen Center, which have threatened lawsuits, blacklisting, and karmic retribution should his given name be printed. Born and raised on a 140-acre estate in the rolling hills of northern Virginia, heir to one of

---

*Throughout this account, the author shall resist the tendency to focus on the salacious details of Calliope's romantic attachments, an obsession which has all too frequently gripped tawdry-minded critics (cf. Harminder Singh, Kristof Meersch, Edwin Decker, et al., whose common gender needn't be pointed out). Despite the suggestive content of her poetry, there is little evidence to suggest these were physical relationships and not the wholly innocent affections in which all young persons indulge.

America's oldest pastry fortunes,* the Beekeeper enjoyed an idyllic child-hood filled with riding lessons, cotillions, family reunion weekends punc-tuated by pats on the head from senators, diplomats, and captains of industry. A quiet, delightful child, his solitary tendencies were apparent early on—he often locked himself in the family library overnight, or dis-appeared from the manor for hours at a stretch, until some family em-ployee or local law-enforcement official found him in the woods miles from home, bivouacked with a blanket, a bag of cupcakes, and his favorite horse, Buckley.

It was on one of these excursions that the boy, then nine, had his first encounter with both the profound solitude and the glaring publicity that would mark his later life, that would serve as the poles of his own strange career. Setting out along a country road on a cool spring morning, the boy dismounted to investigate a pile of stones and fell into an abandoned well. He tumbled nearly twenty-five feet, fracturing his jaw and dislocating both shoulders, before coming to rest wedged tightly between the partially col-lapsed walls and losing consciousness.

"When I opened my eyes, there was no light or sound, no day or night, only the cold and persistent pain," he would tell the roshi, many years later. "I didn't know where my body began and ended. I *was* the pain. It was my only being. I became part of the earth, flesh and blood dissolving, ceasing to exist."†

It was his first experience with the void, the nothingness which would call to him for the rest of his life. By evening, a countywide search for the missing child had been mounted, but it wasn't until early the next morning that a hiker came upon the riderless Buckley, who had not left the spot where his master had fallen. By noon a major rescue operation had been mounted.

Sheriff Willard "BJ" Bojean recalls the day and a half that paramedics, firefighters, and engineers struggled to rescue the child: "Blazing sun one minute, showers the next, wind, even a thunderstorm overnight. It was right Biblical. Had one of my deputies sit by the well all night, reading Hardy Boys

---

*Does the phrase "Snack cakes filled with Grandma's patriotic goodness" ring a bell?
†See also Calliope's poem "Orpheus with Compound Fracture."

so the kid won't be scared of the digging and the drills. Thirty-three years in uniform, I never seen people working so hard, but you know the [Beekeeper's] family, they go back a ways. They draw a lot of water these parts."

American fascination with children trapped in wells being what it is, the site was soon a chaos of cameras, microphones, and spotlights. Household employees and local schoolteachers were interviewed as to the boy's sweet disposition; a local historian estimated there were between eighty and ninety such abandoned wells in northern Virginia alone. CNN reporter Charles Jaco, who would achieve renown a few years later in the first Gulf War, braved the midnight storm to stand with the drill team as they sank a parallel shaft twenty feet away; his encouragement, shouted through thunder and driving rain, would appear on inspirational bumper stickers and window placards for months afterward: JUST KEEP DIGGING!

It was almost nightfall on the second day when the child was brought up—dazed and shivering, but conscious—from the oblivious depths. As he was loaded into the helicopter that would transport him to Inova Fairfax Trauma Center, reporters and onlookers and sheriff's deputies pressed around the stretcher, microphones were thrust toward him, myriad lights played across his dazzled eyes; his name sprang from every tongue, every hand strained to touch him. His handsome face was bloodied, lips white, but his pained grimace gave way to a look of fascination and fear. Just before the helicopter door slid shut, he weakly lifted one arm, palm toward the crowd—either a gesture of thanks and acknowledgment or a desperate attempt to keep the world at bay.

"Was a tricky rescue, no doubt about it," Sheriff Bojean said at the press conference. "Lotta logistical difficulties, lotta surprises." He declined to elaborate, but the questions came in rapid-fire: Why had the rescue taken so long? Why, if the boy was conscious, had there been no answer to the rescuers' calls? Was it true he had repeatedly squirmed away from the ropes and harnesses? "Some of the guys think, you know, it was the victim," Bojean finally allowed. "But I wouldn't want to traffic in speculation. These concussions, people react . . . you know, they do strange things."

Many years later, in a brief conversation with the author, the retired lawman was less evasive. "Had some time to reflect," he said over the phone, "and what seems clear to me is he didn't want to come out. I can't speak to motive, but that boy just didn't want to be rescued."

"Pure, unadulterated nothing," the Beekeeper told the roshi. He had arrived on the front porch of the Mountaintop Zen Center, sixteen years old, having escaped from a prestigious New England boarding school* and hitchhiked all the way to Southern California. In the years since the accident, he had grown increasingly disengaged from the world around him, uninterested in his studies or normal adolescent pursuits. His dreams swelled with the emptiness he had found in that dank and silent cocoon, the sense of his discrete self dissolving into the stone.

"Show me the way back," he pleaded, struggling to arrange his legs in the unfamiliar lotus position. The roshi stood over him, barring the door. The monastery, founded in 197_, was at that time a small training facility for Asian American Zen students. Never before had the roshi taken a Caucasian—nor anyone so young—as his student. "Help me find that emptiness."

"Get lost," said the roshi. Then he turned back inside and locked the door.

The Beekeeper, shivering in the November chill, smiled at the retreating figure. "Thank you," he said.

He sat on the porch for six days and nights until David Roh, the eldest student, took pity and snuck him inside. He shared Roh's tiny cell, sleeping on the floor, eating only the crusts that the older student smuggled from the kitchen; even when the Beekeeper began joining the others for morning *zazen*, sitting for hours in the *zendo's* predawn chill, the roshi would not acknowledge him. For almost five years, he lived and practiced with the other monks, participating in every meditation, every weeklong fast, performing any domestic chore that was asked of him, all without formal acceptance into the community or *sangha*. His name was never spoken—indeed, it was never known to the other students; when he tried to attend *dokusan*, private study sessions with the roshi, the door slammed in his face. He had found the home he had dreamed of: a place where he did not exist.

*Its name rhymes with "bloat."

On the morning of his twenty-first birthday, he strode up to the roshi's table while the master ate breakfast.

"*Kwatz!*" he shouted, in a bid for attention. "*Kwatz!*" When he was still not recognized, he picked up the roshi's bowl and flung it against the dining-room wall, where it smashed, spraying those nearby with rice gruel and boysenberries.

Everyone held their breath. But a moment later, the roshi rose from his chair and bowed to the Beekeeper, who stood with clenched fists.

"Where have you been?" said the roshi.

"You tell me," said his new disciple.

From that day, the roshi was rarely seen without the Beekeeper in tow. The young man proved an exceptional student, devouring the ancient texts, mastering the koans. The roshi could not hide his pleasure; the *sangha,* which had grown to a dozen students and then to twenty, could not miss the evidence of a new favorite. Rumors spread that the Beekeeper was in line to one day receive Transmission—a ritual by which the roshi confers his knowledge and authority upon a student, in essence naming him as successor. This led to rivalries and schisms within the monastery. David Roh, who as the eldest should rightfully have been the roshi's heir, was forced to give up his cell and sleep in the monastery's stable. Six months later he would leave Mountaintop entirely.

"He had just met Calliope," says Roh, who more than three years later cannot hide his bitterness. "It was one thing to be knocked out of the line of succession. But then to see the man who took your place profaning the monastery, sneaking his girlfriend into his cell . . . None of us could sleep! All night they [discussed Zen philosophy]. It's hard to believe the roshi was unaware. But he never said a word.

"Well, the joke's on [the Beekeeper]," says Roh, who returned to Colorado College after leaving Mountaintop and finished a degree in economics. "He thought he'd find emptiness, but then he met that poet. All that time, he was looking for nothing. But she was something. Man, was she something."

———

Calliope's June 4, 200_, appearance on *The Charlie Rose Show* capped an extraordinary year, one which saw the poet transformed from passionate prodigy to scandalous national celebrity. To what degree this transformation was inevitable, and how much of it was cannily orchestrated by the poet and Rhoda Lubinski, may never be known; but the figure who flung herself across Rose's oak table, shoved her tongue in his astonished mouth, and made her shocking declaration, had already embarked upon the terrible path she would follow for the rest of her days. Between her agonizing disappearances—dress rehearsals for her eventual, tragic departure—and her spectacular flameout at UC Irvine and subsequent hospitalization, the public had already glimpsed the fervent butterfly as it struggled from the cocoon. By the next autumn, they would see, close up, the fully spread wings of the Death Artist.

"I would not say she was my most well-behaved guest," jokes the ever-genteel Rose in an e-mail. "She was definitely the only one to wear pink leather hot pants! (lol!) But what I found remarkable was the way she could evoke my sympathy. All of ours. Like a wounded kitten who swipes at your hand when you try to help. Even when Calliope attacked me and my staff, I couldn't help wanting to protect her. From whom? Well, from herself, I suppose."

What were the precursors to that bizarre incident? What were the crucial factors leading to her stunning announcement? To date, Morath Studies has been able to produce only partial answers, vague inferences, fractured narratives; like the elephant of the Indian parable, palpated by a troupe of blind men, scholars have been able to see only that sliver of the beast which confirms their pet theories or conforms to academic fashion. What is clear to this author, however, is that only a comprehensive account can do justice to Calliope's experience. Only a full telling can get at the truth.

Calliope's brief career as a student in Irvine's storied graduate program began promisingly enough, her first quarter by all accounts a tremendously productive one. There was some early confusion regarding the beehives— two colonies she installed outside her trailer, in contravention of rules against winged pets in university housing—but an anonymous donation to the Music Department seems to have greased the wheels of the permitting process. Soon enough, the poet had settled in, and the balmy coastal mornings found her at her desk, watching the lazy rituals of the bees, perhaps dreaming of the Mountaintop existence she had lately given up.

"The bees are my alter egos, my agents," she would tell David Fricke, in the *SPIN* interview the following spring. "When I want to be somewhere, anywhere else, when I want to leave this life behind, I just close my eyes and hitch a ride."

It was a remarkably productive period for the poet, as she labored to complete a manuscript. Her meticulously indexed typescripts show that in the final months of 200_ she completed drafts of "Honey Box," "Uninspired, or *Sui Generis*," "Antigone Among Furies," "Witness Protection Program," and the saucy dramatic monologue that would eventually give the book its title. She also made substantial revisions to "Rigor Mortician" and "Pop Music," two poems from her senior thesis at Mountaintop Arts, and recast "Dancing on the Charles," her tribute to Anne Sexton, as a one-act play in blank verse. Though the less-gifted poets of the workshop could hardly have given her much more than moral support, most scholars agree—if grudgingly—that Calliope benefited enormously from her work with Argentine poet L. Moreno.

Those interested in salacious rumors and crass insinuation have always promoted the view that Calliope and Moreno were lovers. Certainly his role in the disastrous March 31 reading, and the subsequent report by the university ombudsman, have provided ammunition. But this author finds these claims predictable and repugnant. Can a teacher not provide support to a gifted student without being suspected of impropriety? Can he not invest time and effort in her artistic development, can he not promote her work among older, more accomplished poets, include it in anthologies and journals for which he serves as guest editor, laud it in interviews, recite it from memory to colleagues and ex-wives, without provoking a prurient twitching of noses? The reports—if they are to be believed—that Moreno often came to her trailer past midnight, carrying a bottle of tequila, leaving, disheveled, in the early morning hours, are easily explained: Art, true art, cannot be held to a schedule, nor confined to a sterile classroom, and these two gifted poets were driven to continue their passionate debates, to pursue their strenuous analyses to the point of exhaustion. If Moreno brooked no criticism of Calliope in the workshop, if his later volume, *Siren*, was dedicated to *"La Musa, por donde sea que estés,"** these are but testaments to their intellectual connection. To suggest otherwise reveals more about the critic than about the poet herself.

Moreno's patronage was bound to provoke jealousies—among the poets as well as other students vying for her attention, for the privilege of spending an hour or two in her company. Dennis Adams, a member of the workshop who had pledged himself as "Calliope's vassal" in an unguarded moment at a local bar, recalls, "It was hard to get anywhere near her, even when Moreno wasn't around. He had his undergrads watching her trailer, reporting on anyone who went in or out. If she so much as looked at you during workshop, he'd call you into his office and start cursing at you in Spanish, threatening to ruin your career." The experience soured Adams on academia; after the March reading, he would return to Seattle, where he founded the software firm VerSI-FI.

The most visible rivalry, however, was between Moreno and Taryn Glacé, then a doctoral student in her sixth year at UCI. Glacé, whose dissertation purports to be a Marxist analysis of so-called confessional poetry,[†] had adopted Calliope as a kind of lab rat, following her around campus, accompanying her to the library and the local supermarket, cooking for her every Sunday night when the two would meet in Glacé's apartment to watch *The L Word*. Moreno refused repeated requests from Glacé to audit the graduate workshop; in return, Glacé filed a complaint with the School of Humanities and wrote an essay for the journal *Faultline* entitled "Poets and *Peronistas:* The English Department's Dirty War on Scholarship."

That simmering tension flared briefly at the annual English Banquet, a black-tie mixer for graduate students, faculty, and wealthy arts patrons held just after Thanksgiving. The event was better attended than in years past, due to interest in Calliope among the community's elderly philanthropists; Moreno, in his gentlemanly fashion, played escort, shuttling her from conversation to conversation, his arm around her waist, while Glacé

---

*"The Muse, wherever you are."
[†]Though this author finds it to be quite impenetrable.

glowered next to the service bar. After nearly an hour waiting for the poet's attention, Glacé took matters into her own hands, sauntering past the two poets and "accidentally" tipping a plate of hummus and goat cheese down the bodice of Calliope's dress. While Moreno fulminated to the CEO of Taco Bell and his wife, a vicious smile came over Calliope's lips; in the next moment, she took the glass of scotch from her professor's hand and dashed its contents in Glacé's face.

"You Stalinist bitch!" she said, evoking gasps. She then grabbed the cummerbund of Glacé's tuxedo and pulled her close for what looked, to all the world, like a French kiss.

The incident brought a written rebuke from the chancellor's office, and by the end of the following week Calliope had left the campus. At the time, no one knew where she'd gone, though no alarm bells were rung; but Dr. Breve's records indicate that a frantic Calliope called her from Rancho Santa Fe on the morning of December 12 to demand that she "clear [her] schedule for the rest of the week." The analyst informed her that she was soon to leave for her annual vacation in San Miguel de Allende, Mexico, and could squeeze her in only for two evening sessions the next week.

We may never know what happened in San Diego, though the time she spent in her childhood home seems to have been a psychic turning point. Penelope was in Europe, club-hopping and shopping for Paris real estate in the aftermath of Fuck Finn's final breakup (their last album, *The Necro Files,* had sold fewer than 100,000 copies, and their House of Blues tour had been a commercial disappointment); the household staff had been given the rest of the year off. Perhaps it was the strangeness of being alone in that house, where she had always been surrounded by servants and tutors and her mother's companions *du jour,* or perhaps it was merely the onset of winter in San Diego, that brief and startling period when the sky grows heavy, the jaunty palm trees dolorous, windows used to sheets of sunlight are suddenly streaked with rain, and the ocean groans in the tidal pull of regret.

The winter of her discontent, then—by Christmas morning, she had begun to unravel. She spent most of that day making phone calls to her father's former friends, acquaintances, bandmates, and drug suppliers, barraging them with questions and accusations. Marvin Trask, a metal-shop teacher at Santee High School, Brandt's alma mater, answered the phone only to hear a woman's a cappella rendering of "Acid Rain." Gary North, the chairman of NorthStar Records, recalls that the voice on the other end of the phone was distraught and all but incomprehensible.

"Man, it was like, I didn't even know who I was talking to! This crazy-ass chick on the phone, someone tells me it's Brandt's daughter and I'm all, 'What?' Screaming at me that I'm a grave robber, I've ruined her life, and I'm all, 'Yo, you gotta calm your shit *down*, lady!' When she's done screaming, she starts offering me money, millions, if I'll tell her where her father is. And other stuff, too—I swear—she offers, uh, well, let's say she'll give me an *oral exam*? You know, if I tell her."

The specifics of North's recollection may be disputed, but the general tone is in keeping with accounts given by Talia Z, Billy Martinez, and Fuck Finn guitarist Darlene Cream. Of each, Calliope demanded to know her father's whereabouts; each was accused of abetting a fraud, a homicide, an abduction, or some other, nameless horror; each was blamed for having sold Brandt's suicide note to *Newsweek*.

In the days that followed, the poet visited virtually every San Diego locale with any connection to her father. Between December 26 and 30, she checked into over a dozen motels in San Diego's Middletown, Mission Beach, and Kearny Mesa neighborhoods, demanding of befuddled proprietors that they check nonexistent record books for the precise room in which her father had spent a night over a decade earlier. She was spotted in alleys and parking lots, outside the band entrances to every club and recording facility; Tim Mays, owner of the Casbah, was called in during a performance by &%&% and found Calliope attempting to open the pinball machine in the back room with a crowbar. Caretakers of cemeteries from Chula Vista to Sun City recall a red-haired waif in torn blue jeans and a quilted flannel shirt trailing through rows of headstones, and security logs at La Jolla's Golden Slumbers Crematorium show that on the morning of December 29, a guard arriving for the day shift found spray-painted on the building's facade: RISE DIONYSUS!

On the eve of the new year, the poet found herself at the Ocean Beach fishing pier, contemplating the silent structure that stretched like an ambassador to the dark sea. The dilapidated pier had sheltered her father in adolescence—perhaps, she hoped, it still retained something of his vanished essence. Her disappointment is clear from her expression in the San Diego Police Department's Runaway Child Photo Database: an officer having mistaken her for a minor during a routine sweep, the grainy black-and-white image shows a face smeared with soot, eyes stunned and hopeless; surrounded by the humped, blanket-shrouded, inert forms of the desperate and destitute and mentally ill who frequent the fishing pier, there is perhaps no more melodramatic statement possible than that our young, gifted poet fit right in.*

Shortly after the first of the year, an unsigned ad began to appear in the Personals section of newspapers around the world. Addressed cryptically to "Mr. Bath and Rot," the ad reads as follows (with slight variations to accommodate syntax, rhyme, and poetic convention in the various languages):

> O Father who art a bloodstain,
> Hollowed is my world:
>   Come back to me,
>   Nest in my tree,
> Let this bird sing your praises again.†

Although the author claims no special training in psychology, it would seem abundantly clear that the durable surface of Calliope's psychic levee was beginning to show signs of great strain, its concrete beginning to spiderweb and buckle before a terrible flood of despair. It had been almost fifteen years since her father's death, since the silent morning storm clouds lowered upon that house. Not knowing where his body lay, she had not properly mourned him; not having solved the riddles of his life, she could not make sense of the complexities of her own. Perhaps it was then that

---

*The SDPDRCPD photo was reprinted on the cover of *SLAM,* January 16, 200_. The author wishes to reiterate that his association with *SLAM* ended in 199_, and that under his direction such an outrage would never have occurred.

†To date, the author has found the ad in Paris's *Le Monde,* Berlin's *Der Tagesspiegel,* Moscow's *Pravda,* the *Johannesburg Mail and Guardian,* New Delhi's *Hindustan Times,* Tokyo's *Nihon Keizai Shimbun* (both the Japanese and English editions), *Australia Daily,* Cairo's *Al Ahram, El Heraldo de Mexico,* Peru's *El Comercio,* and the *PNG Independent* of Papua New Guinea, in addition to virtually all the major U.S. dailies. This list is certainly incomplete, and does not include magazines or online communities, let alone the radio spots which aired in Cuba.

she conceived of the fantasy that he still walked the earth, and vowed to find him. Or perhaps only then did she begin to accept that he was truly gone, and start preparing to join him in the ocean's deep bosom.

The expression she wore in the SDPDRCPD photo struck an all-too-familiar chord in the author. He had seen more than he wished to of despair, had experienced the extremes of human sadness at no great remove—and it never failed to render him cold, language fleeing his mind as though to articulate such emptiness were to give it a foothold, an embrace. He had known the poet's father in the last years of his life, known him as something more than an acquaintance or colleague, having been close to Brandt in age and circumstance: They had been married in the same year, their careers had risen in rough parallel. At the time of their last encounter, the author had himself recently become a father, a fact he pointed out to Brandt at the conclusion of the band's homecoming concert at the Casbah. They had much in common, he told the singer, they were soldiers in the same army, struggling for the same revolution, a suggestion which elicited a grunt of approval.

"It's a new Golden Age," the author offered, referencing their first meeting, six years earlier. If Brandt recalled the conversation, he made no indication. "Testament to the durability of art amidst a world of materialism, to the power of creativity and exploration amidst a culture of predictability and conformity."

"You were right, Brandt!" he shouted in the superstar's ear. "Dionysus has returned to the forest. All's well in the world."

Brandt peered at him through a haze of smoke, dripping with sweat, exuding the exhaustion of his recently concluded set and of the thirteen long weeks on tour. All around them was the crush of bodies, hundreds trying to crowd into the back room, the Casbah walls pulsing with echoes of the band's encore—a paint-peeling cover of Barry McGuire's anthem, "Eve of Destruction." From the corner of his eye, the author could see the band's manager, Talia Z, struggling toward Brandt, dragging what appeared to be an IV stand. The smell of perspiration was overpowering.

Brandt leaned away from the author, as though to get a better look.

"What the fuck are you talking about?" he said. But behind the practiced hostility, the author could sense the undercurrent of admiration and solidarity which had permeated their relations since their first meeting, half a decade earlier.

"Listen, could you give me a cigarette or something?" Brandt said, leaning against the wall, barefoot, T-shirt bloodstained and torn down the middle. "It's been kind of a fucked-up night." Talia was making little headway, fans swarming around the IV, sporting with the dangling needle, jabbing penknives and keys at the plastic sac. It was not Penny Power herself so much as the seismic wave of her approach that the author saw, the fans and reporters in the hallway flattening against the walls to let the lioness pass.

"You know I don't smoke!" the author said, attempting to punch the musician jokingly on the arm but accidentally elbowing the girl next to him, a harridan in ripped fishnet stockings and improbably caked mascara, who uttered an obscenity and shoved him rudely.

It had been a difficult night for the author as well. Though hotly anticipating the show for weeks, he had arrived quite late, missing more than half the set due to a family emergency, then having to fight his way through the unadmitted multitudes who had turned dreary Kettner Boulevard into a scene from some Latin American *carnaval,* only to be denied entry for another half an hour by the thugs at the door until a promoter friend chanced to wander past.

"So. When should we do the next interview?" the author said. "Should I drop by the studio this week? We'd love to get an exclusive on how the new album's coming. Or the five of us could have a beer, do a casual thing, perhaps *chez moi* . . ."

"What?" Brandt shouted. "Sure, man, whatever. You gotta talk to the label."

"Right, right." The author winked. "Proper channels. I'm hip."

Penny had, by this time, entered the front room and was making steady progress in their direction, as was Talia Z. The roiling sea of admirers threatening to break over him at any moment, Brandt seemed to shrink into himself, into the wall at his back, clutching his glass of whiskey with two hands. Though he stood so tall on the Casbah's stage, on stages in stadiums and arenas around the globe, he was in fact a small man; the author had the momentary urge to put an arm around his delicate, cringing shoulders.

"I gotta get out of here." Brandt stared into the glass. He looked up at the author, his brow furrowed, his eyes gleamed with vulnerability. "This isn't what I meant."

"I understand," the author said. The two stood silently, something like compassion passing between them, the empathy of men struggling against monumental pressures, understanding that despite this shared moment they must each ultimately struggle alone.

"Before you go, could you sign this for me?" the author said gently, handing him the very same cassette demo that Brandt had given him years before. "It's for my son."

Brandt stared at it. "A cassette tape," he said, turning it in his palm. "Fucking analog. Jesus, that was a million years ago." Then he looked up at the author with an expression of total defeat, a forlorn look that suggested all inner supports had collapsed, everything beneath the surface had been hollowed out, rotted away, only a papery shell remained to conceal the absence.

The author was moved. "Brandt, is there anything I can do?" He grasped the musician's forearm, to both of their great surprise, his words sounding silly to him even as he uttered them. "I mean, if you need any help . . . I've listened to what you've said all these years, and your songs, and . . . I think I understand. I feel what you feel. I'm not a musician, nor an artist, but I have a good heart—what can someone like me, who wants to be part of the solution, what can I do to help?"

But Penny and Talia had arrived, and as the latter inserted the needle in the fleshy underside of Brandt's arm, he seemed to grow back into his full stature, closed his eyes, leaned his head against the wall, and smiled.

"Nothing," he said.

And what of the poet's inner life, that strange country of unscaled peaks, arid expanses, wild protean jungles, of secluded moors and churning seas and chaotic cosmopolises knowable to us only through the medium of words, the serpentine vehicle of syntax? For that is all we are left with, what you, the reader, are unarguably confronted with at this very moment: verbal representations of a subjectivity that is not present—a shadow flickering on a cave wall, a ghost.

Any biography quickly comes up against the problem of exteriority, the inability to re-create the particular experience out of the common, primitive material of language.* Like a child reconstructing the Hanging Gardens of Babylon in a jigsaw puzzle—the child suffers for hours or days with the limited elements at his disposal, weeping in frustration, combining and recombining, his triumph upon fitting the last piece into place tragically short-lived once he grasps the awful truth: that this image he has managed to assemble is not, *could never be*, the magnificent gardens themselves.

How then to accurately explain the paradoxes and inconsistencies, how to illuminate the darkest recesses, plumb the deepest chasms of her character? If Calliope herself, as she frequently lamented, was unable to make herself understood, if even the poetry was, in her estimation, a terrible failure that left her feeling like "a hot doomed moth that flames/inside a bulb,"[†] how can an author hope to pierce even the outer battlements of that walled city, with what wooden horse can he gain its courtyards, know firsthand the aspects of its citizenry, end the long, hungry siege along its beaches?

Even a project so blessed with a surfeit of source material—documents, audio- and videotape, newsprint and microfilm, interviews with poets and academics, musicians and fans—is, in the end, insufficient, confined as it is to the orderly realm of language. In the words of Slovenian critic Slavoj Žižek, it cannot leap "from the clear blue skies of the symbolic into the psychotic miasma of the Real."

Žižek, something of a celebrity in the narrow world of literary theory, was the writer of two widely read profiles in the *New York Times Magazine* which appeared the following year. The first, "Missile Defense System," addressed this conundrum of subjectivity as central to any analysis of

---

*In the case of Michael Azerrad's *Make Me*, "primitive" is the operative term.
[†]"Suicide Bomber"

Calliope and her father. In Žižek's telling, Calliope's search for "the real Brandt Morath" was a metaphor for, and a deconstruction of, the human paradox in general: our inability to exit symbolic systems of representation and touch the "hard kernel of the Real." Calliope's entire "life-career" was an attempt to bridge this gap—between form and content, language and experience, the symbolic and that which cannot be symbolized. Her failure was not only inevitable, Žižek seems to say, it was her subject matter all along:

> While art is always organized around the void or center—the hidden unspeakable which Lacan called "the Thing" with correlates in the oozing, undead creatures of film and literature—the originality of Calliope's work owes much to her reckless attacks on this traumatic center, hurling herself into the monster's maw, pursuing the forbidden *jouissance* even as it skitters from her embrace and dislocates along the signifying chain[. . .]
>
> For this reason Calliope's taking the sign of Antigone is absolutely appropriate, her life similarly organized around an unconditional demand. Whereas Antigone insisted on burying her brother, a symbolic act necessary to inscribe him in the text of tradition, Calliope's search can be read as *stricto sensu* a drive to *uninscribe* her father, to disinter him from the fraudulent web—that is to say, the symbolic web—in which he is entangled.
>
> But the dream of escaping the tyranny of signification is the most basic human fantasy, and is itself a product of the symbolic order— the ego, having no other purpose than to protect itself from the Real, cannot produce its own executioner. Both Calliope and Antigone are here at a disadvantage. Their actual suicide is impossible—the *act* is read only as *gesture*, as the symbolic order rushes to express it in language. Like her father (and Antigone's), Calliope is forbidden even the privilege of her own death.*

Note the irony: To lament the impossibility of uncovering the Real, Žižek himself resorts to metaphor, jargon, and obscurantism, adding his

---

NYT Magazine, October 8, 200_, based on interviews conducted the previous summer. However, cf. Slavoj Žižek, "Errata," *NYT Magazine,* November 22, 200_, published after her disappearance.

own strand or two to the "symbolic web" which conceals it. Like the poet herself, he is forced to draw parallels with fictional characters in order to move within striking distance of her factual existence.

Greek drama, postmodernist philosophy, French terminology—such has become the *lingua franca* of Morath Studies, a superheated discourse far removed from the hard-nosed approach the author has taken here. If the "symbolic web" is truly inescapable, then a convincing account of the real Calliope, one which strips away myth and rhetoric to reveal the true subject beneath, may ultimately prove impossible. But this author soldiers on, rejecting defeatism, ever striving for the brute objectivity that leads to the Truth.

"I didn't invent marketing. I didn't design American culture," Rhoda Lubinski would write in her memoirs. "Shakespeare would have starved if he were writing today. Wordsworth? Forget about it. They'd beat him up for his lunch money. He'd be writing ad copy for Pine-Sol. I knew it didn't matter how good the poems were—and they were fucking amazing. We had to use every opportunity, we had to take advantage of whatever we could. That's what I learned at Mountaintop—you take whatever raw material you can find and you discover a new form for it. You *create*."*

By the time Calliope returned to Irvine, in the second week of January, "Operation Calliope" was in full swing. Though Calliope's book was not yet under contract—indeed, though she had not finished writing it— demand grew steadily over the winter months, interview requests rolling in from publications ranging from the weekly *Rancho Santa Fe Ranchero* to the *Village Voice* to *Mirabella*. Her private life—always an oxymoron—was increasingly mentioned in tabloids and celebrity blogs, many of which dredged up appalling old rumors of sexual abuse or scaled new heights of insinuation regarding her courtship with actor Ben Affleck.† The *Paris Review* issue featuring "Sunday on Suicide Row" was out, and a draft of "The

---

*Rhoda Lubinski, *Throwing Pots About Poems: My Work with Calliope* (Random House, 200_), p. xii.
†"Matt Tells Ben: Me or Her!" from *Star*, March 2, 200_, should sufficiently represent these masterpieces of journalism.

Bird and the Bees," much more explicit than the eventual book version, was leaked to *Nerve.com*, photos of Calliope and Connor Feingold at a Malibu fruit stand to the *OC Weekly*. "Publicity begets publicity" was the first commandment of Scambiguity, and indeed the trickle of paparazzi outside the poet's trailer swelled that winter to a creek and then a river, creating still more tension with the university. Offers for talk-show slots—TV and radio, late-night and early morning—began to come in, requests for "sit-downs" with everyone from Diane Sawyer to Tom Green, guest appearances on *South Park* (as herself) and the pilot for *Friends: 40* (as Chandler in drag), an invitation to host MTV's three-day Terrible Children Independence Day Marathon.

"It was as though the poetry *qua* poetry did not exist," says Taryn Glacé. "Calliope was a natural resource to be raped by entrepreneurs, fed for a price to a public whose appetite was to be heightened by any means or trickery possible."

It was around this time, too, that Calliope embarked on her legal efforts against filmmaker Harvey Weinstein, who had begun casting for *The Hanged Man: The Brandt Morath Story*. By the fall, in fact, she would be involved in no fewer than three highly visible lawsuits: the Weinstein affair, the University of California's eviction proceedings, and a damages suit by WNET and the producers of *Charlie Rose*.

"You could virtually see the machinery of multinational capital trying to grind her beneath its wheels," says Glacé, who would finish her degree that summer and take a position at the University of San Francisco. "The system which tried to claim her, the totalized field of corporate depersonalization which can function only because of the unconscious internalization and participation of its subjects, which can only be threatened by the refusal of said subjects. The autonomous entity which resists interpellation. The extant network of laws, created by transnational capital with the sole purpose of protecting transnational capital, turned upon the renegade subject to compel obedience."

Although the author is not unsympathetic to complaints about transnational capital, Ms. Glacé's analysis somewhat willfully ignores the extent to which Calliope, with Rhoda, encouraged and even developed the industry which grew up around her and her poetry. Still, though her hands were not clean, it is true that by the time of the *Charlie Rose* debacle "Operation Calliope" was already growing beyond the artist's control, rather like the lovely bougainvillea, ubiquitous in Southern California, which will, unless tended and pruned with superhuman vigilance, climb frenetically over walls and fences and gates, colonize lawn equipment and a child's scattered toys, invade and obstruct the rain gutters, and force its way beneath the Spanish tile with sheer determination and vegetable strength until even a light rainfall may dampen and darken the ceiling and interior walls and send the mother of the toy-scattering child (who, to be fair, had warned for months of such an outcome) into a paroxysm of tears and recriminations out of all proportion to the actual damage, a paroxysm that may leave her gasping for breath, locked in the bathroom with a stuffed giraffe and a bottle of tranquilizers, while both the child and the child's father stand helpless and guilt-ridden and somewhat bewildered in the water-stained hallway, the one crying and sniffling and wondering what his father has done to provoke such a paroxysm, the other struggling between remorse and anger and a deep intestinal fear at the intensity and duration of the paroxysm, praying he might find a way to defuse it before it escalates even further and destroys him and the child and the house and fecund bougainvillea in the hurricane swath of its wake.

Be that as it may, Calliope had not lost track of her primary quest: to find her father. Her mother was unavailable, having purchased a condominium in the trendy Marais district of Paris, Calliope's contact with her limited to televised images of Penny Power stepping out of limousines onto red carpets in various European cities, rumors regarding her affairs with the disgraced products of various effete aristocracies. Another parent in the process of disappearing—is it any surprise the poet began to see *recovery* as her life's project?

"It was like the whole world had become one giant reference to her father," recalls Dennis Adams. "The walls of her trailer were covered with maps and photos and newspaper clippings. She had pushpins stuck in different cities, places where there'd been a sighting, and she'd scribble the date, the source, whether or not she'd talked to the person—she had a 'reliability scale' to decide which ones to follow up on personally. The fax machine was overflowing, piles of unopened bills on the floor . . . And there were bees everywhere, sitting on the mirrors, the windows, tins of sugar water on every flat surface, just crawling with bees."

Into this psychological squalor dropped the largest contract for a first book of poems in the history of the U.S. publishing industry. At a March 10 press conference, Rhoda announced that Snow Lion Press, of Ithaca, New York, had agreed to pay Calliope an advance "in the low seven figures."*

"Buddhists know poetry when they see it," she told reporters, who were frankly incredulous that a minuscule niche publisher would (or could) marshal such a sum for a book of secular poetry. Snow Lion's three previous releases—*Looking Down from Here: The XIVth Dalai Lama in Dharamsala, Lhasa/Orlando: A Cultural History of the New Tibet,* and *Bardo for Beginners*—had average advances of $1,500 and sold a total of 3,050 copies before returns. "When you've lived so many lifetimes, you start to learn what art really is," Rhoda said, smiling flirtatiously. "It's like karma. Poetry karma."

When pressed to clarify in what way a million-dollar transaction was "like karma," the publicist demurred. "I don't think you're getting the big picture here," she said. "This is a revolution in progress. It's as big as anything her father did. Finally the world is ready for poetry. They're ready for Calliope."

The gathered reporters clamored for Rhoda's attention. When finally called upon, Skip Cárdenas asked whether Calliope felt she had to compete with her father, and whether she recalled his statement at the MTV Music Awards that "the more money they give you for something, the more it usually sucks."

Rhoda was clearly annoyed, and gathered her papers to end the press conference. "I guess you'll have to ask her that," she said.

But of course the poet was not there.

Calliope's first major disappearance, a harrowing nineteen days in March of 200_, has frequently been dismissed as a crude attempt to drum up publicity for the Irvine reading, an event Rhoda regarded as the starting gun for

---

*A source in Snow Lion's public-relations office (hastily established after the announcement of the deal) puts the exact figure at $2.1 million, which included a $400,000 signing bonus, foreign rights, and right of first offer on a second book, but did not include film rights.

"the most important book tour of the new millennium." New to her craft, the story goes, the publicist failed to take into account the volatile emotions of those who knew Calliope—not to mention the poet's own passions— failed to follow her own dicta regarding *t*'s and *i*'s and the orthographic necessities thereof. She overshot the mark, stirred the hive too strenuously; the disaster of March 31, then, as another demonstration of the power of absence, more proof that hunger, once unleashed, cannot be controlled.

Rhoda strenuously denies the charge. "I *wanted* her out there in March. I wanted her face *everywhere*. I had Howard Stern and Jon Stewart sniffing my ass about her. Ben [Affleck] had closed the Continental on a *Saturday night* so they could have a private dinner, photographers everywhere, *kaching!* We didn't have time for a disappearing act. We didn't have time for a bullshit meltdown."*

Taryn Glacé had been the last to see her, early on the morning of March 10, when Calliope purportedly left to join Rhoda at the press conference. According to Glacé, the poet had been "exceptionally energetic" the night before, several times interrupting their study session to check her e-mail. She had packed a large suitcase, larger than seemed necessary for the day trip to L.A., but this detail did not strike Glacé as extraordinary.

"She was a product of her upbringing and context. Money, status, commodity. The *appearance* of capital, the *things* which prove capital to itself," she later told the author, her disapproval tempered by fondness. "It was par for the course."

When Calliope did not arrive in Silverlake, Rhoda didn't think much of it, but by March 14, the publicist began—quietly, at first—to sound the alarm, contacting Penny in France and leaving multiple messages for Connor. By March 18, with still no word, Rhoda took her concerns to the press, and newspapers up and down the coast ran articles that week speculating as to the poet's whereabouts. L. Moreno canceled the workshop and is rumored to have consulted a local psychic; Glacé suggested to the Irvine police that Moreno himself may have been responsible for the poet's disappearance. On March 20 an unidentified person or persons constructed a small shrine—photo, votives—outside the workshop room. On March 22,

*Lubinski, p. 184.

after frantic consultation with the poet's mother, Rhoda requested that the California Highway Patrol activate the "Amber Alert" system to notify freeway drivers of the missing person. The request was denied. In San Diego, KPBS radio reporter Alison St. John organized a telephone and e-mail TipLine, and the house on Azalea Path was besieged once again by newsvans and hysterical fans. The house stood impassive as a monument, its curtained windows and dark gables a mockery of the desire that crept across the lawn.

Any number of theories have been raised over the years, none proven.* Almost a year later, Skip Cárdenas would publish an article claiming the poet spent March 11–26 traveling—under the assumed name of Cal Klein— to Madrid, Fez, Marrakech, Cairo, and Tel Aviv. Though Cárdenas is normally the most levelheaded and reliable of reporters, his theory—that Calliope, wracked by obsession, was pursuing leads as to her father's whereabouts—is based on speculation, the testimony of a nineteen-year-old Moroccan cobbler seeking U.S. asylum, and a partial boarding pass scribbled with a line from Emily Dickinson. Absent more convincing evidence, this, too, must be consigned to the ever-growing heap of unsubstantiated rumor. As with so many events, we may simply never know the truth.

One might speculate that her disappearance indicated a level of ambivalence about the upcoming reading, the poet hesitating on the threshold of a life in the public eye. It is often forgotten that the reading never should have taken place—in fact, almost did not take place. The university had made it clear in a January 9 letter that it did not want Calliope to read on campus and would not grant the use of any facilities for that purpose, citing the disruption and mayhem of her Mountaintop appearance. For many years, therefore, Morath scholars have pondered how Rhoda was able to arrange the event, the account in her memoir being fairly elusive on this point—nor had anyone identified the source of the "confidential" e-mail announcement that circulated throughout the student body and eventually was forwarded to parties in all fifty states, and parts of Canada and the European Union. The return address provided was a "Georges Izam-

---

*The most persistent, and the most inane, regards an alleged Cabo San Lucas getaway with Matt Damon.

bard," the name of Rimbaud's first teacher; after significant effort, the author has ascertained that the sender was Lorenzo Moreno de la Cruz.

In her competent work of biocriticism, *Ashes, Ashes, We All Fall Down*, Sandra Gilbert reviews the many accounts of the Irvine reading, arguing that portrayals of Calliope fall into two categories: that of helpless victim (the intrusion of the protesters, the pressure from Rhoda and Snow Lion, the inexplicable role of the bees) and that of cynical buffoon (her alleged polyamory, rumors of a prescription-drug habit, her love of the self-destructive gesture), stereotypes easily traceable to common views of Calliope's parents. But the more interesting contrast here is that of nature and nurture, private and public, the desperate struggle between the poet's inner turmoil and the needs and desires of those driven to possess her. Is it so difficult to put ourselves in her shoes, then, to imagine how the upcoming reading must have seemed to her: a point of no return, a paradigm, a precipice from which even the steeliest might turn back?

She was next seen by Sebastião Salgado, who arrived at the Malibu home of Connor Feingold early on the morning of March 29, following last-minute instructions from Rhoda's office. Rhoda had handpicked the famed Brazilian photo-essayist to shoot the cover for *SPIN*, having studied his 1990s work with Kosovar refugees. The appointment would indicate that, by March 28, Rhoda knew Calliope's whereabouts.

"I ring the doorbell," Salgado recalled in a 200_ interview in *Esquire*. "She answers after ten minutes, wrapped in a blanket. She looks terrible, just terrible. Unwashed, sunburned, so very tired. She asks can I please wait. Half an hour I am waiting. I hear loud noises inside, screaming. I ring the doorbell. She answers again. Still wearing the blanket."

Salgado's account provoked yet more scandal-mongering: For many, it not only solved the mystery of the poet's disappearance but finally confirmed the reports of her liaison with her father's bandmate. The author rejects that conclusion.

"A man is standing behind her, very tall, completely naked," Salgado told *Esquire*. "They argue. I tell her I do not work in this way. I will leave. She begins to cry. She puts her arms around me. She is very convincing."

The plan was to photograph the poet at the Santa Monica pier, poised for flight above the ocean. Appraising her condition, however, Salgado knew this would be impossible. Before she could delay further, he loaded her, blanket and all, into his Land Rover and drove high into the Malibu Hills until he found the right setting, a wide field of dry heather, needing only twenty minutes to capture the unforgettable image that hit news-stands six weeks later.

From there, the trail goes cold again, the dots unconnected. But there were still two days before the ill-fated reading, two days in which Cal-liope's mental state would only deteriorate further. Any account that glosses over this interval must be considered less than responsible; this author, for one, will not be satisfied until every detail is known, every nu-ance accurately mapped, until the Death Artist, in all her terrifying com-plexity, is understood.

Roshi Lobsang Nobu—or "Roshi Bob," as he is known to his students—descends from seventh-century Japanese warriors who invaded mainland China during the T'ang dynasty. A fleshy, broad-backed man whose scalp and shoulders betray five decades of exposure to the Southern California sun, he sits a horse expertly and, with his fondness for cowboy boots (Nau-gahyde, of course), spurs (rubber), and Stetsons, looks a bit like a robed John Wayne as he mounts a well-marked trail above the monastery. Stop-ping in a clearing, sunshine flaying the author's uncovered head, Roshi Bob smiles winningly and points down at the rooftops of the indoor swimming pool, the Hewlett-Packard Zen Business Center, and the sushi bar newly annexed to the main kitchen.

"This they put up only for the center," the roshi says, pointing across the valley to the black needle that stands from the highest hilltop. "Before this, cell-phone service is terrible! Many people become very angry, which interferes with Zen practice. So finally I ask, Roshi Bob, how can we min-imize the anger and maximize the compassion at Mountaintop Zen Cen-ter? I spoke to Sprint. Soon we have new tower, and persons less angry, able to focus more on Zen Buddhist meditation."

The roshi presses his palms together and bows slightly toward the dis-tant tower. It is mid-afternoon, a hot wind rustling the San Jacinto flora, a solitary hawk wheeling high above. The author leans to remove a razorthorned twig that has wedged itself excruciatingly between his sock and sneaker, clutching white-knuckled at the knob of his horse's Western saddle as the cranky animal shifts from hoof to feral hoof. What had been planned as a quick visit to the monastery has taken up much of the day, while he waited for the roshi to finish morning *zazen* and lead a noon discussion on Internet-based Zen resources. Then there was the roshi's post-lunch swim, during which the author trod patiently alongside the pool while Bob breast-stroked through ten laps, stopping only to adjust the inflatable purple cuffs around his arms.

"So you see, Zen Center is not stuck in past. We do not wish, as some believe, to live in a different world or older world," he says, gently spurring his horse, Dogen. "Nostalgia is a kind of desire, and desire is enemy of Zen Buddhist state of mind."

On a hunch, the author has come to Mountaintop in search of the lost two days in Calliope's life. It is unclear, though, whether Roshi Bob's personal assistant has conveyed this objective, as the roshi's unhurried manner suggests he believes the author to be engaged in a more general kind of inquiry, one which necessitates an exhaustive overview of the monastery and its history.

"Now we have many friends, who help Zen Center to change with the times so Zen Center is not living in past," he says, pulling Dogen's head toward a fork in the path. The author's horse, Sonia, does not respond quite as well to direction, answering each tug of the reins with an irritable snort and a baleful one-eyed glare. "This was not always the case. In early times, when Roshi Bob is first starting Zen Center, we have one building for sleeping and meditation and eating. Eight monks. Now Zen Center is seven buildings, beds for sixty-four persons, and weekly shuttle bus to Santa Monica."

He is clearly amused by this detail, clapping his hands and chortling. The horses come to yet another stop.

"Yes, Roshi Bob, well, but what about Calliope?" the author inquires politely for at least the fifth time. "Do you recall anything about March 29 or 30 of 200_?"

"Zen Center has visitors from all over the world, and exchange program in Osaka, Bangkok, Bilbao, and Woodstock, New York. You know

Woodstock, Mr. Andrew? Jimi Hendrix?" Roshi Bob astonishes the author by turning in the saddle to play an impassioned air-guitar version of "The Star Spangled Banner," replete with quavering, nasal approximations of the melody. The horses stand stoically on the path, only the slightest twitch rippling behind Sonia's left ear.

When he has recovered his wits, the author says, "Yes, it was quite a performance. I'm wondering, though, Roshi—"

"Many many famous persons come to Zen Center, and here they find nourishment of the spirit, focusing of the mind, and relaxing of the body."

"Yes, I recall that from the brochure, Roshi, but—"

"Sometimes I ask, Roshi Bob, what if famous persons do not discover Mountaintop Zen Center? What if L.A. Times does not print article about poet girl that says she loves Mountaintop Zen Center? How would present be different now if many famous persons don't come looking for poet? Maybe they never discover Mountaintop Zen Center? Maybe we still have one building and old kitchen and no T1 line? Maybe there is more happiness and compassion? Maybe less?"

"Well, Roshi Bob, I say, if this present does not happen, there is no place for Roshi Bob to ask such questions about the past." He takes up the reins, gently spurring Dogen toward a descending curve. "We see how the concepts of past, present, and future are not so useful as we think, that it is not straight line from one to the next but interconnected layers. We think of snow falling on grass that is growing in soil: They are different things, but touching and sharing their nature. So I say, Roshi Bob, what is the usefulness of these questions 'what if'? Do you know what is koan, Mr. Andrew?"

"I'm vaguely familiar—," says the author, pulling back hard on Sonia's reins as they jostle down a steep, uneven segment of the path.

"The most famous is 'What is the sound of one hand clapping?' You know this koan?"

"Roshi Bob, please . . . ," the author pants, as the horses emerge at full gallop from the trees, sweeping around the side of the Zen Center and coming to a halt before the stables with a nonchalance that seems, somehow, rather mocking. "Was Calliope here on March 29, 200_? That's all I want to know."

The roshi dismounts and pats the dust from his robes, holding Sonia's reins as the author plants one trembling foot and then the other back on terra firma. Several guests in black robes and designer sunglasses walk past, greeting the horsemen with palms pressed together. A distant, ringing triangle signals the impending supper.

"Mr. Andrew is very goal oriented, do you know this?" He puts an arm across the author's shoulders and smiles. "Why is Mr. Andrew so interested in the poet girl? This is what Roshi Bob wants to know. But Roshi Bob does not ask Mr. Andrew, because Roshi Bob lets go of desire. For this we practice Zen Buddhist state of mind. Perhaps Mr. Andrew does not know why he is so focused on poet girl, and Roshi Bob interrupts Mr. Andrew's path to understanding by forcing him to answer questions before he is ready. Do you know what is Heisenberg uncertainty principle?"

"Roshi Bob," the author says, having brushed the dust from his pants and gathered himself for one last display of superhuman patience. "With all due respect, I am not interested in Zen Buddhist practice, certain though I am of its incomparable benefits to humanity. I would like to know whether Calliope visited the center on the specific dates in question. If you are prepared to answer this query, please do so now, as I have pressing engagements back in San Diego. If you are unable or unwilling to answer, please let me know and I shall leave you to your own numerous responsibilities."

The roshi presses his lips together, and his hand which had been brushing the horse's mane falls to his side. The last edge of the sun slides below the hilltops and the grounds of the Zen Center fall into shadow.

"Mr. Andrew," the roshi says, "you see how desire misleads you? I have already told you what you are asking to know."

After another moment's silence, interrupted only by the stamp of hooves in the dust, the roshi takes the author's hand. "Come, Roshi Bob will show you the Morath Infirmary before supper. Please hurry," he says. "Tonight is Roshi's favorite: soy cheeseburgers. He is looking forward to this all week."

By the end of March, the Beekeeper had been fasting for nearly four months. His responsibilities at the monastery had been gradually curtailed over the course of that winter, as he grew weaker—his regimen apparently consisted of a spoonful of bee's honey and a glass of water each morning; first the gathering of wood and then the washing of dishes and the sweeping of the halls and meditation rooms had proven too strenuous, until finally he was unable even to mount the stairs to his cell or arrange his thin blanket over his pallet without assistance. Once Roshi Bob's star pupil, the Beekeeper was fading before their very eyes. The roshi pleaded with him, offered food from his own plate—but it was as if the Beekeeper were listening to another, more powerful teacher, as though emptiness itself had found a voice.

"Always we must distinguish between reality and metaphor," the roshi told the author, as they relaxed with snifters of cognac in his private study. "We cannot achieve Zen Buddhist state of mind if state of body is unhealthy."

He set down his glass and rubbed two hands over his not-insignificant belly, a belly all the more rotund for the remarkable four and two-thirds soyburgers the author had just watched him consume. "Roshi Bob always takes care of the body, so to better achieve Zen Buddhist state of mind." He invited the author to verify the healthy state of his body. The author declined.

By the time Calliope arrived, the Beekeeper had been moved into the monastery's rudimentary health center—hardly more than a double-sized cell with a few jars of swabs and tongue depressors and an ancient black-and-white television which picked up only a fuzzy signal from Tijuana. For several weeks he had lain there, the last dwindling jar of honey by his side, struggling from his pallet only to perform morning zazen, the rest of the day spent watching Mexican soap operas and occasionally writing in a journal made of tree bark.* His blood pressure was dangerously low, his body temperature hovering around 96 degrees. All his body hair had fallen out, giving the once-virile young man the blank, waxy aspect of a mannequin.

---

*For a time, this journal was in the Texas collection, but gradual desiccation made it virtually unreadable. In August 200_ it was sent to a restorer in Belgium, who stole it.

The roshi, at a loss for how to help his young charge, had written several letters to Calliope, but by midwinter had despaired of response.

Late in the afternoon of March 29, however, her car rattled up the road and skidded to a slushy stop just before the main building, where the roshi and the other monks had just sat down for supper. Though the monks were well acquainted with the poet, her entrance never failed to cause a stir—in this case, a stir enhanced by her haggard appearance, and the fact that she was still dressed only in the bramble- and heather-covered blanket in which she had been photographed that morning, and a pair of duck boots. She carried a small tote bag, and as she hurried through the refectory she made a hurried bow to the roshi, who recalls that the menu that night included macaroni and soycheese and molasses-seared brussels sprouts.

"Always I ask, Miss Calliope, we have supper at precisely 4:30," the roshi recalls with a fond, exasperated smile. "Please time your arrival before or after the eating. Constant interruption of eating is detrimental to Zen Buddhist state of mind!"

Seeing that the Beekeeper was not in the dining room, Calliope vanished up the stairs. The roshi and the others waited, forks suspended above their macaroni, for the inevitable: A moment later, she pounded back into the refectory and demanded to know where he was.

"Is he in the fucking *zendo?*" She gestured at the door. "It's like thirty degrees outside! What's the matter with you people?"

Still no one spoke as the poet exited the building, the door smacking loudly against its frame, the purposeful crunch of her shoes in snow slowly fading. Outside the picture windows, a platinum moon was rising, evergreens sleeved in snow, the world slowly gathering its strength for a spring that was late in coming. Amid the swelling silence, all could hear in their minds the returning footsteps, faster and more volatile and potentially violent, that would soon begin.

She came back shivering, her lips blue and hair wild, one side of the blanket skid-marked with snow. Holding the blanket closed with one hand, she clutched the roshi's robe with the other, repeating her demand. The roshi recalls the intensity of her cold-brightened gaze, the lividity of the birthmark on her neck which pulsed with the regular movements of her carotid artery. He asked for his bowl of macaroni to be kept warm, and led her to the infirmary.

When she saw the Beekeeper, lying with the remote control on his sunken chest, his dull eyes and bony appendages, his withered body barely heavy enough to dent the mattress, the poet fell to her knees; the small room and the hallway resounded with wails.

"Today he takes the last spoonful," the roshi said, indicating the empty jar at the side of the bed. "Roshi Bob has to scoop the last honey with his finger."

Calliope sniffled and laid her head on the Beekeeper's thigh, the only part of his body substantial enough to support its weight. To the amazement of the roshi, who had not seen his student move for days except the merest twitch of the thumb to turn the television on or off, the Beekeeper raised a weakened hand and laid it atop Calliope's head.

"I told you not to come back," he said, a sound closer to the swish of a tree branch in a summer garden than to a human voice.

"I brought you something," she sniffed, reaching into her bag, from which she produced four jars of Moroccan honey.

He closed his eyes. His temples and orbits were darkened with pigment, scaly smudges typical of late-stage starvation. "Don't you see how close I am?" he said. "I can almost feel it. It's right there."

"Young man is very stubborn," said the roshi. "Tomorrow we must bring doctor from Mountaintop to feed young man from intravenous device."

Calliope stiffened but kept her back to the roshi. "No needles," she said.*

"Miss Calliope, young man needs nourishment. If he will not take—"

"I said no fucking needles!" Struck by her vehemence, the roshi pressed his palms together and fell silent.

"Baby, you've got to eat something," she said, smoothing her hand over the Beekeeper's scalp.

"You can't stop me," the specter on the bed exhaled. "You have no idea. Everything is gone, every thought, every formulation stripped away. I'm

*The author opts for a literal reading of Calliope's well-documented aichmophobia, rather than the juvenile interpretation of Meersch and the other Freudians.

alive." Calliope, sobbing quietly, dug dirty fingernails into her forearms. "It's the purest feeling—like a knife slicing through an apple."

"Do you want an apple, baby?" she pleaded.

His eyes turned to her, bloodshot marbles in a doll's head. "It was always right here. Underneath all the noise, all the words . . ."

"I'll get you an apple, baby. I'll buy you a fucking orchard, just please eat something, okay?"

"Why?" he croaked.

Exasperated, she stretched across his body and clenched the blanket. "Because you'll die," she sobbed.

"There is no death." His smile was a thin grimace, revealing a missing front tooth.

She took his chin in her hand. "Then what smells so fucking bad in here?"

The Beekeeper coughed weakly, watching shadows writhe in the TV static. "Your father understood. You have to scrape away the noise to find reality." He coughed again. "Listen to the music, Bird."

The poet moaned. "My father wasn't looking for reality."

"An apple perhaps is not the best solution," whispered the roshi. "Very acidic. A glucose drip more helpful to young man. Perhaps some Gatorade. Perhaps after some days of glucose drip he is ready for an apple . . ."

Calliope changed her tactics, fingertips playing along the Beekeeper's dry skin, she kissed his forehead, the tip of his nose, his Adam's apple. "What about me, baby? Don't you know I need you? What good does it do me if you're dead?"

"I've never been more alive," he said, his shallow breath mingling with the television's hiss. His head lolled. "It's you who's dying, Calliope. They're already burying you."

"After the apple," muttered the roshi, "perhaps some bread, soon young man can eat soyburgers again, help the body recover strength . . ."

Calliope's patience was eroding. "Please have some honey. Just one teaspoon?" she wheedled, moving her hand over his abdomen. "I'll do that trick you like . . ."

With great effort he lifted a hand to touch her cheek. "Now that you're here, I'm ready to take the last step."

Her hand froze at his groin. "What last step? What are you talking about?"

"You had it right. In the *zendo*," he said. "Words are all we have. They're what stands between us and nothing."

Calliope shook her head, terrified. "No." She gripped his arm until he grimaced.

"Only by getting rid of words can we truly experience emptiness. You were right, Bird. You showed me the way."

At the limits of her emotional control, she snatched the remote from his hand and turned off the television. "What's so great about emptiness?"

"It's the truth."

"Well, then, fuck the truth!" She flung the remote behind her; only the roshi's catlike reflexes* kept it from smashing into fragments against the doorjamb. He slipped the remote into the folds of his robe, footsteps in the hallway as the other monks approached.

"Words are the problem," the Beekeeper said. His left arm dangled over the side of the bed. "I'm done with words."

"No," she murmured, touching his face, peeling his eyes back. "Baby, no."

"Thank you, Calliope," he said, and turned to face the wall.

Calliope rocked his shoulder. "Talk to me. Please talk to me, baby." Despite his weakness, the Beekeeper could not be budged.

She pounded a fist into the straw mattress. "Fine, kill yourself! You think that impresses me? I've been there and done that. You shit! You total shit, what about *me*?" By the time the roshi and three other monks could cross the floor of the tiny infirmary, Calliope had climbed atop her erstwhile consort and was raining blows upon his shoulder and back and the side of his head.

"You fucking narcissist, this isn't Zen, it's masturbation!" she said, as the monks tried to drag her from the pallet. She kicked at the well-meaning Buddhists, her fists landing on the Beekeeper's body with the dull resonance of a softball thudding into a beanbag. "What about *me*?"

"Please, Miss Calliope!" yelled the roshi, as one of the monks twisted her arms behind her back, the roshi wrapping his arms around her torso to

---

*N.B.: The roshi asked that the author use the phrase "catlike reflexes."

keep the blanket from falling to the floor. With great effort they pulled her from the bed, the five of them tottering backward toward the door, Calliope's screams giving way to a plaintive moan as her exhaustion at last overcame her. Without warning, her body went limp, the sudden lack of resistance taking them all by surprise so that they tumbled back into the hallway, a black-robed and thistle-blanketed mass, the remote control slipping from the folds of the roshi's robe and dropping to the floor, where it was crushed under a scramble of sandals.

It is interesting to note the discrepancy between the roshi's account and the rendering of this scene in "Foulbrood," the fourth and final poem in Calliope's original "HymenOpera." In keeping with the exquisite melodrama of the cycle, "Foulbrood" presents an aging queen—a tattered, weakened version of the virgin queen of "The Bird and the Bees" who came into her full powers in "Honey Box" and "It's Good to Be the Queen"—at the deathbed of her favorite drone. The poem, one of Calliope's darkest, brings to a crescendo the romance of the first three poems, uniting the themes of love, death, and renewal so ingeniously expressed through the metaphor of apiculture. ("Queen cups" are formations which indicate the imminent arrival of a new queen; "queen substance" is a pheromone by which the queen controls hive behavior.) In the poem, there is no indication of the queen doing violence to the dying male; on the contrary, the carefully constructed sense of claustrophobia ("We are wintered/stuck in supers/annuated past the pale of spring") suggests the workers have confined the drone against his will, cruelly separating lovers who wish only to spend their last moments in sweet reminiscence:

> [T]hese workers turned against their queen
> her whiskered legs substanceless, subpar
> and parceled off to dead combs
> a dark box
> the shock of being stripped by love's
> lacerations, a doom of humming—
> queen cups in the brood announce
> the swarm is coming.

What will this weak woman do?
She hears the sound—can
you?—a distant wind of trumpets
or guitars. Can it be
the spring has come at last?
The past a pile of dry selves
husked outside the hive; tomorrow
they fly in dreams to Shangri-
la, land of silk and honey, but

now, what now?[. . .]

Critics consider "Foulbrood" a pivotal poem in the canon: even while providing a highly satisfying end ("the drawing of the curtain") to the cycle, it introduces a number of themes that would come to dominate her work and culminate fearsomely in "Suicide Bomber"—most importantly the exchange of identities, symbolized by the "dry selves" outside the hive, and the flight impulse, which is transformed from dream to reality through the metaphor of music. Indeed, its very structure—ten incremental stanzas, the first being one line in length, the last being ten—suggests flight and renewal, the dying queen escaping into a wider world of possibility, as Calliope herself would do before the year was out.

But the question is as daunting as it is unavoidable: Which version of these events is the Truth? A faithfully detailed review of the facts—or a highly stylized, impressionistic rendering not only limited to the subjective perceptions of one of the participants, but undoubtedly distorted by the poetic necessity to reconcile action with theme? Can there be a truth based in one to the exclusion of the other? And how is the biographer, devoted to Truth, supposed to distinguish? How is he to know?

In this sense, the project at hand is truly blessed and cursed. The existence of Calliope's poetry, her letters and journals, rough drafts and paraphernalia, provides a crucial counterpoint to the historical version; and yet without the voice of the subject herself, without the speaker's presence, this same paraphernalia—varied and inscrutable and open to interpretation—continually mocks the inadequacy of that narrative, exposing it as a mere construction of words, a literary golem: soulless, jerry-rigged, horrible.*

Dawn found her once again at the Beekeeper's bedside. She had spent a fitful night on the pallet in his empty cell, deposited there by the roshi and his devotees; in the predawn hours, she awoke to the mutter and rumble of monks moving through the old building, filing into the cold for morning *zazen*, sandaled feet crunching through the crust of snow, fading up the trail. She felt her way through dark hallways to the infirmary, dressed in the clean robe that had been left for her, fingertips gliding across bare walls as they had so many happier nights in the past.

Pushing open the door to the infirmary, she discovered her lover staring blankly at the ceiling, shivering, lips moving without sound. His prayer beads had fallen to the floor, but his fingers continued to fidget. His dilated pupils and gray pallor needed no expert medical interpretation. Calliope pulled the blanket up to his chin, wilted to the floor, laid her head next to his, and wept.

It was thus the roshi found them later that morning, having completed early meditation and hurried to the infirmary, stopping only to place a call to the center's doctor and for a brief incursion upon the breakfast buffet. Approaching down the hallway, he could hear her whispers, and stopped just shy of the door.

"I don't know what you want from me," he heard her murmur to the monk's oblivious form. Peering around the doorframe, he saw Calliope sitting next to the bed, filling an eyedropper from a tin of sugar water, depositing droplets on her lover's ruined lips. The roshi, respectful of their privacy, did not announce himself.

"Please. Just one word. I'll do whatever you say." But there was no response. She clasped his limp hand to her forehead. "Why can't anyone just tell me what they want?" she spoke to the floorboards. "Why can't they

---

*Žižek frequently discusses the trope of the "undead" in literary works from *Hamlet* to Stephen King's *Pet Sematary*. Can one dispute the similarity of these ghoulish creatures—leering, suppurating shades of a former life—to biography?

just say it? Everyone wants something. The workshop says they want my poetry—but then I can feel them looking at me, like it's not enough. And Rhoda: 'One more interview, honey . . . one more poem . . .'"

His breathing had grown raspy, but she kept feeding him with the eye-dropper, liquid trickling from his mouth. "'Read my chapbook, Cal-liope,'" she mimicked. "'Come to Paris, Calliope,' 'Take off your clothes and call me *Generalissimo*, Calliope.'" She peeled open one of the Bee-keeper's eyes with a thumb. "Get this: Now the Weinsteins want *me* to be in their stupid movie. They want me to play my *mother*—can you believe that? They want me to be my mother in a movie about my father. It's just gross. There's this creepy guy in San Diego who says he knew my father, now he wants to write my biography.* The Lilith people are talking about a poetry stage next summer, as if I haven't spent enough time on rock tours . . .

"I need you." She jostled his insensate arm. "Don't you understand? I'm supposed to be an artist, I'm supposed to be writing poems, but I don't even know who I am—how can I write if I don't even know what that 'I' means?" She laid the eyedropper on the bedside table and rested her head on the mattress. Her lover took no notice, shaking under the thin blanket, drooling across the pillow. "Mother says, 'Be who you were born to be,' but how do you do that when everyone says you're someone else? Who gets to decide?

"Can't you please say something?" she pleaded.

The roshi stepped into the room. "Miss Calliope, the doctor is com-ing to help young man," he said softly, careful not to provoke another in-cident. "He must have treatment or he will be leaving us I think very shortly."

Calliope looked up, her face swollen with defeat. What the roshi saw in her eyes—a mixture of despair and pride, of sadness and defiance and stubborn fear—moved him to sit at her side and take her hand.

"How could you let this happen?" She rested her head on his shoulder. The roshi put an arm around her, gently rocking to and fro.

---

*Here she is likely referring to Edwin Decker, a local hack vastly unqualified for such an undertaking.

"Desire will always seek its object," he said. "We cannot oppose the desire of another. It will find another path."

"I thought Buddhism opposed *all* desires," she sniffled.

The roshi smiled. "This is our desire," he said.

This made her laugh, a wet hiccup that quickly subsided. They sat in silence for a time, enduring the ominous groans and mutters from the wraith in the bed.

"I'm so tired, Father," Calliope whispered.

"Today you will rest, Miss Calliope. You will both rest."

She hid her face in the folds of his robe. "No. I'm tired of being me. What does Buddhism have to say about that?"

Voices came down the hallway now, the squeaky sound of a wheeled cart. As though sensing an end to his suffering, the Beekeeper fell silent, his arm dangling over the side of the bed.

"Never fear, R. B.," said the doctor, who stood in the doorway next to a cart laden with medical supplies. "We'll get this kid fixed up in no time." He busied himself with a bag of clear liquid, hanging it on a hook above the Beekeeper's bed, whistling a rustic melody. The roshi leaned over his pupil and spoke quietly, laid a hand across his brow.

"What are ya, hogging all the food, R. B.?" said the doctor, who had not yet recognized Calliope as the Mountaintop Arts student whose reading had caused so many injuries ten months earlier. "Looks like you're getting plenty, I see," he joked. "Whyn't you try sharing? Isn't that what Buddhism's all about?"

As he rolled up the sleeve of the Beekeeper's robe and swabbed the loose flesh with alcohol, Calliope backed toward the other end of the bed, her breath quickening. It was then the roshi understood that he had committed a grave error by not removing her from the infirmary.

"Everybody relax," the doctor said. He removed a plastic syringe from its wrapping and snapped the long needle into place. "Everything's gonna be just fine." He looked at the poet then, her mouth open, eyes grown wide, even as the roshi reached out—too late—to stop her. "He's not gonna feel a thing."

Calliope stepped forward and knocked the needle out of his hand. "No needles!" she screamed, and pushed the doctor roughly toward the door, shoved the wheeled cart backward where it crashed loudly into the wall and spilled its contents.

"Get out!" she cried, undoing the sash of her robe; the doctor, now vividly recalling the broken bones and split lips and pepper-sprayed corneas he'd treated the previous June, backed hastily from the room.

"Miss Calliope—," said the roshi, but as the poet turned her furious, dazzling gaze upon him, her robe dropped to the floor. "I'll help him myself," she hissed, her voice crazed and breaking. She opened a jar and scooped a gob of viscous golden honey into her hand, smearing it all over her body.

"Eat, goddammit!" cried the naked poet, covering herself from head to foot, honey smearing over her shoulders and her belly and her long legs, and as the roshi fled the room, the last thing he saw was Calliope climbing atop the Beekeeper's bald, emaciated body, draping her own sticky self over him and sobbing, "Eat! Eat!"

He could still hear her cries as he pursued the frightened doctor down the hall, the thumping of the Beekeeper's bed as she rocked it harder and harder against the wall. The last image was a glowing jewel in his otherwise-ascetic mind, pulsing brighter and brighter as he hurried through the monastery—emerging into blinding winter daylight he suddenly stopped, frozen by what he describes as a miraculous moment of Buddhist enlightenment. After five decades of meditation, Roshi Bob had found an answer to the great Zen koan.

"All my life, I am wondering, Roshi Bob, what is the sound of one hand clapping? Now, because of poet girl, I understand," he told the author, who was by now prostrate on the plush carpet, groggy from the cognac, having given up all hope of returning to San Diego before morning.

"It is loud, thinks Roshi Bob. It is very, very loud."

Early in the afternoon of March 31, Rafael Zuñiga, assistant director of UCI Campus Security, began receiving reports of a crowd gathered outside Carlisle Auditorium and spilling onto the campus ring road, interfering with the smooth movements of faculty and students. Zuñiga, who had earned a BS in Security Management two years earlier, spoke with Facilities Management, which knew of no Carlisle event scheduled for that day. After calls to Student Events and the Music and Theater Arts departments provided no explanation, he signed out an Electric Convenience Vehicle (ECV) from the fleet behind his office and went to investigate.

"This shit happens all the time," says Zuñiga, recalling his initial sanguine reaction. "You don't want to go be overreacting. Usually there's some kinda explanation and shit, so the worst thing is to go in there, all guns blazing and shit, until you know what's up, you feel me? I figure I'll go over, ask the homies what up, send 'em back to class, ain't no big thing. No big thing at all. Shit."

By that time, the "secret" reading had become known to the entire student body and faculty, its original buzz greatly magnified by the poet's disappearance. As demonstrated by its belated response, however, the administration had somehow been kept in the dark.* Arriving at the auditorium just after 3:00 P.M., Zuñiga encountered a boisterous but as yet peaceful crowd of perhaps seventy-five. Many were spread across the building's stone stairs, having laid out blankets and picnic lunches and chessboards; others were involved in a game of Hacky Sack that obstructed the walkway—an explicit safety violation—or had joined the swelling drum circle on the lawn of the molecular biology lab.

"Here comes the rent-a-cop!" shouted one antiestablishmentarian, while executing a tricky, over-the-shoulder flip of the leather beanbag.

"Nice golf cart, dude!" yelled another.

"I pride myself on, like, being down with the peeps and shit, so I figured I'd just hang, find out the story, you know, just homeboys talking and shit," Zuñiga recalls, with a distant, bemused frown. "But these people—man, I'm all, what's up here dudes and they're all, get the fuck outta here, man, and I'm all, yo, I just want to know what's up, and they're all, yo, fuck off."

Unable to elicit from the crowd any information beyond their admiration of his security vehicle, and a prolonged, eyebrow-to-eyebrow recitation from *Leaves of Grass* by one menacing figure, Zuñiga left the scene to

---

*The *Orange County Register* cast doubt on this in an April 5 editorial, suggesting that the chancellor's office ignored the issue in hopes that a public episode would aid long-standing requests for more security funds from the city.

consult the university's *Crisis Intervention Manual;* upon his return to the security office, he found Edward J. Labello, executive director of Students United in Christ, waiting for him.

Labello, twenty-three, was a well-known figure on campus. Under his direction, Students United in Christ had grown from a small weekly prayer group to an outspoken organization of several hundred with a nonvoting seat on the UC Board of Regents. Fiercely activist, Labello could muster crowds seemingly with the snap of his fingers to protest campus events which, according to SUC's literature, "deny the rule of the Lord Jesus Our Savior in favor of smut, materialism, and secular self-gratification." A small-boned man with deep-set eyes and flaxen hair pulled back in a ponytail, Labello was always at the head of the righteous phalanx; while some members of the group favored scarlet spray paint and scripture-quoting placards, Labello's weapon was his gaze. Many an events coordinator, liberal professor, and visiting speaker had been startled into silence by a glance from the crusader. In person he was mild-mannered, with a cherubic complexion and the languid speech of a Wyoming rancher's son. But when his wrath had been kindled, Labello was a fright to behold—across picket lines and police barricades, he regarded the object of his scorn, as though he could see deep inside them and recognize the corruption which burned like an ulcer.

"If you don't shut it down, we will," Labello told Zuñiga, once he had revealed the event's true nature. Zuñiga and Labello had clashed before, most recently outside the Bren Theater during a run of *The Crucible:* SUC had staged a counterdrama entitled *Proctor Burns in Hell,* with Labello playing a chaste, God-fearing Abigail Williams.

"We can't allow our student fees to pay for the dissemination of pornography," Labello told the security officer, twiddling a toothpick between his fingers, staring almost sadly across the small office. When Zuñiga expressed doubts that Calliope's poetry really met that description, Labello produced a draft of "Honey Box," which he must have procured from someone in Calliope's workshop.

"Lick my liquid/Dripping comb to comb, your tongue/stings and tingles, hips/bestride your brow—/How could the mouth/of God be sweeter/filled as it is with love/of Man?" read Labello, raising his eyes to give Zuñiga a preview of his paralyzing gaze.

"No, man," Zuñiga said a moment later. "It ain't like that. She got *bees,* man—she's talking about bees." It was a topic he knew something about, having processed the permits for Calliope's hives. "It ain't pornography— it's metaphor."

Labello stared at the security officer before crumpling the poem and dropping it to the floor. "Metaphor is for the godless," he told Zuñiga, crushing the paper underfoot as he left.

The reading was scheduled to begin at 6:00 P.M. After another unsuc- cessful effort to contact the chancellor, Zuñiga took matters into his own hands and again signed out an ECV, trekking across campus to Calliope's trailer. He knocked at the poet's door for several minutes, but there was no answer, only the faint whirring of her two fax machines, the click and shiver of dry branches, the distant whoosh of military jets tracing a chalky arc overhead. He left a note on the door and climbed back in the ECV. He did notice, in passing, that the beehives which had been installed under a nearby tree were no longer there, two rectangles of flattened brown grass in their place.

"But what do I know about bees?" he says. "You know, it was spring break and shit—people take their dogs when they go away, maybe she took the bees, you feel me?"

At 5:00 P.M., faced by a barrage of phone messages describing the swelling masses outside Carlisle Hall, faxes from Student Events, Facilities Management, and the School of Humanities disclaiming responsibility for an event they had neither sponsored nor sanctioned, and his continued in- ability to reach anyone in the administration, Zuñiga made the decision to cancel the reading. He notified the Irvine Police Department, which de- ployed a woefully inadequate retinue of twelve officers to secure the au- ditorium. According to the police blotter, the IPD officers encountered a crowd of several hundred outside the auditorium, as well as a sizable tent camp spread across part of Aldrich Park. The air was thick with smoke from barbecue grills and smoldering bundles of sage, ringing with the frenetic beat of drums and the din of any number of amateur guitarists crooning Terrible Children songs. Unlicensed vendors had established a small bazaar in front of the molecular biology lab, and the rooftop of the neighboring mathematics department had become an impromptu "rave" party, replete with dancing bodies and whiplashing glowsticks and the tooth-rattling, bass-heavy reverberations of techno music.

With some effort, they managed to clear the stairs of the auditorium and set up a perimeter of flares. Using megaphones and hand gestures, they informed the horde that the event had been canceled, resulting in a torrent of rotten fruit, beach balls, hamburger rolls, and sneakers being flung at their shields, followed by First Amendment slogans and epithets such as "Fascist!" and "Poetry Hater!" No arrests were made, a widely criticized decision that would lead to the early retirement of IPD chief John Wall.

At about the same time, Calliope was arriving on campus, meeting Rhoda outside the trailer, as previously arranged. Rhoda was poring over Zuñiga's hastily scrawled note when Calliope pulled up; as her client shut off the car and sobbed over the steering wheel, Rhoda folded the note tightly and pocketed it.

Calliope exited the car and ran toward the spot where her hives had stood. "Where are they?" she gasped. "Where are my bees? What did you do with them?"

She was pale and bedraggled, dressed in the rumpled black robe she had donned that morning, her skin scaly with dried honey. Her hair in fist-sized clumps, her eyelashes caked, her nose plugged with the sticky stuff, she looked, as Rhoda would later write, "like something the cat had dragged in, batted around, chewed up, pissed on, and left lying in the foyer for its owner to dispose of."*

"We've got a reading to do, baby," she told the poet. "I'm sure they'll turn up."

To believe her memoirs, Rhoda still had no idea where the poet had been for the last three weeks, nor did she know of the tragedy that played itself out in Mountaintop that morning. She had not yet heard of the disturbance at San Bernardino Community Hospital, where the Beekeeper

---

*Lubinski, p. 222.

lay unconscious in critical condition. Since the announcement of the book contract, Rhoda had been obsessed with the reading, with the opportunity to present to the world the radiant, self-possessed Calliope, the awe-inspiring future of poetry. What she was confronted with now, crawling in the dead grass at her feet, swaddled in a filthy robe and layers of dried honey, was a basket case.

"Clean yourself up, for God's sake," she said, yanking Calliope to her feet, shoving her toward the trailer. "No, there's no time. Forget it." She tightened her grip and led the poet away. There was no time for Calliope to change her clothes or comb her hair; nor did she have the chance to listen to the phone messages that had come in while she'd been away, including a series of invectives from L. Moreno which escalated from proud, calm, and aggrieved, to frantic, infuriated, and finally threatening.

In a display of prodigious determination, Rhoda managed to drag the poet across campus, stopping every so often when Calliope's tears and hyperventilation made it impossible for her to continue, retrieving her when she chased a lone honeybee into a copse or through the doors of the science library.

"Baby, I want you to listen to me," she said, as they crossed Aldrich Park, not yet seeing the police officers and flares, only the passionate crowd she'd been imagining for months. "This is important. I need you to pull it together."

Calliope sat on a bench, staring into space as Rhoda fished a tissue from her purse and wiped the poet's nose. In his article for the *Register* the following week, Skip Cárdenas referred to Connor Feingold's past arrests for possession of medication without a prescription, his well-known reliance on the anti-epileptic Neurontin for day-to-day stress management. "Would it be so hard to imagine these old friends, loyal to Brandt's memory and to each other, sharing this as they shared so many things over the years?"*

Whatever the case, Rhoda was growing desperate. "Come on, C—I know you can do this," she said, alternately embracing and shaking the exhausted poet.

---

*In her volcanic April 5 response, Taryn Glacé would accuse Cárdenas of propagating the rumor at the behest of "Big Pharma and other corporate oppressors."

"What does it matter?" Calliope muttered, laying her head on the hard bench. "What's the point? My bees are gone. Everyone. All my pretty ones. Gone."

"This is what we've been working for. This is your whole life, baby."

"O Hell-kite!" Calliope shut her eyes. "What do you know about my life?"

"I know we've got a thousand people waiting for us. I know we've got a book ready to come out, a big advance to earn. We've got interviews, talk shows . . . for fuck's sake, C, we've got *Ben Affleck.*"

"He's a shitty actor," she mumbled.

"*Who cares!* Don't you understand? This is all for you. All those people over there"—she swept her arm to encompass the crowd outside the auditorium, the tent camp, the Hacky Sackers—"this is just the beginning. Snow Lion's expecting you to sell a million books—do you think you're going to do that with just *poems*?"

This comment registered in some remote, still-alert region of the poet's brain. "Poems are all I've got." She opened one eye. "I'm a poet."

Rhoda laughed. "Don't be naive. You are what we tell them you are, what we make of you. You're not just a poet, you're the *future* of poetry. You're art and glamour and danger and no-holds-barred rebellion, you're youth and genius and sex and drama all rolled into one. The formula is a winner, baby. It's working.

"Look, honey," Rhoda went on, hauling her upright, "you know as well as I do that people need to be *led* to the poetry—they don't just wake up and go looking for it. They've got lots of other things to do."

Calliope was stunned. "But they *like* my poetry."

"*Of course* they do," said Rhoda. By now a number of fans had begun to look in their direction, a small huddle conferring some distance away, wondering whether the grubby figure on the bench could possibly be who they suspected it was. "But think about bees—they love nectar, but they have to be drawn to it. That's why flowers are so beautiful—you've got to give the bees a reason to pick *your* nectar over all the others."

"Bees?" she whispered.

"Bees."

"My bees?"

Rhoda took her by the chin and stared into her eyes. "That's up to you." The group of onlookers had drawn closer. "What's it going to be, Calliope? Are you the queen?"

Calliope gaped, shaking her head like a dental patient on Novocain. "I don't know, I don't know!"

It was, as Rhoda would later write, the pivotal moment. All her preparations, the machine she had been building cog by joint by gear, depended on getting Calliope to that auditorium. But the poet was shrinking into herself again, listing precipitously to one side. Another moment, and all would be lost.

Rhoda struck Calliope sharply across the cheek, unleashing the final weapon in her arsenal. "What would your father do?" she said.

Calliope and Rhoda arrived at the auditorium at 6:34 P.M. and were turned away by the IPD. No amount of threatening or coquetry could convince the police to open the doors, and after several minutes of arguing, jostling between the increasingly vocal crowd and the officers' riot shields, Rhoda shoved her way to the side of the staircase, climbed atop a stone balustrade, and waved her arms until she had the crowd's attention.

"Listen up!" she yelled, and when she could not make herself heard, she asked the nearest police officer if she might borrow his megaphone. Inexplicably, he complied.

"The forces of the status quo don't want this reading!" she announced through a blare of feedback.

The rowdy throng replied with boos and a fresh volley of food products.

"The university doesn't want this reading!"

"Fuck the university!" shouted an anonymous fan, to general laughter.

"You know why? Because poetry is dangerous," Rhoda said. "Poetry is the triumph of the individual over the system. It's freedom from tyranny!" While the crowd responded positively to these pronouncements, Rhoda kept an eye on Calliope, who was vacantly examining a large, gluey snarl of her own hair.

"Do you love poetry?" Rhoda shouted. The crowd indicated that they did love poetry. "Do you want to tell the world you love poetry? Do you want to tell the world that Calliope *is* poetry?"

"Fuck yeah!"

"We don't need their lousy building! Poetry doesn't need a roof. Poetry can make a place for itself!" She reached down and grabbed Calliope's wrist, raising both their arms in triumph. *"Poetry can stop the traffic!"* she screamed, pointing toward nearby Campus Drive, and the whipped-up crowd exploded into cheers and turned, as of one mind, flowing across the ring road and past the administration building and the ESL annex, trampling the manicured Perralta Gardens, across the traffic oval and past the towering flagpole toward the busy thoroughfare. Dragging the poet by the wrist, Rhoda mounted the stairs of the pedestrian overpass which connects the campus with the University Center strip mall. The police made only feeble efforts to redirect the crowd; as the screech and squeal of brakes rose into the twilight, Rafael Zuñiga was pulled from his vehicle, taken up in the human riptide which spilled into the four lanes of Campus Drive, indeed stopping the traffic, climbing atop cars and pickup trucks and stamping loudly on the roofs of SUVs, car alarms wailing and horns helplessly honking, a bedlam of metal and headlights and macabre hairstyles and creative facial piercings all turned upward, howling and raising fists to the figure on the parapet.

Calliope stood atop the concrete rail, arms raised, bathed in the headlights. Behind her was the vermilion glow of dusk, the warming windows of condominiums, the neon penumbra of the strip mall. The mad rush to the overpass had drawn her out of her stupor; she waited for the shouting, honking masses to settle into obedient silence. All eyes on her, she waited still another moment, until their loving anticipation stretched toward discomfort and threatened eventual chaos.

"I shall not soon forget the day he died," she began, and the crowd answered with adoring cheers. She paused, expertly, until they once again reined in their enthusiasm. She used no megaphone; nevertheless, her voice carried to the farthest reaches of the gathering, to young attorneys and nurses and middle managers waiting irritably in their vehicles, to the police officers stranded at either end of the overpass, to Rafael Zuñiga, trapped in a tight circle of weeping sorority sisters in identical hip-hugger pants.

"For on that day, I came into myself," Calliope continued, working lan-

guorously through the sonnet which had become her anthem. *"The images colliding in my mind / replaced the man—his kiss, his touch, his breath—/ all lost to me now, like a desert dream / of brambles burning, arid throats unslaked . . ."* and so forth, her voice growing more sure with each quatrain, a feeling of near holiness subduing the crowd.

When the applause for this opening poem had subsided, she introduced a new piece—"Just a little something I jotted down on a cocktail napkin in Giza," she said. "I was thinking about monuments, about immortality. I was thinking about love." No one in the crowd needed reminding of the date—March 31—nor of the grim anniversary that would pass the next day.

"Father died tomorrow, fifteen years / of resurrections, crocodile tears, a daughter's sorrow . . . ," she read, and by now even the police officers were entranced, resting their shields on the concrete and closing their eyes to let the poetry wash over them. Drivers shut off their engines and got out of their cars to hear better; patrons of Starbucks and the Gap pressed against the barricades between strip mall and road. So rapt were the multitudes that no one saw L. Moreno making his way toward the overpass, laboriously pushing a dolly, his face flush, bow tie dangling from his collar.

"You cannot simply say to a person, now I love you, now I don't want to look at your face," he'd said in one of the numerous messages on Calliope's answering machine that Dennis Adams would transcribe and deliver to Irvine Medical Center a few days later. *"Oye, poeta!* I have been very very patient with you. I bring you here to Irvine, I introduce you to editors, agents, I put up with very much bad behavior from you, but you repay me with the talking to the hand.

"You will have to talk to *me, mujercita,*" he said. "When you come back from wherever it is the hell you have gone, you will talk to me and you will listen!"

But Calliope, too, was oblivious to the stooped figure in the houndstooth jacket and the cargo he was arduously wheeling to the base of the stairs. She finished the commemorative poem* and moved on to "For

---

*Critics have customarily referred to this poem as "Anniversary," though no complete transcription has ever come to light and the napkin from which Calliope read was destroyed in the ensuing tumult.

Marshall . . . ," which would only have inflamed Moreno further with its verbal seduction of Calliope's previous mentor, then worked her way through "The Bird and the Bees" and "Honey Box," the first two poems of the as yet unfinished "HymenOpera."

"You know, all the freaking out before and shit, but it was cool, you know, it was super chill," recalls Zuñiga, who upon hearing the familiar lines from "Honey Box" managed to extricate himself from the sorority sisters and clamber atop a Mini Cooper. "She had shit under control, is what I'm saying. It was like, she was all reading us a bedtime story or something. It was like, a hot and sexy bedtime story and shit, but that was cool, you feel me? I didn't know poetry could do that."

Calliope paused and bowed gingerly atop her unsteady perch, reaching down to accept a bottle of water from Rhoda. Though still disheveled, sticky with honey, the poet was back in her element; when she introduced the next poem, all traces of hesitation were gone, only the towering, confident figure bestowing words like benedictions upon the crowd.

"Suicide Bomber," she said.

This was the first reading—partial though it would be—of that storied poem which would cause so much scandal and eventually drive a wedge between Calliope and the public. The poem had never been seen in the workshop; some scholars, following Cárdenas's theory, speculate it may have been conceived during a visit to the West Bank.

"Mirror mirror on the wall / that shatters when I call / his name—the price of fame / is high, but not—"

"STOP!!"

The voice boomed over the crowd, which turned as one to find Edward J. Labello leading the squadrons of Students United in Christ between the rows of cars. Clad in white robes and cowls, bearing torches, the SUC minions advanced to the overpass, halting amid mutters and threats, their diminutive leader folding his arms and fixing Calliope in his awful stare.

Calliope, arms out to the sides, peered down into the glare of dozens of headlights, the flickering torches, squinting through sweat and honey and exhaustion, trying to make out the figure addressing her.

"Who are you?" she said.

But the crusader only planted his torch, tilted his head so as better to take in the figure fifteen feet above.

"Who are you?" she said again, more quietly, uncertainty creeping into her voice. The crowd tightened around the band of Christians. No one paid any attention to L. Moreno, who had by now maneuvered his dolly to the foot of the stairs, dragging off the tarpaulin that covered its cargo.

Calliope tottered slightly and stared at the robed figure. "Why won't you tell me who you are?"

To which the leader of Students United in Christ slowly pulled back the hood of his robe, revealing his long blond locks and high cheekbones, his gaunt but handsome face traced by three days' stubble. They stared at each other, the poet and the apostle, the crowd fidgeting in the growing tension.

"No," she whispered, her head shaking in awe. "No."

What did Calliope see? As she stood fixed in his gaze, in the brilliance of headlights and torches, what vision appeared to her? What can explain the tears that streaked her cheeks, or the astonished, childlike smile that came over her face?

"Finish the poem, Calliope!" cried a woman's voice.

"Fuck you, punk," shouted a man standing near Labello. "Leave her alone!"

"Is it really you?" Calliope whispered, leaning farther out, as L. Moreno slid the covers from the two boxes and a slow, inchoate cloud rose into the reddened sky.

"Go to your mama!" cried the older poet, once the star of the Irvine Creative Writing Program, now eclipsed by his protégée. "Go to her—she loves only you!" But few could hear him over the rising hum of the swarm, the seductive mutter of thousands of bees gathering their attention, each tiny voice joining the others in an angry prelude to speech.

"I love you, Calliope!" he shouted, voice breaking terribly. *"My name is El Moreno!"*

The panic spread swiftly, bodies scrambling over cars, over one another, torches scything through the air to ward off the dark cloud. But the bees were undaunted, having sensed their target: Calliope stood on the ledge, caught in the gaze of the man below. The bees swirled swiftly, quickly concealing the honey-glazed poet, a whirlwind of bees drawn to their keeper like iron filings to a magnet and for just a moment she twirled there, tap-dancing above the human current, caught in a backlit, arm-waving stumble atop the rail.

"Shit, man, it was hectic," recalls Zuñiga, who was standing on the car where Calliope landed and who went into anaphylactic shock as a result of ninety-one bee stings. "It happened so fast, everyone says it was the bees, you feel me? That the bees was stinging her and she lost her balance. They're all, yo, dude, what else would it be?

"There was a lot of bees, I'm not saying that. Shit. It's just, I was watching her. She kept talking to that Christian dude. He wasn't saying nothing, but she just kept asking, over and over, 'Is that really you?'" Zuñiga shakes his head, staring into the distance as though finding there something unutterably sad. "Then he held out his arms. It was right when the bees started covering on her, he held out his arms, like a parent getting his kid to jump off the swing.

"He held his arms out and she came to him. It was like he was waiting for her, you feel me? It's like he knew she was coming. Do you feel me?"*

---

*Whatever the cause, Calliope's hospitalization gave her the chance to finish "It's Good to Be the Queen," the third poem in the "HymenOpera," with the memorable bravura of its final stanza: "Am I the real deal, or smiling fake? O Monalisa, lookalike, sister whore—we shall leave this bed, let the doubters eat their cake." Despite a shattered left tibia, bruised ribs, a broken nose, and multiple contusions, the poet did not suffer a single bee sting.

6.

(EXHIBIT A)

WNET—New York

Transcript: Charlie Rose,
interview with Calliope Bird Morath
Taped 6/4/200_, 1400h EDT, WNET Studio 3

Host (Charlie Rose): Welcome to the program. Calliope Bird Morath is here. She's the author of *(I)CBM*, a new book of poems, released last week by Snow Lion Press with no small fanfare. She's the nineteen-year-old daughter of Brandt Morath, singer and guitarist of the rock band the Terrible Children. Brandt Morath died in 199_, when she was four years old. I am pleased to welcome Calliope Bird Morath.

Guest (Calliope Bird Morath): Thank you, Charlie. It's nice to be here.

CR: What does a poet do to get people to read poetry again? How can poetry still resonate for people, with the Internet and cable TV. Sales are down, generally. The closest some people get to poetry these days is Hallmark cards . . .

CBM: Wow. You don't waste any time, do you?

CR: Can we talk about—

CBM: That's quite a death knell—

CR: —all this excitement around your poetry? It's unusual, isn't it?

CBM: It depends on what kind of historical scale you mean. Is it unusual for today? This decade? Maybe. But poetry's always been around.

It's always been popular. Poets, warriors, royalty—these were the original American Idols.

CR: Not always "American." But I see your—

CBM: Look at Edna Millay. Look at Yeats, Dylan Thomas, Ginsberg. These people were the rockstars of their time. The crowds that came to see them were enormous. We forget that today. It also depends what you mean by "poetry."

CR: Well, that's . . . it's history. Now, today—what about your poetry in particular do you think has gotten so many people interested? What is it you're tapping into?

CBM: Have you read it?

CR: I've read some—

CBM: What do *you* think I'm tapping into? You invited me on the show.

CR: This is true.

CBM: Because it's not for me to say. I just write the poems. I just try to make them the best that I can. I wouldn't let anyone see it if I didn't think it was good. But the reactions they have when they read it, what it says to them—

CR: What it makes them feel? What it makes them see? That's what Conrad said, to make people *see*—

CBM: It's different for everyone. I can't tell them how to—

CR: But you have something to say. You have something to communicate using the poems. This is what you've chosen—

CBM: Did you want me to answer the question?

CR: You're trying to get something across, some emotion or way of looking at—

CBM: Because you're doing a pretty good job, Charlie.

CR: It's interesting to see a young poet—and everyone agrees, nineteen years old is . . . and so much excitement about the first book. Amazon reported close to a million preorders. A million!

CBM: [*yawns*]

CR: [*laughs*] This isn't an interesting subject for you?

CBM: Rimbaud was even younger. The thing is, there's a rhythm to these things, a cycle. Think about music—think about Terrible Children and what they did. Go back and look at the crap people were listening to before *The Hanged Man* came out. Everyone said rock was dead—and it was! But here comes someone, a genius, to bring it back to life. It was a resurrection—rock music crawling out of a cave covered in filth and leprosy, until the Kids scrubbed it down and stuck a lightning rod up its ass. Can it be explained? Analyzed? That's for other people to do. Can I tell you why a million people are interested in my work when Wole Soyinka's last book sold four thousand copies? I'm not wading into that cesspool.

CR: Do you think there's a relationship between rock music and poetry?

CBM: Do I think . . . Are you serious?

CR: You do.

CBM: Jesus Christ, Chuck, what do you think rock music is? Where do you think it comes from? It's the child of poetry, the heir. Bob Dylan, John Lennon, Patti Smith . . .

CR: Brandt Morath?

CBM: Yes, of course!

CR: A poet.

CBM: Of course my father's a poet. Of course. But this is what I'm talking about, you asked me what I'm tapping into—it's this, this energy . . . Call it Dionysus, call it whatever you want. Beatlemania. Kidsophrenia. The artist doesn't create it, she just opens a door.

CR: I want to stay with this question of poetry, what's poetry . . . [*shuffles papers*] What about . . . [*shuffles papers*] Here are the lyrics to "Bingo Slut," a song by the Terrible Children from their—

CBM: Terrible Children.

CR: Pardon me?

CBM: Fire your research person, Chuck—it's not *the* Terrible Children, it's Terrible Children. No "the."

CR: Here are the lyrics: "Gimme that G, ugly ball lady / O, O, O, O, sixty-nine." Is this poetry?

CBM: That's fairly early work . . .

CR: Fine. But is it poetry?

CBM: [*sighs*] Is this a quiz, Charlie? Is this a game show? What do I win if I get it right? [*Host smiles.*] Look. This idea that one thing is poetry and another . . . It's all poetry. Every use of the language is poetry. Who are you to say what's poetry and what isn't? Who am I? If I wanted to sit around an oak table and criticize other poets, I'd have stayed in the workshop.

CR: All right. You left Irvine recently under something of a cloud.

CBM: A cloud?

CR: There was a . . . let's call it a "set-to" at a reading, people were injured, you spent some time in the hospital . . .

CBM: So I'm told. I don't remember most of it. One minute I'm reading my e-mail in my trailer, it's February, next thing you know, it's April and I'm in traction. It wasn't a pleasant time.

CR: You have no memory of the reading?

CBM: No.

CR: None?

CBM: Charlie, what is this? You sound like my mother, or my publicist.

CR: Sorry. You seem to have fully recovered. You're up and about, your book tour—

CBM: I have four pins holding my tibia together. I opted against the nose job. What do you think of the bump? I think it gives my face character, don't you?

CR: "Pins in my tibia." That sounds like a poem. [*Laughs.*]

CBM: Not a very good one.

CR: Touché. I defer to your artistic sensibilities.

CBM: As well you should. [*Touches his hand.*]

CR: Would now be a good time to ask you to read one of your poems? [*Guest shrugs, bats eyelashes.*] Would you be so kind?

CBM: [*clears throat*] Villanelle.

> My father is no longer of this world.
> He sails the seas above us, staring down
> with salt-rimmed eyes at daddy's little girl.
>
> From those sad heights, I wonder if he's heard
> the long laments, the hot tears of this clown.
> My father is no longer of this world,
>
> He left me here, abandoned, bought and sold
> since springing, skull and crossbones, from his brow,
> the arrow nocked—thus, "daddy's little girl."
>
> But now I crawl the shores, a shipwrecked bird,
> the bloodmark on my skin my only crown—
> for my father is no longer of this world.
>
> O Jolly Roger, albatross, my pearl!
> What scarlet tide has tossed you, what strange wind blown
> on your return to daddy's little girl?
>
> Your rudder split, your tow'ring mainsail furled,
> your heavy keel stuck fast in foreign ground.
> I'll find you, Father, somewhere in this world—
> waiting, waiting for daddy's little girl.

CR: The book is *(I)CBM* [*holds up to camera*], the first collection of poetry by Calliope Bird Morath, available this week from Snow Lion Press. [*To guest*] A moment ago, you said, "My father is a poet." *Is* a poet. Would . . . Are you all right?

CBM: [*face in hands, shakes her head*]

CR: Calliope?

CBM: I'm sorry. I can't . . .

CR: [*gestures to someone off camera, shrugs*] Calliope, would you like to take—

CBM: [*sits up*] No. Continue.

CR: Are you sure?

CBM: Let's go, Chuck. The show must go on.

CR: You said, "My father *is*—"

CBM: I'm not going to talk about my father. I told you before the show, I won't—

CR: I just think it's curious that you use the present—

CBM: Charlie.

CR: I understand. But it's you, Calliope, who brought him up. Twice now.

CBM: I'll tell you what, Chuck. When someone you love blows their brains out all over your pajamas, then you get to decide whether or not to talk about it, okay? When someone's blood is smeared on your neck like a tattoo . . . [*Puts face in hands.*]

CR: Fine. Fine. Let's talk about . . . You've grown up under a microscope. Always a lot of attention on you, stories about you in the newspapers. Stories about you in the tabloids.

CBM: [*looks up*] Yes.

CR: Stories about your romantic life. Rumors about relationships. Just today, *Variety* has an article about you and Ben Affleck—

CBM: Is there a question coming? Because I saw a candy machine down the hall and I haven't eaten—

CR: What is it like to be Calliope Bird Morath? Not just the poet: the person. The famous child, daughter of celebrities, the young woman. Trying to make her own way. Do you get distracted by these intrusions? Do you need privacy to—

CBM: What you're asking is if I sleep around.

CR: Not at all.

CBM: I'll bet you'd like to know. [*Puts her legs on the table.*]

CR: No, this isn't . . . ah . . . it's personal information, but this isn't a personal inquiry.

CBM: Am I distracting you? Charlie? [*Wiggles toes.*] Of course it's personal. It's as personal as a hot blade to the jugular. All poetry is.

CR: You like to shock people.

CBM: I think people like to be shocked.

CR: Is that why you wrote "Suicide Bomber"? To shock people?

CBM: You know why I wrote "Suicide Bomber"? [*Stands, leans over table.*] To get on this show. To get close to *you*, Chuck. You drive me wild. That dimple in your chin . . .

CR: Calliope . . .

CBM: —like you got shot with a BB or something. It's so rugged! Mmm . . . I just want to put my lips around it, touch it with my tongue . . .

CR: That's . . . that's very flattering.

CBM: And that smile! Does it drive all the girls wild, or just me?

CR: Do you worry about the personal matters overshadowing your poetry? That some people might think this is why you've sold so many copies already—that people are responding to the persona, to the stories and scandals, and not to the poems?

CBM: [*leans on elbows*] No. The poems have nothing to do with the persona. The poetry is art. Capital-A Art. That's something quite different.

CR: Didn't you just say all poetry was personal?

CBM: Do I contradict myself, Chuckie? I am full of contradictions . . .

CR: [*laughs, points at guest*] Very good. Whitman. Good. Would you like to sit down? [*Guest sits, twirls hair.*] Now, I think you'd have to admit, all the publicity, it's not something, ah . . . not what we're used to in poetry. Interviews on MTV, CNN, cover stories in *SPIN*. Rumors that you've been asked to host *Saturday Night Live*.

CBM: Again with the rumors. You're like a teenage girl.

CR: This was something—forgive me now—but this was something your father was very vocal about, the conflict between making the music, the poetry in your case, and the business side of things.

CBM: I'm warning you . . .

CR: So it's not a distraction. [*Checks papers.*] It doesn't, ah . . . when you sit down to write . . . when you are writing poetry, what goes through your mind? Where do you start?

CBM: It's not really a question of beginning, or of thinking about certain things. The poem is already there. You have to get out of its way. You have to . . . this is where the Buddhists, I think, are very good. You have to empty your mind, or the conscious part of your mind. You have to allow the language, its warp and woof, to take shape.

CR: You have some experience with Buddhism.

CBM: What I'm saying is that poetry is the natural destination of the system called language that we're born with. We're wired for it. It's larger than we are, larger than any individual consciousness.

CR: These are almost religious terms you're describing it in.

CBM: Everyone needs something to die for, Charlie. [*Takes host's hand, presses to side of her face.*]

CR: Your mother. [*Tries to take hand back, fails.*] What's your—

CBM: [*closes eyes*] I don't want to talk about her.

CR: —relationship with her? Her public image is of a rather difficult person, disputes with the press, disputes with your father's bandmates. You must know her differently.

CBM: Not really. She's a complete bitch.

CR: Ah . . . [*laughs*] Ah . . . We, ah . . .

CBM: I haven't seen her in a year. She didn't even call me in the hospital.

CR: And her involvement with the book's publication?

CBM: [*opens eyes*] What involvement?

CR: Well . . . ah . . . now, maybe this is a question for . . .

CBM: [*releases host's hand*] There was no involvement. She gave birth to the poet. Her involvement pretty much ends there.

CR: [*checks papers*] The *Albany Times-Union* is investigating—*investigating,* mind you—a connection between your mother's ties to the Buddhist community in Ithaca and the contract for *(I)CBM.*

CBM: [*pause*] That's absurd!

CR: I thought so, too.

CBM: That's . . . We took . . . My agent and I took that manuscript out to auction, and Snow Lion came back with the highest bid.

CR: I think, well the circumstances . . . the strangeness of a tiny Buddhist press—

CBM: What are you trying to say, Charlie? What's strange about it?

CR: —that's never published poetry before, and they're putting several million—

CBM: Where is this coming from? Who's feeding you this garbage?

CR: —a first book from a nineteen-year-old poet—

CBM: I'll tell you what seems strange—

CR: —and then immediately announce plans to build a new temple—

CBM: What seems strange is that even a quote-unquote respected journalist like you seems totally unprepared to accept me and my poetry without resorting to scandal-mongering and sensationalism. [*stands*] This isn't an interview, it's a high-tech lynching!

CR: Calliope—

CBM: [*to camera*] Are you satisfied? [*Comes closer, hand over camera.*] Is this what you want to see?

CR: Calliope, can you please sit down?

CBM: Help! Rape!

CR: Let's change the subject. We'll . . . we'll get back to the book. Calliope? [*Guest removes hand from camera, straightens clothes, folds arms, stands next to host.*] I'd like to talk about "Suicide Bomber."

CBM: So talk.

CR: [*looking up at guest*] Where did the, ah . . . what was the inspiration for the poem?

CBM: Oh, I don't know, Chuck. What was the inspiration for that tie? Personally, I'd rather be wearing an explosives vest.

CR: Wal-Mart has said they will pull the book from their shelves unless Snow Lion prints a new edition without "Suicide Bomber." [*Guest, standing behind host, leans over and drapes arms around him; host shuffles papers.*] They, ah . . . they say it's . . . ah . . . "needlessly provocative and inconsiderate of national sensibilities." Do you write poems like that to provoke people? To gain attention?

CBM: I have better ways of getting attention, Chuck.

CR: Like at your readings.

CBM: Like this. [*Guest kisses host on mouth.*]

CR: Ah . . . this . . . ah . . . this is . . .

CBM: Do I have your attention?

CR: Ah . . . I . . . can we, ah . . .

CBM: [*to camera*] Do I have your attention? *Achtung!* I've got something to tell you.

CR: Ah . . .

CBM: My father is alive! Do you hear me? My father, Brandt Morath, is alive.

CR: Calliope, could we . . . could—

CBM: Are you listening to me? Are you [expletive] listening to me? [*Guest approaches camera.*] Who are you? Are you [expletive] listening? [*Guest turns to host.*] What are you [expletive] looking at?

CR: Calliope, calm down. Can you—

CBM: I won't calm down! I've seen him! My father is alive!

CR: You're saying—

CBM: [*Balls fists, closes eyes, screams.*]

CR: Calliope, are you, ah . . .

CBM: Don't look at me! Don't [expletive] look at me! [*Walks around table, smacks host across the face.*] Everyone stop looking at me! [*Screams, walks behind host.*] Where are you? What's behind these [expletive] curtains? [*Host stands, extends hand to guest, guest shoves host.*] Get the [expletive] away from me! [*Grabs black curtains, pulls.*] I'm tired of curtains, I'm [expletive] tired of everyone hiding. [*Curtains fall, crew members scatter.*] What are you [expletive] looking at? [*Screams.*]

CR: Please, Calliope. [*Host tries to restrain guest.*] Just . . . [*Guest elbows host in stomach.*] *Oof!*

CBM: [*to host*] He's alive. [*to camera*] My father is alive, do you hear me? [*Approaches camera.*] Are you listening? Brandt Morath is alive!

CR: [*Weakly, clutching chest*] Ah . . . don't touch that . . .

CBM: [expletive] you! [*Unclips microphone from shirt.*]

CR: Please don't . . . ah . . . [*leaning on table, clutching chest*] Can somebody please . . . [*guest's scream picked up by host's microphone*] Calliope, please, somebody . . . [*guest screaming, hand over camera lens*] We'll have to end there [*guest screaming*] . . . tomorrow we . . . ah . . . [*camera shaking, guest screaming*] I don't know where the hell I [*papers rustling, screaming*] . . . hell with it. Security! [*camera shaking, screaming, other unidentified crashes, clatters, thuds*] . . . Jesus Christ, Jesus Christ . . . [*screaming*]

```
[equipment failure]
```

7. JE EST UNE AUTRE

I WOULD NOT CALL IT DARKNESS, although there was no light.

Three years floating in umbilical silence. Faces swam across my vision, voices came across great distance, water-softened, words retained only their barest, simple referents: Eat. Drink. Sleep. Pain.

It was one long day, the walls of the house sliding by—a walk in the backyard with Esperanza, a glass of milk. When night came it was the same bed, the same embroidered canopy that mocked me ("Nothing has changed," it said in its silky flutter), my mother in the tiny rocker by my side, holding my hand, begging, "Please, Bird, say something." I understood: She did not want to lose me, too. I would have helped her if I could. But I was only a pair of eyes, only nerve endings and a hot bloodstain throbbing in the night, whatever had been inside me—will, feeling, self—scraped out like a melon's seedy pulp, a living abortion, the subtraction of Me.

I lay staring at the canopy while she rocked and rocked, her highball glass sweating rings on my nightstand, she stretched toward me, laid her head on crossed arms at my side, and the Nembutal bore her off again. (O mother of mine, how strong you were in your way! How unkind they've been to you, never acknowledging your fear, your determination, never understanding the crazy-making strength of your love.)

And then the room was empty, a terrifying silence lay over me like a coffin lid. How I abhorred that vacuum, how I prayed for a face, a voice, to fill it. There were two of him, you understand: the one who was there and the one who wasn't. She played the music day and night, kept his house unchanged. Nothing was moved, no photograph or framed record, his jeans still folded atop the dryer, his ashtray on the kitchen counter. Only the missing Rimbaud, only the basement door closed and forbidden, a room below that had never existed, a chamber into which no bullet had been loaded, no trigger pulled.

His signifiers surrounded me, they said, *Your father is immortal, your father is One.* In my too-big bed I waited for the signified, the broken promise: gentle lips on my forehead, the warm, unwashed smell of him, cigarette-hoarse voice singing me the nightly lullaby (*"You tell me over and over and over again, my girl—you don't believe we're on the Eve of Destruction . . ."*). I knew, in that long emptiness, that he would come.

I would not call it darkness, just a three-year soft parade, flicker of images one atop the other, the glue between them dried to dust and blown away. Narrative died that same morning, fractured like an orbit, a cranium gone supernova. I learned to suck my thumb to slow my weightless passage through space, to make me feel tethered to something, but that something was only me. Antigone in worn pajamas, I waited for a pardon—loyal daughter, last of a royal line, they would not let me bury him, so I offered myself in his stead. Our house a cathedral that echoed with prayer, I walked the halls at night and heard weeping, peeked past heavy curtains and stared at the field of bodies, candles dancing like fireflies in spring drizzle, a boy and girl huddling in the bushes with a tattered blanket—he brushed the tangles from her hair, kissed her tears. In darkness, I waved to them; the girl looked up, eyes swollen, and waved back. For a moment our faces fused in the glass, and I felt her.

No, I would not call it silence—but what need had I for words? There was one thing only in my world, and it had already been described—who knew what one more word from this wicked whelp might kill? Lesson learned, I wandered, a restless penitent: Children should be seen, not heard.

"Open your mouth, Bird."

I opened.

"Swallow this, Bird."

I did.

O colorless universe in which I moved automatically! O depthless world of things!

A Voice, a Voice: I'd have given my small, stupefied kingdom.

Until that Christmas morning, when sound boomed through the quiet—the seal broken, air whooshed and crackled into the vacuum. His eyes flickered through the flames, his light lit my cobwebbed corners, uncovered furniture long shrouded in solitude. The world burning, he stared at me through the glass: My whole body heard his call, and he a small black core—such power! A whirlwind of sound spun out from him; I rolled in the roar and dazzle and the world struggled back to me: not things but *words*—faster and hotter, the flames spat and what had been dead matter now became a *tree,* and now a *book* and a *stair, paper* and *ornament* and *window* and *heat,* my *toes,* my *breath,* a soft *carpet* with thousands of soft *threads* . . . *red* and *blue* and *yellow* and all their myriad hues, *lights* and more *lights,* the drab sheen of a thousand days seared away by his utterance, made real by his gaze.

Would you believe me if I said I was no longer there? That my body had ceased to hold its place, in the teeming fire of that dream I slipped away, his voice filled the space I left, resounded in my head, it said:

There is no death, but meaninglessness.

Born again, born again: flesh made word made need.

O Daddy, what a good teacher you have been.

But sometimes I recall those silent years, the strange peace I enjoyed—no responsibilities, no misunderstandings, the cool distance between me and the things I could break. I have come a long way since then, plunged into a boggy planet, gushed my verses, lost my head—where is that silent daughter now, that tearless effigy of mourning?

Here I am, Father, tethered to the ground by a thousand stinging stakes—alien people clutching me like an alien god, a fallen incubus running out of breath.

Can you see me down here, among the living?

I should be glad of another death.

*

I woke to a world of polished steel, a sighing, disinfected quiet. A cheery morning sun, faint birdcalls filtered through tall windows. Colors bursting, flowers overflowed a table, the floor, a forest of streamers dangling from silver bubbles cramped like pigeons against the ceiling, throwing a test pattern of helices across my blanket. Blurred shapes slid across a TV screen. In the corner slumped a life-sized stuffed bear in a French maid's uniform; on the table by my side sat a jar of dark red honey.

Air shimmered above the heater, breath danced at the window's border. Awareness and Memory stood on the doorstep of my consciousness, knocking loudly to get in—I held off their rude announcements, savoring the calm. A gauze of cloud crossed the sky, the silent TV tickled my eye. I had no body, no place among these things—how lovely to be invisible again, unobserved, a breathing, opiated nonentity. I could get used to this feeling, I thought. I could search for it across continents. I would pay whoever needed paying.

My self swimming clumsily toward me, a panting dog against an ebbing tide. Something wanted my attention, and now I let my eyes focus on the opposite wall, on a framed portrait that hung there: a ghastly image—who would put such a thing in my quiet world? A long, haggard face—of man or woman, it was hard to be sure—limp brownish hair lit on one side by an unseen light, straggling locks plastered to one cheek, a high, speckled forehead stretched above ghoulish purple eye sockets, mottled blue-black streaks beneath, blurring down to cracked, parted lips and a thin line of drool.

It was an ugly, terrible sight, this haunted face, straight out of Bosch— I closed my eyes to block it out, but my mind was beginning to stir and disobey, drying out and pulling away from me like an orange peel from the meat. A hum of voices outside the door, a bell ringing far away, a sharp odor and a warmth in my leg that would soon, I knew, become unpleasant.

I found myself staring again, drawn by that gaze—so blank it was as if what was behind it had been sucked violently away. It was the face of an invalid, of the electroconvulsively damaged; it was the face of absence, of something vital yet vanished, Bertha Mason marooned in her attic, no language sufficient to express the outrage.

Beyond the door the voices grew sharper, a familiar thread rising from the jumble. My leg beginning to throb, I swallowed thick air and studied that grim portrait. Newly conscious of a terrible itch, I scratched my left arm with my right hand and—would you believe it?—the portrait *moved*, the cold crone swung a claw from one side to the other, trailing a plastic tube across her body like a ghastly puppet string. I gasped—and the red witch's mouth opened wider; I closed my eyes, but when I opened them she was still staring, her gaze all the more pointed for the hollows around her eyes, black buttons on a mauve pillow.

"No, no, no . . . ," said a pitiful voice—and she shook her head from side to side, spittle dragging beneath her chin. Did she have no dignity, no sense of shame? Clean yourself up, girl, I wanted to scream—the innocent should not be subjected to such a one as you! Her face twisted up like strawberry taffy caught in a machine, eyes and lips secreting clear liquid— we regarded each other until a knock came at the door and that awful mouth shaped itself into a dark, startled O.

"Well *hell-ooo* sunshine!" The intruder flung the door wide. She flicked on the lights, flung back a curtain, and dragged a gaggle of balloons to the corner, dropping a packet of papers on the chair and crossing the room in one breathless stride.

"Don't you just look like the sweetest thing, all tucked in and purty?" she said, leaning close to my face. "Did you have a good sleep? Grandma Morphine bring you sweet dreams? We'll get someone in here to clean you up, don't you worry. Doctor says those bruises should clear in a couple of weeks, no big deal. But it's a good look for you, baby, maybe you could audition for KISS or something. We should get Salgado in here, take a new author photo, what do you say?"

Against this typhoon of chatter, I let out a groan, avoiding the intruder's eyes, still drawn to the terrifying face across the way.

"You gave us a pretty good scare," said the little blond lady, someone I seemed to know. "That was one hell of a fall you took—graceful as a swan! Ha! More like Lucille Ball." She fell into the chair at my bedside and crossed her legs. "Could have been worse, kiddo. You should see that poor schmuck of a security guard—his head and neck are swelled up like a beach ball. It's positively *macabre!*"

She paused, pursed her lips, looked down into her lap. "He's going to be fine, in case you were wondering."

But I wasn't paying attention to her, straining to see that face on the wall, to examine her in all her discrete hideousness. She, too, had become more lucid, the whites of her eyes newly visible—and at last she had closed that gruesome, gaping hole.

"Listen, we have a lot to talk about, a million things to do." My visitor walked to the window, stopping to pluck dead leaves from a huge pot of violets. "Your mother sent these. With love, of course. She's in Edinburgh, filming. Couldn't get away." She came back to the bedside, waved an arm before my face. "Hey! Snap out of it, C. We're going to cut down on that freaking morphine. I can't sit here talking to a drooling noodle forever, you know. Too many decisions to make."

"Mor—," I blurted, picking aimlessly at the itchy clump taped to my forearm.

"No more, baby. We're cutting that out fast as you can say 'ibuprofen.'"

The witch in the picture still watching, moving when I moved, blinking when I blinked. She was so simple—that's what infuriated me!—hiding out in her glossy frame, just a collection of lines and colors, a crude icon drawn by a dull child. Nothing complex behind those dark sockets, no ambitions or fears, no unseemly desires. How could they lock me in here with her? We had nothing in common! No, that chippie with her IV tubes and her raccoon eyes, her wet chin and cubist nose, her soulless stare—that terrible, empty vision was nothing at all like me.

"So listen, C—are you listening? Do you want the good news or bad news first?"

"Morphine," I muttered, scratching at the needle taped to my arm. Looking at the spot where the metal disappeared beneath my skin, a fizz of panic stirred in my depths, the hot beating in my leg stepped up its pace.

"Bad news first—and don't get all worked up. They kicked you out of school."

I blinked hard to clear the fuzz, leaned my head against the pillow, a flow of quicksand inside my skull. When I looked up again, she was laughing at me, the bitch on the wall, smacking her gums and cackling with silent glee.

"But whatever, okay? It's not like you need the degree—the book's coming out one way or another. And you know how you always said Moreno was the only part of that program that really, uh, satisfied you? Well, he's gone, too."

She patted my shoulder and walked to the end of the bed, leaning toward the picture on the wall—her own face suddenly leered at me from inside the frame, a polished fingernail dabbed at the corner of Rhoda's mouth as the other one shook and showed me her teeth.

"But look at the beautiful jar of honey the roshi sent!" she said, wiping my face with a tissue. She picked a newspaper off the chair and dropped it on my lap. "Now here's the good news. The press is all over you, C. They're going nuts! I'm getting requests from national media—NPR, Jon Stewart, *The View*—and don't count your chickens, but I think we have a shot at *People*'s 50 Most Eligible. What do you think? You'd have to break up with Ben, of course"—she winked—"but easy come, easy go!"

Blinking away the haze, I looked down at the newspaper. There I was again, on the front page, fuzzy and dark against a dazzling background, standing atop the campus overpass with my arms held high. I squinted until I could read the headline:

DIVE, DIVA, DIVE!
UCI WRITER CREATES CHAOS, LITTLE ELSE

"You're a legend!" Rhoda said, giving me a little shake. But the face in the mirror regarded me gravely. "Listen to this: 'Years of guidance at the hands of accomplished poets' . . . blah blah blah '. . . Ms. Morath's obsessions: her father's suicide, death in general . . . vigorous sexual urges' . . . blah blah . . . 'followers more interested in mystical communion with her late father than the poetry . . . confessional content with punk aesthetics . . . juxtaposition of sex and death disturbing even to colleagues . . .'

"Sex and death, sex and death!" Rhoda danced across the room, stopping to look out the window with a satisfied sigh. "I couldn't have written a better press release." The paper lay on my lap, its dumb, punning headline the pride of some junior copyeditor. I could feel the woman in the mirror holding me in her harlot's gaze, as if to say, "You see, my little verbal surgeon—words, those bastards, cut both ways."

Words, he'd said, *words are the problem.* But it wasn't the noise and confusion, it was the things those words, once uttered, could *do!* Buzzing like a swarm, shredding and reconstructing the world as they pleased. Someone should stop them, I thought in my wooziness—keep them out of reach of children!

"Look at them all," said Rhoda, staring out the window. "They love you. They'll stay there for weeks, just hoping to get a glimpse of you."

Words. Even my father, I thought, a quiet moan escaping my throat—could he possibly have foreseen what his words would wreak, ringing across the radio waves, raining like napalm on an unpacified populace? "Mr. Bath and Rot"—just another innocent game. Could he have imagined the price I would pay, as he sat combining and recombining the letters of his name?

"Where did he go?" I mumbled, my tongue a lump of meat.

Rhoda turned from the window. "What did you say, C?"

My arms were starting to itch like crazy; I scratched my wrists, fumbled to peel back the tape. "Why didn't he say anything?"

"Who, that punk from the reading? Don't play with that, baby." She came back to my bedside. The door opened and a nurse came in, black hair piled in a net atop her head. The tag on her pink scrubs read LUPE. "He's probably out there with the rest of them," Rhoda said, nodding toward the window. "We'll get some lawyers on him, PDQ, don't worry. By the time I'm done with him, eternal damnation will seem like a weekend at Canyon Ranch."

"I couldn't hear him," I said, struggling to sit up, but the spike in my leg pinned me to the mattress. The nurse touched my shoulder, stuck a thermometer in my mouth, pressed down the tape where I'd peeled up the edges; while I watched, terrified, she filled another needle from a vial. "I have to go," I mumbled. "He's waiting."

"You're not going anywhere," said Rhoda. "We're gonna sit tight, rest up, let this thing blow over. No use overexposing you before the book's even on shelves."

"You don't understand," I said, my lips clumsy around the thermometer. Lupe and Rhoda exchanged glances, and then Lupe stuck the needle into the IV tube. Right away the morphine hit—the sour bloom in the back of my mouth, heaviness swirling around me like a magician's cape. I fell back against the pillow and Lupe took the thermometer from my mouth, held it to the light. It glimmered in the back of my eyes.

". . . waiting for me . . . ," I said, turning to the window, the blue, blue sky.

"I know, baby, I know," said Rhoda. "Soon. First they've got to fix up that leg. You can't do a book tour with a broken leg, can you? Just sleep. We'll talk after the surgery. I'll be right here the whole time."

The woman in the mirror was watching, soberly now, almost in sympathy. Already, I had the odd sense that she belonged to me, that barren creature, and I to her—in some way, I knew, I'd be running toward or away from her for the rest of my life.

At least she's silent, I thought, as the drug washed into my brain. A girl ought to know when to keep her mouth shut.

"Do you know what today is?" I said.

"I do." Rhoda ran a hand over my brow. "I do. Try not to think about it."

Eyes closing, voice sliding away, I tried one last time to pull out the needle, in vain.

"It's all I think about," I said.

But no one heard.

*

From the Desk of Calliope Bird Morath

Dear Mother,

So sorry to disturb you, but Rhoda tells me you haven't returned any of her calls. Perhaps you thought she was calling for something publicity related, or to pester you again about the Paris book reception (an idea we've long since dropped, I assure you). No, nothing quite so important, Mom: just that your only child is in the hospital and has been in and out of consciousness for several days and has undergone surgery. I thought you'd want to be at her side in this time of need? Clearly I forgot who I was dealing with. My mistake.

I realize you're very busy—prostituting Daddy's life is a full-time job, isn't it? Yes, Rhoda told me about the film—I'm sure Harvey W. was thrilled with your decision, though I myself find it difficult to stomach. What possibly could be motivating you,

Mommy Dearest? Certainly not money. My friend Taryn says it's because they offered me the role first—something about "capital and alienation of the family structure"—but I assured her you were not so petty. In the end, I suppose, it's between you and your conscience. Is this who you were born to be?

In other news, the book is almost done, though it's hard to feel very excited about it. Rhoda is just beside herself with plans, as you can imagine. It's going to be a very busy time for Calliope, once she leaves the hospital. A coming out. Or a rebirth. I'm beginning to understand what you said about publicity, the strange way you come to think of yourself in the third person, as an object, a commodity. It's easy to say one needn't be complicit, but there are so many little traps, aren't there? Well. The Beekeeper sends his love. Or, he would if he could. He, too, has had his recent mishaps, though I hear he is slowly recovering. The roshi is with him, feeding him baby food, teaching him how to walk again. Rebirth seems to be all the rage, no? We'll see what this new life brings for my beautiful Buddhist. I'm sure he won't change much. He's true blue.

Well, Mother, Bird is due for some morphine in a few minutes, so I should wrap this up while I still speak English. I do wish you would come see me. I'm supposed to send greetings and "a kiss on each face" from Mahmoud, my old teacher from Warren Wilson. I'll have to tell you sometime about my visit. He's very charming. And he certainly seems taken with you. Of course, one prefers to communicate with one's mother, one's only living parent, directly and in person, so perhaps once you're done dragging our name through the Scottish mud you'll come see your poor little Bird. She loves you very much and misses you. You are the best mother she has.

Your adoring daughter,

✩

And what of my suffering mother—you must want to know about her? Penny Power the Bereaved, Penny the Terrifying, Penny the Aggrieved, no account would be complete without a close-up of her face. Perhaps now is a good time for a tangent, while I'm lying in a stupor, broken and bent—yes, a word from our sponsors, let's go far afield, fill in some blanks . . .

Picture Poor Penelope, trapped in the Ithaca of her rock-and-roll fantasy, waiting stone-faced for an impossible return—and I, pathetic Telemachus, bloodied at my father's hand, had no gift to ease her days, not a single consolatory word. Who was left to watch over her? Who would hold her elbow, shrive her soul? Who'd lift the albatross from her shoulders, collateral damage from a vagrant's undiscriminating bow?

You've seen her on your television, in your fashion magazines—but they don't tell of the long vigil on the windy widow's walk, the distant sliver of ocean on which she rested her bloodshot hopes; they don't convey the Babel of lawyers and VPs, police, producers, and debtors; the deluge of claims against him, groupies who swore to god they'd bedded him, were carrying his true heirs; bonds against cancellation in Oslo, Krakow, Sydney, Rotterdam; dealers with cocaine noses, skinny-tied Shylocks demanding their pound of meat; 108 suitors with pens and tape recorders hurling themselves into her moat. What would you have had her do, O disapproving one, don her best sari, make herself pretty, lie down at his side in useless punk-rock *suti*?

Then you don't know my mother.

You think you've seen her, do you? You think that what you read is true, that photos with Hefner, with Bono and Keitel, mugshots and gold records explain this belle in all her complexity—at long last, sir, have you no sense of your own gullibility?

Are you interested in what really *is*? Would you like to try a little quiz?

True or false: She was born in Detroit in the Summer of Love, illegitimate offspring of a groupie and the drummer of the MC5?

False, you fool—you're already failing! They made that one up for the liner notes of Fuck Finn's first EP. Not bad for a couple of girls with no marketing degree!

Number Two (still having fun?): Her mother never told her the secret of her paternity, saving that factoid for the night of her Sweet Sixteen. Spent her adolescence praying to the gods of rock: Iggy and the Stooges, the Dolls and the Thin White Duke, and yes, the Motor City's dissonant quintet, all adorned her walls, watched over her restless futon nights, her backstage dreams, her slippery thighs. Until the night of her birthday, when a leather-clad leviathan stepped through the front door. "Your father," said Grandma—and my mother just gaped, recognized his face from the poster above her bed, the curled lip and dark eyes that had presided over sweaty fantasies. "Daughter," he smiled, and Penelope fled, packed a bag, smashed her piggy bank. By sunrise she'd made Chicago, by the next night Cedar Falls. Hitchhiked her way to a West Coast destiny, holing up at a New Mexico nunnery before arriving at the beach with only the clothes on her back . . .

This story, you say, has got to be true—it fits so well with the face, the songs! It has its own logic—how could it be wrong?

Ah, but it is, despite your surprise—sorry to tell you, bub: You're O for 2.

What about the speed addiction? The psychotic episode? The year in juvenile detention? Strikes three, four, and five—you're out, and then some.

Surely she had an affair with Kim Gordon—that's how she learned to play bass! Surely she lived in a Tijuana brothel, charging fifty pesos just to look at her face?

No, and no again, *mon cher.* Really, I'm surprised—can't you tell when you're being conned, when the machine is manufacturing a star right before your eyes?

Listen closely if you choose—I'll whisper in your ear: She grew up in New Jersey—middle-class suburbs, braces, JV tennis, the whole bit. Daddy's little favorite, groomed for the Ivy League, stealing off to New York on school nights to hear Blondie and the Ramones, smoking pot in Washington Square with her giggling girlfriends. Off to Yale, where she majored in drama, had her first real boyfriend—a doctor's son from Brookline. (My friend, am I boring you yet?) She could have gone on to do anything—law school, med school, family connections on Broadway. But mousy Penelope bought a ticket with her graduation check, and when the plane landed in San Diego, out stepped Penny Power: parentless miracle of self-invention, a fright to behold!

O beautiful Gorgon, how you blazed a trail through the beach clubs and biker bars, walked the streets with a bass strapped to your back, singing your tentative first songs while sitting on some Hell's Angel's lap. Shameless, they called you—and maybe you were: strutting around in a bikini, showing off your assets to frat boys on Pacific Beach, inviting them to your coffeehouse gig with a bat of your eyelashes, a cock of your hips. They came by the hundreds: to the Innerchange, to Ground Zero, to Java Joe's, tiny rooms overflowing every Acoustic Thursday show. (Aha!, you think, my vigilant one: Now this is the Penny I love and know . . .)

She'd start out sweetly—just a girl and her axe, her voice a melancholy whisper over the thrum and the slap, building and deepening, drawing the room in as she stood from her stool and bared her teeth, a howl that seemed to come from somewhere else: a dark planet called Pain. Soon she was flat on her back, thrusting her hips, writhing across the stage—everyone paralyzed, swept up and whirling in the funnel cloud of her rage.

Week after week, they watched her pour out her fury, mesmerized by her spotlit catharses—red-faced, wailing, she rubbed her fingers raw on the strings; in the front row, they could feel the heat radiating from her body, waves of desperation when she stepped up to sing. And though she was beautiful—everyone said so, tall and raven-haired, gray eyes, a model's proud bearing—they all felt they knew her, felt she was speaking to their most private, aching fears, when she sang what would become her anthem, a little ditty you might have heard, called "Ugly Like Me":

> *Tear the shirt right off my back—*
> *Was this what you wanted to see?*
> *Eat my pretty heart out, Mister—*
> *In the dark, you're as ugly as me.*

"We're going to transform the world," she told the slackjawed crowd. Her set finished, she stood dripping in sweat, T-shirt torn and sticking to her chest, face streaked with tears and snot. The hushed room trembled in joy and a palpable terror: that the soul-splitting howl they'd been holding inside might find its way out, that this self-loathing they'd carried around might one day prove the mark of their worth.

"You don't believe me," said Teaneck's erstwhile Most-Likely-To, victim of a profound, hollowing grief. "But it's all going to turn upside down. People like us can be happy. People like you and me are allowed to be happy."

Then she hid her face in her hands and sobbed, shoulders heaving, reflections from her bass shooting prisms of light over mute faces. Every boy and girl, every man and woman in the room wanted to put their arms around her and take her home.

And who's that skinny kid crushed against the back wall, his weak heart pounding with love? He would go to her now, if he weren't frightened to death, pinned by the elbows of the newly converted. Who's that unshaved waif, waiting for a signal all these years, singing his songs to the homeless and the bent, cutting his skin with an X-Acto knife? Imagine the shock when he sees his reflection; imagine what goes through his head as she looks up and hiccups the manifesto of the new revolution:

"Fuck the beautiful," she said.

Well, my astute little punk devotee, you think you know all the rest: how she found three more losers and called them Fuck Finn, how they sailed across the San Diego skies and landed at the top of the Casbah heap, local record companies squabbling over the EP. How she finally met Brandt in the back room one night, two years after he'd first laid eyes; how they married six months later, her belly not yet swelling, the car crash in Ensenada on the way to their honeymoon. Steadily they waged war on the mainstream—my mother always the brains and the drive, working her contacts, seducing booking agents, buttonholing producers and critics alike. Where would he have been without her, that shy kid with the soggy bedroll, angelic delinquent with his pocket Rimbaud? When self-doubt overcame him and he reached for a drink, who smoothed his forehead, kissed his eyelids, who rubbed his tired shoulders and lit his cigarette? When his lyrics rang trite, chord progressions stillborn, who picked up the guitar and said, "Let's try B-flat"?

"Dirtnap," "Kill the Surfers," even "Thorazine Days," might never have been written without her intervention. She had a dream, she could see the future, and nothing was going to prevent its realization: not even her self.

"No one will ever know what your love and belief mean to me," he muttered into the microphone at the MTV Awards. Fidgeting like a fifth grader in his pink tuxedo, Connor and Billy and XXX jostling each other behind him, girls in the audience shrieking on cue. You could hear the quaver in his quiet words, the crowd sucked in their breath—he held the Best New Group trophy over his head and said, "Penny, this is for you."

So don't you dare tell me she coasted on his fame, don't purse your lips, shrug your shoulders, belittle her good name. "Stalker!" "Barnacle!" "Starfucker!" "Yoko!"—she heard it all over the years. But not once did she waver from the course they'd laid, not for a moment did she doubt their ambitions, or underestimate the price that would have to be paid.

Can you imagine what she did for him? The excuses she made up, the distractions she provided, the shortcomings (and drugs) she hid for him? When he was picked up in Pittsburgh, who took the rap? When he wanted to fire their first manager, who made the tough phone call, who let fall the axe? Weeks that she didn't see him, sent Talia to the fishing pier, the fleabag motels, to make sure he was alive; long nights on Azalea Path, waiting for him to come to bed, finding him passed out in the studio in a puddle of vomit—she bathed his face, gently pulled the needle from the vein, and in the morning brought him black coffee, a bottle of Xanax to smooth over the burn.

Who do you think revived him in Mexico City that time? The largest free concert ever held in Chapultepec Park, the triumphant kickoff of the Kids' World Tour, the moment sweet San Diego boy became global wonder ("¡Viva Los Niños!" said La Reforma the next day)—but long after midnight in the Four Seasons, she woke up with a start, the rising star next to her rigid and blueing. She knew without thinking what had happened, knew there was no time to lose: She dragged him to the bathtub, ran the water deathly cold, slapped him and pounded his back, parted his lips and blew air into his lungs—a clock ticking, ticking, tock—and then climbed into the water on top of him, squeezed his body to hers, and started to pray, babbling to a god of whom she'd never asked a thing . . .

A shiver, a cough, glazed eyes fluttered open: "It's fucking cold," he groaned at last, his lips trembling but slowly pinking.

My indomitable mother took his chin in her hand and said, "You won't escape me that easily. We started something, and we're going to finish it."

And after all those years of struggle and hope, after climbing the mountain half-carrying him up the slopes—he left her alone without warning, to stand helpless while his sail breached the horizon, shipwrecked in the suburbs while her hero departed on his foolish, final odyssey . . .

But you didn't know any of that, did you, my friend? You'd heard she was crazy, his unpredictable femme fatale, not untalented but definitely second-tier, she'd lived in his limelight and inherited the farm—such a well-dressed, merry widow, she probably drove him right to the brink . . .

O heartless jury: Don't believe everything that you think.

✶

"Is she here yet?" I muttered.

Rhoda turned from her perch by the window. "Not yet, baby."

Purple dusk, a backlit sky. The hospital hushed, only the mumble of the TV, squeaks of the contraption that held my splinted leg in traction.

"Call her again," I said, morphine leaden on my tongue.

Rhoda leaned her cheek against the glass. "Look at them," she sighed. "Look at them all."

"Rhoda?" I said, the drugs ebbing, fingers of pain that started at my ankle and crept toward my knee like a furtive prom date. But she was watching the crowd in the parking lot, spread on the hospital lawn. She was unstoppable now, she'd had a taste of it—her dreams for my future were an avalanche rumbling toward me. And I an invalid, clipped-winged, too weak to get out of the way.

"Did you talk to her, or just leave a message?" I said. "Maybe it's just really busy on the set . . ."

She came to the bedside, patted my hand. "We should do a reading," she said. Then, to my stupefied expression, "That's it, we'll do a reading! Maybe on the roof . . . No, we've had enough heights for a while. Maybe the atrium? 'The Phoenix Reading,' we'll call it. Or 'Back from the Dead'? Calliope ministers to the sick and the dying, the lame shall walk, the blind shall see . . . Baby, what do you know about handling snakes?"

Just then there was a knock at the door and Dr. Verline came in. I vaguely remembered him from lucid moments of the last few days: tall and distinguished, salt-and-pepper hair, strong chin. He stood over my bed and stared down in consternation, as though what he saw there did not correspond to the clipboard in his hand.

"How are we doing today?" he said. "How's the pain?"

"Great, she's doing great," said Rhoda. "Listen, can I talk to you?

Calliope had this idea for a benefit for the hospital, something to show her appreciation—"

"Calliope?" he said. "Does the leg hurt?" He reached down to touch my ankle, but I shot him a look of such malevolence he thought better of it. "Dr. Markovich said the surgery went well. We should be able to get you off the morphine pretty soon."

"Now," I said. "Get this fucking needle out of me now."

He smiled insincerely, examined my chart. "Has Markovich been to see you?"

"Probably." I turned away. "Is he the one with the big cock?"

He stopped in mid-scribble and looked at Rhoda. "Maybe we could taper it down over the next few days, get you on orals . . ."

"I bet you'd like that," I said. I don't know why I felt the need to be detestable—maybe it was the horrible itching, the hot prickle up and down my limbs. My leg was a rod of fire, morphine pulling back like an evening tide. It left on the wet sand a bright seashell of memory: My mother nursing me through a nasty flu, cold compresses and alcohol rub-downs, nonstop cartoons. When the fever would not let go, she carried me to the pool, backstroking end to end while I languished across her chest; and though it was winter and her teeth rattled, she did not stop until the fever broke, the shine left my eyes, both of us sobbing with re-lief before falling asleep together, wrapped in plush towels in my four-poster bed.

"Just try to relax," Verline said. He patted my shoulder and left his hand there. "Think of it as a vacation."

"A *working* vacation," Rhoda piped up. "Dennis is bringing the galleys over tomorrow, baby. Don't forget, we've got a book to finish."

I glared at the doctor, sour eyes watching me from the wall all the while. When I slept, that monstress invaded my dreams; when I woke she was waiting, her mockery infused with the smell of bleach, the crinkle of starchy sheets.

"Whatever you say, Doc." I closed my eyes. "My family's got a good his-tory with IV drugs. I'm sure your malpractice insurance will cover it."

Verline pursed his lips, withdrew his hand. He initialed the clipboard, hooked it carefully to the bed frame. "Let's see how you do with Percocet," he said.

★

From the Desk of Calliope Bird Morath

Dear Mahmoud,

Just a quick note to thank you and Nura, once again, for letting me stay with you last month. It was ~~so strange to~~ wonderful to see you. It's been so long since my Warren Wilson days, I sometimes have to remind myself that was me, sending you all those purple ballades and sonnets, poring over your ~~wise~~ wise comments. Looking back, I realize how difficult it must have been to work with such an overwrought adolescent (though I would still argue that some comments—"self-obsessed pestilence" and "grotesque advances of a child-whore" come to mind—sacrificed pedagogy for emphasis), but you never let me down or pulled any punches, and I ~~think back with fondness~~ am a better poet for it.

I know it wasn't the most tranquil three days, and I hope you will convey my apologies to Nura and little Hani. Had I not been so preoccupied, I would ~~have been thrilled~~ have ~~happily~~ gladly joined her for an afternoon of embroidery. And again, I was not insulting the goat soufflé: I ~~rarely~~ do not eat meat! ~~I'm sure a Jewish woman living in a Muslim city, married to a Muslim man, understands how important~~ It was wrong of me, really horrible, to tear the head off Hani's Brandt doll—a moment of inexcusable sadism. If by chance you find the old Bedouin who sews them by hand, please buy him a new one. I trust the enclosed check will cover it.

What I regret most is that you and I didn't have more time to catch up, to talk about poetry and life and the old days. The incident on the last night stays with me. I'm sure it was my fault. I think the unremitting heat and all the figs finally got to me. The check should also cover the mirror, and the book. I just thank God it was the Rumi, and not one of your hand-copied Shabistaris, that burned! I'll always remember the beauty of those words, the passion with which you read them to me:

> Go sweep out the chamber of your heart.
> Make it ready to be the dwelling place of the Beloved.
> When you depart, He will enter it.
> In you, void of yourself, will He display His beauty.

You see, Mahmoud, I was listening.

Do you think one can truly "sweep out" one's heart? And how to begin? I wish you knew how tired I am of ~~all this drama bullshit~~ ~~life~~ these incidents. People seem to expect them of me, they say, "There goes Calliope . . ." But that's how I feel, too! Like a spectator . . . How I sometimes wish I could become "void of myself." Do you understand? Do you think we are stuck with ourselves forever, old friend? What do the Sufis say about this? (I wonder now if this wasn't what you were trying to tell me that night, before our little "episode.")

In case you were wondering, the rest of the trip was a failure. The contact in Casablanca turned out to be a teenage shoemaker with terrible acne and a rather rude fascination with my hair. Tangier was no better—no one at the Paul Bowles museum had ever heard of my father. In Marrakech, I was nearly arrested in a tea stall talking to a hashish dealer who was the band's supplier on the "Ottoman Odyssey" Tour. One name strangely keeps coming up, one of the band's sound techs, but no one here has seen him for years. ~~Just another dead end in a pointless~~ The search continues . . .

But it was a wonderful trip, if only because I got to see <u>you</u>. Next time: Paris? I'm still ~~taken aback~~ surprised that you know my mother. I didn't realize you two had ever met. If you should happen to see her before I do, would you please ~~ask her to call~~ tell her send her my regards? And I almost forgot!—thank you so much for the honey from your brother's farm. It was a real lifesaver. I hope to repay you in this lifetime. May Allah watch over you and your family.

Salaam alaikum,

*

For a week I simmered, watching daylight come and go, listening to whispers leak from every corner, seep through the walls and under the door. I lay like a weighted whale in that white mechanical bed, surrounded by papers and books and fan mail, the remote control never far from my hand. Moby Dick with a manuscript, my manic Ahab appeared at mid-morning to harpoon me with ideas and plans, contracts and queries; at noon she wheeled me through dreamlike halls, gabbling about interviews, photo shoots, readings. Every day a new brainstorm: another TV slot, a guest spot on *Love Line,* interviews on PBS and E! She'd never have enough now, I could see it in her eyes: This was bigger than book sales, bigger than Calliope, bigger even than Art and Poetry. At Mountaintop, her projects had been gigantic, unwieldy—like the ill-fated CeramIce Capades (an early spring thaw had put the kibosh on that frigid oeuvre)—curtailed only by lack of time, space, clay. Here, at last, was her unlimited material. Here, the whole enchilada.

"I want to go home," I'd plead, but Rhoda stood fast, staring down at the vigil in the parking lot as though facing an opponent across a poker table. He was out there, I could feel it, the sweet blond boy with kaleidoscope eyes—what was it he'd wanted to tell me? What message had I failed to receive?

"Not quite yet," she said. "Let 'em get a little more desperate." She kept me away from the window for fear they would see me; like my mother before her, she made me invisible, a rara avis, a scarce commodity.

"Get those galleys done," she ordered. "Make sure the poems are perfect. Once we send them to Snow Lion, there's no turning back. It's written in stone."

How that idea frightened me! As I floated in and out of clarity, the poems came to seem downright threatening, my notes unfathomable scratches. What had I been thinking? What had I wanted to say? The words seemed so distant, so clinical. I could not grasp their fullness, nor perceive the spiderwebs of sense that bound them. I couldn't remember who'd written those lines—the lunatic in the mirror?—they swam before me like koi in a pond, glimmering and pretty as a mirage. I reached out and they scattered.

Early each morning, after Verline's rounds, I dragged the galleys from under the bed. *Today,* I told myself, in the cool flush of the day's first narcotics—today I would focus, make the hard decisions. I would hear the music, regain my mojo. But soon I'd look up to find that hag watching— did she never sleep?—and my hands trembled. I tried to ignore her, to read the poems aloud, but that only amused her more, her eyeteeth showing, the cackle of her learned critique filling the room.

"Lupe!" I'd cry, stabbing the button at the bedside. The nurse finally ambled in, looking none too alarmed. "Lupe, I need a pill." I tried to smile sweetly. After two days, I was a convert to the Church of Percocet. A true believer. "I think the other nurse forgot."

"Let's see . . ." She'd pick up my chart with one hand, take my pulse with the other. "No, you had two pills at six. It's 7:15 now."

"A mistake," I gasped, shedding honest-to-goodness tears. "It never happened."

"Says right here—"

"Words!" I cried. "What do they mean? Who can trust them?" I clutched at her scrubs, pressed my cheek to her arm. "She could write anything she wants!"

"I'm sure she'd never—"

"Maybe she gave it to *her!*" I said, pointing at the witch on the wall, who returned my accusation, fierce and red-faced. And it was true: none of it meant anything—the words on my manuscript, the signs on TV. "Mother," I whispered—but there was no mother, only a cold, echoing hospital room; "Daddy!" I thought, careful never to utter that murderous moniker. "Lover," "beekeeper," "art," "home"—what good were those sounds if they could not produce the *thing,* if they invoked nothing but a titter from my gruesome roommate?

Even "Calliope"? What on earth did that mean? A Bird is a bird is a bard. A bored. Nonsense, babytalk, gobbledygook—yet somehow it had come to signify: for the writers of the *Orange County Register,* the mob camped on the lawn. What relationship did those syllables bear to my being—or were they only a synonym for the void? A placeholder, nothing more, a mat of rushes laid over a deep trap—one false step and you tumbled into darkness, a wormstinking pit of anonymity, never to be heard from again.

You think I'm being dramatic, *mon cher*, perhaps overstating my case? Day after day I languished, a twisted punctuation mark amid sterile whitespace. In the corner the brainless bear gawked—it would not look away, though I stuck out my tongue, shook my fist. While outside, the vigil continued, the starving masses, barbarians at the gate—they would stay until they got what they came for, what the words on their placards and banners declared: the battered, benumbed body that went with this butchered name.

"Calliope?" said a voice, slipping into the room. "Uh, Miss Morath, I mean?" Rhoda and I looked up—she from Sudoku, I from an intense exploration of the lines on my palm—to find a young man standing with his back to the door. He was much younger than Verline, not much older than I—mussed, bleached hair, a pinched, narrow nose, and a dark soul patch beneath his lower lip. Under his white coat he wore jeans and flip-flops, a faded T-shirt that said WHITE STRIPES.

"I'm Dr. Silverstein," he said in a stage whisper. "Your regular doctor couldn't make it. He's on vacation."

"He was just here," I said. "About an hour ago."

He walked to the foot of the bed and picked up the clipboard. "It was a sudden vacation. Family emergency. He asked me to come in and run some tests."

Rhoda took off her glasses. "What kind of tests?"

"Tests," said this doctor, bleached eyebrows knitting. "You know, just regular tests. To make sure she's healing." He squinted at the chart in his hands, flipped the pages, turned it upside down.

"So, I see you're taking Per . . . sock . . . Persocket—how's that doing for you?" He looked up and smiled brightly; finding two flat stares, he fumbled at the clipboard again.

Rhoda put a hand on my shoulder. "What did you say your name was?"

This doctor peered at the bag of saline, traced the plastic tube with an index finger. He would not meet my eyes, his gaze skating over the top of my head.

"When is my mother coming?" I asked him. I was suddenly sure this fellow had information, a message to be given in signs, secret handshakes.

"I'd like to test your hand-eye coordination," he said, producing a pen from his breast pocket. "Do you think you can write?"

"I wrote her a letter. Did she read it?" I reached for his arm. I pulled until he bent toward me, holding the rail for balance. "I know who you are," I said in his ear. His eyes widened. I had to whisper so the bear couldn't hear. "The roshi sent you, didn't he?"

Rhoda stood. "Her coordination is fine. What's this all about?"

"Ma'am, you never know, do you?" said my new doctor, my secret messenger, my I-spy. "We want to make sure there's no, like, hidden damage."

I lunged for his lapels, the witch on the wall again demonstrating her displeasure. "There is!" I pressed my face to his middle. "There is damage!"

"Here." The doctor offered me the pen. "Why don't you just try writing your name?" He took something from his coat pocket and laid it on my lap. "Maybe sign your name, you know? Or . . . let's see, maybe first write, 'For Billy.' That ought to tell us everything we need—"

"Okay, that's it," said Rhoda, scurrying around the bed. "You're done. This is a hospital, not a poetry workshop. You can't harass people in here." She grabbed him by the arm and pulled him away, but he hooked a foot on the bed rail.

"Please, just sign it," he said. "I paid a lot of money for that! I'm a huge fan!"

As Rhoda wrestled him toward the door, I looked down to find a CD case—a photograph on the cover of my father onstage, eyes closed and spittle flying, his hair a radiant nimbus. *Japanimosity*, read the title, in crude lettering dripping blood, a dagger stabbing the heart of the O.

I remembered hearing about this recording, the limited-edition '80s bootleg, revered by collectors as the pinnacle of the Kids' pre-NorthStar sound. Their popularity just blooming in the United States, in Japan they were already gods—an Osaka convention hall packed to the exits, four teenagers trampled at the foot of the stage before my father jumped into the crowd to help clear a space.

But the pièce de résistance was the encore, one they'd never played before—Barry McGuire's "Eve of Destruction," at the end of which my father crawled inside XXX's bass drum, huddling silently as the curtain fell. I'd like to think he chose it with his baby in mind, the ruddy one-month-old he'd had to leave behind but to whom, each night over the phone, he'd sing a scratchy lullaby.

"Don't you understand what I'm trying to say? Can't you see the fear that I'm feeling today?" The lyrics were printed on the back cover, subtitled in Japanese, across an image of my father taken from behind, stagelights dazzling, guitar strap across his back like a bandolier: a rock-and-roll guerrilla leaping into the fray.

"Where is he?" I said, throwing off the sheet. Pain rushed through my leg as I twisted toward this improbable messenger. "The frets on the guitar," I said. "Tell me what the words mean!"

"Baby, you stay in bed," Rhoda warned. She had him pinned to the wall now, one arm barred across his chest.

I tried to lever myself up against the nightstand, heat searing in my hip as I twisted. "Did he send you?" I said, leaning on the page proofs. "Mr. Bath and Rot, did he give you that pen?" But the papers slipped under my hand, and down I went like a sack full of kindling—papers and CD case, books and letters all rustling to the floor.

By the time Rhoda and the fake doctor got to me, I was laughing like mad. My cheek pressed to cold linoleum, my broken leg propped at an angle against the bed.

"Shhh!" I told them as they bent to help me. "Don't say anything."

"Let's just get you into bed," said Rhoda. "It's okay, C, upsa-daisy . . ."

"I'm really sorry," the fake doctor kept muttering. "I'm so sorry."

"They're listening," I tried to tell them, pointing with my eyes to the television, the crazed painting on the wall, the stuffed bear. I'd heard the signal—but there were others desperate for the information I now possessed. "They're trying to find him, too. They want to get there first and *praise* him," I said.

They managed to haul me into bed, the prize still clutched in my hands. "You won't talk about this," Rhoda told the man in the white coat. "Not one word. Don't fuck with me, or my lawyers will be on you like Jack the Ripper on a bad-hair day. Trespassing, harassment, impersonating a doctor . . . we'll get the AMA so far up your—"

He shook his head, stared longingly at the CD case. "I didn't want to cause trouble," he said. "I just wanted an autograph."

"If she signs that for you, will you keep your mouth shut? You didn't see her like this. She's perfectly lucid, working on her manuscript night and day . . ." He nodded frantically, like a child offered a sweet. Rhoda squinted, then smiled shrewdly, as though she'd found a new angle. "She's consumed by her art." Rhoda straightened his coat for him, laying on the charm. "You've never seen such dedication. She's even planning to do a reading for the other patients . . . a sneak preview of new poems, never heard before. But it's closed to the public," she added.

I turned the CD over, looked closer at the image on the back. "Who is this?" I said.

The doctor took the bait. "Do you think maybe I could come?" he said, and sucked his soul patch, eyes lit with hunger. "I'll totally be quiet, you won't even know—"

"Who is this person?" I demanded, holding up the case. At the side of the stage, visible over my father's shoulder, stood a vision of beauty: statuesque Penelope, waiting in the wings, holding in her arms a white-swaddled, red-tufted bundle.

Rhoda looked briefly at it. "That's you, baby," she said, pinching my cheek. "You and Penny." She turned back to the faux doctor. "Sorry, pal. Patients only. Catch a terminal disease, and then we'll talk."

But I hadn't gone to Japan, and neither had my mother. I knew that much for sure. We'd stayed behind in the tiny apartment, my mother browsing real-estate listings, her infant sleeping fitfully. In the wee hours, exhausted, she'd walk out to the ocean, rock me in her arms until the waves put us both to sleep.

"It's an impostor," I said. "I wasn't there!"

The photo had been doctored, or was an out-and-out fake. An image from another concert, overlaid with Japanese words. And what about the music, I wondered, my fingers trembling on the plastic—what if that, too, was bogus? Songs from another concert, another tour—maybe another band! Why would my father have sent something so false, I wondered. Was he still playing tricks on me after all this time? Furious, I flung the CD across the room; it struck the wall, splintered, and fell to the floor.

"Hey!" said the doctor. "That cost me six hundred dollars!"

"You're not my father." I glared at the poor boy.

"All right, this little game show is over," Rhoda said, leading him to the door. "Thanks for playing. You get a lifetime supply of Turtle Wax . . ."

"This is bullshit!" he said. "I ask for an autograph and you assault me and break my CD? How about I go down there and tell everyone about this, tell them how you asked me to lie—"

"Where did you put him?" I roared, pointing at the terrible image on the wall, the livid visage with the drool-shined chin. "Leave us alone," I told her. "You're not me!"

"Look, we'll get you a new one," Rhoda promised. "She'll sign it. No problem. Just go." Behind her I babbled and sobbed, pulled the sheet over my head so the eyes could not locate me. With everyone watching, I'd never find my father, never crack the code. That's why the hag in the mirror had come, I realized: to throw me off track. She had to keep tabs for Mr. Bath and Rot, take notes on my progress and report back.

Rhoda was still trying to soothe the fake doc. "She's fine, really, just a bad day . . ." He grumbled his doubt and she tried another tack. "Listen, we'll prove it—tell them to watch the window tonight, after dark. She'll come to the window and wave, they can take pictures, whatever. Can you tell them? I know they're worried about her, they want to see their poet and make sure she's okay . . ."

At this he started to laugh, a sound both pitying and cruel. "Wave?" he said. "You think they're waiting for Calliope to wave?"

Rhoda said nothing, and in the starchy white world under the sheet, I fell still.

"They don't want her to wave," said my accuser. "They want her to jump."

✶

From the Desk of Calliope Bird Morath

Dear ~~Mother~~ Mom ~~Dearest~~ ~~Penelope~~ Mommy,
   Where are you? Did you get all   those messages?

Your the best mother   I have and I ~~need~~ would like to see the
real you now

                                        Love ~~always,~~

✶

My friend, can't you see me, pinned at the hip, frantic and disheveled, losing my grip? Alone at night, only my precious pink pills for company, I fretted over poems, scratched out whole stanzas, crumpled up pages and drowned them in my private sink. I wrote meandering letters to teachers and friends, full of non sequiturs, exclamation points. Not ten minutes later, I couldn't decipher what I'd written. I wrote to Ben Affleck, to H. D. and Ezra Pound. I wrote to the shaman, my mother's old chum, to the regents of the university, to my new friend Sebastião. I wrote to XXX, to Taryn, to Talia Z at her ashram. "Darling," I wrote the Beekeeper, languishing in his own bed, "Rescue me, please, from this oppressive stuffed bear. If you call at my window, I'll let down my hair. . . ."

My father was everywhere, an electric chlorine ghost: a whisper of Muzak, a televised wraith. He was trying to reach me, but I couldn't yet understand the words. I feigned sleep, one eye on the door. I moved in and out of memories, the squeeze of his hand so real I could see its imprint on my skin. The TV showed tributes and old interviews, cloying *In Memoria*. I saw my house surrounded by police cars; an empty Casbah stage; a lonely fishing pier, even the seagulls flown; a grainy, sleepwalking Penelope, fifteen years younger, closing the curtains one by one.

"We're not interested in making a lot of money," he told Downtown Julie Brown, his sad voice stretched to a whisper. He sucked on a cigarette for dear life, absently swept ashes from his lap. "I mean, that's our whole thing is just looking at how screwed up the world is, you know? Money has a lot to do with that. We just want to play our music . . ."

But Brandt, you're a star—that's got to feel good! Everyone loves you. Don't tell me that's not what you wanted.

Sometimes I wish I could just be alone. That I could be the person I was before all this started, and not this . . . rockstar. Or, you know, that I could disappear, change my identity, go back to being someone nobody gives a shit about.

Your daughter would miss you so much, Brandt. You'd ruin her life. She'd grow up not knowing what was real and what wasn't.

But she'd know in her heart, Julie—she'd know I hadn't died. Can you hear me Calliope? I'm not dead . . .

I blinked in the Clorox brightness, gasped a wet breath. The TV was off, Verline at the foot of the bed, reading my chart to a gaggle of students. They stared at me as though I were Icarus himself, crash-landed and pathetic, the fall not half as humbling as the laughable convalescence.

"Did you see him? He was right there!" I pointed to the corner of the room, but found only the slumped, glassy-eyed bear.

The students whispered behind their hands. Verline scratched his chin. "Maybe it's time to take the Percocet down a notch."

"You killed him, didn't you?" I said to the doctor. I gripped the sheet in both hands, tried to tear it with my teeth. "You killed him with your fucking words."

"Maybe two notches. Maybe we'll try Tylenol," he said, to the general laughter. Then he leaned down and whispered, so the others wouldn't hear: *It's me, Bird, the one you've been looking for. Don't you recognize me after all these years?*

The week wore on, my calvary continued. The flames in my leg slowly dulled, doused by time and synthetic opiates. The squeaky pulleys disappeared, replaced by a pistachio-colored cast, signed in Sharpie by Lupe and Verline and someone named Sam. Taryn and Dennis came to visit; the roshi called with daily updates. Hour by hour, Rhoda sat at my side, looking at schedules and proposals, dashing off torrents of e-mail. Madame Defarge with a BlackBerry, she devised a far, far better scheme each day—as I listlessly read and reread my poems, she sat knitting a revolution but left out my *liberté.*

"At last, at last," she beamed, when I finally handed her the book. "Thank God Almighty! This will go out tomorrow. Ithaca's all abuzz . . ."

But I felt no victory, no surge of pride. The words were a black-and-white jumble, a scrapheap of symbols I'd moved back and forth. The pages so full of groaning effort; not what I'd dreamed of creating, not what I called art.

"And what a story!" she said to herself as she flipped through the pages. "I'll put it in the press kit, and I want you talking about it in interviews: how you had to finish the poems from a hospital bed, whacked-out on pain-killers, how you suffered for your art, et cetera.

"This is just the beginning," she said, exactly what I dreaded hearing. "The tour's going to be spectacular. *Charlie Rose* is all set, I'm talking to *The View* as we speak. With all this hoopla, you're a lock for the Yale Prize. And what's that other one, starts with a P?"

"I can't," I said, watching the empty sky. I knew she wouldn't listen. The euphoria of the pills had given way to grimy fatigue. I was dissolving into the dirty sheets, my awareness losing sharpness and resolution, losing my crystal-clear sense of Me.

"I'm working on a grand finale. Something unprecedented." She went to the window, spied once again on the crowd. "Give me a day or two—I can't tell you just yet. Right now let's concentrate on the hospital reading. If our friend Dr. Feelgood does his job, we might have a *slightly* bigger crowd than expected . . ."

"I can't!" I said to the mattress. I heard a soggy, keening sound that turned out to be coming from me. "I can't do it. I wrote the damn poems, what else do you want?"

Rhoda settled back into her chair, pushed her fake reading glasses higher on her nose. "Grow up, C. The poems are just the beginning," she said. I curled into a one-legged fetal position. "That's what I keep telling you. It's not just the lines, it's who wrote them. It's not just rhyme and meter, it's context and history, the circumstances of their creation, the motivation . . . That's all part of the experience people have when reading them, or buying them, what it says about *them* that they even *own* your book."

I tossed my head and moaned—*no, no, no*—though deep down I feared she was right. After all that work, they wouldn't even be reading my poems—not the way I did. "It's a waste," I said. "A joke. I won't do it." I could feel the bitch on the wall giggling in triumph.

Rhoda sat back, shuffled the pages, tapped the edges. "Yes, you will." She smiled her most dangerous smile. "You owe me. And this book is just the beginning. What we're selling is much, much bigger."

She bent to kiss my forehead, lips lingering in benediction. "Don't you understand?" she said, too close to my ear. "These words aren't the real poem: *You* are."

*

We tried, for a time, to be unremarkable—average suburbanites, a minivan, trips to the mall, prearranged playdates. Just imagine our poor neighbors, picking up the phone: "Hi, this is Penny Power—can I borrow a couple of eggs? Some sugar?" She sent Esperanza through the neighborhood, to find other children my age—now that I'd rejoined the world of the living, she was determined I be properly socialized.

"Stop rhyming!" she'd shudder. "Do you want your new friends to think you're abnormal?" I'd stare at her across the dinner table, her sweating gin and tonic, a stack of legal papers for review. What was normal, I wondered over chateaubriand. What passed for average outside that house of nine gables?

There were two of her, as well: one who stumbled around upstairs at night, strewing articles of clothing, slurring my name; the other vigilant as an eagle, shrieking her way through our gloomy days. It was as if we'd both been transformed that Christmas—the flames that enveloped me had burned away our shared history: The house had no basement, her child had no father. We never spoke of it. Do you disapprove? Walk a mile, O happy anonymous one, before you condemn her unconditional love.

Weekends at the studio in Manhattan Beach—my mother remastering tracks for the box set, remixing and splicing while I read Ovid or Keats. See her standing at the mixing board: so beautifully focused, chic eyeglasses and a chignon, twirling the knobs and adjusting the levels, her calm determination to make the final tracks come out *just so*. ("Think the Tower of Pisa, the Great Wall, the Kremlin," she said. "When this collection comes

out, there'll be no confusion. The world will understand what they lost.")
At night she dropped me at Connor's for pizza and videos, the two of them
greeting coolly, she wouldn't pass the front step. God knows where she
went those nights, what she did or with whom; but the next morning she'd
pull up to find me playing outside, practicing headstands in the grass next
to his enormous bronze Buddha. I remember the smell of her in the hot
car: smoke and toothpaste, something vaguely antiseptic, the whiteness
of her knuckles on the wheel.

"Be who you were born to be," that's what she always said. But who
was my mother? What had she become? Did she sleep at night dreaming
of a New Jersey bedroom, of Friday-night football, playing clarinet in the
marching band? Did she recall skating in Rockefeller Center in winter, a
mother's prudish makeup tips, a father's loving hand? She'd wake in the
mornings, a widow, and wonder: at the giant house, peculiar daughter,
strange familiar photos on the walls; she'd see herself on the evening news
with a beautiful boy whose memory was starting to fade. Did she clutch
at her pillow then, stifle a scream; did she wish she could take it all back and
go home, sad woman and her crumbling butterfly dream?

I sat one afternoon in the Markers' playroom, with my brand-new acquaintance: a seven-year-old boy named Terrence. A large, airy alcove just
off of the kitchen, billowing curtains and a view of the pool, bustling
sounds of birds in the trees and household help preparing for a party. Terrence was lovely, docile, and kind, content to zoom his LEGO car around
a LEGO town while I prattled "Ozymandias" and "The Emperor of Ice
Cream." I was having a very pleasant afternoon, despite my mother's misgivings. After years of cloistering, I was full of energy, delightedly tickling
young Terrence, chasing him around the room when he pulled on my
ponytail, inventing a game I called "Pirates of Penzance." Under those high
ceilings, the breeze moved gently, jasmine slinking inside like a recalcitrant
cat—even breathing was easier, away from the mortified silence of my
home. Already the burdens of my childhood were lightening; I looked forward to a future filled with such neighborhood chums, a ready-made audience for the poems I was learning, my budding ideas about line breaks
and poetics. But as was so often the case, my joie de vivre was just prelude
to gloom and gathering dread.

My mother was to pick me up at six, on the way home from her acupuncturist. Perhaps impending separation had made Terrence and me anxious; or perhaps, sensing the future as children do, we were simply determined to make the most of those last minutes. Suffice it to say that when Mrs. Marker came to fetch us—in heels and a tight green cocktail dress, platinum hair freshly pinned—she found us in a state of some disarray: little Terry's pants around his ankles, and Calliope, swashbuckler, brandishing a plastic scimitar!

"Alan!" she screamed, when her hands had dropped from her mouth. "Alan, get in here right now!"

The only sounds were of a jet passing overhead and Terrence's sniffling, rapid breaths. Seconds later, a stumbling clap of shoes hurrying down marble stairs.

"What? What's the matter?" gasped Terrence's father, red in the face, his thin comb-over somewhat disheveled. He was short and a little chubby, one strap of paisley suspenders fallen over his blue pinstripe sleeve. He was much older than his glamorous wife, who glared at him with unmitigated disgust.

"What's the *matter*?" she said. "Didn't I tell you this was a bad idea?"

Mr. Marker scratched the side of his head, took a step forward, and pulled up his son's pants. "Okay," he said, pressing the air. "Okay, no harm done. No big deal, Stevie."

"No big deal? I've got five software geeks and their boring-ass wives coming in an hour, the caterer is late, and your son is being molested by that slut's daughter. You call that no big deal?"

At this, of course, Terry started to cry, and his father knelt down to him, put a hand atop his head. I was still holding my plastic sword, stunned into paralysis. "Sweetheart, no one's being molested. They're just kids," her husband said. "It's just play—right, Calliope?"

"*She's holding a fucking sword!*" Mrs. Marker hissed, with which she reached out and yanked it from my hand, then deposited the toy through the open window. "I knew something like this would happen. This is what you get for letting your son play with those people's kid."

"He's your son, too," Mr. Marker said quietly, ruffling his sobbing son's hair, flashing his wife a smile of appeasement.

I wanted to tell her my mother wasn't a slut, though I didn't yet know what it meant. And in any case, I couldn't say a word, couldn't even shake my head.

"Are you going to *do* something?" Stevie asked her hapless husband.

Mr. Marker, very tired, hitched up his errant suspender and stood. "All right, Terrence, go to your room," he sighed. "I'll be up later and we'll talk about what happened. Calliope, honey, let's go wait in the kitchen. Your mother will be here soon."

"Oh, wonderful," said the wife, arms crossed over her ample chest. "So not only do I have to endure her child trying to castrate my son, but now I have to have that woman in my *kitchen*? Why don't we just invite her to the dinner party? Why don't we invite all of her degenerate friends, Alan? I knew this would happen . . ."

Mr. Marker, hand on my shoulder, listened to this tirade with the forbearance of a man used to listening. He led me into the kitchen and pulled out a chair, Stevie click-clicking behind us in her heels. I bit my lip as hard as I could and repeated to myself, *Don't cry, don't cry, do not cry*, knowing how my mother hated to see my tears.

A few minutes later, a tap on the screen door: There she was, in a lavender suit and sunglasses, wearing a smile she must have poached from a waiting-room magazine.

She strode inside, offering her hand. (How I loved her at that moment, her determination to be just another wealthy lady on the block.) "I'm Penelope. You must be Stevie and Al—"

"Can you just take your brat and go home?" Mrs. Marker dragged on a Virginia Slim, placing it in an ashtray on the counter, the filter rimmed in hot pink. "We're very busy."

My mother looked from face to face and finally at me: round eyes, flushed cheeks, blank stare. "What happened?" she said, her artificial mood fraying. "What did you do, Bird?"

She came and knelt before me—*don't cry, don't cry*—touched my forehead, shook my shoulders. Behind her, Mrs. Marker blew smoke at the ceiling.

"Talk to me," said my mother, her hands starting to squeeze. "Please say something, baby. Oh God, not this again! Oh please, not this again!"

"Everything's fine," said Mr. Marker, trying to avert catastrophe. "There was just a little, er, inappropriate play, and we had to separate them. I'm sure everyone's going to be just fine." He shot his wife a pleading glance. "No need to worry."

He pulled a handkerchief from his back pocket and handed it to my mother, who was still crouched before me.

Mrs. Marker snorted and tapped her cigarette ash. "Inappropriate play, my ass."

When my mother had composed herself, she stood and took my hand. "I'm very sorry," she said to Mr. Marker. "Nothing like this has happened before. I hope you won't hold it against her—she doesn't have many friends."

"It's okay." He held open the door, hoping to hurry us out before the next eruption. My mother smiled sadly and shook his hand. Then we were out on the walk. I could smell the chlorine from the pool, I could see our car parked—so close!—in the driveway.

". . . nice evening . . . just forget it, everyone will be here soon," we heard Mr. Marker pleading inside. His wife said something inaudible, and he replied, "Well, she seemed very nice to me."

"Very *nice!*" Stevie's scream carried into the backyard. "Do you even know who she is? Do you know who her husband was, that scumbag and his bullshit band . . ."

That's when my mother stopped and looked up into the sky. A terrible calm overcame her. "Wait here." She patted my head and forced a smile, then turned and walked back inside.

"I know you, don't I?" she said to Stevie, caught with her mouth open. (Of course I was following close behind.)

"Excuse me?"

"You used to live in Ocean Beach, right?" My mother's sweet smile seemed to put Stevie off guard, though I knew what was coming. I almost felt sorry for her.

"I lived there for a year or two after college. Why?"

"I remember you now. You were always down at the beach with the surfers, right?" She turned and smiled at Alan, who smiled right back, a field mouse smiling at a plummeting hawk. Before Stevie could answer, my mother said, "My husband hated surfers. You know what he used to call surfers? Hemorrhoids! He said if you scraped away a little extra muscle, all that was left was an asshole."

Mr. Marker let out a chortle, prompting a stern look from his wife.

"He wrote a song about them," my mother said. "'Kill the Surfers'? Maybe you heard it? It was number one on *Billboard* for eleven weeks?"

"I remember it!" said Mr. Marker, and while the two women looked at him, he started to sing the chorus, ticking his index finger back and forth in the air like a metronome: *"Going out with the tide/absolution is mine . . ."*

"Alan, shut up," said Mrs. Marker.

"But I guess you knew them all pretty well," said my mother. "They really seemed to like you. You know what her nickname was, Alan? They used to call her Stevie the Blowfish. Do you want to know why?"

"Excuse me!" said Stevie. "I don't know what you're talking about. I want you out of my house, and take your ugly little puppy with you."

But my mother didn't miss a beat. She moved a step closer to Mr. Marker and snaked an arm around his back, leaning up to whisper loudly into his ear. "I'll bet she doesn't give you the kind of service she gave the surfers," she said, to his stricken expression. "I'll tell you where you can get better. *Much.*"

Poor Mr. Marker, he'd never been in such a position before—his wife glancing around wildly, my mother pushing him against the counter, breathing into his collar. Even I knew she'd never seen Stevie before in her life, but Alan looked as if he wanted to run and hide, flushed and stammering. As she pressed her body against him, his hand rose for balance to the small of her back—it was too much for shrill Stevie, who crossed the kitchen and shrieked, *"Alan!"*

She sprang at my mother, grabbed her by the hair, and pulled her away. I could see my mother beaming, eyes narrowed in triumph. By the time it was over, Mr. Marker breaking it up with the bug-eyes of a heart-attack victim, Stevie was sobbing, wedged into a corner of the kitchen, holding the edge of the table as her shield and protection. As for the shimmering green dress she'd put on for the party, it was torn down the front, sequins dangling, exposing the tattoo just below her navel: a calligraphed

"TC" wrapped in sunflowers, the insignia from the back cover of *The Hanged Man*.

"I think you should leave now!" gasped poor Mr. Marker. "Please, you've done enough."

"If you ever say a word about my family again, I'll break your jaw," my mother calmly told Stevie. "Come on, Bird." She pulled me through the door.

"It must have been hard, having such explosive parents," said Michaela, years later, when I coughed up that story like a nugget of phlegm. She asked if I felt threatened by my mother, if I worried she might turn that anger on me.

"Not really." I shrugged. It wasn't explosions I feared but her cool appraisal, the contempt she turned on me when I hadn't met her expectations, when I hadn't been "who I was born to be."

"Do you feel you have to live up to their example?" my analyst tried again. "Do you feel your emotions must be manifested this way, in your poetry, your performance?"

Ah, dear Michaela, you always tried so hard. But that's too easy, too neat—and simplicity isn't a traditional Morath trait. No, Dr. B, what kept me awake that night, what I've thought about ever since, was the look on Stevie's face as my mother walked out: not fear but confusion, the woman before her incomprehensible, a raging chimera in a slightly mussed lavender pantsuit.

"Who the fuck do you think you are?" Stevie whimpered through the screen, as we walked down the path into that ruined summer night.

But I knew exactly who I was. I was Calliope. I never had a choice in the matter. That flaming phantom in your newspaper clippings? That terrible child on cable TV?

No question about it, my cool auditor. You know as well as I do: That's me.

✶

"Okay, everyone, here she is!" Rhoda threw back the door with a flourish and wheeled me in. "I hope you realize how lucky you are. This is something to tell your grandchildren about, a real coup for this hospital. A real treat for you!"

The lecture hall was buried somewhere deep in the hold of that giant, sterile ship. Stale heat slinked at my ankles as the heavy door slammed shut, cutting off the hollers and alarm bells—dozens or hundreds who'd snuck in through the hospital lobbies and garages, the cafeteria loading dock, emergency exits flung open by their cohort in a desperate, rubber-soled run. Security was overwhelmed, chasing them through the wings and stairwells like mice through a silo. As Rhoda pushed me into a service elevator, the thud of a nightstick just around the corner, she'd beamed satisfaction, another scheme come to fruition: poetry pandemonium *par excellence.*

"Do you know how many people would like to be here today?" she said now. Beyond the stage, all I saw was the dazzle of a spotlight, the dark windows of a projection booth along the top row of seats. The room smelled of textbooks and corn chips, the boredom of students, the musk of sickness. From a balled-up tissue, I snuck a pill I'd been hoarding since the night before, stuck it under my tongue, and sucked on its bitterness.

"But Calliope was adamant: Patients only! She wanted to be here just for *you.* What do you think of that?"

From the invisible rows came an uneasy grumble. I straightened the blanket on my lap and wriggled in the flat heat. Again, I had the sense of being only partially present, as though I were flickering and fading, a shadow body gliding through a dream.

Rhoda finished the introduction, eliciting a few feeble claps and mut-ters. In the silence that followed, I could hear my own, low pulse. In front of me, a woman cleared her throat; air whispered through a tank. I clutched my note cards and closed my eyes, the clamor still banging, muffled, through the halls. Someone snored lightly. I waited for the pill to kick in and, like Alice's potion, make me very, very small.

"I shall not . . . ," I started, my voice a rusty squeak. I swallowed hard, blew my nose. "I shall not soon forget the day he died." It was the wrong choice—I felt it immediately!—a stirring in the audience, a col-lective sigh.

"I'm sorry," I said. "Give me a minute." I looked down and shuffled the index cards, words inching across them like caterpillars. I turned to Rhoda at the side of the stage. "Can you do something about that light?"

She fiddled with switches and knobs, and at last I could see them, my adoring fans: four dodderers planted in the front row like potted petunias in a window box. Three ladies, in thin gowns like mine, tucked into their seats like crumbly pastries, one fast asleep; and a man in a wheelchair, a fierce and dignified look on his liver-spotted face, scalp stringed with white hair, one hand resting on an oxygen tank. Rhoda stood at the side of the stage, pleased as punch, one hand holding the other as though to keep it from flying away.

"You'll have to forgive me," I mumbled, flipping the cards. "I haven't been myself." The old man unsettled me: his ramrod posture and lucid eyes, pale lips moving with a slight palsy under a thin plastic tube. Over his head the dark windows looked on, mute and impassive.

"This is the one from the *Paris Review*," I said, knowing as the words left my lips that no one cared. But I pushed through all six stanzas, wincing at the images and rhymes in which I'd once taken pride, occasionally looking up in hopes of finding a smile, a raised eyebrow, some vague acknowledgment. My listeners just waited, faces blank as gourds, a gray tableau: Still Life with Oxygen Tank.

As I read the last couplet, a sound came from the front row, like a cough crossed with a belch.

"Arthur, don't be rude," said a rouge-cheeked woman. The old man sat up straighter, fixed me with red-rimmed eyes.

"Is this almost over?" His voice was surprisingly hale. "It's almost time for supper."

The woman gave him a poke. "Let the poor girl read. It's better than bingo, isn't it?"

The woman next to her, bright silver hair and a face like a fist, leaned across to tell Arthur, "I won six dollars last week."

"Don't you want to give something back?" Rhoda had asked me earlier that day. "These people are sick, they're old, they're desperate. They need someone to bring joy into their lives. Isn't that what poetry is all about?" She'd really warmed to the pitch, convinced herself that she cared. If all went well, she was considering a mini-tour: hospitals, hospices, old-folks' homes. "Poetry as the Fountain of Youth!" she said. "Might really help our sales in the sixty-five-and-over demo."

But the four people in front of me took no joy from my lines. To them, the poems were a distraction, a dim blip on the radar of dull days.

"What's that mean, anyway, 'the coroner always rings twice'?" said the old man, repeating a line from the last stanza of "Sunday." "Rings what?"

"It's poetry, dear," the woman next to him said. "It can mean anything you want it to."

"How about something cheerier?" Rhoda suggested. "Maybe one of the bee poems, something with a little sex appeal?"

"I don't care if it's poetry, it's wrong," said Arthur. "The coroner doesn't make appointments, young lady."

I nodded, searched through the cards, but found nothing suitable, no secret password or magic spell. That morning I'd thought I had figured it out, the real motivation for Rhoda's big production: The reading was a pretext, a poetic Potemkin village. Once we got there, the truth would out: the old Daddy-jumps-out-of-the-cake routine, the Big Reveal, the Percocet Prize.

But now, foiled again, I slumped in my wheelchair, heat prickling along my arms, up the side of my neck. Was he coming for me now? What would he think when he saw me parked onstage, disheveled and stuttering, wrapped in a flimsy blanket, a poetess strangely beside the point?

"Let's get on with it," Arthur grumbled. "We're not going to live forever, you know."

"Now, Artie." Rhoda descended from the podium with her most flirtatious smile. "You never rush a lady. I'm sure a handsome gentleman like yourself knows that." She perched on the arm of his chair and touched his cheek. His lips pursed and twitched as though he were sucking on a marble, but he fell silent.

"Calliope, my dear," she said, "how about the poem you were working on the other day, the new one about Marie Antoinette?"

"How nice!" said the rouged woman. "Something brand new?"

"I just love their pies," said the other woman.

"No, dear, that's Marie Callender."

I searched through the cards until I found what I needed, squinting at the lines someone had printed in my hand. "It's Good to Be the Queen," I said, but my voice seemed to flee, echoing somewhere behind me. My fingers and toes tingled, the air in front of me had begun to pixilate. Could they see me changing before them, my molecules rearranging, my skin sloughing off?

Be who you were born to be. How I'd hated her every time the words left her mouth. What if there'd been some mistake, a baby-switching, or theft by wolves? What if you were born to be someone else?

My mouth hung open, words stuck beneath my jaw. Somewhere above, I could see my reflection: a brownish smudge with an outsized sense of its own importance.

"*You're doing great!*" whispered Rhoda from the seats. "How about a little show of appreciation for Calliope?"

"Is it true you jumped off a bridge?" asked the old man.

"Arthur!" said the woman next to him.

Rhoda slapped his shoulder, shook a finger in his face. "Where did you hear such a thing?" But I was above them, stretched between the dark windows and stage, a balloon whose owner had let go the string. My mind was a bubble, a whitewashed prairie—from its cold center came someone else's voice, words I'd forgotten I knew.

"*Why art thou silent and invisible—Father of jealousy, why dost thou hide thyself in clouds from every searching Eye?*"

I could see them all: the rag doll in her wheelchair, the grayhairs in the front row, the bright-eyed chaos swirling in the halls. Blake's imprecation had always terrified me, but now I hovered beyond harm.

"*Why darkness and obscurity in all thy words and laws,*" the voice continued. "*That none dare eat the fruit but from the wily serpent's jaws . . . or is it because Secrecy gains females' loud applause?*"

Silence. The audience was gone, but I sensed bodies all around me, muttering voices and elusive, dissonant music. It was a sensation distantly familiar, the faint trailing of an old dream or vision, the reflection of stars in a dark pool. A strange heat, sultry but comforting; a strong odor: rich, biological, sweet.

As I drifted through the old dream, the voices grew rowdy, bodies rushing past me and colliding, laughter rising in volume and pitch. I was hemmed in, claustrophobic. I remembered this feeling, remembered nights in the house on Azalea when I'd cried out in my sleep, the certainty that somewhere in that delirium my father was waiting for me, and the hot fury that I had failed, again, to find him.

"He is not ready." The shaman sat in moonlight at the edge of my bed. "When he is ready he will reveal himself, and you will call him by his name."

And then he, too, vanished, curtains billowing, a shivering girl alone in the bed, soaking the pillow in confusion and rage.

"Calliope!" A cold shock across my face brought me back. "Are you with us, kiddo?" said Rhoda. She shook my chin until I shuddered, saliva running over my lip.

"No napping!" she joked, for the benefit of my four listeners. Then, through her teeth, "Come on, baby. You're freaking these people out."

"Where is he? I heard him . . ." In my lap lay a few index cards, the rest in a messy arc across the floor.

"Just give her a minute. It's all the damn pills." Rhoda leaned to my ear. "One more poem, C, okay? Finish the new one and I'll take you back to your room."

I smacked my lips, squeezed my eyes until I saw spots of color. I had not thought about that dream for years—somewhere along the line it had dissolved into quiet Mountaintop nights. But I was sure now my father was ready for me to find him—he'd said so on the TV! He'd sent his best friend, Verline (*Verlaine!*), to guard me. I had to get away, resume the search. First, I had to get out of this room.

"It's good to be the queen, that shoddy velvet biddy, that freest flying lady, shamaness of drones and dreams," I began, holding the wheelchair, wincing at the cheap sonics, the nursery-rhyme cadence. "No glorious straight arrow, a purring grape marked by sorrow, flying suicidal into that cold cauldron . . ." I ventured a glance at my audience—the women's eyes wide, hands clasped politely. Arthur glared at me, skin pale, knuckles white on the sides of his chair.

"Am I a jane-come-lately, or god's lioness true? Medicine man, consult your images, that I may know which dance to do. For death lies in autumn's clover, and I a lady long past summer—"

"Death!" spat Arthur, sitting back with a jerk and a cough. "More god-damn death." The woman at his side reached out, but he shook his head. "What does she know about death? What do you know, young lady? I want you to tell me."

Rhoda shot me a look, stepped off the stage again but Arthur's gri-mace stopped her. "All these poems about death and suicide." He hunched forward, a wheeze filtering his every word. "Is that what they teach you in school?" He sucked on the air, his eyes bulging, and broke into a volley of wet retches and heaves. Each bellowing cough shook his shoulders, brought more scarlet to his ashy cheeks.

When the fit finally passed, he raised his head, flecks of spittle on his chin. "I'll be dead in a month or two," he said. "You sit here and talk about suicide. If suicide is so interesting, why don't you just do it?" With that, he hacked deep into his throat and spat on the floor—a viscid, black gob veined with crimson.

Rhoda groaned; the old women cried out and hid their eyes. Just then the door flew open and a small crowd burst into the room—teenagers and security guards, two nurses carrying needles, pill bottles, plastic sacs of saline. They overran the floor, the small stage, one girl diving for the cards at my feet only to be tackled by two men twice her age. Hands scrambled to touch my wheelchair, my face, clutched at my broken leg. Across the room I saw our friend the fake doctor, held in a half nelson, his cheek pressed to the wall.

"Invitation only!" Rhoda shouted. But behind her frantically waving hands, her eyes shone in grim ecstasy. We'd make the papers again to-morrow—the reading may have been a disaster, but the show was a smash-ing success.

"I'm so sorry," she called to the old women. "I think she's been over-medicated. I told them she was still too weak . . ." The noise was terrific, the melee swirled around me. The windows of the projection booth danced with reflections as though, behind the glass, someone were laugh-ing at all of this.

The nurses finally reached Arthur, refastened the oxygen lead under his nose, and wheeled him toward the door, while security guards rounded up the intruders, shepherding them out amid Rhoda's high-pitched appeals.

My head lolled, my eyes closed again, but the vision had receded, the dream fled beyond my reach.

Then the door clanged shut and the room was empty. Cards strewn on the podium like leaves at the base of a statue; a forgotten white cardigan on one of the chairs. The brownish lump of Arthur's sputum was smeared three times its size, treadmarks visible from a nurse's sneakers. Exhausted, I stared at the empty rows. My head felt light and clear for the first time in a week.

"After great pain, a formal feeling comes—," I said. It was a poem by Emily Dickinson, a favorite I'd learned in childhood. Again I saw myself in the house on Azalea, book in lap, locked in my bedroom on a long-ago rainy night. From downstairs came the sound of dishes smashing, pots and pans clamoring, exclamations in Spanish as Esperanza tried to calm my mother. It was their wedding anniversary, though by then he'd been gone for years. As I sat under the canopy, reading the poem again and again, I felt silence sprouting inside me like a seedling. With each crash, each escalation of my mother's violence, the silence grew larger, until I could curl inside it, disappear into the poem.

"The Nerves sit ceremonious, like Tombs—," I went on, taking a deep, clean breath. My voice did not quaver. I sat up straighter, cleared my throat. Every empty chair in that empty room took note.

> This is the Hour of Lead—
> Remembered, if outlived,
> As Freezing persons, recollect the Snow—
> First—Chill—then Stupor—then the letting go—

*

Is it any wonder, O friend of mine, what happened after that? The calamities that came to pass, the travesties and sleights of hand? Don't believe the gossip or wild surmises, forget the nonsense on the Web. Remember this and this alone: I was trying to get to him, I'd heard the call. I'd go anywhere I had to, in this world or the next.

Once, if I remember well . . .

I woke in the last throes of a setting moon, the House of Lysol grumbling in slumber all around me. Only the whish of air-conditioning, whoosh of nurses moving through the hall. A distant tin clatter, faint as déjà vu, the tap-a-tap of a keyboard, hushed announcements spreading under my door like a slick; sickly violins filtered down from the ceiling in a cloying mist.

The drugs had worn off, the pain in my leg gathering and focusing my mind. I drank in the sense of immediacy, of being present to myself again. In the thin light I surveyed the room, littered like the aftermath of a disappointing birthday party. Wilting violets lined the windowsill, shrunken petals dark as ink; the floor scattered with manuscript pages, crumpled and aborted poems and letters; half-deflated balloons hovered pathetically at eye level. Someone had draped a shawl over the frightful mirror, but the giant bear still watched from the corner, a glint in its eyes that made my palms itch. On the silent television, the old video for "Dirtnap" flickered, my father laid out in a coffin wearing a prom dress and purple lipstick, Liv Tyler sobbing into a handkerchief while the other three rocked on the altar, dressed as medieval priests.

Awkwardly, I hauled myself from the bed and stood by the window. The hills of Orange County were spotted with lights that shivered in the predawn. On the grounds of the hospital, they still waited: sleeping bodies arranged behind police tape, a tent or two, a newsvan parked and darkened. My lights were off, I waited in shadow as the world kept up its vigil, insensible to my observation, ignorant of the eye above.

I could not stop thinking about Arthur, the creeping death in his lungs. And the women who'd sat with him: Who knew what cancer was eating their organs, what failing hearts or withered synapses sapped the last of their strength? Among these tragedies my own was mere mockery, Sturm und Drang, the clumsy flailing of a duckling in a puddle. I was a fraud—that much was clear to me. I'd been a fraud all along.

"Every substance contains its essence," the shaman once said. Nights I wandered into his laboratory and watched him bent over his books, sweating in the glow of the crucible. He beckoned me to his bench, dropped in my palm a hot, heavy nugget no larger than a cherrystone, its surface smooth and impervious: pure gold. "All contamination must be distilled and then purged," he said. "This is the only search that matters. This is the one true art."

Standing in the window, I could feel my own contamination, feel the masks and camouflage, the poisons in my blood. And not a pebble of truth to show for it all. No father, no mother, no poetry I cared to claim. Only everyone's expectations, greater than I could bear. Once, I'd been a poet; now I was a whore.

The night was losing its grip, my reflection in the window beginning to fade. For a moment I could almost see him—his face in the outline where mine had been. His baby blue eyes, shy smile on parted lips. I closed my eyes and kissed him, but when I opened them it was the hag who stared back. Ugly and mocking, horribly scarred. I was not very surprised—I'd suspected the mirror couldn't hold her for long. Now she'd gotten loose in the world, determined to spoil everything she touched. She'd stop at nothing, follow me forever, a dark kite hovering over me, waiting for the merest drop in the wind to fall upon my head.

You lose, she said.

But I would not concede so easily, would not let her keep me from my goal. With a small cry, I limped back to the nightstand, took a nail clipper, and popped the balloons one by one, Mylar wilting in my hands, slipping to the floor like silvery fish skins. I ripped the petals from the dying violets, strew them across the bed. Then, with cruel joy, I fell on the stuffed bear— her agent, no doubt—dug into his plush face and tore out his little plastic eyes, flung them into the bathroom with a whimper of triumph. There would be no witnesses, no more judgment of this feckless bird, no one to snicker at her awkward last flight.

Then I stood in the middle of the room, breathing heavily, listening to the music that fell lightly from above: first the strings, then the piano, the soft backbeat tugging at my consciousness. I strained to hear the melody— it was gelded and sweetened almost beyond recognition, but I already knew what it was:

You tell me over and over and over again my friend . . .

It was his sign. At last I was on the right track. The light outside was spreading. There was no more time to lose. I flung the blankets from the bed, stripped the sheets and laid them end to end, found another set folded on a shelf in the closet. My hands steadier with each second, I tied the sheets together, straining and yanking to tighten the knots. Wobbling on my bad leg, I wrapped one corner around the bed frame, looped the free end over the bathroom door and passed the whole bundle through the vent above the lintel, stretched my makeshift rope as far as it would go: not far enough.

"Don't you understand what I'm trying to say?" I sang under my breath, watching the clock. It was 5:47—they'd be coming for me soon—but calm had taken hold of me. Careful as a seamstress, I measured out another sheet. *"Can't you see the fear that I'm feeling today?"*

I looped the end of the last sheet, cinched it tight, pulled until my forearms shook, until I broke a sweat. Out the window, the vigil was stirring, two people standing at the edge of the lawn, faces turned toward my window. Straightening my hair, my gown—a girl wants to look her best!—I made the final test: grabbed the rope with both hands and pulled with all my strength. The bed frame behind me creaked and groaned; the knots contracted but did not give way.

"You tell me over and over and over again my friend . . ."

I dragged the nightstand far enough to climb up on it, my plaster cast knocking as I clambered atop. There were a dozen faces turned up toward my window, pale smears in the chalky dawn. How would they react when they got what they wanted, a victory they never really expected, bigger than a glimpse of a poet, better even than my name?

". . . you don't believe we're on the eve of destruction."

I took a last look at this room that had held me, shed skins and discarded papers, the ursine Oedipus in the corner, the unsent galleys on the armchair. The book would not be finished, but Poetry would survive without me—that tyrant that had long controlled me, used me as its mouthpiece, its shaky amanuensis. Here, then, was my resignation, effective immediately.

"Here I come," I whispered, and held my breath.

"Oh my god!" cried a voice, startling as a car wreck, the door flying open and smacking against the wall. "I am so freakin' happy you're awake! I couldn't wait any longer, I just had to tell you, C, I've got the most unbelievable news!"

Perched on the nightstand, wretched sheet clutched in my hands, I stared at Rhoda as she walked in a tight circle, flapped her arms, buried hands in her hair.

"You're gonna shit your pants. I just got off the phone with New York. NBC." She shook her head, covered her eyes, sat on the edge of the bed. "You have no idea how much legwork I did for this. *No* idea. Are you ready? Do you want to know? Can you say *Saturday Night Live*?

"It's not totally in the bag yet, but we're close." She jumped to her feet and hurried to the window, slipping on a dead balloon. "There are concerns on their end, something about 'editorial review,' but I told them, 'Forget it, nobody tells Calliope what to read.' I don't think it's going to be a problem, but I'm flying to New York this afternoon."

She squinted into the window, daylight spreading like jaundice over the crowd. "What the hell happened to that bear?" She screwed up her face, dug in her purse, and sat in the armchair, immediately got up again. "Anyway, it's good news all around today. I just got a text message from the roshi: Nature Boy's out of the hospital, so you can stop worrying. Apparently he's been eating cheeseburgers!

"Oh, and *here's* a little tidbit," she said. "Guess who got arrested in Scotland? Hah! Assault and attempted mayhem—seems old Penny attacked Macaulay Culkin on the set, tried to claw his eyes out. Jesus, C, and I thought *you* were volatile . . ."

She trailed off at last, the gusts of that tropical storm sputtering. Her hands fell to her sides. I couldn't say anything, couldn't make a sound, holding on to my security blanket, the long knotted rope angled across the room.

"Baby," she said. "What are you doing?"

I swallowed hard. "Rhoda—" My body started to shake, my chest tightening and sobs rattling out.

"Calliope?" she whispered, moving closer, taking my hand. Gently she pried open my fingers, flung the sheet away. Her face went through many contortions, her lips opened and closed, a million calculations running through her head.

"You were trying to escape, right?" Her voice was thick and motherly. She held out her arms. "You were going to go out the window, try to get away?"

My teeth began to chatter. I nodded, lowered myself into her embrace.

"You know, that rope isn't nearly long enough, baby." I pressed my face to her body, heard her heart beating furiously, felt her hands on the back of my neck. "And these windows don't even open."

"Rhoda . . . I wasn't—"

"Shhhh. I know how hard it's been. I know how much you want to get out of here." I rocked in her arms and she squeezed me tight. "Okay, C. We'll take you home. We'll take you home today."

"He's waiting for me," I said.

"That's right."

"I have to go. Please." She nodded and stroked my back. Sunlight slanted through the window, cutting a slash across the covered mirror. "All the readings, interviews, everything . . . I don't have time," I said. "You have to get me out."

"Baby—"

"I can't!" I said, growing hysterical. "Don't you understand? He's waiting."

The door opened again, the sound of many feet entering. "Good morning, ladies," said Dr. Verline, with sarcastic cheer. "I see it's another tranquil day . . ."

He stopped a few steps into the room, and they bunched up behind him, crowded for a view. Like a naughty schoolchild, I hid my face while they took in the sad disaster. Now I'd never get out of that place, I thought. They'd find me a room with no windows; they'd take away my pills. Sobbing in Rhoda's arms, I waited for the doctor to prescribe my punishment.

"Oh, bravo, Calliope!" Verline started to clap his hands. He kept clapping until one by one his students joined in, then the nurses, an orderly who happened to pass by. "Bravo, bravo! We're very impressed." The applause was contagious: Outside they pumped their fists in the air, cameras pointed at my room, shouts and whistles rising four floors.

The ovation continued, bracing as a splash of alcohol in the eye. "You've outdone yourself this time. Encore," he said. "What a show!"

I looked up into my publicist's drawn face. "Rhoda?"

She glanced at the crowd, the hanging sheets, the galleys. She closed her eyes, nodded slowly.

"Give me some time, okay?" she said, her voice thick. "I'll take care of everything. Just give me time to figure something out."

*

From the Desk of Calliope Bird Morath

Dearest Michaela,

Yes, I'm still here. ~~Not that you care. In case you want~~ I don't know how much longer I can take this. The length of the days, the bleachy sunshine and ticking ticking ticking ticking of industrial clocks. ~~This is Hell, I think. Only the pills make it bearable.~~ How cruel you are. Still, I would like to speak with you, to see your ~~lovely~~ ~~nasty~~ stylish familiar face at the door. Why won't you take my calls?

Though spring has come to Orange County, it is winter ~~in my soul~~ ~~lonely hospital room~~ here. I am sharing the room with a very interesting person. I wonder what you would make of her. She frightens me, but at least ~~I can count she's always~~ she's here. In loco parentis. Ha ha. Do you remember the time you asked me to draw a picture of my mother? I think you were rather shocked at the results. Do you know what I would draw now? Here it is:

~~They were perfect twins, both~~

You won't be surprised to know I took that trip after all. Of course you were right: I learned almost nothing. ~~I managed to alienate yet another teacher. I don't know why what happens, the minute I feel safe around a man~~ I talked to a woman in ~~Cairo~~ who had some provocative ideas. I'm still trying to locate DG, but no one knows where he is.

~~I find no peace, Michaela, only an eternal drowning. Won't you~~

~~speak to me? How does one~~ I feel as though ~~I am~~ drowning or already dead.

The nurses don't like me. I hear them whispering outside my door. The only word I recognize is <u>tonta</u>. Rhoda came this morning with a new list of events, my twentieth summer to be spent shuttling from TV studio to radio station, shopping malls, amusement parks, six dates on the Lilith Tour. I'm locked in, Frau Doktor, I'm not me anymore.

<u>Je est un autre.</u> That's what Rimbaud said. I understand now, watching from outside, holding my breath: Who is this howling, red-haired horror, why is she living this farce of a life? ~~My father says What would Lacan~~

Maybe I should have been a lawyer. An aerobics instructor. A call girl. Anything other   [unreadable] like the soul-ravaged Sufis O to be taken over by god, filled by his love until there is nothing left of ME   to wander in the desert until I've forgotten my name until it means nothing no one remembers me not even me

I know, dear Michaela. These are only fantasies. You taught me the difference very well. I see all of it now, all of <u>you,</u> through a long telescope, as though it's happening far away, to someone else. It looks so ~~nice lovely odd~~ real.

Adoringly, from Room G-32 (just past the vending machines),

*

P.S. I wrote a new poem today. Try not to analyze it, please.

Poem to an Unconceived Child, Hopefully

Your mother never knew you, her life was fast and full
of nonsense, wordgames, dull as a cracked bone or TV
static—change
the channel, would you?

8. THE SILVER CORD

WHY SUICIDE? Why the universal fascination with this darkest act—the ultimate rejection, a denial not only of life and its possibilities but of the very subject making that denial? A survey of suicide in the arts is beyond the scope of the present work; but it may be safely said that literature has long cherished the subject, wallowed in its abject grandeur, its limitless debasement, as though having an illicit affair with a dangerous lover whose cruelty and perversion are the true source of the sexual charge. And yet one can't deny that such ugliness has often been the wellspring of beauty, the darkness has enabled many an artist to see, at least briefly, the dazzling light of inspiration—as though for some the affirmation of love and life is to be found only in the sweaty embrace of death.

The obsession has perhaps been strongest among poets, the self-proclaimed guardians of the language, for whom that language is both a garden of delights and a hellish dungeon. Žižek:

> What is suicide but an attempt to disengage from language, to put one's existence beyond the reach of signification, to uninscribe oneself from the (con)text of the world? American culture in the new millennium is literally dying to escape its own monstrous symbolic order, which it has created and relentlessly exported to far-flung regions of the globe in Hollywood films, in sneakers made by Malaysian children, and in the nose-cones of "bunker busting" artillery.*

---

*Žižek (MDS). Žižek is discussing the appeal of Calliope's poetry, as this first article was written months before the events in San Diego.

An "opting out," then, a principled withdrawal, almost an ethical decision. In this formulation, suicide is the end of an argument between the subject and the "symbolic order," a speech act directed at the language itself. Taryn Glacé follows suit in *Karl. Che. Kaliope*, seeming almost to celebrate "the refusal to participate in the communal fantasy, a refusal for which the apparatuses of capitalist ideology are ill-equipped." In her view, Calliope stood heroic before these "apparatuses" which had exploited her and, with one swift blow, brought them to their ideological knees.

But what can be ethical about ending one's life? What triumph is to be found in the renunciation of one's life's work, in the erasure of relationships, the desertion of one's family? With their pristine logic, Žižek and his ilk would have us believe that the suicide is solitary, isolated, that she snuggles up at night and warms her feet only against the cold surface of the "symbolic network." They would ignore those that suicide leaves behind, those who loved her and would have moved heaven and earth to help her, to keep her here. The impact, in this version, is no more than that of a distant star winking out.

Even the author's wife tended toward this kind of intellectualization. In her brilliant, unfinished dissertation, she examined what she called "suicide's performative dimension," anticipating Žižek's later description of the act as a kind of speech. Though not concerned with the art world per se, the highly original analysis leverages Durkheim's seminal investigation of suicide against postmodern theories of personality to argue for suicide as a singular kind of performance, an art form all its own. When the author first met her, in the spring of 198_, she had just begun the prospectus for the dissertation, which focuses on the deaths of 913 people in Jonestown, Guyana, in 1978. She frequently recalled the day of the tragedy, the mix of horror and awe she'd felt while watching news footage of smiling cult members in the months before their deaths intercut with images of their bodies heaped one atop the other.

It was, she explained to the author during a romantic walk through La Jolla Cove, "a perfect example of the Kantian sublime," and went on to explain that our fascination with such an event stems from the impossibility of getting one's mind all the way around it, the confrontation with "the abyss in which the imagination is afraid to lose itself."* Willingly or not, she claimed, the suicides in Jonestown had created a giant "installation"—to confront such a work is to experience the same swooning paralysis one feels when gazing at the *Mona Lisa* or listening to a Beethoven symphony.†

The author takes her point, and yet resists the glorification, the sublimation, of self-destruction into something of great social value, as though it were only a matter of contributing to history, with no dire consequences for the survivors! Can such a view apply to someone like Calliope, whose life and art touched so many? What solace does such a theory offer in exchange for the warm, living body?

Though no one disputes the sublimity, Kantian or otherwise, of her art, by late 200_ the poet could hardly have dreamt of getting "beyond the reach of signification." Her entanglements only proliferated after her release from UCI Medical Center, the publication of *(I)CBM* sparking a publicity marathon the likes of which the poetry world had never seen. Her increasingly volatile behavior only intensified the public's adoration, her gestures and insinuations of impending flight only induced her fans to tighten their clutches, only strengthened their determination to hold her.

The book itself seemed designed to fuel this struggle, the shadow of suicide immediately cast by L. Moreno's lengthy introduction, excerpted on the book's cover: "To read these poems is to feel the beauty of desperation, the headlong dash to the finish line, the laughter of the condemned man who runs into a burning building."

Her readings closely followed this theme, her antics growing more disturbing with each passing week. She often began by lighting candles, asking the audience to join hands and close their eyes while she read from *The Tibetan Book of the Dead* and attempted to contact her father's "living spirit." In New York in July, she took the stage at KGB Bar with a noose around her

---

Critique of Judgment, §28.
†The prospectus, "Notes Toward a Reading of Public Suicide from Masada to Jonestown," can be found in the UCSD library (microfiche only).

neck; in Santa Monica, she held what she claimed was a live grenade for the length of the reading, the safety pin rolling ominously on the table. Often, she could not finish the program: In San Francisco, she broke off halfway through "Uninspired, or *Sui Generis*" and ran out of the store, lying down in the middle of Haight Street; in New Haven, police arrested the poet midreading, charging her with inciting terrorism by reading "Suicide Bomber."* Each alarming act, each new outrage brought a spike in sales; organizers were forced to move the readings from bookstores and small clubs to theaters, civic auditoriums, and minor-league ballparks.†

"This is the source of her erotic charge," wrote Žižek, who argued that her bizarre behavior was a shrewd attempt to bridge the gap between subject and language, to reunite the Symbolic with the Real.

> When Calliope pantomimes suicide, she enacts the desires of every person in the crowd. She forces the listener to confront his own repressed fantasmatic background, tearing the fabric of symbolization in an attempt to penetrate to some authentic center—the sexual act *par excellence*.‡

If the readings became unpredictable, her interviews hewed ever closer to one topic: her father. One day she might repeat the allegation she first aired on *Charlie Rose*, viz., that Brandt was alive; the next she might recount the morning of his death, the level of grisly detail escalating beyond what some interlocutors could stomach.§ Critic Jacqueline Rose (no relation) suggests that this oscillation and increased gore point to the poet's growing doubts, a semiconscious attempt to assure herself

---

*The case never went to trial, as witnesses disagreed as to whether the poet had in fact read "Suicide Bomber" or the metrically similar "310."
†The poetry boom extended beyond *(I)CBM*, particularly in the coveted 15–24 demographic. In the third quarter of 200_, Amazon.com reported that sales of *A Season in Hell*, Keats's *The Fall of Hyperion*, Anne Sexton's *Live or Die*, and *This Plane Is Going Down: Haikus of the Japanese Kamikaze Pilots* all rose by nearly 800 percent.
‡Ibid.
§E.g., "the splash and ooze of gray matter, which smelled like someone's feet," the last straw for *The Late Late Show*'s Craig Ferguson.

that she had witnessed the event at all.* By Labor Day, it was clear to nearly everyone that Calliope had entered a terra incognita of instability, one that could not fully be blamed on her expulsion from UCI or the rumored addiction to painkillers, though both figured prominently in the anguished letters recovered from her hospital room and auctioned on eBay by nurse Guadalupe Morales.† With the arrival of autumn, one sensed the poet's behavior building toward a climax, a terrible collision between that part of her which affirmed life and that which cleaved to death.

History was repeating itself, as no one was in a better position to appreciate than the author. As he worked on the biography that summer, keeping abreast of Calliope's activities with growing alarm, he often thought of the morning of Brandt Morath's death and the awful days that followed. He had received the news at the *SLAM* offices; in one of life's minor ironies, he had that very morning put up a seven-foot poster promoting *The Fisher King,* the singer's leering face looming over the editorial desk. At first he mistook his wife's hysterical phone call for an April Fool's joke—one conceived and recounted in incredibly poor taste—but when he understood the grim truth he was overcome by a strangely personal fear which soon gave way to dreamlike detachment. He stayed at his desk for some time, the phone sitting before him, his wife's voice small and distant, and stared into the glaring blue eyes of the poster. He remembers feeling as though there were something he wanted to ask that pale face, some knowledge the singer could only now impart, but he could not find the right words; after some time, he stood, hung up the phone, and walked out into the flat, merciless heat.

She found him that night on the sands of Ocean Beach, his shoes lost and a half-empty cigarette pack in his hand, surrounded by many hundreds who had congregated so as not to be alone in that terrible hour. But as he explained to her then, and as he maintains today, such are normal human responses to shock and sadness, unrecognizable in the sterile theories of

---

*"Agamemnon's Heirs: Morath Family Tragedies and the Instability of Recovered Memory," *Abnormal Psychology Review,* 41:3.
†Morales reportedly fetched close to $40,000 for the lot, which also included torn and charred galley proofs, an empty honey jar, and the soiled remains of an unidentifiable stuffed animal.

Kant. It was his close relationship with the deceased and his love of the music which had brought him there, his empathy for human suffering which bade him stay. The yawning "abyss" of her academic considerations was nowhere to be found.

Humans have a need to mythologize, of course, to find or create the sublime in our brief, pedestrian lives. But if we can learn anything from Calliope, it is the danger of such mythologizing, the wounds it inflicts on those already wounded by loss. For that reason the author takes it as his sacred mission to avoid revision and romanticism in this work, German philosophy be damned! For that reason, he has set himself a simple, if arduous, task: to objectively recount the factual existence of the poet named Calliope, who was born to spectacle, existed in spectacle, and was destined from the first to disappear into the burning glare of mythology.

After she left the Muse, Cassandra Beers agreed to be interviewed about the events leading up to September 28, 200_, when Calliope hosted the season premiere of *Saturday Night Live*. At the time of their meeting, Sandy was once again in New York, living at a halfway house in Greenpoint, Brooklyn. Her job as assistant producer and talent coordinator was, of course, long gone, but she expressed hopes that a childhood friend would take her on as caretaker of a beach home in Montauk, where Sandy might lead a quiet existence by the ocean, reading poetry and contemplating her strange experiences. She and the author met at a restaurant on Manhattan Avenue where, over a plate of pierogis, she spoke softly and hesitantly, sometimes preferring to write her thoughts on a notepad, as she had not yet fully recovered her voice.

"It was all so exciting," she said, as the author leaned forward to hear her. A girlish figure with dark hair held back by plain barrettes; her narrow eyes and stick-straight nose gave her a severe look in contrast to her ample, brightly painted lips. "We were talking about it all summer, you know. Lorne was a huge fan—he used to come to our breakfast meetings and recite lines from 'Honey Box' or 'Rigor Mortician.' He said we were going to make TV history, that something amazing was going to happen."

She swallowed hard and continued. "Tina was the most anxious. She tried to remind Lorne about Irvine, the lawsuits. He wouldn't listen. The Weinstein story came out in mid-August.* Lorne didn't even blink. Tina would take me aside and complain. She thought Lorne and Seth and Darrell had a big crush on Calliope that blinded them to the problems. 'Seth just thinks he's gonna get his dick wet,' she said once. 'And Darrell thinks he'll get to watch.'†

"My concern was just about the poetry." She switched to her notepad, occasionally glancing up at the author with a distant, puzzled look, as though confused to find herself across the table from him, to find the both of them in a noisy Polish restaurant in Brooklyn, so far from the silent world of the Muse.

"That was the thing about Calliope," she wrote. "She behaved badly at times but still seemed so well meaning. Like a child. She won you over with vulnerability. Won me over. You overlooked the danger. It was like she needed you to help her. And you did."

Beers was, indeed, won over, though it has never been established just how far she was taken into the poet's confidence in the days leading up to the broadcast. Certainly the network took their close relationship as proof enough of her complicity; but the former rising star of *SNL* production, presumptive heir to Lorne Michaels's thirty-year rule, maintains she was as surprised by Calliope's actions as anyone. As for the rumors of a sexual tryst between the two, the author takes this as merely the worst kind of New York tittle-tattle—and never mind the photos in the Sunday Styles section!‡—unworthy of even the briefest consideration here.

By the second day of rehearsals, the two women were thick as thieves. Michaels saw the value in allowing Beers to "handle" the volatile young poet, and relieved her of her other duties so that she might serve as a per-

---

*"A Bird in the Ointment," *Playboy*, September 200_. Interview in which the studio head discusses *The Hanged Man: The Brandt Morath Story* film project, describing the threats and outright sabotages by which Calliope attempted to halt production.
†In addition to Lorne Michaels, executive producer of *Saturday Night Live*, Sandy is here referring to Tina Fey, the former head writer, and cast members Seth Meyers and Darrell Hammond.
‡Photos can be doctored, or even fabricated, of course—has the reader learned nothing about the amoral voraciousness of the publicity industry?

sonal assistant of sorts, shuttling Calliope to and from her Chelsea hotel, obtaining her meals and other necessities.*

"She would find me at rehearsal and whisper, 'Let's get out of here,' and we'd jump in a cab and spend an hour at her hotel, or walk up to the Sheep Meadow and lie in the grass. I knew everyone would be freaking out, but I didn't care—it was so much fun to be with her. People would come up and ask her for an autograph, and instead she'd quote them a stanza from Pound's *Cantos* or sing a Robert Johnson song.

"I never had a sister," Beers wrote, her hand shaking, likely as a result of the three cups of coffee she'd ordered, each enhanced by several packets of Splenda. "Being around Calliope was like being a kid again. Most guests were nice to me, but everyone was so concerned with their image, what skits they'd be in, calling their agents six times an hour. Calliope didn't care about any of that. She was just <u>there.</u> She was alive."

While Beers paints a relatively carefree picture of the poet, others with whom she came into contact that week saw things differently. Anthony Tetrazzini, the night clerk at the Hotel Gansevoort, a posh establishment in New York's Meatpacking District, recalls Calliope as "scary looking, like some kinda [. . .] *Night of the Living Dead.*" According to Tetrazzini, the poet spent her nights wandering the halls like a Victorian apparition; twice, in the early morning hours, he was summoned by the occupants of room 310, where the poet had been knocking incessantly, asking for her father. Leading her back to her room, the young man was touched by her distress. "Her eyes were just [. . .] empty," he recalls, "like she was just [. . .] gone."†

On the night before the show, according to her memoirs, Rhoda

---

*Fey would later tell the *New Yorker's* Susan Orlean ("Talk of the Town," 10/21/0_) that those necessities included "buckets of pills—Xanax, Percocet, Viagra, you name it. She was insatiable. A time bomb. Every time she came to rehearsal we cringed, waiting for her to lose it completely. I practically needed tranqs myself by the time it was all over." Beers denies this emphatically: "There were no drugs. Not even Advil. Calliope was already cleansing herself of contamination. She was already becoming pure."

†Whatever sympathy he might have felt was likely dispelled on the morning of September 27, when, according to Tetrazzini's affidavit, the poet asked him to procure for her a bushel of apples; upon being informed that the hotel did not provide grocery service, she allegedly assaulted the clerk with a telephone.

Lubinski found Calliope on the roof of the hotel, dressed only in a satin nightgown, clutching a photograph of her father and a copy of *Goodnight Moon*. September had been, if anything, more tumultuous than the summer, her escalating legal troubles and the dustup with Wal-Mart taking their toll. Sales of *(I)CBM* were robust, but the adverse publicity surrounding "Suicide Bomber" had the normally placid lamas of Snow Lion Press twitching with anxiety.* The day before, the *Times*'s David Brooks had called for a "teleboycott," arguing that regardless of whether Calliope performed "Suicide Bomber," her persona had become toxic, a symbol of what was wrong with America:

> Don't the victims of real suicide bombings deserve our sensitivity? Should their grief be used as material for confessional poetry? [. . .] Liberal, conservative, or mainstream, middle-of-the-road like me, we can all agree the people's airwaves aren't a platform for hate speech.

Perhaps most troubling for the poet, earlier in the month the University of California had won its lawsuit and evicted her from the trailer; with the help of Rhoda, Taryn Glacé, and security officer Rafael Zuñiga, Calliope spent Labor Day weekend moving her belongings to a storage facility in nearby Costa Mesa. Despite the luxury in which she had been raised, she had adored the shabby trailer, had seen it as a blinking light on the map of her mind, always beckoning her return. Now, for the first time in her life, Calliope had no place to come back to. She was homeless.

Even before the first rehearsal, Sandy Beers had received several e-mails from NBC executives, insisting that Calliope not read "Suicide Bomber."† Though the network had agreed, the previous May, to a non-review clause in the contract with Lubinski Management, they argued

---

*After Pat Robertson said, on Fox News's *The O'Reilly Factor*, that "Suicide Bomber" was "what you get when you allow non-Christian publishers to disseminate heresy in the United States of America," Snow Lion and Ithaca's Namgyal Monastery received numerous threats and, ominously, an anonymous shipment of a thousand umbrellas.

†These e-mails, and Sandy's diplomatic replies, are accessible through the interactive kiosk in the collection at the Ransom Center.

now that they had not been shown the published version of *(I)CBM*, nor could they have foreseen the summer's controversy: readings canceled in Bloomington, Columbus, Denver, and Eau Claire, following the New Haven arrest. They were receiving seven hundred phone calls a day protesting Calliope's appearance. The Brooks editorial was the last straw; on Friday morning, Beers was instructed to present Calliope with a pledge, drawn up by NBC's lawyers, which the poet was to sign by 5:00 P.M. If she did not sign the pledge, or if she broke it on national television, it was implied, Sandy Beers would lose her job.

"I was terrified," she recalled, smiling wistfully, almost placidly, despite the violent shaking of her knee beneath the table. "To think that I cared so much about something so . . . meaningless as a job. But that was a different me, an old self."

She stared for a long moment at the author, then surprised him by taking his hand across the sticky, cluttered table. They shared a long, probing look. With her free hand she once again picked up the pen.

"This is what she taught me: Truth is all that matters. Truth is very small, and very hard; around it is wrapped the world of appearance, which is not Truth. Our only mission in life is to discover Truth and expose appearance for what it is."

She halted and squeezed the author's hand, scanned his face in a way that made him somewhat uncomfortable. He found himself unable to reach for the check or sip his decaf or excuse himself to the restroom.

"What is your Truth, Mr. Altschul?" she wrote. "Have you made Truth the focus of your life?"

The author cleared his throat, several times. The restaurant was infernally hot. "What about beauty?" he rejoined. "Must we reduce poetry to mere fact-finding? Is this what art has become?"

Beers made no reply. The author signaled to the waitress, intending to complain about the inexcusable heat, but was ignored. Cassandra's glimmering gaze was intolerable; though he tried to look elsewhere, his eyes kept returning to hers.

"So, am I to understand that she didn't sign the pledge?" he finally asked, his own voice having hoarsened considerably.

Sandy released the author's hand and sat back. She again raised her coffee cup, only to find that it was empty. She set it down gently, a distant smile on her lips as though recalling some intimate pleasure.

"You are simply to understand," she said.

The season premiere of *Saturday Night Live* garnered a whopping 58-share in the Nielsen ratings, the equivalent of 31.2 million viewers, setting an all-time record for a late-night broadcast and shattering the mark set the previous winter, when Hillary Rodham Clinton served as host. Like many of those millions, the author watched from the comfort of his living room, where he was spending a pleasant evening with his son, enjoying the kind of bonding all too rare in the turbulent days of a child's late adolescence, when peer pressure and media culture combine so virulently with raw biology, often resulting in the kind of parent-child schism the author was determined to avoid.

Ah, those Saturday nights when the two would enjoy a game of Scrabble, a six-pack of root beer, and a bag of Sun Chips, the son affecting a mute sulk, the author gamely attempting to keep up appearances, to play the role of the stern parent, while in truth overflowing with affection and the nostalgia that accompanies a child's impending, though not yet actual, adulthood! How the author misses such simple moments!*

By the time the program began, the game was nearly finished, only a handful of tiles remaining to each competitor. The author was clinging to a slim lead, and as the opening skit unfolded he laid his final word on the board, building C-O-R-T-E-X off a tight cluster near the top (he had been hoarding the X for most of the game), gleefully totaling his points and daring his son to pull off an act of last-minute alphabetic heroism. On the television was a "Breaking News" story in which Brandt Morath had been spotted heading south on the Santa Monica Freeway, stowed in the back of a white Ford Bronco driven by his wife; as helicopters and police cruisers

---

*On this particular Saturday night, it should be said, the author's son had been grounded, as consequence for his latest suspension from school, where he had disrupted English class with what even the teacher admitted was an impressive display of flatulence—a reaction, undoubtedly, to the class's benighted response to a poem he had written and set to music.

followed the car, news anchor Amy Poehler was able to establish a cell-phone connection with the fugitive, who maddeningly answered her questions with snippets of pop songs sung in a raw, digitally unstable voice.* It was an immensely clever start to a show all America had been anticipating, though given what was to come later that night, one has to wonder if the decision to trade so brazenly in the legend of Brandt's death—to foist upon the poet's precarious mental state further proof that her life and career were inextricable from his—wasn't a rather poorly thought out and ultimately counterproductive one.

"Dad," said the author's son, as the Bronco skidded and fishtailed at the side of the freeway, and an alarmed and neurasthenic-looking Calliope slid into the empty chair next to Poehler. The author sat up straighter, having seen the poet before only in photographs, the live image provoking an emotional response of a nature he could not precisely describe.

"Dad, I won," said the author's son, as the Bronco flipped over several times, slammed into the concrete barriers, and was struck from behind by several police cars in succession, squashing up like so many tin cans, the back windshield misting over with crimson and shattering. "I beat you, Dad. Look."

"Be quiet!" the author said, perhaps a bit sharply. His son folded his arms and under his breath muttered an epithet which, in different circumstances, might well have earned him a time-out. Overcome with remorse, the author patted his son's knee and glanced at the board to discover that his son had indeed won the game, capturing the last triple-word-score square with the high-value D-O-U-C-H-E.

"Brandt!" cried Poehler, as the cameras zoomed in toward the wreck, focusing on the mangled blond head in the Bronco's rear compartment. "Brandt! Are you all right?"

"*Ommfaaadddinn. Ughalak,*" muttered the broken voice on the cell phone. Next to the newscaster, Calliope had gone white, fingers stroking the birthmark under her jaw.

"Hey," said the author's son. "She kind of looks like Mom."

---

*E.g., "Where have you been for the last fifteen years?" was answered with "Under the Boardwalk"; "Why have you decided to make contact after all this time?" with "I Just Called to Say I Love You," etc.

"Brandt, are you alive? How badly are you hurt?" asked the frantic newscaster. Calliope was now glancing toward the side of the stage, where Sandy Beers, unseen by the viewing audience, made soothing hand gestures.

"Ammdying. Amgonnadie," groaned the voice in the car.

"She looks a little like Mom, don't you think?"

"Brandt, your daughter Calliope is here. Is there anything you want to tell her?"

"Don't you think she looks like Mom?" repeated the author's son.

"Certainly not," said the author.

"Brandt, Calliope is with us," said the newscaster, rising from her chair in agitation. The front of the Bronco had burst into flame. "She's all grown up now. Do you want to say anything to her, Brandt? Do you have any last words for your daughter?"

That's when the bloody blond head moved just enough to look straight at the camera, which zoomed in past the flames and shattered glass to focus on his bright blue eyes, and next to the newscaster Calliope lurched to her feet and bolted off camera, hands clamped over her mouth.

"Live from New York," shouted the dying man. "It's Saturday night!"

To say, as Lorne Michaels did on Monday, that Calliope's breakdown was "absolutely unexpected and unpreventable," ignores Cassandra Beers's many attempts to warn of impending catastrophe. All afternoon and evening, Sandy had felt a sense of foreboding, a nearly paralyzing fear that the carefully orchestrated *tour de force* could blow up in their faces. But preshow jitters were not uncommon on the *SNL* set, and for much of the day she held her tongue. After the opening skit, however, her anxiety began to build toward something like panic.

"My phone started ringing as soon as we went to the music, and Rhoda is chewing me out so loud I can barely understand," Sandy recalled. "I'd never even met her, and she's calling me a tramp, threatening to tear my eyes out, at the same time I'm watching Calliope walk out onto Stage 1, all houselights up, glowing around her . . .

"For a second or two, everything went silent," she said, stopping in the middle of the sidewalk, where she and the author had been taking a postprandial stroll. "I could see this aura around her, like the lights and the band and the audience became more solid than she was, for a minute. Like the sun's corona during an eclipse? And in the center, the actual Calliope was becoming indistinct, like she was going to just . . . disappear."

The vision startled Beers enough that she called Michaels, who told her to "stop being a worrywart" and inquired as to the current phase of her menstrual cycle.

Calliope had somewhat recovered her poise when she came out for her monologue, wearing a tight black T-shirt which proclaimed: "He's Alive. I'm Dead. Up Yours."* The audience responded rousingly, standing on their seats and waving copies of (I)CBM and tossing roses at the poet's feet. One lovestruck gent had to be escorted from the studio after lighting a copy of Friday's *Times* on fire and sprinting, naked, down the aisle. Watching from home, the viewer could see that Calliope was taken aback; though no stranger to adoring crowds, she had been shaken by the "newscast" and perhaps dazzled by the glare of the stagelights. For a long moment, she squinted at the camera, one demure bead of sweat tracing her jaw.

"You know, I was pretty nervous about coming all the way to New York to read my poetry," she finally picked up her lines. "Everyone says New York audiences are so unforgiving. But then I asked my father what to do"—she paused for laughter—"and he said, 'Fuggetaboudit . . .'" Her middling imitation of a Bronx accent provoked laughter and applause. She launched into an uproarious two-minute history of suicide in the arts, beginning with the Greek poet Sappho and touching on Chatterton and Van Gogh, Woolf and Hemingway, recounting each vignette in one or two heroic couplets.† Offstage, Sandy Beers paced and wrung her hands, trying to decide whether to barge into the control booth and plead with Michaels or stay at her post and care for Calliope when the inevitable came to pass.

---

*A reference to a shirt made by Sex Pistols manager Malcolm McLaren, after bassist Sid Vicious was indicted for the murder of Nancy Spungen. Vicious's shirt read: I'M ALIVE—SHE'S DEAD—I'M YOURS.

†E.g., "Virginia filled her coat with rocks and sand/While Leonard, the wise virgin, stayed on land."

At the end of the monologue, Calliope walked to the edge of the stage and whispered to the audience. "To end this life, move on to something new—/I often dream it fondly. How 'bout *you?*"

The audience fell silent.

"Come on," she laughed. "Haven't you ever thought about it?" She blew the audience a kiss, cocking a hip and drawing a pistol from the small of her back.

"You're all liars!" she said, and raised the gun to her temple. "Byron said, 'No man ever took a razor into his hand who did not at the same time think how easily he might sever the silver cord of life.'" Offstage, Sandy Beers was suddenly overcome by light-headedness and clutched at Seth Meyers, who shook her off in irritation.

Calliope closed her eyes, her brow creased—until Tina Fey flew from the wings and tackled the poet, sending the gun skidding harmlessly beneath the band riser.* The drummer, obligingly, played a rim shot, and at the crowd's relieved laughter they went to commercial, the control room erupting in celebration, Michaels leaning back in his armchair and bellowing, "She's killing them out there! She's just killing them!"

"I'm going to my room," said the author's son, leaving the Scrabble board and empty bottles on the coffee table, in contravention of household expectations.

"Stay and watch with me," said the author, who felt unaccountably melancholic—almost maudlin—in contrast to the televised hilarity. "Don't you think it's funny?"

"It's bullshit," said his son, breaking yet another house rule. "I'm outta here."

"Sit down," the author said. "We are going to watch this together, like a family."

"Some fucking family."

"What did you say?" cried the author, as the commercials came to an end.

The early segments of the show proceeded without further incident, though backstage Sandy Beers had all she could do to keep Calliope from

---

*The author has been unable to corroborate the rumor that the gun was loaded.

storming out of the studio. The chain reaction which had begun with the phony newscast had left the poet in a condition of extreme agitation, such that she began wandering the halls backstage and, according to the story in the *New Yorker*, asking crew members for Percocet or Xanax. She found her way to the control room and had to be escorted out by two technicians, and vigilant viewers might have glimpsed her face peeking in an interrogation room window during a spoof of *24*. Sandy tried to guide Calliope to her dressing room, but she was herself still in the grips of the strange spell that had overtaken her.

"I had done a little coke right before we started, so I thought maybe it was reacting with my Zoloft or something," she said quietly. By now she and the author were facing each other across a bar table in Williamsburg, each sipping from an outrageously overpriced pomegranate martini. The author was touched by her honesty, by the air of survival she gave off, of someone who had not succumbed to trauma, who had returned, sadder but wiser, to tell of it.

"I just kept having this feeling that she was, you know, <u>gone,</u>" Sandy wrote, chancing a glance at the author and playfully streaking the back of his hand with the tip of the pen. "I'd look at her, but all I'd see was a Calliope-shaped space, surrounded by blazing lights. When she went out to read the first poem, I just sat on a crate and cried."

Though the reading of "I Shall Not Soon Forget the Day He Died"—during which a film montage of Brandt Morath was projected on a screen behind the poet—went off uneventfully, the six-minute "Electra" skit served as the proverbial last straw.

"Tina was really excited about that segment," Sandy recalled. "She was working on it up till that morning. Everyone knew it would be the highlight of the show—viewers love Greek tragedy, and who better than Calliope to bring it into the twenty-first century?"

Who indeed? The Moraths' fondness for invoking Hellenic drama as metaphor for their own lives is well documented,* and under different circumstances one can imagine Calliope being quite pleased to play the role

---

*Cf. *Bringing Ulysses Home*, Jimmy Iovine's memoir of his work with Fuck Finn, as well as Žižek, Rose, Gilbert, et many al.

of the prototypical grieving daughter, her life stunted by her father's death and her mother's callousness. In rehearsals, Sandy describes her as "wildly enthusiastic," even "jubilant" at the return of Orestes, Electra's long-lost and presumed-dead brother, who had come out of hiding to help her take revenge.

"When Seth would pull back the hood of his robe and speak his line, it sent shivers down my back. The first time, Calliope jumped into his arms and shoved her tongue into his mouth," Sandy recalled with a giggle. She and the author were now on the G train, Sandy having offered to help him find his way back to his great-aunt's home in Park Slope. "I think she was doing it to make me jealous. Poor Seth didn't get it. He thought he was in love."

But the producers had a surprise in store for Calliope, a surprise they had purposely kept from Sandy, fearing a conflict in her loyalties. Imagine, reader, the gasps and squeals of the audience at the crucial moment: the hooded figure, confronting his long-abandoned sister before their father's grave, the sister bedraggled and only casually attached to sanity, her attention pricked by the sweet familiarity of the voice—"Dearest of women, here is Orestes, that was dead in craft, and now by craft restored to life again!"—the hood drawing back to reveal none other than Ben Affleck.

"In their defense," Sandy said, "we were all misled. I mean, it had been in *all* the magazines for months, all the gossip shows—Ben and Calliope this, Ben and C-Bird that . . . And Ben never said a word at the secret rehearsals. I mean, his agent *loved* the idea! How were any of us to know the two of them had never even met?"

Viewers began to suspect something was wrong when her "brother" swept Calliope into an embrace, only to be shoved roughly backward and stumble over the gravestone. Calliope stood shaking her head. "Until now I have held my rage speechless," she finally said, something like terror on Affleck's face. "But now I have *you*."

And no viewer could resist a shudder when, a moment later, "Electra" drove the knife into the throat of Tina Fey as Penelope/Clytemnestra, Fey's eyes bulging in discomfort as Calliope whispered her final line:

"Did you take so long to find that your names are all astray, and those you call the dead are living?"

———

During the final commercial break, Sandy found Calliope in her dressing room, all the lights out, one vanilla-scented candle lit before the vanity. The poet sat studying a photograph of her father, reading a letter on thin airmail paper, all the frenzy of the Electra skit having given way to resignation. Standing in the doorway, Sandy again had the sensation of not being able to see Calliope—the glimmer of light in the mirror threw the poet's face into shadow, her voice echoing against bare walls.

"How could you?" she whispered to Sandy.

"I didn't know what to tell her," Sandy said tearfully, again facing the author across a table, this time at a popular breakfast spot in Park Slope. Taking the author's hand, she sobbed, "She thought I knew. She wouldn't let me explain. I tried to put my arms around her, but she pushed me away and said, 'It's time for the last act,' and shut the door in my face. She thought I'd betrayed her."

The author, never sure how to respond to such surges of female emotion, allowed his hand to be held, staring out the window at the passersby on busy Seventh Street as his companion wept. After a long moment, Sandy withdrew her hand and blew her nose loudly into a napkin, reaching for her notebook.

"Human destiny sucks," she wrote. "We're only happy for a short time before bad luck wipes it out. Knowing that's inevitable, joy becomes cause for sorrow, almost as much as sorrow itself." She tore out the paper and left it on the table. Then she rose from her chair with great dignity, stopping to kiss the author's cheek before leaving the restaurant, blending into the crush of humanity on the street. She had not paid her half of the bill.

After months of anticipation, the moment had arrived. In her dressing room, Calliope sat silently in candlelight, applause ringing in her ears but failing to bring the satisfaction it once had. She had achieved, at nineteen, more than most artists achieve in a lifetime—a bestselling and critically acclaimed book, attendant riches, high romance, international celebrity— but it was not enough. The world would always demand more of her— more poems, more performances, more complicity in its endless exploitation of her family history. The world had become for Calliope, as it had been for her father, a house of mirrors; she wandered its hallways in search of her father, but found only images of herself. Who, in time, would not seek to quit the house entirely? When the knock came at the dressing-room door, her final introduction booming through the studios, she took a breath, made her decision, and blew out the candle.

It would have been a source of great concern to Lorne Michaels and the NBC lawyers to see Calliope take the stage wearing a shining gold burqa, its silken folds shimmering beneath the stagelights, only the poet's eyes visible through its eye slot. As she stood demurely at center stage, hands folded beneath the glowing cloth, the crowd came to its feet and began to chant *"Bomb-er! Bomb-er!"* while the rest of the cast, watching from the wings, held their breath. Michaels had an assistant sit with a finger above the Camera 2 button, prepared to cut away if she spoke even a single line of the forbidden poem. Viewers at home moved closer to their sets, captivated by the drama unfolding on live television, trying their best to ignore the complaints and sullen profanities of teenagers who had perhaps been threatened with revocation of driving privileges if they left the room. Surrounded by darkness, the gold-shrouded Calliope glinted like a candleflame, the air around her all but vibrating with excitement.

"Tonight, I've been told what I can and can't read," the poet said quietly, provoking a thunderous volley of boos from the audience. She waited until they quieted before continuing. "There are people who think words are dangerous"—she smiled beneath the stifling burqa—"and I suppose in a way they are.

"But poetry . . ." Her voice faltered. "There are more dangerous things than poetry. Poetry is just a way of searching for the truth. Are we the enemies of truth?" she asked. "Are we?"

From the back of the studio, a lone woman's voice cried, "No!"

"Poetry is not the enemy," Calliope said, and paused, blinking back tears. Everyone in the control booth rose to their feet as she drew a sheet of paper from the folds of her burqa and thrust it at the cameras.

"Fight the real enemy!" she cried, as 31 million viewers beheld a photograph of her father, a photograph they had surely seen many times before and which the author was stunned to recognize as the very same image which had once graced the walls of *SLAM*.

"*Fight the real enemy!*" Calliope cried, hiccuping through tears as she tore the photograph into a thousand shreds, flinging them outward so they fluttered around her and fell upon the stage like snowflakes, the flame of her gold burqa guttering as she stomped and danced among the debris.

"This is bullshit." The author's son strained against his father's grip. "This is such bullshit, I can't believe you're making me watch this." But the author could not respond, could hardly breathe, the poet's self-destruction unfolding before his eyes.

"This is so fucked-up!" his son shouted, his voice rising a full octave. "You just think she looks like Mom. You're totally fucked-up!" he cried, at last freeing himself of his father and running from the room, but by then the author must admit he had ceased to care about anything but the sad, radiant form of Calliope dancing forlornly on the stage, an image which would stay with him—which would invade his dreams—for weeks and months afterward, though in another second the producers recovered their wits and pressed the button, the screen fading to black so that it was as if, for the millions of Calliope's fans—as well as for Sandy Beers, who finally succumbed to her visions and fainted into Ben Affleck's waiting arms— the poet had, at long last, disappeared.

"It was a negation," Taryn Glacé wrote in a widely quoted article,

> a brilliant blow aimed at the heart of the superstructure. The crowning achievement of her jihad. A suicide bombing as the deadly collision between ideology and the human body upon which ideology acts. The explosive provided by the theoretical force enabling the collision. A collision capitalism always works to prevent, making itself invisible and everywhere present so that the subject cannot take aim at it. The "suicide" of the subject, certainly, but insofar as the subject is the *subject of* capitalism, of capitalism itself[. . .]

Calliope-as-jihadi brought into view the cultural apparatus which deployed her father as a form of currency. Exposing that currency before an audience of millions, she committed the only truly forbidden act: she tore up money.*

The author has elsewhere affirmed his great respect for Dr. Glacé, as well as his gratitude for the generosity with which she has answered the author's queries. And, though it verges on the hagiographic, he would not deny the influence of her two-volume study, *Karl. Che. Kaliope.* Nevertheless, as he told Dr. Glacé herself at their one brief encounter, a hurried exchange outside her office at the University of San Francisco,[†] the political consciousness and agency she ascribes to the poet is not justified by the evidence, and thus serves as obstacle to a true understanding. Why must a young poet—burdened by history, besieged by the terrors and vicious pains of the world—be drafted to represent a particular philosophy or historical movement? Why must she be made into a standard-bearer? Why must the Taryn Glacés of the world impose coherence upon such a creature, why must the radically inconsistent jumble of her words and deeds be reorganized, shaped to a particular agenda, repackaged and gift-wrapped and affixed with a small card that reads "Calliope"?

We properly honor a life only by telling the truth. Not some self-serving version of the truth, not some airbrushed narrative or fawning rehabilitation,[‡] but the Truth, that immutable nugget which is impervious to human desire. If we insist on cloaking sloppy reality in a false mantle of narrative integrity, on making a discrete object out of nebulous subjectivity, then how can we expect to know her, to really *know* her?[§]

In its way, Dr. Glacé's analysis stands as a scholarly cognate of the general uproar which followed *Saturday Night Live.* As passionately as the public had embraced Calliope in the period before publication of *(I)CBM,* and stood by her throughout the scandal-plagued summer, so now did the fervor of the masses begin to turn against her. The demonstrations began

---

*"Metastasis." *Modern Marxista,* Winter 200_. Reprinted with changes in *Karl. Che. Kaliope.*
[†]From which she has been on sabbatical since December 200_, a mere four months after her hire.
[‡]And not, clever reader, Sandy Beers's variety of truth, which in any case was never clearly defined.
[§]And is this not the supreme challenge not only of biography but of all human relationship?

the next morning, as unruly groups gathered outside NBC studios and the Hotel Gansevoort, flinging copies of *(I)CBM* into the gutter and filling the puddled streets with their shouts: *Three-five-seven-nine, Calliope has crossed the line!* A mock courtroom was set up on the sidewalk, barristers in powdered wigs demanding that Calliope answer for her actions. But the poet was nowhere to be found.*

On Monday, after giving a brief statement suggesting that the incident was the result of a "choreographic misunderstanding" with *SNL*'s producers, and that Calliope was suffering from "sixteen years of grief and exhaustion" and would be unavailable for comment, Rhoda flew to Ithaca for a tense meeting with the board of directors at Snow Lion, who were understandably rattled by the television appearance and incipient fallout.†

The parade of denunciations from the press began in earnest on Tuesday and continued throughout the week, with every New York daily condemning her actions. Both the *Paris Review* and *Poets & Writers* issued statements declaring they would publish no more of Calliope's work until an apology was issued, and the *Chicago Reader,* which had been preparing a cover story in anticipation of Calliope's scheduled reading at Northwestern University the following week, not only canceled the story but went to the extraordinary length of stripping the poet of her title, conferred by the previous month's Readers Poll, of "Chicago's Favorite Poet." Despite repeated phone calls to Marky "Mark" Lipschitz, current editor of *SLAM,* the author was unable to convince his former colleague to tone down that magazine's reaction; thus San Diego's most trusted chronicle of the arts, which had once, under different leadership, considered itself a friend to local artists of all stripes, blasted Calliope in her hometown with its lurid, tabloidesque cover copy: "Petty Poet's Patricide."

---

*According to hotel records, Calliope had checked out at 3:08 A.M. Examination of the security films, however, shows that it was Rhoda who gathered the poet's belongings and settled the bill. Calliope would not be seen again until the terrible night in San Diego, thirteen days later.
†Wal-Mart announced it would remove all copies of *(I)CBM* from its stores, while Barnes & Noble took Calliope off their coveted "Discover" list of new writers. Her sales ranking on Amazon.com, which had risen as high as 70, plummeted Monday to 31,226; public sentiment perhaps can be summed up by a customer review posted that day by "A Disgusted Lover of Brandt," who wrote, simply, "This selfish b**** can go to hell."

Perhaps most painful was the response being prepared by *Rolling Stone,* which had played such a key role in Terrible Children's ascent to the rock pantheon. Editor and publisher Jann Wenner had been a close friend to Brandt and Penelope since before the first album was released; photos taken on Wenner's yacht during a trip to Nevis—Penelope eight months pregnant, her hair waist-length, Brandt looking healthy and relaxed after his first detox—are among the most idyllic images of the couple ever made public. In 199_ *RS* had run a special-edition tribute to Brandt featuring Wenner's stirring obituary; now, Rhoda was informed, the incensed mogul was drafting a scathing response to the *SNL* incident, a quasi-obituary to read, "The Career of Calliope Bird Morath: 199_–200_."

Only William Logan, whose June review of *(I)CBM* in the *New Criterion* had crucially validated Calliope's work among the poetry establishment, came to her defense, offering a spirited plea for clemency in the *New York Review of Books:*

Confessional poetry having long since lost its power to shock or in-spire critique of any complexity, Ms. Morath has driven the final, long-overdue nail into its self-adoring coffin. She has dared readers at last to confront her poetry as poetry, not as peep show or ritual purge. If this last proves impossible, it is we, and not the poet, who are to blame.*

But nothing captivated the media so much as the *fatwa.* Opposition in the Muslim community had begun upon publication of *(I)CBM,* but when Snow Lion agreed to print a version of the book without "Suicide Bomber," the grumbles had subsided. As a further olive branch, Calliope had made a July stop at an Islamic community center in Detroit for a read-ing and extended Q&A, impressing the crowd with her intimate knowl-edge of the Sufi poets. The *SNL* affair, however, went too far: Muslim women made up a significant contingent of the protesters, many dressed in burqas and holding placards declaring, MUSLIM WOMEN LOVE BRANDT! The weekly paper *The Prophet* deplored "the rampant disrespect shown by American artists" to their faith, and on October 3, Imad al Din al-Rashid, imam of the Queens Mosque of the Faithful, issued a statement declaring

*October 10, 200_.

that "for insults to the dignity of Muslim women and the righteous cause of the Palestinian people, all valiant Muslims are called upon to extract punishment from Calliope Bird Morath without delay, so that no one henceforth will dare insult Islam."

The edict might have gone unreported, were it not for Rhoda's uncharacteristically impolitic response. "*Fatwa*, schmatwa," she snapped at a stringer outside her Silverlake condo the next day, a comment that earned her a down arrow in *Newsweek*'s weekly "CW" item. "This shit is good for sales, anyway. They're doing us a favor."*

It was in the midst of this furor that the idea for the present work, conceived in the abstract some time before, began to gather shape and momentum and the kind of inevitable force which every artist recognizes as the clarion call of inspiration. The author found himself unable to sleep, entranced by persistent thoughts of the poet in her golden robes, by the challenge of delving beneath that glimmering surface and returning to the world with the Truth in hand. His agitation achieved such intensity that he began to borrow cigarettes from the packs in his son's jacket pocket, which he smoked on the front stoop in the chill of dawn, a practice in which he had not indulged since the later days of his marriage. He spent several mornings sifting through boxes for old Terrible Children notes and transcripts and eventually managed to gain entry to the Rose Canyon storage facility where *SLAM*'s archives were housed; he had a DSL line installed in the house (to the great delight of his son, who had been on home/school restriction since the night of the *SNL* broadcast, a punishment several times extended due to his insistence on greeting his father each afternoon with an obscene gesture), ordered subscriptions to several of the better literary journals, and began to compile a list of potential interviewees and source materials to be tracked down. The spare bedroom of their home, locked and untouched for several years, was opened and aired out, old clothes and

---

*In an instance of "collateral damage," Moroccan poet Mahmoud al-Shakil, spending the month in Paris, was asked by *Le Monde* to comment on the affair. His refusal to condemn the imam's statements drew widespread disgust from human-rights groups and is largely viewed as the beginning of the end of his career.

textbooks stowed neatly in the closet—into this newly breathable space the author moved a desk and computer, above which he hung the name-plate he had removed from his office door on his last day at *SLAM:* ANDREW ALTSCHUL, EDITOR IN CHIEF.

Even as the drumbeat against Calliope, and the questions as to her whereabouts, rose toward crescendo, he began to plan his attack. After a week, he had outlined several chapters, the floor of the Calliope Corner turning into a sea of articles and transcripts, books of poetry and literary criticism borrowed from the public library, photographs and news clippings and small, colorful adhesive notes upon which he had scrawled flashes of insight. He began at 7:45 each morning, when his son left for school, and was usually still hard at work, typing and clicking and poring through material, when the boy returned, slamming first one door and then another, in the afternoon.

By mid-October, though understanding full well that he had months, if not years, of work to do before he might approach a true understanding of the poet and her life, he could not resist the urge to start writing. Gripped by urgency one evening, he wrote the opening lines of the first chapter—the story of Calliope's Christmas combustion; working through the night in a kind of wild fever, stopping only to brew coffee, by the time his son came home the next afternoon the author had concluded the scene.

"Listen to this, listen to this," he said, waving off his son's habitual hand-greeting. He waited for his son to finish rifling through the refrigerator, then cleared his throat and read the first paragraph. Not surprisingly, his prose was met by a bored glower; sensing the keen interest that glower was meant to conceal, he read on.

When he had finished the chapter, he looked up. "Not bad for a 'washed-up old dude,' is it?"

"I thought no one's supposed to go in that room," the son muttered, gesturing with a half-eaten salami sandwich in the direction of the Calliope Corner.

The author smiled at the attempted diversion. "I really have something here, don't I? It really captures the sense of magic, the larger-than-life *aura,* as it were, of the poet, don't you think?"

"You said that was Mom's room. So what, now it's like some kind of library or something? What the fuck is that?"

"Drew, please don't use profanity," said the author, beginning to feel the cumulative effects of inadequate sleep and excessive caffeine consumption.

"I wanted to put my stereo and guitar amp in there, but you were all, *That room is the storehouse of memory.*" He rolled his eyes far back in his head and creased his brow in a mocking imitation of his father. "Now you're in there writing some stupid book about that fucked-up girl?"

"Please. I am asking for your opinion of your father's work. Can you put aside your adolescent pique for one moment and try to give a fair evaluation?"

For a long while they stared at each other, the son struggling between the natural love he felt for his father and the exigencies of teen rebellion. The author's exhaustion was a series of heavy fishing weights attached to his muscles, his joints, his scalp. He wanted nothing but to lie down a while and return, refreshed and resolute, to the project.

"Larry says I'm supposed to talk to you," said his son. Larry being the high school's morbidly obese and mildly effeminate guidance counselor, with whom the administration had mandated twice-weekly meetings. "He says we're supposed to talk about stuff."

"That's precisely what I am trying to do." The author nodded, clapping a hand on his son's shoulder which was quickly rebuffed.

"I think he means, you know. Other stuff."

"Anything you want. There's nothing a father and son can't discuss. But Drew—" The author leaned heavily against the doorframe, feeling the irresistible pull of the project as a presence, as though someone were standing directly behind him, calling him to return, as though were he to turn quickly he might yet catch a glimpse of her face. Against this sensation, he clutched the pages and waved them at his son.

"I need you to understand that this means a great deal to me," he said. "I'm sure your mother would understand."

At this, his son's mouth opened slightly and closed again. They watched each other, father and son, the salami sandwich and subliminal rattle of the still-open refrigerator filling the space between them. In his profound fatigue, the author felt a brief sensation of vertigo, and gripped the pages like the guard rope above a frothing waterfall.

"Whatever," the son finally managed, turning for his bedroom.

"Not whatever," croaked the author. "Not whatever!" And he might have followed his son through the house, might have grabbed him by the shoulder and spun him around and thrust the pages at his sullen face, if not for the fact that at that precise moment, slumped against the doorframe and watching his son's form recede, the first sentence of the next chapter fluttered unbidden into his tired mind and he turned back to capture it before it flew away.

From the thirteen days between the disastrous *Saturday Night Live* broadcast and the "Death of Poetry" reading, as Calliope's last appearance has come to be known, two crucial documents have survived. The first is the "Blindness Letter," received by Marshall Vaughn, Calliope's Mountaintop Arts mentor, now on permanent display in a humidity-controlled and bulletproof case at the Ransom Center in Texas. The elderly poet, who had retired, for health reasons, to San Francisco, received the letter some four or five days after the *SNL* broadcast; though the postmark is from Malibu, the letter is typed on Hotel Gansevoort stationery, making it impossible to determine the precise date of its composition. That it was not discovered among Vaughn's effects until over a year later, after the first appearance of the Muse, further stymies interpretation; some scholars consider it a "manifesto" of sorts, a more eloquent version of the message the Muse would leave in the smoking rubble of her path.

The letter is remarkable both for its apparent renunciation of the art to which Calliope had devoted her life, and for its sophisticated discussion of identity. In it we find traces of the Zen Buddhism and poststructuralist theory to which she had been exposed at Mountaintop and Irvine, respectively. Also present is a rebuke to Taryn Glacé, et al., who were constantly co-opting Calliope and her poetry in support of the political stance *du jour*. Ironically, many interpretations of the letter have continued in precisely this vein, invoking the document to allege her affinity for one school of poetry or another, her passion for particular social causes such as the alleviation of world hunger, the campaign against genital mutilation, and the ethical treatment of animals.* But for those who are able to put biases aside and read Calliope's words in all their heartfelt purity, the "Blindness Letter" stands as simply the most cogent statement of her poetics, a poetics she painstakingly stitched together from the multivaried swatches of experience's cloth.

"If brass wakes up a bugle, it is not her fault," she said, invoking Rimbaud.

> The world has things in store for brass that she could never have anticipated, over which she can exert little control. But—*But, Marshie*—does poor brass have to resign herself to remaining a bugle forever?[. . .]
>
> The world's silly insistence that one "be" some *thing* demoralizes our little brass victim[. . .] though she be a bugle today, she might be a doorknob tomorrow—or a banister, or a barber's chair, or a breadbasket. Or she might wish to be none of these, to renounce altogether the burdens of *thingness*[. . .]
>
> The soul becomes monstrous through exposure to the horrors and indignities of the world. All the forms of love and suffering which surround it, the corruptions of language and culture inflicted upon it, must be withstood—not by defending against them but by passing through them untouched, as a stone passes through water. It is a kind of blindness I'm suggesting[. . .] the poet must make herself blind by a sudden and painful detachment. She must forsake the ecstatic flight, renounce the world of things, to become—in the world's eyes—*nothing*. Rimbaud said the poet is the thief of fire; I say she must give the fire back!

Provocative words from a poet whose career to that point had been, precisely, an ecstatic flight—from the Christmas fire to the Irvine reading and her dramatic leap. Vaughn, whose objection to Rimbaud was well known, must have been pleased at Calliope's repudiation of the poetics of self-aggrandizement. But what must he have thought of the letter's final paragraph? This lion of American letters, whose 196_ volume, *Spoke,* had

---

*And who can forget their sense of surreal outrage during the 200_ Super Bowl, to hear the letter excerpted in an ad for Monster.com?

been lauded by T. S. Eliot as proof of "the limitless potential of the word," what must Vaughn have made of Calliope's terrible conclusion?

> The problem is *words*, dear one—there are too many! Words are too vulnerable and changing, they have no rights of their own. The new poetry must be as silent as the poet is blind[. . .] The only honest number is zero. A poetry without words will at last approach the truth. It will be pure.

A pure poetry, not subject to misinterpretation or misuse. A poetry that has mastered its context and stands indisputable, immune to the indignities of subjective reading. It is here that Calliope embarked upon her greatest quest, for that Holy Grail of all art: that the ideas and emotions and observations of the artist, the complex and nebulous feelings provoked by her movement through the world, be not *explained to* nor *illustrated for* the listener but actually *communicated,* body into body, blood into blood, that the poem should thus achieve the status of revelation.

We dream of knowing the artist—but is it not also the artist's dream *to be known?*

Of course, anyone who reads the "Blindness Letter" can see that the purity-through-silence of which she dreamed, the "painful detachment," referred, terribly, to more than words.* No one who witnessed her appearance on *Saturday Night Live* could doubt that the poet was in distress, that if the end of her rope had not yet been reached it was, at least, dangling in plain sight. It is hard to disagree with Jean Baudrillard's literary autopsy, which interpreted the destruction of her father's image as "a ritual or imitation of ritual by which she translated herself into the realm of the simulacrum—pure image, no longer accessible via traditional hermeneutics[. . .] One could thus say the subsequent event was a pseudo-event, that it never took place at all."†

---

*Only Edwin Decker's incomprehensible work, *Sordid Tales of a Terrible Grandchild,* seems to miss the analogy here between Calliope's poetry and her life.

†From his keynote address to the Modern Language Association at their annual conference held in Phoenix that year (December 27, 200_). The remarks were repeated the following day at a panel entitled "(Ab)uses of the *Oresteia* and the Responsibilities of Theory," though the author was unable to attend the panel due to a mix-up regarding conference registration.

The relationship between the two events was best summed up by Rafael Zuñiga, whom the author visited the following January. Having taken disability leave from UCI following treatment for severe depression in the wake of Calliope's disappearance, Zuñiga was living with his brother, a U.S. Marine sergeant, in Oceanside, spending his days writing poems and tending to a starter hive of honeybees he had built in his brother's garage.

"Soon as I saw her with that photo, I knew what was going down, you feel me?" Zuñiga muttered. We sat on his brother's back porch as the sun set over a Pacific of corrugated tin, a slight chill and wash of color in the sky disturbed only by the drone of bees returning to the hive. "It's like, that was the end of everything and shit. Anything after that didn't matter, you feel me? Like that Oedipus dude, you know, how he comes to Colonus to die and shit? But he's already dead—he'd already offed himself like way long ago, and then just wandered around and shit."

He paused, resting forehead on knees. The author, though mindful not to interfere with the recollections of interviewees, placed a hand on Zuñiga's shoulder and looked away until the moment had passed.

"I'm saying she was already gone," Zuñiga moaned. "After that nothing else mattered. San Diego was just like punctuation and shit, you feel me? The TV show was the real suicide. What happened next was just, like, the acknowledgment."

The second document, the startling poem "In Clover," was found in Calliope's car, which was recovered on Niagara Street in Ocean Beach, fifty yards from the fishing pier. A striking coda to the "HymenOpera," "In Clover" has been included in later editions of *(I)CBM*—a decision that elicited cries of tampering from several corners.* The poem, more rigidly formalist than its predecessors, seems to support both Baudrillard and Zuñiga: Its static central image suggests nothing so much as termination, the absence of vitality, the "white, windless plain" symbolizing the loss of all heat and color, the failure of seasonal renewal, even as it recalls the cold clearing in which she

---

*"Yet another rape," proclaims wilma planck in her essay "Confession, Submission, and the Meaning of the Poetic 'No!'" (Included in *The New Concord: Contested Lives of the Poets,* Ronald Bosco, ed., UC Press, 200_.)

had met the Beekeeper so long ago. With the stark beauty of a marble sculpture, the poem—likely the last she wrote—reveals an eye for composition and balance not seen in earlier work; its understated dignity gives answer to the critics who reviled her verse as flashy and uncontrolled.

There is no ignoring the presence of death in the poem, the final flight of the "robeless" queen, Calliope's alter ego through all five poems of the sequence. Nevertheless, something haunts the poem's funereal silence, a presence which suggests continuation or metamorphosis, the persistence of voice after the body has breathed its last. This "splitting off" or double consciousness gives the poem its odd, final note of triumph and recalls the cry of the Beekeeper on a bright spring morning: "There is no death!"

> The queen is perfect,
> Lying robeless, chaste
>
> As the day she came
> From her cups. Virgin,
>
> Sphinx, at last you've flown
> The coups, buzzed your grace
>
> Beyond the babble
> Of towering truths.
>
> Your royal blood cools,
> Exhausted body
>
> Small and black against
> The white, windless plain,
>
> Quiet and final
> as a period.
>
> Daughter, mother, soul:
> That pale sun has seen
>
> Your last flight. Usurped,
> Unbowing, behold
>
> Your new home, silence;
> Speak your new name: Wind.

For thirteen days, there was no word. The world held its breath, unable to exorcise from its mind's eye the image of the broken poet in her gold burqa, unable to shake the sense of dread the scene had so viscerally conveyed. Just as her image had been replaced by blankness on 31 million television sets, so was her presence supplanted by absence—albeit an absence more tangible, more agonizing, than the visibility she had previously enjoyed.* One could scarcely pass a newsstand without seeing her face; coffeehouses and taverns, public squares and water coolers and chat rooms resounded with argument, speculation, elegy, conspiracy. In New York City alone, Emergency Services reported over two thousand calls to 911: Calliope passed out in a Coney Island storm cellar, Calliope in protective custody of an antiterrorism unit concerned about the *fatwa,* her image materializing in a water stain on the wall of the Holland Tunnel. On October 8, acting on an anonymous tip, the NYPD raided the Mosque of the Faithful, but found neither the poet nor the underground "jihad command center" in which she was supposedly being held. Aaron's Gulch, a hamlet in Pennsylvania's Amish country, experienced brief renown when a group of children reported a strange girl sleeping in a stable, sobbing and muttering nursery rhymes; the media descended like a sandstorm, only to find that the "strange girl" was a seventeen-year-old boy who had been driven from his home in a nearby town after disclosing his homosexuality.

What distinguished this disappearance from those that had come before was the silence from Lubinski Management. There were no press releases, no tearful appeals—after her statement to *Newsweek* on October 4, the normally strident publicist fell silent. For those who loved Calliope, who had followed her life and drawn inspiration from her poetry, for all those whose hearts responded to a young woman in pain and whose nights were spent wondering what they might do to soothe that pain, the silence was, simply, unbearable.

---

*This paradox, absence/presence, has been explored at length by J. Hillis Miller in his recent monograph, *I See BM* (Routledge, 200_). But, in fact, no one was more conscious of its power than Calliope herself, who chose Emily Dickinson's ode to absence as the epigraph for her book: "To disappear enhances—/The man that runs away/Is tinctured for an instant/With Immortality."

"When she arrives on this morning, Roshi Bob is not surprised," recalled the head of Mountaintop Zen Center. "We have prepared for her the same room that young man lived in so many years. Roshi Bob even makes a small floral arrangement for poet girl, that he gathers on evening ride with Dogen, and sets extra place at supper table. When she does not arrive, Roshi Bob has no choice but to eat her portion of shiitake risotto—in Zen Buddhism we do not waste that which is provided for us."

The roshi and the author were sitting, once again, in the roshi's study, some two months after the author's first visit to the Zen Center. The roshi had been unsurprised to see him, knowing that the puzzle of Calliope's existence would inevitably lead the author back to that quiet redoubt; the author, for his part, refrained from asking why the roshi had failed to relate this part of the story during their last conversation, having neither the time nor patience to listen to a history of Zen Buddhism or litany of koans.

"She must have been very upset when she arrived," prompted the author. "She must have needed your wise counsel, Roshi."

The roshi leaned back on the couch. "When Roshi Bob is first starting Zen Center, he is new to United States, new to the culture. We have one building for sleeping and meditation and eating. Eight monks. No electricity. No digital cable."

"Yes, yes, Roshi. Of course."

"For years there is not interest from outside world. The only contact with outsiders is when sheriff sends inspectors to ask questions about sanitation or when someone puts a large cross in *zendo* in middle of night and lights it on fire.

"But Roshi Bob understands these things. The unfamiliar is threatening to the undisciplined mind. This anxiety is natural result of immersion in the world of things." Fearing that interruption would only goad the roshi to greater acrobatic feats of digression, the author made himself comfortable.

"Roshi Bob sees so much of the anxiety and ambition, so much noise of daily life. Where is the space in this culture for *dhyana,* for living in the moment?, Roshi Bob asks. How can Americans learn to appreciate the world-as-it-is, to overcome fear of death?"

"How indeed?" sighed the author.

"Soon, thinks Roshi Bob, soon many American persons will come to Zen Center. One day Zen Center will need more beds and a larger kitchen and state-of-the-art wireless infrastructure. Can you imagine, Mr. Andrew, until very recently we do not have cell-phone service? So Roshi Bob calls Sprint—"

"Yes, I recall this story, Roshi. It's quite impressive. Did you ever tell this story to Calliope, perhaps?"

The roshi looked momentarily confused and glanced out the window of his study, rolling his cognac glass between his palms. "The poet girl," he said wistfully. "So much of the desire. So much pushing against the world, as if the world can be moved by one person! As if the world is a stubborn water buffalo and person only must put her shoulder to its flank to make it do as she wants!"

The roshi threw back his head with laughter, cognac sloshing over the lip of the glass. He licked the drops off his knuckles and pointed mirthfully at the author, who smiled and nodded at the amusing metaphor.

"Stubborn buffalo!" the roshi repeated.

"Yes," said the author. "Quite right."

She had come in search of the Beekeeper, knowing of nowhere else she might escape from the deafening roar. Amid the public outcry, how appealing the idea of the Zen Center must have been—an oasis of safety, where she might rest in the Beekeeper's embrace and the calm, daily routine of *zazen*. For just as the artist dreams of being known, the celebrity dreams of anonymity; as the artist wills herself into existence, *sui generis*, the celebrity longs for annihilation: *sui cide*.

"Father, please tell me where I can find him," she said to the roshi, her voice small and deferential. Having interrupted morning meditation, she knelt before the roshi and, in a show of humility, touched her forehead to his sandals. Though he had watched the entirety of *Saturday Night Live* with great concern, the roshi was unprepared for the woman before him, trembling and insubstantial, defeated.

"I need him, Father. Please." He tried to ignore her, to preserve the sanctity of *zazen*, but Calliope lay prostrate on the hard earth of the *zendo* and began to sob, shaking the concentration of even the most experienced monks.

"Miss Calliope," said the roshi, leading her down the path toward the monastery, "young man is not here. He has not been here since your last visit."

She leaned against him, rubbed her nose on his robe. "When is he coming back?"

The roshi looked again at her face: pale, stretched, desperate. "Miss Calliope," he said gently. He took another step down the path, so their whispers would not be overheard. "Roshi Bob has not seen him since he leaves San Bernardino Community Hospital. Roshi Bob is thinking perhaps he is with Miss Calliope."

Calliope's mouth opened, her watery gaze meeting the roshi's. They could hear the monks stirring, the shuffle of sandals as they began to make their way down to breakfast. The roshi tried to extract himself from her embrace so as not to lose his honorary place at the head of the meal line.

"But he loves it here," Calliope said. "He never wanted to leave."

"Perhaps young man is changing." The roshi peeled Calliope's hand, finger by finger, from his arm. "Perhaps he becomes more interested in outside world. This is normal for young persons. Outside world can be very attractive, very seductive."

She shook her head. "Not for him."

"Miss Calliope, desire, too, is impermanent." The roshi chose his words carefully. "Young man from early age desired emptiness. But this desire is like any other, which turns to smoke and disperses."

At this, Calliope peered into his eyes. "What are you not telling me?"

He pursed his lips, bowed slightly. "The Heart Sutra tells us that form and emptiness—"

"Fuck the Heart Sutra!" She shoved the roshi away from her. "You know where he is. Tell me what happened to him." But the roshi was already making his way down the path, gently shouldering past the other monks on his way to breakfast, leaving Calliope to ponder the silence which was all that remained of her sanctuary.

For four days she sat in the *zendo*, refusing food, stirring only to sip from a small thermos of ginseng tea and avail herself of a chamber pot the roshi had brought to her. She neither shivered in the nighttime chill nor sweated in the afternoon heat. From time to time she let out a small gasp, and her eyes flickered open, her head turning slightly as though attending to the whisper of a nearby voice. After a moment's indecision, she shook her head as though to clear it of unwelcome distraction, and lay the palms of her hands on the earth. Thus steadied, she closed her eyes and returned to her thoughts.

The monks did their best to maintain their schedule, despite a natural fascination with the figure in their midst, a figure who in the past had been the herald of disruption but who now seemed the very avatar of quietude. Their early morning walks to the *zendo* were punctuated by whispered chatter as they contemplated the young woman's vigil, speculating as to its duration and the circumstances of its inevitable end. In the *zendo* itself, their very seating patterns were now oriented to Calliope, as though she were a pebble that had fallen into their still pond, they the ripples of disturbed water; the dining room became the locus of arguments over the nature of her visit, factions of supporters and detractors refusing to break bread together, their debates filling the room with unfamiliar tones of righteous anger as the roshi struggled to keep peace and smooth over disagreements, the food on his plate inexorably growing cold.

On the fifth morning, having spent one of the only sleepless nights in his thirty years of presiding over that idyllic community, Roshi Bob resolved to speak to Calliope and offer what help he might—both to dissuade her from traveling the same road of self-deprivation that had ruined his erstwhile dharma heir and to protect the integrity of the Zen Center, which was under more pressure each hour she remained in its midst.

He walked up the path at first light, but when he stepped into the stillness of the *zendo,* he was surprised to find Calliope fully awake and standing at the edge of the clearing, backlit by the orange dawn. As he approached, clearing his throat and stepping heavily so as not to startle her, the roshi was further stunned to find that the poet, whose long, tousled hair was as recognizable as the splotch of pigment on her neck, had shaved her head. She was bald.

"You're a liar, Father." Her voice was husky, without resonance, no more alive than the leaves scattered at their feet. "You've got them working so hard for something they can't have. But you just let them keep hoping."

"Miss Calliope, perhaps now you will eat something? Roshi Bob has breakfast prepared early. Refusing to eat is not healthy for body or for Zen Buddhist state of mind. Of all people, you know this to be true."

She turned to face him, and the roshi drew breath at the starkness of her appearance—her pale face seemed more angular, her dimpled chin and thin nose haunted, the birthmark in furious contrast to her flesh.

"You talk about desire. This place is a monument to desire," she said. "You talk about striving toward emptiness—but there's no such thing as emptiness. There is no nothing. Only death."

She took his hand and the roshi shivered, suddenly recollecting the images of wrathful deities on the tapestries woven by old women in his village.

"No matter how far you go, there's always something," said the poet, "even if it's just the sensation of nothing. There's no peace, no escaping the noise. Once you've created something, it can't be destroyed.

"You're stuck with it." She closed her eyes. "For as long as you live."

"Miss Calliope," he said, "you have had a difficult meditation. Please join Roshi Bob for meal of soybuttermilk pancakes. Then we will sit in Roshi's study and talk about what you will do after departure from Zen Center—"

"I want to know what happened to him."

The roshi sighed and looked away, dawn breaking in earnest, sending a glimmering test pattern through the woods. He had been dreading this moment, through the long summer while he waited for some word from his former student. It was his own karma, he had decided, the result of overconfidence in his abilities as a teacher, his own unconquered ego. He had lost his heir, and in the drawn face before him he saw another sentient being slipping into ruin.

"Roshi Bob does not know," he said. "In his hunger, young man encountered questions with no answer, questions Buddhism has struggled with for thousands of years."

"What questions?"

"Always we are asking, 'Whence birth? Whither death?' Buddhism has many answers to these questions." Catching a whiff of warm buttermilk on the air, the roshi's stomach rumbled. For once, he ignored it. "But *who?* Who is the one that asks these things? Who is the one that suffers for not knowing? This is the harder question. In the hospital, young man is begging Roshi Bob to answer this question, and Roshi Bob can tell him only that there is a place where birth and death have no authority. No teacher can show the way. You must go into the depth of self to find this place."

Calliope dropped his hand. "I've heard that one before."

"In the hospital, this question becomes very important to young man. As soon as he can sit up, he is meditating on this question and on his own nature. And then one morning he tells Roshi Bob he has had a vision. He has seen the image of a well with no bottom, and a child that climbs on the edge of this well and falls. And no matter how the child cries out or tries to reach for something to stop himself, he cannot. 'He's still falling,' young man says to Roshi.

"That afternoon, while Roshi is at Planet Tofu, young man checks out of San Bernardino Community Hospital. Roshi Bob has not seen him since."

The sun was risen, inching up behind the trees red and intrusive as a newborn. Monks passed on their way to the *zendo,* throwing backward glances and whispering to one another. Calliope stared at the roshi, her icy blue eyes wide, and he was suddenly overtaken by the certainty that this would be their last conversation, that after this exchange and perhaps a few shared niceties over a hearty breakfast, he would never see her again.

"What does it mean?" she asked.

"Miss Calliope," he pleaded, "you must have patience. You must understand that your life is a movement toward enlightenment, and this enlightenment is already a part of you. In time, you will learn to see this part truly. In time, the other parts of you will seem as they are: distortions of the truth."

She closed her eyes, ran her fingertips along the curve of her skull. "That's Blake," she murmured, a sad smile on her lips. As the last monks disappeared into the *zendo,* she once again raised her eyes to his.

"I don't have that kind of time," she said.

———

The Arizona Café sits unassumingly between a car-glass warehouse and a bicycle-repair shop, in a run-down section of Bacon Street, only a block from the ocean. Strolling by, one might well overlook the establishment, the windows of which display only tattered blackout shades and glass frosted by decades of motor exhaust and sea salt, much as locals had overlooked it until *SLAM* named it "Best Dive Bar in San Diego."* For many years after Brandt's suicide, locals continued to fill its threadbare barstools and two tattered booths to bask in the watering hole's aura of glamour and nostalgia, their patronage attesting to their punk aesthetics, their politics, their attitudes toward humanity: in a word, their Brandtness. In time the aura faded, and the Arizona Café reverted to the grungy anonymity that was its destiny and its best nature.

Entering through a set of swinging doors—one of which has not swung for many years, the other of which rumbles and sticks across the threshold—one encounters something resembling the long-neglected rec room of a veterans hospital or Soviet gulag. An ancient pool table, felt faded to a patchy ocher, one missing leg replaced by two 1983 telephone directories, stands to one side of the room, whose walls are papered in red velvet. Behind the bar, which boasts no beer taps, hang yellowed sketches of regulars from an earlier era, all of whom seem to have suffered from pattern baldness and interesting skin lesions. One's shoes stick sickeningly to the floor. The jukebox's most recent offering is Al Stewart's "Year of the Cat."

In an alcove used to store broken chairs and tables, a spinet piano missing all its black keys, metal music stands, and the chassis of rusted bicycles, a single halogen illuminates the bar's prized possession: a black Fender Stratocaster hangs on the wall, its body chipped and gouged, a long crack running erratically up the length of its neck, two machine heads missing, and a large bolt driven into its headstock. Across the white pickguard is scrawled in what seems to be lipstick: *Hey Joe, Where you going w. that gun in yr hand? xoxo BM.*

---

*"The prospect of sharing a libation with the likes of Charlie Ware, John Reis, or Brandt Morath more than makes up for sticky countertops and unspeakably backed-up toilets. If you've never been to the Arizona, you might as well live in Arizona." (Andrew Altschul, *SLAM*, July 24, 199_.)

It was in this alcove that the Arizona Café hosted the only concert of its long existence, the brief debut of four local ne'er-do-wells who would go on to shake the world to its very foundations.

"I remember it like yesterday, seeing as I was just about the only one here," smiles Joseph McAdderly, the proprietor and nighttime bartender at the Arizona Café since 197_. McAdderly is a gruff, burly Irishman with snowy hair and a sardonic smile; only his rolling brogue and the size of his gnarled hands attest to his former life as the "Galway Grabber," the enchanted isle's professional-wrestling hero.

"These hooligans come stumbling in, all piss and vinegar, causing trouble with the regulars. They asked me if they could play a concert and I say, 'Nah, we don't go in for that sort of thing here.' But they just come right on in anyway, kicking over the chairs, swinging their guitars at each other's heads . . . They were shite, you know. Just fucking shite. You knew it from looking at them. Then Brandt goes and knocks himself senseless with his own bloody guitar!

"The dumb cunt," McAdderly laughs fondly. "I thought he'd gone and killed himself for sure."

In *Throwing Pots About Poems,* Rhoda Lubinski recalls the process of choosing a venue for Calliope's last reading. Though she first suggested the Hollywood Bowl or Tijuana's Agua Calientes Racetrack, Calliope insisted upon the tiny Arizona, drawn to the last by the powerful symbolism of family history.

"That's where it all began," she said, brooking no argument. "And that's where it all shall end."[*]

How shall history understand the final appearance of the poet named Calliope Bird Morath? If one event encapsulates all the difficulties of the project at hand, one event at which the ambiguities—and Scambiguities—that lie like faulty masonry beneath any account of her life become exposed for the disaster-in-waiting they are, it is the October 11 reading. If there is a chapter in her story that is unrepresentable, that mocks the would-be biographer's dream of completeness, of expertise, it is

---

[*]Lubinski, pp. 424–25.

undoubtedly the night that poet and critic A. Alvarez called "the Death of Poetry."*

The last, pitiable cry of a woman haunted by history, by a father from whose shadow she could not emerge, hounded by a culture that fed off her poetry and her life and threatened finally to tear her apart and consume her like Orpheus at the banks of the Hebrus? Or—as the case has been made forcefully by Wally Weeks in his as-yet-unreleased documentary, *Helicon Lost*—the most elaborate and stunningly executed of hoaxes, a terrifying masterstroke that elevates Calliope and Rhoda to Himalayas of cynical genius? A final confession or the ultimate manipulation—we may never know.

What cannot be disputed is that the woman who entered the Arizona Café on October 11 was not the Calliope the world had known. A hollowed-out, hairless version of her former self, her once-glimmering eyes were dull and blank, the sternness of her features emphasized by her baldness and by the birthmark, which seemed to have crept farther up the curve of her jaw.

McAdderly remembers the feeling he had when he saw the poet: "Me grandfather used to frighten us little ones with stories about soul-stealers, that if you didn't behave they'd come to suck your soul right out your throat and you'd go without a soul forever. When [Calliope] come through the door, I had a shiver, thinking, that's what Granddad had in mind—this one's already dead."

The calls had gone out that morning—to Taryn Glacé and Dennis Adams, to the former members of Terrible Children and Fuck Finn, to Skip Cárdenas and Talia Z and NorthStar president Gary North, to former Rancho Santa Fe neighbor and current regional skateboarding champion Terrence "TT-Fly" Marker and housekeeper Esperanza Medina Blumstein and ex-roommate LaTonya Hammond, to Marshall Vaughn and deirdre v. deirdre and a handful of others from Calliope's past.† Some had not seen the poet in a decade or more, but all felt bound to her by history, by the role

*From "Requiem," published in *Poetry London,* Spring 200_.
†The author is certain he was meant to be included in this list, as he had recently sent a proposal and sample chapter to Lubinski Management, along with a query regarding authorization for the biography.

each had played in the family saga. Crucially, all could be counted on for their discretion.

"I had no idea what was going to happen," Rhoda recalled in her memoir. "How could I? [Calliope] was tired, that much was clear. She needed time away. I owed her that much. When she told me she wanted a chance to 'say good-bye,' I just thought she was being melodramatic. I thought she was being herself."

Given the short notice, some were unable to attend. The most notable no-show was the Beekeeper, who could not be located despite the extensive efforts of Rhoda's assistant, Leigh Mulgrew. She couldn't have known that he did not wish to be found, was in fact already holed up in a derelict schoolbus in Alaska's Denali National Park, where he would spend the next seven months furiously writing the book that would bring him such renown.

By 8:00 P.M., the Arizona Café had begun to fill—not with the usual assortment of palsied veterans and bike-chain-wielding misanthropes, but with a more urbane crowd who threw bemused glances at the decor before taking chairs, fidgeting and whispering at the small tables. McAdderly had not been notified of the event, and stood in frank disbelief as one well-dressed patron after another stepped tentatively inside.

"You live around here, then?" he asked one woman, upon returning from the basement, where he'd managed to dig up a bottle of white wine.

"None of your business." Her small mouth twitched to release the syllables and reverted to a tight smile. The woman wore an austere black suit, her blond hair pulled back into a bun, blue capillaries visible at her temples. "And I don't appreciate the crude attempt to discern my socioeconomic status via my address," she informed the Galway Grabber. "One of the more perverse products of capitalism is the practice known as 'slumming,' which reinforces and fetishizes racial and class divisions, acknowledging their power by the energy required to transgress them. I do not engage in this practice. Make of that what you will."

McAdderly considered this before sliding the wineglass across the bar. "That'll be three dollars," he said, adding a 50-percent markup to the usual price.

It could hardly have surprised anyone that Calliope was late. No one had seen her for thirteen days—not even Rhoda, whose contact had been limited to two hurried phone calls. There is no way to know what the poet did in those last hours, whether she may have visited her childhood home, or her old school in La Jolla, long since converted into a Pilates and T'ai Chi academy, whether she cruised the downtown motels her father had frequented one last time, or parked in front of the Casbah while jeweled airplanes whooshed overhead to land at Lindbergh Field. Was it she who broke into the condemned apartment building on Abbott Street, leaving cigarette butts and a used syringe on the linoleum? Was it Calliope who purchased a $300 gold-plated crack pipe with a picture of Brandt set in an enamel disc, as has been claimed by a clerk at Ocean Beach's venerable head shop, The Black? We may never know.

But certainly she made her way to the fishing pier, there to huddle in gullshit-speckled shadows and contemplate the ocean, much as her father had done in times of trouble, throughout his short life. Waves crashing in darkness along the seawall, a trash-can fire flickering in the adjacent parking lot, Calliope drew her knees to her chin and leaned back against cold concrete. All her struggles had come up short, her quests led to empty grails. She had been born into a story already in its third act, shaped according to the dictates of that story ("She answered its summons," as Žižek memorably put it); she was an icon, her fame still growing, her name known to more high school students than that of the vice president of the United States.* Yet that night she was but a scared child staring out to sea, not knowing, in the end, who she was.

"Tonight is a very special night," Rhoda told the twenty-five invited guests. It was nearly ten o'clock, and Calliope sat motionless at one of the tables, wearing only a thin white shift, her strange appearance assuring all eyes stayed on her. Behind the bar, McAdderly turned off the jukebox. Tom Jones's "Delilah" faded out.

"Someday you'll tell your children about this event," said Rhoda, winking at Esperanza Medina Blumstein, eight months pregnant, who blushed and ran her hands over her belly. The shuffle of feet and sliding

---

*According to a Pew Research Center survey taken on September 15, 200_.

of glasses slowly quieted. Gary North, standing next to the jukebox, turned off his cell phone and slid into a booth next to Taryn Glacé, whose perfect posture did not so much as quiver. Leigh Mulgrew blew a kiss to Joe McAdderly, who winked in return. Connor Feingold's six-foot-seven frame towered over the rearmost tables, the African robes he had taken to wearing in recent years lending his silhouette the air of a benign specter.

"What Calliope has accomplished is unprecedented. It's only been four months since her book came out"—here Rhoda held up a copy of (I)CBM, which elicited mutters of appreciation—"and already she has changed people's ideas of what poetry can do. Like her father, she has changed the world."

At this Dennis Adams, Calliope's staunchest defender in the Irvine workshop, burst into passionate applause. Adams, who had withdrawn from UCI to protest Calliope's expulsion, would the next day become the briefest of media stars, making himself available to Paula Zahn, Katie Couric, Larry King, et al. (though refusing, with an uncharacteristic burst of profanity, to speak to Charlie Rose).

"Breaking the news to those people would be the hardest thing I ever had to do," Rhoda wrote in Throwing Pots About Poems. Though Wally Weeks traces Rhoda's movements in the week before the reading, uncovering numerous phone calls to France and Canada, and a mysterious midnight visit to the Center for the Study of Pain Management on the campus of UCSD, Rhoda maintains that she stayed in her Silverlake apartment "on the verge of catatonia," contemplating the end of her only client's career:

> I decided just to give it to them straight, and we'd get through it together. We were the closest people in the world to Calliope. Of course I hoped she'd change her mind. I'll never forgive myself for not seeing what was really happening. She was my best friend. I should have understood.*

---

*Ibid.

The dismay that surged through the room when she made her announcement was profound, almost operatic, a collective groan breathing through the already-sultry air. Esperanza, perhaps hormonally oversensitive, burst into tears and Spanish prayers. "What the fuck?!" spat Terrence "TT-Fly" Marker, as Connor slid down the back wall into a crouch. Dennis Adams was a vision of pain, hands clutching at his hair, while Taryn Glacé bit her lower lip and secured an errant blond lock behind an ear.

"Tonight is not an end, but a new beginning." Rhoda opened her arms. "For the last time, please welcome: artist, icon, revolutionary, Calliope."

The ovation carried everyone to their feet. While Joe McAdderly looked on in wonder, Fuck Finn guitarist Darlene Cream let out a volley of piercing wolf whistles and high-pitched ululations, Talia Z at her side pumping both fists in the air. Billy Martinez, who stood in leather pants and vest, no shirt, a cigarette dangling from the corner of his mouth, dragged Connor Feingold upright until he, too, applauded. At the bar, Skip Cárdenas was trying to somehow clap and take notes at the same time, a task made all the more difficult by TT-Fly, who was slapping both hands on the countertop in adulation.

In the gloomy alcove, the author's son tilted his chair back and leaned against the wall. "This is just the biggest load of shit," he said.

The author stiffened. "Please," he hissed. "Try to restrain yourself."

"It's like, are these people even paying attention? Do they realize how ridiculous they look?"

"Drew—"

"Is this some kind of act? Are these people for *real*?"

The author refrained from dressing his son down in public, something he had been informed by the school guidance counselor could have "negative consequences" for the teenager's self-esteem. "I don't expect you to understand this now," he said evenly, covering his son's hand with his own, "but maybe once you've grown up a bit. This is a very important event, and we are lucky to be here to share it. So when you are tempted, as you inevitably will be, to make a snide remark, ask yourself what your grown-up self would do—and then do it. Ask yourself whether you'll look back one day and be proud of how you've behaved. Can you do that?"

The applause began to wane; the crowd took their seats. "Can you do that for me?" The author squeezed his son's hand and was answered by a baleful glare. "This is a very important night for us."

The teenager scowled. "Who the fuck is 'us'?"

Calliope rose from her chair and turned to face the room. Her blank expression did not waver, though one could see her jaw muscles clenching. Her eyes moved from one adoring face to another, as though hoping to draw strength from the onslaught force of their love. Hairless and robed, she might have been a mannequin in a store window, or a child's cherished doll, if not for the unforgiving blot across her throat. A tiny shape flickered in the light around her; those closest were able to make out a lone honeybee circling the poet's head.

"Hello," she said. "This is the first poem in the book. You've heard it before."

She cleared her throat and the audience shifted expectantly. "I shall not soon forget the day he died." Her voice was devoid of intonation. The once-incendiary line was delivered with such apathy that the listeners could only squint.

"For on that day," she said, in the monotone of a stone falling in a sepulcher, "I came into myself." Silence expanded into the room's corners. Gone was the emotional punch of that second line, its prophetic force and metaphysical claims, replaced by a cruel irony: The figure reciting the lines appeared to have no identifiable "self" left. Though the sonnet's desert imagery and Old Testament allusions remained intact, its heartrending final plea—*Why have you forsaken me?!*—unaltered, the poet's flat delivery drained it of all power and beauty.

When she finished, she stood blinking at her audience. The honeybee swooped intermittently, droning eerily in her orbit. Dennis Adams once again jumped to his feet to applaud. Rhoda whispered encouragement from a few feet away, and Terrence Marker slapped the bar and cried out, "That was *phat*, C!" The author closed his eyes and twisted his wedding ring, whispering his encouragement: "You can do it."

By the end of the first long stanza of "Sunday on Suicide Row" ("My house has no basement / A barren womb marked by traces / of a beautiful mind—my own/foundation, my kind/red spirit," etc.), the assembled few were casting glances at one another, at Joe McAdderly, at Rhoda. A hum of discontent arose among a group of ex-roadies. Gary North stole a look at his cell phone, and Skip Cárdenas replaced the cap on his pen. Connor Feingold hugged his knees.

"Lepers, tax collectors line up at Heaven's Gate," read Calliope. "Father, who will cleanse my sacred temple/what profane wax can seal my fate?/Eternity lives at a different address/and the coroner always rings twice . . ." She went on, but the lines could not overcome the want of a speaker, could not achieve their intensity without the poet's presence. Calliope knew it. With a last look at her gathered friends, her hands fell to her sides. Whatever tiny spark had thus far animated her performance wavered and gave out.

"He's not coming, is he?" she mumbled. No one responded; a few heads turned toward the door. Only the roll and wash of the ocean a block away, the faint whine of the honeybee in its orbit. "Is he?" She turned to Rhoda, who looked at the floor and shook her head.

It was as though the last support, the last thin twig propping her up, snapped. She turned her face to the wall and cried into the worn velvet, first a few sniffles and then a tide of sobs filling the room.

"Oh, what the fuck is this?" exhaled the author's son, dropping chair legs to the floor. "Can we leave?"

"We most certainly cannot," gritted the author.

The poet dropped to her knees, her profile visible beneath the spotlight, her shift slipping off one shoulder to reveal the pale, freckled flesh. Her cheek had turned wet scarlet, as though the birthmark were rising like bathwater, her face twisted in distress.

The crowd was paralyzed, all except for Gary North, whose love/hate relationship with Brandt and Terrible Children has been well documented, and who had spent many a long night in the early '90s tending to the Moraths' histrionics.* "Come on, kid," he said. "Stop wasting my time." He stood and stabbed the keypad on his phone, leaning against the de-

---

*Cf. L. Cleopatra Vanis. *North by Southwest: How Brandt Morath Built the Gary North Empire* (Random House, 200_).

crepit jukebox, the lights of which pulsed in broken syncopation. The honeybee sailed in frantic figure eights, its anchor lost, its centered universe in shreds.

At last Rhoda made her way to the poet, bending to help her to her feet. But Calliope shook her friend's hand away, shoved at her legs until Rhoda backed off.

"What the fuck are you looking at?" Calliope sobbed. Her face shone in the spotlight. A bubble of drool at the corner of her mouth crowned and spilled in a slow-motion spider's web. The audience now could clearly see the livid birthmark, which seemed to stretch toward her right ear, one hot tendril just touching her lower lip, another vanishing along the back of her neck as though it would choke the very life from her.

Rhoda advanced again. "Come on, C, let's take you home."

The audience was riveted, unable to comprehend whether the spectacle at hand was performance or authentic breakdown. Concern mixed with anxiety, empathy with irritation and fear; and racing beneath it all an undeniable voyeuristic charge and its backdraft of shame.

"I feel you looking at me." Calliope stretched her arms against the wall, fingers gouging at the velvet. "Why won't you leave me alone?" Dennis Adams tried to come to the poet's side, but was held back. The author's son sipped at his soft drink, the straw making slurping noises in the bottom of the glass.

"You're always looking at me," she said. "Everything I do, you see it; everything I say, you said it first." She smacked her palms against the wall, pressed her mottled cheek into the wallpaper. "Well, *fuck you*," she spat. "I don't even know who you are."

"I'm out of here." The author's son pushed back his chair.

The author clutched his wrist. *"Sit down."*

"I'd rather go home and jerk off. This isn't poetry, it's masturbation."

"I just want to write poems," Calliope sobbed. "That's not enough for you, is it?" She hauled herself to her feet. No one dared breathe, so strong was the sense of approaching catastrophe. An unsettling smile passed across the poet's lips, a dry and mirthless laugh escaping. "I know what you want," she whispered.

She took a step closer, the spotlight sliding across her features. Then she closed her eyes and with both hands clutched the light muslin of her shift, gritting her teeth until the dress tore down the middle and fell in a puddle at her feet.

"Holy shit!" said the author's son. Heads turned to glare at him, but just as quickly looked away.

She stood before them, naked and trembling, narrow-hipped and knobby-kneed and finely freckled, brow knit in concentration. No one could look away, nor escape implication in what was taking place. All had seen her performances, all knew her penchant for drama—but the Calliope they had known and cared about was gone, replaced by this grotesque, vulnerable creature condemned to perform her most private agony for their Friday-night enjoyment.

"I killed him," she said.

She said it quietly, a toe creeping past a threshold. "It was me. I killed him." Her eyes widened at the sound of those three words: "I killed him."

She stepped forward and cupped her breasts. "Look at me!" she said. "Go ahead, look at me. That's what you want, isn't it?" Standing before the nearest table, she leaned toward Esperanza and Dennis Adams, proffering her flesh. "I killed him. Do you hear me? You want my confession? I killed him."

"Oh, mija." Esperanza bent over her belly. "Oh, my little one . . ."

"Please, miss," coughed Joe McAdderly, his face ruddy. "I could lose me license."

"Dad? What the fuck is going on?" said a shaky voice at the author's side.

Rhoda snatched a coat to cover the poet, but Calliope froze her with a glance. "They want to look at me. So look!" She clapped a hand between her legs and thrust her hips toward the back of the room. The clench of her jaw had loosened, her rapturous smile suffused with the bloodstain's bright emanations.

"What do you see?" She clutched her groin, shaking her shoulders. "A poet? A woman? A murderer?" She stood on a chair and spread her arms. "Who am I? Tell me what you see!" A few patrons tried to head for the door, but she called them back. "Look at me, dammit! Look!"

They looked: at her glossy skull and the fine hair on her midriff, her unshaven legs, myriad freckles like a strange system of punctuation across her body. They examined the smoothness of her shoulders, the light heft of her small breasts, the serpentine mystery of her navel, her undimpled thighs. They tried to glean what they could from the image before them, burn it into their retinas.

"Somebody stick a fork in her," Gary North grumbled. "She's done." Taryn Glacé silenced him with a smack across the cheek.

"I don't get this." The author's son had gone pale. He rubbed his palms together, his eyes darting from his father to the apparition beneath the spotlight. The poet began to shiver, her eyes rolling back, her flushed face all but glowing. "What is she doing, Dad? What's the matter with her?"

But what was happening in that room was beyond explanation, beyond the comprehension of anyone present. The poet's distress radiated to the farthest reaches of the room, a contagion of the kind one might expect to find in some clapboard Pentecostal church in a Southern swamp. At the end of the bar, from where she had been making eyes at Joe McAdderly, Leigh Mulgrew suddenly stumbled off her stool, shaking from head to toe, grunting spastically. No sooner had the others taken this in than Connor Feingold, who had been crouched in a yoga pose, rose to his full height, palms pressed over his head, lips trembling, eyes closed. Rhoda pressed a hand to her forehead, the other hand clenching and unclenching at her side, while Taryn Glacé struggled out of her suit jacket and started to unbutton her blouse and Calliope gibbered breathlessly: "He's dead . . . he's dead . . ."

"This is fucked-up." The author's son stared at the floor. "This is fucked-up, Dad. This is totally fucked up." He leaned elbows on knees and gulped for air, an occasional groan escaping his lips.

One by one they rose, shaking, from their seats, fear in their eyes, while the poet twitched before them like a charismatic. The air crackled with energy. Finally Terrence Marker, Calliope's childhood friend, leapt atop the bar and cried into the silence:

"O Captain! my Captain! Our fearful trip is done!"

He crouched there, in corduroy board shorts and a bright pink tank top, feet spread wide, sunglasses perched on his frost-tipped hair and half-crazed amazement in his eyes. "The ship has weather'd every rack, the prize we sought is won!"

Gary North's cell phone dropped to the floor with a crack. "What lips my lips have kissed," he called out, "and where, and why, I have forgotten . . ." He stepped forward, hands held toward the poet in supplication. "And what arms have lain under my head till morning . . ."

"When I have fears that I may cease to be"—Connor lunged away from the wall into the Warrior II pose—"before my pen has glean'd my teeming brain, before high-piled books in charact'ry hold like rich garners the full-ripen'd grain . . ."

"Call the roller of big cigars, the muscular one, and bid him whip in kitchen cups concupiscent curds!" cried Taryn Glacé, who had stripped down to her bra. "Let the wenches dawdle in such dress as they are used to wear . . ." Talia Z stared at Taryn's midriff and hiccuped. "*Cuerpo de mujer, blancas colinas, muslos blancos, te pareces al mundo en tu actitud de entrega.*"

"Can we go, Dad?" the author's son whimpered, scratching his forearms and rocking. "Please, can we leave?"

One by one, they began to recite, each directing their words toward Calliope, who shook harder with each passing second.

"Let us go then, you and I, when the evening is spread out against the sky like a patient etherized upon a table," said Billy Martinez, whose voice was drowned out by a cry from Darlene Cream: "Wee, sleekit, cow'rin', tim'rous beastie, O, what a panic's in thy breastie!" and Esperanza, who hauled herself from her chair and said, "Who, if I cried, would hear me among the angelic orders?" No one in that room was immune to the strange energy, the author found himself in the grip of a hot turgor and fumbled in his pocket until he was able to produce notepad and pen and began to scribble ideas for chapter titles, footnotes, point-of-view experiments, as well as a startling insight into the relationship between poetry and beekeeping, most of which would be illegible when he looked at the pages the next day.*

The author's son squeezed his palms against his ears and rocked in his seat. "Why do we have to stay here? This is totally the kind of shit Larry

---

*Only this last note was readable, though incomprehensible: *"nihil/Zing < > sting??!! ask R.B."*

keeps talking about. He says you've got problems, Dad. He thinks *you're* the problem." But the author would not be distracted, creativity swirling in his breast, rushing into his throat, his extremities.

"Do I dare disturb the universe?" called Billy Martinez. "In a minute there is time for decisions and revisions which a minute will reverse!"

Connor Feingold, holding his yoga pose: "And when I feel, fair creature of an hour, that I shall never look upon thee more . . ."

"You're supposed to be my father." The author's son shook his father's arm, ruining one valuable observation. "You're supposed to be taking care of me."

"Stop it, Drew," the author panted.

The few who would ever speak of that night were unanimous: They did not believe they'd known the poems they recited, and certainly not by heart; they resisted the suggestion that they had perhaps learned them in grade school, or at the lips of lovers past. Even Taryn Glacé could not find a theory adequate to the night's events.* Those who were there recall only the uncontainable passion, the sense of a dam crumbling inside them, the ecstatic relief of the flood.

"I can't believe you," sobbed the author's son. "I'm so sick of this shit. You don't fucking care about me. You're just obsessed with this weird girl, like some fucking robot. I wish Mom were here."

The "weird girl" still shook under the spotlight, her face red and luminous as the poetry spoke around her, the babble having a rhythm and syntax all its own.

"O heart! heart! heart! O the bleeding drops of red . . ."

"In my heart there stirs a quiet pain for unremembered lads . . ."

"Thy wee-bit housie, too, in ruin! Its silly wa's the win's are strewin!"

"Are you even listening to me?" said the author's son. "You don't even talk to me about anything, I have to talk to that fat queer at school. Mom used to listen to me!"

"Break, break, break, on thy cold gray stones, O Sea!" moaned Skip Cárdenas, who had a hand at Esperanza's back to support her. "When

---

*In later comments, she would point out that all the poems but one were written by men, a clear example of artistic sexism—but whether Calliope's or the audience's, she could not say.

longing . . . overcomes you," Esperanza panted, "sing of women in love . . . for their famous passion is far from immortal . . ."

". . . to have squeezed the universe into a ball, to roll it toward some overwhelming question . . ."

"*Cae la hora de la venganza, y te amo.*"

"On the shore of the wide world, I stand alone—"

"Mom would never do this to me." The author's son banged a fist on the tabletop, tears streaming down his face. "This is bullshit!"

"Drew," gasped the author, "Drew, please—" His pen continued to move furiously, breathlessly, across the page, now apparently writing declarations of a personal nature.

"She wouldn't do this to me. She used to care about me. More than *anything*! But you don't give a shit. You don't want to talk to me. I wish she were here, she would never act like this, you freak—she would never make me—"

"Your mother is dead, Drew," said the author. He put down the pen, turned to his son, and clasped him by the shoulders. "She's dead. What is there to talk about?"

The author's son did not finish his sentence. His stared at his father, his face a rictus of misery, one tear curling through his faint mustache. His eyebrows drew together as they had when he was a toddler and his mother snapped at him for disorganizing her textbooks. His mouth opened and closed. The author turned back to his notes, straining to keep up with the torrent of language, to keep one eye on the poet, though her form had begun to blur in the heat.

"These beauteous forms, through a long absence, have not been to me as is a landscape to a blind man's eye," said Rhoda, covering her face with both hands. At the other side of the room, Joe McAdderly was locked in Leigh Mulgrew's embrace. "Ah, love, let us be true to one another!" he told her.

"Let the lamp affix its beam," said Taryn. "The only emperor is the emperor of ice-cream."

Lost in the babble, the author was not aware that his son had left the table, until a loud clatter and crash cut through the chaos and startled the room into silence. Calliope gasped, her eyes opening, everyone following her gaze to the very alcove in which the author sat. As he turned, the author felt that queasy dread familiar to all parents: the certainty that their child, left to his own inadequate resources, has committed some minor atrocity that will have as its result not only public disgust but the full weight of the public's opprobrium falling upon the head of the innocent parent.

Drew faced the back wall, his hands wrapped around the neck of the black Fender Stratocaster, struggling to remove it from the brackets and bolts upon which it had hung for two decades. His face was dry, the shriek of hardware pulled from plywood and plaster, the crumble of grit showering to the floor. Scimitars of light flashed from the instrument's stainless-steel pickups, slicing through the stunned audience. The room's heat was a sensual throb across the author's neck, his underarms. Everyone was silent, shocked into immobility by this sacrilege.

In another moment, Drew had freed the guitar, slung its ancient strap over his shoulder, and turned to face the room, the fading inscription only partially visible: *Hey Joe, where you goi*—. The veins in his forearms stood out as he gripped the neck and, squinting, arranged his fingers on the frets, mouth set in concentration. Someone—perhaps Joe McAdderly—breathed from the bar, "Lad . . . ," but said nothing more as the author's son fished a plastic pick from his pocket, drew it across the rusty strings, and slashed a rude, fearsome sound into the silence.

"The joyous howl of manumitted slaves, the indignant shriek of the faithful into a godless cosmos," is how Robert Christgau, in his 199_ review of *The Hanged Man,* described the immortal first three chords of "Dirtnap."* But as those chords tore through the air, in the same room where they had first been heard, what those in the bar experienced was neither liberation nor loss of faith, but the abrupt jolt of a door being slammed. What they felt, in their exhaustion—the music so familiar that their minds anticipated each note, heard each note before it was struck—was the concussive force of history folding upon itself, and the searing, surly certainty of death.

What happened in the next moment has had to be pieced together from brief glimmers of the author's memory, fragments that have entered

---

*Village Voice, October 21, 199_.

his dreams like splinters working their way to the skin's surface. The caustic melody repeating, refracting from the walls and the jukebox and the dusty bottles, darkness dissolving into flash and movement, he woke to the vision of a fountain of light, burning in the spot where the poet had stood. As he watched, that lovely blaze flickered and gathered unto itself and let out a last desperate cry, a forlorn scream that melded with the music and crushed the author's heart all at once like an aluminum can, then began to move swiftly across the room, sweeping past the bar and toward the exit. The author leapt from his chair, stumbling over music stands and pocketbooks and tables in a mad dash to apprehend her, to prevent some terrible and nameless future from finding them, all of them, pursued her through the swinging door and into the damp night, and he might have overtaken her at last, might have laid a hand on her bare, unhappy shoulder, had he not been struck from behind and driven to the sidewalk, the full weight of the Galway Grabber barreling down upon him and forcing all the air from his lungs so that he could only watch in hypoxic anguish as the glowing poet receded up Bacon Street and into the shadows of starlimned palm trees. "Calliope!" he wheezed into the terrible night, his lungs spasming, the others crowding through the doorway behind him. "Please, come back," he said, the last lines droning from the bar as though drawn in their mistress's wake:

> Exult O shores, and ring O bells!
> But I, with mournful tread,
> Walk the deck my Captain lies,
> Fallen cold and dead.

Few will forget where they were the next morning—a starkly beautiful autumn morning, chill sun splashed on a canvas of astringent blue—in what humdrum act they may have been engaged when they first heard the news. Few will forget the images of Coast Guard cutters in the waters off Ocean Beach, the ragtag flotage of Sunfish, surfboards, catamarans, Jet Skis, private yachts, inflatable rafts, and inner tubes, private citizens snorkeling the shallows near the fishing pier. An hour or so before dawn, Calliope's car had been discovered on Niagara Street, fifty yards from the entrance to the fishing pier; soon enough the pier was packed with mourners and tragedy addicts, each dreading the moment the poet might be raised, lifeless, from the waters, yet each harboring a secret desire to be the first to see her, the first to cry out, to bring the news to the world. The media followed, in vans and cars and choppers—satellites were fed, blogs posted, file footage found and spliced. Police cars and ambulances crawled the streets and parking lots of Ocean Beach, medevac helicopters lingered in the perfect skies as though reluctant to touch the ground, lest by touching it they make the unfolding tragedy real.

They watched from living rooms and kitchens, they crowded around the display windows of electronics stores, they listened to car radios, congregated in grim silence in high school cafeterias, bookstores, coffeeshops, college quads. Candlelight vigils sprang up in front of the Casbah and the Rancho Santa Fe mansion; NBC's New York studios were vandalized with spray paint and rotten food; at the Namgyal Monastery in Ithaca, New York, morning *puja* was brought to a halt while the lamas conducted impromptu prayers for the poet.

After years of false alarms, everyone knew that this was *it*. Hadn't Rhoda announced that the reading would be Calliope's last? Hadn't twenty-nine people at the Arizona Café seen a distraught, lifeless woman, heard her final, defeated cry?* The logic was plain. She had come back to San Diego, followed her father to the only place she had not yet pursued him: along the fishing pier that had sheltered him, to the ocean that had comforted him, and at last into the wide, welcoming arms of death.

But she had one final surprise in store. At 9:16 the search near the pier broke off. Word spread quickly: a note had been found, certain other personal belongings, at the base of the lighthouse at Cabrillo National Monument, the rocky promontory at the tip of Point Loma. The multitudes

---

*Police were able to question all except the author's son, whose whereabouts the next morning were not known, and Esperanza Medina Blumstein, who went into labor following the reading and gave birth at 3:42 A.M. to a healthy girl, Dolores Pájara Blumstein.

charged across the peninsula, the helicopters and Coast Guard ships and flimsy flotilla arriving soon after, all churning around the small stub of the lighthouse like a carousel turning upon its hub. The note had been in the form of a letter to her father, some speculated, or a letter *from* her father, or a hastily composed sestina; it had been written in Italian, or Arabic; it had been written in crayon in a four-year-old's scrawl; it had been signed in blood. Others claimed to have it on authority that among the items left on the shore was a wig made of Calliope's hair, or a new poetry manuscript, or a rib encased in Lucite, or a photograph of Calliope at the Great Pyramid, hugging a gaunt man with a bushy beard and striking blue eyes.

As the hours passed the scene grew circuslike: séances and conspiracies, tales of spacecraft hovering in the night, the poet transported aboard in a beam of light. Arguments and scuffles broke out. A twenty-four-year-old waitress was beaten unconscious for stealing a copy of *(I)CBM*. Two exhausted surfers were rescued by Coast Guard divers. On television, dull footage of the unyielding sea shared time with split-screen interviews: Billy Martinez spoke of his long friendship with the family; Skip Cárdenas gave a somber analysis of media fascination with Calliope; Taryn Glacé talked about death and labor exploitation. Dennis Adams reliably broke down in tears each time he was asked how the poet had touched his life. Geopolitics and natural disasters took a backseat that day—from Bangor to Bangladesh, Calliope's disappearance upstaged all other concerns, and San Diego was again, for a brief moment, the center of the universe.

At 4:10 P.M., the search was called off. No body had been recovered, but a visibly startled spokesman for San Diego Fire and Rescue told reporters that one of their vessels had encountered something bizarre: About two miles off shore, spread across the surface of the sea like a golden carpet, were millions upon millions of dead bees.

The spokesman scuffed the gravel with a shoe. "Impossible as it seems, Calliope Bird Morath is gone," he said over the crash of waves. "We got to give her up. We got to let her go."

And so the mourning began. Condolences poured in from around the globe, flooding the phone lines of Lubinski Management, UC Irvine, NorthStar, Snow Lion, the Library of Congress, even the U-Leave-It storage facility in Costa Mesa, where the poet had rented a locker the previous summer. Hastily produced tributes hit radio and TV and Internet, home video footage accompanied by Terrible Children songs, tributes from classmates and acquaintances, assessments of Calliope's artistic legacy. MTV ran the Queen Latifah/"I Shall Not Soon Forget . . ." video nineteen times in a row—once for each year of the poet's life. From Córdoba, L. Moreno gave a telephone interview to NPR's Linda Wertheimer, only to break down in sobs of rage; Marshall Vaughn, speaking to a San Francisco news anchor, voice shaking from late-stage Parkinson's disease, said, "I never had another student like her." CNN's Larry King held up a copy of *(I)CBM*, Poet Laureate Thomas Lux by his side, and declared, "Art. Immortality. *La poète est morte; vive la poète.*"

The day had the air of unreality. Some simply could not believe she was gone, that this uniquely fascinating figure could pass from the earth. They sat dazed before the television, arguing with Wolf Blitzer, resenting the public's credulousness and lack of faith. They paced empty houses, finding bottles of vodka at the back of kitchen cabinets, pouring generous shots while trying to transcribe their racing thoughts. They knocked on bedroom doors, thinking to commiserate with absent children, shouted denials at passing cars from their front stoops. They convinced themselves they had only dreamed it. Nothing short of the written word could cement the tragedy, only the gut-wrenching headline could drive it home:

FAMOUS POET LOST AT SEA

By midnight the vodka was gone, the last cigarette lay in an ashtray on the living-room floor, a tendril of smoke swimming up into darkness like a soul reluctant to leave the body. Somewhere in the house was an empty bottle of Ambien, somewhere the pathetic beginnings of a manuscript which now seemed repulsive and sad in its inadequacy. Slumped against the couch, the author clicked stubbornly through the channels, dutifully absorbing the last coverage. Mayor Horneiwicz commended the rescue squads for their efforts. UC Irvine's School of Visual Arts announced a contest to design a memorial. In Denver, LaTonya Hammond played "Taps" on the flute. Edward J. LaBello, former head of Students United in

Christ, led a prayer for the prodigal soul, who would "find love and for-giveness in the bosom of the God she abandoned."

Just after 3:00 A.M., CBS cut to its affiliate in Anchorage, Alaska. Re-porter Ali Reed had arrived by snowshoe at a windy vale in the heart of De-nali National Park. A gray and ghostly wilderness given visual depth only by the ruined shell of an old bus, windows lit from within. When Reed knocked, the door was opened by a monk in a red robe with a yellow sash, who led her inside where a small covey of monks sat with a thin, shivering man wrapped in a sleeping bag. He had dark, bushy hair and a cruelly hooked nose, a strong jaw covered in stubble, a prominent Adam's apple. The ticker at the bottom of the screen identified him as "Anonymous: Has just signed multimillion-dollar deal for as-yet-untitled memoir."

Lips blue, eyelashes edged in frost, he beckoned the reporter to him. A manual typewriter sat on the floor amid a sea of paper. The wind howled against the metal walls. Reed crouched at his side and waited for some comment on the day's tragedy, some pronouncement on the poet's life and her sad end.

The Beekeeper wiped an icy tear from his cheek. "I guess some people just take themselves too seriously," he drawled.*

And in Paris, Penny Power leaned against the door of her Marais con-dominium, pale and ravished, beautiful in grief. The narrow street lit only by gas lamps, the stone facade of her building blank but for black shutters and boxes of violets, she stared into the BBC camera and struggled for self-control. Her hands clenched as though she would gouge the old stones. At last, pulling herself together, the former queen of punk lifted her face and smiled a terrible smile.

"She's gone and joined that silly sorority now," Penelope said. "I love you, Bird. I hope you found what you were looking for." She was led back inside by an unidentified man in silk pajamas,† who held his palm to the camera lens and briskly shut the door.

---

*When it was learned that Reed, a thirty-one-year-old junior reporter, had attended Cornell Uni-versity in Ithaca, New York, questions were asked about possible connections to Snow Lion Press, raising the specter that the interview was orchestrated, the first salvo of publicity for the Bee-keeper's memoir.
†In *Helicon Lost,* filmmaker Wally Weeks identifies Penelope's companion as Mahmoud al-Shakil.

The night, by then, had grown quite cold, a starlit chill that sliced straight into the young woman's bones. At the old lighthouse, under a sky so clear it seemed painted on, she hugged herself and stared toward the horizon, the unfeeling constellations, waiting for her breathing to slow. At last she was alone, the crowds left miles behind. The dark ocean lashed the promontory, again and again, its ceaseless movement confirmation of her own insignificance. *Do as you like,* the ocean whispered, *it will not change a thing.* And this was a comfort—no one would misunderstand her words any longer. Her deeds would speak for themselves.

She took a few tentative steps, testing the feel of the ground against bare feet, her skin stippled and damp with mist. She swallowed cold air in gulps, spread her arms and let the wind raise and drop them. At the foot of the lighthouse she left her prizes, the few treasures she'd wrested from a greedy world: a gold-plated cigarette lighter, engraved with her father's initials; a plastic bag containing a necklace of human teeth; a photograph of herself and the Beekeeper exulting atop a San Jacinto ridge; her copy of Blake's *Songs of Innocence and Experience,* its binding tattered, pages dog-eared and teacup-ringed, the inscrutable note tucked inside. Resolute, she walked out along the headland, shedding desire and adoration, splendor and fantasy and winged persuasions. The hard-won emptiness wrapped itself around her like a small child shivering out of a bath. She had fought with all her strength—to find her father, to be loved on her own terms. Like Shelley's Adonais, she had withstood the wolves of criticism, the ravens and vultures of misinterpretation and doubt, only to be conquered, in the end, by the dragon coiled in her own breast.

O weep for Calliope—she is dead!

The Greek tragedians put their dying offstage, perhaps to protect audiences from unbearable fear and pity, perhaps in admission of death's insoluble mystery, its ultimate unrepresentability. Compare, for example, the bloodbath at the end of *Hamlet* to Agamemnon's last bath, to Oedipus's unseen undoing, the quiet demise of Antigone, swinging in darkness. At the end of her tragedy, Calliope, too, left the stage, understanding as well as Sophocles that the mind always struggles to fill in the blanks, but the heart knows only what it can touch.

We will not look away, reader. We will not deny her or turn our eyes from this passion. How could we lay claim to the truth of her life without recounting her last, terrible act? Like all history's bit players, we are doomed to bear witness, though our every muscle strain to reach out and stop her, to strangle this new world in the throes of its becoming. For is it not true that in the end we cannot save one another, that once the seeds of self-destruction have been sown in the garden of private despair no love or devotion can breach the space between us?

He was waiting for her, somewhere in that distance. She would know him now, as the blood knows the oxygen which gives it color, as a lyric knows the melody which shapes it. Was that his image, traced by the ghostly constellations? Was that the sound of his voice, singing faintly across the tides of time? She closed her eyes, filled her lungs with salt air, felt the spray upon her cheeks. Everything was simple now. Everything clean. He had loved the ocean, and it had loved him back. And she was his daughter.

With a last glimpse behind, she passed fingertips over her scalp, pressed her hand to the heat of the birthmark. Then, opening tired arms to oblivion's embrace, she began to run. The wind lashed her skin, the mist stung—the last mortifications of the flesh. Can you hear her soft footfalls, swiftly fading? Can you see her, bright against the moonless sky, burning through the inmost veil of Heaven? Your mouth fills with ash; your desperate lunge clutches only air. She is growing smaller. She has left you now, your voice cannot call her back, nor the strength of your love dissuade her.

And yet there is beauty here, still there is hope—don't you feel a lightness in your heart as you watch her? Though your tears spill into the dust, though your soul trembles, do not grieve: only draw breath and wonder as Calliope lifts off at last, as her pale form rises into the night, leaving you here on the silent earth to remember.*

---

*The text of the note would not be made public for several days, its meaning a source of hot dispute in Morath Studies ever since: "Goo goo g'joob" she wrote. "Who is the Walrus now?"

The Great Gig in the Sky

It starts on a beach. High sand dunes and strings of black kelp like severed tentacles, transparent bulbs pulse in a tangled pile. There is no one else in sight. The tentacles are malevolent, suckers that want to drag me under. I try to run, but have no traction. My feet sink in sand up to the ankles, the knees. I crawl up the dunes, which have become very steep, strewn with pebbles and shale, broken clouds racing overhead. The sky is a color I've never seen. The smell of something burning. Now the beach is gone. I'm at the base of a mountain. Someone is calling me back, but I can't see the path. I keep climbing, cut by stones, thorns. Trickles of blood run down my thighs.

There is a sound, a vibration. I feel it in my belly, under my jaw. It seems to come from everywhere, exuding from every rock and blade of grass. The rhythm is familiar, maddening. I should know it. The sun burns my shoulder and scalp. As I climb, the sound grows louder, hugging me like a glove. Below, the world is covered in creamy fog; above, the sun rages, emblazoning the cold peak. Then I've arrived, barefoot and bleeding, at the end of the path.

The cave mouth is narrow and dark, strung with spiderwebs which sway gently. A smell of rotten meat, a flock of crows perched on the rocks above the opening—dozens of crows, sitting side by side and watching me like the robed justices of a grim tribunal. Their eyes are nervous white discs with sickly yellow centers. The vibration has grown deafening, emanating from that opening. I know that once I cross that threshold I can never go back.

Where am I now? A dark tunnel, dim blue light with no source. The ground is sticky. It sucks at my feet. I feel bodies moving, jostling past me, sudden whispers in my ears, but I can't see their faces. In the distance, voices are crying, moaning, laughing; the vibration is all around, unbearable. I swim through sound, through colors that flash and kaleidoscope in that narrow space. My nightgown soaked through. On hands and knees I inch forward, finally tumbling with a gasp into a wide cavern and the touch of a woman's cool hands.

"Who are you, little girl?" she says. Behind her a bedlam of bodies and lights, shadows gliding overhead like prehistoric wings. "Who are you?" she asks again. I have no answer. She smiles; her eyes glitter. Her dark hair is perfectly coiffed, bobbed at the shoulders. She crouches next to me, in a red dress tight at the chest and hips, painted toenails winking from gold sandals. Her voice is low, musical, and dangerous. "Are you here to confess?"

I start to cry. "It's hard to be a daughter," she says, running a hand through my hair. "Impossible, really." She stands and walks through the crowd, to a man in leather pants with a thick beard and cruel eyes, who leans against the wall with a bottle. She tilts her pale neck under his chin. The music swoons louder and louder—guitars and cymbals, a martial bass-line beating like a pulse. The walls are hung with thick skins, animal pelts, some with the heads still on, teeth bared in a death grin. I've made the wrong choice. I should have stayed on the beach. I try to turn back but the passageway has vanished.

Throughout the giant cavern there are stages strung with streamers and balloons, strewn with dead violets. On each stage, musicians play different instruments, a different song. Hundreds of melodies come from giant speaker stacks, the sound weaving and clashing like sirens. I stand alone, shaking with terror. Someone is waiting for me but I don't know where. On one stage I recognize a tall black man with dandelion hair and a sweaty bandanna, coaxing a squeal of desperation from a flaming guitar. I recognize two drummers with shaggy hair and crazed eyes, who bash their kits in tandem, sweat flying in every direction. Two guitarists standing back to back, one in a plaid cardigan with thick glasses, Boy Scout hair; the other thin and blond with sensuous lips and psychedelic clothes. A wildman prostrate over a piano; a woman making love to a violin that glows with her heat. Some of them look sadly at me, others take no notice. I know them, but their names are nonsensical in my mind. A woman howls into a microphone, bent over double, her face ecstatic and sweat-red as a newborn. A skinny coffee-colored woman croons toward the roof of the cave, her voice low and smoky, unyielding as iron. The air above her lips sighs as though the darkness itself were weeping. In the shadows a man blows into a saxophone, fingers caressing the brass, belling forth gusts of apocalypse. A fat graybeard hunches over an electric guitar, colors spouting from his fingers, dancing around his form. An old cowboy weeps over a dobro, each slide a slippery, erotic gasp.

I know them, all of them: but they're not why I'm here. I try to move forward but the music holds me, every melody distinct from the others and yet blending into clouds. No one talks to me. At some point, I realize I am naked.

Between these stages, people gather at cocktail tables and lecterns, chatting and drinking straight from the bottle. Spotlights play across their faces. Their laughter, disembodied, frightens me. From their mouths flow strange sounds and rhythms, bursts of hollers and applause. When the spotlight finds a willing face, it stops to let them speak their lines, strike their poses—the others hoot and hiss, shout and wolf-whistle, mob around. The cave is breathing like a lung. I know these people, too—the poets—but they don't see me.

My friend in the red dress appears—one hand on her hip, the other dangling limply. I can't understand her words. Her voice makes men and women moan. They reach for her body, grope the insides of her legs until she is pulled back into the crush. A thin, nervous man takes her place. Corduroy jacket, Coke-bottle glasses, and a messy beard that he scratches repeatedly; he blurts his lines without raising his eyes, giggles to himself while the crowd cries, "Huzzah!" He wipes the sweat from his eyes, points to a tall man in a wool vest and tie, who makes his move.

A wild-eyed man in an English suit, Irish brogue booming, drinks from a flask and wipes his mouth with his sleeve. A tiny woman with thin lips, hair pulled into a tight bun, twists her hands fiercely and blushes—her sentences hyphenate, double upon themselves and break their own meaning. A handsome lad with shoulder-length hair and a bright, melancholy smile; a woman whose face is hidden by bows and ribbons and dark, tight ringlets; a brooding boy with a feverish brow and lips sheened in blood; a woman in a long coral robe, hair bound in garlands, thick brows over eyes like polished stones. I want them to help me, but still I am unseen. I know I'm late. I'm supposed to be somewhere. I'm letting someone down.

The crowd's movements grow wilder, more dangerous; the music louder, like a scream. A reedy woman streaks naked across my path; a dark-browed man, slumped against a riser, offers the sweet, oily smoke from his pipe to all who pass. *The man in the leather pants is on the prowl—women in black fall upon him, gouge his flesh with their nails, their teeth. A tall woman in a house-dress clutches two small children, her eyes ablaze, she opens her mouth and lets out a fearsome roar. I can't breathe.*

I'm panicking, searching for a way through the crowd. Tears, sweat, drip-ping down my nose, the risers shaking, people falling to the ground, punching one another, tearing out their hair—and I know it's because I haven't found what I'm there to find. I fight through hands, step terrified over humping forms. I stumble, fall to my knees, and look up to find gray eyes watching me, a cruel brow, mouth twisted in a sneer. The man—a boy, a child—leans on a makeshift crutch, one leg of his pants pinned at the knee. The others are [inaudible . . .] *his bare, filthy foot but he doesn't acknowledge them. While I stare, a thin man with a white beard reaches a hand into the boy's zipper, only to be chased off with a whack of the crutch. The boy holds me in his gaze, his lopsided sneer squeezes my throat in ice. They grab his clothes, his hair, cover him in saliva and blood and urine, their howls rising as they pull his body apart piece by piece, limb by filthy limb; but even as his body disappears, his eyes keep watching me, he opens his teeth and laughs and that's when I understand that I've died.*

Then the music stops. I'm kneeling at the foot of a silver door. The jambs are carved with twisting vines of ivy, golden snakes writhe along the lintel. My hands are stuck to the floor. Everyone behind me lies with their foreheads touch-ing the stone, and overhead a voice moans in agony: Ohhh! Ohhh! I reach one hand forward and then the other, each movement excruciatingly slow. I can't . . . [41 seconds inaudible, subject weeping . . .] *I'm the only one left. I'll never get there. I keep trying to reach that door. I have to find out what's inside. My arms and legs are being pulled out from the joints. I'm so frustrated I have to scream but it makes no sound, nothing comes out, there's no one to hear me anyway.*

And then it's over.

And what's behind the door?

[Session #81, April 2, 199_; 1700–1750h.]

SECOND ACT

The progress of the artist is a continual self-sacrifice, a continual extinction of personality.

—*T. S. Eliot*

Where in the world is Calliope Bird?
Tear away my shroud (these words)—
The poet will soon be heard.

—*The Muse*

9. THE HANGED MAN

ON A BREEZY NOVEMBER AFTERNOON, one of those autumn days when the invincible Southern California climate suddenly seems fragile—ocean winds biting pleasantly, palm trees shaking spastically at the side of the freeway, the sky a crisp cobalt infused with longing—the author maneuvered his car through the narrow streets of Del Mar Village, humming a tune as he searched for a place to park. Light clouds brushed the horizon, pink and grooved like a palate, feathering and dissolving as they rose above the sea like something struggling, but failing, to enter the world.

Eventually finding a space, he sat for a moment looking over his notes. Well-heeled pedestrians moved along the sidewalk; snippets of their conversations, bubbles of tossed-off laughter, seeped through the window. When he emerged, they barely took notice, eyes ticked across his face before returning to their own, unknowable concerns. He had arrived early, and to pass the time he lit a cigarette and set off along the promenade, shoulders hunched into the unexpected chill. He strolled past clothing boutiques, real-estate offices, and yoga studios, a gift shop selling sandstone replicas of Renaissance sculpture, a Thai noodle shop. Passing picture windows, slowing briefly to glimpse the patrons inside, he had the strange feeling he sometimes had when visiting an unfamiliar place: that what was happening inside had greater weight and presence, that its existence was somehow more secure, than what was outside. His role in the tableau was spectral, that of a mere eye.

In the not-unpleasant moments before his appointment, his thoughts turned to the passage of time, the brevity of human existence. The uncounted billions whose lives flicker into the history of the species, winking out with all the fanfare of a stray spark—how few make any real mark upon the world, their flame burning long enough for even one other person to take notice. How blessed is he who sees that light and remembers.

The wind gusted, twisting the smoke from his cigarette. High tide, the ocean roared distantly, its spangled surface stretched toward a fading sun. He wondered how many times Calliope had strode along this very sidewalk, what desperate moments she might have weathered, standing where he now stood. Perhaps she, too, had leaned against this seawall, stared toward the horizon—the ocean before her, which had so often been a comfort to her father, was the same body of water before the author now, and yet it was ever-changing, affording only the cruel illusion of permanence.

What is memory? he asked himself. What is this thing that seizes the mind's eye? We step out of time temporarily, we see and feel what is no longer there. Blinking, we come back, and the world is as it was. If our memories cannot affect the present, what purpose do they serve? What advantage is bestowed by their sweet, unfulfillable desire? If it means, in the end, nothing at all to envision something in the mind, to recall to existence that which no longer exists, then is not memory itself a kind of lie, a delusion? Do we who place such faith in it not suffer from a kind of insanity?

So absorbed in these thoughts was the author that he twice passed by the office of Dr. Michaela Breve. Realizing his blunder, he stood another moment outside the door, shielding his eyes against the glare. He checked his watch and took a last, deep inhale from the cigarette before stepping inside.

It was an unremarkable suite: brushed stucco walls, a fake fern potted in the corner, black-and-white photos of the La Jolla coastline at various stages of development. Outdated copies of *Highlights* and the *New Yorker* on simple end tables. A sedate, instrumental version of "The Way We Were" lightly infused the air as the author stepped to the front desk.

"Help you?" said the receptionist, not looking up from his monitor. He was a light-skinned black man in his twenties, with a shaved head and a ruby stud in the side of his nose. His fingers, festooned with gaudy rings, tapped ruthlessly at the keyboard.

"I have a four o'clock appointment with Dr. Breve."

"Yeah?" The young man leaned over his workstation, the colors of the monitor flickering in his eyes, then clutched at the mouse, jerking his torso one way and then the other in an attempt to influence whatever game he was playing. The maneuver unsuccessful, he looked up with a peevish expression. "Say again?"

"Four o'clock."

"Right. Alt . . . Alshuler?" He clicked twice on the mouse and peered again at the screen. "Two hours?" He raised his eyebrows. "Must be some emergency . . ."

The author smiled, but did not stoop to a response. He had turned to look for an appropriate magazine with which to pass the wait when the man called him back and slid a clipboard across the counter.

"How will you be paying?"

"It's not that kind of appointment," the author responded firmly, turning the clipboard back to the insolent receptionist.

"Says right here: 'Make him pay.' " He turned his monitor toward the author and, indeed, the offending phrase appeared, boldfaced, in the 4:00 P.M. slot. "You have insurance?"

"Well, no," the author said, holding a copy of *Condé Nast Traveler* guiltily at his side. "I wasn't expecting—"

"Visa, MasterCard, Discover." The young man smiled sweetly. Too sweetly, in the author's opinion. "No Amex. ATM down the street, take a right at Häagen-Dazs."

Speechless, the author stood, magazine in hand, as violins swooped into the maudlin bridge of "The Way We Were." He had the sudden urge to find the hidden speakers and damage them. It had taken the better part of a year to secure permission to speak to the renowned psychologist— working through the disorganized offices of Lubinski Management, the publicist in turn needing to run the request by Penelope Morath, who had been, since Calliope's suicide, cloistered in a convent outside Aix-en-Provence, forbidden contact with the outside world. Dr. Breve had been unable to fit him in the schedule for two months more—although it was dawning on the author that this delay may have been the mere whim of the factotum at the front desk. In any case, he was not about to let the matter of payment stand between him and the priceless insight he hoped awaited him behind the Japanese screen. *Veritas* over all, he reminded himself, taking a card from his wallet. What cost too high for the Truth?

"Andrew, it is a pleasure to meet you at last," came a voice from the hallway. Melodious yet sharply enunciated, her consonants crowded like a freeway pileup, Michaela Breve's words were a hatchet through the still air. "Has Jerome offered you coffee?"

The author straightened his tie and shook the doctor's hand. Though she stood a good six inches shorter than he, Michaela Breve radiated command of the room and the situation. She wore black pants and a maroon turtleneck sweater. Her face was round and shiny like a doll's face, her short hair the color of stainless steel. Delicate helices of gold hung from her ears, twirling when she moved her head.

"He has not." The author smiled his tolerance.

With a flicker of her eyes, she wiped the smile from the receptionist's face. "I was just about to." He pushed away from the computer. "Cream, honey? Sugar?"

"Black will be fine."

"Fine is right," Jerome muttered. "You don't know the half of it."

She led the author around the screen and down a short hallway, into an office which seemed a cross between an English study and an exotic dance club. Bookshelves lined the walls, an expansive mahogany desk sat before blinded windows, its surface uncluttered except for a telephone and blotter, a small stack of books. To the left of the door, a high-backed leather chair stood next to a small lamp table, upon which sat an antique clock, a notepad, and a beige coffee mug which read: "Ph.D-*lightful!*" In the center of this old-world charm, however, sat a plush chaise longue, jade upholstery on a cherrywood frame which inclined at one end (the end nearest the armchair), with intricate scrollwork under where the patient's head would lie. Set into the floor alongside this settee were what appeared to be halogen floodlights; when Dr. Breve flicked a switch, their thin, powerful beams were reflected in a mirror that covered much of the ceiling, so that the chaise longue appeared to float inside a chamber of light.

"Very impressive," said the author.

"The mirror is one of the most intriguing human inventions," said the psychologist. "Some believe that its appearance as a common household item was a watershed in the development of consciousness, that without it large-scale cultural changes such as the Protestant Reformation, the Enlightenment, the Industrial Revolution, might never have happened."

"Is that so?"

"Jacques Lacan believed the onset of subjectivity occurs when the child sees its reflection—that the splitting of *je* and *tu*, the thing I feel and the thing I see from outside, is a trauma which opens the space for language. Please—." She waved at the chaise longue, her unpainted lips parted slightly and smiling. She settled into the armchair and lifted her coffee mug, eyes flickering as she sipped, helices atwirl. Seeing nowhere else to sit, the author perched on the settee and faced her as best he could.

"And what if a child is raised with no mirrors?" He set his own mug on the floor. "Does he not develop subjectivity?"

"Ah, you're very astute."

"Well, I try—"

"The mirror is a metaphor, of course. We are constantly mirrored in the world around us—the mother's eye, the true *I* of the *be-hold-her*, the name we are given, the expression on another's face, our treatment by peers and teachers, the expectations placed upon us. All serve as powerful messages as to our identity."

"But a metaphor is not the same," said the author, warming to the repartee. "Lacan's child does not look into a metaphor, he looks into an actual mirror. You cannot touch a metaphor, cannot see—"

"Nor can you 'touch,' as you say, the subject. This, too, is a figure. A figure of speech."

"I see." The author nodded. "Then the subject is a fiction, merely a container for others' expectations, a repository for their various conceptions."

Dr. Breve pursed her lips. "That is a simplification. But no matter—"

"And in the case of someone like Calliope, the wildly mixed messages, the father's graphic exit, the images of herself on television, the mother shutting her away for years, the demands that she live up to the celebrity which spawned her, all these would not only have *influenced* her, you're saying, but in a way *constituted* her."

"Not precisely . . ."

"Not that there was some whole, pristine *Calliope* which was buffeted by fame and grief and the demands of the world, corrupted by her father's abandonment and her mother's stifling love and an obsession with poetry, but that fame and suicide and heedless possessive love actually created her, they were the reality into which her, her subjectivity was born, the what did you say *space for language* and so of course these were the obsessions of her poetry because poetry was the way she used language to communicate with the world."

"You might be more comfortable lying down," said the doctor.

"And so all of the flamboyant behavior, the promiscuity, or alleged promiscuity I should say, the suicidal gestures—these are not *symptoms* in the sense of some underlying disease that can be cured, but rather she behaved this way, she wrote what she wrote, because it was what was expected of her, the mirror of her world had shown her precisely that self. Her existence could hardly have taken another shape."

"I see you're interested in Lacanian theory. I'll be happy to recommend some reading for you at the end of the session."

"And so, for example, when Calliope meets the Beekeeper in the woods and he says, 'You're that famous poet,' he serves in that moment as a mirror, and the degree to which this corresponds with her inner sense of who she is is the degree to which she feels *known* by him, *known* and therefore *loved* . . ."

"You're speaking of the article in *Seventeen*. I'd just remind you—"

"And so yes, of course, her love for him is, in a sense, love for herself, and so it makes perfect sense that when she is most confused, at a crossroads, she comes to him because he *is* her, or at least he is the keeper of her identity—"

"Perhaps we should get started?"

"And to watch him waste away as he did, to watch him starving would have been, at some level to watch her *self* withering and eventually disappearing, when she went back to the Zen Center and he wasn't there, and the roshi said he might have given up Buddhism—how that must have sounded to her . . . and in the midst of all her confusion and the backlash from *Saturday Night Live,* all the pressure to perform and 'be who she was born to be,' in her mother's words, and out of all that noise she had chosen *him* to trust, *his* input to believe in—"

"Andrew—"

"And yes! Of course! She must have heard about the memoir, the execrable memoir—and this at the very time she needed him so, needed his wisdom and his . . . *mirror*, to find out that he had sold out utterly, and in the process invaded her world, invaded her lifelong refuge in literature—and moreover invaded it with that most sordid of literary products, a *memoir* . . . why, it must have seemed to her as though she'd never really known anything about him to begin with—"

"I'm sure you'll be more comfortable—"

"And if she didn't know anything about *him,* then of course she hadn't known anything about *herself.* Yes, I'm seeing it very clearly now, Dr. Breve, the whole last week, the reading at Arizona, everything. You've been immensely helpful already."

The doctor put down the coffee mug and folded her hands in her lap.

"I have no doubt whatsoever that it was worth the wait." The author beamed at her. "There's just so much to figure out about Calliope, so much is not as it would seem to the untrained eye. I'm quite sure you'll be the perfect cipher."

"I'm glad you feel our time together is valuable."

The two of them were silent for a moment, the one catching his breath, already mentally integrating the new material into the biography, the other watching him with no expression, steel eyes blinking at what seemed an abnormally slow rate. After a moment, she touched a switch on the underside of the lamp table and the overhead lights dimmed, stranding the author within the silvery veils reflecting from above and below.

"Now," said Dr. Breve, "what is it that you'd like to talk about?"

The shock had worn off slowly, if at all, the world emerging from the fever dream to find its hallucinatory vividness faded to quotidian drab, its sense of epochal urgency retreated into disappointment and clinical depression. Much as Calliope's stretches of frantic productivity were often followed by melancholy troughs, life after October 11, 200_, returned to the sameness that had marked the days before the poet had gripped the imagination. Op-ed pages and talk shows, tabloids and high-traffic blogs reverted to sex scandals, political arguments, speculations about celebrities' spiritual inclinations; magazine covers were once again graced by movie stars and supermodels who, for all their beauty, could not compete with the flawed, dimple-chinned urchin who had filled, for so short a time, the howling void in the American soul.*

It was within the insular and sensitive world of poetry that the blow was felt most acutely. Of the eight poets remaining in the UCI workshop now headed by James McMichael (who had been dragged out of retirement to replace L. Moreno), five were unable to complete the fall quarter. By January, three had withdrawn from the program, and one had transferred into the university's MA program in environmental studies, leading to questions about the future of one of the country's most prestigious workshops. Commercially, too, poetry went into a tailspin: Although in the weeks after Cabrillo Point sales for poets from Sappho to Sexton soared, by early the next year sales had returned to pre-Calliope—which is to say, minuscule—levels. Snow Lion raced through nineteen additional printings of *(I)CBM* over the next six months, but the financial windfall was offset by the reported $2.7 million advance the Buddhist press had ponied up for the Beekeeper's memoir—which, come summer, was still unfinished, untitled, and with no set publication date.

Not everyone could move on so quickly as the lamas. While the culture industry—what Taryn Glacé refers to as the "poexploitation machine"—is driven, by nature, to find the Next Big Thing, poets and academics are given to commemoration, analysis, nostalgia. While publishers and starmakers scoured art academies and MFA programs and the spoken-word circuit,[†] literary journals churned out tributes and eulogies,

---

*Exceptions prove the rule: *Star*'s November 200_ travesty, "Poet Abducted by Aliens: Calliope's Extraterrestrial DNA Experiments," alleging that an army of Brandt clones was being manufactured in Roswell, New Mexico; and *American Eye*'s grainy photos of a cabin cruiser in choppy seas, two crewmen pulling a nude figure from the water, with the unfathomable headline, "Calliope's Tempest in a Teapot."

[†]E.g., Copper Canyon Press reportedly held a weekend of "auditions" at the University of Iowa, interviewing and screen-testing poets in the Writers Workshop.

reprinted old interviews and file photos, and launched contests under Calliope's name. The University of Memphis's psychiatric quarterly, *Death Studies,* devoted its entire spring issue to the poet's demise, including a twenty-four-page "roundtable" with Dr. Breve and three experts in the field. Memorial readings were held in libraries and on college campuses, a network of "meet-ups" sprang up on the Internet. At the time of this writing, a Google search for "calliope bird morath poetry death" yielded about 1,270,000 hits.

Glacé spends a chapter of *Karl. Che. Kaliope.* discussing the relationship between death and capitalism, a morbid synergy with ample precedent in Calliope's family history. Glacé proposes a simple formula: The distance between celebrity and fan corresponds to the energy (and capital) the consumer is willing to expend to possess or "own" that celebrity. In stardom, as in love, in other words, we reach out most desperately for that which recedes from us. Death here figures as the ultimate distance—and *self-inflicted* death precipitously tilts the slope of the graph until the y-coordinate (devotion, money, what-have-you) begins to approach something like infinity. Suicide, according to Glacé, is thus read by the public as a supreme act of withdrawal—the throwing of a gauntlet, the nonpareil of provocation.

Glacé recounts the story of *TC,* the second full-length Terrible Children album, released six weeks after Brandt Morath's death. For a year, Brandt had fought bitterly with the record label over the new material, much of which was a departure and maturation from the raw anarchy of *The Hanged Man* and *The Fisher King.* Brian Eno had replaced Steve Albini as producer, giving the album's eleven tracks* a more layered, multi-instrumental feel, and bringing Brandt's vocals forward in the mix so his lyrics could be more easily discerned. The label had balked, demanding a complete reengineering and the exclusion of the melancholy bassoon-driven ballad, "Acid Rain"; Brandt refused, threatening to exercise an option to buy back the masters and release the album at his own expense. When *TC* came out, unchanged, after the suicide, the ensuing hysteria forced the

---

*Plus two hidden tracks, one of which, "Exeunt," was comprised of nine minutes of freeway noise, ending with the sound of one car passing at high speed, the squeal of tires as its brakes locked.

label to hold an online lottery for copies while they pressed millions more; after a week, these "first editions" were selling on eBay for $1,200, and UPS refused to deliver the new copies to record stores after several of their drivers were assaulted. And, while "Take My Life, Please!," the most caustic punk song on *TC,* was the first single promoted by the label, it was "Acid Rain," with its haunting instrumentation and premonitory chorus,* which became the album's breakaway hit and held the No. 1 chart slot for thirty weeks.

Would *TC* have been such a success if Brandt's death had not intervened, or would the band's fans have felt alienated by the new songs' introversion and subtlety? Glacé's thesis is that it is not only impossible to say, but that the question itself is nonsensical. Death, she maintains,

> is the ideal and the *telos* of capitalism, and the forces of poexploitation have always sought to control its commodity value. *TC* showed that the obstacles to such control are ethical, not practical, a lesson which was not lost on Calliope. We cannot know what the record's true value would have been if Brandt had lived, nor do we care. As Engels liked to say, "If my aunt had *hoden* [testicles], she'd be my uncle." (615)

In Calliope's case, however, there was no posthumous masterpiece to slake the world's thirst; the culture industry had to look elsewhere for the commercial potential of her death. Two examples should illustrate the scope of their efforts. The first is the "Poet's Death Mask," introduced by Inconnue Industries of Dana Point, California. The mask, made of light, laminated plaster, resembled Calliope's face to an uncanny degree, though with none of her flaws or asymmetries, giving her the enigmatically peaceful expression of a Greek sculpture. Thanks to a clever cross-marketing campaign with Urban Decay cosmetics, the mask quickly caught on with American teenagers and was soon all but ubiquitous in high school corridors, shopping malls, and skate parks.

But what began as an innocent fad soon led to strife, as the Death Mask was adopted first by the so-called Lady Crips, the female contingent of one

---

*"Nothing can forgive me / Leave me here, outlive me / Anyone can take away my pain . . ."

of Los Angeles's deadliest street gangs, who painted the masks blue and wore them to parties and clubs and, according to police reports, a rash of convenience-store robberies. Not to be outdone, their rival gang, the Ruby Reds, donned red masks, which led to a number of violent skirmishes that left a sixteen-year-old Inglewood girl paralyzed from the waist down. High schools in Southern California and then nationwide implemented zero-tolerance policies for the Death Masks, which led, predictably, to a spike in sales and to student protests. In September, Amanda Breen, a seventeen-year-old National Merit Scholar, class valedictorian, and varsity volley-baller, staged a march on Northern Highlands Regional High School in Allendale, New Jersey; news coverage captured eerie images of the faculty standing sternly behind a row of locked glass doors while masked students gathered on the sidewalk, waiting to be allowed into school.*

More disturbing is the story of Shaylene Hicks, whose meteoric rise both paralleled and parodied Calliope's. Hailed as a "poetic diamond in the rough," Hicks was a virtual unknown until May of 200_, when her book, *Wet,* was brought out to great fanfare. Bret Easton Ellis provided a much-quoted blurb, which announced the twenty-two-year-old Hicks as the quin-tessential poet of her generation: "Here, in 41 burnished gems, is America: its vulnerability, its depravity, its unspoiled innocence." According to press materials provided by the International Creative Management agency, Hicks had been raised in the remote hills of Kentucky with no electricity, no indoor plumbing, and no mother. Her father, a coal miner and Viet-nam veteran, had refused to send the girl to school, leaving her in the care of seven brothers, six of whom sexually abused her ("The Seventh, too Bashful/Content with midnight masturbation/Set to the soundtrack of my tears"†); at sixteen she left home and hitchhiked as far as Charlottesville, Virginia, where she lived on the streets and practiced survival sex, stashing her hastily scrawled poems in a bus-station locker until she was discovered by the poet Charles Wright. From there, her trajectory was a familiar one: a national reading tour marked by huge crowds and the poet's unpre-dictable tantrums, wrecked hotel rooms, New York parties attended by the

---

*At present, *Breen v. Board of Education* is before the U.S. Third Circuit Court of Appeals.
†From "Snow White in Appalachia."

local literati, heated debate about the quality of the poems, and speculation as to the nature of Hicks's relationship with the much older Wright.

Hicks was blond and lanky, with startled eyes and a fondness for tank tops and cutoff shorts; a photograph on the cover of *Maxim*, for which she posed in a barn, lying across a pile of blankets, chewing on a stalk of hay, seemed to make the essential point: Here was a poet with no inconvenient scruples about mingling art and sex, a beauty with no blemishes to bedevil a marketing campaign. Rather than wrestling with family ghosts, she was a self-made orphan; rather than hiding in academia's cloister, she was a child of the streets, a heroine of the underclass. She was a dream come true for the post-Cabrillo world: the anti-Calliope.

But the culture industry's giddy celebration was to be short-lived. While Hicks was filming a video with the pop band No Doubt, who had set her poem "Coal Miner's Fodder" to music, a disgruntled intern at ICM leaked internal documents identifying Hicks as a thirty-one-year-old actress from Ventura, and laying out the meticulous strategy—including the ghostwriting of her poems—by which her career had been created and promoted. Charles Wright, under fire at the University of Virginia, denied any knowledge of the hoax, and in an open letter published in the *Los Angeles Times* deplored Hollywood's "cynical attempt to colonize the last frontier of innocence in Western civilization."* Hicks's own denials were as unconvincing as would be expected from an actress who suddenly finds that her script is missing pages; after a few months of guest spots on *Deal or No Deal* and *The Howard Stern Show*, the erstwhile ingénue disappeared from the public eye, reportedly settling down to write "her side of the story."

An unsettling episode, certainly. But is art really "the last frontier of innocence"? Does art aspire, in its highest forms, to a purity removed from the sordid workings of the world? Certainly the Greeks believed otherwise— why should the poets be ejected from the Republic if not for their inherent corruption, the threat of its contagion? Nathaniel Hawthorne, a fierce critic of New England puritanism, declared that the purpose of art was to explore "the truth of the human heart"—hardly the territory for a poetry that

---

*August 5, 200_.

functions at Wright's cool remove. This would seem to be the conundrum for artists of all eras: the artist must hold herself outside the mainstream of human congress and commerce, her art is valued based on its purity of motive, its unbiased honesty—and yet we demand that art faithfully represent its subject, that it know the world more intimately than the world knows itself. How can the poet keep her hands clean, when her calling demands she immerse herself in something as impure, as blind and biased and ultimately untrustworthy, as "the human heart"?

"The world asks of us a certain *aplomo,* a kind of auto-mesmerism, as though we were not also human beings, as though we did not need to eat and sleep and shit like human beings," said Lorenzo Moreno, speaking with the author by telephone from his family's sheep ranch outside Córdoba, Argentina. "People don't want to see their poets in the *supermercado* or on the next treadmill at the how-you-say, fitness center, they don't want to think about the poet balancing his checkbook or jerking off or God forbid falling in love. Human but not human—I ask you, is this something that can be demanded of a person? That he leave his natural functions and desires in a small box outside the vault of poetry like it is a goddamned coat check?"

Their conversation took place in August 200_, ten months after Calliope's suicide. Moreno, still seething over the University of California's treatment of him, claimed not to be following developments in American poetry; when the author told him of Shaylene Hicks's rise and devastating fall, he was both amused and unsurprised, recalling that in the course of his career he had encountered any number of "little girls with their hot pants and their quote-unquote *free verse,* for whom the poetry is only a means to capturing the virile, experienced poet of their fantasies."

"I think you're somewhat missing the point," the author interjected, attempting to steer him back to a discussion of the poet's cultural position. "My point is that it might not be quite so easy to draw the line between art and commerce, between innocence and experience. It's a rather complicated issue to determine who *is* a poet, who embodies the qualities necessary to *be* a poet, and who does not. If one is to judge the poetry on its formal merit, then what does it *matter* how the poet lives her life? Isn't it just as likely, hypothetically speaking, that someone like Shaylene Hicks could produce immortal poetry as someone like Calliope, regardless of—"

"There can be no question whatsoever!" shouted Moreno. "To compare Calliope to this, to this *prostituta* you are telling me is an insult to poets everywhere." Behind his voice, through the intercontinental static, the author could make out the sounds of bucolic life—sheep bleating and antipodal birds singing, the silver thread of a woman's voice calling, "*Loreeeen-zo! Loreeeen-zo!*" like the velvet tug of memory.

"Let me tell you, a poet knows a poet, *Señor*. I have seen many many students who wished to be poets, who believed that the key to being a poet lay only in the writing of the lines, as though the key to being a great *futbolista* is to kick a ball between two sticks. No, one must learn to *be* a poet, not simply to do what poets do. One must see the world as a poet sees it, to move through the world as a poet moves—more deeply, more consciously, always tuned to the language of our experience, and yet untouched by the world, throwing it off with a flash like a salmon sheds glimmers of water as it leaps—"

"Yes, but this is precisely my point. Is it reasonable to expect—"

"You are not listening to me. Poetry is not a career choice. It is not something someone decides. It is something which happens to the poet, which is born with them and incubates in their soul until the day it can no longer be contained and then bursts from them and into the world—part of them, but more than them. They can choose to ignore this gift, but always it will haunt them, itching them like a how-you-say, phantom limb.

"You would not understand this," he went on. "You wake up in your comfortable bed each day, with your comfortable family and your comfortable life, and you say, 'Well, I would like to write a book about someone. Perhaps this Calliope, who seems interesting and like a good,' how-you-say, 'market niche,' and so you spend a few hours reading about her or talking to the people who loved her and write down what you have heard. You are a secretary, *Señor*. At the end of the day, you come home and take off your hat and kiss your wife and you have changed nothing in this world, no?"

For a moment there was no sound but the rattle of cars outside the author's house, the rustle of livestock on a Córdoba hillside. The author, already several hundred pages into the biography, was by now used to the unpredictable give-and-take of an interview, well schooled in the need to give the subject free rein, to let the conversation go where it may, and to wait for the nugget of Truth to wink from the rushing current. But he was always taken aback by the emotion with which Calliope's friends and loved ones spoke of her. It was indeed as though there were something inside them, some pulsating force that could not be controlled and only temporarily contained; it was this force he wished to know firsthand, this fever he hoped to understand.

"You must miss her terribly," he said to L. Moreno.

The sigh was audible through a spate of bleating. "When Calliope wrote her poems, it was beautiful to see. She was taken up like Leda in the beak of inspiration. She glowed with the poetry. All day, all night, writing the poems, even driving in her car or during my workshop: always writing. The other students of course found this to be quote-unquote *distracting*. But their own work was not worth a damn.

"This is poetry, my friend. When everything else dulls next to the shine of the language. She could not function. She did not bathe. Her trailer was so disorderly, dirty dishes and laundry and dead bees, a smell I would not want to describe. At these times a person could be in the same room, but it is as if one does not exist. She is so consumed, she will stop in the middle of whatever she is doing with this person—even if it is something that should never be stopped in the middle—and get up to change a line break. And this person, maybe who feels he has done so much for her, he can be angry and say things he does not mean, things he may never have the opportunity to take back."

The author noticed, as though in a trance, that the tape in his microcassette recorder had run out. But he was unconcerned: the artist's words rang like grace notes, engraving themselves in his mind.

"But this, of course, is what art does to you," said Moreno, two continents of lonely static whispering over the line. "First it destroys your life. And then it destroys everyone else's life."

Connor Feingold was seventeen years old when he was expelled from Michigan's prestigious Interlochen Arts Academy, where he had spent two years studying strings and jazz theory. Johann Walthausen remembers the young Connor as "deliciously talented, a prodigy in the nineteenth-century style," and twenty-five years later still expresses regret that Interlochen had been unable to properly channel the young man's energy.

"You must understand—and this is what we told his poor mother—the school was simply not ready to accept a Sex Pistols medley for harp as a thesis," recalls the former headmaster. "We could not overlook extensive lipstick damage to a 1911 Steinway concert grand. And when he played his cello solo in the Winter Concert stark naked except for a tube sock over his . . . well, I'm afraid he quite sealed his fate."

Feingold came home to Ocean Beach and took a job at Cow Records, which was where he would meet Brandt Morath a year later, when the starving runaway would come to the store's back entrance and plead with Feingold to let him sleep in the storeroom.

"We'd hang out in back after closing and I'd buy him a burrito and we'd go through some of the records together and we'd be like, 'Man . . . !'" Feingold recalled in a 199_ interview.

> There was so much great shit just rotting in the bins, shit *no one* knew—the Vaselines, the Slits, Saccharine Trust, the Dragons, Ass Fixation. But Brandt knew all of it. He ate it up. He had this piece-of-shit Peavey guitar, one pickup was blown and it couldn't hold a tune for shit, and one night I walked out into the alley to take a piss and when I came back in he had this killer progression going, just singing, "Woke up in your satin sheets / Didn't know my name / Mirrored stranger staring back / Heaven's not the same," and I was all, "No shit, man!" I sat down and picked out a harmony and twenty minutes later, *boom*, "Shave Me, Shrieve Me."*

Within a few short years, the Glummer Twins, as they came to be known, would be writing songs in five-star hotel suites and limousines, recording in the sumptuous Manhattan Beach studios of NorthStar Records, in the basement of the Rancho Santa Fe mansion, or in the studio-cum-yoga loft on the top floor of Feingold's Malibu A-frame. By all ac-

---

*Andrew Altschul, "Ocean Beach: Not Just for Dimebags Anymore," SLAM, May 4, 199_.

counts, Connor was more than a close friend—best man at Brandt's wedding, he was at the wheel of the creaky Nissan when it collided with a pickup truck full of day laborers outside Ensenada, in Baja California, on the way to the honeymoon villa; it was Connor's well-intentioned efforts to compensate the injured parties that led to the trouble with the Mexican government and the lawsuit against the band and NorthStar. When Brandt disappeared for two days during the 199_ Japanimosity tour, it was Connor who somehow tracked him to Hiroshima; in Paris, on the World Tour, he coaxed Brandt off an eighth-story window ledge by putting on a video of *Beavis and Butthead*. Marriage counselor, public conscience, godfather to Calliope, Connor's steadfastness was the glue that held Terrible Children, and Brandt, together.*

But with Brandt's death, Connor, too, came apart. The photograph of the devastated bassist carrying the swooning four-year-old Calliope up the stairs from the scene of the suicide remains one of the iconic images of that morning. After the terse press conference announcing the band's breakup ("Sine qua non," he muttered, and took no questions), Connor retreated to Malibu and accumulated a small cache of firearms to discourage paparazzi. He had food and supplies delivered monthly, he conducted all business—including the fierce legal battle over the box set—through proxies. If he wrote or recorded any music over the next decade and a half, it never made it to public audition; he devoted his energy to Ashtanga yoga, according to one source at NorthStar practicing up to six hours a day in the A-frame's now-empty loft with a view of the ocean.

It was Brandt's daughter who coaxed Connor back to the world. Much has been speculated about his relationship with the troubled teenager, much of which this author considers to be beneath contempt or

---

*That Feingold's relations with the press were so warm perhaps explains why so little has been written about the "intervention" rumored to have taken place at the Days Inn Airporter on March 31, 199_. Conspiracists including Edwin Decker have suggested that Calliope's poem "310" refers to the room number in which Connor, Billy Martinez, and Talia Z confronted Brandt about his drug use; whereas scholars tend to see "310" as referring to the area code for Malibu. Either explanation raises complicated questions about how to interpret a line like "Moving lights pass over me / Firstborn, lambsblood, ecstasy / My friend, you know what's best for me."

comment.* What is inarguable, however, is that their friendship returned some measure of life to her father's best friend, that the infusion of energy and ambition she represented lay behind his reconciliation with Penny, as well as his musical resurrection as the driving force behind the bestselling *12-Bar for Darfur* benefit compilation. He gave a handful of interviews and began offering yoga instruction in his home to local children. The Connor who appeared with Billy Martinez and XXX for a surprise reunion and performance at the 200_ Grammy Awards was much changed: His thick beard and colorful robes, his serene expression as he powered through the instrumental medley of Terrible Children songs, came as a shock to fans. But he was alive, his thundering bass chops unspoiled by time, his presence testifying to the resilience of art and hope he had imbibed at Calliope's fountain.

All of that came to an end after the Arizona Café. Like an endangered sea turtle that has braved the shore in search of food and a mate, only to find a burning village, crazed natives engaged in wanton slaughter, the flipped, helpless bodies of its turtle brethren littering the beach like flung coffee saucers, Feingold beat a hasty retreat, scuttling plans for *Darfur II* and shrouding himself once more in the robes of solitude. After a brief period of renewed media fascination, during which the rumors of his sexual involvement with Calliope were exhaustively revisited[†] and a group of zealots tried to break into his home, claiming he had abducted the poet and was keeping her drugged in a basement "dungeon," the air around the A-frame once again grew silent.

The approach to Feingold's property is an unmarked and perilously pitted track that branches off State Road N9, shadowing the high ridge which marks the boundary of the Santa Monica Mountains National

*For his insinuation that "[t]he relationship constituted, for each, a powerful consummation with the only true love of their lives: Brandt," Harminder Singh deserves to lose every nickel of the $7 million for which Lubinski Management is suing him. What kind of black heart is required to malign the wounded? What sadism or sense of gnawing inadequacy makes a writer take the innocent for a target? From one writer to another: Living people figure everywhere in this story, Harminder, and some things are more important than revelations about poets. Take care that in divining their souls you do not sell your own!

[†]With no less a spectacle than Sandra Gilbert's essay for *Ms.* (January 200_), which essentially rehashed the theories about Calliope's "aural fixation" first elaborated in *Ashes, Ashes.*

Recreation Area. As you climb through a dense wood of pine and euca-lyptus, the flat spring sky seems to lower upon you, driving away all thoughts of vulgar Los Angeles and the interminable freeway. A solitary hawk's lazy circle passes with regularity through your field of vision. After a time, out the driver's-side window, the forest thins to reveal the ocean, afternoon sunlight dancing across its distant texture. It is a place of true serenity, a perfect counterpoint to the ferocity of Terrible Children. Ghosts tread these paths in somber contemplation, their footsteps cushioned by history's pine needles.

Emerging at last into the wide clearing, the author was momentarily blinded by the sun's reflection in the A-frame's windows. He parked in a graveled circle, the hub of which was a large bronze Buddha sitting in a meditative pose, surrounded by clutches of violets. The house stood silent as a temple, an angular thrust of wood and glass that blended into the trees and the rocky ridge above; shading his eyes, the author was startled to see a figure in the upstairs window, indistinct behind the mirror image of ocean and woods. Such was the trick of the light that the reflected pine trees appeared as the dark bars of a prison cell behind which Connor stood motionless.

The author quickly gathered his materials and got out of the car, wav-ing at the figure in the window. But the window was now empty. He stood in the driveway, surrounded by silent woods, waiting for some sign of wel-come from a man whose career he had helped to launch. He turned to the Buddha and admired the smooth dignity of its face, the fine detail of its body, its hands cupped in its lap. He tried to replicate the figure's serenity, to steel himself for a difficult interview. The lonely man in the window was no predator, he told himself. The sad figure who had crouched on the floor of the Arizona Café was incapable of cruelty. Eccentric though Con-nor may have become, lost in his obsessions, proper due must be given to the power of grief. Anyone who has not stood next to tragedy, not served as its witness and attendant, cannot begin to fathom the ways in which it seeps into the soul and festers, emerging at its leisure and only in disguise. Though the world may have judged Connor harshly, the author admired his strength, his determination to channel pain into productivity, when the most enticing thing would be to shrivel up in despair.

"You can't read, motherfucker? You think this is fucking Yosemite?"
Connor stood in the doorway with a large-caliber rifle. "Get back in your
fucking car and get the fuck out of here." The erstwhile rockstar stood on
the topmost of three stone steps, one eye hidden by the rifle's sight. Two
children stood with him, a boy and a girl of nine or ten, each clutching a
corner of his multicolored robe.

"Connor, hello," the author said, raising his hands in front of him and
taking a step toward the house.

"Are you fucking nuts?" Connor yelled, jerking the barrel of the rifle
to indicate the author's car. "I told you to get out of here!"

"I'm sorry to intrude. Were you busy?" The author dropped his hands
to his side. "I would have called, but . . ."

"No phone here."

"Precisely," said the author, modulating his voice into a soothing tone.
"Surely you remember me?" he said. "The interview in '8_? The OB 'Orgy
Beach' fête? The Casbah?"

Connor did not lower the rifle, but raised his chin slightly to get a
closer look. The children drew closer to his side. The key here, of course,
was to remind him of their past working relationship, the bygone days
when "Kidsophrenia" afflicted only a ten-by-ten-foot practice studio in El
Cajon, and a hungry young journalist came to interview the man who had
thrown up on his desk.

"I'm sure you recall the following," smiled the author. "'Behind the
rough terror of Morath's anguish rise Connor Feingold's ghostly har-
monies, trembling and vulnerable, a filthy Phoenix struggling from the
ashes.'"* The rifleman squinted but did not lower his weapon. "Does the
word *SLAM* ring a bell?"

"You're a fucking reporter?" Connor once again lowered his eye to the
rifle sight.

The author pursed his lips and glanced at the Buddha. "Not anymore."

Hands at his sides, the author explained that he had recently redirected
his literary energies to a project of much greater scope than mere rock
journalism, a project for which the bassist's insights would be virtually

---

*Op. cit.

priceless. Connor whispered something to the children, who glared briefly at the author and disappeared inside.

"I ought to shoot you in the ass right now," Connor said.

The author laughed, shading his eyes and peering up at the majestic house, the towering trees and the ridge above. "She did love such places, didn't she?"

Connor squinted. "Who?"

"Such bombast in her work, and yet the places we truly come to know her have this quality of stillness. I suppose one might think of it in terms of *yin* and *yang* or somesuch. But I can't help thinking how, well, out of place she would seem to me here."

"Are you here for an autograph or something?" Connor lowered the rifle and stood it inside the door. From a table in the foyer he took a band photo and offered it to the author. "You people have no fucking shame."

"I'm here to talk about Calliope."

This, at least, seemed to have some effect. Connor stood for a moment with his jaw moving, the sinews of his forearms twitching.

"Without your perspective, I will have no biography worth the paper it's printed on. I understand it's an immensely painful topic. I know the wound is still open. But I ask you to think, for a moment, what it means to the world. Ask yourself: Can you grapple with your grief for long enough to impart it to others who loved her? Though every fiber of your being says it's too soon—isn't it precisely *now* that your thoughts are the most pure, your emotions most powerful?"

Connor leaned against the doorframe and crossed his arms.

"You owe it to the world, Connor," said the author. "You owe it to Calliope."

At this he snorted. "You don't know what the hell you're talking about. What makes you think I'd talk to you about her? Why would I talk to anyone, after the things they've written about me. That I *raped* her? That her father and me were like some kind of Satanists that sacrificed her as a baby?"

"Shameful," the author agreed.

"What's the point of talking? You'll just write whatever you want to write, whatever will sell."

"I want to write the Truth."

"Ha! Which truth is that?"

"There's only one," said the author. "That's why I'm here."

Connor gaped at the author as though the latter were a ghoul or hallucination. Frowning, he sat on the stone steps and let the afternoon sun dapple over him; the author was surprised to note the considerable linings and loosenings of age discernible in his features, a perceptible downturn of the mouth, silver veining through his thick reddish beard. But what was most noticeable to someone who had known him in his youth, who had seen him strut across the stage in the throes of his art, was that the brightness in his hazel eyes had decreased to a mute twinkle. As though sadness had become the surface of his life, the ferocious joy of an earlier era driven far underground.

"Look, uh . . ."

"Andrew."

"You're supposed to arrange this kind of shit. You can't just come barging in up here. Even if I wanted to talk to you, how am I supposed to know who you are?"

The author explained that he was, indeed, a serious writer, that he was in the midst of complex negotiations with Lubinski Management to secure authorization for the biography. He added that he had already spoken to Moreno and the roshi. "This is not some fly-by-night project," he assured him. "This is my life."

Connor, hands on his knees, debated with himself. "What's it called, the book?" he said after a moment.

The author sat next to him on the stoop. "I'm toying with *Dazed and Bemused: The Troubled Life of Calliope Bird Morath*. What do you think?"

Connor sucked his teeth. "It's not more Kama Sutra crap, is it?"

"You're referring to the Beekeeper's memoir," said the author.

"Did you read those excerpts in *Vanity Fair*?"

"Awful. Pure trash. Surprising, too, considering how intelligent he's said to be."

A hummingbird hovered in front of the Buddha's face. It buzzed there a moment, green and red contrasting bronze, made a series of feints at the unforgiving metal, and zoomed away. "It must be very difficult reading for you," the author said. Feeling the musician stiffen at his side, he tried a different approach. "Certainly, to someone like me, it's rather shocking to read some of the more, well, explicit material. Difficult to reconcile the, shall we say, *outré* proclivities he ascribes to her with the poet of *(I)CBM*."

"Difficult to believe they pulled that shit off in a six-by-eight monk's cell," Connor grumbled.

"You don't believe it then? You think he made these things up? Hard to imagine Rhoda would sit still for it—especially since she figures so, er, viscerally into the scene in the *zendo* . . ."

At this Connor turned to the author. "Rhoda? You think Rhoda cares whether something's true or not? Jesus Christ, for all we know she wrote it for him!"

The author considered this. "Scambiguity," he said. "Yes, of course." He picked up a pebble and tossed it lightly at the bronze statue.

"See, that's what's so fucked-up about what you're doing, about you coming here. You think there's some *truth* I can tell you, something real or objective or whatever, and when I tell it to you you'll know it for what it is. But man, they'll just be words leaving my mouth. Words don't mean shit. I could tell you she and Penny and I used to get it on in Brandt's studio, I could tell you she was a virgin, I could tell you she was a hermaphrodite, or she wasn't really Brandt's daughter—how are you going to know?

"And check it out—" He turned to the author with a smile that seemed almost brutal. "Even if it's true, and even if you believe me and print it, how's it going to compete with the other truths out there? There'll always be someone who believes something else. Who are you that anyone is going to place a higher value on what you say than on what someone else says, or what anyone feels like imagining?"

"Well, that's the point of the authorization—"

"You don't get it, do you? Nothing's true. It's all true. It doesn't matter! This *is* Calliope now—whatever the Beekeeper guy says about her, what you say about her, what fucking Moreno or Rhoda says. It's all the 'truth' because it's lodged itself in people's opinions of her, their whole understanding of her. That's all that matters—not what kind of toothpaste she used or what her favorite color was. Nobody cares about that shit. They want stories. They want to construct a fantasy and call it Calliope. The actual person just provided the vessel for them to pour it into. That's who Calliope *is* now—she's the name all these stories are attached to. She's where they fit.

"It was the same shit with her father." He shook his head. "Enough to make anyone want to get as far away from it as they could."

"You mean suicide."

Connor leaned back and closed his eyes against the glare. "Call it whatever you want."

The sun was now visible as a white smear through the trees as it spread against the horizon, igniting the ocean in blood and quicksilver. The author stood and trod a circle in the gravel, pausing to run his fingertips over the Buddha's surface. At his feet the brilliant violets shivered in a late breeze.

"Well, in any case, I do believe in the Truth, and I believe it's a writer's responsibility to discover that Truth and represent it in as forthright and faithful a way possible. It's why I'm here, Connor, and I should think Calliope would want it that way. I should think *you* would want it that way."

Connor nodded. "It doesn't matter what I want. And it doesn't matter what *you* want."

"I disagree."

They were silent, the one watching the other in the onrush of dusk. For the first time, the author could hear the ocean, its rhythmic moan and gasp—at this distance more a suggestion, taken on faith, than a sound.

"Sometimes I try to remember things," Connor said. "I mean, I have photos and news clippings and titanium records and all that. But sometimes I close my eyes and try to pretend I'm there—at the first gig at the Arizona, at Brandt's wedding, at Calliope's birth, Brandt's . . ." Still staring through the woods, the author heard Connor rise from the steps. "I picture it down to every detail, I try to see everything, so I know I was *really* there, you know? So I can be sure it wasn't something I saw in a video or a dream, or something I made up. Because the thing is, we can't be sure, you know? Our brains treat it all the same way—just a set of details and impressions and feelings. There's no, like, filing system that separates what's real from what we imagine."

"No," the author heard himself whisper.

"We just move through this stuff. It ought to change us somehow, inscribe itself in our bodies. But it doesn't. You can think about it all you want. You can write it all down. But that won't change the fact that it's gone."

Now Connor came and stood next to the author. The latter did not turn, only stood in the presence of that tall shadow as the Malibu night willed itself into being.

"So there's no way I can give it to you, you understand? I can't even have these things for myself."

"What you're describing is a desolation," the author said. "Knowing is my business. It's what a biographer *does*."

"I empathize, man." Behind them, the house's silence was funereal. "You were caught up in something, just like we all were. Something much bigger than you. It changed you, rewired you. And then one day it vanished. Now you can't figure out how to wire yourself back."

The author felt but did not meet Connor's stare, only turned to examine once again the Buddha's serene face, in the last cooling of sunset.

"But nobody else can ever know that," said Connor. "Not like you do."

"No."

"It doesn't matter how many ink marks you put on a page. You can't make it real. I mean, seriously—how will you even know that you're here, now, talking to me?"

At this the author faced Connor and crossed his arms. "I thought that we were having a serious discussion."

"I don't mean *this* you," Connor said. "I'm talking to the you who's going to go home and transcribe this tonight, the you who's going to write it into your book and describe the scene, maybe add in a couple of discreet details you can't quite remember—like what kind of flowers are planted in my driveway, whether I'm barefoot or wearing sandals*—smooth out the dialogue so we both sound like intelligent human beings. And by the time you're done, *this* will be gone, and all you'll have is *that*. *That* will become your reality. It will supplant this real moment in every way."

---

*He was barefoot.

From the window above, two shadowed faces were watching. The author clenched his fists and squeezed his eyes shut, willing the moment to enter him somehow, to impress itself upon him like a handprint in wet concrete. He thought if even the smallest stone from the driveway could stay with him permanently—not in its physical body but in its *presence*, its *Truth*—it would validate his entire project.

"I'm talking to your readers." Connor kept on, his voice low as the breath of the forest. "How can they be sure this scene really happened? How do they know you were really here?" The lanky musician placed his hands on the author's shoulders. "How do they know I even existed?"

The clearing was dark. There was nothing more for the author to gain, and so he thanked Connor and dug for his car keys, already imagining the long ride back, the surreal beauty of the coast road, the abrupt affront of Los Angeles. The difficult task of incorporating the interview into the biography was still a ways off; he did not feel he had gained any useful insight or information, did not feel that his subject had been illuminated by the effort. And yet to ignore the conversation, to excise the event from the record, would be, in a way, to endorse Connor's sickening proposition. The paradox was already clear: Only by including this inane discussion of the truthlessness of memory and text could the author's text achieve something like truth.

"Connor?" the author said, back in the car. "Could I, in fact, have that photograph? It's for my son."

With a sigh, Connor retrieved the photograph—an ancient publicity shot, the four comrades leaning against the rail of the OB fishing pier, hair damp from sea spray, all except one looking into the camera.

"Do you want me to sign it? What's his name?"

The author told him, ignoring the bassist's smirk. "He's really quite a fan. He and a few of his more highly functioning chums have put a band together." The author cleared his throat. "If I'm not mistaken, all they play are versions of your songs."

"A cover band," Connor nodded. "Tell him we're honored."

"It's really quite unlistenable," the author confided.

Connor capped the pen and handed the photograph to the author. "You know better than that."

"Indeed," the author muttered a moment later. But by then the clearing was empty. As he sat in the driveway, both hands on the steering wheel, the lights on the top floor came on and out of the corner of his eye the author saw three backlit figures staring down at him. When he turned to look at them, they were gone.

A more exhaustive catalog of the rumors, myths, inventions, exegeses, and dreams that attended Calliope's suicide will surely be compiled, perhaps by an expert in such affairs as Skip Cárdenas, whose 200_ series for the *Los Angeles Times* did so much to clarify Brandt's status in the cultural memory. Theories were legion, narratives proffered from the sublime (the poet achieved enlightenment at the base of the lighthouse, her leap into the sea not a suicide but an embrace of what Buddhists call "nirvana") to the ridiculous (the poet was several months pregnant and desperate, unsure whether Connor, Moreno, or Ben Affleck was the father). Still more audacious accounts clashed factually with what the author knew, firsthand, to be the truth—e.g., the story told to *60 Minutes II* by former soundman Danny Grier, who claimed Calliope had shot herself at the Arizona Café after receiving a letter from her father, and that Rhoda and Gary North had covered it up and paid exorbitant hush money to all in attendance.*

Other scenarios involved foul play: Calliope murdered by drug dealers to whom she—or her father—owed great sums; an argument-gone-wrong with XXX over the latter's attempts to license "Dirtnap" for use in a laundry-detergent commercial; violent death at the hands of Moreno or *Saturday Night Live* writer Tina Fey or the poet's own mother; in every case, the Arizona reading dismissed as fiction or imposture.

And then there were the sad souls who denied her death entirely, fed by the fact that there had been no body and no funeral—more echoes of

---

*Grier was paid $90,000 by CBS, and provided documents and photographs to prove his claims. After Lubinski Management threatened to sue, CBS retracted the story, admitting that the documents could not be verified. Of course, the media frenzy over CBS's embarrassment served only to keep the story alive, conspiracists now claiming that the retraction was but another piece of the cover-up. The whole episode ended tragically: A year later, Grier apparently went on a methamphetamine binge with his ill-gotten gains and was found dead in a room at the Joshua Tree Inn in Twentynine Palms, California.

Brandt. Supernatural intervention was a pervasive theme: claims of alien abduction, a cover story in the *Astral Gazette* theorizing that Calliope had been rescued from watery death by "walk-in spirits," a clairvoyant in Iowa City who claimed that the spirit of poet John Berryman had dissuaded Calliope from the fateful leap. Imam Imad al Din al-Rashid told *Wahhabi Weekly* that the prophet Muhammed had wrestled with Calliope on the promontory until she submitted to Allah. Terrestrial narratives included abduction by the CIA and imprisonment at Guantánamo Bay, Cuba, all as a consequence of "Suicide Bomber"; a change of identity, courtesy of the Federal Witness Protection Program, in exchange for testimony against Gary North for racketeering; a midnight helicopter ride to Las Vegas, the poet whisked off the headland and deposited at the Cupid's Shotgun chapel, where she was eagerly awaited by . . . Ben Affleck.*

It would take a veritable Joseph Campbell to analyze this multiplicity, to discover what our stories about Calliope tell us about ourselves. But one common thread is clear: the poet as subject to forces beyond her control, incapable of choosing the course of her own life—a pawn, a dupe, a damsel, a victim. "As early readings of *Antigone* focus on Creon's cruelty, we are tempted to read Calliope as prey to the powerful," wrote Slavoj Žižek, one of a dozen contributors to a feature in the *New York Times Magazine* marking the one-year anniversary of her suicide.

> The agency implied by suicide, the subject's demand *to no longer be a subject,* is an obscene blot which, because it so nearly matches our fantasies, cannot be acknowledged. Calliope's suicide, *qua* suicide, is thus impermissible. Camus said, "There is only one liberty: to come to terms with death." By this we take him to mean human beings can never achieve liberty, only subject-hood.†

But fantasy and falsehood are not the subject of the present work—this author is concerned only with the facts and what they can tell us about the historical Calliope. It is a truism to say her death posed more questions

---

*Variations on the "secret wedding" story include L. Moreno in Nassau, Bahamas; writer Sebastian Junger/Montauk; XXX/Puerto Vallarta; and Tina Fey/Northampton, Massachusetts.
†"The Poet, the Big Other, and the Fountain of Youth," October 12, 200_.

than it answered, and nothing infuriates a biographer quite so much as a question mark. By nature he cherishes completeness and accuracy, a full reckoning, he despises phrases such as "more or less" and "as far as we know" with their louche attitude toward the Truth. That not all writers hold themselves to the same standards was, by the spring of 200_, already evident in the profusion of literary distortions, impressionist accounts and tell-alls, "nonfiction novels" and audio-montages and error-ridden "wikis," any number of questionable techniques employed in attempts to represent the real Calliope.*

Though confident his project would stand head and shoulders above this dross by virtue of its unstinting devotion to the Truth, the author deemed it essential to secure the sterling imprimatur of the poet's estate, and early that year he stepped up his pursuit of authorization.† He had several conversations with Leigh Mulgrew, Rhoda's assistant, but the publicist herself seemed constantly to be out of the country. Letters and e-mails went unanswered. The abbess at the Convent of the Holy Virgin in Aix-en-Provence listened patiently to his request, but Penelope's vow of silence, and the author's poor French, fairly doomed the attempt.

Undeterred, the author carried on, sparing no effort to discover Calliope in her true form. Progress was slow. Each area of inquiry gave rise to a half dozen others; each stream of analysis branched into tributaries of examination and anecdote. Much time was taken up pursuing interviews—with former students at Mountaintop Arts, former monks at the Zen

---

*Perhaps the worst of these is Edwin Decker's "life portrait," *Sordid Tales of a Terrible Grandchild*, in which the writer goes so far as to imagine "scenes" in which he and the poet have conversations about life, death, poetry, etc., while walking on the beach at sunset, sharing margaritas in Tijuana, or riding the roller coaster at San Diego's Belmont Park. In one widely quoted passage, Decker claims Calliope made a pass at him in a movie theater, "her hand clutching the manly bulge in [his] pants like the gearshift of a Porsche" (211). Must it be said that the author finds this shameful? Must he point out that Decker is only projecting his adolescent fantasies upon a defenseless woman, an act tantamount to necrophilia?

†It would later occur to him, in a dark hour, that even this devotion to Truth might fail to lift his efforts above the others, not because the devotion would be insufficient but because the product—the Truth—might well be indistinguishable to readers from untruth, exaggeration, vendetta, etc., that words printed on the pages of a book look the same regardless of their "truth value," a reader hasn't the ability or even necessarily the inclination to "get behind" or "dig beneath" or "open up" those words to divine their status, a realization which inspired several unhappy days of reading in Nietzsche and Derrida, reading which the author does not have the strength to summarize here and which, in any case, he does not recommend.

Center; with poets and critics within academia and without; with family friends and former employees of Terrible Children and Fuck Finn, cooks and gardeners from the Rancho Santa Fe mansion; in short, everyone whose path Calliope had crossed who might add something, however trivial, to the record.

While many gave generously of their time and recollection, others were more reticent, or refused outright. Ted Ainge, Calliope's former swim coach (and cousin to former NBA star Danny Ainge), demanded a $5,000 "contribution" to his Aquatic Youth Fund; LaTonya Hammond, Calliope's onetime Mountaintop roommate, insisted upon a percentage of royalties. Gary North, most likely thinking to shore up his sagging empire, hinted at a possible publishing deal with NorthStar; but when the author made it known that he would not relinquish any creative control over the project, the record mogul stopped taking his calls.

Most frustrating were the figures whom the author never managed to track down. After reading the letters Calliope wrote from Irvine Medical Center, he briefly began his own search for Danny Grier, but got no farther than a shabby condo in Palm Springs, where the former soundman had been seen only sporadically in recent years. Mahmoud al-Shakil did not respond to letters or telegrams, nor is it clear that it was Shakil himself who answered the phone number in Fez and unloosed a string of Arabic imprecations.

He spent inordinate energy trying to locate the Inca shaman, whose presence at the Christmas fire promised a unique perspective on both the source and expression of Calliope's passions, but who had exited the Morath demesne in 200_. Esperanza Medina Blumstein describes the shaman's last months at the mansion as tumultuous, Penelope and her former spiritual adviser arguing about Calliope's upbringing and education: "He wants to have a say in what the girl is reading, who she can visit, even what she wears. Like he is Calliope's father!" The last straw was apparently a dispute over Calliope's application to Mountaintop Arts Academy, during which Penelope smashed several pieces of laboratory equipment and burned a priceless Egyptian scroll. The shaman left for good the next day.

He seems to have become something of an itinerant jack-of-all-trades: The author was able to trace his path through the homes of two other wealthy widows, a failed biodiesel enterprise outside Colorado Springs, and the Bellagio Hotel in Las Vegas, where he offered spiritual counseling to compulsive gamblers. His last known address is the Esalen Institute, Big Sur's venerable center for psychospiritual exploration, where for a time he taught a highly esoteric workshop using the principles of alchemy to effect "ego transmutation"—but after an incident involving the transgendered child of a Berkeley city councilmember, he was asked to leave. From there, the trail grows cold—as though the shaman had simply shed his identity, walked out of his own life and into history, as though the man Calliope knew in her childhood had simply ceased to be.

In the face of these challenges, the author strove to steel his will, to "step up to the plate," as it were, to match his work ethic to the rigors of the project. He continued to rise before dawn, sitting down with a mug of coffee and a sheaf of Calliope's poems, typing and clicking furiously until breakfast. He was usually able to work uninterrupted for several hours before the onset of "The Racket"—the daily invasion of blistering feedback, wanton banging, and paint-peeling howls emitting from his son's bedroom. Afternoons were spent perusing news clippings and videotape, arranging and conducting interviews, or researching in the public library. On quieter days he might manage a catnap, arising in the evening to wrestle with the angel for another few hours before joining the nightly battle with insomnia. Though the pages accumulated, he couldn't help but feel the thinness of the words and sentences, was sometimes arrested by a vision of their essential emptiness, an emptiness that could be filled only by authorization. As he sat in his small yard, among dying roses and the riotous, infernal bougainvillea, he was haunted by the knowledge that others were beating the same bushes, poring over the same materials, hoping to be the first to bring out the definitive Calliope. The race was on, the last heat of summer humming a command: *Hurry! Hurry! Hurry!*

It is tempting to see a parallel here between the author's dedication and his son's daily attempts to shatter every window within a four-block radius, tempting to note that father and son were each engrossed with their artistic pursuits, the latter having inherited the former's capacity for hard work, thoroughness, etc. It must be said, however, that the exploits of Bratworst, as the obstreperous quartet had come to call itself, amounted to no more than commonplace outpourings of teen angst, thwarted longing, and narcissistic dreams of fame. As Buzz Matapan, the so-called drummer, eloquently phrased it, the group was conceived from the first as a "blow-job magnet."

"Time was when aspiring musicians took themselves somewhat more seriously," the author rejoined.

"You're tripping, Mr. A.," said the young man, a squat and muscular Filipino with several vaguely sinister tattoos and what can only be described as an Eddie Munster haircut. Despite his tragic lack of rhythm, he was the most amiable of the four, the only one capable of interest in things other than his own petty discontentments. "We take this shit *mad* seriously. What could be more serious than getting the betties?"

He elbowed the author, who could not help but smile at the young man's exuberance. It was late September, a balmy evening, a thin haze softening the starlight. As he pulled into the supermarket parking lot, the author was struck by how still the world seemed, how unremarkable—Calliope's whirlwind having passed over the horizon nearly a year ago, one could almost convince oneself it had been a dream, a story picked up at a cocktail party; Connor's vision of a world in which all stories were equal and thus equally insignificant felt all too credible.

"What about you, Mr. A.?" Buzz said, as they trailed down the beer aisle, the drummer hauling two cases into the cart, tattoos dancing. "Any betties in your life?"

"Betties?"

"You know: ladies. Babes."

The author paid for the beer, and they strode out into the night. They were eager to get back—Buzz to the band's rehearsal, the author to a passage in the biography that had been vexing him for days.

"I'm serious!" Buzz grinned. "Lotta betties dig that older-man shit. You could be getting *mad* tail."

"I'll keep that in mind," said the author.

"We've got a gig at the Arizona in a couple months, you should come, find yourself some hot surfer betty, you know?" He reached into the backseat and, with one hand, tore open a case of beer, extracted a can, and popped the top, rudely slurping the foam. He offered a sip to the author, who declined. "Shit, Mr. A., I know it was hard. But life goes on, you know? Don't you think about getting back in the game?"

"I'll pass, Buzz."

The drummer stared at the author's profile. "Don't you think, you know, Mrs. A. would have wanted you to be happy?"

"With a 'betty'?"

Buzz laughed. "With, like, seven or eight betties!"

They were turning now into the author's street. Over the sound of the engine, the author imagined he could already hear the cacophony emitting from his son's room, could see the steady glow of the computer screen through his office window.

"The truth is, Buzz, I already have a very special woman in my life, and I don't have room for others, tempting though you make it sound. She requires all of my concentration."

"You mean that poet? Morath's daughter? Drew told us about that shit. Weird."

"Nevertheless."

"But Mr. A., I mean, I hate to break it to you and shit"— Buzz took another sip and then squeezed the can in his fist, dropping it on the floor of the car—"but she's dead."

They parked and walked to the front door, but Buzz blocked the author's entrance. "I'm not trying to get all up in your shit or anything, Mr. A.," he said. "But what's the big deal about this chick? What's it got to do with anything? Don't you think it's kinda messed up?"

"Time was, Buzz, that musicians and poets were part of a common enterprise. Time was that musicians took inspiration from poets, when they looked to them for lessons about art and life, when the poets were the eyes of the world. Your hero, Brandt Morath—don't you understand where his songs came from? Do you know nothing of the lineage of rebels and misfits of which he was the most recent incarnation—the London punks, the Situationists, the Dada movement, Rimbaud and the Paris Commune? Have you no sense of whence your own traditions derive?

"This is important, Buzz. You and your chums can cover the songs. You can play at the Arizona and pick up as many 'betties' as you like. But if you don't understand where it comes from, you'll be nothing but a soul-less reflection, a simulacrum of that which you hold so dear."

The young man raised his hands in surrender, grinning and stammering. The author wanted to continue, to explain about the Sex Pistols and the Living Theater, about Keats's negative capability, Baudelaire's debauchery, and Lowell's skunk hour, about Bertolt Brecht and CBGB and *The Drunken Boat*, but when he paused for breath and looked through the front window, he saw something which stopped him cold.

"Excuse me, please," he said, pushing through the door, already certain that a new and as-yet-inscrutable chapter was opening in the tragedy he had determined to record.

His son and the other miscreants were lounging on the couch, their shoes soiling the cushions, snorting idiotically at one another. As the author entered the room, Drew picked up the remote control and aimed it at the television.

"Put that down!" the author said. He set the beer on the floor, which served as sufficient distraction for him to take the remote from his son and claim a seat. On the television, Penelope Morath was being interviewed by a French reporter. It was early morning in Aix, and the erstwhile queen of American punk rock stood at the stone gates of the convent in a simple pink dress and white cardigan, the abbess and four sisters of the Holy Virgin arrayed behind her.

"And I just know he would have seen it as a wonderful tribute," Penelope was saying, her voice melodious and demure, "a way to honor his life and his work. Everyone was really respectful of that, Bob and Harvey and Oliver, everyone understood that this wasn't just a *movie*, it was a cultural document, a true time capsule."

The reporter's question was not audible, nor was the voice of the off-camera translator. Penny leaned forward attentively, the sweet smile on her face baring no trace of her erstwhile savagery. Her hair, once a jet-black serpent's nest, was groomed and layered and slightly graying, held back by plain barrettes.

"Of course," she shrugged, "it will always be difficult. I don't wake up a day without thinking of him. But the press exaggerates." She batted dark lashes at the reporter. "Macaulay was wonderful. We got along very well. He's extremely talented and sensitive. Brandt would have felt honored."

It was a new Penelope who stood before the flashbulbs, hard-won poise accentuated by a gentle Gallic sunrise. The author searched desperately for a pen and paper; the would-be musicians ceased their clowning and stared at the screen.

"Yo, she's fucking *hot*, man. She's a total milf!" said one.

"Man, if I had that shit in my bed, I wouldn't go blowing my head off, you know?" Buzz replied.

"She's way hotter than her daughter," said another.

"Yo, Drew, didn't you say her daughter looked just like your mom?" said one, his laugh deteriorating into animal brays.

"No," said the author's son, with a glance at his father.

"Hey, that's fucking cold, man," Buzz said.

"That's enough!" The author turned up the volume.

The cameras followed Penelope on her last stroll through the convent gardens, beneath a vine-covered arbor and finally out the gates. A white sedan awaited, an amazon in full livery holding open the door. The former field general of Fuck Finn stood breathing the morning air, lifting her face to the new sun. Birds twittered. She hugged each of the nuns, and whispered something to the abbess before gathering her skirts and getting in the sedan; as the engine started, Penelope rolled down her window to wave her last good-byes. A shouted question caught her attention, and the serenity on her face changed. For a brief moment, the old, feral energy was visible, eyes flashing Medusa-like at some unlucky soul.

"Don't you ever talk about her," she hissed. "Do you hear me? Don't bring her into this." The nuns clustered in whispers; the driver put the car in gear. Penelope leaned out the window, hair slipping out of one barrette.

"You have no right," she said. The author perched at the edge of the couch, nearly paralyzed with expectation. The sound of a beer can opening near his ear startled him so much that he knocked the can out of Buzz's hand and it lay foaming on the carpet. "You will never, *never* understand how much I miss her," Penelope said, a tear squeezing from the corner of a mascaraless eye as the tinted window occluded her face and the sedan pulled away.

On the couch, the author and the members of Bratworst sat in silence. Beers were sipped, his bandmates stealing uneasy glances at the author's son.

"We ought to invite her to the show," said Buzz, to mutters of derision. "Drew, man, we ought to invite her and introduce her to your dad. What do you think, Mr. A.?"

But the author's son had risen from the couch, one hand shoved in a pocket, the other holding a guitar pick, scratching it absently on the hip of his blue jeans. The stare he threw his father was baleful.

"Drew," the author began, but he could not think of the next thing to say.

What all of them, in their own ways, sensed that evening was that a transition was under way. Autumn had begun to coalesce, the world bracing itself again. It had been a long year, Calliope's absence had bled into the world like a sunset and then become part of that world, one of its cherished stories. The world had gone on, as the world must.

But her absence had fallen especially heavily on the shoulders of those who had loved her best. Daughter, partner, inspiration, Calliope had blazed through their lives and called forth the best parts of them, brought color and caprice into a rote existence, allowed them a glimpse of happiness before her flame rose too high and consumed itself and was snuffed out. She had left them, then, to crawl through darkness, desperately trying to remember light, clinging to the cinders of the only warmth they'd known.

And then she came back.

"But if you could have seen her face, the sheer anguish, the *inhumanity* of it, with her newly shaven head and that birthmark which—well, fanciful as it might sound, seemed to grow larger and more vivid as her self-control, her very sanity, unraveled, as though it were the dermatological equivalent of a mood ring—"

"Yes, I've heard it was quite a traumatic event."

"And the inexplicable behavior of the audience, the total lack of restraint . . . Certainly I make no claims to expertise in this area, but one has to imagine it would make a fascinating study in group psychology, along the lines of the Milgram experiments or the tragedy in Guyana. Have you considered writing a paper about the event?"

"Not my field, really—"

"Because it seemed to me as though—and please don't think me superstitious, I'm only relaying to you the *effect* of the thing, the way it might have seemed to someone less critically aware—it was as though she cast a spell of some kind, that once she said those awful words they were all swept up into her private drama or fantasy world or . . . well, I don't know what to call it, exactly, reality or hallucination or some kind of literary narrative sprung to life. You can see how this becomes one of the central formal problems with the biography."

"Would you like to talk a little about the biography? What it means to you, what interested you in the project in the first—"

"'*I killed him.*' It was heart-stopping. Can you imagine? Oedipus is turning in his grave! Was there ever anyone so . . . it was really a gift, I think, this ability to mythologize, to enter the body of tradition in this way. Others dismissed her as a hysteric, of course, a drama queen. But I think it was extraordinary."

"The subject's ability to symbolize what he perceives, to use language to capture and control it, is the prerequisite of what we refer to as 'sanity.' Language as a mediation between reality and the Real—without it, the Real overflows reality, leading to psychosis. It sounds as though symbolizing the event at the Arizona Café has become a stumbling block?"

"I have only just begun trying to write about that incident. I admit, I feel a kind of trepidation, trying to map out the attack, as it were—the strangeness, the gaps in my knowledge, in *everyone's* knowledge, despite the fact that I was there to witness it—"

"I'm interested to know how you happened to be there."

"—and then the *coup de grâce*, shall we say, the showstopper: '*I killed him.*' Incredible!"

"Are you familiar with the term 'radical responsibility'?"

"I don't believe—"

"Radical responsibility is one way the subject reacts to a face-to-face encounter with the Real, an attempt to symbolize and control that trauma, to get on top of its monstrousness, in a sense."

"By fantasizing one's guilt in the matter?"

"Not guilt, responsibility. Responsibility as another word for *agency*, for *significance*. Here we have a crucial moment in the process of subjectivization: the subject—the self—has come to accept itself *qua* subject, as bounded and defined by its place in the symbolic order and therefore as a *signifier*, but now must confront that place where the signifier *doesn't signify*, where it is, literally, *insignificant*."

"Ah. Yes. Yes, I see where you're going with this. So she fantasizes that she has killed her father, because the reality is too difficult to bear—"

"Not reality: the Real."

"But why would the thought of killing her father be any easier?"

"And not fantasy. This is crucial. We are not talking about a fantasy in the sense of something which overlays objective history, which distorts it for some end. We are talking about the experience itself, the encounter with the Real, understood *in the moment* as an answer to a summons, or a wish. The subject, to preserve its significance, to reassert the integrity of the symbolic order, subscribes to a cause-and-effect: There was a wish; the wish was granted."

"A wish?"

"A wish."

"You can't expect me to believe she wished her father dead."

"Come now—is it that shocking?"

"She worshipped him."

"Yes."

"She defined her very existence by him."

"Don't we all, from time to time, harbor unseemly desires? Don't we resent our loved ones, imagine the world without them, imagine our liberation?"

"Do we? You're the psychologist."

"Have you never felt hatred for those close to you? Have you never imagined yourself as *free*?"

"Could we get back to the incident at the Arizona Café?"

"And given that we have these thoughts, when trauma occurs, we retreat into responsibility, for responsibility does not challenge the symbolic order. It is a comfort, relative to the disintegration of the subject threatened by the Real."

"These lights are quite hot. Could we perhaps turn on the overheads?"

"Please lie back. Try to relax."

A moment passed while the author stared at his reflection. Lying with hands folded on his chest, surrounded by cushions, he had a brief, vertiginous sensation of being suspended above himself—inverted, the room turned on its ear and his muscles tensed against this sense of falling: falling into himself.

"Well, then, the—ah . . . the birthmark."

"Yes, the birthmark. The 'bloodstain.' A guarantee, of sorts. A thumbtack."

"I don't follow."

"A piece of the Real that confirms the omnipotence of the subject. How else to be sure that the communication has been heard? There is no intersubjective communication possible without something from the *outside,* some excess which guarantees it. Otherwise we are merely moving signifiers around."

"'Daddy.'"

"A trade was made: the signifier for a little piece of the Real."

"Surely you don't believe—"

"Often in psychoanalysis, the key to understanding rests with some piece of the Real, some object or image which bridges the—"

"But what, then, if you say Calliope harbored these horrible, this hatred . . . What could be the . . . are you saying that the rumors were true, about Brandt, that Calliope might have fantasized a kind of *revenge?*"

"I'm saying no such thing."

"So there was no abuse?"

"I can't discuss such matters with you, Andrew. That was our agreement."

"But then if . . . well, I suppose it's irrelevant, you'll just tell me that whatever she *thought* was true—or real . . . and probably that, too, was subject to change. But if the bloodstain—the birthmark 'guaranteed' the symbolic order, then how could she continue . . . why was she so convinced she would one day find her father alive?"

"Maybe we could talk a little about your background: family, upbringing, occupation—"

"Is it merely the case, perhaps, Doctor, that the symbolic *cannot* be guaranteed, only sustained, propped up—"

"—because I know your budget is limited, and I don't want to use up—"

"—and so in order to maintain the fantasy, as Rose implied, she would need to find ever more convincing 'little pieces of the Real,' ever more grandiose, to disguise the disintegration of the symbolic order, to forestall acceptance of the reality of his death!"

"You confuse reality with the Real. The Real does not *exist* in a positive sense."

"Does not . . . but then, you said it is traumatic—are you saying all these traumas are *imaginary*?"

"The imaginary is something else entirely."

"Doctor . . ."

"There is nothing outside the symbolic, and yet the symbolic is hopelessly inadequate: its gaps and exclusions, that which it contains but cannot represent, this is what we call the Real. It is what the symbolic is structured around. There is language, the Big Other, and there are its limitations, its failures, its death."

"The Big Other?"

"You mentioned that you have a teenage son. Perhaps you'd like to talk about your relationship while we still have a few minutes?"

"It's akin to what Žižek said in the first profile, that Calliope rips away some veil, she forces her audience to confront the . . . well, the Real, I suppose he must have been saying. Is this right? And that this confrontation was what produced such—what was the word he used—*jouissance,* that her fans experienced *jouissance.* Is the Real synonymous with *jouissance*?"

"Ah, Slavoj. The Lion of Ljubljana. How I have always adored his attempts to bring Lacan to the average mind. It's very Eastern European, this democratic compulsion—"

"You know Žižek?"

"Back in Paris, I used to call him the Bono of Psychoanalysis. The man is a born performer; he cannot resist the spotlight."

"I found his articles quite compelling."

"Of course he wasn't as heavyset back then."

"I'm sorry?"

"But it's clear that this is what drew him to Calliope, this deep narcissism. In a sense, he was writing about himself, all the rhetoric about 'bridging the divide' is merely self-congratulation on his dumbing down of Lacan. And while he is on his book tours, or writing for the *New York Times*, the real theorists are left behind to toil in small offices, publish in obscure journals, endure conferences in Liverpool and Perth—"

"It seems psychoanalysis is as incestuous a field as poetry."

"Tossed aside while graduate students make fawning documentaries—"

"You are the poets of the psyche, wouldn't you say?"

"Yes, fine. Andrew, we're nearly out of time. Would you like to set some goals as to what we'll discuss next time? We should narrow the focus—"

"Let me . . . I'd like to get this straight. The Big Other is dead."

"You must understand, these are metaphors, illustrations—"

"And language is the Big Other."

"I feel we're going in circles here. Have you spoken to Jerome about scheduling the next appointment?"

"And so if the symbolic network is structured around the Real, if it mediates between the subject and the Real, to keep—how did you say it, to keep the Real from overwhelming reality?—wouldn't that make language itself a kind of defense mechanism? A neurosis? And then Calliope's obsession with language, with poetry, her feverish writing and her fixation on the topic of herself, of her father's suicide, couldn't this be understood as a symptom, an anxiety or desperation in reaction to the insufficiency of the language, the proximity of the Real?"

"But this is one definition of art, isn't it? The Big Other looking at itself through the eyes of the artist, the artist using language to get the attention of the Big Other. Even Freud saw this."

"The Big Other conceals the Real, the subject represses the Big Other's death. Where in all this is the Truth? It's a dog chasing its tail, a futile circle."

"*In girum imus nocte et consumimur igni.*"

"Sorry?"

"'We turn in circles in the night and we are consumed by fire.' It's a palindrome. Calliope often quoted it in her trances."

"Trances?"

"She was quite taken with its apocalyptic tone. She liked to say her life was palindromic. She said it would make a fitting epitaph."

"But then Doctor, if the poetry was neurotic, if the insufficiencies of language were at the heart of the problem, then what . . . well, of course, then the cure would be *silence,* would it not? Yes, it makes perfect sense!"

"I once suggested that she stop writing poetry."

"It would seem she took your advice."

"There seems to be some disagreement over that."

"Are you referring to this ludicrous graffito? Dr. Breve, you surprise me—tell me you aren't succumbing to this mass delusion, this wishful thinking. *Et tu?*"

"'The poet will be *heard,*' Andrew. The course of her career as a demand to be heard. A demand for the attention of the Big Other, which in the narrative she told herself took no notice."

"And so the ever more outrageous performances as flamboyant bids for—"

"This is the human condition. Bounded and located by the symbolic order, we are deprived even of the certainty that it is aware of us."

"Like a father."

"Indeed."

"And so *Saturday Night Live*—"

"Yes."

"So that's why she destroys the photo of Brandt. To get his attention. Even though he's . . . Oh, goodness, seen this way it is so . . . sad. The desperation. The pathos."

"Our time is up for today, Andrew."

"A moment . . . please. I'm just recalling . . . and how it backfired . . . The suffering child—all she wanted was for him to acknowledge her. Just to get his attention . . ."

"Tell me, Andrew. Whose attention are *you* trying to get?"

The room still dark, the glowing hands of the clock on the lamp table had made their rounds. The author had the sensation of time outside the room having stopped.

"We're not really here to discuss me, are we?"

Across the halogen veil, the doctor stared her peculiar stare. "Lacan was quite fond of saying: 'A letter always arrives at its destination.'"

The world premiere of *The Hanged Man: The Brandt Morath Story* was conceived from the first as a gala event to match the phenomenon the late singer had sparked and piloted. The festivities—including red-carpet reception, cocktail hour, tribute speeches, and a fifteen-minute short feature chronicling not only the making of the film but also of the premiere itself—were to be held at San Diego's Spreckels Theatre, a gilded old-world auditorium built in 1912; in a landmark partnership between the Weinstein Company and the city, the theater was refurbished at a cost of $13.2 million, part of which was raised by adding a controversial twenty-five-cent "culture contribution" to movie tickets in San Diego County. Luxury skyboxes replaced the lower balcony, and overall seating was reduced from 1,460 to 1,150; plasma screens were installed throughout the lobby and on the building's facade, a cluster of boutique kiosks was designed on the ground floor, and a helicopter bay built on the roof. The Broadway entrance was expanded, and a thirty-foot-high glass guitar designed by I. M. Pei erected, beneath which arrivals passed on their way into the theater.* Weinstein Company reserved the top floors of the nearby Pan Pacific Hotel for press suites and after-parties, and arranged a three-hour "Terrible Children Tour"

---

*Cf. Matt Potter's award-winning series for the *San Diego Reader* detailing the relationship between Weinstein marketing director Stan Fliegelbaum and San Diego City councilmember Brucie Markham. In early 200_, Markham was lavishly wined and dined and twice whisked away to Prague on Fliegelbaum's private jet, allegedly in an effort to influence her vote on the public financing package. The revelations stirred outrage in the weeks before the opening, a result which, according to Edwin Decker, was the true goal all along, Markham's vote having been expendable to the 7–1 council decision. By accusing Potter of being "a pathetic pawn in the marketers' malodorous game," however, Decker goes too far.

for the afternoon of the show, which took invitees past the Casbah, the OB fishing pier, the Arizona Café,* Cow Records, and the Abbott Street lot where the Moraths' first apartment had stood. A whisper campaign hinted at a surprise performance by the surviving members of the band, with Penny Power filling in for her husband on vocals.

"The world's going back to 199_," Harvey Weinstein told *Variety*. "We're digging him up and bringing him back to life, rebuilding him out of his own stories and letting him loose. It's gonna be a hell of a show."

For Penelope, of course, the December 18 event would be a crucible of complex emotions, and public curiosity as to how she would handle herself contributed in no small part to the advance "buzz." For a year she had been out of the spotlight, living a life as extreme in its solitude as her former life had been in its drama. She had lost the two people closest to her, whom she had long ago described as "my reasons to go on living, to take care of them and keep them safe. Beware the she-wolf!"† European tabloids had first outed and then eulogized her relationship with Moroccan poet Mahmoud al-Shakil, who in the wake of the *fatwa* incident had left Paris in disgrace, denouncing Penelope and her "infidel offspring" and returning to his job at the University of Fez; unless one is to believe the tabloid stories of "bestial sex orgies" in the Convent of the Holy Virgin, Penelope had spent the long months face-to-face with no one but herself. For the first time in her life, she was alone.

"There had always been an emptiness," she told Mark McGrath, co-host of NBC's *eXtra* and former heartthrob leader of the pop band Sugar Ray, in an exclusive interview aired the week before the premiere. The two sat in high-backed leather chairs before a fireplace, the warm glow of embers playing in their eyes.

Penelope: There was a hunger inside of me, which I tried to fill with sex, with drugs, with Buddhism. You name it.

McGrath: Anger?

---

*Where, coincidentally, the somewhat less notable Bratworst World Premiere was to be held that same night.
†*SLAM*, August 23, 199_.

Penelope: Anger was what came out. Anger was the sound of that void going unfilled. It wasn't a part of me as much as a byproduct of how we lived—the world promises you everything, tells you you *have* everything, and you can't understand why you feel so empty. That's what the sisters helped me to see.

McGrath: So you wouldn't consider yourself an angry person anymore?

Penelope: I was never an angry person, Mark. I was always a lover, not a fighter.

McGrath: Me, too! That's so cool that you say that. But seriously, people always saw you as angry. That was one of the things they loved about, uh, about your band.

Penelope: We were kids! I mean, Darlene was seventeen when we started. Yeah, we were angry. But we were also having fun. It was a persona. It made us a lot of money. But the anger's a trap. You have to turn it on anytime someone puts a nickel in the jukebox, to keep up the image they have of you. You start to feel like a whore.

McGrath: [*nods thoughtfully*]

Penelope: You know what I mean, Mark. I remember how you used to look in those Sugar Ray videos, so healthy and sexy—

McGrath: Those were the days!

Penelope: But really some part of you must have felt misunderstood, like the hunk in the videos was different from who you really were? [*Interviewer stares.*] Don't you feel more, I don't know, *complex* than that image? [*Interviewer stares.*] Well, anyway, that was the old Penny Power. Now it's Penelope.

McGrath: So you've changed your name?

Penelope: [*bites her lip, pats interviewer's hand*] Yes.

She had undergone a transformation, or so she claimed, had pulled off that most American of feats: reinvention. Perhaps the change was genuine, a progression toward emotional health in the aftermath of a years-long ordeal. In the cool, dim hallways of the convent, where the only sounds were the gentle *plink* of water in stone fountains and the distant echoes of punk music in the shadowy nightclub of her mind, who could say Penelope had not found the strength to put the past behind her? Who could say she had not found, in her austere room with a view of the tulip garden, the inner peace she sought?

Some had their doubts. Indeed, the ad campaign for *The Hanged Man* seemed designed precisely to remind the world of Penny Power's erstwhile explosiveness.* What degree of cynicism attended her compliance, to what extent was she a willing participant in the marketing of her own personality, the very personality she was trying to slough off? If she had indeed changed, how must it have felt to see her past exploited in this way, even as she struggled to convince the world of her newfound serenity? Would not her compliance, in that case, represent a grotesque compromise, a denial of her new self so decisive as to negate the very transformation she claimed in the first place? Did Penelope herself know the answers to these questions?

The appearance of the Coronado Bay Bridge graffito on December 12 was not immediately linked to the ongoing preparations, though the strange message was clearly legible from the roof of the theater. Duly noted in the local press, the foreboding message was nevertheless dismissed as merely the latest in a year of rumors, sightings, and harbingers. Though the poetry world still mourned their fallen idol, the general public's emotional investment was waning, their fascination with new mysteries and insinuations attenuated by what Skip Cárdenas calls "Morath Fatigue."

Nevertheless, scores of the curious gathered along San Diego's Harbor Drive, on the piers of downtown's Seaport Village and in the fortieth-floor bar of the Manchester Hyatt, as well as Coronado's Tidelands Park, to view the message. Airline passengers landing at Lindbergh Field were able to watch the strange verse unscroll along the bridge's graceful northwest sweep. Lane Thisselbaugh, a twenty-six-year-old former surfing champion, whose career had been cut short when he lost part of his right arm to a tiger shark, offered ninety-minute "Poetry Cruises" in San Diego Har-

---

*One trailer, for example, offered a glimpse of the legendary scene at NorthStar Records when Penelope assaulted Gary North (played by Oliver Platt) with his own desk chair in a dispute over Terrible Children's contract, while Brandt lay unconscious on North's desk.

bor; under clammy December skies, his thirty-two-foot vessel, *The Shredder,* raced out into the winter chop, Thisselbaugh's captaining clearly influenced by his surfing style such that passengers were rewarded for their $45 with a crippling case of seasickness. The excursion set out from Shelter Island, heading north and west past the North Island Naval Air Station for a glimpse of Cabrillo National Monument and the lighthouse where, in Thisselbaugh's telling, "the crazy chick offed herself." Turning in a hazardously tight sweep, *The Shredder* sped back into the harbor toward the Coronado Bay Bridge, which snaked bright blue against a steely sky, the defacement visible first as a blood-red streak, growing in clarity as the onlookers approached. At a quarter mile, Thisselbaugh cut the motor and *The Shredder* bobbed, even the most jaded, green-gilled passengers drawing breath at the message stretched across the sky:

> Where in the world is Calliope Bird?
> Tear away my shroud (these words)—
> The poet will soon be heard.

The letters were eight feet high, written in cursive along the girders. A few commuters, tiny spots along the roadway, leaned over the rail to view the message from above. The nineteen unforgettable words were followed only by a strange calligraphic mark, an intricate symbol or ideogram; but no one who read them, rocking gently in the silent harbor, could doubt their author.

"The rhymes, the aggressive meter, the self-aggrandizement, all point to Calliope. Cf. Morath's affinity for parentheses in 'Suicide Bomber' and other late poems," wrote Vassar College professor Donald Foster, in a report to the San Diego Police Department. Foster, an expert in "forensic linguistics" whose experience in textual authentication ranges from Elizabethan diaries to the infamous note in the JonBenét Ramsey murder case, was flown in three days before the premiere to calm the nerves of city officials; his conclusion that there was a "high probability" that the graffito had been composed by Calliope understandably had the opposite effect.

"As far as the glyph in lieu of signature," he went on, "it bears resemblance to symbols found in the *Ars Chemica* and other sixteenth-century alchemy texts. But as for a specific source or translation, this linguist is at a loss."

The report was promptly leaked to the *San Diego Union-Tribune*, which ran an editorial challenging the SDPD's preparations for the upcoming event. But when it was discovered that Foster had previously served as a consultant to the Weinsteins for a film about the Ramsey case, his report was dismissed as a cynical ploy in the *Hanged Man* publicity campaign. Even Rhoda Lubinski, hardly one to undermine a story that could further promote her late client's fame, expressed skepticism:

"People just can't accept reality," she told NPR's *Morning Edition*. "Calliope writing poems from the great beyond? So what, now she's not only come back from the grave, but she's brought climbing ropes and spray paint? Pull my other leg, please! I've made up some whoppers in my time, but this is too much."

The message was thus dismissed as a hoax or a joke, orchestrated by the Weinsteins or perpetrated by a Terrible Children fan, many of whom had long cast a jaundiced eye on the film for its reported exaggeration of Brandt's mysticism, his rumored dabblings in Santeria, his death wish. Only Cassandra Beers, the disgraced *Saturday Night Live* producer who had landed a job as a best boy for the Spreckels extravaganza, took the graffito seriously. Before dawn on the morning of December 18, Beers forced her way into Bob Weinstein's suite at the Pan Pacific to deliver an urgent message. She managed to rouse Weinstein from sleep, but when he came into the sitting room he found the young woman gesticulating wildly, clutching her throat. He tried his best to calm her, but Beers was unable to speak. After several frenzied moments, Weinstein finally thought to bring a pen and paper, upon which she scrawled "SHE'S COMING!!!" before swooning onto the sofa.

Weinstein spent the next hour on the phone with his brother, but in the end they agreed that the multimillion-dollar production could not be halted on the basis of a best boy's hysteria. Whatever Beers's prophecy meant, whatever inscrutable disaster it foretold, flights were already landing at Lindbergh Field, limousines fueling in L.A. In a matter of hours, the guests would arrive. It was too late.

The stars began pulling up at 4:30 P.M., pausing to wave at the fans corralled behind police barricades and to answer preapproved questions in front of TV cameras from nineteen countries, before passing beneath the giant glass guitar and into Spreckels Theatre. The weather was vintage San Diego, crystalline skies and a light breeze off the harbor rustling perfectly groomed palm trees—"Just like we ordered it," joked Oliver Platt, to the general laughter. The steady stream of actors and rockstars,* in tuxedos and idiosyncratic dresses, lingered in the lobby and stairwells of the reno-vated theater, pausing to admire the high-definition plasma screens or to pick up an ounce of perfume at the Givenchy kiosk before finding their seats. Reporters accosted limousines as far away as Horton Plaza, at the corner of Broadway and Fourth Avenue, and the Front Street freeway exit ramp. By shrewd calculation, Penelope Morath arrived by helicopter, waving at frustrated reporters from the roof of the theater while cam-eramen frantically scaled the fire escapes. At 5:10, a mere five minutes be-fore showtime, Macaulay Culkin's limo arrived, and the actor, whose career had been resurrected when he landed the role of Brandt Morath, stepped onto the carpet escorted by model/talk-show host Tyra Banks. Culkin seemed unsteady on his feet, his eyes painfully bloodshot, his hair still shoulder-length. When he spoke, it was in the pained, self-effacing tones of the late musician; a three-day scruff of beard and a lapel pin that read FUCK CORPORATE ART further emphasized the blurring between actor and role.

"What was it like working with Penelope?" shouted a reporter.

"Wow," said the actor, flashing his boyish smile, seeming to both nod and shake his head simultaneously. "It was way cool. It was an adventure."

"Is it true Brandt came to you in dreams? Were you intimidated by the role of someone so adored by his fans?"

"You know, I felt him working with me," he replied, pausing to make odd clicking noises with his tongue. "It was like, wow—like I became Brandt. Like he, I don't know, inhibited me or something.

"I am Brandt," he said, opening his palm before his face. Banks said

---

*Including guitarist Billy Martinez, drummer XXX, and all the original members of Fuck Finn. Connor Feingold was a notable no-show.

something the cameras did not pick up and tried to steer the star into the theater. "I'm Brandt. Brandt's me."

The lights of the theater began to wink, scattered applause greeting the pulses of neon that shot through the neck of the glass guitar. As Culkin and Banks moved toward the entrance, a squeal of brakes drew the onlookers' attention, and a black BMW convertible came to a crooked halt at the curb, the driver leaping from his seat onto the red carpet. Out of breath but smiling irreverently, the Beekeeper stood beneath the glass guitar in a three-piece white suit and dark sunglasses, casually checking his pocketwatch and speaking into the nearest microphone.

"Am I late?" he quipped.

The lights blinked more quickly, the show about to begin. "Sorry, friends, no time to visit," he drawled. "We'll catch up later. Enjoy the show!" Then he, too, disappeared into the entryway, cameras following him through the doors, the news crawl on TV screens identifying him as "Anonymous Author of Tell-All Memoir about Calliope Bird Morath, *A Gut-Wrenching Tale of Crippling Hunger.*"

The audience having at last settled into their seats, champagne brought to all 1,150 in attendance, the long-awaited show got under way. Speeches were delivered by Harvey Weinstein and San Diego mayor Barry Horneiwicz, who presented a key to the city to Brandt's widow. Gary North spoke about discovering the band back in 199_, sleeping under the fishing pier with Brandt for nearly a week before convincing him to sign with North-Star ("It was like talking to Hamlet, waiting for him to decide: To rock or not to rock?"), concluding with a passionate denial of the federal racketeering charges recently brought against him. The final speech came from Terrible Children manager Talia Z, who brought the audience to tears with fond memories of Danny Grier, backdropped by a photo of the late soundman. Throughout the speeches and the brief documentary, cameras panned through the audience, now lighting on Penelope, who wore a highcut gold gown and sat unescorted, hands folded in her lap, now on Culkin, who slumped closer to his date with each passing moment. The Beekeeper sipped champagne, sunglasses still on, turning occasionally to chat with Jack Nicholson in the row behind him.

"If Brandt is in Heaven, looking down on us tonight," said Penelope, in the monologue that closed the short film, "he'd be proud and honored to feel all our love. We miss you, darling—but I know you'll always be with us."

Lights went down, the last warm glow fading from chrome balustrades and gilded turn-of-the-century molding. The anticipation was profound, in the darkness each person remembering the first time they'd heard "Dirtnap"—whether watching MTV, or walking through a record store, or leaving the office and popping an unmarked demo into the car stereo, hoping only for a few moments of distraction before confronting the personal horrors of home. They recalled the keen edge of Brandt's guitar, the irresistible rasp of his voice, how the music swept away everything in its path and reminded them of what they had perhaps, in the grind of their lives, forgotten: that art, true art, conquers all. It is unassailable, a world unto itself.

A single guitar chord rang out—pure, sustained, tense. A thin bright line shot horizontally across the black screen, slowly expanding until its brilliance lit the entire theater, a thousand silhouettes revealed in perfect stillness. It was a sunrise, white desert light washed across an empty highway, the night sky still ablaze with stars. From the road's vanishing point appeared a solitary figure, a dark smudge before the rising sun. The guitar chord still sounding, the figure slowly progressed and grew, the night sky seeming to purple and dissolve before his advance. Though there could be no doubt who this vagabond was, nothing could suppress the crowd's shiver of recognition as he neared, the splinters of a broken guitar slung over his shoulder, his army-surplus jacket and shredded jeans distorted by the shimmer of asphalt heat, the sound of his voice, when it came, elicited the nearly orgasmic thrill of a collective wish fulfilled.

"The sky was made of amethyst," the voice insinuated the darkness, the first of several voice-overs digitally altered to match Culkin's voice more closely to Brandt's. "The stars flashed like the souls of lonely fish through the sea-void of the night."

In the theater, a thousand fans squirmed in delight, transported back in time. Several people fainted, others hyperventilated only to be shushed by their neighbors. The waitstaff, standing at the top of the aisles, forgot their duties, mesmerized by the rough music of Brandt's voice raised from the dead.

"Misfortune was my god," he continued, the words culled from Brandt's diaries and "dramatically enhanced" by Associate Producer JT LeRoy. "Everything was permitted me, burdened with the contempt of the most contemptible hearts."

Everyone knew the story: Brandt's first guitar, bought with money saved from his minimum-wage job at a medical-waste disposal site, destroyed by a gang of surfers at a keg party in Santee while they chanted lyrics from Guns N' Roses's *Appetite for Destruction*. The film's genius, already apparent, was in its ability to reference such stories without fully dramatizing them, a cinematic shorthand dependent on the audience's prior knowledge: Whatever was shown on the screen, what the audience was really "seeing" was an intricate conflation of memory and narrative, a highly satisfying synergy resulting in a delicious déjà vu, a sense of intimacy and wonder akin to the fantasy of witnessing one's own birth.

Another moment, and the disheveled figure had arrived, the screen filled with his bruised, battered face—a face which, in a synaptic flash, *became* the face of Brandt Morath. None who saw it would ever again look upon a photograph of the real Brandt without its seeming, in some way, wrong. He looked straight into the camera, lips trembling, as the guitar chord faded out. At last he spoke:

"O may it come, the time of love: the time we'd be enamored of."

The audience burst into applause and wild hoots, celebrities embracing in their seats, clinking champagne glasses and settling back with the happy knowledge that the show had only just begun. Darlene Cream and Billy Martinez engaged in a lingering, openmouthed kiss, while in the next row Tyra Banks shook Culkin awake and hauled him up for an impromptu bow. In the window of their luxury skybox, Harvey and Bob Weinstein could be seen celebrating, the most important project of their careers already an unqualified success. The image of the grown brothers dancing and high-fiving was the last before the screen—and the theater—abruptly went dark.

It took several seconds for the audience to realize that this new darkness was not part of the show. As they waited for the next scene to begin, the only sounds were the clearing of throats, the distant slam of a fire door, a muffled shout from the projection booth. When the houselights suddenly came on, the audience squinted in confusion, muttered to their neighbors, a few giving voice to their annoyance in vulgar exclamations. A gasp went through the front row, a shriek—and then a thousand pairs of eyes snapped to the front and beheld stark impossibility.

There she stood, before the blank screen from which, a moment before, her father's face had gazed. Bald and flawless as a newborn, Calliope stared at the audience with wide blue eyes and the blank expression of a mannequin, her hands clenching and unclenching at her sides. Some would later report that she wore a bodysuit of black leather; others swore she was dressed in a long golden gown; still others said the poet was naked, discomfitingly hairless from head to toe. A minute ago overcome with joy, all were now paralyzed in disbelief and the giddy, nauseating arousal one feels in the sweaty borderland between dream and waking.

For nearly a minute, the theater held still. Those in the frontmost rows recall studying the strange figure—though there was no doubt who she was, there was nevertheless something unfamiliar they couldn't put a finger on. It was difficult to hold her steady in one's gaze, to confront her directly, even the balcony cameras seemed to waver and skate over her pale form. Lips pressed together, eyes narrowing, she scanned back through the rows. Halfway to the rear of the theater, she found what she was looking for, and a grim smile slicked across her features.

"Suspect may have entered by Second Avenue stage entrance, some signs of tampering evident, no prints, no witnesses," the police report would read, despite great pressure from City Hall to determine precisely how Calliope managed to disrupt the show and hijack what had promised to be a major financial windfall for the city. "Projection-room employees did not see anything, equipment malfunction remains unexplained. Officers' response time satisfactory. How suspect got out of the building with hostages is currently under investigation."

Gripped in the fist of her daughter's stare, Penelope slowly rose from her seat, mouth open and manicured hands fluttering to the high collar of her dress. Though a few reached out to stop her, most scrambled out of her way as the Morath matriarch moved into the aisle. At the end of the carpeted path waited the bizarre figure, her smile widening as her mother approached. Witnesses recall the sensation of trying to move—whether to intervene or to escape—but finding their limbs too heavy, the air around them a gluey, impassable medium.

"Baby?" Penelope whispered, stopping ten feet away. "What's the matter?"

Calliope gave no answer, her eyes locked on the unsteady figure.

"It's okay, Birdie." Penelope lapsed into a whisper. She shook her head once, twice, as though to clear cobwebs. "Mommy's here." She offered the poet a trembling hand but came no closer, struggling to smile, her breathing quickening. "Everything's going to be okay, sweetheart. I'm here. Mommy's here."

Apparition or resurrection, miracle or monstrosity, Calliope stared unblinking at her mother, who grew more anxious with each second, looking to the faces on either side, all of whom turned away.

"Don't you like the movie?" Penelope said, slipping into a mother's babytalk. "Sweetie McC, don't you think Daddy would like it?" She took a step forward, but stopped midstride, as though pulled equally in both directions by invisible forces. "I think he would like it. He'd be proud of us, don't you think? He'd be so proud.

"Say something, baby." But Calliope only cocked her head. "Talk to me, please? Don't do this to Mommy. You know she loves the sound of your voice."

But there was only the same empty stare, the same bloodless pursing of the poet's lips. "Say something," her mother pleaded. "Why won't you talk to me?" She tried to take another step, but instead fell roughly to her knees, as though shoved. Behind her, eight women rose from their seats and trained their eyes on the pair at the front of the theater.

"I protected you," Penelope whimpered. "I took care of you. I didn't know what else to do. You're my only baby. The only one. Remember? And I'm . . . I was your only mother. Remember, Bird? Who's the best mommy in the world? Who's the best—" She choked off and sobbed, snatched at her throat, while behind her the eight women—including her erstwhile bandmate, Darlene Cream, and Cassandra Beers—

regarded her with expressions that mirrored Calliope's: unswerving, un-yielding, empty.

"I don't understand," Penelope keened. "Why won't you talk to me?" Her hands flew to the side of her head, ripped the diamond studs out of her earlobes and flung them feebly at her daughter's feet. Two trickles of blood seeped along the line of her jaw.

The audience was beginning to buckle under the strain, sobs and moans from all corners. In the city's skybox, a junior aide to the mayor fell to the floor in an apparent seizure. "Just say something. You're like my damned therapist . . . why won't you say anything?" Struggling for breath, she started to crawl, an excruciatingly slow progress toward her daughter's feet. Behind her, the eight women stepped out into the aisle,* while in the projection booth the master reels of *The Hanged Man: The Brandt Morath Story* began to smoke and shrivel. "What is this, some kind of inquisition?" said Penelope through gritted teeth. "Some adolescent revenge? What?"

One hand after the other she crawled, the file of women following. "What was I supposed to do?" She stretched along the carpet and squinted up through tears. "I was a young woman . . . this huge house . . . every time I looked at you, I saw him. Do you have any idea what that's . . . you wouldn't say anything, just like now . . . I looked at you floating through the house and I saw him *every fucking time.*

"He ruined *everything.*" She raised herself again to all fours, shouting at her daughter's impassive face. "We had a story. We had a beautiful story and we made it happen. And he ruined it." She clutched at Calliope's ankles, makeup smearing down her cheeks, the muscles of her neck stand-ing out like piano wire. A clear pinkish liquid ran from her left nostril. "Why shouldn't I? Why shouldn't I get to live it again? It's *my fucking story*! Why should I have to see someone else in my story? It's *mine,* don't you un-derstand? It's *mine* . . ."

If the poet understood, she made no outward sign, only regarded the pathetic figure at her feet with complete detachment. As the women

---

*Several witnesses claim the eight women "levitated," but the author assumes this description to be a byproduct of group hysteria.

gathered around them in a semicircle, Penelope wrapped her arms around Calliope's legs, pressed her cheek to her daughter's knees. "Baby . . . my baby," she wept, her body wracked with sobs, as the windows of the projection room filled with flame. The audience all at once released from paralysis, before the houselights shorted out the last thing anyone remembers is the sight of Penelope pulling herself hand over hand, as though climbing up her daughter's body, Calliope closing her eyes and raising an arm, palm open, above her mother's terrified face.

By the time the ensuing pandemonium was brought under control, the magnificently refurbished Spreckels Theatre was in ruins. In what experts in mob psychology have referred to as a "collective catharsis," and what SDPD captain Eugenio Sanchez called "demonic goddamned possession," the crowd of a thousand ran amok in that elegant space, tearing velvet curtains and plush carpeting to shreds, slashing leather upholstery and smashing champagne glasses and hors d'oeuvre trays, destroying the new movie screen and wrenching speakers from their casings in the theater walls. In the lobby, plasma screens were shattered and torn down, the Givenchy kiosk was reduced to fragrant rubble, carved banisters were kicked and smashed to splinters; the theater's six restrooms were flooded, sinks and urinals pulled from their fixtures; throughout the building, century-old molding was chipped and pried and ripped and, in one place, apparently bitten off the walls. The Weinsteins' skybox was irreparably vandalized, windows and wet bars smashed, furniture burned, walls smeared with excrement. Above the doors to the main hall, the theater's pride and joy—an original mural of Greek nymphs dancing on a stage, commissioned for the 1912 opening and preserved through various renovations—was defaced by blood-red paint,* a simple message covering the old image like a palimpsest: TRUTH.

But those watching at home saw none of this; the balcony cameras were early targets of the vandalism. The last images they captured were of stunned, mute audience members trembling in their seats as the emergency lights flickered dimly on. Calliope was gone, as were Cassandra and

---

*Forensics later confirmed the paint as chemically identical to that of the Coronado Bay Bridge graffito.

Darlene and the other six women.* The silence was like that which precedes a tornado, all the oxygen sucked away, as they turned to one another
to verify what had just taken place, to wordlessly ask what it all could mean.

There was a strangled shout, and the Beekeeper leapt from his seat in
the twelfth row and stumbled into the aisle, dropping and then stepping on
his sunglasses in his panic. People on either side rose to help him, but
stopped a second later, hands over their mouths. Stunned and shaking, the
Beekeeper turned in place, arms flung wide, staring down at himself with
a groan—across his white jacket and vest was scrawled, in bright red, a
warning: SHHHH!!!

In the next second, the last before the theater erupted, he turned his
back to the camera, whereupon millions glimpsed the second half of the
Muse's terrifying message:

I'M NEXT.

---

*Penelope was later found, curled fetally in the second row, by paramedics and transported to
Scripps Medical Center, where she was admitted in a persistent catatonic state.

10. SONG OF MYSELF

LET'S JUST SAY I WAS testing the bounds of Calliope.

Let's say I pressed my nose to the window and found it wanting, the glass enclosure of my life, my words, my body, too restricting—let's say I picked up the only rock I could find and smashed it to slivers, stepped lithely from those ruins.

Can we say that, friend, and leave it there? I know you wouldn't dream of intruding, you wouldn't want to pry—let's save the rest for Christmas cards, retrospectives, let's just say, "On such-and-such a date the poet died . . ."

What a surprise: You aren't satisfied. My heartfelt explanation doesn't live up to its billing. What else do you require? Fishes? Ashes? Front-row tickets to the mercy killing? You've heard all the stories of the haunted House of Morath: my father, the wasted angel; my mother, fearsome Valkyrie; my sad, transparent self, born to splashy disaster and death. You've sucked on my misfortune like a sweet-and-sour candy. What hunger still remains to you, what datum still unknown to you, what bird still sings unnoticed in this tragic family tree?

Pray tell, my mawkish lookalike, what more do you want of me?

Is it merely my confession, the final will and testament of this pure gold baby—must you hurl me in your crucible in the name of prurience, of alchemy, will it only be my dying shout—*I'm melting!*—that knocks you out?

All right, my magic mirror—this fair lady aims to please.

I, Calliope, being of sound and furious mind—and no body—bequeath my history to the heartless, my memories to the murderous, my childhood to the pry-

ing. To the brokenhearted I leave this bloodstain, my father's final autograph, splashed across my childflesh with a fascist's cool panache; to the salacious, my years of solitude, sealed inside our lonely home, the mourning masses camped in the yard, paparazzi tangled in the tree limbs, servants selling their memoirs for six figures or more. To the maudlin I leave my mother, the tiger-fury with which she swaddled me, my teenage struggles to break free, the chilly silence at the other end of the phone; and to the Peeping Toms, my poetry, the years of notes and diaries, doomed efforts to translate my life into language, to read my own story like spilled tea leaves—if you can make sense of this jumble, I hope you'll share it with me.

Alas, I know it's not enough, O Prurience, O Empathy. You want to see the scar tissue, you need to feel the blade. Experience is the name of this game: mine? yours? What difference anymore? There you sit with your spectacles, your chardonnay, you think my verse might do the trick—each syllable a new sensation, each diphthong a tiny death. The transmutation of this leaden Bird, her anguished words to your hot gooseflesh. I hate to burst your bubble, pal: The signs are everywhere, but everywhere they're meaningless.

So let's just say I was curious—curious to see what could happen. That's all I was, after all, what I had become: a curiosity, a clown. My foolishness knew no bounds or borders: a buffoon, a knave, a jack with just one eye, chasing after the suicide king. Let's just say I wasn't playing with a full deck. Let's say it wasn't fun anymore.

Please don't pout—it's so unbecoming! Were you expecting fireworks, ticker tape, standing ovations? Were you expecting Virgil's gentle hand, a white-robed choir, Revelation? Abandon hope, my paramour: In the end, my story's not so special, just a lonely girl ISO her father, wanting to know the truth. Don't be disappointed—it could only happen this way. You make someone a hero, launch them skyward, and watch them tumble. Admit it, kid, that's the real rush, the big thrill: fear and pity, gravity and death—not rapture, not trumpets, not singing dogs or pearly gates.

Katharsis, my dear acolyte: the bloody binge and purge.

Anything more is just religion.

★

The letter arrived the evening before the big show, a sharp knock on the door of room 503. I didn't answer, of course—I was, *comme on dit,* caught up. Autumn sun slicing through the window, across the small plush room and the rumpled bed, my clothing strewn over every surface. I stared at the ceiling, sweaty and exhausted: All day I'd been rehearsing, babbling my lines, hitting my marks. I'd had to run through Rockefeller Center to avoid the hungry autograph hounds, the outstretched hands and flashing bulbs—my bad leg throbbing, sweating in the humidity and heat. All I could think of was this quiet room, a precious pill, a few quiet hours tending to my needs.

Another minute and the knock came again. "Do you need to get that?" Cassandra looked up, that expression on her mousy face—annoyance mixed with fear—that I'd already grown to dislike.

"I'm sure it's just a reporter, or worse," I said, and draped an arm across my eyes. The air-conditioning hissed and whispered, tingled pleasantly across my belly. "Do you know that man at the reception desk, the big palooka with the hooked nose, the Aqua Velva? He asked me on a date this morning, can you imagine?"

Cassie propped herself on an elbow, dark hair strung damply across her cheek. "What did you tell him?" she said, her voice taut with nonchalance, reaching for the cigarettes on the nightstand.

"I'm pretty sure this is a nonsmoking room," I said.

"Like you care."

"I'm a stickler for the rules." I shrugged and wrapped the sheet around me. Like candy from a baby: I knew I'd get a rise. I was already tired of her, you see—three days of romping through Midtown, through the East Village, hiding from photographers, from Rhoda, from her boss. Fun fun, games games—but here's the truth, *mon cher:* It was boring. It was *all* boring—and the worst part was I was only doing it because it was expected of me, because I'd made a deal. A big, splashy mess—typical Calliope. To do otherwise would confuse the critics; it would fuck up Rhoda's plans.

Dear Cassie: It wasn't you, it was me.

But there I was, trapped in a swank Chelsea hotel, a thirty-year-old TV producer stuck in my orbit, chattering about leaving her fiancé, about running away with me to Key West. The *Times* op-ed had come out that morning—in a kitschy diner around the corner, Rhoda swooned over grapefruit: "I knew I could count on David Brooks," she said, eyes aglimmer. "Talk about money well spent!" I looked across the diner and saw a dozen others flapping their newspapers over yogurt, over eggs and bagels. "Third-rate doggerel," was what they'd read on A23. "Hate speech." "Decadence." Worst of all, he'd called me "confessional," the boor! So much for compassion, I thought, and balled up the paper, threw it on the floor.

Was it worth it, I wondered. But of course I knew the answer: It didn't matter anymore. The wheels were in motion; the train had left the gate. New York was the crucial phase of the Lubinski Magnum Opus, Zero Hour of Calliope's Great Escape. She'd been putting it together for months: the bank account in Bermuda, the condo in Montreal. She had a doctor in La Jolla, one of my father's old suppliers (the OxyContin King, they'd apparently called him, which explained the mysterious liner note from *The Fisher King*—"OK rules!"): A few threatening suggestions and he was putty in her hands, no match for my Polish pugilist; we'd have a signed death certificate, a year's worth of Percocet scrips. It would be the Stunt of the Century, Rhoda assured me, the Apollo 11 of the New Scambiguity.

"Suicide right on the stage!" she crowed, and faces at the counter turned her way. She lowered her voice, leaned across the table. "It's foolproof, baby. I've outdone myself. After tomorrow, no one will doubt it: the pressure got to you, the bad reviews, you couldn't take it, there was no other way out, yadda yadda . . ."

I plunked my spoon in the oatmeal and sat back. "Just like my father."

"Just like your father."

"Spare me the gloating, okay, Rho?"

She took my chin in hand, lifted my eyes to hers. It was a scene we'd been repeating, verbatim, since May. "This is what you wanted, Sweet Pea. Don't forget. You begged me. In the hospital. Remember?"

"It's what *you* want," I said.

"I want what's best for you. And for your career."

"Because you get fifteen percent."

Rhoda signaled for the check, took out her compact, and touched up her powder. "Don't insult me, C. You want another agent? Go for it. See who'll put up with you. Why don't you call your beloved Beekeeper's agent? See how well she's done for him?"

"He hasn't finished writing the book yet, Rhoda."

"I'd have sold that thing before he uncapped the pen." She snapped the mirror shut, threw a fifty on the table. "By the way, did you ever find out what it's about?"

"He wouldn't say. I'm sure it's about Zen and fasting and all that."

"Big audience there."

"You might be surprised," I said.

We walked out into the mild heat, Ninth Avenue's dull luminousness stretching forever in both directions. I had to be at NBC in twenty minutes for what promised to be a long day of rehearsals—the Electra skit just wouldn't come together, the vibe wasn't right at all. When Clytemnestra shouted at Orestes, it was unconvincing, flat, as though she were talking to the wrong person. I stood at the corner and squinted uptown, a veil of haze stretched between the jumble of buildings, truck gears grinding on the cross street and the smell of fresh diesel and stale pretzels, one gleaming airplane floating silently behind the fray.

"Look, kiddo, we can always turn back," Rhoda said, in the smug tone she took when playing her trump card. "Keep doing your little performances, keep signing your autographs and playing the fool. I hear they want you to host *Fear Factor,* maybe be the next *Bachelorette.* Or you could make a sex tape, leak it to the Internet. How about that kid at the front desk? He looks like the type . . . People love you, C, they love crazy and unpredictable—you can be crazy and unpredictable forever, right?"

I didn't answer, waving for one cab after another. They all passed me by, rolled-up windows reflecting flashes of my face. The cabbies could see my fraudulence from five blocks away. I felt leprous.

"It's your life, Calliope. Your career. Don't do it for me."

Crazy and unpredictable—was that even possible anymore? Were there any surprises left in Calliope's repertoire? I looked into Rhoda's eyes, tried to remember our teenage Mountaintop days—long afternoons of Scrabble, biking into town for ice cream in the dog days of July, smoking joints on the Terrace and comparing our love lives. It wasn't so long ago, I thought. Who were we now? No one I recognized. In that sense, I thought, I had already disappeared. In that sense, I'd already died.

"I can't stand myself," I said. I had the urge to sit right there on the pavement, lie across the sidewalk, wrap myself in cardboard, and let the pedestrians step across my body, let pigeons peck my hair.

Rhoda sucked her teeth and looked away. "Skip the waterworks, please. Save it for the show."

A taxi pulled up at last, and I quickly got in. Rhoda stood on the curb with arms folded, sunglasses perched atop her head. "Just leave me a little self-respect, Rhoda, okay? Try not to rub my nose in it."

She leaned close to the window, pressed her hands on top of mine. "This is what I do, C. Don't ruin it for me—this is *my* art."

She slapped the roof of the cab and the driver put it in gear. "And read your contract again, dear. Fifteen percent is for earnings while *living*," she called as we pulled away. "For posthumous I get twenty-five!"

Nine hours later—ten? who cared?—I held a pillow over my face while Cassie babbled on, that insistent perkiness in her voice papering over deep panic. "Do you think Lorne suspects something?" She nudged my knee for attention. "I'm fucked if he catches me fooling around with the host. It'll be the end of my career, the end of everything. You don't think Amy saw us coming out of the broom closet, do you? She's always had it in for me—"

"No," I said, for at least the fifth time.

"Good, because I don't even know what I'd—"

"Cass." I laid the pillow aside, pressed my palm against her face. She closed her eyes and leaned into my hand, and I traced her lips with the pad of my thumb. A long sigh, her body went soft and curled into my side.

"Yes?" she whispered.

I wanted to say something terrible, something cutting and cruel, just to see the betrayal on her face. Or maybe it was my own surface I wanted to shatter, throw off the jade veil that had lain over my shoulders these past months. How many readings and junkets had I done? A marathon of publicity, a blitzkrieg of bullshit: interviews, nine-minute TV slots, reading my poems like an automaton, leaping about like a lunatic, like a *crazed monkey*, faking orgasm for an insatiable public—and all the while watching from above, rolling my eyes at this pitiful performance, wanting to shout at the harebrained harlot below, "Be quiet! For the love of god, *shut up!*"

All summer I daydreamed of freedom, floated on Percocet and imagined soundless mornings, silent nights. "Soon, baby, soon," Rhoda would say when I pestered her for the promised plan, the long-awaited exit strategy. "I'm working on it."

The knock at the door came again, sounding both more urgent and final. "What if it's someone from NBC?" Cassie murmured.

I leaned down and whispered, "All the more reason to keep quiet, my sweet."

Knock knock!

Who's there?

Daddy!

Daddy who?

Daddy gonna leave you and ruin your life!

Ha ha.

Daddy gonna mess with your head so baaaad . . . you'll never figure out who you are or where you came from, never know your true history!

Very funny.

Daddy gonna blow his brains out, mark you for life. Daddy gonna leave you high and dry so you can never have a real relationship, never be satisfied—

That's a good one. I get it.

Daddy gonna—

Enough!

Enough? It's never enough, Birdie-B! This is the show that never ends. That's why they call it the afterlife!

Past the windows, a twilight of rose and pearl seeped across the Hudson like strong tea in water, a bejeweled cruise ship slid downriver, across the bright punch card of New Jersey. The knocking stopped, a swish as something passed beneath the door. I rolled away from cloying Cassie, swiped the pills off the nightstand, and went to fill a glass of water.

"You just took one of those," she said.

"Did I? I thought that was hours ago, at the studio . . ."

"It was here. As soon as we got back. Remember? You were worried the maid would throw out the bottle? When you found it on the dresser, you fell to your knees and thanked Jesus?"

Water glass in one hand, I bent to pick up the manila envelope lying just inside the door, tossed it on the bed. Probably more clippings from Rhoda—late reviews of the book, editorials about the upcoming Chicago reading, hate mail from Hartford and New Haven; or maybe it was from the brawny kid downstairs, a Bronx-style love letter, his proposition looking better by the minute.

"Isn't it dangerous to take too many?" My worried escort reached idly for the envelope, undid the clasp. "Even allergy pills can mess you up, you know, and we want you in top form tomorrow."

"I'll be in top form tomorrow."

"I want you in top form *tonight*," she teased, pulling something out of the envelope and studying it. "Who's Danny Grier?" she said.

I downed the pill and snatched the envelope from her hand. After a glance at the contents, I ran to the door and flung it open, dashed into the hallway—yes, naked, my bright *observateur*—but all I saw was a closing elevator door and two blue-hairs in crepe de chine, one of whom raised a pair of opera glasses to get a better look.

"Sorry," I mumbled, and stepped back inside.

Hey kid, read the note, in a teenager's slovenly hand. It was clipped to an old-fashioned airmail envelope: red, white, and blue edges frayed, a riot of postmarks and colorful stamps. *I hear you been looking for me. It's a long time since I saw you or your mom. Not long enough, if you ask her.*

"What is it?" Cassie kneeled on the bed and tried to peer over my shoulder, sniffing my neck playfully until I walked to the window.

I shouldn't be giving you this, the note went on. *But I figure you're old enough to decide for yourself. Keep it real,* he signed off—*Uncle Dan.* The airmail envelope was addressed to him, at an address in Palm Springs. The handwriting sent a shiver up my back, a splash of warmth across my chest—*Once, if I remember well . . .* —I leaned against the air conditioner while the room began to buck and heave.

Cassandra was watching me like a puppy unsure if it's about to get fed or kicked.

"Get your clothes," I said.

"What's the matter?"

"I need to be alone. Go! Go!"

She crossed her legs and stared at me, cigarette quivering between her fingers. "What about dinner? Are we still going to Dojo . . ."

"Forget it. Get out." She made no move, only watched me with a wounded look that made me savage. My mother's child, as it turned out: Pathos made me vicious, the scent of a wound made me cruel. "Out!" I cried. "I don't want you here!" I grabbed her arm and pulled her from the bed, the terror on her face almost funny as she stumbled across the room. I stood by the window while she scampered, whimpering, for her clothes. I had to quell the urge to kick her bare behind. The sky had grown dim, patterns of light from neighboring buildings flooding the room like a diorama, our own spotlit shoebox open to audiences in Weehawken, Fort Lee. It was perfect, I thought, Rhoda would be sorry she missed it—another tawdry episode, courtesy of Calliope.

Cassie stopped at the door, still buttoning her blouse, shoes clamped under one arm. "Can I call you later?" she said, bravely raising her chin. I closed my eyes and took a breath, wondering when the pill would kick in, seep sweetness into my bones. Biting my lip, I put my arms around her, kissed the top of her head.

"I think I'm in love with you," she said, staring in stunned misery. I reached for the doorknob—there just wasn't time!—but still she clung. "Is this about Ben?"

"Ben?"

She squinted, squeezed my arm. "How many of those pills did you take?"

I shook her off, pushed her into the hall. "Right. It's Ben. He's so jealous, Cass," I said, brandishing my fingernails like a claw. "Be careful: He won't neglect his vengeance." Her perplexed eyes staring back, I shut the door.

And then I was alone, the terrifying thing in my hand. I drew the curtains, clicked on a lamp, and held the envelope to my nose, breathing in its foreign scent. How far had it come? Over what mountains and oceans—what deserts of absence, what rivers of death? The handwriting, that childish scrawl—it was his, it had to be—a tremor spread up the backs of my legs, into my armpits, my elbows. Damned Percocet—never as fast as you needed it to be! I took another pill, but my hand still shook when I tried to slide the onionskin letter from its pouch—so I took one more, for good measure, splashed water on my face, sat cross-legged on the floor, and tried to steady my breathing.

Wait for me, my girl, he'd said in his previous communiqué. Fifteen years, with not even a peep. And how I'd waited! Reached out for him, prayed for him, sent my messages through time and space. As I gently squeezed the envelope, two slips fluttering to the carpet, I realized I'd never expected an answer: Searching was simply a part of my life, sending my summons to the silent universe. And here was the universe's reply.

"I wanted you to see this," the letter began—no salutation or ceremony, no shaft of heavenly light. I was already hyperventilating, my head swimming. I turned the AC on high, pulled on a nightgown, and slumped beneath the window. I slapped my cheeks and blinked the fog away.

Keep it. I've got three more. See? She did love me once. That was a long time ago. Why should I fuck up her life anymore? I won't ask her for one cent. I brought this on myself. It's a fitting end. The farce is almost finished.

I looked at the other slip: a tiny photograph, black-and-white, cut from a photobooth strip like you find at the mall. There he was—my stunned and anxious giant, caught once again in too-bright lights; and clinging to his neck, her back to the camera, a squalling, diapered baby. His expression was almost comical, one hand between her shoulders, the other beneath her pampered bottom—and though I'd known it all along, it wasn't until that moment that I understood how young he'd been, the vagrant in the photo not much older than the woman holding it now.

De profundis, Domine. What a fool I am! I don't like your plan, that's final. Leave her be. She deserves to be happy. I'm going upstairs to wait. It won't be long now. If you have news, send to J, general delivery. Mr. Bath and Rot.

De profundis, Domine—from the depths, O Lord! cried Rimbaud, who knew a thing or two about Hell. The phrase scared up a morning from my scarred memory, like a covey of crows taking flight. Where were we—the beach? my new bedroom? My father held me in his lap with the battered book before us, the smell of him surrounded me, his voice low and cigarette-rough. "What a fool I am, Birdie," he quoted his patron saint. "A *fool*, get it? Like a court jester. Some translations say 'ass' or 'beast,' but that's not the same. Get it?"

I craned to see him. "Yes," I lied.

"An ass is ugly and stupid, something people make fun of." He made a gloomy face. "A fool is someone who makes fun of himself." He stuck out his tongue and touched it to the tip of his nose. I squealed. "Which would you rather be?"

A difficult question, over a toddler's head. I thought very hard and said, "Which one are you?"

My father stared for a minute, then hugged me tight, growled in my ear, lifted me over his head. "From the depths," he said, and pulled me down, blew into my neck, and made a farting sound. "From the depths I am crying out to you."

All grown up, I leaned into the hotel air conditioner, heart beating a tango, and read the letter over and over. I stretched across the floor, held the photograph to my forehead. From what depths was he crying out? What had he brought on himself? Who on earth was "J"? The farce was almost finished, he'd said, a line that spiked me like an icicle to the small of the back. Stupefied in twilight, I tried to get it straight: He was in some kind of trouble. Was he broke? Was he sick? Was he—ohgod—*dying*? (*Not again!*) What was Danny's plan and why did my father find it unacceptable?

None of it made sense. But one thing was clear: The terrifying letter was the sign I'd been awaiting, his song of ascent, if sung sotto voce: Mr. Bath and Rot lived!

I had to do something. It was all happening so quickly, it didn't fit with the plan. In twenty-four hours I'd be on national TV, reading my poetry, trafficking in his myth—but here were his words clutched and crumpling in my fist, here was his need, so tangible I could taste it, filling my mouth like sweet ether, swimming through my opiated brainpan. O Mr. Bath and Rot! How could you think I'd be happy without you? Now that I'd seen your words, now that I'd (almost) found you? Whatever the price, I'd pay it to reclaim you. Just tell me what to do. *Come back, Uncle Dan!*

Someone in the room had started to moan, making quite a ruckus— I remember thinking I had to get out of there, find somewhere quiet to think! Like Jane Eyre in her Red Room, I was cruelly confined—a strange little figure suffering so, the spirit of her dearly departed hovering close. Pulling myself up on the bed, I chanced a look in the mirror—and there she was: the horrible hag with her hollow eyes, her broken nose, the shrew who'd followed me around all summer, hiding in closets, squeezing into my suitcase, attacking me in the bathtub with psychotic delight. The pills did a middling job of keeping her at bay—but now she stared back with something like pity. The sight of her was too great a shock—her hideousness knocked me flat; my ears pulsing and ringing, I suppose I had a species of fit.

Then I was on the roof, humming to myself in the warm night. The sound of traffic was a kind of wind—but in that aerie, walled in by glass panels, nothing stirred. Light spangled on the surface of the swimming pool, rose in towers on every side, and was absorbed into a dun and starless sky.

"Who are you talking to, Bird?"

"Who?"

"You said, 'I'll be right there.'"

There were gentle hands under my shoulders. There was a picture of my father in my hand. Colored lights danced across the river, and every horn below honked at me.

"What am I going to do?"

"You'll be brilliant. Don't worry. You'll knock 'em dead."

I could hear the sound of running water. "Dead?"

"It's okay, baby. Let's not talk now. Let's get you in the bath."

"Alive," I said, every nerve ending thrumming. The feeling was reaching for me again, the dark claustrophobia I'd felt in the hospital: bodies crowding around me, noise and frenzy pressing me forward. "*De profundis . . .*"

"Shhh, just relax. I'm right here."

Spider legs brushed my face, my neck. At the back of the cave, someone was waiting. "Crying out," said a drowning voice.

"*De profundis,*" I heard. And then, "*Alive.*"

*

Here's how it was supposed to work:

Halfway through reading "Suicide Bomber" I would shed my golden skin, revealing my brand-new fashion sense, Calliope's mind-blowing fall line: explosive vest, bandolier, grenade belt, all strategically arranged over my naked body. A tasteful ensemble, it was sure to set off tabloid fireworks, the fashionistas would be blown away, the millions aside the catwalk casualties of my devastating Daisy Dukes.

"Front page of *USA Today* for sure," said Rhoda. "Maybe the cover of *Cosmo!*"

"More like *American Mercenary.*"

"Just make sure you look dangerous, darling—give a little suicide vogue."

"Armageddon chic?" I offered.

"Talk about a plunging neckline."

"These hems are going sky-high!"

The outcry would be instantaneous: I'd be a prisoner in my hotel, pinned down throughout the week while the scathing reviews proliferated. I'd try to sneak out once or twice, the news would show footage of an endangered Bird: hounded out of Barnes & Noble, her taxi pelted with garbage, protesters chanting and holding up the Qur'an. Demonstrations in Queens, in Ithaca, with any luck in Hebron. When I made my triumphant return to KGB the following Thursday, I'd be a nervous wreck, shaken and wan. No one would doubt it when I passed out mid-sonnet. Early the next morning, the press would be summoned to a hotel room splattered in blood and vomit, the body already on a plane back to San Diego, the unimpeachable doctor's certificate: *Causes of Death: 1. Broken Heart, 2. Percocet.*

Later a tape would surface: a cell-phone caller to a suicide hotline, an anonymous voice slurring, "Daddy . . . Daddy . . ." before passing out on the line.

It was all very elegant, as fake suicides go; but as I watched Rhoda work during the late summer weeks, listened to her thinking aloud, I felt as though I were already vanishing, shrinking into a hard, leathery nut somewhere inside myself. Across her desk in Silverlake, or in the next seat in first class, her eyes would grow wide, hands dancing in the air, stopping to write furiously on a cocktail napkin, draw a diagram—I felt myself deflating moment to moment, retreating from my outer edges like the pit of some slow-rotting fruit. I shrank farther and farther until her voice seemed to come from above. Like my beekeeper trapped at the bottom of his well, I was surrounded by silence, locked in solitude—while up above, the dry husk continued to speak and agree independently of me.

But—and here's the rub, my chickadee, the grim conundrum of Calliope's *To Be*—who was *really* doing the talking, signing on the dashes? Who practiced the lines, who helped pick out the dishes? That dull, nodding automaton: Could *that* be the real me?

"I'm in here! Help me!" I tried to shout, but my voice disappeared in the dark. "Make me stop," I cried in dreams, lone rider in a speeding subway car. I'd bang on the glass of that steel coffin, I'd struggle and scream: "Let me out!" As Rhoda described the condo, imagined the shock of my eventual return, the book deals, the inevitable miniseries, I'd browse swatches of wallpaper and wonder: Which Calliope would survive the metamorphosis, and which would slough off like snakeskin, cease to exist?

He loves you so much. If you want to help him, you better hurry, said the note that arrived the next morning, sliding under the door with the first sticky daylight. I opened one eye, saw Rhoda slumped in the blue padded chair; with all the stealth I could muster, I slid from the bed and whisked the thin envelope away, locked myself in the bathroom. *I can't explain what's happening,* wrote Danny. *You'll have to see for yourself.*

There was a number at the bottom of the page: a dollar sign, lots of zeros.

I stretched on the bathroom tiles with my bottle of pills, my leg a lance of flame, and tried to regard this new message calmly. Staring at the strange words, my mind began to empty. What last night had seemed a phantasm, a shot across the psychic bow, in the still morning took on body and consequence: The paper in my hands was real, the words real. I needed to think it through, understand what they asked of me. I needed to survey the new landscape, plot a new course. (*O dear Mr. Sulu, where are you when I need you?*) I needed time, but time was the one thing denied to me.

"Baby, you okay in there?" Rhoda knocked on the door. "How're you feeling? Shipshape? Let me in—we have to talk about tonight."

I stared at the paper, the poorly penned demand, the creepy signature in scrunched letters: *Love and kisses, U.D.* I could feel Rhoda's excitement through the door: It was the big day. I was surprised she'd slept at all. She was my best friend—"your number-one fan," she always said—she'd been by my side for years. I couldn't let her down, I thought—and yet already, in the pit of my throat, a new MO was struggling to form. I tried to keep it from growing, willed it to wither on its disloyal vine. But there were the letters, the old photograph, undeniable. The words swimming in my mind: *Wait for me, my girl . . .*

"Cassandra Beers just called my cell," said Rhoda. "She sounded upset. She said she needs to see you before the cast dinner. I'm sure it's something about the pledge. I don't know, C—maybe you should just sign it. It's hard to sue the dead, right?"

My leg was throbbing, pain stabbing into my groin. I levered myself standing, avoiding the sight of myself in the mirror. I opened the pill bottle and closed it again. I slid both letters back into their envelopes and hid them under the sink.

"She wants to meet you by the duck pond at six. You've got Žižek at five, so maybe you can just make it. Try to keep the big tyrant on schedule, okay? Remind him *you're* the one who's supposed to do most of the talking . . ." The doorhandle jiggled. "Are you okay in there? I think Cassandra's a little strange, don't you? The way she follows you around like a little kitten. It's like that security guard all over again, that kid at Irvine? What was his name? Ronaldo? Roberto?"

The cacophony in my brain drowned her out, a garble of questions, of possibilities stretching to countless horizons. I held my breath, tried to think clearly. With each minute my betrayal was ripening; with each heartbeat my true loyalties were swelling, weighing down their branches.

"Listen, baby, I had another idea. Let's rearrange that bandolier—*tastefully*, of course—let's give them a quick nipple-shot when the burqa comes off. What do you say? We'll call it a 'costume gaffe,' something like that . . ." She stopped, and I could feel her staring at the door. "Are you listening, C? Can you say something, please?"

Sitting on the toilet, one leg outstretched, head in my hands, I lurched from despair to grief to resignation. Rhoda would never let me go—that was obvious. She had put in too much work, too much scheming; she'd never let me break cover, blow the house of cards down. A week from now I'd be a shut-in Canuck, living on grocery deliveries and TiVo; the clock was ticking—*T-minus thirteen hours, twelve*—while far away, my father suffered, heartsick and broken. I'd found him at last—and he didn't even know!

The irony fell on me like a bag of wet sand: It was *I* who was the patsy; the Scambiguity was on *me*.

"One other thing—and I promised I wouldn't say anything, but I think you ought to know, so you don't overreact." She spoke more quietly, like the silken voice of my conscience. I wanted to beg her to be quiet. "In the Electra skit—and I swear this was not my idea—but they're planning a little surprise—"

Just then the phone rang, an intrusion so merciful I nearly burst into tears. I hauled myself standing, splashed cold water on my face, pulled my hair back and tried not to meet the eyes in the mirror. When she hung up, I knew, I'd have to come out. There was no time for dallying: the apple had fallen; *sont fait, les jeux*. But I would find a way, I'd already decided. In the meantime, I needed to give a sign, something to let him know I'd gotten the message. What word or gesture could I possibly send him? What signal could I expect him to see?

"That was Cassandra again," called Rhoda. "I do think that woman is a little unbalanced. You better call her back." She rapped on the door, rattled the handle. The ache in my leg was a thread that pierced the sole of my foot, drawn by a hot needle out the top of my head. "Okay, C, we've got to get moving. No more fucking around."

I set my jaw and stared into the mirror, found the hag's dark eyes staring back. The resemblance was striking: the nose and chin, the freckled arms, worried brow. How could I separate this decrepit creature from Calliope? How would I ever sort it out?

My father would know, I told myself. He'd sired me, bathed my new-born body, pampered and powdered and fed and diapered me. He would know his own daughter from a conniving fraud—he'd settle this once and for all.

Rhoda pounded. "Open this door. It's time to go."

A new course of action was slowly forming: Call it a detour; call it Plan B. I'd figure out the details as I went along. But I would need my wits, my nerve—above all, I'd need clarity. So I opened the bottle of Percocet, shook all the pills into my fist. Gritting my teeth, I dropped them in the toilet, watched them swirl out of my life.

Composed, I turned the handle, opened the door. My old friend looked me up and down. "You win," I told Rhoda. "Let's get on with the show."

✳

Breathe, now, my dear one—you're looking so pale! Get ahold of your-self, go powder your nose—there's plenty more to this tale.

No reason to get excited, though you fear for me, think I'm unwise. This mystery letter, it's too much, you think; it smells of a trap, it feels con-trived. Just another false alarm, you're sure, another of Calliope's pathetic gaffes—she's being groomed for calamity, fattened up like a golden calf . . .

But don't jump to conclusions, my sweet. Don't roll your eyes or write me off. You think you've got it figured out, but you don't even know the half! Of course I appreciate your heartfelt concern, I value your insight, admire your gumption—but it will take a bit longer to get to the heart of this tangle. *Caveat auditor:* Proceed with caution!

✳

It was a beautiful night to drown in, velvet sky vaulting overhead like a bonnet, land's heavy shadow receding. Every star urged me onward, every benign constellation blessed my journey. With each long stroke of my arms—how they remembered the rote work of childhood, the silent af-ternoons in the pool coded in lung and muscle!—the world I'd known dropped into the past, a huge and shady future looming ever closer though I never could quite touch it.

The moon had risen, bulging and gibbous, tired light stretching the air. I looked for the clear pathway, the silver carpet, but her beams splintered and danced like snowflakes. When I raised my hand before my eyes I caught them briefly on my fingertips—winking and darkening, enjoying a brief and bodiless existence before dissolving. I floated on my back, let that moon-mother bathe me, waited for the hot ache in my shoulders to abate. My sea-lover surged and thrusted, lifted and fell, and I was almost content.

The lighthouse shrank to a pale nub, San Diego's gold corona quivering at the horizon like an upper lip: *Never to return? Did you say never?* The sea-stench raw and antiseptic, filling my head with midnight's vapor. Can I tell you, my friend, about freedom? Can I sing a song of Whitmanesque wandering, the shores of the living world ever receding, and with them the facts of my existence? I was large, and growing larger! My multitudes molting, my contradictions slipping out with each sea-heave! Only the pins in my leg held me together, cold and prickling, my skin becoming porous. In time, I was everywhere—but Calliope, shrunken to the size of a word, was nowhere.

For hours I swam, my scissor kick keeping at bay the enormity of what I'd done. When fatigue overtook me, it was stealthy and diffuse, of a piece with the water and the cooling air. Tumult and terror slipped into my wake; clamor lifted like mist and dissolved. Loneliness and confusion, orphanhood and rage, all seeped through me and were sucked away. I knew then why drowning is the best way to go: What could be more natural than this exquisite embrace? In the end, I understood, it would feel like love.

Somewhere in a distance without direction or coordinate, a tanker's throaty horn hummed. From a pocket of moonlight, a quick flock of winged creatures fluttered past. I could hear my breath, my groans and grunts, could feel tears warming my cheeks. When I could swim no longer—my arms rigid and burning, my legs dead as drumsticks—I stopped and sculled under a sky grown hazy, fringes of wool filtering the moonlight. It was a plan of brazen simplicity, a Houdini-like escapade—when the rescuers sifted through the wreckage, when all the rubble was cleared, they'd look up in alarm, shake their heads, cry to one another:

"She's not here!" The audience would gasp, Rhoda would leap to her feet: like a bathing-suit beauty in a jeweled lacquer box—first they'd seen the poet ripped in half, and then she'd bloodlessly disappeared.

Rhoda.

For a moment I thought of my poor friend, my patient tutor—only now would she know how well she'd taught me. How confused she'd been, back at the Arizona Café; how terrified and distraught she'd be tomorrow. To the last I'd pretended I was still with the program—nothing but jitters, second thoughts, a last-minute switch from Manhattan to San Diego when KGB canceled my reading (as I'd known they would). I was sorry about the burqa, about my little improv—but we were still moving forward, all systems still go . . .

O forgive me, my darling, my booster, my guide: It was all I could do to get on with the show, to free myself at last from this life of deceit.

You fool! You dumb bunny! You deceived her, didn't you?

At first I thought the sound was the play of ripples, another flock of night birds. But as the cloud-veil pulled away from the moon, I looked into the depths and saw her: that nightmarish face chiseled from marble, the awful eyes, the cracked and sallow lips.

You deceived everyone—and in the name of truth, to boot! Falsehood, thy name is Calliope!

She swam sneering up at me from who knew what watery hell: my own bloated Fury demanding reverence. I flinched before her arrival, but the churning water could not obscure her purpose. Like a sucker punch, I felt the futility, the laughable sham of my well-laid scheme. I'd lied to my closest friend, strewn heartache like rose petals in my efforts to heal my own wounds. I'd been the recipient of love unbounded, benefactor of the world's encouragement and trust—and what had I given in return? Cheap histrionics, self-pity and bile—they'd opened their arms, but I'd flipped them the Bird.

Calliope, you entered the world as the Champion of Truth; but you left it as Handmaiden to the Lie.

All this came to me as I bobbed there in the blank, limbs aflame. My sickening sister did not look away; her gaze knew neither shame nor pity.

I cringed to think what she might say next. But when she moved her lips, all that came out was a droning hum, so low it might have come from the deepest abyss; I shivered in the glare of a moon turned against me, spotlighting my jetsam triviality. She blinked once and wrenched her mouth into a smile of pure cruelty.

Then I was swimming again, fast as I could, fleeing that vision with all the strength I had left. What good would it be—to escape the torments of life, only to be hounded unto death by such a horror? What use, to show up at my father's doorstep trailing this misery, this conjoined twin? Stroke after stroke, my shoulders seizing, back beginning to spasm—she kept pace too easily, her dizzy moan growing louder. Her fingers snatched at my fluttering toes, my calves. The moon disappeared, the black ocean rose against me, water trickling into my mouth, up my nose. I had to stop to cough it out, bright spots dancing in my vision—my momentum broken, the bitch got a grip on my ankles and started to pull!

The drone was deafening, filling my ears, the moon a harsh disc dancing overhead. I flailed and gasped, nearly blind, but the hag yanked me back. I felt my muscles freeze; the black water gripped me and pulled me down.

Down, slowly down, the circle of light above grew smaller as the hag stole back to her lair, dragging home this sad trophy. I had no struggle left—as the last air bubbled from me, I wondered if this even deserved the name "suicide," or whether death in the course of faking death—death by the utmost folly—wasn't something of a different kind, an act without honor, without gravity, the destination of tragedy:

Here lies Calliope, a bald and bloated punch line.

When the green translucence parted and churned, and strong hands hooked my arms, I almost resented the interruption. Light speckled and shot in every direction, a riot of bubbles, I was buffeted like a waterlogged rag doll. The hands wrenched me from the witch's grip, a hand clamped itself hard over my mouth, fingers pinched my nose tight. A scream rattled through my skull but had nowhere to go. I tried to turn around but was held fast; as consciousness fled me like a flock of birds into the night, the thought entered my mind: *He's found me at last!* I could still see her face—a pale and leering smudge shrinking back to the depths—as the troubled blend of light and darkness pulled hoodlike over my head.

*

The return address on the airmail letter was only the name of a town: a strange conglomeration of syllables in an unrecognizable language. I had not heard from Danny again; I did not know this "J." There was no way to send word to my father in advance. No matter, I thought: If he'd seen my signal, he'd know I was on my way.

The farce is almost finished, he'd written. Through the long nights I'd lain awake, running endless interpretations through my head: His health was failing, his body consuming itself in romantic agony; or he was about to be exposed, perhaps worse, by enemies or debtors, or a foreign government enraged by his subversive activities. He could have been on drugs again, of course, the pure and potent strain of some tropical infusion gnawing his brain; or beset by enraged locals, the lord of the manor whose munificence has run its course.

Always as night weakened, the first seepage of dawn, I'd light upon my favorite, unbearably sweet, scenario: He was ready to come forward, to finish the farce himself. His daughter by his side, he'd return to the world of the living, announce to the faithful: *I never left you. I am I.*

But first I'd have to get to him, to step outside the design. Back in San Diego, I called a number from an old business card.

"Knew I'd hear from you sooner or later, kid," RT Dunleavy said. "I got men on every continent. Women, too. I got nine-year-olds on payroll. They make the best little spooks. Just come down to my office, and bring your checkbook. We'll find that s.o.b., don't you worry."

But that brashness I remembered from the day he crashed the workshop dissolved into grumbles when I explained what I needed. It was outside his expertise, I had to understand. He was a detective, not a babysitter, nor a rescuer of dames. What I was asking blurred the boundaries, it pushed the envelope of professional ethics—though he had to admit it sounded like fun.

"Think of it as a new horizon," I said. "A work of detective art."

"I want art, I go to the museum. This is business," he said.

"I wouldn't have called if I didn't think you were the best man—the only man—for the job." I heard him hesitate, heard the rasp of his stubble as he stroked his chin. I went in for the kill. "I'll pay you anything you want."

"Anything?"

"I'm sure you know, I'm a wealthy girl, Mr. Dunleavy."

"Please," he said after a pause. "Call me Dick."

✱

"Can you hear me?" said a voice, pushing through a layer of hot aquamarine cotton. "Say something, Calliope. Can you hear me? Are you okay?"

I felt myself shivering, felt the weight of heavy blankets on my skin. My head was enormous; my jaw felt wired shut. I was propped up against a cold metal wall, the floor beneath me vibrating, the muscular hum of the boat's engine rattling my body. It was the same loud buzzing I'd heard in the water: my saline persecutor's ghoulish drone.

A face loomed toward mine, out of focus, a low forehead and wide, pockmarked nose. "That was some lucky timing, kid—another minute and you're shark bait," he said. "Thought you said you were a strong swimmer. I got insurance to worry about, you know . . . What did you do to your hair, anyway?"

I closed my eyes, lulled by the slap and splash against the hull. "Hey!" he said, and I felt someone shake me, my head heavy as a gourd. "You with us? Can you speak?"

I sucked sweet air, savored the warmth of the scratchy blankets. Activity bustled around me, men with tanks and pontoons peeled themselves out of wetsuits. I felt the reassuring weight of Dick's hand against my forehead, my cheek. Yes, I could speak. Everything seemed to be in working order.

But why should I bother? What good had words done me before?

I thought I'd try silence, at least for a while. It couldn't get me in any worse trouble, after all! As I sipped from the coffee Dunleavy gave me, warmed my hands on the tin mug, I felt certain this was the right course: To get to my father, I would have to start listening, learn to be all ears. Slowly my body stopped shaking, the pulse in my ears faded. All that prattle and chatter, all those profligate lines—plastic pearls thrown before gluttonous swine. No, I thought, no more waste, no more babble or fuss.

Dear Daddy: Get ready—my next word is for you!

The cruiser ran all night, chugging its lightless way south through the chop while Dick sat at the wheel and squinted into the stars. "Nothing like running dark, kid," he breathed, hiding even the glow of his fat cigar from the keen eyes of the Coast Guard, of drug lords, of pirates. "Last thing we need is the fucking Mexicans stopping us. They're worse than the Americans. Shit, they're almost as bad as the Vietcong. I tell you about the time I was running smack in and out of Saigon?"

Finally warmed, dressed in clothes from the suitcase delivered to his office the week before, I huddled in a corner of the wheelhouse with a mug of tea while he reminisced about the war. Testing out my vow, I said nothing, and he took my silence as encouragement, rambling through tales of his two marriages, his brief stint as head of security for the L.A. Lakers. I could feel the engine straining, the propeller turning, but as I drifted into exhausted stupor all the sounds blurred and melted together, coalesced into one sentence, the raw magic of a fatherly voice: "Hello, Bird."

And then it was morning; we were bobbing at a small pier. The sky was a pot of milk-blue paint; spikes of sunlight poured upon rooftops of Spanish tile, stalks of bare rebar stuck out of windowless cubes of concrete. Two shifty fellows stood holding the ropes, chatting with Dick in Spanish, watching the quiet seaside street. No cars passed, only a beat-up taxi, engine running, waiting for me at the end of the dock.

"Nice doing business with you," said Dick. He gave me the suitcase and put a hand on my shoulder. "Remember, if you ever come back, if all this comes to light, make sure you give the Dunleavy Agency a plug. We specialize in runaway kids, wandering wives, philanderers . . . it's all about keeping families together—"

I grasped his broad shoulders and gave him a kiss on his craggy nose. He blushed, waited for me to speak. When I didn't, he waved and turned back to the boat. "That's all the thanks I need, kid," he called.

Four more days of travel—on buses, on airplanes, hours in filthy depots, sterile transit lounges. Dick had helped me lay out the bewildering route—a crazy squiggle of loops and double-backs and discontinuities to throw off any intrepid pursuit. I was unshowered, sore, bored literally to tears, only the two books I'd packed to entertain me: a crisp new copy of my beloved Blake, and my own slim volume, which I couldn't even look at anymore. My limbs cramped in growing discomfort (it had been two weeks since I'd abandoned my little pink friends, getting by on meditation, yoga, and buckets of naproxen). Long blurs of time in which I couldn't say if I was awake or dozing, jerked into awareness by a soulless voice that came from all sides. My pulse quickened, my tongue stuck. How could she have followed me? Did she, too, have a fake passport, forged traveler's checks? But it was only an announcement over the airport PA, the last call for my flight: *Good evening, Ms. Klein . . . Right this way . . .*

As I doggedly approached him, traversing the globe, I thought less and less about New York and Irvine, about Moreno and the Beekeeper and poor, sweet Rhoda. They were panels in a long-finished fresco, exquisitely detailed but unconnected to me. For a few excruciating hours, overcome with remorse, I fixated on the desire to call my mother. But that, too, passed soon enough. She would miss me, of course, they all would—but they could take care of themselves. All the excitement and anxiety of the past years, the frustration and lust, ecstatic spurts of writing, sterile weeks of block, unendurable anticipation—I could remember the moments, I could give them dates and names. But the feelings themselves fell from me like old scales; at 37,000 feet I was as cool and smooth as a pinball, nothing stuck to me anymore.

How strangely simple—this must have been what he'd felt all these years, the silence of total detachment, a derangement of the senses, an airborne *zazen*. Not emptiness but anonymity, I realized; not no-thing, but no-one.

My thoughts flew ahead to the moment I'd arrive—what would I feel, I wondered. What words, if any, would come? Would I crumble into childish tears, or stand stoically for his greeting? Would I scold him, pour forth all the pain he'd caused me, or forgive all in an instant, surrender to his embrace? In the bathroom, as the last flight began its descent, I washed my face, put on just a touch of makeup. Would he startle at my baldness? Would he even recognize me? I'd never before had to worry if my father would find me pretty, but cramped in that plastic cubicle I was paralyzed by the starkness of my appearance. I stared at the light streaks of my eyebrows, my too-long earlobes, the rough bump in my nose. Why oh why had I shaved my head? Had I really experienced such a depth of self-loathing, or had it been just more performance, vamping the role of the hysteric, the crank? I couldn't quite remember.

"Miss, please come out now." A flight attendant pounded on the door. "Miss, we are about to land!"

I forced myself to breathe, to look away from the mirror. None of it mattered. All the fatherless years were about to end, I thought, buckling myself in for the last time. My damned hair would grow back.

✶

Half an hour later, I was standing on a sidewalk in the full glare of a cold afternoon sun. A parking lot ringed by bulletin boards for cigarettes, cell phones, cable TV, a high fence of thick iron rails and beyond it a smoggy chaos of taxis, a gas station, stiff-backed police futilely blowing whistles. Behind it all rose the mountains, parched to the color of potatoes, vaulting one over the other in a race toward the cobalt sky. Through the haze of exhaust and my own stunned fatigue, the mountains proliferated, the most distant capped by winks of white. I pulled my thin sweater tight. The air was thin, my eyeballs buzzing; an ineffable silence somehow overlaid the noise.

I scanned the crowd moving past me, but saw no one I knew. For the first time I wondered how different *he* might look, what ravages or disfigurements time and chance had wrought. But I shook it off: Of course I would recognize him. He was my father! No disguise could fool me, no change throw me off.

My leg screamed in pain, my joints hot and itchy. I waited, teeth chattering, and scanned faces: backpackers and tourists, local businessmen in cheap black pants. I waited for a beautiful vagrant to materialize, but saw no one who fit the bill. The rush of passengers drained past until there was nobody left—just a couple of soldiers smoking by the gate and a bald, exhausted bird, trembling after her final flight.

"Hey, you," said a voice, almost frantic, its owner racing out of the airport's glass doors. "What the shit, man? I am waiting by the gate. What are you doing out here? I didn't know where the shit you were!"

He was a teenager, twenty or twenty-one, tops, dressed like a cross between hippie and mountain guide: loose, too-long cords over beat-up brown brogans, a heavy wool zip-up sweater with sleeves too short to reach his thin, braceleted wrists, and a thick knitted scarf twisted into a knot at his neck. He was tall and skinny, his dark hair shoulder-length, one layer clipped back to keep it out of his face. He wore small, rectangular sunglasses with green-tinted mirror lenses. His face raced downward over a sharp, straight nose to a point at his beard-dusted chin.

I watched him, my tongue heavy and still. "Jesus and the saints, man, you almost stop my heart!" he said. "I am worrying. I think, Shit, maybe I lose her!" He stared at me a minute longer, shifting from foot to foot. "What's it, does the cat have your mouth?"

Then he lunged at me, pulled me into a surprised embrace. "I'm just so happy you here." He leaned back to look at me. "It's so very good to meet you!"

I gently extracted myself. The man—the boy—peered into my face. "You don't look so much like him." He examined my smooth head, the new bump in my nose, the rusty stain across my throat. His breath was sweet and smoky, like clove cigarettes; his hair gave off the smell of dust. I stood as though for inspection, tried to still the shaking in my bones.

"You don't bring warm clothes? You think this is the Bahamas or something?" In one motion, he pulled the heavy sweater over his head and handed it to me. When I put it on, the shivering started in earnest.

"We go now, okay? Better we get in the road before sunset." He picked up my suitcase and I followed him across the parking lot to a small, dilapidated white van. The tires were bald, the windshield had a long, desultory crack across its upper half; inside, the rear had been stripped, a couple of black cases strewn across the bare metal floor.

He held open the passenger door, but I stopped and gripped him by the arm, raised my eyebrows questioningly, pointed at his chest.

"Oh!" he said. "You don't know? I'm Jacobo." He extended his hand and I shook it. "Of course I know your name," he said, hurrying around to the driver's side, starting the engine with a tinny rasp. "You're like a famous person for me, like a movie star. I want to meet you ever since I know about you . . . And now you are in my truck!"

He reached for a pack of cigarettes and offered it to me but I shook my head. I tried to focus on my aching leg, to use the pure, cold fault line of pain to center myself. "You are lucky I have the friend in the capital," he said. "She works in the airport. Maybe you see her? She says, 'Jacobo, I think this girl you are asking about is on the next flight.' Now I owe her a big favor. Otherwise, what are you thinking to do? Where do you go?" He tried to sound scolding, but he could not hide the eagerness in his voice. We pulled past the iron gate, the van lurching and squeaking on its struts. A policeman waved us on with a bored flick of his arm. The sun was foundering on the crests of the mountains, spreading like an egg in a skillet. Every pedestrian was my father, every face in every window, every taxi driver. Somewhere in these ramshackle avenues, or behind those hills and billboards, he was waiting. I almost wanted Jacobo to pull over, to suspend the delicious moment, the last gasp of fatherlessness, a threadbare virginity I was ready to lose.

"I have something to tell you." Jacobo jerked us into traffic, taxis blaring and zooming around us. "A message I am waiting very long to give." I watched his face as a dog watches the stranger who adopts it off death row. He tossed the cigarette out the window.

"Calliope," he said, "welcome home."

*

I dreamed of the dark cave, the razorflash of bats swarming blindly around me, a whirlwind of round, blank eyes. I raised my arms to ward them off, but one got past my defenses, tore the flesh from my leg, left veins dangling like bright, bloody worms.

A hand shook me, and I startled awake. Jacobo was staring with almost-comic concern, one hand on my shoulder, the other on the steering wheel. Beyond the weak headlights was a night as black as pitch; the van was a tiny ship, unaccompanied in that vacuum, fragile as a bubble. He raised his voice above the straining engine. "Jesus and the saints, you making some noise! It's the altitude. Everyone has the bad dreams at first. After a week or two maybe it stops." He pointed to his temple. "Not enough oxygen, so the brain, it does some things, you know?"

The van strayed and he jerked the wheel, veering us back into the lane. "Good, Jacobo." He shook his head. "Maybe you drive the truck into a ditch, and then she comes so far only for an accident."

We were crossing a plateau, high grass or grain undulating in moonlight, broken up every so often by the hunched silhouette of a lone hut— thatch roof, glassless windows, perhaps the weak flicker of a candle inside. Train tracks ran beside the road, peppered with litter, weeds sprouting between the ties. The tracks would shadow the van for a few miles, then dip off into a valley or a glade of thin, improbable trees, reemerging minutes later like a loyal puppy. I pressed my nose to the cold window, shifted on the uncomfortable seat. When I tried to stretch my leg, a knife seared into my hip.

"You cold?" He reached behind the seat for a thick, musty blanket. I wrapped myself as best I could, scratched my arms and throat under Jacobo's itchy sweater. With a frown, he ground the gearshift down, and we struggled into a long, curved incline, my ears popping and ringing, the doors rattling, the ticking whine of the engine rising. "Not so much longer," he said.

As we swept up and around the incline, the flat landscape heaved up a jagged line of mountains that rushed toward us. Dark against the star-soaked sky, keen and irregular as broken bottles, the mountains dominated the panorama, the quarter moon barely outlining its edges. The tallest peak, crowned by a glacier, threw back a dull gleam.

I touched my fingertip to the windshield, pointed at this stern, towering rock. Jacobo glanced at me once, and back at the road. "This is Old Maker," he said. "The old people say it is a holy mountain. They pray to Old Maker for water, when the snow is melting in the spring. Then the old men go to climb and bring back the special water. Only in that time is it allowed you climb Old Maker. Otherwise he get angry . . ." Jacobo rolled his window halfway down; the air whipped my cheeks like a lash, woodsmoke and eucalyptus chasing the odor of gasoline and rust through the van. "You know, the old people believe strange things. But yes, it is dangerous to climb Old Maker. Too much dangerous," he said, as though I'd already put on hiking boots. "Maybe in spring I come and we go to climb together, okay?"

I nodded, wrapped myself tight. It had taken half an hour to wind through the cramped and convulsing city, Jacobo prattling nervously, as though at the next corner I might bolt from the van, dash into the crowd. A puzzle of winding streets, soaring steeples, and fallen tile roofs; outdoor markets, every stall covered by a blue tarpaulin; narrow cobblestone passages trod by women in heavy mantles and broad-brimmed hats, carrying infants in shoulder slings, leading goats by frayed ropes. Men in ironed pants and shiny shoes stood talking to children in rags; old men with tangled beards and tire-tread sandals begged before jewelry stores, got shooed away from restaurants by waiters with slicked-back hair. Teenagers in bright T-shirts lounged on benches; a shriveled woman played a small nutshell banjo. Water from a stolid bronze fountain spouted and prismed in the dusk. Behind this plaza rose an enormous stone cathedral, two bell towers and tall wood doors belted with iron; carvings ran along the cornices and the two iron clocks on its facade told different hours. I pressed my face to the window, but soon the cathedral had disappeared around a bend. We bounced over cobblestones and cracked pavement, the road rising with each curve until we were circling the rim of a great basin, all that tumult blended into a mosaic of maroon and ocher below.

"Okay, so you ready to say something? Like maybe, 'Hello, Jacobo, it is also nice to meet you finally'?" I shook my head, and he shrugged, downshifted as the grumbling van continued to climb. We drove into dusk, late sun drawing a pink glow from the landscape, the fields above the city faded to moss green and fuchsia.

Turning in my seat, I examined the black boxes that slid around the back of the van—instrument cases, like the ones that had crowded the spare closets of my childhood. Jacobo saw me looking at them. "He taught me how to play a little bit, you know. But I'm not so good, even if I practiced every day." He took out another cigarette. "It's not so much my bag of chips. I don't have the gift. I play the songs he teach me, but it sounds like I am pretending to be him."

He turned to me with disarming seriousness. "You must have the gift, isn't this true? If you don't have the gift all you are is pretending, like you are imitating the person with the gift. No?" For a moment I believed he was talking about me—had already seen through me, divined my inner falseness? Had I come so far only to be quickly sized up and dismissed?

But he went on talking, while the last signs of development dropped behind us—small, uncompleted houses, roadside vendors, gas stations festooned with paintings of gods and saints. When he'd stopped trying to play the guitar, he said, he found he could listen to other musicians and pick out their errors, show them techniques that he himself had not been skilled enough to play. He could make suggestions for different sounds, intonations—and not just for guitar, but piano and horns, violin, even the drums his next-door neighbor built from old crates and scrap leather. By watching and listening, humming along, he could find the inner melody or rhythm, tweak the structure of any composition, bring out what the others hadn't known was there. Soon every musician in the village, young or old, was asking his advice; Jacobo could hear something in his head— their ideal, their aspiration—and show them the way.

" 'You are a producer,' he tells me. He helps me open my studio in the city, behind this café, just a couple rooms, but good equipment, man! He sends to the capital for some of it, to Boston, to Berlin . . . Then Danny has to come and set everything up, teach me how to use it!"

I looked up sharply and he said, "You remember Uncle Danny, yes?" I nodded anxiously, hoping he'd say more—the first hint of connection to that world I'd lately left, the first continuity from those strange letters to this dilapidated vehicle, this washed-out landscape.

He swerved to avoid a mule being led at the side of the road. "Now all the musicians come to my place. They say, 'Jacobo got the touch!' I always tell him he have to come play the music, but he doesn't. He says he won't play anymore, not until Calliope comes." He stared at me, and I watched the passing landscape, emaciated cows grazing on the tracks, dwellings of mud and tin. Soon—*soon* we would come to the turnoff, the golden gates opening wide to reveal my father's gleaming palace.

"And now she is here," he said.

But now, how many hours later, I still shivered in the rattle and fumes, tried to see into the distance past the weak headlamps. The road was rougher, long curves wrapping into the foothills, the mountains themselves craning above like sentries. Though my leg tingled with pain, my brow feverish, I found ease in silence — as though my words had been the source of all trouble, not merely its expression. "Pardon me," he said when I caught him staring. He fiddled with the knob of the broken radio. "He says, 'Don't bother her, Jacobo. Don't ask her so much things. Let her rest.'" He rolled his window down, back up, reached for the cigarettes. "But I wondered about you, you know, such a long time. I am waiting all this time to meet you."

We pulled slowly onto a dirt road, crept past the boarded-up storefronts of a small village. Everything perfectly still, no one moving about, low stone structures leaned over the van as it crawled up a constricting passage and eventually emerged into a tiny square. There was a derelict car or two, ancient bicycles standing against crumbling walls. In the center of the open space, what may once have been a garden had surrendered to dust, trash heaps, stray dogs scavenging through piles of wide, dry leaves. The tallest object was an unlit streetlamp, which stood out with hallucinatory clarity against the slate sky, its shadow reaching toward me like a long finger.

We got out and closed the doors. The dogs looked up, then bolted between two decaying buildings. *Here?* I thought. *My father lives here?*

Jacobo hauled down my suitcase, and I limped behind him into a flagstone alley. On either side, squat stone houses breathed with sleep. A gentle trickling whispered around us as we went, narrow water channels, no wider than my hand, cut into the stone on either side of the passageway. At each door, an even smaller stream branched off to bring water inside. I bent down and trailed a finger, the water so cold it tingled and stung up to my wrist. With each step my heart pounded louder. Up ahead, I could see the end of the narrow lane; beyond the last house the mountains sat like giant animals keeping insomniac watch. What if my father was angry I'd come? What if he'd hoped for someone slightly different? I hadn't been that diapered baby for so long — would he accept this grown-up version with all her compromises, all her complications?

Jacobo stopped at the last house and waited for me to straggle up. I held my breath as he opened the door and ducked below the lintel, stepping down onto a dirt floor. For an instant I fought the urge to turn and run, but he took my elbow and pulled me into a small room lit by a single candle— no furniture, nothing on the stone walls, only a few large sacks leaning in a corner, a couple of empty metal tubs, a waist-high rack filled with jars. Above the smell of dust and wet stone was a familiar odor: waxy and earthen, reassuringly sweet.

"It's okay," Jacobo said. "She is . . . shit, I don't remember the word. She doesn't hear anything? I show you your room, no problem. You want coffee?" He held his wristwatch close to the candle, shook his head. I stood shivering. *She?* Had he remarried? Had the rumors been true? From the street came the faint sound of an infant crying, a dog baying in the hills. "Shit, man, I have to go soon. Come on, this way. Maybe you just want to sleep now? You get settled tomorrow—no hurry, right?"

With new urgency, he picked up the suitcase and went through into a small courtyard half-lit by the setting moon. On three sides were doors, one of which we'd just come through; on the fourth stood a washtub and a sink, an ancient icebox and propane stove. A small table and chairs sat in the middle of the courtyard. Jacobo vanished through another door—*No hurry,* he'd said, as though I'd be waiting here for some time. I pulled a chair from the table and sat. A reef of cloud passed overhead and threw the courtyard into shadow. Maybe this was a way station of sorts, a safe house where my father would find me when the coast was clear. Despite my confusion, my vow of silence held—I'd given my word (so to speak); if I broke it, who knew what could happen? Exhausted and nauseated, I reaffirmed it: Only when I'd found my father. It couldn't be much longer.

I may have dozed again. When I opened my eyes, I saw her, shuffling from the farthest door into the light: a bent creature not five feet tall, her face rectangular and puckered with wrinkles, her eyes two dark holes bored into ash. Her mouth was sunken, one side twisted, as though she had already taken my measure and I was not what she expected. She moved deliberately toward me, examined me eye to eye. When her lips moved, only a low moan came out. I shook my head. She moaned again, breathing thickly, took my face between her hands—palms dry as sandpaper, fingertips light as a landing fly—and turned my chin to the side, examined the stain at my neck. She muttered her fascination, pinched and prodded the skin as though examining a bruised fruit. She did not frighten me, despite her strange appearance. Her indecipherable sounds were tender, almost good-humored. I surrendered to her scrutiny.

"The bed is not so comfortable, but it's okay," said Jacobo, ducking out of the doorway. "Oh, good morning you old crow." He bent down to kiss the top of the old woman's head. He tried to embrace her, but she shrugged him off with a grunt. "Yes, I love you, too, you pile of wrinkles!" he laughed. He turned to me. "I got to be back by nine, there's this polka band coming in to make the tracks for their first album. I know"—he nodded—"polka, not so cool . . . but these guys have the talent, man! Maybe not so together yet, so coordinated, but Jacobo will fix that.

"Plus," he said, "it's fifteen people in the band, and I charge per channel." This made me smile, and Jacobo flushed with pleasure. Hands in his pocket, a wide grin, he seemed less anxious, almost handsome. "I put some candles and a towel, anything else you need she gets for you in the morning, okay?"

I stood and took his arm. He couldn't leave me! He avoided my eyes. "I want to stay also. But I'll come back soon, okay? Maybe in the weekend. She take very good care of you, right, old lady?" He bent down to her again and leered. She took his face in her hands, yanked on his long hair with both fists, and grumbled. Jacobo leaned toward her, smiling painfully, trying to pry open her fists.

"She wants me to cut my hair. She says I'm looking too much like *him*." I, too, clung to him. I could not grasp the idea of sleeping alone in this place, no one to speak to me, no idea when my father would show his face.

"You got to sleep," said Jacobo, as I trailed him into the front room. "I forget how long you are traveling, and you get sick easy up here if you are not used to it. You should have seen him, when he came back . . ." He whistled, a sound that made the old woman look up. "He lose so much weight, sweating for days, talking crazy . . ."

He stopped in the door to the street, moonlight behind him. How long would I have to wait? I had known Jacobo only a few hours, but already I thought of him as my friend, my guide. *Take me with you,* I wanted to beg. But would I have gone if he'd offered? Probably not. I had a date to keep, after all.

He hugged me stiffly. "Don't worry! Now you are with your family. Just rest yourself. You don't got to do anything."

I stood a moment longer, listening to the dull clop of his boots receding. After a while, I heard the van's engine start, gurgling and fading through the narrow streets. Silence breathed up the alley. I steadied myself, blew out the candle, and went back inside.

✳

She came into my room toward dawn, small steps accompanied by grunts and moans. I didn't know how many hours I'd lain awake on the low, lumpy bed, shivering under blankets of horsehair or raw wool, watching shadows shift in sinister configurations across stone walls. Mystified, bone-tired, my heart tapped out all the unanswered questions, every misgiving rattled in the weary bag of my body. A frayed cloth of red and black and gold, dulled by the sun, covered the glassless window to cut the icy wind. Each flutter revealed a glimpse of the mountains, the ominous Old Maker sticking up like a tooth. Something howled on distant slopes; something rooted outside, a stray dog or pig. I curled close to the wall, huddling against the delirium I felt creeping up on me, the queasy fever of withdrawal, slumped into a daze in which I was always falling, flinching back to myself.

The old woman put a ceramic bowl and pestle on the nightstand, motioned with her hands for me to sit up. There was a hitch in her breath, a distant ticking, as though a wooden wheel were turning in her chest. Her fingers palpated my neck, squeezing and rubbing while those dark eyes narrowed, colorless lips moving in her private language. She stirred with the pestle, lifted a dripping piece of cloth and pressed it to my skin, patting and smoothing the edges. The cold paste warmed me under my chin, a tingle that spread to my cheeks, my scalp, down the backs of my arms. I watched her eyes while she applied this potion: like bullet holes, the singe spilling over onto her temples; I could see no iris or pupil, only an inky depthlessness that was nevertheless perfectly aware of me.

Muttering, she pressed her poultice to my bloodstain. She must have thought it was a rash or bruise, some exotic disorder of the skin. How could she know my condition was permanent? The room was bare but for the bed and nightstand, my suitcase by the wall, a small Last Supper hanging from a bent nail above my head. Who was she, I wondered, as sleep's arrow sped toward me again. Why hadn't my father met me himself, why bring me all this way to leave me with strangers? What task or tribute did I still need to perform?

As new light leaked through the window, fatigue swamped me, fever plugged my ears. She removed the cloth, dropped it back in the bowl. I could smell soap and dust and a whiff of camphor on her skin. With a grumble, she kissed the top of my head, and went back out to the courtyard, shutting my door. I heard water spattering in the basin, the clack of the dish in the rack. Another door closed. The house was still, and I was wide awake.

✳

In daylight, some of my terror abated; the knitting needles in my innards lay still. I woke to shouts in the street, children's voices lifting and falling, a rattling sound of plastic scraping against stone. The sun was high over the mountains, the sky even more brazenly blue than it had been the day before. Sunshine slanted through the window and drew the scent of damp clay from the stone walls, to mix with the eucalyptus and jasmine outside.

I limped into the courtyard, but the old woman was gone. Through an open door, I saw a room almost identical to mine: a bed and nightstand, a tall bureau with two drawers missing. Her window looked out at open space, yellow and beige scrub running straight at the mountains, piles of rock humped like sleeping hogs. A latchless door led to the bathroom: pink tiles, a lidless toilet, a rusted pipe protruding from the wall. There was a plate in the kitchen sink that she'd left for me: a pair of sweet rolls and half of a strange green fruit; when I bit into it, the tangy juice coated my lips and chin, the surprise of it almost choked me. Under the plate was a glass of milk which I drained in one draft.

Back in my room, I hauled open the suitcase and took out the few articles of clothing, two books of poetry. From a rolled-up T-shirt, I took a thick pouch wrapped in tape: my father's ticket out of whatever trouble had found him. I unzipped it, counted and recounted the crisp, bundled notes—his payment for the piper, his ransom or cure. Satisfied, I rewrapped the parcel, returned it to the suitcase, which I slid under the bed.

The town seemed even smaller than it had the night before, the wide unknown reined in by power lines, cobblestones, my steps buoyed by generous light and fresh confidence: I'd have a father by sunset; I'd be an orphan no more. Storefronts on the tiny plaza offered shelves of soap and candy bars and bottled water; glass cabinets crammed with ancient rolls of cookies, bottles of shampoo, half-crushed boxes of maxi pads, decks of cards and rusted spark plugs, fin de siècle sardine tins. Barrels of small potatoes sat on the sidewalk, cardboard boxes of fruit, a few tables where flies congregated around sugar bowls—all struck in thin mountain light. From each corner led a narrow street like the one the old woman lived on, stone houses standing shoulder to shoulder—each alley branched into small cul-de-sacs before petering out, one ending at a steep crevasse that dropped to a squirrel-colored river, another giving onto a sprawling heap of trash. Men in heavy sweaters conferred in doorways, playing dice on tabletops; young boys tripped over each other, chasing a plastic jug down the street. Women trudged by bearing heavy sacks, grimacing with each lurching step.

Strange, bald stranger in a strange, parched world—I covered the town's quarters in less than an hour. I searched for my father around each corner, behind every counter, under every bench in the drab square. I kept watch for the battered van, waited for Jacobo to hop out: *Are you ready?* he'd say, arms spread wide. *He's waiting—climb in!*

My leg ached, my joints uneasy; I could feel the altitude scraping the well of my lungs. I sat at a table on the square and somehow managed to procure a cup of lukewarm, gritty coffee, my bubble of cheer deflating with the lowering sun. A jagged shadow-line angled across the square. On the air was the smell of burning rubber, the far-off clanging of someone working on a car engine. I thought about trying to write something, but had neither pen, nor paper, nor any ideas. The thought of creating something worthy seemed as far off as Old Maker's peak. Even my old poems seemed churlish to me now, the noise of an infant banging her high chair with a spoon. In all my life, had I ever written anything valuable? Had I said one thing that was true?

What if I was in the wrong place? I thought, as shadow overswept the table. What if Jacobo had confused me with someone else? A cold vacuum opened around my heart. I wiped sweat from my brow, fought nausea and this thought: Maybe my father had already seen me, watching from the shadows. Maybe he'd decided I wasn't the one.

I fought the swelling desire to turn back, hop the first flight to my old life. Maybe it wasn't too late to repent, I thought, as I limped back to the old woman's house. I could call Rhoda from the airport, prostrate myself with apologies, beg her for another chance. My stomach clenched, the setting sun's chrome ached behind my eyes. I barely made it through the courtyard and into the bathroom, fell to my knees just in time to lose the coffee and bread, the strange green fruit, some lingering bit of my crestfallen soul, down the waiting mouth of the toilet.

I sat against the tiles and gulped for breath. A second later, I retched again, the last pale specks of breakfast stringing from my lips—like a trumpet blast, a blinding racket set up in my head, a pulsing sound like all the world's car horns blaring at once. I clutched my ears, pressed my cheek to the tile. But the shrill noise grew louder, pounding and resolving into sick laughter.

You fool! You ass! Did you really believe it? That nasty, familiar voice filled my skull, ringing louder and growing steadily more vulgar. *My word, what a sucker! You thought a couple of plane rides, a late-night swim would save you? Did you really believe in this fairy tale?*

Idiot, she cackled, *did you really expect this little game to work?*

I lay still and waited for the spasm to pass. But her giggles insisted, and when I opened my eyes there she was, the hideous nag: floating in the uneasy toilet water, ringed by fruit and phlegm. How could she have found me here? I'd left her at the bottom of the ocean!

He's not coming, she gurgled. *He doesn't want you. Never did.* Her voice bubbled off the fixtures, drove between my ears like a spike. With a splash she lurched up to grab me, tried to pull me down to her level. *Go back where you belong,* she sneered. *Lie in your damned bed. Your father never gave you a moment's thought—not now, and certainly not then.*

Shut up!, I gagged, and grabbed at the knob on the wall. Freezing water gushed from the pipe, soaking through my clothes, stinging my skin, and squeezing all the oxygen into a ball in my chest. The hag shrieked in fury; her face collapsed on itself. The foul water swirled and swirled and finally swallowed her with a prolonged, appropriate belch.

By the time I made it to my room, shucked my clothes into a wet pile, and wrapped myself in blankets, my teeth were chattering so violently I had to clamp my jaw for fear they'd splinter. My scalp clutched my skull with a thousand tiny pins, full-blown fever pulsing in my temples. I pulled the blankets over my head, shivered and wept until my eyes throbbed. Was there ever such a fool, I wondered, ever a more pathetic sight? No, never did a daughter deserve a father less—the hag, my callous stalker, was right.

I had not found my father, but *she* was here. The irony was unbearable. As I squirmed in pain's fist, I wondered why no one had told me about her: my parents' other daughter, this feral and twisted stepchild. Who had they been protecting? When she said "Calliope," who was my mother really calling? Then, worst of all: Which of his daughters was my father expecting?

*

Now I had entered my own wordless year. I note for you here my entrance, however queer, the exact voltage of my voiceless tenure, the frequency of my fear—it moved through me as I lay on that lumpy bed watching light slide from one wall to the other, slant down the stones like a camera's slow shutter. For days—or weeks—I lay brittle and quivering, time marked only by the rhythms of fever, the careless moon's passage across a glassless window, alternation of darkness and fever dreams, grainy films that flickered across memory's screen. My few lucid moments were punctuated by pain: pain pulsing through my leg, my pelvis, pain concentrated into a state of mind so sharp it felt like desire. Pain was a tiger asleep at my side—I could not scream, for the slightest sound would be enough to wake it, the slightest movement a provocation. I lay like a corpse, unbreathing, in hopes the predator would not notice me.

At night, the mountains presided over my sweaty ordeal, irregular shapes scissored out of a glittered sky. Animals snuffled at the door, their cries spiraling up and breaking into long and terrifying silences, an ice floe of silence, I was pinned like Gulliver to its frozen face. It was a ghost world, a cold catacomb, I dreamed of thieves and harlequins, I dreamed my limbs detached or turned to wood. I dreamed of prison, cruel guards dragging me under freezing water while I struggled and screamed. Again and again I entered that hidden cave: the colors and bodies colliding, shadows swift and terrifying, the music I could never quite identify. And always I could sense him there, behind the silver door, marking my progress. I could not reach him, though I thrashed like an animal in a trap. I woke in fury, terrestrial hands shaking me, my arms and legs burning with the strain.

"It's okay, Calliope," said a voice nearby. "You will be okay, I am promising." A strange man sat next to me, a patchwork clown with hair on his chin and green eyes as big as a bug's. Beside him stood a small, eyeless creature who sang a terrifying song. I scrambled back, pulled the blankets close. "Don't you remember me?" He reached huge hands toward my face. "Don't you know who I am?"

"You blew it, kiddo. Killed the golden goose," Rhoda said, sitting in lotus on the windowsill, limned by afternoon sun and the mountain's outline. I struggled to touch her but fever's hot collar cinched me back.

"Have mercy," scolded Marshall, leaning on a crutch, his face painted like a red-light-district whore. "Dive deeper," he beckoned. "Come and make the grade."

"Beam me up, Birdie," said Dennis, a kicked-dog grin on his face. He wore a black leotard and held a long pole, wobbling on a tightrope that stretched all the way home. "Remember the Prime Directive: Let lying dogs sleep."

They visited me singly and in pairs, jumped out from dark corners: my beekeeper, dressed as a race-car driver; my mother in a purple burqa, shrunken skulls in a garland around her neck; T. S. Eliot, holding a baby with long cat's whiskers; Michaela, crawling on all fours. From the corner he watched them all—my father, hunched over a bagpipe, a sad grin at the corners of his mouth. He clutched that bundle as though nursing a child, cleared the room with a blast of sound and dropped me into darkness.

In cool moments, brief respites when I was able to sit, the old woman spooned applesauce into my mouth, rice pudding, helped me sip from a glass of tart red liquid. She sat at my side and smoothed her balm over my skin, lips moving slightly, palm on my forehead cool and dry as spiderwebs. I lay unmoving, empty as a phantom. The sheets stank of me, my limbs weak as dandelion stalks; while she sat with me I was safe, my body sank beneath the blankets and the gossamer spores scattered to the wind.

Can you imagine the fury, the stifled self-loathing that seared me where I lay? Morning and night, I stewed in that pot, muscles atrophying, memories fading, the tattered scraps of my old self slowly blackening and burning away. *The farce is almost finished,* he'd said—but my own farce had just begun: I'd given up everything, left my life floating in Coronado Bay, only to come ashore in this world where no one knew me, infirm and failing, my father as absent as he'd been since Day One.

But all that time I was being prepared, tended like a rosebush, fattened like veal. It shouldn't surprise you: All my life I'd been a chess piece, a plaything for others' desires and dreams. Why should it be different now? After years as a pawn, why had I thought I could snap my fingers and be made queen?

"You looking pretty good, not so bad." Jacobo stood in the doorway in a dazzle of sun. "Shit, when you are getting up from that bed? Enough of this lazy stuff, the jet lag can't be so much!"

I sat up slowly and the bright day sliced clean to the back of my skull. My head felt weightless, my mouth stuck shut with a salty paste. The fever had broken, my breath felt cleaner, my limbs sore but functioning. Out the window the sky was unbearably blue, the browns and gaudy greens of the landscape mixed from the palette of a child's crayon set. The stone wall next to the house crawled with white jasmine, an explosion of goldenrod shuddering in the breeze. A hummingbird zoomed into the frame, hovered and buzzed a moment, and darted away.

"So you can say something? Now you talk to Jacobo?" He stood by the nightstand as I eased my legs over the edge of the bed. His smile brought creases to his cheeks; his eyes shone with relief. His long hair had been brushed, pulled back in a ponytail, his scraggly beard neatly trimmed, a shaving nick under one side of his jaw. When he reached into a pocket, I noticed the creases in his pant legs, his button-down shirt wrinkle-free, as if he'd ironed everything just for me.

"Everyone says the fever takes your voice. But I say no, she just waits for the right time to say something good!" He leaned toward me, peered into my face. "It's true? You say something good? Like maybe, 'Hello, Jacobo, how are you?'" I couldn't help but smile. Seeing this, his eyes lit up and he laughed, a pure and gladdening sound. "I don't stay so long today. I got to be at the studio tonight—the polka band, you don't believe the hassle! Fifteen people, and some of them play more than one instrument. The studio looks like a home for retired instruments, all the cases and sheet music, other shit all piled up. I can't have no more bands come in until the record is finished. No space!"

A gold frame glinted around one of his eyeteeth—for some reason, it filled me with tenderness. I wrapped a blanket around my shoulders, pulled Jacobo toward me and kissed him on the cheek.

"I know I am bothering you," he said, blushing. I shook my head. "But we are worried, we don't know how to help when you are so sick . . . and she is here all alone, with so much to do, and her health is also not so good." At my puzzled expression, he tapped his chest. "She has the condition, sometimes she doesn't able to breathe. Sometimes she has an attack and is sick for days. She has some herbs, she boils for a tea that helps. I will show you, later."

He picked up the Blake from the nightstand, eyed the cover, put it down. "When he tells me you are coming, I think, good! Now she don't have to do so much alone. Now someone is here if she has an attack, who can take care of her. Now I don't have to drive so far all the time to know she is okay.

"She raise me, you know. She is like my mother." He tried to hold my gaze but grew shy, knitting his fingers at his waist. His forehead wrinkled as he mulled over what he wanted to say, and that's when I resolved to trust him. If he hadn't brought me to my father yet, there had to be an explanation. I would be patient; I'd bear with him, this kind boy with the familiar smile. After all, I had nothing but time.

"You aren't so much like I thought." He sat on the bed a mile or so away. "You know, he only tells me about you last year, when he comes back from the States. He say, 'Jacobo, soon you will meet her.' So now I am trying to know you, right?"

I leaned forward, shook my head sharply. *Last year?* What was he talking about? My mind began to bob and weave; confusion staggered me like a swift body blow. But that was nothing compared to what he said next: the unexpected sucker punch, the TKO.

"That is the first time I know I have a sister. You believe the shit?" He laughed uncomfortably, as though surprised by his own audacity. Then he stood to go. "So if I bother you, just say, 'Jacobo, leave me alone!' But I want to know my sister now. So okay?"

He walked to the door, left me reeling, a croak caught in my gullet. I heard a bird flutter and perch on the wall outside, heard the boys kick their plastic ball down the alley. I barely registered what he said next, words bouncing disembodied between the stones.

"I am happy you feel better. So now you can help her. I forget to ask you: Do you ever know something about bees?"

✳

That night, after the old woman had gone to bed, I wrapped myself in a blanket and limped out to the courtyard, gulped glass after glass of cool water, nibbled on a piece of bread. I recognized the kitchen only distantly—the ancient basin and propane stove, the stacked crates filled with jars of honey. The cold air soothed and fortified me. I rubbed my arms, touched my lips, my ribs, my sore legs and knobby knees. I was a new woman, scoured clean—exposed to a new world, ignorant and ready for imprinting.

I lay atop the kitchen table, stared into a sky taut as cellophane. The air was filled with the sweet scent of woodsmoke. *Brother,* I thought. Brother? I have a brother. I turned the word over and over in my mind. How? And who? And when? Where had my father been last year—and why? I ran my hands over my head, felt the wisps of itchy hair that had begun to grow. None of it fit together, nothing yet made sense. *If you have news, send to J,* said the letter—at least one small riddle was solved. But with each answer the image grew blurrier, lost resolution. No more words, for god's sake, no more explanations—just give me a body to throw my arms around!

The farce is almost finished. But my father still had not shown himself. I'd survived the journey, the sickness and withdrawal, only to wake to another mystery. Or maybe it was all a dream, I was still delirious, this midnight date with absence the only reunion I'd ever get. It occurred to me then how fitting that would be: It was, after all, for absence I was best suited, knowing it so intimately as I did.

Back in bed, I took out his letter, read it another hundred times. I held it to the light in hopes of finding a hidden map, some invisible clue. But they were only words, a ghost's careless scribbles. Who was that bare-backed baby in the photo: the horrid changeling I saw in the mirror, or the one I'd always thought of as "me"? I'd seen so many newsclips when I was younger, seen Wally Weeks's documentary, footage of a newborn in a guitar-shaped bassinet. Photographs I'd pasted into scrapbooks: my mother, pregnant and topless on the Riviera, or cradling a bundle on the cover of *Elle;* my father, hair snarled and held in barrettes, sharing an ice-cream cone with a pinafored kid at the corner of Haight and Ashbury; parents and toddler, backs to the camera, on a black-and-white London street, all reaching back to give a paparazzo the finger.

Was that really me?, I used to wonder, staring at the girl in the pictures. She had my name—all the captions said so! But that child was not father-less; her skin was clear as a new can of paint. All these years I'd had the sense of doubleness, of performing someone else's life, of separation be-tween the girl everyone talked about and the self I felt behind my eyes—but now I had the answer: It was *her* all the time. And she'd stuck with me even in death, using me to lead her to the father she'd lost. When I found him, she'd muscle me out with a gnash of her teeth, wanting him all to herself.

It was her birthright, after all.

I leaned against the stones, ran my hand over my neck, sensed there the bright birthmark, its faint pulse of heat. For the first time in my life I was grateful for the mark, the blemish that clutched my jaw like a wretched red hand. At least he would know me. Though I'd grown somewhat taller since he'd seen me last, my freckled hands long and bony, my skin a bit thinner, my haircut austere, he would not hesitate to stake his claim. There was no denying this bloody ID, my indelible calling card, his true greatest hit.

When I found my father, there'd be no question who I was: his daughter, his creation. Finally: his.

II. ♭, OR THE MURDER OF THE THING

THE READER MAY WELL IMAGINE the challenge, the inexpressible chaos into which the present work was thrown by the events at the Spreckels Theatre. What had begun a year earlier as a straightforward—if difficult; if, at times, utterly exasperating—biography in the course of one night transmogrified into something far less easily identified: a narrative transcending the familiar, necessary limitations of biography (*bios*=life, after all!), gazing into that world beyond the grave, faithfully recounting and, when possible, explaining the actions of the poet *after* all action had become impossible, *after* her life, as it were, had ended.

Of course many biographies offer a postscript or "epilogue," summarizing the long-term consequences of the subject's life or revealing the fates of secondary figures or even (in narcissistic fashion) of the biographer himself. Make no mistake: What was required here was not such a collection of afterthoughts, not some "mop-up" operation, but an altogether new movement, a continuing and ever more complicated chronicle of the poet's path, the scorch-marks she continued to leave as she blazed through the world—*the very world she had already left!* No longer life (*bios*), then, but death (*thanatos*); as of December 19 no longer a biography but a *thanatography*.

It was unprecedented. An author begins any project with certain unknowables, of course—variables of theme and emotion, details and surprising revelations which will only be made constant by assiduous pursuit of the Truth. Still, in the case of biography, he has one crucial "knowable," viz., that the study of a life is bounded by the limits of that life, he is guided by the widespread assumption (at least in Western cultures) that life in the protagonistic sense ends, irrevocably, at death, an assumption without which no account could be concluded, no book closed—and therefore none opened, no story begun, nor even conceived. An author thus embarks upon the journey without knowing all its detail, but confident of its *nature*—he sets sail upon stormy seas fully aware of the maritime hazards which may lay in store, but with Polaris's bright beacon always overhead. When that guiding light disappears, when he is left tossing on the dark, inchoate seas of imagination—reader, what is he to do?

In the case of this author, he had no choice but to shorten the sails, lash himself to the mast, and sail on. The uproar that began on the morning of December 19 and almost immediately reached a pitch of hysteria allowed little time for hesitation or theorization, demanding of those who would write about the Poet Formerly Known as Calliope a journalistic agility that brooked no delay. Apart from its urgent metaphysical ramifications, the catastrophe at the Spreckels Theatre raised numerous practical questions, the most immediate of which was: *Where is the poet now?*

No expense was spared, in either the public or the private sector, to ascertain her whereabouts, nor those of the eight women who disappeared from the theater that night.* The San Diego Police Department opened a crisis center behind the ruined theater and set up a telephone hotline and Web page for tips, rumors, and theories. The FBI, invoking obscure provisions of the USA PATRIOT Act,[†] on Monday sent a team of agents to San Diego, a development which SDPD captain Eugenio Sanchez bore with barely concealed indignation, remarking drily to KUSI news anchor Kimberly Hunt, "Find me one [FBI] agent who even reads poetry and we'll talk. Those boys from Washington don't know a sonnet from Shinola."

The tension between local and federal investigators would only grow in the coming days, the former relying on community relations and a strategy of voluntary cooperation while the latter resorted to wholesale detentions and interrogations; by Christmas Day it had degenerated to

---

*Five of the eight were identified the next morning in the *San Diego Union-Tribune:* Tyra Banks of Los Angeles, Cassandra Beers of New York, Taryn Glacé of San Francisco, Darla Krum (aka Darlene Cream) of El Cajon, and Trinh Ngo of San Clemente. Two others—Maria Oropeza and Leigh Mulgrew—were subsequently identified from photographs. The eighth has never been identified.
[†]A justification later found to be legally questionable by the Justice Department's Inspector General.

outright antagonism, a fistfight breaking out at Hodad's Hamburger Shack in Ocean Beach when a local police officer told an FBI agent to "go back to Waco."

The media, too, were in a frenzy, newspapers and magazines and cable outlets tripping over each other to be the first to locate the Muse. Though local sources such as the *Union-Tribune*, *SLAM*, and the *Reader* would normally have had a head start on such a story, the national media already had "boots on the ground" for the premiere of *The Hanged Man;* thus, the press suites in the downtown Pan Pacific Hotel were transformed, the next day, into "war rooms" that would not be "decamped" until January 21, when the whole entourage, like a flock of pigeons wheeling together on some unheard command, "redeployed" to Portland.* Of course, none of the hopeful Woodwards and Bernsteins would meet with success, and so the column inches and ninety-second segments and ticker items and cover copy set aside for the Poet Formerly Known as Calliope were filled with analysis, overanalysis, meta-analysis, and official pleas for calm. Her absence opened the door to all manner of substandard news product, of which Edwin Decker's idiotorial in the *Peninsula Beacon* serves as a representative example:

> Please please please please please please please *please,* Calliope—or however you pronounce that glyph thing—please tell me where you are! I need you! Here's my number: 555-5996. Call me! We'll meet anywhere you want. Lunch, drinks, whatever. My treat! I'll write whatever you want me to write. I'll make you look good, I promise. Come on, lady—you know you want to!†

---

*The military metaphors belong to Geraldo Rivera, who made a silk purse out of a sow's ear by reporting on the media itself: the fruitlessness of its search, reporters' boredom and frustration, the rivalries, sabotages, and collusions between networks, etc. His special report, *San Diego Under Siege,* in which he appeared in full battle fatigues and combat helmet, prowling with flashlight through the basement corridors and laundry rooms of the Pan Pacific, was the most highly rated cable program of December 24.

†January 6, 200_. Whatever his crimes against journalism, literature, and the English language as a whole, Decker was the first to point out that the figure who disrupted the premiere of *The Hanged Man* was missing Calliope's prominent telltale birthmark.

The sudden reappearance of the poet provoked a monsoon of mixed emotions in those who had known her and worked with her, and their public expressions of bewilderment, longing, and grief were as varied and unpredictable as had been their relationships with her. Dennis Adams, who had been such an eloquent memorialist a year earlier, returned to the national spotlight with a cathartic appearance on *Live with Regis and Kelly* that left host Regis Philbin speechless.

"I knew she'd never leave us," said the CEO of Seattle-based VerSI-FI, which had recently gone public on the strength of its poetry-based fantasy-gaming software. Adams, a devout Unitarian, fell to his knees before the camera and gave solemn thanks. "I knew she'd come back. Thank you, Calliope. Thank you, God." In an apparent surprise to Philbin, as well as to the University of Texas, Adams announced that he would donate $2.5 million to seed a permanent collection of Calliope's papers, poems, and effects at the Harry Ransom Center for the Humanities.

This emotional display would be surpassed in a commercial produced and financed by actor Ben Affleck. "Calliope, honey, I miss you," he said, sitting on a couch in his home in the Hollywood Hills, hands folded in his lap. He wore a dark turtleneck, which emphasized his somber mood against the hundreds of white roses arranged through the room. The spot aired only once—immediately preceding the finale of *It's a Wonderful Life*—in every major U.S. market. "Fly back to me, Bird," Affleck said, his voice unsteady. "I forgive you. Please come home."

Snow Lion Press capitalized on the appearance of the Muse with a one-two punch of publishing prowess. On December 21, it was announced that a new, limited edition of *(I)CBM* was in the works: leather-bound and gold-leafed, *(I)CBM and Beyond* would include twenty-four color-photo plates, facsimiles of handwritten drafts of many of the poems, and line-by-line explication by Camille Paglia; the volume, scheduled for an initial print run of twenty-five thousand, would be priced at $599. At the same time, the Buddhist publishing house was preparing for the release of *A Gut-Wrenching Tale of Crippling Hunger,* the Beekeeper's long-awaited memoir, which had already racked up six-digit presales on Amazon. The Beekeeper himself was deep in the throes of the prepublicity campaign—of which his appearance at the film premiere was meant to be a linchpin of sorts; in the weeks between the Spreckels incident and the book's scheduled release, he was all but ubiquitous, his attitude oscillating between that of jilted lover and terrified prey.

"Hell hath no fury . . . ," he said to reporters massed in the parking lot of the Mount Baldy Zen Center, outside Los Angeles. He pursed his lips, looked off into a chilly mountain twilight. To either side, a bodyguard scanned the parking lot, occasionally mumbling something into his wrist-watch. The Beekeeper had ostensibly come to pay homage to poet and songwriter Leonard Cohen, who had made the monastery on Mount Baldy his home since 199_, and to seek Cohen's blessing for the success of the memoir. But few in the media had forgotten the rumors that an urn containing Brandt Morath's ashes was housed in a vault in the monastery's basement—and so this "private errand," when leaked to the press, aroused suspicions that the Beekeeper was hoping to find an altogether different poet than the gravel-voiced Canadian songwriter.

"You know, friends, after everything—all the infidelity and the mayhem, after the pills and the home videos and the humiliation . . ." He trailed off, staring out over the L.A. basin. "I would still take her back. She was the most remarkable person I ever met."

He bit his lip. "Bring it on, C. I'm ready for you."

Reporters clamored for details regarding the pills and the home videos, neither of which had been mentioned in the excerpts in *Vanity Fair* the previous summer. "You'll have to read the book," he told them, the set of his jaw indicating memories too painful to utter. "It'll be out on January 20."

The displays only grew more bizarre. On New Year's Eve, Southwest-erners United in Christ held a candlelight vigil at Cabrillo Point, where eighty people gathered around the lighthouse to pray for the souls of Calliope and the eight women. The group's leader, Edward J. Labello, the former leader of UC's Students United in Christ, had founded the regional grassroots organization a year earlier, and already claimed a membership of sixty thousand. Though still a blue-eyed firebrand, Labello had cut his hair and retooled his public rhetoric for more mainstream appeal; the new group's mission statement made no mention of "Holy War," nor of the "incineration of blasphemers and hedonists beneath the sword of the

Avenging Christ" which figured so luridly in the student group's literature. Instead, SUC$_2$'s brochure featured images of happy Californians of all colors, frolicking on pristine beaches and climbing mountain trails, beaming faces raised toward a white cross on a hilltop.*

"Listen to the voice of one who does not know God," Labello told his followers, who huddled at the base of the lighthouse, sheltering their candles as a winter rainstorm pelted the promontory. "'Love me like Lazarus/My humid cave sealed tight, waiting/for your rigid exploration/the tip of your digit beckons me—/gasping: *Jesus*—/to the light.'"†

He held the flock in his irresistible gaze, an irate sea growling and smashing around them. "Though mired in sin and poetry, she felt the power of God and it took her breath away. If Jesus can reach out to a blasphemer like Calliope, if He can quiet the voice of sin and replace it with the silence of virtue, then who can't Jesus save [*sic*]?"

Who can say these ardent prayers were not heard? Who can say the poet, biding her time in whatever unknowable redoubt, was not moved by these outpourings, by the awesome need of those she'd left behind? Who can say that behind that cold visage there did not still reside a sensitive soul, capable of regret, longing for the loved ones who called to her across death's chasm.

"Lay her i' the earth!" cried Penelope Morath, bolting upright in her hospital bed at 3:00 on New Year's morn, conscious for the first time since the night of the premiere. In the brief lucidity that followed, she told the floor nurse that her daughter had appeared in the room as a small child, trying to clamber into her mother's bed. "Lay her i' the earth!" she shrieked, terrified, for several hours, gaping into the mirror on the opposite wall until she was administered a dose of Haldol and subdued.

That same day, the doorbell interrupted the author's customary mid-morning hiatus from writing. He arose from the neatly made bed in his

---

*"God gave us this beautiful state. Don't we owe Him?" reads the brochure. In its first year, SUC$_2$ devoted most of its energy to lobbying for harsher penalties against major polluters, encouraging public schools to include the Bible in literature syllabi, and promoting a ballot initiative to close state and county parks on Sundays to non-Christians. As of this writing, the initiative, "California for Freedom of Worship," was scheduled for the November 201_ ballot and expected to pass by a wide margin.
†From "Rigor Mortician."

son's room, where he had nodded off while meditating on the prophetic last quatrain of "Electra Returns to Azalea Path," to find a man in a dark suit and expensive sunglasses at the front door. The man—tall and fit, of Asian descent, an apparent enemy of the friendly handshake—identified himself as Carlton Lum, an FBI special agent. The visit came as no great surprise to the author, who had suspected that the authorities would eventually avail themselves of his expertise. He invited Agent Lum inside and offered to put on a fresh pot of coffee. The agent declined.

"I have to warn you in advance, I have no firm knowledge of Calliope's whereabouts, though of course I have my theories," the author said. "Nevertheless, it would be irresponsible of me to voice these without more thorough investigation."

The agent had not removed his sunglasses. "I'd like to speak with Drew," he said.

"Most people call me Andrew."

"Your son, sir." The agent sat on a stool at the kitchen counter, taking in the entirety of the modest home with a quick swivel.

"Certainly he can't tell you anything. As close as we are, I don't permit him access to my work in progress. You'll have to deal with me."

"Is Drew at home, sir?"

The author, sipping casually from his mug, informed him that his son was not, in fact, at home. "Have you made much progress with the investigation?" he asked, subtly suggesting it might be of mutual benefit for the agent to share whatever leads he might have obtained. The ongoing attempts to secure authorization for the thanatography having not yet borne fruit, it occurred to the author that cooperation with the authorities might provide an alternate means of access to the principals in the case.

"What can you tell me about the events of December 18 at the Arizona Café, sir?" Agent Lum asked.

"The Arizona? Hah!" said the author. "I assure you, Carlton: adolescent tomfoolery, crass imitation, nothing more. But as offensive as the performance may have been to people of discriminating taste, surely it doesn't warrant the attention of the federal government? On the other hand, I've spoken with one of the concessionaires at the Spreckels, who claims to have found a snippet of graffiti—a limerick, from the sound of it—in the wreckage of the men's room. I could, perhaps, give you his name . . ."

"A Joseph McAdderly tells us that Drew spoke with Ms. Morath that night." He flipped open a small notepad. His mouth had not approximated a smile. "That the poet . . . *appeared* to the lead singer and gave him some kind of message?"

"Agent Lum." The author took a long sip and burned his tongue. "Surely you don't intend to traffic in this kind of silliness? 'The lead singer,' as you call him, had just beaten himself unconscious with his own guitar in the basest attempt yet to impersonate his musical hero. Whatever he might have said to Joe, his claims were obviously some combination of publicity seeking and hallucination brought on by a near concussion."

"So he told you about it?"

The author waved a hand at the living-room furniture, the stacks of books on the couch, spilling onto the floor. "He mentioned something. I gave it no credence."

"Did he tell you what she said?"

The author and the agent regarded each other across the counter. The agent leaned back and his jacket opened slightly, exposing the edge of his shoulder holster: a veiled warning to the author.

"He did not."

"Where is Drew now?"

The author nodded vaguely at the front door. "I'm sure he's 'crashing' on the couch of one or another of his putative bandmates."

The agent asked for the addresses and phone numbers of the other delinquents and stood to leave. "You don't know when he'll be back?"

The author shrugged. "Do you have children, Carlton?" he said, explaining that the only effective way to deal with rebellion was by a careful, casual disregard, lest the mutinous child be encouraged by the oppressive parent's discomfort. Then, thinking to cultivate trust between them, he recounted what Drew had told him on the morning of December 19 while shoving dirty T-shirts into a bookbag.

"Apparently, there was a man at the Arizona who identified himself as a representative of some obscure record label. There was some discussion of a brief tour of Japan and South Korea." The agent raised his eyebrows. "Of course the man was a charlatan," the author hastily added. "I'm sure you'll find Drew lounging in Buzz's garage, playing one or another of his atavistic video games."

"We'll check it out. If you hear from him, please give me a call." The agent left a card on the counter, buttoned his jacket, and reached for the front door.

"Listen," said the author. "You're barking up the wrong tree. I have been following this case for nearly two years. I have made unprecedented strides toward a true understanding of the poet—her fears, her ambitions, the unconscious forces which drive her. No one knows her better than I do. No one." He followed the agent to the door and put a hand on his arm. The agent regarded the author's hand. "If anyone can reach her, I can. Let me help. Before it's too late. I'm certain we could work out an arrangement that doesn't compromise your investigation. Think about it: One needs an artist to catch an artist, *n'est-ce pas?* Perhaps you could speak to Ms. Lubinski about, shall we say, *facilitating* the authorization process? Let's not compete, Carlton. Let's scratch one another's proverbial backs. What do you say?"

The agent smiled for the first time, removing the author's hand with gentle, but undeniable, force. "We'll be in touch," he said.

"Why don't we start by talking about you. Tell me a little about your life. How would you describe yourself? What are the words that come most quickly to mind?"

"Here's what I don't understand. The little girl sees her father commit suicide in the most grisly of ways. She has a birthmark which she believes, however misguidedly, to be the evidence of that event, the . . . I'm sorry, what did you call it? The guarantee?"

"I think it would be most useful if we put aside for the—"

"And indeed, through much of her adolescence and young adulthood, she conducts a very public search for his remains—tragic, really, but consistent with her belief in his death—and certainly her poetry doesn't lack for corroborating imagery. For goodness' sake, 'Sunday on Suicide Row' takes the word 'cerebral' to graphic new heights . . ."

"I'd like to get back to the question of audience. As I was explaining last time, a symptom is a kind of message, a plea which cannot be spoken aloud, translated into the language of the body and repeated, in hope that the desired audience will understand."

"But so then, if she believed in his death, believed so unshakably that she was marked by it, that in a sense her physical reality *originated* with it—"

"Andrew—"

". . . I'm still not clear why she spends such tremendous energy looking for her father—her *living father*—later on, why the ads in all the papers, the disturbance on *Charlie Rose,* the alleged trip to Egypt . . . She can't have believed both things, can she?"

"Obsessional behavior is another such message. It has its own grammar and syntax and, like a letter sent by registered mail, it can only fulfill its function when it has been signed for. Otherwise, it simply keeps repeating itself. Lacan called this 'The Agency of the Letter.' The word has a mind of—"

"It's almost as though she believed in two fathers—two different men, one of whom died that morning in Rancho Santa Fe, the other of whom absconded, pulling off one of the great scams in history and spending the next fifteen years in ignorance of his daughter's pain, her longing . . ."

"It's an interesting point. Lacan—"

"Or . . . *or,* Doctor, not ignorant, but fully *cognizant,* no? Isn't it likely this would have crossed her mind, that her father, passing his days in some tropical paradise, surrounded by bathing beauties, having squirreled away a small fortune, siphoned it off for just that purpose . . . wouldn't she come to imagine him living out this fantasy of anonymity and luxury *despite* the knowledge that his grieving wife and daughter were still in San Diego, their lives shattered, and this would then inevitably seem to her a kind of *mockery,* wouldn't it? Wouldn't this in a way be more painful than his actual death?"

"If I could get a word in?"

"By all means."

"Lacan speaks of two fathers. One, the lawgiving father of the Oedipal cycle, the figure of taboo, of proscription, corresponding to the strictures of language, what Freud called the Reality Principle. The other, the Obscene Father who enjoys what the children are forbidden, unlimited *jouissance* not bound by language or taboo, and who jealously guards this privilege, whose name cannot be spoken without psychosis as its result."

"I see."

"Do you follow?"

"Two fathers?"

"This is of course rather complex—and far afield, I might add. Let's . . . you mentioned that your son is no longer living with you. Is that something you'd like to discuss? While we're on the subject of ruptured familial relations?"

"Hardly a rupture. Just another flamboyant bid for attention. No doubt he's lounging in his friend's garage, secretly hoping his father will come to collect him and cause some angry scene to confirm his warped idea of me and justify further misbehavior."

"And why don't you?"

"Why don't I what?"

"If what your son needs is attention, why don't you give it to him? What do you gain by withholding it?"

"Doctor, really. I'm surprised. Of course there's positive attention and negative attention, and you know as well as I do the consequences of the latter. But back to this matter of the two fathers—"

"I'd really like to discuss just this one, Andrew."

"Aha, yes, *touché*. But if Calliope had two fathers—the one of 'obscene enjoyment' and the other being the 'law,' as you put it, the Reality . . . well, then, if Brandt Morath was her lawful father—and we have no reason to believe that he wasn't—then his suicide was, in a sense, the application of the law, no? In the sense that it structured her life, gave focus to her language, her poetry—"

"You might consider what I've said about symptoms needing to be read when thinking about your son's behavior and your relationship to it, to him. He, too, is writing a book. And whatever the consequences, you will eventually have—"

"The question then, of course, is, 'Who is the other father?'"

"What do you think that book says, Andrew? Have you read even the first chapter?"

"Who, Doctor? You've opened quite a door here, quite another, shall we say, *dimension* in the story of her life. Of her death, as it were. This might be precisely the linchpin I've been looking for, the key to her duality!"

"Andrew. Listen to me. If he is crying out to you, you must hear him. You *do* hear him, of course. Who else can he turn to? He has only one father."

"Ah, but Doctor, are we not talking about two fathers?"

"No, we are not. This is theory. It is metaphor. Lacan himself would be the first to admit that it is merely a particular reading of the Big Other, a kind of game. We can no more look for a second father than we can locate a region of the brain called the unconscious, walled off from the rest of the organ by structures of repression and denial. You of course understand the concept of denial?"

The author sat straight up on the plush divan, momentarily dazzled by halogen glare. Behind him, Dr. Breve sat in shadow, entirely still except for one ringed finger which tapped tinnily against her coffee mug.

"I don't understand." He rested his hands on his knees. "If we're not talking about reality, if we're not trying to get at the Truth, then where are we? If all of this boils down to a word game, what good is it? If we're only talking about some purely conceptual realm. What bearing does it have on the life of the flesh-and-blood subject? Where does it touch down?"

"This is precisely what Lacan wants us to see! Precisely! That the place where it 'touches down,' what he referred to as the 'quilting point,' is not some pure, originary space that has been distorted by the symbolic but on the contrary, a *product of* the symbolic, developed through a kind of alchemy between the Big Other and the individual's need to reconcile—"

"Did you say 'alchemy'?"

"This is not unrelated to the concept of the guarantee we have been discussing—a way to limit or manage the chaotic play of signifiers—"

"That's very interesting, very . . . Of course. Alchemy."

"Derrida referred to the 'Transcendental Signified,' the end of the chain of referents, a center of meaning that anchors the entire system. A fantasy, of course—"

"The Philosopher's Stone."

"Excuse me?"

"The Philosopher's Stone. The pure substance which culminates the alchemical process. As I understand it, a kind of mysterious catalyst, a Holy Grail, as it were . . ."

"I see. Well, we are indeed far afield. Might we—"

"No, you see, I've been reading up on Jung, his discussion of alchemy as a metaphor for human—"

"Oh for heaven's sake, you're not going to bring *Jung* into my office—"

"Don't you see the analogy here, Doctor? The alchemists believed metals could be infinitely transformed, heated or dissolved or what have you . . . but what they were really after was the end stage, pure gold, a substance that has been *perfected,* that brooks no further transformation. But they needed the Philosopher's Stone to get there. Does that not sound like your 'transcendental signified'?"

"I thought we had all graduated from Jung's fairy tales. Twaddle. Shall we also read tarot cards?"

"And so the shaman's experiments, this idea of 'ego transmutation' . . . then what would be the equivalent, the stopping point, what would halt the endless movement of—and you said the subject is a signifier, so what is its transcendental . . . We're back to the guarantee, aren't we? What is the guarantee, isn't that the question?"

"Andrew, listen to me. I'll grant you a superficial resemblance, but—"

"But what, Doctor? But what?"

"But there is no Philosopher's Stone," she said. "No one ever discovered it."

He shook his head in the intransigent spotlights, but the shadow play only stunned him further. The figure in the armchair sat motionless. "Then what you're saying is that there is no reality, no Truth, everything is entirely subjective and without authority . . ."

"Of course not."

"That my attempts, for example, to tell the truth about Calliope are themselves some kind of game. That she, herself, is a mere symbol, that she doesn't—or didn't . . . I have to tell you, I reject that view utterly."

"Andrew, we are talking about strategies by which the psyche attempts to fill the lack inherent in the symbolic. But of course it cannot be filled, only hidden. Getting back to the case of the fatherless child, the father's absence becomes a representation of *lack itself,* his return fantasized as a return to completeness, the oneness with the world that precedes the self/other split. The father becomes what Lacan called the 'phallus,' something to fill the lack, or cover it like a veil, postponing grief and the acceptance of subjecthood. In your son's case, we might look at—"

"I'm sorry, did you say 'phallus'?"

"—representations of absence in his own symbolic matrix, we might ask what his unconscious offers as replacement. Which brings us back to the two . . ."

"But this is . . . well, if the phallus . . . it's . . . this certainly brings up certain issues in Calliope's childhood . . . the persistent questions of abuse, though I know you'll refuse to discuss this with me, but of course it's all too easy then to jump to the rumors of her promiscuity in later . . . all too easy then to give credence to the scurrilous accusations, the unpalatable acts described . . . I have to say I'm disappointed in you, Doctor, lending your authority to such nonsense. Garbage."

"What are you feeling right now, Andrew?"

"What possible relevance can that have to the topic at hand?"

"Humor me."

"Well. I'd have to say. Somewhat . . . insulted."

"Go on."

"I feel attacked, insulted. As though you wish to believe, wish others to believe, things that aren't true. It's like I've been counting on you for solidity, objectivity, and you perhaps are not quite the rock . . . the authority . . ."

"You feel I'm misunderstanding you?"

"Yes! No . . . not me. Misunderstanding, misrepresenting *her.*"

"Who?"

"All this talk of symbolic structures, of veils and penises—"

"The phallus is not the same—"

"Whatever! Penis, phallus, *whatever!* All this talk of the Big Other and quilts and transcendental . . . as though discussion of the real person were forbidden! As though we can't say anything authentic, we aren't in possession of the proper vocabulary and so have to dance around it and create narratives that have nothing to do with the real person."

"Please. Continue."

"As though we have locked the real person away, as though she were locked behind a door and only by getting inside . . . but we can't get inside because the key has been misplaced, left in the back of some kitchen drawer full of crap and all the while she's in there . . . in terrible need . . . and I can hear her . . ."

"It means a great deal to you to say something about the real person."

"It's my job! It's my purpose."

"Encountering such difficulty must be frustrating."

"I feel as though we are doing some kind of harm to her! As though this very conversation were a kind of betrayal."

"Lacan would agree with you."

"He would?"

"'The symbol is the murder of the thing,' according to Lacan. Do you see?"

"But . . . you said *everything* is symbolic. That the only access to the real is *through* the symbolic."

"Yes."

"So everything, every word or act, every poem—her whole life, then, an ongoing . . . murder. Of course. This is how she must have felt: *I killed him!*"

"But how do *you* feel? Who is behind the locked door?"

"But if one's whole life is symbolic, an ongoing homicide . . . If the symbol is the murder of the thing . . . then what happens when you murder the *symbol*? Wouldn't it make a certain desperate sense to think that killing the symbol is the only way to get the *thing* back? And if the symbol, so to speak, is your *life* . . ."

The doctor set down her mug. "And that," she leaned forward to dim the halogens, the softer overheads dawning upon the author's squinting form, "is why Lacan insists: The only act which is not a failure is suicide."

———

Truth.

Splashed in red acrylic over a century-old mural. A painting. A work of art. As though to say, "Even this is not pure. Even this: a lie."

In *The Republic,* Plato prescribed the expulsion of the poets, dismissing their work as "representation"—mere imitation of the eternal and perfect things, essentially corrupt. Poetry as a symbol of human falsehood, our inability to *be,* rather than *seem*—and thus a mockery of our strivings for perfection and Truth. A lie.*

The mural at the Spreckels Theatre, depicting as it once had a scene from classical Greece, was a natural target for the Muse. How better to start demolishing millennia of lies? How better to tear out, from the roots, the vast cultural vegetation of a Western tradition that had borne, as its fruit, her father's life and career as well as her own sad history, ensnared them in the brambles of dishonesty and artifice, how better, in one red stroke, both to announce the revolution and demonstrate the might of its principal weapon? *The only honest number is zero.* The New Poetry which Calliope had declared in the "Blindness Letter" to Marshall Vaughn had been unloosed, the strike at Spreckels was the Boston Tea Party of the movement. The battle was joined. It was war.

The author's efforts redoubled in the new year as he struggled to make his own contribution, to stand apart from the gaggle of cheap versions spat out like so much pabulum, to produce a thanatography worthy of its subject not only in the sense of representing that subject but in understanding her down to the molecular level, in knowing her, making her accessible, flesh and blood, to the reader—in the sense of "getting it." Winter's drear lying over his home, he felt the Truth circling ever closer, rustling through the shrubbery like a stalker. Some mornings, the house blissfully empty, this sense of nearness was so strong he'd throw open the Calliope Corner's curtains expecting to see a face staring out of the nebulous dawn. It was the precise character of this face he longed to know.

---

*The artist might respond: Poetry is in fact a *more* perfect representation, able to transcend human frailty: complete, undying, unmarked by the desires and degradations of the flesh. Symbolic, yes, but suggesting that if, indeed, the symbol murders the thing it does so by *exceeding* the thing. Might we not then understand ♀ as, at the same time, the murder, suicide, and perfection of Calliope?

Dr. Breve's analyses were moving him ever closer to the Truth, her revelation of the two fathers an invaluable piece to the maddening puzzle. Who was this mysterious other figure? When and how had Calliope learned of his existence? And what relationship, if any, did he have to the "Walrus" alluded to in the suicide note? For weeks the author pored through public records and newspaper archives, tracked down former cooks and gardeners from the Rancho Santa Fe mansion as well as the manager of the apartment building on Abbott Street. He interviewed teachers at Mountaintop Arts, executives at NorthStar Records, pediatricians and neighbors, none of whom could shed the slightest light on the poet's complicated parentage. His letters to Connor Feingold went unanswered; he thought it best not to hazard another visit to Malibu just yet.

Fighting on all fronts, the author intensified his efforts in pursuit of authorization. After the Spreckels debacle, the offices of Lubinski Management had fallen even farther into chaos, due both to the typhoon of media inquiries and the disappearance of Leigh Mulgrew, Rhoda's longtime assistant.[*] The agency went through a string of temps, none even remotely qualified to handle the phone, mail, and fax traffic; paradoxically, it was easier now to get Rhoda herself on the phone, as the harried publicist was often the only one in the office.

The author chanced to reach her on or around January 1.

"Jesus Christ, what the hell do you want now?" Rhoda said, falling quickly into the banter which had developed between the two professionals.

"First, I'd like to wish you a very happy—"

"You think I have time for this bullshit?" she quipped, her voice echoing thinly over the speakerphone. "I've got NPR calling me in an hour, I've got half a dozen lawsuits to keep up with, Jim Jarmusch is on his way over to pitch a documentary . . ."

"Ah, the life of the much-sought-after," he said sympathetically.

". . . I've got a champagne hangover and a dead client running around

---

[*]Mulgrew was listed as a missing person from December 21 to January 22, with suspicion falling on the Arizona Café's Joe McAdderly. When the SDPD learned of an outstanding 196_ warrant for a bar fight in Galway, McAdderly was arrested and held until after the Portland fire, when the first photographs of the Muse surfaced.

vandalizing bridges, and my receptionist decides *now* would be a good time
to go on a bender . . ."

"I wondered whether you'd had time to think some more about my proposal. There've been some, ah, developments you might be interested—"

Now he heard the click as she picked up the handset. "I told you, I can't
think about this now. Penny's a vegetable, the Beekeeper's doing junkets,
Snow Lion won't let me anywhere near him—it's not up to me," she said.
"What developments?"

The author recounted his interview with Agent Lum, taking care to
gloss over the issue of Calliope's "visitation" at the Arizona Café, not to
mention the new information regarding her paternity. His relations with
Rhoda were cordial, but he could not yet trust her to honor his exclusivity,
not until he had been granted the authorization he sought.

"It seems likely," he said, "that I—that *we* can count on the FBI's
cooperation."

"Terrific. If they find her, can you tell her I'd like to speak with her,
please?"

"Well, that's just the thing." He paced tight circles in his living room.
Out the front window, the apartment buildings and bungalows of Ocean
Beach crouched under a sad winter sky. At the end of the block the author
could just make out the garage door of the Matapan family, erstwhile practice studio of Bratworst. "If they find her, I doubt they'll give you access,"
he said, with only the subtlest of emphases on *you*. "I'm prepared to act as
a go-between . . ."

"Very generous. And in return?"

"Authorization."

The sound of a drawer being wrenched open, slammed shut, a long
pause. He imagined Rhoda staring at the hills of Los Feliz, tapping a pen-
cil to her lips. A canny young woman, she was bound to recognize a check-
mate when she heard one.

"We both want the same thing, you know," said the author, slackening
the line a bit, preparing to reel in the catch.

"And what's that?"

"To understand." Out the window, he watched the postman turn up the path toward the front door. A moment later, a small avalanche of mail poured through the slot and slapped to the terra-cotta tiles. In the silence he had the sense of imminence, that the universe would perhaps finally relent in just this one thing, unbar its pitiless door.

But in the next second, he heard a man's voice in Rhoda's office, heard her muffle the receiver, heard the protests of her desk chair, rumbles of laughter—*Jim, baby, you look fabulous!* "Ms. Lubinski?" the author coughed. Though he strained to make out the conversation, the author could hear only the incoherent burble of friendly voices.

After a moment, she took up the phone and said breathlessly, "We'll have to do this some other time. Call me in a few months—"

"Ms. Lubinski"—he was determined not to lose the moment—"you must understand: I will see this through. Why not work with me, have some hand in the process? I'm not going anywhere, Rhoda. I will get to her one way or another."

But even as he spoke, he could hear the emptiness across the line: She had hung up.

So close! Authorization was nearly his! In a sweat of agitation, a restlessness not unlike that of a hopeful swain on a first date who has won the coveted invitation into the house, who has patiently borne chitchat with overprotective parents and siblings in braces, who has cooed over the family's quivering and misanthropic Jack Russell terrier and laughed at some insipid late-night rerun and at last finds himself alone on the couch with the object of his desire, the lights dimmed, the shag carpet lying invitingly at their feet—the author walked through all the rooms in his house, trying to control his breathing, slow the workings of his mind. How could she not see the logic, the inevitability? How could Rhoda not recognize Calliope's rightful biographer, not hear the beating of his pure, authentic heart?

At loose ends, needing to occupy his hands, the author picked up the sheaf of mail from the entryway: credit-card offers, coupon packets, another notice from the bank—junk mostly, not even a postcard from some distant land to break up the meaningless deluge. At the bottom of the pile, he found an envelope addressed in an unfamiliar hand. He turned it over and over for some clue to its origin, distractedly thumbed open the fold and shook out its contents: two creased articles—no note of explanation, nor indication who had sent them.

SECOND TERRIBLE CHILDREN RECORD WRAPPED, read the first headline, above a photo of Brandt and Connor standing in the driveway of the Malibu A-frame. The photograph, two decades old, projected an innocence that seemed almost anachronistic: the quasi-brothers, grinning as they emerged from the house where they'd done the final overdubs for *The Fisher King*. Their faces were unlined, Brandt's not yet showing the ravages of the coming years; Connor, standing a good nine inches taller, hugged the singer close as though to protect him. The background emphasized this two-against-the-world symbolism, the musicians isolated but for the house, the empty driveway, the overarching sky.

> MALIBU—NorthStar Records announced today that the second album from San Diego punk rockers Terrible Children, will be released on December 7, in time for the Christmas rush. The band, fronted by guitarist Brandt Morath, smashed sales records in 199_ with *The Hanged Man,* a six-song EP.
>
> "We put everything we have into this one," said bassist and cofounder Connor Feingold. "We felt like we had something to prove. We're not one of those one-record bands. We are here to stay."
>
> The band, which also includes guitarist Billy Martinez and drummer XXX, originally finished recording in May at NorthStar Studios in Manhattan Beach. Mr. Morath, unsatisfied with the sound quality, fired producer Jim O'Rourke and holed up with the master tapes in Mr. Feingold's home studio, where the two remixed several of the tracks.

The author skimmed through the rest of the piece, its well-known account of the feud between the band and O'Rourke and the resulting chill that came over Brandt's relationship with the influential New York outfit Sonic Youth, early champions of Terrible Children.* Finding nothing new,

---

*Giving rise to one of the more inane but persistent conspiracy theories: that SY guitarist Thurston Moore arranged to have Brandt murdered. A variation sees the murder as revenge for a rumored affair between Penny Power and Moore's wife, SY bassist Kim Gordon. The 200_ album *sonic bØØm* is said to be a response to, or a wink at, these preposterous narratives.

nothing to suggest why the article had been sent, he moved on to the next, which was in color and printed on glossy magazine stock, the name of the magazine and issue date torn away. This article, too, offered a photograph of Connor's house, though here in Brandt's place was Penny Power. She wore an expensive black suit, sunglasses perched atop platinum hair, and all but radiated health. Holding hands with a robed, much-aged Feingold, she leaned over to the enormous Buddha in the center of the driveway, kissing its shiny bald head. TC BASSIST AND MORATH WIDOW RECONCILE; BOX SET TO BE RELEASED NEXT YEAR, read the headline.

Like the first piece, the article which followed told the author nothing new, rehashing the legal and emotional issues which had bedeviled the box set. There was nothing to be learned here, no clue as to the identity of the second father, no insights regarding the nature of the Muse. Perhaps some amateur sleuth had sent the articles, angling for an acknowledgment—or even coauthor credit! If so, the pretender had underestimated the author's research skills, the degree to which he was already steeped in Morath lore, as well as his autonomy. He worked alone.

Still standing by the front door, the author looked at the two articles, considering their juxtaposition: one from the distant past, the other fairly recent; antediluvian vs. post-; Penny vs. Brandt, male-female, Connor as the constant . . . Was there a message? What mote of vital information lay in (or between!) those lines? Why these two articles, of the thousands that had been written? And why now? He picked up the envelope and peered inside, squinted at the illegible postmark. There was no message, no startling insight, just two flimsy pieces of paper signifying, as the bard said, nothing.

In the kitchen, Rhoda's rudeness still rankling, the author flung the useless clippings toward the recycling bin. They fluttered and glided to the floor. Stooping, he took a breath, reminded himself that frustration was an occupational hazard for those who would seek the Truth. He picked the articles up and laid them atop a stack of clippings on the daybed in his office. All things in time, he thought. He would get back to them.

Though Powell's City of Books, a 68,000-square-foot behemoth on Portland's busy Burnside Street, was no stranger to celebrity, having hosted, in

over three decades as the most prestigious bookseller in the Pacific Northwest, such controversial luminaries as Henry Kissinger, Gloria Steinem,
Salman Rushdie, all three Clinton authors, Louis Farrakhan, and Dr. Phil
McGraw (in the turbulent, class-action-suit days), the week leading up to
the book-release party for *A Gut-Wrenching Tale of Crippling Hunger* saw an
unprecedented level of anxiety and preparation. Thanks to Snow Lion's
relentless publicity campaign—including full-page ads in the *New Yorker,*
Vanity Fair, Tricycle, and other national publications, picturing the Beekeeper
in his now-trademark white suit and top hat, grinning and holding his cane
in the air while a nude red-haired woman knelt before him with her back
to the camera—the Beekeeper's memoir had broken records, online and
off-, for presales. Powell's had constructed a temporary high-security area
in their underground storeroom to guard the first shipment; by January 15,
five days before the event, the Portland Police Department was estimating
attendance at 7,000–8,000, with 240 tickets available.

"We thought it was just fabulous, we thought it was wonderful won-
derful wonderful," said Tommy Rosen, 59, who had owned and operated
Powell's since buying the store from founder Walter Powell in 200_.
"Books! All this attention to books! Not politicians, not teenybopper pop-
stars, not that dreadful Brad Pitt: a writer. And such a good-looking boy . . .
I was so excited, it was all I could do not to strip naked and run around
Courthouse Square."

The author spoke with Rosen in early July 200_, nearly five months
after the Beekeeper's reading; though the insurance settlement had left
him a rich man, Rosen still appeared stricken, hollowed out by his own encounter with the Muse. "Of course we wanted to make sure there were no
problems—god forbid!—but I never imagined . . . We thought [the] San
Diego [incident] was just kooky California stuff," he said, responding to
charges he had declined sufficient police protection for the event. He
reached across the table in a Pearl District Starbucks and tapped the back
of the author's hand. "Besides, who can't appreciate a little scandal?"

The author gently reminded him that "little" was hardly the proper
adjective to describe the events of January 20; Rosen sighed, and his frame
seemed to collapse, the purple and chartreuse flowers on his Hawaiian
shirt crumpling. "Who would have dreamed?" He clutched the rhinestone

collar of his deceased Siamese cat, Mitzi, wrapping it tightly around his wrist and unwrapping it again, squeezing his flesh a deathly white.

"Why on earth would anyone want to do what she did?"

On January 14, Portland Police Department's Special Envoy for Civil Disobedience, Maris Taranakis, paid a visit to Powell's to discuss security arrangements. Taranakis had made her reputation during the 199_ World Trade Organization riots in Seattle when, as deputy to the city's police commissioner, she came under fire for excessive use of force. "Anarchy works both ways," she told federal prosecutors, who refrained from bringing charges against Taranakis in exchange for her voluntary transfer. "You don't fight terrorism with the Eighth Amendment. The protesters defined the playing field. They chose the game. We suited up."

Taranakis had spent two days on a bench across the street from the bookstore, wearing sweatpants, an FBI sweatshirt, and an NYPD baseball cap, eating sunflower seeds by the bagful. "I hadn't the foggiest idea who it was," Rosen said, recalling the austere figure with military-grade binoculars and a walkie-talkie. "My staff thought it was a lunatic, some paramilitary book hater, stalking us all!" On the third day, Taranakis entered the store, demanded to see the owner, and listed the security precautions she recommended for the Beekeeper's reading, including metal detectors in every entrance, rerouting of city buses, background checks of all employees, and a cadre of snipers on Powell's roof. Rosen was taken aback. It was out of the question, he told her, he refused to turn the bookstore—"a place of harmony and community"—into a bunker. Taranakis might do whatever she deemed necessary to protect the city as long as his customers were not inconvenienced, the feathers of the celebrated memoirist not ruffled.

"I'm not sure you understand who you're dealing with," she said.

"*Whom*," replied the prickly store owner, whose distaste for authority went back to his UC Berkeley days. "It's an object, not a subject. 'I'm not sure you understand *whom* you're dealing with.'"

Taranakis, who stood several inches taller than Rosen, did not blink; the tone of her voice remained businesslike. "You're a foolish little queer," she reportedly said,* laying her service revolver next to the cash

---

*Taranakis, now retired and living in Coeur d'Alene, Idaho, declined to respond to Rosen's account.

register and cleaning her sunglasses with the hem of her sweatshirt. A nineteen-year-old cashier, Ananda Mehta, started to defend her boss, but one look from the "Protest Czarina" silenced her. "She's going to come in here and she's going to tear that Buddhist pipsqueak limb from limb," said Taranakis. "She's going to wreck your business and humiliate my department.

"And that, Sally"—she poked Rosen in the chest—"is the kind of bullshit up with which I will not put."

In the event, Rosen threatened to deny police access to the property, and Taranakis countered by threatening to declare the reading a menace to public safety and cancel it altogether. After the bookseller placed a phone call to Portland mayor Sam Winograd—the two were old college buddies—a compromise was reached: no metal detectors, no snipers, no officers inside the building; but concrete barriers would be placed in a fifteen-foot perimeter around the Burnside entrance (the Couch Street entrance would be sealed) and police would search all bags before allowing customers into the store. Additionally, the reading was moved from the third-floor art gallery to the more easily secured children's-book section at the rear of the labyrinthine Rose Room. When asked by the *Oregonian* if she thought the precautions sufficient to stop an intruder who had, a month earlier, materialized out of thin air and destroyed a theater without using any weapons, Taranakis replied, "I'm a public servant. It's not my job to think. In theory, someone else is doing that."*

The Beekeeper arrived at the City of Books at 3:00 P.M. in a rented Buick Skylark, having opted not to call attention to himself by bringing his BMW roadster. Wearing jeans and a "Free Mumia" T-shirt, L.A. Dodgers cap pulled low over his eyes, he entered through Powell's loading dock, accompanied by two monks from the local Dharma Rain Zen Center who seemed to function not as a bodyguard but as moral support, rubbing the Beekeeper's shoulders and whispering encouraging words in his ear. Rosen recalls that the handsome young writer was pale and temperamental, constantly looking behind him and swallowing Tums by the handful.

---

*"Powell's Owner Prepares for the Best," January 18, 200_.

"The poor boy was absolutely *terrified*," Rosen told the author. "Sweating profusely, any little noise made him jump. And on top of that, to have to project such debonair calm to the world—it was amazing. I watched him later in the office, meditating with the Buddhist fellows—it was like watching a star athlete get ready for a game. That white suit was his uniform, like a superhero donning his cape!"

The small entourage moved through the dim underground corridors, past the high-security area where nine crates marked with Snow Lion Press's saffron-and-black logo rested atop pallets behind floor-to-ceiling wire mesh. The Beekeeper stopped and took off his hat, regarding the shipment which had arrived by Brinks van earlier in the week. He stared at the crates, perhaps allowing himself a moment's satisfaction, perhaps wondering at the path that had brought him from the bottom of a lonely Virginia well to the peak of public renown. When he stepped forward, Rosen lunged for his arms to prevent him from touching the electrified wires.

"My god!" the bookseller gasped, wrapping his arms around the stunned memoirist, shuffling him into the opposite wall. To ensure the Beekeeper made no more false moves, Rosen held him there, squeezing tightly, until the monks peeled him off and the group proceeded to the freight elevator.

By 5:00 P.M., the crowds gathered outside Powell's for the 7:30 reading had accomplished what Maris Taranakis could not: the closure of Burnside Street. Thousands rumbled and surged against the barriers, making normal traffic flow impossible all the way to the North Park Blocks, where scalpers were fetching up to $750 for passes to the nominally free event. Mounted police waded into the throng, horses snorting and steaming in the damp January chill. On the triangular island formed by the intersection of Oak Street and Burnside, avid fans clambered over the kinetic sculpture called *Pod*, a thirty-foot tripod of steel and titanium whose insectile arms seesawed slowly overhead. That morning while opening the store, Ananda Mehta had gasped when she looked out the window to find the message spray-painted across that teetering wingspan: *Where in the world is Calliope Bird? Tear away my shroud (these words)— The poet will soon be heard.*

"Isn't it wonderful?" Rosen said to Taranakis. They stood just outside the entrance and stared at the crowd, the one beaming like a proud parent, the other flatly scanning faces, hands, bags, pockets, keyed to any incongruous movement, any glint of light from the windows across the street. "He'll be so pleased. When he sees how much they all love him, he'll never want to leave."

A team of paramedics hustled by, attending to five victims who had fallen before the barriers. Two officers sent to clear the giant sculpture came back unsuccessful, covered in rose petals and strands of dried yak cheese.

"You sure you don't want a few shields inside?" Taranakis spat a barrage of pulped sunflower seed husks at Rosen's feet. "Last chance."

"Look at these people, Maris. They love him. Nobody wants to hurt him—they want to hear what he has to say."

The cacophony of anticipation gusted around them, streetlamps patterning the dusk. Taranakis crossed her arms, the last levee against a tsunami of human passion. "They could give a fat fuck what he has to say." With a jab of her nightstick, she felled a fanatical woman who had been sneaking behind her toward the entrance. "They're here to see his destruction. They're here to see the Muse."

When the Beekeeper emerged from Rosen's office at a few minutes past 7:00 P.M., he seemed momentarily stunned by the scene that confronted him. The children's-book section was filled to overflowing, people sitting atop seven-foot bookcases, crouched on tables previously covered with coloring books, squeezed into the plastic cubes of Poopie Playgrounds.* Darkness having fallen, the windows doubled the multifarious crowd, whose rowdiness threatened to drown out Rosen's unassuming voice. Several times during his introduction, the two monks had to quiet the room; Rosen, almost swooning, stuttered and dropped his notecards,

---

*The report by the Portland Fire Marshal assigned partial blame to overcrowding, estimating that over four hundred people had been allowed into the Rose Room. "Nevertheless," states the report, "had the emergency exits not been sealed, safe exit would likely have been possible for most." Despite sworn testimony from three of her officers, Maris Taranakis continues to deny that she gave the order to seal the exits.

fumbling to continue until the Beekeeper put a hand on his shoulder and whispered his thanks. Rosen turned a stricken crimson and took a seat to one side of the lectern.

"Friends, I am just so happy you're here," said the Beekeeper, his voice hoarse to begin with but taking strength from the audience's enthusiasm. Twice he opened his mouth and closed it; the encouragement was loud enough to rattle books from their shelves. He stood leaning on his cane, one hand adjusting the top hat which he eventually removed and handed to Rosen. The Beekeeper's hair had been shorn close to the scalp and dyed magenta. His face was drawn, his normally ruddy skin sallow, the restiveness in his eyes belying his reputation for self-assurance, as though what he was about to do—what he had planned for months with Snow Lion's PR department, rehearsed down to the last word—were stealing his breath like a succubus, afflicting him with the same awful hunger that had haunted his youth.

The crowd quieted. "I want to talk for a minute about art," he finally said. "Anybody here know anything about art?" He stared to the back of the room, one hand fiddling with the gold handle of his cane. "Anybody think they know what art is? Think they can tell the rest of us what's art?

"Good," he said, before anyone could answer. "Me neither. Fact, I'm kind of glad we're not in that old art gallery tonight. I'm not here to tell you what art is, what's good or bad, what's smart or dumb. That's the difference between me and some other people, who say literature has to be complicated to be worth anything.

"I think you people are smart," he said, slowly regaining the sly, easy smile that had landed him at number 4 on *People*'s 200_ "Most Beautiful People" list. "I think if a lot of you like something, it must be pretty smart. It's like Louis Armstrong says, 'If it sounds good, it *is* good.'"

Applause resounded, four hundred people and their reflections shifted their weight. The heat they generated had begun to steam the windows, rivulets tracing paths of black clarity through the fog. "Poetry . . . ," The Beekeeper shook his head sadly. "That's the worst of it. I used to date a poet," he said, eliciting shouts and hoots, the rolling thunder of heels beating against table legs and low shelves. "Boy, did she ever try to tell me what was what . . . and then I'd go read her poetry and I'd say, 'What makes this good poetry? What makes this smart?'"

The crowd had fallen under the dream-spell of his honeyed voice. Tommy Rosen leaned starry-eyed against the knees of a seated monk, his Siamese cat, Mitzi, slinking through the chairs. At the store's entrance, Maris Taranakis, listening to the reading through a wireless earpiece, popped some sunflower seeds and started to relax.

"I'd say, 'Hey, babe, I'm your number-one fan! I'm your ideal reader! If you can't even show *me* a good time, who else do you think's gonna give two ticks off a dog's belly about your poems?'" The Beekeeper strolled before the lectern, running fingertips across his clipped purple curls. "The worst part of it is, she said she was a Buddhist." He winked at the two monks, with each moment his voice slipping farther into his native drawl. "But Buddhism and art . . . they just don't mix. You see, I know a thing or two about Buddhism. It's about denial of the ego, about selflessness, being one with everything around you. But art, least the way these people do it, it's all about the so-called *artist*. It's all about *me*.

"Least that's what my friend Freddy Nietzsche says." He held up a much-worn copy of *The Birth of Tragedy*, waving it sardonically overhead. The crowd leaned forward, one clumsy teen sliding off his chair to the general laughter. "Know what else?" He flipped through the pages and stopped at a bookmark, which fluttered to the floor. "The lyric poet's the worst of all. The confessional poet. The poet who thinks the only interesting subject is herself."

To the boos and hisses, he held up a patient hand. "'How is the lyric poet at all possible as artist?'" he read. "'He,' or *she*, 'who always says *I* and recites the scale of her passions and appetites? Isn't she for that reason a *non-artist*?'"

It was as though he were daring Calliope, taunting her across the divide of death. Like a gospel preacher in some frayed tent pushed outside the city limits of respectability, the Beekeeper worked the crowd into a revival-grade uproar, pounding his lectern, then held his cane overhead in perfect imitation of the revolting print ad that had already sold millions of his books.

"Let me give you some of why you came tonight." He waited for relative silence. "Let me read a little something from these memoirs I jotted down." He took an unjacketed copy of the book from beneath the lectern. "This comes from a chapter toward the middle called 'I'll Huff and I'll Puff and I'll Blow Your Damn Mind.'"

The crowd settled back. The Beekeeper sipped from a glass of water, then took off his jacket, revealing blue-and-yellow striped suspenders, a white shirt darkly stained at the armpits.

"'It was a thirty-minute drive down to Hemet, and a twenty-minute drive back,'" he began, reading from a section that detailed Calliope's use of a variety of inhalants to enhance sexual stimulation. According to the Beekeeper, the poet had a number of connections in Hemet whom she visited several times a week to replenish her supply of amphetamines; accompanying her on one such trip, the Beekeeper claimed she had, under the influence of amyl nitrate, performed an act of fellatio upon him while speeding back toward Mountaintop on the treacherous curves of Highway 74. The anecdote, ludicrous and libelous though it certainly was, was shrewdly chosen for a reading that already conflated the two celebrities (and their combined sales-power), sampling the powerful fusion of art, commerce, substance abuse, and sex that gave his otherwise-worthless scribbles their base appeal.

But he would not arrive at the climax of his cynical screed. While he read his amateurish descriptions of Hemet's soulless commercial district and clinically depressed trailer homes, while Tommy Rosen hugged his knees and sighed, while Maris Taranakis stared down the legions of the unadmitted, Rafael Zuñiga, the former security officer at UCI, who had paid $600 on Craigslist for a pass to the reading and arrived at the store at 9:30 A.M. to assure himself a seat, casually removed the brown Rockport loafer from his right foot and unscrewed the cap of his water bottle. As the Beekeeper paused for effect, having just lyrically described the deftness with which Calliope could unzip a zipper, Zuñiga lurched to his feet and made a limping, one-shoed dash to the front of the room.

"*Huff this, motherfucker!*" he cried, splashing fluid across the stunned Beekeeper's chest and flicking a cigarette lighter against the sole of the loafer in his hand.

"I couldn't take it, you know, this *pendejo* running her down and shit," Zuñiga would later testify. "Homeboy probably never even *met* her, you feel me? Thinks he can just say whatever and ain't nobody there gonna do nothing. It wasn't kosher, man. Somebody had to stand up for her, you feel me? Somebody had to set things right."

But Zuñiga's crazed act of chivalry was not to bear fruit. In contravention of the agreement she'd made with the mayor's office, Maris Taranakis had placed several plainclothes officers in the crowd, disguised as Reed College creative-writing students. Between them, they were able to wrestle the sputtering Zuñiga to the floor, where he continued to blow pathetically on the tiny flame of his lighter in a futile attempt to ignite the explosives in his shoe until he was dragged out of the room to jeers and sputum and the hard-edged impact of pop-up books used as projectiles.*

"Lost a customer there," the Beekeeper quipped, eliciting a collective chuckle of relief. The tension that had been building since the night of *The Hanged Man*'s premiere peaked and burst and finally dissolved into hilarity.

He put his jacket back on, straightened his tie, and picked up the book once again, Zuñiga's hysteria echoing in the distance, all present smiling uncontrollably as the nervous excitement slowly worked its way out of their systems. And if they believed the worst to have passed, if they believed themselves and the white-clad charlatan they adored to be out of danger, it was only because no one present, the Beekeeper included, had a sufficient understanding of the Muse. No one understood the Truth.

Though undoubtedly the most dedicated, the purest of heart, during this frenzied period the author was by no means the only pilgrim struggling hungry and exhausted toward the Muse's hidden altar. By early 200_, writers as varied as Slavoj Žižek, David Foster Wallace, Marjorie Perloff, Edwin Decker, Tama Janowitz, and Jon Krakauer were preparing their own assaults upon that summit, though none had yet reached the peak, none had

---

*In the night's most tragic irony, the room in which Zuñiga was held and allegedly subjected to torture at the hands of Maris Taranakis was directly across the hall from the secure area where the crates from Snow Lion sat. But Taranakis, focused on the task at hand, did not hear or see anything.

discovered her, none *gotten her*, any more verifiably than had the author. If the symbol is the murder of the thing, all that can be said is that these megabytes of description, discussion, dialectic, extemporization, and paean amounted to just so many attempts at a definitive symbolization of a thing none could truly possess. In that strange season preceding the horror at the Graveyard, those determined to know her mapped out ever-closer approximations to the perfect murder.

Žižek, whom readers will recall from his swaggering articles in the *New York Times Magazine,* returned with a rushed, incoherent essay in the February issue of *n+1* which tied the Muse to that unchartable region between the symbolic and the imaginary, what Michaela Breve had referred to as "the quilting point." Relying on the somewhat-less-elegant metaphor of "suturing," Žižek's own insecurities are on parade, his insistent references to castration saying perhaps more about his own nature than Calliope's:

> [Castration] is the precondition for subjectivity. The alternative is psychosis, estrangement from the Big Other, loss of phallic function. Yes, it is ironic: that the subject must be castrated, must enter the symbolic, so as to achieve a functioning sexual identity [. . .]
>
> The problem of the Muse is the problem of *noncastration,* of a phallic function (*phallicité*) run amok to penetrate the social order. Here we see why she takes as targets those industries—publishing, film, music—which rely most heavily on the codes and conspiracies of commerce. Thrusting into the loins of symbolic practice, she becomes "the Other of the Other," the unspeakable thing (*das Ding*) that works its way into the fabric, loosening the sutures until the garment lies in shreds.*

Whatever the excesses of Žižek's discussion, he at least makes an attempt to grapple with the ramifications of the New Poetry, the silence which Calliope injected into the babble like a saboteuse. The essay elicited charges of literary necrophilia from feminist quarters: "Let's not bemoan

***

*"Extimité," February 200_.

the shredding of Žižek's garments any more than that of the Emperor's robes," wrote Judith Butler:

> The tedious insistence that castration is the determinative act, reifying a priori gender roles, ignores the performative, protean nature of Muse's gender. It exposes the true purpose of the categories "imaginary" and "symbolic," for in the one we find her a prostrate, virginal victim, in the other a dangerous, gender-bending whore. Having at one time been castrated, then, do we assume that the Muse's phallus is of the "strap-on" variety? If so, let's hope Žižek's sutures are as durable as his rhetoric.*

It was perhaps in response to such bickering that poet and critic William Logan, one of Calliope's early defenders, wrote "You Are Balanced on a Razor's Edge," published a week before the Graveyard Riot. Solemn and prophetic, the forty-four-line dramatic monologue speaks in the voice of Tiresias, the blind prophet who foresaw the falls of Oedipus and Creon, casting Calliope less as a bruised, suicidal Antigone than as the unyielding spirit of Fate, the instrument of the gods, the Muse thus equated with a kind of disembodied wrath, the very spirit of suicide:

> Beware all things you find
> in language's bright cavern. My counsel:
> Calm your tongues and keep
> a better mind
> lest your own dog-nature murder you in sleep.†

But the most audacious discussion came from David Foster Wallace, published as a lengthy "folio" in *Harper's*. Like Edwin Decker, Wallace most likely hoped to use Calliope's fame to put his own name on the literary map.‡ The essay seemed designed precisely to maximize this attention, describing the writer's imagined "vision quest" into the canyons and ravines

---

*"Don't Praise Antigone, Bury Her!" *Psychoanalytic Dialogues*, March 200_.
†*New Yorker*, March 28, 200_.
‡His use of his middle name, for example, seems a clear, if ham-handed, imitation of the poet.

of Death Valley in search of the poet and her "family." With winks and nods to *Helter Skelter*, Vincent Bugliosi's account of the Charles Manson case, Wallace's article weaves discussions of sociology, German aesthetics, French semiotics, and Francis Fukuyama's "end of history" into a hyper-intellectual confection of the kind often produced by writers unable to get at the simple Truth. Most difficult to swallow is the essay's 5,500-word "intraview" in which ♀ utters not a single word. In turns smirking, sentimental, and imaginative, Wallace's piece says nothing useful about the poet, affording insights only of Wallace himself.

ME: Are you comfortable out here? I mean, the black leather must get pretty hot. Do you have a problem with chafing? I find even blue jeans on a hot day can, well, you know . . .

HER: [. . .]

ME: Still, I've got to say, you look very healthy, very fit. Death's been good to you. What's this new perfume you're wearing? 'Cause I smelled it before I saw you, when I was climbing over that manzanita back there. I mean, it's just this really good smell.

HER: [. . .]

ME: And but so the silence thing—what are you trying to say?

HER: [. . .]

ME: Here's what I'm thinking: "Death of the Author." Am I right?

HER: [. . .]

ME: You know, how Barthes formulates the postmodern author as a kind of nexus for cultural and historical reference, a sort of filter or clearinghouse, a "neutral, composite, oblique space where our subject slips away, the negative where all identity is lost."

HER: [. . .]

ME: So then if your literary product is the absence of words, that means that the references are also absent, null and void, that what the culture has produced until now in all its cacophony and complexity amounts to nothing, in the Faulknero-Shakespearean sense.

HER: [. . .]

ME: You following me?

HER: [. . .]

ME: Or maybe the point is to let the world babble on while you take it all in, to fill up the vessel, the "oblique space" of the Muse, and learn something crucial and gonad-bruising about ourselves by what goes in. Is that it?

HER: [. . .]

ME: Because it does get annoying. The silence.

HER: [. . .]

ME: What if I try it? How would you like it?

HER: [. . .]

ME: [. . .]

HER: [. . .]

ME: Okay, that didn't work.

HER: [. . .]

ME: Ever read Benjamin?

HER: [. . .]

ME: Okay, forget Benjamin. Jeesh, what's the point, anyway, other than for me to show you how knowledgeable I am, how agonizingly inca- pable of directly experiencing this moment and conversing with you human-to-human, or human-to-um-posthuman, trapped in the Escher- like convolutions of my own overeducated U.S. thought patterns, and so even in this moment of trying to free myself from those thought patterns and have exactly that human-posthuman interaction I'm stand- ing here wringing my hands in the blazing sun and tragically recount- ing my difficulty in doing just that and pretty much illustrating your point about cacophony, while you . . . what are you doing, anyway?

HER: [. . .]

ME: Is that a ratchet?

Reader, the insufficiency, the futility, need not be belabored. Unlike these others—obsessed with comparison, driven to historical reference or abstract theory—the author never abandoned his quest for the real ♀. He seems to have been the only one to understand that biography, like poetry, "seeks to be . . . an unvarnished expression of truth."* It was for this reason Calliope brought us the New Poetry: to strip away the varnish, to show us to ourselves. And in precisely this sense, her life, her death, had become the poem itself: image, language, idea, scandal, needing only the sensitive soul to arrange the elements into something coherent, something incomparable, undying.

"Writer. Thinker. Former journalist. Artist, after a fashion. Father. Loving father. Doting father. The kind of father who would do anything for his child, who puts his child's welfare above all else, to the point that he's willing to disappoint the child, cause the child temporary unhappiness in the interests of the child's greater long-term good. Sacrifice. Of the child's esteem, the child's affection—willingness to give these things up simply because he knows what is best. Selflessness, is what that is. Selfless, then. Taking the long view. Unwilling to depart from what he knows is best, is right, for short-term gratification. Unwilling, though this very unwillingness might be taken for rigidity, providing still further motivation to relent, to take the road more traveled: the easy way out. Allergic to the easy way out, you might say. Determined. Self-assured. Are these the kinds of words you're looking for, the—what did you call them?"

"Master signifiers."

"Yes."

"I'm not looking for any words in particular."

"Thinker. Did I say that? Analyst, of a sort, though not as credentialed as yourself . . . Depth. Complexity. Compassion. Yes, certainly compassion, else how can one put oneself in the place of another, understand what it is to walk that terrible mile in those tattered shoes? Empathy, then.

---

*From *The Birth of Tragedy*.

Above all else. Empathy. The ability to understand another, to inhabit, if you will. Empathy as the necessary foundation of human intercourse. To feel the pain of another—not just hear it, understand it, soothe it, but experience it. To enter their reality, however distant it might seem, leave your own troubles and really *feel* what they are feeling. To *get it*, as it were. So you can know them. So when their pain becomes so great they can't stand it anymore, you experience that pain, too, and perhaps have the strength to see them through it, so that she won't be alone in her hour of need, will know that someone understands, that all is not so bleak and unremittingly hopeless. Do you understand, Doctor? What I mean by empathy?"

"I think so."

"Certainly not the wishy-washy feel-good version in the greeting cards. Certainly not the half-assed nonsense children are taught by guidance counselors. I mean real, honest-to-goodness understanding, the kind that takes hard work, utter devotion—only this kind of empathy can have the desired results."

"And what are those desired results?"

"I'm sorry?"

"What results are you referring to?"

"Well, of course I mean . . . I'm speaking abstractly, of the need for us to understand each other."

"You used the word 'results.'"

"Rhetoric, Doctor. I didn't mean anything—"

"And yet you said it."

"Yes, fine. I said it. Could we perhaps get back to the subject at hand?"

"Which is?"

"Calliope, of course. The Muse. Here's what I'm thinking now, *as per* our previous discussions of the Real—"

"Let me try this another way. If there are 'desired results' of empathy—and I'm using your words now—then what might result from a *lack* of empathy?"

"You talk about the Real as something traumatic, unspeakable, overwhelming our ability to symbolize it. I'm thinking of Portland, of what happened when the Beekeeper opened his mouth—I'm thinking of the orgiastic frenzy at the Spreckels Theatre. I'm thinking of Brandt's death, the abject and gruesome shock . . . Aren't these in some way equivalent? Is this not some kind of . . . *theme?*"

"Well. There's a crucial difference."

"What's that?"

"We don't know what 'really' happened the morning Brandt died . . . just as you haven't told—"

"Excuse me?"

"We don't know what really happened. All we have is Calliope's memory of what happened, the memory she recovered—and any close reading of the various interviews and transcripts quickly shows the evolution of her—"

"I'm sorry, did you say 'recovered'?"

"Well, yes. You can't—"

"Doctor, do you mean to say that all this time we've been discussing a so-called *recovered memory*, that the entire foundation of the thanatography—the first chapter, for heaven's sake!—is built upon something—"

"I can't see how you would have been unaware. I published the entire case study in *Psychanalysis Aujourd'hui!* I gave a major paper in Perth."

The author stood and walked quickly to the far side of the office, the blinds which kept the room in cryptlike darkness. Uniform slats of light wood outlined by chrome sunshine. At every turn, she escaped him. At every step she danced away, a free soul fleeing the prison of the finite body. Closing his eyes, he tugged on the drawstring and the windows' wood eyelids opened. February sunshine gushed coldly into the room.

"Andrew, isn't every memory, in a sense, recovered? Each time we access it, don't we fill in gaps, revise details, remember things which had previously escaped us?"

"No."

"Don't we re-present the world, even to ourselves, every time we present it? Is there so much of a difference here?"

"It's impossible," he said, touching the cool glass. A few palm trees waved pathetically against the unquiet ocean, the seawall, and parking lot, a white sun sinking—all seemed without scale, a sliding jumble of empty figures, no ground.

"What's impossible?"

"It's impossible. It's impossible. How am I to . . . how can anyone?"

"Go on."

"Russian dolls. I'm trying to say something about her, she's trying to say something about that morning. Her recollection, my representation . . . and now you tell me she doesn't even . . ."

"That's not precisely—"

". . . and what is a *reader* to think, Doctor? With yet one more layer, one more degree of separation, as it were, all of this collapsed into print on a page and her inability to touch . . . or, I mean, to know the truth of it."

"To touch?"

"A figure of speech!"

"To touch?"

"And the Russian dolls—yet another metaphor. Pathetic!"

"Andrew. To touch."

"*Me,* all right? To touch me. Where am *I* in all this? Sandwiched in between Calliope's fabrications and the physical fabrication of the book, the *product* . . . What do I become but some kind of specter, unavailable, unknown—anonymous. Dead. Like exactly that—I don't even remember the phrase—that *empty space* he's talking about. Who is there to . . . Do you understand?"

"Can you say more about that? Andrew?"

"No."

"No?"

"I refuse to believe it. Perhaps she, I don't know, perhaps she wanted to please you. Perhaps she was ashamed. At first, ashamed, frightened of . . . look at this office—who could blame a child for withholding, feeling intimidated, even a child accustomed to grandeur, who could blame her—at first—for keeping it from you?"

"I'm not sure I'm—"

"And then slowly, as she began to trust you, piece by piece filling in the awful . . . yes, of course that would sound to you as though it were being recovered rather than a literal transcription of truth. Doctor, really, this might be quite valuable to you, I think, to understand this about the psychoanalytic dynamic, the discontinuity of the . . . transmission. *Static,* then,

static interference. Under such conditions what *wouldn't* sound like something recovered, pieced back together—looked at this way, what *isn't*? But
that doesn't change a thing! Not a thing!"

"Is that what you're doing now?"

"I'm sorry?"

"Are you feeding me pieces, rather than telling me the truth?"

"Well. Certainly I . . . this has nothing   "

"You said something once I found very interesting. You said memoir
was a . . . let me check my notes . . . a 'sordid literary product.' Do you believe memory is sordid? Do you think talking about yourself, revealing your
own history, is shameful?"

"Of course not."

"It sounds as though you consider it a sign of weakness, or narcissism.
I wonder if that doesn't account for some of the . . . determination to write
biography."

"Not at all."

"Then why the disdain?"

"It's really quite private, isn't it? One's secret desires, griefs, et cetera.
Something for the therapist's office."

"You're in one of those offices now."

"I'm hardly a patient, Dr. Breve."

"You're here, you're lying on the couch, you're paying for the appointment—"

"As a courtesy!"

"Look in the mirror, Andrew. What differentiates you from—"

"I'm not here for myself! I'm talking about someone else."

"Aren't we always? That's what Lacan would have us understand."

"Please, Doctor—"

"Are you familiar with Rimbaud?"

Again to the window. Again pulling the shade: opened, closed, a blinking. The whimsical notion of sending a signal to someone watching from
some hypothetical craft offshore. The author did not know semaphore,
nor any other visual code. And of course there was no recipient. He sat
again on the divan, sensing but not seeing his double settle upward into his
own comfort—identical and yet unidentical, without purpose or soul.

"I'd like to talk more about biography. Is that all right? How did you become a biographer? You mentioned you'd been a journalist."

"Yes."

"For a newspaper?"

"More or less."

"Can you talk about that?"

"*SLAM.*"

"Again?"

"It's a local arts magazine. Culture. Music. Once quite influential, but it's sunk rather low of late."

"Since you left?"

"The new editor, Mark Lipschitz. Incompetent, really. Skilled only in politics, in sad little palace coups. No creative energy of his own. Must we talk about him?"

"You dislike Mr. Lipschitz."

"Where was he when Terrible Children was just two ragamuffins writing songs in a stockroom? When Penny Power was crawling across Java Joe's stage? He was a child, a high school student, collecting baseball cards, bottle caps—where was he when giants walked the earth? While the real journalists are at the Arizona Café, watching the heartrending, the self-destruction . . ."

"You never told me how you happened to be at Calliope's last reading."

"Instead he fills the pages with imitation, he comes along after the real work has been done, with his firm handshake and his communications degree, with his trumped-up accusations . . . I trained him, Doctor, he was my intern! We were a team, a band of brothers!"

"You feel betrayed."

"Look at it now—worthless! There are bands out there, starving, unnoticed, bands with something *new* to say, but *SLAM* puts cover bands on the cover. *Cover bands!* Validating the very proposition that these are *artists,* that this is art, simply to please industry bean counters who work tired formulas until . . . Why not send reporters to look under fishing piers, instead of lavishing on oneself a ticket to Tokyo to follow a gang of ventriloquists? Why not put on a showcase for local talent, instead of cosponsoring this . . . monstrosity, this daylong festival in the middle of nowhere? Was this why we started it? Was this the reason for our sweat, our sleepless nights?"

"I'm afraid we're going to have to stop for today. Have you talked to Jerome—"

"No one understands teamwork. No one understands loyalty. It's like a marriage, the need for people to work together, to weather the disagreements, the frustrations. They can't simply lock the door, clear out the desk, revoke the parking permit . . . they can't simply shut each other out!"

"I'd be interested to pick up here next time—"

"Of course there are problems, different ways of looking at the world. Impossible—to breach the outer hull, to see inside . . . but you don't simply lock the door, drown it out as though ending your involvement entirely. You don't simply write the other off, decide for all eternity that they just don't get it, that all is hopeless! We're in this *together*. You cannot cut the line and drift off on the tide never to return. How selfish. How ultimately cruel and selfish."

"I wish we could continue. I do. Could you come back tomorrow? I'll have Jerome move things . . . Andrew, are you all right?"

"I'm sorry."

"Don't apologize. This is real progress."

"I'm sorry, Doctor," he breathed.

"Please. Call in the morning. We'll see what we can do."

"Yes. Yes, I think I almost have her now."

The doctor nodded stiffly, hands spread over the arms of her chair. The lights came up slowly.

In the dimming parking lot, early winter sunset, the author watched the movement of cars—waiters, lawyers, yoga instructors, manicurists on their way home. How to know, from looking at them, which shape was full and which empty? One couldn't simply grab them by the elbow and inquire. Each had their own story, each in need of their own biographer, however thankless and brutal the task. As the author pulled out of the lot, a woman in a Lexus honked her horn. He smiled. She gesticulated strangely, and the author rolled down his window to hear what she had to say. But the glass remained raised, her lips forming an exaggerated syllable.

Lies, he thought she said at first; but after a moment he realized he had not turned on his headlights. He thanked her with a wave as she pulled off.

According to Richard Dunleavy, a private investigator based in Long Beach, Tommy Rosen had several times refused to post a uniformed officer outside the storage area in Powell's basement, where the crates from Snow Lion Press sat for several days. "Books are not the problem," Rosen told Maris Taranakis, in one of many discussions caught on tape. "They aren't the enemy. Go catch a rapist or a drug dealer. Don't ask me to militarize a bookstore."*

In footage of the press conference Portland mayor Winograd gave on January 21, Taranakis at his side, one can see incredulity and rage playing across her bruised face. "I don't think anyone could have imagined that the Muse would hijack a shipment of books," the combative mayor told reporters. "These were supposed to be book lovers. What happened to all those books? That's what I want to know. Why don't some of you amateur sleuths get on *that*?"

Still, it's hard to imagine even a small battalion stopping the Muse. Had the poet not shown us in San Diego the awesome power of the Truth? Literature, art—these were not meant to lie. The language could not be made to serve one man's corrupt purposes with impunity; for this ♀ had become, in some strange way, the language's conscience, its furious superego, come to cleanse base commerce from the steps of its temple. As though the Beekeeper's perfidy were a beacon, his disregard for truth a glowing **X** on the map of the living, she had set her sights and was even then speeding with a mute shriek toward the target.

"Well, I wouldn't say 'nympho,' exactly," the Beekeeper told the audience at the City of Books. He had finished reading the chapter from his

---

*Dunleavy, founder and president of the RT Dunleavy Agency, had been hired by an unnamed party to find the Poet Formerly Known as Calliope. In the week before the Beekeeper's reading, Dunleavy bugged the City of Books; though the tapes were later declared inadmissible as evidence in *City of Portland v. Rosen,* Maris Taranakis successfully used them to challenge her dismissal and have her pension reinstated.

memoir and was now taking questions. He had already put his jacket back on, placed the top hat over his magenta stubble; he leaned against the lectern and rubbed his jaw, a cloud passing across his features. Tommy Rosen stood to one side, stroking his Siamese cat. "See, that's the sad part— at least with a nympho you think, hey, she's getting what she wants, she must be enjoying it. With a nympho, it doesn't so much matter who *you* are.

"At least, that's what I'm told." He winked, and a ripple of laughter passed through the room.

"But Calliope, well . . . It mattered. It mattered who you were." He squinted as though just now understanding. "And I'll tell you, sometimes I wasn't sure she knew. Sometimes I'd see her looking at me and I'd think she was seeing someone else. I don't want to speculate. I'm not a psychologist. Let's just say, I think she wouldn't have been too upset if I'd had a guitar in my hand, and leave it at that."

He took his cane from one of the monks seated next to the lectern, and Rosen announced that the Beekeeper would be happy to sign copies of *A Gut-Wrenching Tale of Crippling Hunger,* which would be brought up in the freight elevator during the wine-and-cheese reception.

"Are there any other questions?" The Beekeeper scanned the room. "I want to thank you all for coming out. This book would be nothing without you. I mean that. See, unlike some people, I think art is made by the audience. I think it's not art until someone *else*—"

He was interrupted by a gasp from the back of the room, a clamor as a young man in a Trailblazers sweatshirt, sitting atop a bookcase, jerked and scampered and tumbled from his perch. The woman he'd been sitting next to let out a moan and froze, staring at something on the shelf. A small furor grew as people rose to assist the dazed young man; two of the faux–Reed College students, having returned from the basement, sprang alert in the doorway.

"It stung me," the young man was heard to say. He lifted himself to all fours, shaking his head violently. Atop the bookcase the woman, an Asian American in her thirties whose wool skirt and horn-rimmed glasses gave her a lawyerly air, began to hum an eerie high-pitched melody. All had stopped to look up at her in confusion when a shout brought their attention back to the front of the room.

"Oooh! My goodness!" Tommy Rosen exclaimed, stumbling over the chairs recently vacated by the Buddhist monks. Mitzi slunk from his arms and disappeared behind a set of shelves. He clapped a hand over his mouth and pointed toward the lectern, where the Beekeeper stood stock-still, clutching his cane, eyes turned upward trying to look at his own forehead.

A dark black spot had appeared on the Beekeeper's top hat, a fingernail-sized stain against a bright white background. Even as those in the front rows leaned close, the strange wailing floating overhead, the honeybee rotated and moved down toward the hat's brim, wings flickering in quick spasm and folding against its dark thorax.

"Folks," the Beekeeper said in a hoarse, high voice. "It's nothing to worry about . . ."

Gasps and squeals issued from every corner as bees appeared atop shelves, in shirt cuffs and handbags, moving lightly across the spines of books. People tripped over one another in their panic, sprawled over folding chairs and low plastic tables, slipped on picture books. The young man who had fallen was standing now, his face blank, empty. With each cry of pain, another fan stood to face the Beekeeper, as though bringing solemn judgment to bear upon his testimony.

"I have a question!" the Asian American woman sang out, and immediately resumed her spectral humming. Trembling, the Beekeeper turned his eyes to her as the honeybee navigated the underside of his hatbrim and neared the bridge of his nose.

"Okay," he croaked, eyes watering.

But she said nothing further, her gaze boring upon him from the height of the bookshelf, the odd noise flowing from her lips, rising in pitch and blending into the mirrored space until the very air trembled. "What's the question?" hissed the Beekeeper.

The bee moved twitching to the tip of his nose, ducking down into the whiskered indentation of his philtrum, and as they watched everyone in the room became aware of a presence—the Poet Formerly Known as Calliope and her eight sisters arrayed silently at the room's perimeter. In the next second, the honeybee crawled across the Beekeeper's lips and unleashed its pitiless sting.

He could not move, only squeal in pain, his face red and sweating, eyes fixed on the face of his erstwhile love. A gloss of tears trailed from the corners of his eyes. His cane clattered to the floor. The nine women looked on, the wailing sound a high-pitched memory ringing out of time.

"Okay," he muttered. "Okay, listen . . ." as another bee crawled up from beneath his collar and stung him beneath his left ear. Shaking now, he whimpered like a frightened child, his bloodshot eyes darted from corner to corner, across shelves and emptied chairs. "Don't," he panted. "Please don't. Listen, just let me . . . Please just listen."

Honeybees swooped lazily through the empty space like scavengers over a wreckage, and the Poet Formerly Known as Calliope stepped to the center of the room. The others fell back from her like water from a heavy stone; mute, bald, her neck unblemished as a virgin page, she held the Beekeeper in her gaze as he sniffled and tried to see the bees which moved up his sleeves, under his chin, across his forehead as though scrawling there an invisible message in the language of death.

"Okay," he said, when she stopped before him. "It's just, don't take it so seriously, okay?" His voice had risen to a near babble, veins pulsing at his temples, his lips swollen grotesquely. "You always take everything so seriously. But that's just it. That's the whole thing, what I finally figured out. Are you listening? Are you . . . just wait . . ."

She had not blinked. Four hundred faces watched this extraordinary confrontation, a static picture enlivened only by the desultory bees. "The old texts, you know . . . I read all of it . . . up in Denali. The whole thing, it's not real, that's the thing. None of it. Not even nothing." His body ached toward her, each sting causing his eyes to throb. "Even nothing's not real. That's what I . . . And so if nothing isn't real, then neither is *something*. Or, what I'm saying is, *something and nothing are the same.*

"There's no such thing as Buddhism. No poetry, no music, no sex or politics or fast cars . . . And if none of those are real, then neither are *we*. Neither am I. I'm not really here, babe, you know? You understand? I'm not really me. I'm not anyone.

"That's why the book's anonymous, get it? It wasn't written by any particular person. Being a particular person is just a way to make something out of nothing. I'm just trying to be honest here, understand?" His voice quavered, but the Muse's expression had not changed. "I'm nobody, so nothing really comes from me. You see?"

Another bee stung him beneath one eye, the flesh of his face growing puffy, his voice hoarse, his breath wheezy. "If I'm nobody . . . then I get to do anything, say anything. 'Negative Capability.' That's Keats. That's what art is, right? Not to attach to one . . . idea, one particular version of the world. One identity. But if there's no identity, no *you*, then no one reaches enlightenment. It's a sleight of hand, Calliope. The whole thing. It's a scam—nirvana's a scam."

She took a half step toward him and every muscle in his face betrayed his desire to back away. "So these things I wrote," he said, each word a labor, "they're not about anyone . . . It's just a story . . . it doesn't matter if it really . . . happened, people understand . . . truth isn't about facts . . . there's another . . . truth, the emotional . . ."

She closed the distance, sobs leaking from the Beekeeper's mouth, his lips and earlobes and nose discolored. His top hat had begun to shake strangely, and now the Muse lifted a hand and removed it to reveal hundreds of bees, wriggling and seething across the colorful crown of the Beekeeper's skull.

"There's no . . . bottom," gasped the terrified Beekeeper. She reached out and pressed a hand to the side of his face, and he dropped to his knees. "The well . . . has no bottom. You fall . . . forever, nothing to stop you. Do you know what that means?" He looked up into that terrible gaze. "You're not really falling . . . Understand? If there's no bottom, you're not . . . falling."

He pressed his face into her palm and closed his eyes. The bees crawled over the back of her hand, her bare arms, his scalp and eyelids, now lifting briefly into the air, now settling with a twitch of gossamer. At the room's periphery, the audience climbed over chairs, knocked shelves of books to the floor in a dash for the exit. Their cries reached Maris Taranakis, who bolted up from the basement, plainclothed officers in tow.

"Not falling," the Beekeeper wheezed, his eyes swollen nearly shut. The bees drifted between their two bodies, several alighting gracefully on the crown of her head. "Not falling . . . see? Not falling . . ." He could bear it no longer, dissolving into sobs. Calliope held her hand above his head briefly, as though in benediction, then turned away. As if to call out, to stop her from leaving or beg forgiveness, the Beekeeper mustered his remaining strength for a last, desperate speech—but when he opened his mouth what came out was a dark and terrifying torrent, a horde of bees pouring forth like hell's own minions or the small, deadly shrapnel of his soul.

"Everybody stay where you are!" shouted Maris Taranakis, who had blockaded the entrance and stood, hand on her service revolver, facing ⚥. But there was no controlling the hundreds of witnesses, whose fear gushed upon the air like the black bees that still roared from the Beekeeper's throat. "Miss Morath, I'll need you to come with me—" Taranakis strained to be heard over the tumult, strained to keep her eyes on the poet, and we shall never know whether the poet might have gone along peacefully, we shall never know whether calamity might have been avoided or whether it was Calliope's intention all along—for as the Beekeeper's spent and useless frame collapsed face-first to the carpet Taranakis drew her gun and took steady aim at the leader of the Muse, who merely smiled in return and opened her mouth and in that very instant a brown Rockport loafer, forgotten and unattended at the bottom of what was now a mound of paper and cloth, surrounded by 68,000 square feet of books, for no apparent reason, exploded.

Less noted than the loss of the City of Books was the loss, in the same week, of Marshall Vaughn, who died in his sleep in his home in San Francisco at the age of eighty-four. Though his artistic heyday had long since passed, he was deeply mourned by former colleagues and students, including Poet Laureate Thomas Lux, whose open letter to *Poets & Writers* pointedly recalled "a time when our word was our bond, Marshall the merchant with the guts to hold us to it. Silence was not an option. Silence was surrender."

The reference was clear. Though the Muse had appeared only six weeks earlier, the crisis had already begun to churn in the halls of academia. Sympathy for her cause was not hard to find—though her methods were problematic for a field based on the reproducible, analyzable speech act, based on ideas and their expression in language. The "Blindness Letter," sent to Vaughn more than a year before, was made public upon his death, its claim that "[t]he soul does indeed have to be made monstrous" used as a rallying cry by both sides in the debate. Prudently, Vaughn's widow kept private her husband's own last word, scrawled in red ink across the text of the letter as though correcting his student's work one last time: *Abomination.*

Vaughn's death also threw the author's project into some distress. He had that week been expecting news from Lubinski Management regarding authorization for the thanatography, but Rhoda, who had twice taken and twice failed Vaughn's workshop, absconded to San Francisco to attend the funeral and could not be reached for days.

"She must have a cell phone, a pager," the author strove with her new assistant, who declined to give her name. "She would want to be kept in the loop on this matter. Word to the wise: If you enjoy your job, you'll get her the message."

In the meantime, it was more waiting, more infuriating mornings in the Calliope Corner, pounding away at the computer, staring at piles of books and journals, loose papers strewn across the daybed like the disheveled nest of some inelegant, logorrheic bird. At times it seemed so much noise, so many meaningless marks—how to sort through all the documents, sift through reams of language for the gleaming pebble of Truth? Some nights, assaulted by the unruliness of it all, the author felt frustration creep hotly up his neck, a violence in search of some target less pliable than paper. Some early mornings, the skies out his window an underwater blue mottled by shadow, it must be said he experienced despair.

Such mornings, he revived the habit—dormant since the later days of his marriage—of walking on the beach, sometimes covering several miles until the sense of futility, of helplessness before a nameless affliction, was carried off on the salty breeze. Returning home one such morning in mid-February, he opened the front door to find his living room crowded with unfamiliar objects—large black crates on wheels, metal appendages, suitcases spilling clothing. His first impression was that the house had been ransacked, his next thought of Carlton Lum and the FBI. The crates reached nearly to the ceiling, the living room was a labyrinth. He quickly made for his office, the Fourth Amendment on his lips, but tripped over a cymbal stand and lay on the floor clutching his ankle and cursing.

"Hi, Dad." The author's son emerged from his bedroom. From his vantage point, the author could see shadows moving, a thick cloud of smoke through the doorway. "That shit'll be out of the way soon."

"You're back," said the author, jaw clenched in pain.

"Yeah, well. Not really. Just getting my stuff." From his son's room, the author heard first one adolescent titter, then another. The smell of marijuana was unmistakable. "I'm taking this, okay?" He held up an ancient cassette tape, the autographed demo version of *The Hanged Man* given to the author decades earlier. "We need it."

"Now just a moment," the author said, attempting to pull himself to his feet.

"I don't want to get into it, Dad. We just got back from Japan, and I'm fucking jet-lagged, and I can't deal, okay? I'm taking the tape and the rest of my shit. I'm moving out." From behind him, again, the mindless laughter of teenage girls. His leg throbbing, the author limped toward his son, who stood with hands shoved in the pockets of his jeans, barefoot, throwing glances over his shoulder. The author looked into that face, familiar but unfamiliar: the lovely pale eyes hooded by heavy lids, the prominent lower lip he had inherited from his mother. In the silence, the author realized his son was taller than he, wondered how the boy could have grown taller in a mere six weeks.

"Would you like to introduce me to your friends?" the author asked. For a brief second he entertained the fantasy of sharing their marijuana, perhaps even putting the tape in the stereo and regaling them with the old stories, their faces intent, their attention undivided.

His son bit his lip and squinted. "Listen—"

"How was Japan?"

His son pulled the bedroom door shut behind him. "It was fine," he said.

"You look hungry. Shall we go to the diner, father and son, like old times?"

"When did we ever do that?"

"When you were quite young. I admit, it's been a while. Sometimes when your mother was, well . . . when she wanted to be alone, we'd leave her here and—"

"Dad, did you hear me? I'm moving out."

"Yes, I heard you."

"Do you have anything to say about it?"

The author sat at the kitchen counter and ran his palm across the cool surface. Through the door to the Calliope Corner, he could see the answering machine blinking—most likely a message from Rhoda, most likely the authorization he'd been seeking for over a year.

"It's been quite a month, as you can imagine," he said slowly. "You probably didn't hear all of it in the Land of the Rising Sun, but it seems Calliope"—at the look on his son's face he stopped. "I've worked very hard, Drew," he said quietly. "I thought perhaps you'd be, I suppose, proud."

His son shook his head sharply, as though to clear water from his ears. "You're incredible, you know? Fucking-A."

"Drew—"

"I'm leaving you a ticket." He flung open the door to his bedroom. "We're doing this big concert in the desert. There's gonna be like a billion people there. Come, don't come—I could really give a shit."

"Wait—" The author reached for his son's retreating figure, but stumbled badly on his sore ankle and collided with a hardshell guitar case. In agony, he leaned against the wall as his son and two Japanese girls in half T-shirts, high heels, and obscenely tight black pants whisked through the living room, his son loping heavily, the girls' steps clipped and precise.

"Buzz'll come by with the truck later. I gave him a key," Drew said. At the front door, he turned to face his father. "I gotta get out of here. It's like being buried alive." He left the door open and strode down the path. The girls hesitated, then waved sympathetically to the author and followed.

It was nearly noon. The sun had not yet emerged from the heavy layer of fog; the breeze brought in from the ocean the sharp, sweet smell of a sewage spill. The author took a moment to regain his composure, then went to listen to Rhoda's message. But the voice on the answering machine was inquiring as to the author's cable-television viewing habits, and before it had played through he had pulled the machine from the desktop and thrown it to the floor, where it bounced once and divulged its microcassette and emitted several urgent beeps before falling silent. He kicked his desk chair—a mistake, considering his recent injury—and then with a cry swept a pile of books from a shelf, stumbled onto the daybed, and landed atop myriad papers which he pulled from under him and flung into the air, a guttural cackle filling the room. Slowly the papers snowed to the floor. When he opened his eyes again, he saw atop the pile the two clippings sent anonymously the month before, the photos of Brandt and Penny, each outside Connor's home, the two stories straddling an era of great art, great tragedy. *Like being buried alive.* The house was silent but for the sound of a car alarm coming through the still-open front door. The author stood and straightened his clothing. He took up the articles with renewed interest.

12. *TU VATES ERIS*

WE WAITED ON THE *front step at dawn. One nightingale purred in the shrubs. The truck came up the shadowed street, growled in the driveway, and we got in, shivering. Connor squeezed an arm around my shoulders while he drove and my mother stared through her thin reflection in the window. East by northeast, through suburbs, ranchland, the sun swelled up ivory and amethyst, horses stood at fences and watched us pass. We parked by a row of concrete huts, woodpeckers hammering oblivious overhead. Men in white coats frisked us at the door. My mother set her jaw, held me against her legs. She's just a fucking baby, she said. Down a hallway to the open door, where a man stood next to a metal cot, hands at his side. He wore a beige gown that stopped at his knees. His legs were pale and hairless, thick scabs on his ankles and the backs of his hands. Blue, bloodshot eyes watched me, terrified. Don't you recognize Daddy? my mother whispered. She pushed me into the room, a wide slant of light cutting through a high window. He shook when he held me, his chest vibrating, a choking sound. He smelled so different. I waited for him to sing, but he didn't sing. I wriggled away and said, You're not my daddy, and he sat on the bed with his face in his hands. My mother slapped me so hard I didn't cry, sent me out to the hot truck where I waited alone, listening to the uncaring woodpeckers, hating her for the trick she'd tried to play.*

★

It was the worst attack I'd seen, a bolt from the blue that brought the old woman to her knees on the rocky path. One minute we were heading home from the beehives, exhausted and sticky with wax and creosote, helmets and veils under our arms and chilly gusts of early spring sliding off the slopes to slap at our cheeks; without warning, she dropped her armload—tools clanging on stones, tin smoker spilling a smoldering clump of leaves and pine needles. She pressed a hand to her breastbone, a fierce and desperate light in her eyes that I knew and had learned to dread. The tick in her lungs tightening, her throat muscles wringing out the air. With shaking fingers she tried to unzip her coveralls, looked up at me with bluish lips, her knees buckling, a fat vein pulsing at her temple.

For months I had listened to her nightly struggles, the crackling and straining of her lungs, her clumsy shuffles into the kitchen where she boiled water to make her tea. On a shelf above the sink she kept a jar of rare, tiny flowers—pale cups of five petals, a dark red center like the inside of a mouth—gathered from the slopes of Old Maker. Many times I'd watched her crush the flowers between her fingers and sprinkle them into the pot—she held her face above the pungent steam and her dark eyes shone and wept. Eventually her breath loosened, her color came back, and she wilted to the floor, semiconscious and wracked with coughs, sputum bubbling at the corners of her mouth.

"She don't want to come to the city to see a doctor," Jacobo had told me, in the days when I'd first left my sickbed. "Maybe there is another medicine, or maybe an operation, but she is so stubborn! She say she can't go because of the bees. The old crow," he lamented, "she say the bees will die without her."

Winter was the worst, he'd warned, a double whammy: the air so cold and dry even healthy folks had trouble breathing; the pink flowers even rarer, autumn stockpiles dwindling week by week. But we all survived the winter, the long months of cold that stabbed into my marrow, short and pallid days that seemed to be over by lunchtime, as the old woman and I dragged along the mountain paths with jugs of sugar syrup, tins of antibiotic powder, traps for intrepid mice who built nests in the warm hives. Though numb and listless ourselves, we'd gone nearly every day, clearing frost and debris from the black-paper coverings, sometimes building small fires to help the bees stay alive. In the ache and shiver of those months, I had almost gotten used to the waiting, the endless deferral of my father's arrival, learned to exist in the urgency of *now*. My life took on the rhythm of her life: one foot forward, then the next, my most pressing goal the warm bed that awaited me at the end of each day.

But as the winter weather eased, her attacks came more frequently, her distress grew deeper. Often, on the long dawn walks out to the hives, she had to stop and lean against a boulder or fallen stone wall. She'd stand with fists clenched, breath whispering in her chest, staring furiously down as though the ground itself were stealing her oxygen. I stood by helplessly while she pulled in each breath by force of will, pushed it out through puckered lips. I had not told Jacobo about these morning crises, nor about the nights she sat awake, a pot of flowers on a low simmer, guarding against the spasms that came one behind the other. I did not want him to take her to the city, did not want to be left alone. Her company seemed natural now, like the dry mountain air, the muscled rush of the brown river we could see from the path. When Jacobo asked about her seizures, when he tried to tend to her, she waved him off with a grumble and a shake of her head, feinting with an open palm while I rocked with mute laughter.

Now she was crouched on all fours in the dust, wheezing hideously, short gulps of air rattling like stones over a washboard. I knelt at her side, tried to unzip her coveralls, rub her back—but she slapped my hands away. I looked for something, anything, to help her, but saw only the stern mountains, the hives a dozen yards off, pollen-heavy bees drifting home and funneling into the brightly painted boxes. The flowers grew much higher up, too far to climb; the town was almost two miles distant—even if I ran all the way, there was no one who could help, no way to bring them to her fast enough.

The rasping faded as the fist around her throat tightened. She sucked tiny breaths, her back arched, arms trembling with the effort to keep herself from collapsing. In tears myself, I glanced around wildly: at the copse of scrawny eucalyptus where we often sat to take our lunch, the lean-to where we kept spare frames and supers, the uncaring mountains, slopes still dusted with winter. The pink sky arched and curved away, clouds gathering at the horizon. Her silence clenched and terrible, the old woman put one arm forward, and with a groan pulled her shrinking body toward the beehives.

She crawled with raw determination, shoved a gloveless hand into the dark entrance of the first hive. Sentries zoomed out and circled her, frantic, alighting in her hair, on her shoulders, the back of her neck. She pulled her arm out, covered to the elbow with bees; the air filled with the sound of their anger and the thin, antiseptic scent of fear. Dark eyes bulging, she unzipped her coveralls, unbuttoned the top of her sweater, plucked a bee between two fingers and stuck it roughly to her skin at the notch of her clavicle. As I watched, the bee curled its abdomen and plunged its stinger into her skin.

She let out a choked whimper and the cords of her neck jumped. I bent down to her, bees zoomed toward my eyes, crawled along the crest of my ears, through my thatch of hair. She brushed off the dying bee, plucked another with a palsied hand, then a third, each twitching briefly along her collarbone and unleashing its venom. In another moment her muscles went limp, like a high-tension wire that loses its juice, and she sank heavily onto her side.

I dropped to my knees, bees crawling along the back of my neck. I shook her shoulders, took her face between my hands. Slowly, in twos and threes, the rest of the bees lifted off her clothing and drifted back into the hive. I sat wide-eyed and useless, clasped her limp, bony hands between mine.

Soon her muscles began to relax; I heard the sweet sound of air moving through her throat. Her eyelids fluttered and squinted, the sickening blue drained from her lips. It was quiet all around us, only the muttered bustle of the bees storing pollen, the cackle of birds newly returned to the valley. I rested her head in my lap. After a moment she blinked her eyes. I squeezed her hand. With a cluck and a grunt, she got her legs beneath her, dusted off her coveralls—I helped her to her feet and we took tentative steps back to the path, where she bent down to gather the tools she'd dropped.

She was pale and shaky as we picked our way back to the village, along the tall granite ridge that sheltered her many hives, through the eucalyptus groves and haphazard rock gardens that speckled the foothills. The sun was nearing the mountain rim, scattering platinum across the peaks, slicking new grass in oily shadow. Between rocky patches, spring blooms were exploding, white and orange clusters carpeting the ground, the air filled with the scent of crocus and hazel. She would not let me carry her pack, nor so much as hold her arm, muttering to herself each time she stumbled, as though cursing the legs that refused to carry her. After so many months, I could not imagine life there without her, could not imagine that stark, empty house of stone. I'd been absorbed into her world, my old self fading until it was almost unrecognizable. At night I stared at the black-and-white photograph of my father and me—the adoration and surprise on his face, my arms flung around his neck. Would he still know me?

By the time we reached the cobblestone streets, the sun was down, the low houses crouching in dusk. In a few windows, weak electric lights glimmered, but most were lit only by candles, or not at all. I eased her over the threshold, helped her undress and climb shivering into bed. Her breathing was shallow but clear, her forehead dry and too cool. I put water on to boil, eyeing the jar of pink flowers, which had gotten dangerously low—spring had only just begun, the first blossoms shy and remote. We'd plucked a few handfuls earlier in the week, but were waiting for a warmer day to venture higher and gather more. I put away the thermoses and tools, pulled on Jacobo's heavy sweater. When I checked on her again, she was sleeping; I tucked the blanket under her chin and walked to the square to buy food for our dinner.

The tiny plaza was alive and well lit, more active than usual for this time of day. A dozen old men stood in the bare garden, slapping each other on the backs, clinking beer bottles and tipping their hats. The spring festival was beginning—in a few days they would put on traditional costumes and set out at dawn to climb Old Maker, returning late that night with chunks of ice from the glacier, heavy jugs filled with freezing water, the first runoff of the new year. Jacobo would be back to watch the small parade with me, to wait at the edge of town for the pilgrims' triumphant return. Part of me looked forward to the spectacle, something to break up the sameness of days; another part regarded it reluctantly, another season passing into history, and I as fatherless as I'd ever been.

As I ducked into the bodega to buy rice and vegetables, perhaps a little meat, something caught the corner of my eye, a face at one of the tables, just a blur as I passed by—it was not yet recognition, not quite, but a fizzle began in the far corners of memory. It worried me as I stood on line, chose tomatoes from a basket, scooped rice from a fifty-kilo sack. As I pulled some coins from my pocket, I found my hands were sweating, my fingertips gone numb. I dared not think it: After months—decades!—of waiting, at long last someone had come.

He was still there when I came out, watching the door, leaning back in a rusted chair with his legs propped insouciantly against the stone wall. His jeans were faded, fraying at the knees, his workboots spotty, black leather jacket dusty and worn. He wore a strange hat—dark leather with a wide, drooping brim—but I could see the deep hollows under his eyes, the scarred pallor of his skin. He smiled, revealing rotted-out eyeteeth, lips thin as lengths of wire. From that part of the brain where nothing is lost, memories mothballed and packed into trunks, came the name I was looking for:

Danny Grier.

"Hey, kid." He rose as though to embrace me. I stood blocking the doorway, paralyzed, two boys squeezing behind me to get out of the store. I clutched the groceries to my chest as though he were a mugger looking to steal my rice.

"Well, you're all grown up," he said. He dropped his arms and leaned against the wall, looked me over in a way that felt as if I were being spattered with cooking grease. His eyes were bloodshot, a subtle twitch in one lid, his two-day beard patchy. When he lifted his hat to scratch his head, his sandy hair was thin and dull. He nodded slowly. "I can see your mom in you. Not that she'd let you get away with that haircut." He laughed. "Guess it's true you haven't talked to her. Smart. Let the old battle-axe think you're dead. Not a bad idea, all things considered—though I'm sure she'd prefer it was me."

He brought out a pouch and sprinkled tobacco into a folded paper, twisting the ends without taking his eyes off me. "Old bitch has probably tried to have me popped a couple of times, I'm sure. But Uncle Dan's too smart for her, y'know? Keeping one step ahead . . . just like you."

I didn't know what he was talking about, had only vague memories of him coming by the house a few times, and one unpleasant Thanksgiving when I was eight or nine. He'd gotten drunk before the turkey was even served, sat on the living-room couch and railed at the shaman, who answered with a silent stare. Next thing I knew he was weaving out the front door, lurching off in a battered Karmann Ghia. My mother didn't say a word for the rest of the night, she and the shaman at either end of the table, trying not to meet each other's eyes.

"Here. You look like you need one." He held out the lit cigarette. I took it before I could think twice, sucked the dusky smoke in anxious ecstasy. If Danny was here, it must mean my father was ready—he'd sent a messenger to prepare me. Would it be tonight, I wondered, nearly swooning. Was there time to go check on the old woman, to leave Jacobo a note? Stupidly, I looked in the bag and wondered if I had time to cook the rice.

"All right, enough with the tearful reunion," he said, resting his hat on the table. "We've got business to take care of." He pulled out a chair and I sat across from him, still pinching the cigarette. In the plaza, the old men had begun to dance, arms across one another's shoulders, doing a skip-step and swaying to a rhythm someone slapped out on a bench. Danny leaned back with that lupine smile, as though he'd been waiting a long time to say what he said next.

"So, kid. You bring the money I told you?"

Of course I still had it, bundled and wrapped, stowed beneath my bed. Each night I brought it out and recounted it by candlelight, sat on the floor and read a poem from my book. I'd made it my own little ritual: the money my solemn offering, the poem my prayer. The hard-packed dirt beneath me was my father's silent altar, the dark mountainscape his numinous image. I hardly thought of it as money anymore, only a prop in the silent Cult of Brandt. But Danny's bored expression reminded me of the truth: It was still real to him, the token demanded of me for a glimpse of my father, the price of admission.

But I would give it only to my father—not to his lackey or consigliere. It was for him I'd brought it, for him I'd given up all. I shook my head, stubbed out the cigarette. Danny sucked his rotten teeth and leaned back.

"Figures," he said. "Chip off the old block. I should have known." He took out his pouch and rolled another cigarette, but did not offer me one. We listened to the old men's revelry, bottles clanking and rolling on the stones. One man stumbled into the road, chased two dogs off with loud barks while the other men hooted. The stars had come out, storekeepers closing up shop. I thought of the old woman, sick in her bed. Could I risk bringing Danny back to the house? Did he know her? The idea of that man standing in the place we lived filled me with nausea, like a dirty hand slipping into my underwear.

"Look, you want to see the old man or not?" he said. "You think it matters to me? I could really give a shit, you know. I'll just walk out of here, go the fuck home. I been doing his bidding a long time, dragging my ass all over the world. Fucking Guatemala, Bangkok, Cairo . . . Calcutta, what a pain in the ass. You never seen such a fucking shithole. And these people with their mystical bullshit, their fucking hocus-pocus . . . I'll be glad when this shit's over, kid." He blew a cloud of blue smoke up toward the street-lamp. "I had a life, too, you know."

He leaned forward. "You gonna say something, or what?" He looked me over, then flicked his cigarette into the street, where the men had begun to wander unsteadily home. "Suit yourself." Danny stood up. "I told him this wasn't gonna work."

He dismissed me with a wave and took a step from the table. I caught his arm and squeezed. *Tell me where he is!* I tried to write it across my face. But Danny only sighed and pulled his arm away.

A creaky old minibus rattled up the road and parked at the curb. "Tell you what," he said. "It's bargain day at Uncle Dan's. Give me half the money now, give him the rest when you see him. How's that?" Still I hesitated, and he shoved his hands into the pockets of his leather jacket. "Look, Calliope, that's the last bus. I'm not spending the night in this fucking back-water, so you want to get this taken care of I suggest you do it now. Half the money, period. Yes or no."

For another second I stared, my heart pounding hot and fast, as though the very air were squeezing me. Then, before I could talk myself out of it, I was running back to the house, the bag of groceries left behind. Up the quiet street, the only sound my footfalls and the trickle of water in the canals. I yanked the suitcase from under my bed, pawed through old clothes until I had the thick packet in my hand. No time to count it, I eyeballed the stack, split it in two, and shoved half under my sweater. On my way out, I stopped in the old woman's room—she was still sleeping, a bit of color back in her cheeks. I kissed her forehead and straightened the blanket, then dashed through the courtyard and back to the square.

"Smart," said Danny, thumbing through the wad of cash. The combie was idling at the corner, the driver honked once and then again. "Hey, it's only money, right? You people are rolling in it. What do you care?" He took his hat from the table. I thought he would try to hug me, and I stiffened. He sniffed and stuffed the money inside his jacket.

"Listen, kid. It's not what you think." He spoke lower, and for the first time I saw how exhausted he was, as though he'd been fighting something dark and invincible, his stamina worn away. "I just want out, you know. It's been a long time . . . it's too much. Whatever the hell he's doing up there, I gotta walk away. I deserve a little something, right? For everything I did, everything I gave him?

"Good luck to you both. I mean that. He's been waiting a long time. You have, too." He took my chin, held it when I tried to turn away. "Just keep your eyes open, okay? Listen to your uncle Dan. That's all I'm gonna say."

Then he turned and hailed the combie, which had begun to move away from the curb. Before he could get on, I pulled him back, stared hotly into his face. *Where?*

Danny looked at me with pity, as though he'd always believed I'd grow into someone smarter. "You mean you haven't figured it out?" He laughed to himself. "Poor kid." Then he shook my hand off and stepped onto the bus, hanging on the sliding door as the engine sputtered and the driver pulled into the street. As the door slid shut, he banged on the metal roof and called across the plaza: "Why don't you go ask J?"

★

Those flowers were darker, rich and symmetrical around their black button, purple and shocking as a hand to the cheek. They floated on the surface of the bath like lily pads, soaked and darkened, bobbing nervously around my mother's body. Her hair hung in wet strands, trailing small wakes in the water, her head bowed. She didn't hear me come in. Silent mouse, dazed and truculent daughter who ghosted that dazed house, I stood in the candlelit bathroom while she wept into the bathwater, knees drawn to her chest. The window open above her head, the top of the jacaranda grazing the night sky. I thought: She's a little girl, just like me. With a splash, she snatched a handful of the floating violets and forced them into her mouth, chewing miserably through sobs. Then she looked up and saw me, sucking my thumb by the medicine cabinet. She closed her eyes and sucked on that cud and I thought, She'll die now. She'll die, too.

★

He was my friend, my guide, my brother. My only source of information. In the months since my fever, I'd listened for Jacobo's footsteps in the alley each night as I sat down to silent supper. I imagined his narrow, worried face lit by the weak glow of the dashboard, hurtling toward me through dark, mountainous space. I'd sit up in bed at the sound of a door clicking shut, filled with nervous gladness, a shyness I didn't understand.

He came smelling of clove cigarettes and soap, brought me clothes from the city, a woven belt, a bottle of cold beer. He slept on a mound of blankets at the side of my bed, refusing my offers to share. We'd stay awake after the old woman went to sleep, sipping beer or tea, listening to the faint sounds of the town: a cart clattering over cobbles, the mutters of men walking home, the distant lilt of an accordion from the feedlot that doubled as a bar. All these months, I'd somehow kept my promise—though my father had not yet kept his. How odd it felt to stay silent while Jacobo prattled on, like a walkie-talkie stuck on *receive*. What a new way of being, to listen without comment or resistance—how easy it was, and yet how unlike me!

He told me about his life in the city, spent shuttling between his studio and the room he rented in an artists' quarter, the meals he took alone in a dingy eatery across the street. I liked to imagine him there, sipping soup at a table by himself while pedestrians passed by, perhaps listening to a soccer match on the radio, or reading from a paperback. He worried endlessly about the polka band—told me of the hundreds of hours of tape, dozens of versions of each track he'd comb through, fifteen personalities he had to coordinate and cater to. He reminded me of my mother, the years she'd worked on the box set—the tremor in his voice when he talked about it, as though the music were a lover, teasing him, infuriating him, stealing his sleep.

Throughout the autumn, he wrestled the cacophony, struggled to find the band's true sound; by midwinter, a few songs were nearly finished, others starting to take a fragile shape. "Maybe it's close now, I don't know," he said, sitting with his back to my bed frame, flattening a cigarette between two long fingers. His voice was distant, distracted, as though he were arguing some technical point with himself. "Maybe by the spring we have the first mix. Not mastered or anything. But only so I can hold the tape in my hand and think, yes, you do this, Jacobo. This is something you help to make."

He looked at me over his shoulder, and I combed my fingers through his hair, a few strands of colored string woven into skinny braids at the back. "Always there is more to do. Always I can make it sound better. Like there is a perfect song somewhere, and I am just trying to see it a little, so I can get closer, you understand?"

He took a sip of beer, leaned back into my hand. "When I am still very young, I remember he brings me an old radio from the city, a cassette player someone gives to him, and a box of tapes. I listen every day. I don't speak so much English then, so I don't know who is the band or what the songs are meaning. I just listen, and in my head I make up the story. I try to sing along, but it's the story I am deciding in my head."

He rested an arm on the mattress, brought his face close to mine. "Do you ever think of this?" His dark eyes wavered in the candlelight. "How many things are in a song: the melody and the harmony, all the different instruments, the rhythm, the emphasis? So many things to decide—how the words will sound, what they will repeat, the effects on the guitar, the kind of microphone or amplifier . . .

"You can change one thing, and everything else is different. There are infinite combinations, and each song is a new thing no one has done before." He started drumming lightly on the mattress, climbed to his knees in his excitement. "But if you are lucky, you make all these things come together, just so perfect, the voice singing and the guitar, the piano, a cymbal hitting in the same instant as the chord . . .

" 'She sayyyyyy,' " he sang, off-key, half-whispering, his hands slapping the beat on his blue jeans, " 'I don't wanna like to be dead . . .' "

I burst out laughing, and Jacobo stopped, grinned abashedly. "It's like a miracle, you know?" he whispered. "So many things, but when it's finished, you only hear the one thing. You think it could never have been different."

He fell silent, sipped his beer. *A miracle.* I remembered when I used to feel that about poetry: the endless striving for perfection, the joy of hearing a poem arrive at its true sound. Somehow I'd lost that feeling, buried it under other considerations, severed my connection to the work. Afternoons at the hives, while the old woman sipped coffee, I'd stare at the pages of a notepad, blinded by sunlight on blank paper. At night I scribbled a thought or two, a fragment of a dream, a memory that suddenly worried at my heart. But they were too simple to call poems—no rhyme or meter, just plain description, stripped and literal. I kept them tucked between Blake's pristine pages, told myself I'd at least written something, even if it wasn't quite art.

Jacobo was reading my book of poems—after months of objection, I'd finally relented. Each night he read one or two, mouthing the words silently while I huddled in the corner and hid my eyes. I'd listen to him laugh or mutter to himself, secretly rejoice when I heard him finish a poem and take in a satisfied breath.

"I think this is so good." He prodded my leg under the blanket. I kept a sheet pulled up over my face and pretended not to hear him, but he yanked it away, forced me to listen while he read one of my poems out loud. I never read them anymore, could not bear their bombast and pique; but when Jacobo knelt at the side of my bed and spoke the lines, I sometimes heard a glimmer of something: call it energy, or honesty, call it naïveté—from my brother's lips the words sounded almost true.

"I have this idea," he said one night. "When the polka thing finishes, you come to the city and read the poems, okay? We can record them in the studio." I looked at him blankly and he fiddled with the loop of plain yarn around his wrist. "Maybe with music . . . yes, we will record the poems with music! Oh, I know some people who can write music to go with the poems."

He nudged my shoulder, poked a finger into my ribs until I squirmed. "This is a good idea, okay? Believe me—I am the producer." He thumped his chest until I smiled. "It will be a whole new thing, you get it? Like a completely new shit for the world!"

But when I would not answer him, he turned away to hide his disappointment. This is how we were with each other: each waiting nervously for something the other could not give. Though I looked forward to his visits, they always left me unsatisfied—despite the gifts and trinkets, he had not brought me what I wanted most. Each time I saw him duck through the door, I tried to see past him, in case that long trailing shadow should take a different form. He rarely spoke of my father, never said where he was or when he would come for me. Sometimes it seemed the man was no more present to my brother than to me: a floating signifier lost among mountain shadows, while two lonely readers pined for the signified.

"One time he comes into the studio," he said one night. "Maybe a year ago. Maybe less. I am just starting with things, learning the equipment." Late winter, I'd grown edgy and truculent; I sat at the kitchen table and ignored him while sewing a button on a sweater. He twirled a toothpick between his lips, leaned back under a sky of black ice. Perhaps it was a bribe—he would draw me out with a glimpse of what I lacked. I put down the sweater and folded my arms. "There is a singer I am recording, just a guitar and vocals, like a hippie. But I think, okay it's not so bad. Nothing so complicated. I ask him to tell me what he thinks, you know? I play the tapes all the way through. 'Please,' I say. 'Tell me if it sounds good.'"

Jacobo brought his chair forward until the legs touched the floor. "He puts a hand on my shoulder, so serious! This is what he says: 'Jacobo, it sounds like you.'"

I watched his face for some clue as to what it meant, whether criticism or admiration, whether even Jacobo understood. He watched me, too, perhaps hoping I had the answer. But I was tired of this game, this mute bait-and-switch, tired of frost in the mornings, of cold showers, tired of my brother's solicitous need. When he said nothing further, I folded the sweater and went silently to my room.

But later that night, Jacobo snoring softly, I thought I understood. It was not a judgment, just a statement of fact: The finished record *was* Jacobo—it described him better than any story or photograph, his true self present only in the thing he'd made.

Hadn't my father taught me this, too? I picked my book off the night-stand and held it close to my face, smelled the pages, felt the edge of its spine. *Calliope Bird Morath,* said the cover. But what did that mean anymore?

Did this poet still live? Soon—*soon*—I would hand it to my father, let him read what I'd written, let him decide.

"I'm proud of you, my girl," I imagined him saying, as he read it cover to cover. "Now I understand everything."

*

Though nights were still my father's, the days belonged to the old woman and her bees. From the first weeks after my illness, through the back-breaking autumn honey harvest, I'd spent all my sunlit hours at her side. We trudged through brass dawn carrying thermoses of coffee, a midday meal of bread and cheese wrapped in paper. The land rose slowly toward the foothills of Old Maker, growing more uneven as the river valley dropped behind, until we came to the broad plateau where her apiary strung out at the base of a high granite ridge. She had dozens of hives, simple one-body boxes painted bright yellow and blue, spaced in threes among eucalyptus groves and the rubbled foundations of ancient stone structures. There was some distance between hives—to walk from the first to the last took nearly an hour; we might finish our work in two of these clusters—lifting off the supers, the honey-laden chambers stacked atop the hive bodies; nailing together new frames of pristine comb—before the mountain shadows swept across the plateau and the cold took over. Our joints stiff and rickety, backs aflame, we stacked the dripping supers on an old cart that we'd coax home along the rocky terrain.

Despite myself, I grew used to our routine, the days' exertions muscling out the clamor of my impatience. As the weeks cooled, thoughts of my father damped to a constant mutter, like a radio left on faintly. I kept a jar of honey at my bedside, my index finger perpetually sticky with the spicy, musky stuff—so different than the crude treacle of the Mountaintop bees. I marveled at the muscles that swelled at my arms and shoulders, traced the veins from my elbows to my wrists. The days shortening, we hurried to finish repairs, build new hive bodies, wire in new sheets of wax foundation, driven by grim urgency and the bite of the wind. We carried the warm thermoses next to our bodies as we cleaned the hives of dead larvae, moth eggs, spiderwebs, brushed them clear of leafblow and grit, mouse droppings and the occasional gray carcass. We combined some of the weaker hives to make sure they'd survive the winter, re-queening the least productive with powerful young queens Jacobo brought from a supplier in the city. I watched admiringly as the old woman smoked the bees into submission, hunted the old, failing queen and unceremoniously killed her with the sharp end of a hive tool.

Rain came in cold, ragged bursts each afternoon, sheeting out of black clouds that sliced across the river valley. We huddled under the lean-to, among stacked frames and rolls of screen, old cans full of nails and brackets and brushes, odors of kerosene and creosote thick as a wad of cotton. Fog gathered around Old Maker, slowly erasing it from sight, until the old woman and I were stranded in a hushed gray chamber, rain washing in rivulets off the tin roof. I came to love those moments in that wind-worried burrow: their cool serenity, the resignation of haiku. Across the wet clearing, the stolid hives steeled themselves, hummed their *Om* and braced for the yearly ordeal. We stayed with them until we could no longer stand up straight, until the first stars cut brightly through the dispersing clouds. We leaned on each other as we shuffled home, fortified by the necessity of our tasks: Once the hives were covered for winter, there would be little more we could do.

Friends, survivors, can you see this seasoned bird, thinned and sinewy, her frecklish skin grown somewhat leathery, reddish hair creeping back like memory, standing in the shadow of that cluttered topography? I wore thick, shapeless sweaters, stiff dungarees that rustled like cardboard. My sturdy boots grew supple as old gloves, one sole starting to detach at the toe. My lips chapped, my fingertips split open as though I'd run them across a razor. Clear mornings, I'd sometimes imagine my father was watching—a giant eye staring as I bumbled inside a glass globe. At night I lit my candle and lay rigid under the blankets, listening for the quiet footfall, the unexpected whisper.

I'd wake to find the old woman at my bedside, pressing the damp cloth to my neck. Her ministrations brought strange comfort, though I saw no tangible effect—unless it was the sense of my old life being rubbed away. Who, after all, was that girl who breathed fire, who grabbed the world like the bars of a cell? Who was that poet who roused rabble, caused scandal, who gobbled pharmaceuticals, played a mean kiss-and-tell?

She was me, I supposed—my mind knew this to be true. But those days had come to seem like old dreams about strangers, an alternate universe, a vague reflection at the bottom of a deep well.

But my other companion—she who hid behind mirrors, skittered around corners—she would not let me forget. *Impostor,* she sneered, *who do you think you're fooling? Traitor, Judas, you don't belong here!* I hung a cloth over the bathroom mirror, avoided standing water, averted my eyes when I walked by car windows. But she was clever, that one, she always knew where to find me—lurching from a glass storefront on a bright Sunday morning, scowling like Picasso's demoiselles on the curve of a knob.

Stupid child, you haven't changed a whit. You're still empty-handed, a fatherless wonder. Go back home, hang your head, wear the shoe that fits! She whispered to me in the shivers of dawn, her cruel singsong from behind the cloth: *Oh sweet child,* she said, her voice vinegar laced with tears. *Will you never learn to live for the truth? Accept it, dear sister: He's been dead all these years.*

But I would not accept it, not when I was so close to the goal! Teeth chattering, half-naked, I yanked the cloth from the mirror and picked up a sponge. While she tittered and spat, I ran freezing water, dumped in blue scouring powder, and scrubbed with all the strength in my arms. Ruthlessly I swirled the sponge over the glass while she gurgled and choked, rubbed the mirror to a high shine. When I'd rinsed off the lather, dried it until it squeaked, I stood panting, staring at the face I saw there: empty, lifeless, spent. For an instant I thought I saw sadness in her eyes, something small and afraid, like regret. I flung the sponge at the mirror, where it left a soapy smear. I ran from the bathroom, shut the door tight.

The world was overrun by drear—drear crept over the mountains, stole into town while we slept. The water channels glistened with ice, faucets sputtered and clunked before admitting a trickle so cold it burned. Jacobo came home more often, shivering from the interminable drive. His worried eyes followed the old woman everywhere, oppressing her, until she turned on him and brandished a skillet or boxed him around the ears.

On the night before we were to close the hives, she had a mild attack in the front room, where she'd been washing clothes in a tub. Jacobo ran to her, wrapped her in a blanket, while I boiled the tea; we both waited out the spasm uselessly, sprawled on the dirt floor, our clothes heavy with washwater, smeared with mud.

"Please," he said to her when she sat up. "Just one day, you come to the city and see the doctor. Calliope will take care of the bees for one day." But the old woman only straightened herself and went back to the wash, wringing out wet clothes until her hands were white. "Now it is winter, what do you do?" he said, pacing the room's perimeter, his shoes squelching in the soapsuds. "You don't even have so much flowers to last until spring . . ." He reached for her shoulder but she shook him off, flapped a pair of dungarees, and spattered him with water, pinned them on the line to dry.

"So stubborn!" he moaned. "You like so much to suffer?" He tried to hug her, but she groaned and struggled like an animal in a trap, stamped hard on his foot with the thick sole of her boot. As he leapt around on one foot, grumbling in pain, I couldn't help but giggle at the three of us, bedraggled and shivering. His glare pinned me where I sat.

"You are saying something? Good, then you can talk to her, tell her to stop being so foolish." My mouth dropped at the sharpness in his voice, his unfamiliar sneer. "No. Of course. You don't say anything. No one say anything. Why nobody says anything? Why nobody talks to Jacobo?" He looked at me, then at the old woman, who pretended not to notice. "Why do I even talk, then? Only a crazy person talks to himself, no?"

He raised his two hands before his face, chattering birds facing beak to beak. *"Can you understand what I am telling you?"* said the one hand to the other. *"No. Can you understand what I am telling you? Why are we talking at all?"* He looked up, startled at his own anger. Then he flung open the front door and disappeared down the alley.

It was late when he finally came in, found me lying pale and still, walloped by cold. He sat on the edge of the bed and took off his shoes, slid the lump of blankets from underneath and spread them on the floor. He smelled vaguely of beer, strongly of cigarettes. In a stupor, I pulled the covers back and he stared, blinking in moonlight, then slowly, as though a sudden move might break me, lay down at my side. I wrapped us tightly, sensing the tremor in his body; when he whispered in the dark his voice was stretched with a child's fear.

"You know, my mother dies when I am three years old," he said. "I don't remember so much, only the shape of her, the way she smells, some old clothes I keep. No pictures." He did not turn around. I watched his long fingers spinning the loop of yarn around his wrist. "She is sick for a long time. In the end, she doesn't recognize me.

"Only I remember she is in the bed, and I am trying to lie down with her. But it hurts her too much, so my grandmother puts a chair next to the bed and holds me in her lap, but still I am trying to climb on the bed with my mother—" He turned and stared into the shadow between us. I held still, watching a glimmer of candlelight like a shard in the corner of his eye.

"This bed." He touched the mattress.

I touched my palm tentatively to Jacobo's cheek. He pulled away, sat up with his back to the wall. "He isn't here when she dies," he shrugged. "Maybe he doesn't care, I don't know. I don't see him for almost two years. He comes, stays a week, then he is gone again. Always like this. She is the one who raises me. She does everything. So when he says he wants to help me starting a studio, he will buy the equipment, I say no. I don't want to leave here. How do I leave her, when she always takes care of me and now she is sick?"

He lit a cigarette from the candle and closed his eyes. "One day she puts my clothes in a suitcase, some things in a box, and she gives me a bus ticket. You see what she is like—she won't listen, almost she is pushing me out of the door." He laughed bitterly. "So I go. Soon I have the studio and everything is working, and it makes me happy. But I think it is wrong. I surrender very easily, don't you think? Maybe in secret I wanted to go and I am just waiting that she decides for me."

Before I could reach out for him, he stubbed out the cigarette and pulled the blankets over him, turned his back to me. "Always I can feel her here, you understand this?" he said. "Like there is a string from this house to me, and it goes everywhere I go. But she is more sick every year, and so I think, what if she is not here? What if this string breaks? If there is not this house, if she is not here when I come. I can go anywhere, yes, but also maybe I just float away."

I hugged myself and watched the back of his head. But what ran through my mind, no matter how I tried to hold it back, was, *The farce is almost finished.* I blinked at the shadows and stifled a tremor of anger. My father had treated them no better than his other family. And I—I was as useful to them as a sack of stones, taking up space all these months, unable even to comfort my brother. *Here's your real farce, Daddy,* I thought. Maybe the hag had it right: Maybe I should just go home.

"Then he tells me about my sister. So I am happy, because now someone looks after her when I am not here. But I am also happy for me, because now this is another reason I am coming home. Like another string."

I slid an arm around him, pressed close to his back. We had to be up in only a few hours, to load the cart with rolls of heavy black paper, spend one last, long day with the bees. "Because it is hard, sometimes," he said. "Do you understand? Hard always to talk to someone who doesn't talk back."

I lay awake listening to the scavengers outside, watching the quarter moon set. I thought of all those balmy nights in San Diego, when I'd watched the branches of the jacaranda through my window, stared until the shadows took form and came inside.

Of course I understand, Jacobo, I thought. *I've been doing it my whole life.*

★

In the morning, we made our way slowly to the hives, the cart jostling with the clumsy paper rolls. The air was a milky glaze over frozen ground; no movement in the brush, no birds chattering, only the ripple of a late-migrating flock speeding toward a vanishing point in the bright sky. We stretched paper over each hive, cut corners and secured them with ropes, rubbing our hands furiously. Breath clung to our faces. Even Jacobo was silent, his every movement determined, economical. As we finished one cluster and tromped off to the next, I felt my joints clenching like fists, my cheeks tingling. The air felt empty, as though it were missing something—the world's heat gone, the awful cold just another kind of absence.

When we came at last to the farthest cluster, I knew right away that something was wrong. I heard nothing, could not feel the subliminal rumble the bees made in my throat. The old woman knelt at the first hive, ran her hand across the ground. Dozens of small, shiny corpses littered the area around the box, sick bees carried out and left to die. All three hives were silent—when we lifted the covers, a gagging stench leapt out. Bees moved listlessly over the frames, their legs sticking in a slimy residue, brood cells plugged with mucus and withered larvae. It was foulbrood, something I'd heard about but never seen. In another life, I'd dared to write a poem—about a renegade drone's romance with a dying queen. But what I saw before me now was no poem. It was death—simple, unromantic. This once-sweet, thriving world was not art: It was over.

Holding our breath, we took the hives apart frame by frame, pried up the boards and piled them in a ring of stones. We worked quickly, scarves wrapped around our mouths and noses. I could not look away from the combs, where sick bees clung to empty cells. I was sure they understood what was coming. Soon there was a high stack, and Jacobo returned from the lean-to with a jug of kerosene. We watched black, oily smoke gust into the sky, wood and wax and wire crackling, warping the air between our three faces. A knot of old pine burned with a long, whistling shriek. When the fire had reached its peak and shrunk to a smoldering ruin, the old woman gathered her tools. Jacobo and I watched the dead hives burn a while longer, not looking at each other, then took the frozen path home.

*

Lookathat, will ya? said Old Joe. Like a fucking maniac, isn't it? He laughed and smacked the head of the wooden doll on the bar and it bobbled crazily up and down, side to side in strange angles, plastic blond hair and a scruffy beard, miniguitar with a gold monogram: BM. Like a fucking monkey, Joe laughed, and my father lay his head on his arms, eyeing the sweat on the side of his beer glass. Bone-white sunshine seeped around the door, glowed behind dark green windowshades. Whaddaya think of your father, Birdie girl? said Joe, and I waited for my father to knock over the stupid doll. A row of them on the top shelf, next to tall, clear bottles: Billy and Connor and XXX still in boxes, each with the vapid smile of a marionette. He hit the doll's head and said, Whaddaya think of your old man now? I whispered to my father, It doesn't look like you, and he raised an eyebrow, regarded the doll again. Tell him it doesn't look like you, I said, and he sat up slowly. He smiled at me, opened his mouth, and widened his eyes, nodded his head ghoulishly up and down, side to side, nodded and nodded while the bartender hacked with laughter and I burned on my barstool, tears too hot to fall from my eyes.

★

You again? Does your nose know no bounds?

Well, in truth I suspected you'd stick around—you've been more than patient, it's true. Endured the slow climb, the long-rising action; now you must have your payoff, lest anticipation kill you. You demand to see Calliope's quest succeed or fail—it hardly matters which, Lord knows! As long as you get to thrash around, moan your climax, then light a cigarette and bask in the selfish afterglow.

But how should *I* feel while you're arching your back? Imagine the pressure to make it worthwhile, to arrange my life so it satisfies *you*! In the end, I'm no more than a cheap entertainer, Scheherazade with a haircut and a G-string, spinning round a greased pole, giving a lap dance on cue. My story's not over until it's been told—only once you've heard it does this tale become true.

O darling foe, O intimate friend: What, in the end, does that say about you?

★

After Danny left, I went back to the house and sat with the old woman, listened to her light snores and watched the night clarify out her window. With the passing of winter, the world had lost some of its painful sharpness, the mountain silhouettes softening in the milder air. Again, the brush behind the house rustled with mice and voles digging their burrows; again the streets muttered with men playing dice on stoops, husbands and wives who leaned against each other on the way home. Tonight, or tomorrow—whenever my dear brother showed his face—I would take Jacobo by the collar, shake him until his beard fell out. I would tie him to a chair and inflict any torture, until he told me what I wanted to know, put an end to the farce, coughed up my father.

What a dope I was, what a stooge! For months I'd waited while he worked his angle. All autumn and winter he'd fattened me like Hansel—my thumbs plump as Cornish hens, my meat lean and succulent—waiting for the right moment to slide me into the oven. What was his cut, I wondered. When would Danny slip him the vigorish? All the stories he'd told me, the strange inconsistencies, details that didn't quite fit—now it made sense:

He'd say anything to keep me there—the truth was just his raw material! Scambiguity was transnational, Jacobo just another skilled practitioner.

But I had him now—or I would any minute—and nothing else could stand in my way. He'd tell me the truth if I had to pull out his fingernails, thrash him within an inch of his life—he'd have no defense against this furious sister!

But he didn't show up that night, nor all the next day. I paced that house inch by inch, wore a path from the front door to the town square. Too restless to eat, I cleaned the rooms with a vicious hand, swept the dirt floors and scoured the fixtures, washed clothes and cleaned honey jars, scraping off the soft amber with my fingernails. The old woman slid in and out of sleep, sitting up weakly and moaning until I brought her tea. I had to help her to the bathroom, where she sat shivering with her head in her hands, skin pale and rubbery as dried paste. Small spasms came one after another; the flowers dwindled—soon there would be only a pinkish powder dusting the bottom of the jar. When her lungs relaxed, she shooed me away with a flick of her arm. She wanted me to go to the hives, which had begun to overflow with spring vigor, frames full of first nectar and velvety brood. If they got too crowded, the hives would have to be divided, new supers built and sealed. The day she fell ill, we'd spotted a few queen cups, waxy lumps where new queens were being bred, a sign that the bees were preparing to swarm. Our diligence would amount to naught, the homes we'd tended become empty boxes, tasty snacks for rodents and wild pigs.

When there was no more cleaning to be done, no chore to occupy my hands, I sat with my notepad, but could not put my thoughts into lines. I lay on the bed and tried to imagine myself in the *zendo* on a quiet autumn day. I breathed deeply, envisioned emptiness—I *was* empty, a clear vessel, on the verge of being filled. I thought of the lines Mahmoud had read to me in Fez. Never had they seemed more true: All this time I'd been sweeping out the heart's corners, preparing a chamber for my beloved, as the Sufi poet said.

When at last I heard the front door open, I sat up quickly, already dressed. I lit a candle and waited, suitcase at my feet, the bundle of money in my lap.

Jacobo tiptoed into the room, beamed with pleasure at finding me awake. "Good, I am happy to see you!" he whispered. "Look what I am bringing." From behind his back he produced a CD in a blank case. The metal caught the candlelight and flung it against the ceiling. "You know all this time, they drive me so crazy . . . but now we finish, twelve songs, and I think maybe it is very good." He offered it to me. "Now you will listen, like you promise? In the morning, you tell me what you think?"

He put it on the nightstand and took off his jacket. I sat still as glass, resisting the urge to dash the CD against the wall. "What is wrong?" He touched my elbow, sucked his teeth. "Is something happening? Is she—"

I stood and shoved the brick of money at him, pushing him backward. While he turned the packet over and over, I took out the old letter, thin paper worn smooth. I pointed stiffly at the bottom line: *Keep it real*, it read. *Uncle Dan*.

He looked up slowly, struggling for comprehension. I railed and waved my arms, snatched at his sweater, brandished the brick of money in a furious game of charades. Jacobo sat on the edge of the bed, hands flat on his knees. When my vehemence was depleted, I stood over him and waited. I already knew I would accept his apology—I'd forgive all his deceptions if he told me what I needed to know.

But he looked up with hard eyes, a stern chin. He put out his cigarette in the saucer on the nightstand. When he stood, his face glowed orange in the candlelight.

"No," he said.

He walked past me and out to the courtyard, opened the door to the old woman's room. I was right behind him, tugging his elbow, incredulous. *No? No?* This was not part of the plan!

He sat at the edge of her bed and watched her sleeping quietly, stared at the saucepan of cold tea on the floor. He picked up her hand and stroked it, kissed her cheek; she grumbled and pulled back her arm, wrapped the blanket around herself. He went out to the kitchen, picked up the glass jar, and shook his head at the pathetically low stock of pink flowers. When I rapped on the table to get his attention, he shot me a look of warning, bade me follow him through the front room and out to the street.

The plaza was deserted, the garden a sepiatone image of decrepit benches and dead shrubbery. A few handcarts and animal pens on wheeled platforms sat on the sidewalk, decorated with ribbons, paint, and colored flags for the spring festival, covered with tarpaulins to await the weekend procession.

He sat on a bench and stared straight ahead. "So you don't like to hear the music? Or you don't want to listen to what your brother is doing?" I started to protest, but he waved his hand. Two dogs ranging among the strewn trash raised their heads. "Okay, maybe it's not so important. It isn't why you come here. You don't care about the polka band, or anything like this."

He lit a cigarette, threw back his head, and blew smoke into the air like a geyser. "When you are sick for so many weeks, she sits with you, she washes your face and feeds you with a spoon. You remember this? How you are sick on your clothes, on the sheets, and she cleans it up? You have fever, so she takes you in the shower when it is so cold outside . . ." He watched an old car sputtering into the square, its headlights dimming and brightening with each stammer of the engine.

"But maybe you don't remember," he said, poking the tip of his cigarette at me as he talked. "Maybe it's like a dream, maybe this place we live"—he waved his arm across the storefronts, the alley mouths, the mountains—"it's not so real to you. Maybe she is also like a dream, not like a real person."

Across the plaza a door slammed, the scrape of metal as someone fumbled with a padlock. "When I am not here, do you think about where I am?" He stopped my answer with a raised hand. "Because I think about you. Even if I am in the city I think about my sister. I can see you in your room or with the bees, or sitting here"—he slapped the wood bench—"in the plaza maybe. But when I leave, in your mind maybe I only go to an empty place, like a blank page. When I come back, I come from nowhere, no?"

I turned to the empty street. "We are like people in a book for you," he said. "Not real people. When you close the book, we are gone."

I hugged myself in the cold and my eyes drifted from bright constellation to heavy shadow, from orange streetlight to a distant radio antenna, blinking red on a hilltop.

"He told us you will stay. He says, 'Jacobo, if you make her your family, she will *be* your family. She will stay.' But now you want to leave. You think because you have this money, you can do anything. You don't even know why you bring this money. You bring it for *her*!" He stood and nodded at the package in my hands. "Oh, yes, Danny takes something. This is what he asks, for arranging everything. My father says, okay, no problem. There is so much more than she needs! Maybe two bills, maybe three, is enough for a doctor, so let Danny take—who cares?"

He laughed, a sound like an old motorcycle failing to start. "But she won't take it! This is funny, right? She won't go to a doctor, so all this money is worth nothing. If she won't take it, you have nothing to give us."

He turned back toward the house, but I chased him to the alley and jumped in front of him. I tried to thrust the money in his pocket. He was right: It was worthless to me. He could use it to bring a doctor from the city. He could hire a whole medical team! He could use it for the house—to put in glass windows, a roof on the courtyard, electricity. There was so much he could do with it, I thought. If my father really needed it, I'd find a way to get more.

But Jacobo shoved my hands away, so roughly I stumbled. The rims of his eyes shone in the sickly light. He left me in the alley, scraping my fingernails against a wall and staring at the yellow face of the moon, queasy shame heating my gut. Black mountains loomed over the rooftops, noting my failure once and for all.

By the time I got back to the house, he was down on all fours in the courtyard, one arm wrapped around the old woman's waist as she crawled and spat into the dust.

"Please!" Jacobo cried, nodding at the saucepan which lay overturned on the floor, a dark and steaming stain spread around it. "The tea," he said. "Boil more water, please!"

The sound of her breath was terrifying, a wail of pain crammed into a cold marble. Her back rose and fell like a cat's. I filled the pot, my hands shaking—the water from the tap would take forever. While the propane stove labored and the old woman croaked at the floor, I ran to my bedroom and dragged blankets from the bed, tried to drape them over her and Jacobo, but he shook them off.

"Just the water." He grabbed my wrist and pushed me toward the stove. "I am helping. Hurry."

It could not come fast enough. Her body was clenching and bucking, the awful sounds fainter with each breath. When I knelt next to her, her eyes were already glassy; her shoulder blades shuddered like a small motor against my palm. Jacobo sat against the icebox and cradled her head against his chest. By the time the first wisp of steam appeared above the pot, the first pathetic bubble, she was nearly unconscious, her lips puckered into an asterisk, one hand clutching Jacobo's hand like a claw. I snatched the jar of flowers, unscrewed the lid, dumped every last petal in.

The steam was so thick and pungent it brought tears to my eyes, pins and needles to my throat. My arms shaking with the pot's weight, I gagged as I stooped to her, water sloshing over the brim and sizzling in the dust. Jacobo tried to lift her, but her limbs were loose and heavy. I set the pot on the floor and lunged for a blanket, pulled it over both our heads and cinched it close. My temples were pounding; colored lights flashed in my vision; my hands burned where water splashed them. I dragged her limp body closer and pulled the blanket as tightly as I could. My eyes streamed and my nose ran freely; I wrapped my arm tighter around her waist, tried to hold her face directly above the steaming pot. The vapor stank of camphor and tamarind, ginger and dung; I choked on it, my sinuses opening like a balloon expanding, but I did not let go. I could hear Jacobo sobbing outside the blanket. My brain was on fire, my back muscles screaming, but I held on.

At last I felt her shiver—once, and then again—felt her buck and recoil from the hot steam. Still I held her, until she began to cough, drew a croaking breath and vomited weakly, thick spittle spilling to the floor.

When, after several minutes, she was able to support her weight, I pulled off the blanket and collapsed by her side. I gulped cold air, blinked at the bright stars and the colored streaks between them. The last steam wended skyward, rising from the pot on the floor and dissolving before my eyes.

Jacobo's face was gray, his jaw muscles working. He did not know whether to touch the old woman or let her be. She slumped against the icebox and wiped her sleeve weakly across her face. Her brow was ashen, her eyes pressed into deep dimples. Slowly her breathing smoothed and color crept back into her face.

When I could stand without the shaking in my legs betraying me, I took up the brick of money from where it had fallen. He would not meet my eyes. I bent down and shoved the whole thing in his coat pocket. He could take it or throw it out; he could give it away. What did it matter anymore? For the first time in months, I thought about leaving, jumping on the afternoon jitney and making my way home. There would be something fitting about it, I thought, something appropriate, as though failure had been the most likely outcome all along.

As I walked to my room, I heard Jacobo say something. I stopped but did not turn. Cold air burned up and down my chest. I wanted to cry out, but knew better.

"Okay, you go," he repeated. "If it is more important, go."

*

This is not the true world, said a voice in the dark. Rain in San Diego, the sky an elephant's loose skin, fists of cloud swelling in from the ocean. I drifted through that exhausted house, sniffles from my mother's room, monks sleeping on mats in the living room. Incense smoke hung in the air in ropes, clove and cinnamon, jasmine and wood; voices muttered prayers in the kitchen, the dining room, at the bottom of the stairs. This arises from desire, said the voice. All this suffering is only the flare of a match. When I pulled the curtains aside, it was like a city skyline: hundreds of lights in the darkness, pinpricks across the lawn, rain-soaked fans camped under the sad jacaranda. The boy and girl had made a small shelter, a tattered blanket strung across two hedges, soaked and drooping in the middle. I watched him stroke tears from her cheeks, untangle her hair. I waved, she sensed it, looked up and waved back, our two hands shadowing each other in the faint reflection. The monk touched my shoulder. This is not the true world, he said. His brown, puckered face slid across our doubled image. Don't confuse the two, he said, before the yellow sash of his robe receded into the grainy darkness inside the glass.

*

From the mountainside the town was a gray mosaic, drab squares of stone roughly fitted, a rust splash of Spanish tile roofs like dusty jewels in an antique brooch. Beyond it the river bowed and twisted through its channel of green, a silty hieroglyphic I squinted to decipher—no Rosetta stone, no binoculars, I sat on a ridge and listened to the human sounds around me: none.

Smoke hazed the empty space like light frosting on glass, the faint smell of burning wood ubiquitous on the air. The afternoon sun struck flat against my face, but my hands cramped in the cold, the tops of my ears stung. When evening came, shadow crossing these slopes like a scythe, the temperature would plummet. Jacobo's heavy pullover would not protect me. I had no hat or gloves.

I had brought only a hunk of bread, a jar of honey, a bottle of water. As I'd put these things in a sack, Jacobo sat smoking at the kitchen table, legs crossed and chin resting on his hand, staring as though I were a specimen of bug, an unsightly creature heretofore unknown. He was not angry so much as amazed, like the old farmer in Aesop protesting to the treacherous snake. *O Brother, forgive me for biting your hand—but you knew what I was when you first took me in.*

By the time the sun was up, I'd passed the beehives, pushed past familiar stone outcroppings and into the foothills. At noon I sat in a meadow blackened by a recent fire, my legs trembling and twitching, my lungs whistling, listlessly eating my simple meal. The afternoon sharpened to crystal, the overgrowth dwindled and drabbed until only a few stunted trees clung to the slopes. The pale blue sky slid across the back of my eyes, sun inching precariously close to the peaks.

He'd said to keep climbing until there was no path to follow. I could hardly miss it, he'd said. As the dying light slung along the ridge, I wondered if Jacobo hadn't had the last cruel laugh, hadn't managed to do in his prodigal sister. Wind mugged me under my clothes, sweeping off the glaciers. My knees were aflame; my bad leg stiffening with each step. Looking back, I knew there was no way I'd get down that path in the dark, even if I were inclined to try. My course was set, each moment the mountainous world grew dimmer, a dark mouth of shark's teeth—and I, a dumb goldfish, kept swimming into peril.

As the first star emerged, a pick-mark in pink-blue ice, I sat under an overhang and drank the last water, hugged my knees to my chest. I didn't think I could go any farther. The whole thing was ridiculous, a farce through and through. But I could not go back until the farce was finished— I had betrayed everyone, stabbed friends and lovers in their sleep. I could not turn from this foolish path until I knew what it had all been for.

Hungry, teeth hammering, I gave in to gloomy visions: my innards shriveling like fists, eyelashes caked; my bones found decades hence, picked white by dispassionate wind. Too exhausted even for regret, I stared out over the valley, broken up by wisps of fog, and started to laugh. It was perfect! It was too rich! I lay back and laughed at the glaciers, the moonless sky. I laughed at the image of an underdressed child, huddled among the oblivious stones. I remembered my mother's command—"Be who you were born to be"—and rocked with hilarity. Who in the world was born to be *this*?

O Mother, I thought with a pang, it's been far too long. Where are you now, what's become of your own strange life? Despite myself, I'd missed her—her raging storms, her terrible calms. She'd been so young when the story of her life overtook her, when great events crept up and blew through her, discarded her like a rag doll at the side of the stage. I knew now what it meant to look at your life and not recognize it, to think your history a stranger's dream.

Lying on that frozen ground, I made a silent promise: I would see my mother again. If I made it off this mountain, I would get word to her some-how. Drifting toward sleep, I let myself imagine it: my father's warm wel-come, the speeches, the feast. *Daughter,* he said, *I'm so pleased you've come . . .* I saw myself at a rolltop desk, my father at my shoulder as I wrote her a letter: *Dear Mother, I found him. Come home.*

When the crow's cry came, I sat up so quickly I nearly slid from the ledge. The honey jar slipped from my hand and hit the stones with a ping and rolled rattling over a small shelf and flew out and away into wide si-lence. Another squawk, loud and liquid—I inched out from under the over-hang, squinted until I could see it a dozen yards up the path: an ovoid shadow standing in relief against the heaped world, one yellow eye mov-ing in twitches. Unnaturally vivid, its black beak opened, black worm of its tongue shook; the sound arrived an instant later, as sharp as if it were perched on my shoulder, complaining into my ear.

The wind hummed while I stared at the crow, confused by its brash jabber—hypoxic or delirious, I was sure there was sense to be made here, some message to decode. I took a step but the bird did not fluster, answered with a warbling murmur. I took another; its wings beat once and it hopped higher, prehistoric claws scrabbling on stone. Again it shouted its garbled instructions. In a daze I followed, past the last scrawny eucalyptus, toward the peak of Old Maker, glowing in anticipation of moonrise. Here and there, the crow stopped to make sure I followed, peered at me and pecked the ground, peered some more, twisted its neck, and stammered at the stars.

The wind squalled and faltered, squalled, faltered, and whipped at my sweater. I clutched at outcrops, found crevices with my fingers, worked boot tips into narrow grooves. The crow's odor dragged back to me: richly stinking, an old man's cigar with a hint of vinegar; grimy and humpbacked as a pervert, the bird blasted its strangled blare at the forbidding peak. For an hour I followed, until the tremor in my ankles and knees took on a life of its own—a subterranean rumble with a rhythm lingering just beyond hearing. I knew I was being stupid, but I didn't care—with each step the scene began to feel more familiar, the crow's nervous gargles coming as if on cue. The stars proliferated like bright stones on velvet, the air astringent with the smell of broken rock. In a trance I hauled myself around a hillock and came at last into a clearing, a wide mountain pass shaped like a saddle, squashed by the sky's dark fist.

I stopped, struck by impossible recollection. The crow cried once and flew up to a ledge, bits of dust and stone showering to the ground. When I blinked, there were a dozen or more of them, a row of grim birds chirring a black chorus. The music I'd been hearing grew clearer, its beat insistent, the distant scrape of a detuned guitar. Déjà vu closed my throat. I shook my head. I could almost name that tune.

Can you guess where I was? You're always a step ahead, or two . . . Of course you remember that disquieting dream. "The great gig in the sky," my beekeeper once called it, lying on the river stones on a warm Mountaintop night. He held my chin in his hand, banished the dream with his lips. "I told you, Calliope—no one ever really dies."

Now the dream was here before me: a narrow, slanting cavemouth partly concealed by a boulder. Above it, the birds babbled, shook their legs, rained grit, shat blithely on the spattered stone. This was it—the end of the path. Jacobo must have been here, I realized. Maybe recently. While I toiled, unsuspecting, in the apiaries below, he'd been conspiring with my father to keep me away. I wiped my nose on the back of my sleeve, blew into my hands. A whirlwind of questions and fears churned in my head, but I refused to listen. In the driving music, the dark gap appeared to pulsate like the drum of a speaker. I looked back once more at the valley blanketed in shadow, dim lights where the village must have been. You know what happened next: I shouldered my pack, took a breath, and went in.

Ready or not, Daddy, I thought, *here I come.*

At first I could hardly see a thing, the blackness vibrating and sliding with the hard pound of music, music so loud I could not get the sense of it, could not tell each beat from its various echoes. Something squelched under my shoes, a thick muck that clutched and sucked with my every step. My eyes unadjusted, as though I'd swum into a bowl of pitch; I waved my arms every which way but they struck nothing, I bit my lip to keep from panicking. I could have called out, but no one would have heard me over that racket. I took another tremulous step, half-expecting to plunge into a chasm, to fall for miles until I landed, broken, in Hades's lap. Something winged and light flashed by my ear and I batted my arms wildly, lost my balance, fell to all fours. When I stood, mud clung to my wrists warm as an armpit, a sharp smell like urine that gagged me when I brought it to my nose.

I could no longer make out the cavemouth, just a faint brush of gray that might easily have been my eyes' trick. Step by shuffling step, I moved into the screaming dark, heading toward the faintest of lights, a pale blue glow that danced like water. I could feel the cave hemming in around me, my shoulders brushing against uneven stone walls. I was in a tunnel, the roof lowering until I was forced almost to a crouch, the music both pulling me forward and trying to punch me back. It was suicide, I thought as I moved forward—soon I would work myself into a spider hole or crevasse from which I could not get out. As the space squeezed, my terror whirled into a scream, I slapped stupidly at the rock walls and ceiling—the mountain and its loud pulse compacted me like a filthy, snot-glazed diamond, I put one foot in front of the other until suddenly there was nowhere to step and I stumbled, pitched, fell headlong into brightness—a blast of color as I crashed onto a hard bed of mud and rock and every gasp of breath flew from me.

I squinted and moaned, twisted onto my side in dazzling light.

With a squeal and scrape the music stopped, leaving behind it an echoless ring like a fingernail against fine crystal. "Are you all right?" said a startled voice.

My body ablaze, one leg turned beneath me—I clambered to my knees, squinted into the harsh light, my hand landing on something flat and smooth as I tried to find the source.

"Oh!" he gasped. I could hear my breath, my animal whimpers, the thump of my pulse. Someone was coming toward me, a blur in all that light. "It's you? How . . ."

I felt him touch my shoulder and I flinched, scrambled until I felt the hard wall at my back. My hand closed on the flat object and I held it before me as though it would protect me. The ringing in my head persisted, the white dagger of fear stuck in my throat.

"It *is* you," he said in wonder, kneeling before me. "It's really you." His face swam before me, so terrible and strange I had to look away. "I can't believe it." His voice broke. "My daughter. I've been waiting so long."

His grip on my arm was tight, his breath so close I could feel it on my cheek. I could not look at him, squinted instead at what I found in my hands. It was a book, of course—thin and battered, the binding shot, held together by a filthy rubber band. I wiped the cover with a trembling thumb. When I made out the title, I burst into uncontrollable sobs.

Can you guess it, my stalwart? I think that you can.

Arthur Rimbaud, read the relic. *Une saison en enfer.*

*

Something was crawling, scurrying in the darkness. Beneath the gloom lumped shapes shifted and moaned, the night's backlit glow barely illuminating the space in which they lay. Behind us, the winter ocean pounded, smashing white plume against the broad cement legs of the fishing pier. The shadows smelled of garbage, ammonia. I clutched his two fingers, the skin rough at the knuckles, fingertips calloused hard as pebbles. Don't ever go in there, Bird, he said, and took his hand away, lit a cigarette, cupping the match against an outburst of wind. No matter how bad it gets. He held me close to his hip and shivered in the salty chill. Under the pier a huddled form threw off a filthy sleeping bag and took a step toward us. My father's head was huge against the cloud-blotched sky. A cracked voice echoed: Hey, man, can you hook me up? The figure moved toward us and my father squeezed my shoulder. You hook me up, bro? You remember all that shit I gave you? My father didn't answer. Hey, the voice said, what's your problem? Don't you recognize me? He shambled forward in dirt-smeared jeans, a Terrible Children T-shirt, the awful smell—Did you forget where you come from, bro?—and a little girl shrieking as arms reached around her.

★

"What do you think? You like the studio? It took a very long time to build. Very long. Just to find it, the right space, the dimensions. It was so difficult!" His voice rang into the cave, each syllable full and precise as a musical note. "And then to get everything inside, piece by piece, haul a generator in and wire everything. You can't imagine how difficult, how *fucking* difficult.

"Danny must have told you about it," he said. "He was very helpful at first. Then he met the girl. From the city. Did you meet her? Well, I think her brother is a dealer . . . You know Danny. He got greedy." I cowered against the wall, still trying to make sense of what I saw. When he spoke again it was slow and exact, as though he were sounding out someone else's lines. "What an asshole," he said. "What a colossal prick."

He laughed, a reedy laugh that was taken up by that rough-hewn space, captured and focused by stone walls, lost under the high, shadowed ceiling. Enlarged and resonant, his voice smoothed itself over my skin like syrup spread on toast.

"It was all worth it," he said, and reached for the guitar that stood against a table: a battered old Peavey, rusted frets and a cracked pickup, black letters written in marker along the neck: G-O-F-U-C-K-Y-O-U-R-S-E-L-F. Of course I recognized it, though I was too dazed to feel more than dull nausea. He lit a cigarette, cupped it under his palm like a soldier smoking in the rain, then stuck it between the strings of the headstock where it trailed a white stream into the darkness.

His face was grotesque, too hideous to look at for long. His broad cheekbones and once-handsome features had grown too sharp with age, his high forehead bulged, the shiny black hair I remembered was gnarled into clumps and shot through with dull silver. Most horrible the thick black lines that crossed his brow and cheeks, the ridge of his nose, curved along his chin and jaw. Broad and raised like keloids, these lines traced a matrix over his face and neck, back behind his ears. Their edges were dry and scaling, small blisters swelled along their length—as though some barbaric surgeon had marked him for the knife, or had already begun to cut.

"Listen," he said.

When he swept his hand across the strings, sound washed around us as though splashed from a giant bucket. The chord built in waves, a diaphanous bubble expanding to the edges of the cave. My larynx vibrated in sympathy, my molars tingled as though I were chewing tin foil. The sound rolled and rolled, each individual note cleanly audible in the whole. When at last it faded, there were no echoes, only that same faint ringing, so delicate it seemed made of light.

"Phil Spector, eat your *fucking* heart out," said the shaman.

He smoked his cigarette, and the suck of his cheeks made those black marks wriggle, like fat earthworms across his features. His eyes, once keen, looked bleached, faded to a sickly pinkish brown—they scanned me carefully, as though I were a shipment received, and he were checking the lading. He wore tattered, mud-struck jeans, his bare feet cast in muck; an ancient flannel shirt, all the buttons missing, threads sprouting from the seams. His skin shone like tarnished pewter in the candlelight; when he moved, his shirt fell open, and I glimpsed the black marks that crisscrossed his chest.

"I've been able to get so much done here, to get everything ready," said the shaman, crouching next to an iron stove. He looked at me over his shoulder. I could not look away from those bizarre markings, the lower brow and wider cheekbones described by those lines, the dip of the chin, as though another face were being mapped there. "You'll be proud of me, Calliope, won't you? I always knew you'd understand."

The cavern was the size of a small lecture hall, rough-hewn walls covered with shaggy animal skins, long faceless furs that fluttered in the stale air. Along two sides, worktables stood end to end, covered with bottles and jars and burners, odd implements scattered everywhere, a small mirror in a wood frame propped on a shelf. A few books lay open, fat and yellowed tomes; sheaves of paper scattered among beakers and canisters and burlap pouches. The burners spat blue rings of flame, blackening the bottoms of glass vessels—some short and spherical, others long and tapering to graceful swanlike necks. Inside, flames danced over liquid or small piles of sand. The air smelled of electricity and lye, sulfur and hot stone. It sizzled in my nostrils, covering the reek of cigarettes and body odor.

Along the other walls were speaker cabinets and stacks, amplifiers and mixing boards, enough sound equipment to crumble a nightclub's walls. Everything was smeared with dried mud, red and green and white indicators blinking in code, coming in and out of sync: on, off, on and on again, off. When he touched the guitar, the speakers gave a temblor of sound; when he put it down, they simmered and hissed with ambient noise.

"I've learned so much. So much. I've written some good songs." He struck a long wood match against the tabletop. With a groan of metal and a dull baritone roar, fire arose in the belly of the stove. "Some really good *shit*." He looked at me sidelong, and again I had the sense he was practicing his lines, trying out another voice, checking to see if he'd gotten it right. "Do you want to hear?"

My heart beat hot terror, but my thoughts were trapped in wet cement, my eyes stuck to his grotesque face.

He picked up the guitar, the amps and stacks coughed as he pulled the strap over his head. A chord came screaming out, and then two more, a dark progression with the force and momentum of a subway train. He stroked the neck, yanked a hand across the filthy strings, threw back his head, and the muscles of his neck leapt taut:

One thing, one thing, truth without lies.
Certain truth—from this thing all things arise.
All things below are like all things above,
One thing, baby—give me your love.

As he sang—a tight and nasal howl, melody scraped from the pit of his throat—dismay gathered in my fingertips, the roots of my hair, hardened into an irregular lump in my gut.

"Not bad, right?" He nodded at the dusty books on his workbench. "It's old alchemy *shit*. An invocation to the goddess. It says, 'All things arise from one thing: a simple act of creative adaptation.'

"Transmutation, you get it?" he said. "It's some *heavy fucking shit*."

He swiped something from the table, clutched it in his hands, and came toward me.

"I was not expecting you just yet. But I'm ready. Calliope. Birdie. Birdie-bird. Everything is ready." I could feel stone against every square inch of my back, could feel the pulse banging in my throat as I tried to squirm away. He stopped in front of me, touched the bridge of his nose, tracing a line down the center of his lips, his chin. "I can feel it working. You can see it, right? Can't you?"

He touched my neck with the side of his hand, ran a fingertip under the line of my jaw, traced the outline of my bloodstain. "It's working on you, too."

I tried to push back, to escape into the mountain, but the wall would not take me in. He unclenched the thing in his hands: a hat, soft suede lined with fleece, smeared in the cave's filth. When he pulled it over his head, the dirty lining and crumpled earflaps made a frame for those hideous black scars, a few snarled locks of hair clung to his cheeks. His voice grew halting, a too-familiar mix of melancholy and mockery.

"I've got enough new *shit* for a whole new album." He sat before me, guitar facedown in his lap. "It'll be the comeback of the century. The greatest story ever told. You have no idea.

"My daughter," he whispered. "I am *so fucking happy* you're here."

Then he cupped my face between his hands and I started to scream, thick hiccups lurching from the pit of my stomach. The marks on his face swam out of focus, the dazzle of color swirled up and sacked me, exploded across my vision.

When I came back to myself—exhausted, my throat burning—the shaman was at his worktable, adjusting the many burners. On either side, the bright vessels made a strange, colorful menagerie—flames danced and flared, one moment threatening to burst their containers, the next dampening and dying, disappearing entirely. He took a test tube from a rack and inspected its contents, uncorked it and poured it into a heavy crucible, sparks fountaining and hailing onto the tabletop. Along the shelves, glass piping whined and whooshed, the vessels grumbled, the occasional pistol-crack and flare of light. He shoved more wood into the potbellied stove, and the light from the door lit his features in bronze: two faces briefly competing for resolution.

Quietly, I pushed myself to a sitting position, clamped my jaw to slow my breath. I needed to think clearly, but I could not see the tunnel through which I'd come—as though the walls had closed behind me, sealed us in the mountain's hot gut. On the floor lay the book: *A Season in Hell.* One eye on the figure at the table, I opened the cover. The pages were dog-eared, crossed out, slipping from the spine, scribbles in almost every margin. *Fascism in the 18C,* scrawled one annotation. *No shit, dude!!!!* in another. *Earthbound=strong.* The shaman rattled glass jars, fed the fire. Sentences were underlined, circled, highlighted—*I am so utterly forsaken* and *Ah, that life of childhood!*—arrows and cross-outs, shapeless doodles, a glowering pair of eyes. If I had any doubt this was the lost copy, the one my mother had sought for years, it vanished when I read the chorus, scribbled—for the first time?—in my father's hand:

> Nothing can forgive me
> Leave me here, outlive me.
> Anyone can take away my pain.

"He was interested in alchemy. Did you know that?" said the shaman. "'Ce fut d'abord une étude. J'écrivais des silences, des nuits, je notais l'inexprimable. Je fixais des vertiges.'" He lifted a beaker and poured a thin stream over each of his forearms. It steamed and sizzled over his skin, dribbled to the floor; I gasped, but the shaman's expression hardly changed. "It's all in there," he said hoarsely. "'As I wept, I saw gold. And I could not drink.'"

A sweet smell of burnt skin twisted through the chemical reek. My teeth began to clatter as he held the beaker before his eyes and the shine inside dulled, the liquid clarified and congealed into a translucent splinter.

"You see? It's the 'Alchemy of the Word.' Rimbaud knew." He set the beaker down and turned to me. The lines on his face had widened, their edges raw and split; the deep shadows under his eyes highlighted their eerie pallor. "'A long derangement.' This is how it begins: confusion, searching. 'He exhausts within himself all poisons and preserves their quintessences.' The nigredo. The—" Suddenly he swayed, slapped a hand on the tabletop to steady himself. "The *fucking* nigredo," he said.

"Of course he is destroyed in the ecstatic flight. Of course! That's the whole point!" His eyes rolled white and his lips pulled back in a grimace— along his arms the skin was simmering, peeling from the burn. He shrugged out of his shirt, his torso a grid of black marks, picked up another beaker and streamed liquid onto the muscles of his neck and shoulders, down his back, sickly smoke lifted off him while I gagged and spat on the stone floor.

"It's all there." He gritted his teeth, nodding at the book in my hand. "Everything but the stone. What is the stone? Thousands of years . . . powders and metals, a virgin's blood, a king's semen . . . everything . . . but *nothing fucking worked*." The shaman unbuckled his pants and dropped them into the mud, laughed again in that strained voice. "Do you know how long it took me to understand? If it's an alchemy of words, then *what is the fucking Philosopher's Stone?*"

I shook my head, pulled myself to my feet, and wandered the perimeter of the cavern. Keeping one eye on the shaman, I ran my hands along the walls, searched for a door under the heavy pelts.

"It's more than the body," he said. "You understand? The body can be changed; metal can take another shape. But what about the soul?" I nodded, just to keep him talking, bumped against a table. He was naked now, his legs striated with wounds, his penis half-erect and raw red. "This is what you want to know, too: *Where is he now?* You've been asking this your whole life."

His hand darted out and wrenched my arm, drove me to the floor. I sat hard in the mud, my head swimming with the gasoline stench, my face close to his scarred and blistered feet. I could see the pulse beating at his ankle. He lifted my chin, forced me to look into the disintegration of his face.

"He's almost here," he said.

Releasing me, he turned back to the table, unstoppered a glass jug that he pulled from a shelf. He took two clay cups, unpainted and with no handles, and filled them with clear liquid. I recognized the smell immediately.

"They weren't thinking about the mind," he mumbled, swirling the liquid. I crawled away but had nowhere to go. "The alchemy of the *word*. They did not account for it. They thought it was only metaphor, that they could change the soul without changing the body, without *sacrifice . . .*"

I nodded frantically, tried to scamper away but he had me cornered. "Everything contains its essence. Unlock the compounds, take them apart. A new form. You can be *fucking* pure." He grasped my wrist, pressed one of the clay cups into my palm. With a slight gesture, he lifted his cup and bolted down its contents. "We'll both be pure," he said.

I dashed the liquid at his feet, flung the cup against the wall. I wrapped my arms around my head, expecting him to strike me, but the shaman went back to the table, turned over another cup.

"The stone rolls away, the dead return . . . Just think what it will mean, Calliope, what we will have. What we can *fucking be . . .*"

The feedback from the wrecked guitar was spiraling into a caterwaul. I raised myself to a crouch, ready to stab my fingernails into his wounds, gouge his eyes. "We'll exhaust the poisons. Find the essence. We'll be *pure.*" I lunged, but he was faster—stepping quickly to the side, he pushed me past and I sprawled again on the floor. My thoughts a fire-white babble, I grabbed the book and brandished it at him, as though Rimbaud himself might appear, crippled and filthy, to protect me.

With a sweep of his arm, the shaman knocked it from my grasp. It flew and fluttered like a shot bird, pages scattering and drifting in the hot breeze. His fist flew out and clutched my hair, yanked my head back; with his other hand he smashed the cup against my lips until my teeth parted and the vile brew filled stinging into my mouth.

"The farce is finished," he said. He tossed the empty cup away and stroked my throat. I tried not to swallow. The backs of his hands were raw and pink with old scars, pale patches where he'd been burned on a long-ago Christmas morning. In the flickering light, his eyes appeared ice blue.

"Do you know what the stone is?"

I could not look into those eyes. I could not look away. *No,* I shook my head.

"*It's you,*" he hissed, then crushed my windpipe until I swallowed, held my jaw shut as my stomach tried to vomit the liquid back out.

When I was still, he released me. I coughed and spat and wept for breath.

"It's you, my girl," he said quietly. He pressed a gentle hand to my cheek. Then he turned back to the flickering beakers, the stove's white heat, the word bouncing cruelly in my brain: *Me?*

✶

I will see you again, said the shaman. It will not be for a very long time, but I will see you again. I stood in the doorway of their bedroom while he folded clothes, laid them in a suitcase. His belongings were piled in the foyer, crates of equipment brought down from the laboratory. One day you will help me, he said. As I helped you. I held the doorframe, confused by the desire to run at him, pummel him with eleven-year-old's fists. The fire that touched you, he said, taking shirts from my father's closet. It touched me, too. It is only the beginning. I followed him from the bedroom, trailed him down the long sweep of stairs. Mother was in the kitchen, picking dead leaves from her precious violets. How I hated her for not stopping him! He turned in the front door and took something from his pocket. This is yours now, he said, laying the necklace over my head. The teeth rattled lightly against my collarbone. The backs of his hands were smooth and speckled where he'd been burned, patched like a quilt. I will see you, he whispered in my ear. I give you my word. He opened the front door and the day exploded. He was a shadow negated in sunlight. I hid my eyes until I heard the front door close.

✶

How shall I describe what happened there? How can I make you *see*?

What can be said of this family reunion, this distillation in the mountain's crucible, the last transmutation of dear old Calliope?

Daughter of Memory, give me your song: an end to this long soliloquy!

I was clearheaded, perfectly calm, filled with a prickly breeze that began in my calves and flowed up the chimney of my body and spread along my limbs. I felt my uvula shudder as this wind passed through, felt the roots of my hair tingle in its electrical draft. The ayahuasca traveled my veins, sizzling like sparklers on the Fourth of July—but none of this alarmed me, none of it brought confusion or pain. My thoughts were under my control, my attention keen.

The shaman's thumb moved along my neck, my jawline, pushed into my mouth and probed behind my teeth. The flesh of his face, his chest, was peeling and swelling, his mouth twisted into a feral grin. His brow slick, the pitiful hat soaked in sweat and filth. When he spoke, the lines of his face moved strangely, skin splitting like a melon rind, the bloody new face pushing through.

"*Unum ego sum et multi in me*," he said. He made a design in the air with his index finger, then palmed the back of my head and brought his lips to mine. His hot breath yawned into my mouth and nose, crept into my ears and around the stem of my brain and passed down my throat like a root seeking rich soil. I stiffened, drifted back against a speaker, slid lower in the muck. *I contain multitudes*, I thought. The shaman's furrowed face rose above me like a planet. Behind him, light beat white and hot.

"Whitman knew. But it's older than Whitman," he said. "It's *so fucking old* . . ." My mouth hung open, a spill of drool stretched to the floor. "The old alchemists. They understood. They just didn't know how to break it apart." He held the guitar before him, played a few chords. I could not stop myself from sinking, the heat and the mud claiming me cell by cell.

"The texts . . . the forty-two sacred texts. The *Secreta Secretorum*. Words!" he said. "The Book of Venus, the Emerald Tablet . . . Millions of words. The alchemists only *read* them. But you, Bird—you're a poet. You know what words can *do*."

Multitudes, I thought. How many times had I read Whitman without really *listening*?

The shaman poured another draft and bolted it back, refilled the cup and handed it to me. I stared into the dark liquid, where slivers of light trembled and vanished in concentric circles. When I drank, I felt those curved blades whirl inside me, slicing me to ribbons. He picked up the guitar and played a familiar progression—the sound wrapped around me and forced a shiver. He watched my face as one watches a feverish child, waiting for some response; he struck the guitar again, rattling jars and beakers on their shelves.

"*At the top of my game, strike a bargain with shame, give me someone to blame, what's my name? What's my name?*" The last squeal faded to a chime. He clapped his hands over the strings and silence punched into the cave. He looked in the small mirror, pulled his lips back to expose the gums.

Heat gusted from the potbellied stove, the pelts on the walls billowed in the convections. Again he knelt by me, again I felt his breath push through me.

"Every substance contains its essence," he said. "I told you, Bird. It's *pure*. The music . . . that's where you *create*—" He held a hand before his face—his fingernails were shriveling, detaching from the skin. Droplets of blood seeped up in the pale flesh they left. "You fuck yourself up any way you can, try to scrape something genuine out of your veins, something *honest* . . . but then they make you copy it, perform it over and over like a trained monkey until you're sickened by it. Until it's not *pure*."

He puffed his cheeks in and out. Behind him the glass vessels were changing colors, the flames rose and quieted, a slow and ominous dance.

"You hear yourself in every idiot's mouth. What the *fuck* do you do then?" He pounded on the guitar until the air shimmered with the vibrations, until the cave walls seemed ready to burst. "You destroy it. That's all you can do."

As his breath spread inside me, a furious light began to dawn. Listen: It was not something I could see. I could not name it, only felt it, *understood* it: a bright plane that spread through me, taking on the exact size and shape of my self. It moved through my organs, suffused muscles and joints, swept across my thoughts and burst into the cavern until its edges were the edges of everything—a transparent sheen across every object, a subtle tint to every color, a glimmer in every thought.

I could still see the shaman, anointing himself from another hot vessel, could smell the skin burning, hear the guitar. At the same time, I saw hairlines forming in that sheet of glass, spiderwebs that crept in all directions, deepening as they spread. I felt myself separating into pieces, a deathly dark in the spaces between. I wrung my hands, tried to keep myself whole, but the drift could not be reversed.

"Not destroyed," said the shaman. "Dismantled. Split into its elements, until someone puts it back together . . ."

I swam in a geometry of broken glass, silver-limned figures reflecting and moving away from each other. When I breathed, the sound was amplified, dislocated, as though someone were breathing with me. I felt myself teetering on the edge of a chasm, felt the edge rolling up under me. I screamed silently and fell in.

I flailed my arms but made no contact, swallowed a bitter bubble of ayahuasca. I forced my breathing to slow. In one of those bright shards I saw motion, the image of a face. Swimming closer, I saw a small boy on all fours. He looked up at me, and in the next breath I was back in a familiar room: cold stone walls, stone floor, glassless window, a curtain of red and gold. I knew this room. I watched the child, but at the same time I *was* the child, smothered by boredom, sullen with afternoon's eternal emptiness. The boys outside would not let me play. I dug with a stick between stones and opened the dark cavity, my secret trove, took out my treasure: a sack filled with tiny bones. I'd found them scattered at the riverbank, left there by some predator who'd first stripped every shred of flesh. I sat against the bedpost, arranging and rearranging the fragile bones, pretending they belonged to one creature or another: a field mouse or a dragon, a miniature spirit or an unborn bird sucked sleeping from the egg. I listened for my mother's footsteps—if she caught me, she would pinch my face, throw out my precious bones. She did not like me to play with dirty things.

"'A systematic derangement,'" said the shaman. "You see? But after he is destroyed, what re-creates?" I saw the shaman and did not see him; I recognized the music and did not recognize it. Still, I was in that room. I looked at the child at the same time I looked out from his eyes—I was both seer and seen. "The music is not enough, the formulas. Only the stone . . .

"Look at me!" His voice was tormented. When my attention snapped to, I lost the boy, felt that pane of glass drifting off. The shaman strummed a low minor chord that brought tears to my eyes. He crouched low, crooned to me: *"Hanging back, shutting down, take myself down to the ground, when you gonna teach me how to play?"* But I was already turning to another image, already entering it. *"Ask you for a hand to hold, wrap myself up in the cold, sky is crying tears of acid rain . . ."*

We were at the hives. My mother's hands smelled of creosote, her wrists were crusted with honey. How I hated the taste of honey, the grubby smell of it! The bees made me impatient with their stupidity, their mindlessness, all the buzzing effort just to keep alive from year to identical year. She pulled out a sticky frame and laid it atop the hive, pointed to a bulging cell cupped with a dome of wax: a queen cup, where the new queen would soon be born. I tried to touch it, but my mother slapped my arm. The queen would emerge, gigantic, frightfully colored—the bees had proclaimed it so. I dreamed the boys dragged me to the river and wrapped me in dried grass, laid me in a canoe and shoved me into the current. They stood on the banks and urinated into the water. When I pulled off the shroud I was tall enough to straddle the river and they clung to my legs.

"It's working, I know it's working," said the shaman. He put wood in the furnace, went back to the mirror. His voice was thin and self-mocking, his movements stiff and ungraceful. He drank from a beaker of blue liquid that ran over his chin, down his neck and chest, bubbling in the furrows of his skin, doubling him over.

Now he wandered through a covered market, a young man far from the village where he'd grown up. Rain pelted on blue plastic tarpaulins, heaps of sneakers and stacks of metal tubs, towels, dishes, transistor radios. A row of colorful spices in heavy burlap sacks, oranges and browns, deep red, a yellow I could taste. I wanted to plunge my arms in, smear those colors across my face. The air reeked of urine and meat. A hog's head hung on a hook, dripping thin pink blood. Later, walking the city streets at dusk, hair wet, clothes clean—I stepped into a store, drawn by jewels in the window. A soldier swung in front of me, pushed his rifle crosswise against my chest, but the man at the counter laughed and the soldier let me pass. The man took out trays of necklaces, earrings, small figurines; he let me touch them. *Gold*, he said, when I rubbed at a dull lump of rock. His voice was so strange, I dropped it on the glass, ran past the soldier and back into the street.

"You can't destroy it. Only put it back together in a new way." He knelt astride my hips, hot breath in my face. His arms, laced with gashes, held my shoulders to the ground. "Birdie," he pleaded. "Give me your word."

The ayahuasca crawled million-legged inside of my skull, tiny blue insects that flared and shriveled in the heat. I closed my eyes and found myself in a cinder-block room, no windows. A row of men sat barebacked before square mirrors, the frames lined with round lightbulbs, many brown and dead. While I mopped the floor, cleaned a toilet, they took jars from paper sacks, brushed color onto their cheeks, glued long eye-lashes to their lids and painted them black. When one caught me look-ing, he batted his eyes, rubbed his hand in his crotch. Their skin grew pale, sparkling with glitter, fingernails bright red. They zipped one an-other into tight dresses with birdlike movements, deep voices changing to giggles. One by one they walked out into a hallway that echoed with music, rowdy cries, the sound of glass breaking. *Ernestina* was my friend's name—each night he brought me a piece of fruit, kissed the air near my cheek. After the last set I found him slumped at the dressing table, sob-bing. He looked up with haunted eyes and spat at the mirror, saliva run-ning down the smear of his miserable reflection. When I touched his shoulder, he shouted and drove me away. I saw myself in the glass behind him: dark hair, brown skin, black eyes.

"Your *fucking* word, my girl," the shaman said. He lay next to me on the muddy floor, the guitar standing against a table and feeding back in a shrill and oscillating wail. He reached around me, pulled my sweater over my head. I did not resist. It was happening to someone else. "An act of cre-ation, you understand? No one can imitate it."

The images swam like grains in the bottom of a kaleidoscope. I felt no more fear, only a deep, shivering pressure: I did not know what he wanted, but I could sense it inside me. I shut my eyes tight to find it.

A bus station, music from cheap speakers in the front of a store. What was it that grabbed me so, what froze me to the spot? "Dirtnap," I realized, though the shaman had never heard it before, never heard this angry melody wedded to sweetness and loss. I stood listening again and again until I missed the bus, until the storekeeper cursed me, turned the radio off. I spent the rest of my money to buy the tape; Ernestina found me an old tape player and I carried it with me through the streets, played it in the dressing room when the girls were gone. I pressed my tongue to the back of my teeth, fought the desire to throw up or howl. Later, I saw him on television for the first time, studied his eyes. Later still: a concert, the screams of the others, hot sweat of skin on skin, he cried his lyrics to the room and I sang along with him, shredded my throat. When he leapt from the stage, I clutched at every inch of him—touched the back of his leg, his bare foot—I wanted to eat his foot, pull him to me, possess every inch of him.

How long did I lie there, caught in these visions, while the shaman writhed next to me, his fists clenched white? What did I see: his memories or dreams, or a delusional collage we were creating together? A black-and-white television, my house, footage of the morning my father died. Mourners sprawled on a beach, lights strung along the fishing pier, a girl with an acoustic guitar. I saw my mother's face, gasping in orgasm, heard the name that she called him as he thrust into her. I saw a desert bazaar, a shop full of leather that hung in sheets, a familiar-looking Arab boy took a heavy book from a chest; when I offered him money he squeezed his hand open and shut: *More.*

The shaman clutched my arms, my backside, pulled my hips close. "Baby girl," he moaned. His face streamed with sweat. "He's almost here." I did not pull away. *"Aurum non vulgi.* You see what we can do . . ."

Heat pummeled our bodies; feedback made our eyes bulge. I stared at the open door of the stove, the white fire of that furnace searing into my eyes. I saw flames bursting at the base of a tree, flames all around me, brighter than the molten metal at the bottom of the crucible, brighter than anything I'd ever seen. I stood on that high balcony, staring down at the child, the air burning without sound. Someone pressed sharp nails into my arm as the fire burned brighter, the little girl's passion feeding it like gasoline: *Fire! Sire! Liar!* It was a message directed at *me*—something was beginning, a door cracked open. When the child raised her arms, caught me in her gaze, I did not hesitate. She opened her embrace and I shook off the clutching hand and raced to feel it, to enter that heat, join it to the flames sputtering to life in my every cell. I walked into that fire and came back to me.

I was lying next to the speakers, naked and coated in mud. The guitar was quiet. The stove rumbled and shook on its base of bricks. The shaman poured the last of the beakers into one large vessel; with the addition of each hot liquid, the light dimmed and shrank until finally there was only a boiling black mixture, thick and shiny as oil.

"It has to work," he said. He reached for the mirror. "It has to."

He set the beaker on the table and picked up the guitar, shrugged the strap onto his shoulder. Then he stood over me, his skin shredded and blackened, his abdomen twitching and rippling like the skins on the walls. His legs shook, his penis stiff as a mainmast.

"*What's my name?*" he sang, slashing at the strings. One speaker after another shrieked and sparked. His face was sad and broken, his eyes forlorn. "*What's my name? What's my name?*"

I knew what he wanted of me. After sixteen years, at last I understood.

He reached for my arm and pulled me standing, but I twisted away, leaned panting against the table. *No!* I shook my head. *No!*

When he came toward me I reached for the beaker—the glass seared and smoked against my hand. He took another step and I threw the beaker at him with all the strength I had left. It missed him, smashed against an amplifier, and a burst of sparks rose out of the mud and caught on the bottom of a long, shaggy pelt.

A ripple of flame crawled up the wall. It wavered in the crossdraft and caught on the next skin, quickly devouring them both. The shaman pulled me toward him, feedback screeching. The smell of burning hair was overpowering as the fire ringed its way from pelt to pelt and surrounded us. The jars on the table began to shatter, sent splinters of glass whizzing past me, nicking my shoulders and back.

"Please, Calliope." He held my face to his chest, his words barely audible. He tilted my chin and his lips moved again: "Daughter."

Whose eyes stared at me with such damaged innocence? Whose voice implored me, lost and disconsolate? Whose hands held me so tenderly?

I wouldn't want to say.

All I know is I recognized his face: the impossible desire, the pitiful need. It was like looking in the mirror: This person looked just like me.

"Be who you were born to be," I heard my mother say. I'd been so many people since then, but my first role would always reside in my bones. I still remembered my lines.

The fire surrounded us, greasy smoke snaking up our legs. The speakers gave a last earsplitting screech. I relaxed in his arms, pulled the hat from his head, and cupped his face between my palms.

"Daddy," I said.

He shuddered. The stove coughed white flame. Pools of liquid on the table ignited, puffing colored gasses into the air. Fire snaked in streams through the mud; the very floor seemed to burn.

"Daddy," I said again, into one ear and then another. I kissed his bloody cheeks, his blackened eyelids. "Daddy."

One of the burning skins detached from the wall and fled upward, illuminating the dark as it rose. I could feel my own skin stiffening, the hair on my body sizzling. He held me and I heard his heart hammering, both of us shaking as though possessed.

"Daddy!" I called, sobbing and laughing, the word too delicious on my lips. How long had it been waiting there? I said it again and again as he stroked my face, the nape of my neck—just to feel it on my tongue once more. We sank to the floor, he laid me on my back, his eyes streaming. He kissed me again—*Daddy!*—his weight pressing me into the stone. He smeared a hand in the muck and brought it to my forehead, drew a strange shape on my flesh.

That's when I saw her, standing behind him: a white silhouette backlit by the blaze. She was laughing, her face as horrible as I'd ever seen it, her voice a chaos of electricity and heat. When her mouth moved, the last speaker shrieked and blew. The tables were burning, the walls burning, everything about to be consumed—but the hag had time for her final taunt. She'd be free of me at last, I thought. And why not? Why, in the end, shouldn't we all get what we want?

"*Solve et coagulum,*" said the shaman. Again he made the sign on my forehead. The hag watched us with bright eyes, bald and monstrous, her stern features twisted in triumph.

"*Solve et coagulum,*" he gasped, marking me one last time. Then the hag puffed her cheeks and a hard blast kicked him in the spine and he collapsed on top of me.

"Now you are a poet," he groaned.

I lay gasping beneath him, still whispering his name as the fire blurred my vision. The last thing I saw was my horrible other, who snatched my clothes from the floor and blew me a kiss, then slipped wordlessly through the gap in the wall.

★

Once, if I remember well, my life was a feast where all hearts opened and all wines flowed. One evening I seated Beauty on my knees. And I found

The pen runs out of ink.

A man looks at it in disbelief, scribbles on the yellow pad, throws the pen across the room. It skids under a chair. He opens a sideboard drawer and finds another, writes slowly. It is almost daylight, a cream-colored dawn outside the dining-room windows. His arms itch like madness: old tracks trying to heal.

When he has finished, he reads over what he has written. His skin is sallow, his eyes serene. He finds an envelope, a book of stamps, writes out an address in tidy block letters, sits staring at the white rectangle on the polished mahogany. For a moment it seems he might relent, tear it into pieces, abandon the whole plan. But then he looks up, sees on the wall a framed photograph of himself, and smiles.

But where is the child? From what vantage is she watching? Upstairs in a four-poster bed, canopy billowing like a sail upon gentle seas. Perhaps she is dreaming of his music, his hands in the small of her back as she floats in the shallows, swells lifting her toward the sun. Pushing back from the table, he takes up the envelope, slips out the front door and hurries barefoot across the dew-slicked grass. Somewhere in the house, a grandfather clock strikes. The sleeping child tosses, cries out, but her father does not hear her. He pauses under the jacaranda, stares at its mangled branches, touches his palm to the slate trunk one last time. Thousands of buds are bulging from the branch tips. Soon they will burst, ablaze in lilac, and the spot where he stands will be covered in their shade.

The child is awake now, though she doesn't know why. She whispers his name, but she can't see her father, can't stop his last errand: a blue-jeaned vagrant opening the mailbox, kissing the envelope, raising the flag.

Does he think of his daughter as he turns back to face those high walls? Does he look to her window as he walks, resigned, across the lawn? Can he hear her calling when he comes back inside, her prayers answered by the sound of the door opening, a moment's bright hope before it clicks, quietly, closed?

✷

I am the ghost of an infamous suicide, born and born again each time my father died. Stepped beyond the stagewings at the stirring of a ghost; strangled by the silence of my own outrageous quest 'til a long-caged word flew out and made the mountain ring—

[*Curtain down, music swells*]

—the double play's the thing.

But you, pale and quaking, mute audience to this mess—why are you still in your seats? What more grows from this rubble, what else is left to say or guess? We've reached the climax, *Exeunt all,* they've bid the soldiers shoot. . . . O Hunger, you don't believe we're through? You need exegesis, shining light, the soft snowfall of epiphany?

Perhaps my soul approached that region, but what souvenir could it fetch to fill you? A T-shirt? A snow globe? A bumper sticker to mark the mileage?

Loose lips sink ships, my love. (And I should know.)

Repeat after me: *The rest is silence.*

✷

Shivering and scoured, I struggled from darkness into cold day. Wind stuttered across the pass, stirring nothing; overhead a purple sky stretched depthless and final. Into those two dimensions I limped, naked and singed, covered only by crumbling, baked mud and the rank, smoking hat on my head.

I picked my way over pebbles, gasped with thirst. The empty moonscape gusted, the mark on my forehead stung. Beyond a stone shelf the crow waited, murmuring and stabbing impatiently at the carcass of some alpine rat, stringing off its bloody sinews as though sewing those gruesome innards. It fixed me in its yellow eye, cawed once. I rested a moment, cold air against my blistered skin. I heard the scrape of the crow's beak on stone. Behind me came no footstep, no hoarse plea, no song. Though my every bone ached, I waited. My eyes would not close.

The crow ruffled its wings with a spray of dust and feathers. I hauled myself up, half-hopping on my stronger leg. Slowly, we made our way down Old Maker's hard spine, the dark crow in the lead, the weaker bird sunk into stupor, kept awake only by cold, bloody feet. It was hours before I saw the town emerge—the brown, wending river, the first distant sounds rising from the valley like an afterthought. High noon, I came upon a field of flowers—bright and fragile pink cups spread over a shallow basin, color delicate as a feather bed, surrounded by walls of high rock. They must have bloomed in my absence—I was certain they hadn't been there before. I bent down, aching, to pick a handful, but I had nothing to hold them. A shiver of grief clutched me then. I knew without turning that the crow was gone.

Down into the foothills, the day slowly warming, a sky clouded over and gone peach-pale. At last I came to the ruins at the mountain's base, the hives like toys left out by a fastidious child. Only when I stepped into the first clearing did I notice the stillness, the grass undisturbed by the bees' industry, the air untroubled by their sound. I lifted the first cover and found the hive empty, the combs full of nectar but every last worker and drone gone. I did not need to open the others—every last bee was gone. I gulped from a water drum, gasping and shivering, stomach clenching on the freezing water, coughing half of it back up. I dunked my head, scrubbed at the paste of ash and filth—I tried to see the mark he had drawn on my forehead, but in my reflection there was nothing there.

At the lean-to, I covered myself with overalls and limped on. It was almost dark when I came to the edge of town, the laughter of children in the streets and the sound of men arguing. The cobblestones were covered in streamers, empty bottles, dead balloons; carts and floats left in various states of disassembly, the aftermath of the spring festival that had come and gone in my absence. How long had I been gone, I wondered—and with that thought, the stinging grief hit again. I shouldered the walls anxiously. When I made it to her door, I was not surprised to find the crowd milling, village women ducking in and out bearing jars of honey, their lips moving in prayer. Votive candles were arrayed on the stoop, shining on loose flowers and drawings of saints, glinting in the channel of water below. I felt myself slump to the ground, too exhausted to cry. I pulled the hat low on my head; one of the neighbor women recognized me and helped me to my feet, put an arm around me, and led me inside.

The house was tidy and swept, as though the town had cleaned it together. When I saw her empty bed, stripped and narrow, my knees turned to custard, my heart nearly gave out. I collapsed into the arms of strangers. They slapped my cheeks, brought me water—but when they led me to the other bedroom, I would not lie down. There were a dozen women or more bustling through the house, offering me food, wine, looking to me for permission to claim her few possessions. All I could do was stand between those walls—my books sitting uselessly on the nightstand, my clothes piled in the suitcase. I had known—of course I had known, had felt it even as I walked away that morning, how many days ago? What would I do now, without her kindness? Who would I be without her? They watched me from the doorway, whispering to each other, but I stood apart. So this is what grief really feels like, I thought—every face that stared back at me was her face, every pair of eyes belonged to her. It was I who had changed: The person I'd been to the old woman could no longer be.

Later, they helped me out to the street, dressed in a clean blouse someone found for me, a pair of old jeans from the bottom of a drawer. All I could think of now was Jacobo, the look on his face when I'd left that morning. *If it is more important, go.* I had to find him now. Even if he would not speak to me, I had to see his face again—though I didn't know what to say to him. Flimsy words could not change what I'd done.

In the plaza, a rickety truck stood gurgling at the curb, thin exhaust rising into the orange glow of the streetlamps. The truck bed was piled high with hay bales, sacks of grain, one scrawny sheep tied to a rail. The women argued briefly with the driver, and soon I was being lifted into the back, settled into a nest of blankets, the town drifting back in clatters and squeaks.

The road stretched toward a marbled horizon, the night sky a black beach covered with shiny leavings. I jounced and wept with every pothole, closed my eyes but was afraid to sleep. I tried to keep Jacobo's face in my mind, tried not to think of the cavern, the fire, the last look I'd seen in the shaman's eyes. I could feel everything trying to come together, to organize and explain itself in my mind; I stared at the receding mountains and tried to keep it at bay, but the pieces were drifting inevitably together, raw experience coalescing, forming the story I'd soon have to tell.

After an hour of frightened bleating, the lamb lay down and folded its forelegs, nibbled a hay stalk, and watched me sideways. I hugged the blankets around me, pulled the hat over my eyes, and hid from the wind. I nodded into nervous sleep, waking when we pulled off for gas, the driver's shoes shuffling on pavement, the radio muttering in darkness. He checked on the lamb, nodded at me, and looked toward the paling horizon.

"Soon," he said.

In the dawn, the city was magnificent, sprawled across the basin like the rusted innards of a complex machine. The streets were grimy and ordinary, ordinary people going about their necessary tasks. The driver left me in the main plaza, and I stood gaping in a patch of sunlight: traffic scurrying and bunching on every side, horns honking, the shouts of cabdrivers, a huge bronze fountain spouting arcs of water, mist tingling against my face. Storefronts opened with a clatter; old men in aprons splashed buckets across the sidewalk. Women swept dust into the gutters. Schoolchildren in clean uniforms followed a pretty young teacher across the square, waiting at a corner when she held up a hand. No one took note of me as I eased myself onto a bench and waited—dazzled and depleted, another shabby migrant come in from the sticks. I didn't know how to find Jacobo, only the name of his studio. I pictured his dour face, his nervous eyes. Would he speak to me? Would he blame me for what happened, hate me for not being there when she died?

He was not my brother, I'd realized, the thought dawning calmly on that long stretch of empty road. I didn't yet know how to say what he was. But I needed him near me now—to tell me his stories and listen to mine, to wave his hands in excitement, to tease me and make me laugh. I had no family left, had lost what was left in the hot guts of Old Maker. I could not yet say what I'd gained in return.

Across from the plaza, on a wide stone platform that took up a whole block, sat the cathedral. It vaulted skyward in massive certainty, obscuring the hills and the neighborhoods behind. Its solid walls glowed pink in the morning light, towers and buttresses etched against the impossibly blue sky, framing the clouds, as though the sky had not been complete before those towers were there to describe it. Pedestrians walked across the wide terrace, crossed themselves, checked their watches against the iron clock-faces. The cathedral had been there for centuries, Jacobo once told me, but looking at it now I felt sure it had been there forever—before the cars and cafés, before TVs, before e-mail, before roads, before short-lived people had come to call this place their home. This plaza, these streets, were there only to give it a setting. The town itself was unimaginable without the authority of its presence.

Can you remember how you felt when you first heard music, the first time you learned a song you loved? Do you recall how the world shrank around you, the universe squeezed into a tiny, infinite burst of joy? That's what I felt as I gawked up at the cathedral, a feeling I had forgotten somewhere along the way: This was art, I thought, petrified before the vast handiwork, three iron bells motionless in the highest tower. The men who had made this—imagined it, brought it forth from nothing with decades of labor, teams of workers who'd cracked stone, sacrificed sleep, broken their backs, mothers whose children were pressed into the service of a dream—where were they now? Who remembered their names? And the dreamer himself, who'd watched it grow stone by stone, loyal to an image in his mind—he, too, was buried and long forgotten. He was no one.

And who was I, after all? Would I ever make something as lasting as those pocked and mortared walls? Would I ever know that great sigh of completion, ever stand back to admire my handiwork, then smile a satisfied smile and disappear from memory?

It was something to hope for, I thought, gathering myself to go—the possibility of making something real and alive. Something necessary.

As I roamed those warming streets, I could feel the incomprehensible past struggling for coherence. How to make sense of it, this collection of incidents, these dark thoughts and strange accidents, wild urges and images? A million little pieces, each contradicting the last—could I ever reconstruct it with any integrity? My life had been a great confusion, constantly changing in tone and in diction—to put it together and make it presentable, I'd have to smooth out the borders, trim the frayed ends and package it nicely, price tag still on, shrink-wrapped straight from the factory. I already knew it was an impossible task. I could never be just one person, one self, a ballistic missile with just one trajectory.

I shall be free to possess truth in one soul and one body, Rimbaud said, returning from his hot season, a fierce invalid with a chip on his shoulder and a history to found. I no longer believed him, though my father had taken him at his word. Truth had never come to me that way. I didn't see why it would start now.

After a time I managed to find where I was going: a quiet café at the end of a maze of alleys, across from a small public garden. It was an unassuming place, picture windows and two tables on the sidewalk, a couple of white saplings held up by wires. I mustered my courage, bit my lip, pulled the hat lower on my head. But something stopped me as I crossed the sidewalk, froze me before I went in.

Through the window, I saw him in profile, the only one inside: his long hair gathered back neatly, his white shirt wrinkled but clean. He sat in front of a computer screen, eyes swollen, face ashy, beard grown a few days too long. He pressed a hand to his forehead and leaned on an elbow, eyes glazed and unfollowing in the light from the monitor. My heart began to thud; my throat closed and stuck. Sweet, burdened Jacobo—I wasn't sure I could face him. I almost turned and ran.

Then, as though he'd heard my thoughts, he looked to the window and saw me standing stupidly outside. How can I describe the look that flooded his face, the sad smile that flowed out to meet me? If I had the language I would write that poem, if I only had the necessary skill: I'd describe how he rose, slow and stiff, as though tugged by invisible strings. I'd say he came to me with a pure and open heart, forgave everything in the first footstep's instant.

Would you even believe me? Would you know what it meant?

And what about Calliope? What, after all, will you think of her? Take a long, last look at the red-haired girl, the awkward, excited fool—rushing to the doorway, stumbling in secondhand shoes, her too-large blue jeans and borrowed shirt, the soot-black hat slipping from her head . . .

Stop the presses! Here she comes: Lady Lazarus, back from beyond, stories to tell of the living and the dead, ready at last to speak her mind, without any clue how to put it in words, or what it might sound like when she finally did.

13. MORE TERRIBLE
THAN SHE EVER WAS

"THE MOST IMPORTANT IS THE CHEESE. One must search for the cheese which melts evenly and retains creamy consistency. Many soycheeses when melting turn to lumps and fibers, very unappetizing, and there is much hot oil which can soak through wax paper and make problems with the handling, and also perhaps give second-degree burn when running over your wrist. This is destructive to the very idea of the vegan cheesesteak, and not conducive to Zen Buddhist state of mind.

"But you will say, 'Roshi Bob, is it not flavor which is most important? How can Zen Buddhist who is concerned with inner essence and not with outward appearance be also so concerned with aesthetics of soycheese and how it is melting and in what consistency? Is not flavor the true essence of the soycheese? Is not its soycheeseness the most important?' To which Roshi Bob says, 'Such a distinction is illusion of *samsara*. Soycheeseness is not something hidden within the room-temperature-only body of the soycheese. Soycheeseness is not "soul." It is the range of possibility for the soycheese, encompassing its various states of being as well as transitions between them. What is the aesthetic realm but the sensual expression of soycheeseness? What is soycheese essence but the potential for rich flavor and creamy consistency?'

"Many misunderstand Zen Buddhism as rejecting the sensual realm, but this is not so. Mr. Andrew has been to Mountaintop Zen Center, has he not? He has seen beautiful environment and state-of-the-art Morath Infirmary and recently expanded sushi bar. How to appreciate such things if one rejects the sensual realm? Roshi Bob thinks this is unfortunate myth regarding Zen Buddhism. Has Roshi told for you story of cell-phone tower which Sprint constructs in San Jacinto Mountains?"

"Yes, Roshi, I believe you have," said the author.

"Ah," he said, and momentarily fell silent before picking up again in his description of the ideal vegan cheesesteak, the search for same being the task in which he and the author were presently engaged. "Then, of course, there is question of the seitan, which one hopes has been texturized to hold the melting cheese like tree branches hold falling snow. Not like rainwater running off a roof. And also the proper elasticity for mouth to believe it is experiencing actual shaved rib-eye beef. So we see it is no one thing but an important combination of factors contributing to vegan cheesesteakness. Then we ask, well, what *is* this vegan cheesesteakness? Is it the seitan? Is it the soycheese or the perfect hoagie roll from Philadelphia, Pennsylvania? Can vegan cheesesteakness be found in any one of these?

"It cannot. Only in combination and balance do we find vegan cheesesteakness. To consider one aspect separate from others is error of non-Buddhist state of mind, and in this way we fail to achieve understanding of vegan cheesesteak. Roshi Bob has enjoyed perfect vegan cheesesteak only once, in the city of Chennai, which perhaps Mr. Andrew knows as Madras. Mr. Andrew has been to Madras?"

"I, um, don't . . ." The author shook his head, by now only peripherally aware of the roshi's monologue as it mingled with the crunch of their footsteps, the silent breath of hot wind.

"Mr. Andrew usually asks many, many questions." The roshi slapped a hand rather hard on the author's back. "Today Mr. Andrew listens. Roshi Bob thinks, well very good! Perhaps Mr. Andrew is learning to be less goal-oriented, to concentrate on process and not so much on product. In this way Mr. Andrew becomes teachable. In this way Mr. Andrew observes the world without his attention snagging on illusion of discrete things, like cloth flowing down river which becomes stuck on a twig. How will this cloth come to understand the river? So intent was this cloth on finding where river ends that it was not aware of twig in the first place!

"So we see that Zen Buddhist state of mind is like the water, flowing around the twig, and not like the cloth which becomes snagged. Zen Buddhist mind is already part of the river, and does not need to seek understanding."

"Yes, Roshi," said the author. "Indubitably."

The silence, and the vast emptiness that stretched around them, was haunting for the impression it gave of fullness and presence. The wind was largely responsible: hot and transparent, each step he and the roshi took passed through a layer of resistance, a membrane. The sun was almost overhead, banishing the last shadows from the Mojave Desert; only the slow, steady movement on the horizon, a glinting line of cars snaking soundlessly east, broke up the sepia stillness, the queasy shimmers of air pretending to motion like the shifting contours of memory's unreliability. The author's neck was burning, his back sweat-soaked, his shirt plastering his skin, chafing beneath the strap of the small bookbag he carried. The roshi, though draped in a black robe that buttoned at the throat, was dry, his face shaded by the wide brim of a black gaucho hat.

Behind them spread the 130-acre fairground, as yet still calm but for the hunched movements of the forty-odd monks who crawled like red and black insects over the hardpan. On its swift journey to the northern horizon's odd, lithic monuments, the eye was stopped only by the enormous stage—an intricate metal superstructure hung with kaleidoscopic light arrays and flanked by 60-foot-high video screens, the clusters of trailers that would shelter the performers and their entourages, as well as the press and various other important persons, scattered to one side and behind the stage like miniature supplicants before some obscene and technological god. All stood at the ready, all sound- and sight-checks having been conducted that morning. The only ongoing task was the slow and meticulous fabrication of the sand mandala—a masterpiece of brilliant color and byzantine design whose diameter spanned some 425 feet between the east and west banks of portable toilets, and whose circumference passed through stage and concession stands and Piercing Palace and soundboard and skateboard half-pipe and security posts alike. The monks of Mountaintop, coached by Tibetan lamas visiting from Nepal, had been at work on the giant mandala for eight days, moving in shifts across the desert with their metal *chakpur* sand funnels, sleeping only three hours a night. A small fleet of dump trucks, once loaded with colored sand, at last stood empty, the last bags in wheelbarrows that rested at intervals on the tarpaulin pathways that transected the huge work of art. Not until the last bag had been emptied, the graphic representation of the cosmos completed, would the gates be opened for the estimated 90,000 ticket holders who would, with their flip-flops and Keds, their filthy blankets and benighted attitudes, their garish tattoos and wanton body piercings and thong underwear, their fuch-sia hair and their tablets of Ecstasy and mandatory scowls of persistent apathy, trample and scuff the immense mandala into incoherence in a matter of minutes.

"Roshi Bob remembers Mr. Andrew's first visit to Mountaintop," said the voluble monk as the pair drew close to the Jeff Buckley Vegan Village, one of three sprawling food bazaars, which already reeked with a jarring combination of odors, resounded with sizzles, each tin-roofed stand emitting its own heat shimmer under the imperturbable sky. "Willful as the horse Sonia!" he cried, and briefly removed his hands from beneath the conical black robe. "He is like the man who stands before ocean with a sword. And Roshi thinks, Roshi Bob, here is a test for you, someone who maybe is very far from Zen Buddhist state of mind, who maybe cannot learn to let go of desire and understand interconnection and respect for all sentient beings. But Mr. Andrew *is* learning interconnection and respect. Mr. Andrew's mind is opening, and with initiation of Yamantaka Mandala this afternoon Mr. Andrew maybe will take first step on path to enlightenment."

"But the Muse, Roshi," the author muttered, not so much to remind the roshi as to keep his own mind focused against the tidal onslaught of his companion's discourse, keep his object squarely before his eyes like the heart into which the dagger seeks to plunge.

The roshi turned his head but kept walking, hands hidden in the black robe which draped to the ground so that the impression was of an austere chess piece gliding of its own power across the board. Almost noon, the sun seemed to pulse, irate, in the sky.

"Oho!" the roshi laughed, but did not elaborate.

It was not true that the author had forsaken his goals, nor the single-minded sense of purpose needed to achieve them.* If anything, he had come to this barren oven 140 miles from San Diego with a renewed sense

---

*Which is not to say that the author was not at the same time an open-minded, accepting person with a firm investment in the happiness of all living beings; in other words, a Buddhist in spirit, if not in practice, which he most certainly was.

of such purpose, a renewed appreciation for the rewards that accrue to dedication, loyalty, love. In the two months since the tragedy at Powell's, it can honestly be said that that purpose had taken over his life, become his life, had led him like a blindered horse down strange roads, the fruit it bore both unexpected and tantalizingly sweet. And in a matter of hours—and, of this, certainty imbued his veins like liquefied iron—he would at last come face-to-face with its object.

Those who had predicted that Portland would be the Muse's last appearance, that her appetite for Truth would be satisfied by the exposure of her former lover and her mother, were woefully ignorant of the poet's appetite.* As any intelligent observer might have guessed, the catastrophic Powell's fire and the "auto-assault," as police had termed it, upon the Beekeeper had signaled an escalation in the cruelty and deadliness of the Muse's attacks; no longer content to punish only the speakers and promoters of falsehood, it would seem, the Muse now sought to sweep up the willing, hungry consumers of falsehood in the bale of her deadly gaze. This inclusiveness could certainly be testified to by the attorneys, defendant, judge, and jury in record mogul Gary North's racketeering trial, were not the majority still in intensive care as of this writing; by poets Shaylene Hicks and Charles Wright, not to mention Fritz Meers, the owner of the Rockville, Maryland, motel in which the Muse visited them; by the surviving members of the rock band Creed; and perhaps most gruesomely by actor Ben Affleck.[†] Preceding each terrible incident, the graffito had appeared, as though to taunt anyone who might doubt her resolve; in the wreckage of each was blazoned the monosyllabic call to arms, as though offering the corrupt and the insincere, the treacherous and the selfish and the merely foolish, one last chance to open their hearts to the Truth.

"How is he?" the author inquired, wrenching his attention back to the monochrome world, shifting his bookbag from one livid shoulder to the other.

---

*Notable among them were the editors of *SLAM*, embarrassed by their own feature retrospective entitled "Life After Life After Death" (February 18, 200_), and Edwin Decker, who published a farewell sonnet in the *Peninsula Beacon* entitled, simply, "Whew!"

[†]Though Anthony Lane's suggestion that Affleck's casting as the lead in *Maid in Manhattan II: Re-Maid* was the Muse's ultimate revenge must be taken with a grain of salt (*New Yorker*, August 30, 200_).

The roshi lifted his face, briefly, to squint at the sun. A hot blow of wind tore away his first words. "—to hope for young man. Of course Zen Center is happy to provide a home if it brings peace to young man's mind."

"Then you find him improved? Has he spoken?" The author removed his sunglasses to pluck a recalcitrant grain of sand from one eye. "I should dearly like the opportunity—" He could not finish the sentence, a sudden bubble of wind stuffing his mouth like a warm sock. The roshi stopped to let this gust blow through, then continued his glide.

"Young man is much the same. Silent, without expression. In the mornings Roshi must rouse him from his cell, where he lies in corpse pose on sack of brambles and stares at ceiling. Roshi must lift him from pallet, which makes some trouble for Roshi's sciatica and causes Roshi to be late for breakfast of fresh corn bread and poached Egg Beaters."

"In a sense, this is what he wanted," the author offered, as they stopped at the first of what would turn out to be seven vegan cheesesteak vendors, the roshi determined to sample each of their wares before settling on the perfect meal. Other than the sounds of food preparation, the chatter of concessionaires each adorned with his or her own laser-encoded security badge, there was no activity in the Jeff Buckley Vegan Village; the author and the roshi moved from stand to stand unobstructed, like survivors at some post-apocalyptic picnic. "In a sense, this is the emptiness, the enlightenment he sought."

At this the roshi stopped, cheesesteak suspended en route to his mouth, sallow oil spattering the hem of his robe, searing the sand at the author's feet.

"No, Mr. Andrew," he said. "Not enlightenment."

They had brought him to the door of the monastery—mute, bald, his scalp still swollen and ablaze with stings, the skin of his face and neck pockmarked and skeletally drawn, legs too weak, nine days after the fire, to support his weight. Gone was the easy, seductive grin, gone the smooth arrogance of his fasting days; in its stead was a terrible vacancy: The Beekeeper's eyes following whatever movement or shiny object crossed before them, he had to be led by the arm through the hallways and chapels of his former home, led haltingly up the path to the *zendo* where, if left in full lotus, he would remain for days, insensible to heat or cold or inclement weather, until one of his brothers came to fetch him.

"He's like some kind of fuckin' zombie, yo," said the monastery's newest novice, Terrence Marker, who to the roshi's great consternation insisted that the other monks address him as "Brother Fly." "Dude, we should like sit his ass on a pile of papers, like a human paperweight! We should paint him bronze and put him out at the end of the driveway, like 'Dude, Welcome to Mountaintop.' Totally fuckin' phat, yo."

"Brother Terrence," the roshi began, putting down his fork, a gesture which provoked gasps around the table.

"Fly." Terrence leered at the others for approval.

"Brother Terrence," said the roshi, "young man is not paperweight and not Buddha lawn jockey. Young man has belonged to Mountaintop Zen Center many, many years, since you were small, impertinent child. When young man first arrived, there was one building, eight Zen Buddhist monks. No Hewlett-Packard Center. No cell-phone reception. Path to *zendo* was lined with broken glass, covered in snow many months in year, and monks forbidden to wear shoes. Young man never complained about hardships of Zen Buddhist way of life, or questioned Roshi's teachings. Young man was never arrested for hitchhiking back to Zen Center from Anza Beer & Bowling. Young man does not wake Roshi up at night with sound of skateboard in Zen Center hallways and stairwells.

"Young man always will have place at Zen Center." The roshi glanced down suddenly, as though just remembering the half-eaten stack of pancakes, ascertaining that his plate had not been mistakenly cleared, nor pilfered. "Brother Terrence will be his assistant, to help young man with his duties and gather fresh brambles for his pallet and clean young man's chamber pot."

"No fuckin' way, dude," said the pupil, waggling a finger at the roshi. "TT-Fly doesn't clean any fuckin' chamber pots. Fuck that. You get one of these other cue balls—"

"Brother Terrence!" shouted the roshi, surging to his feet and overturning the remnants of his breakfast. "Roshi Bob has listened to enough of ignorance and disrespect!" Terrence shook his head and made to stand,

but the roshi struck him a swift blow to the side of the head and the former skateboard champion woozily sat. "You should meditate on possibility of ever being one-tenth the pupil to Roshi that young man once was.
Respect for all sentient beings. Respect for all life, regardless of its form of
expression or its incontinence. This you will learn at Mountaintop Zen
Center, so long as Roshi Bob is your teacher. If you do not wish to learn
Zen Buddhist state of mind, you may take skateboard collection and Bill-
abong robes and hitchhike your bitch ass back to La Jolla!"

Amid the ensuing turmoil, the roshi gathered his robes and swept from
the room, carrying a plate from which he would personally spoon-feed the
Beekeeper his breakfast.

In the weeks that followed, the Beekeeper was slowly integrated into
life at the monastery, coaxed into performing such menial, repetitive tasks
as sweeping the hallways and porches, dusting the monitors and keyboards
in the business center, and brushing Dogen and Sonia. Although Marker
complained of the injustice of his assignment throughout morning and
afternoon *zazen,* he kept quiet during mealtimes to avoid further encounter with the roshi's wrath. Guests of the Zen Center grew accustomed
to the silent figure who wandered the grounds during off-hours, now standing next to a tree as though engaged in silent conversation, now in the
middle of the driveway so that arriving motorists were confronted with
his lifeless apparition. The monks grew used to his shadow's slow movement through the hallways, the appearance of his swollen features behind
them in mirrors before he slipped away like a wraith; the cooks, to finding
him in the kitchen before dawn, staring at the refrigerators. In that place
that had seen so many extraordinary dramas, the Beekeeper's presence became simply one more testament to human endurance, one more caution
against the ego's stealthy desires.

"Dude! Uh, Master Roshi dude . . . sir!" Brother Terrence bounded into
the roshi's private chambers late one night. The roshi was reclined on his
couch in sweatpants, shirtless, watching the second season of *Lost* on DVD;
so startled was he by the unprecedented intrusion that his snifter of cognac flew from his hand and shattered against a bookshelf. Readers needn't
be importuned to imagine his displeasure.

"Brother Terrence," he said evenly, "Roshi is wondering, why would least-favorite student at Mountaintop Zen Center interrupt Roshi's private time? Knowing that Roshi finds *Lost* to be program of incomparable interest, very conducive to Zen Buddhist state of mind, why would slow-witted novice intrude—"

"That's totally what I'm trying to tell you, bro, if you just—"

"Also he is wondering, why can Brother Terrence not learn proper forms of address for Mountaintop Zen Center to show respect for elders? Roshi Bob has seen many students, some with mental impairments much greater than Brother Terrence's—"

"Hey!" shouted Marker. "Just fuckin' shut up for a minute, yo. I just thought you'd want to see what I found buried under his pallet."

With this, he held out to the stunned roshi an unkempt stack of papers, one timeworn book, and a sheaf of ancient parchment, curled and worn soft as an old sock, bound into a split length of bamboo. Cobwebs dangled from the yellowed pile, dirt and grit showering to the polished parquet floors of the roshi's sitting room. As the roshi pulled on a T-shirt and fumbled for his reading glasses, the novice tried to clean off the scroll, scraping dust and pebbles haphazardly from the pages.

"Why would he, like, bury this shit, uh . . . sir? I mean, what the fuck's the big deal about these old books?"

"Get out," the roshi said, attempting to take the papers from his student. His student did not relinquish them, and the roshi's eyes grew wide.

"Just tell me. Are they some secret, forbidden shit or what? Is it like, Buddhist porn?" He winked, but the roshi's eyes were now closed, his lips moving inaudibly. "Guess he wasn't such a great student after all, yo, if he's like keeping shit secret from the roshi. You don't see TT-Fly keeping shit secret, do you? No way, dude. Brother Fly gets with the program. Maybe he doesn't talk like the rest of these pencil-necks, but at least he's not burying porn under his pallet.

"Maybe there's a lesson here for *you*, dude," said the student, he and the roshi each still holding one side of the filthy sheaf, the roshi's low chant growing louder. "Maybe you're a little too focused on form over content, you know? Not so Zen Buddhist state of mind, yo. I guess that swollen-up motherfucker . . ."

But here Brother Terrence broke off, brows knitting, and stared down at his hands where they touched the old texts. The roshi's eyes still squeezed shut, his lips forming the strange incantation, as the young monk stood bewildered he believed he saw his own hands begin to redden, believed he suddenly smelled the sweet, acrid odor of burning flesh, until in the next instant the roshi's eyes opened and Brother Terrence saw his hands flash into flame.

"There is no distinction between form and content, Brother Terrence," said the roshi, clutching to his breast the books and papers the younger monk had released. Brother Terrence was gasping for air, his hands, whole and unharmed, raised before his eyes. "Now leave Roshi's sight, please."

Upon close inspection, the roshi's fears proved well founded. The bound leaves and parchments, written in Sanskrit, comprised ancient, illicit commentaries on a first-century text called the Mulamadhyamikakarika,* a radical analysis of the metaphysical underpinnings of Buddhism. Written by the brilliant scholar Nagarjuna, the MMK addressed itself to contradictions in the doctrine of Dependent Arising, the Buddhist theory of death and rebirth, and found them irreconcilable, thus invalidating Buddhism's very foundations before moving on to render all theories of any kind to be worthless.

"No things whatsoever exist, at any time or place," declares the first verse, which renounces positive concepts of existence in favor of the term *sunya:* emptiness. All things are empty, said Nagarjuna, even the theory of emptiness itself, an epistemological paradox which the MMK both embraces and sees as a grave danger. For this reason, its teachings had been diluted, the more provocative commentaries suppressed for millennia, for fear that students would be ruined by exposure to this, Buddhism's dark heart: "The feeble-minded may be destroyed by the misunderstood doctrine of *sunyata,* as by a snake ineptly seized."[†]

"Many times, Roshi Bob warned young man against dangers of incomplete understanding, of taking literal meaning of the words without grasping the sense which binds them together." Having devoured the final vegan cheesesteak, the roshi had led the author up a gentle rise, at the top

---

*Hereafter referred to as "MMK," for reasons the author trusts are obvious.
[†]MMK, XXIV:11.

of which the two friends now stood, sun lashing the backs of their necks, looking down at the magnificent array of color and design that made up the sand mandala, its brightness sharply contrasted by the monochrome desert and the ominous stone formations which gave the venue its name.

"Roshi Bob pleaded, 'Do not presume to be your own guide.' Young man believed he did not need a teacher. So we see that hunger for truth can be misleading; desire for enlightenment can lure the impulsive from Zen Buddhist state of mind. Even if the goal is noble, those motivated by impure desires of the ego can find themselves imprisoned, bound by their own rope."

Understanding at last where the Beekeeper had left the path, the roshi went to his former prodigy's cell, his silent padding through the monastery's dark halls interrupted only when he tripped over a derelict skateboard. In his arms he carried the bundle Brother Terrence had unearthed: the fragile scroll of the MMK, the suppressed commentaries, and a copy of Jacques Derrida's *Of Grammatology,* overdue at the University of Virginia library since November 199_.* In his other hand he carried the bottle of cognac.

"I have failed you, my disciple," he said, sitting by the Beekeeper's pallet. In the place of the brilliant student he had cultivated, the roshi found a disfigured shadow staring forlornly at the ceiling. "In my pride I put myself above you as teacher and forbade you to read [MMK] and so gave focus to your ambition. Better that Roshi sits with student and travels road with him, explains concept of *sunya* emptiness and its double, fullness, perhaps invites young man to chambers to share cognac and see how snifter is full when empty, empty when full."

As the Beekeeper moaned pitifully in the dark cell, the roshi arranged the books and papers into a small pile on the stone floor, took the stopper from the bottle, and, with one last appreciative sniff, emptied the cognac atop the heap. "Young man was searching for enlightenment"—the roshi took his hand—"but Roshi directed him to ego and nihilism instead." The roshi closed his eyes and again began to intone the strange words, the

---

*Though the author knows little of ancient Buddhist texts, he has enough familiarity with the Derrida volume to attest to its gravely disheartening effects, not to mention its cavalier attitude toward standard spelling. In combination with the MMK, it is little wonder it provoked such deviance in the Beekeeper.

resonance of the stone walls filling the space with echoes. He clapped his hands and the papers kindled, flames dancing over and within the curled pages, casting their wisdom upon the walls as writhing shadows.

"In this we see that it is young man who is teaching Roshi Bob, and not Roshi Bob teaching young man." The Beekeeper slowly turned to face the fire, the glimmers reflecting in his eyes, mouth opening slightly and closing again. All his striving for emptiness, for detachment, had come to this: nothing.

"The student has surpassed the teacher." The roshi prostrated himself before the Beekeeper in the esoteric ritual known as Dharma Transmission. "Now we see who is true Roshi."

The precious texts curled and sent sparks into the air and at last collapsed with a small sigh. In the Beekeeper's eyes flickered the terrible, inescapable pain of one whose dearest wish turns out to be his undoing—that is to say, of all humans.

"Blow out the flame," pleaded the Beekeeper. But the roshi could not.

That night the troubled roshi was visited in dreams by the Muse herself. They sat atop the monastery's horses—Calliope upon Dogen, the roshi upon Sonia—backward in the saddles as they crossed a flat landscape, a surface of glass. At a sign from the dead poet, the horses stopped, the two riders staring through the clear ground into the hollow center of the earth, where glowed a vision of the Yamantaka Mandala so perfect that the roshi had to turn away. The Muse, now sharing the one saddle with him, put her lips to his ear and whispered a message, one which gave the author an electrifying start when he heard it repeated from the roshi's lips.

"But what does it mean, Roshi?" he asked, heart thudding in the scorching heat. "What do the words mean?"

The roshi stood unmoving, eyes trained on the realization of his dream's vision as it neared completion on the desert floor. "Always Mr. Andrew is focused on individual words, and not overall truth. This is not Zen Buddhist way. Would Mr. Andrew prefer to eat the words, 'vegan cheesesteak,' or the delicious thing itself?"

"Roshi, I am a writer. Please."

"Take, for example, the word *sunya*, which has caused so much confusion to young man. This word is translated as 'emptiness,' but in fact it is closer to 'hollowness' or 'swelling.' Empty but also pregnant, a potential for coming-into-being. All things are Buddha things, all things are *sunya*— does this mean there are no things? From one eye we say yes, from other eye we say no. Does Mr. Andrew understand?"

"I . . . I'm not sure what you're trying to—"

"Sometimes we must separate the thing from its name, in order to return to the nature of the thing, its essence. For example, Yamantaka Mandala. What is this Yamantaka Mandala?" He gestured over the empty space, sweeping his arm across the milky sky. "Yamantaka is 'Opponent of Death,' but to concentrate on this name is to ignore the perfection of the image, to limit understanding of its meaning. In another example, sometimes we see stories with pictures, sometimes perhaps in newspapers or magazines, but if we focus only on words we may have incomplete understanding of the images . . ."

The author squinted at the mandala, attempting to synthesize the riot of geometric shapes and lurid pictograms into some larger, coherent sense. "That's interesting, 'Opponent of Death.' Can you say more about it?"

"Sometimes we receive such stories through U.S. mail, but we are too focused on old ways of understanding to experience full meaning . . ."

"Roshi," the author said, suddenly struck, turning to take his arm but finding only a handful of black cloth. "Are you saying she is pregnant? The Muse is pregnant? That would be . . . my goodness, what a new . . . I had never even considered . . ."

The roshi closed his eyes, bowed his head, perhaps in tacit admission that the author had successfully navigated the labyrinth of his locution. They stood that way a moment longer, the conical black figure lost in thought, the other holding in one hand the robe, in the other the bookbag in which he carried the incomparable treasure, acquired at great personal risk, whose rightful owner must even then have been speeding her way to that desert basin not imagining that such a gift awaited her. In the distance, beyond and between the five thin, wind-carved monuments known to geologists as the Tombstones, dark smudges had appeared in the sky's lower quadrant, moving swiftly across the desert.

"In Mahayana school of Buddhism, it is said there are many who reach enlightenment and break cycle of rebirth, but some few who wait on the threshold to help others across," said the roshi. "It is said that this helper will not cross until all sentient beings have reached enlightenment. This one is called 'bodhisattva.'

"This person you call the Muse," he said. "Perhaps she is such a one."

"A *bodhisattva*."

The roshi looked at the author and then away. "Perhaps."

"Calliope?"

"For this she is returning, to bring others to place of *sunya*. The *bodhisattva* does not rest or desist. Not until the grass itself is enlightened."

The author did not point out how little grass was to be found on the desert floor, how much less would remain after the evening's inevitable "moshing." He shielded his eyes against the spectacular colors; the coat of oil that held the sand in place against the mercurial wind glared like a bore to the back of his retinas.

"I've heard the word, Roshi. *Bodhisattva*." The author took a notepad from his back pocket. "What is its literal translation?"

"Mr. Andrew, do you not listen to Roshi Bob?"

"Yes, yes, of course. Words cannot tell the whole story, et cetera, et cetera. But it is words I have to work with and I'd like to get them right. They are the indicators, the placeholders of Truth, and it is Truth I am hoping to assemble here. Think of it: Calliope's poetry—words; Brandt's lyrics, his note, all of the criticism and scholarship, her graffito . . . The eyes may deceive, Roshi," said the author, nodding toward the mandala, from which even now the monks were retreating, its form complete but undulating under a sheen of heat, "but words cannot. They are what they are. They *mean*. They are permanent."

"You are wrong, Mr. Andrew." The roshi's shadow was a long, thin wedge aimed at the heart of the dazzling mandala. "The Diamond Sutra tells us quite clearly: Words cannot express truth. And that which words express is not truth."

With that he turned and strode back toward the Jeff Buckley Vegan Village, leaving the author to contemplate the tableau, still motionless, of the Graveyard. Though they had immediately been torn away by wind, the roshi's words nevertheless lingered, given new resonance by the arrival of the helicopters, rotors beating a rhythm in the clear, hot sky, the author momentarily dazed, queasy, as though his eyes were perceiving more dimensions than usual, and each dimension was empty. He stood as the helicopters executed a tight sweep and settled upon the hardpan behind the trailers, small figures emerging from their bellies. The sun was unbearable. A small dust storm was brewing beyond the south gates. Bratworst had arrived.

When she returned to the University of San Francisco, in the early hours of April 24, 200_, Assistant Professor Taryn Glacé found her office on the third floor of Campion Hall locked, the door plastered with police tape, her nameplate missing from its frame. She sat in the hallway, nearly catatonic, until discovered at approximately 7:20 A.M. by a startled custodian. From the first, the university had been unsure whether to treat Glacé's disappearance as an abduction or a dereliction, and so had simply handed over her spring classes—a survey of Modernist poetry and a senior seminar entitled "Althusser and You: Examining Your Own Apparatus"—to adjuncts, leaving aside questions about her status until her hoped-for return. Her mailbox overflowed with messages regarding the Lone Mountain Marxists, a student organization she had revived after a twenty-year dormancy, requests for independent studies, and invitations to speak about her book, *Karl. Che. Kaliope.*, already a minor academic classic. Though undeniably the cause of administrative difficulty and campuswide consternation, Glacé's disappearance had nevertheless given rise to some measure of apprehensive pride: the English Department's junior professor swept up in a living experiment with profound—if still unclear—ramifications for contemporary poetry and culture studies; the university's glamorous *feminista* plastered across tabloids and post-office bulletin boards nationwide: an outlaw, a glittering refutation of criticisms about literature's irrelevance to life.

By eleven o'clock that morning, the bedraggled and semiaphasic professor was being interrogated by Carlton Lum of the FBI, who had flown up from San Diego and now sat across a table in the student center while Glacé shoveled handfuls of dry cereal into her mouth.* She remembered

---

*Although the Justice Department's internal investigation is ongoing, no one has ever answered the question of *where* the alleged "waterboarding" and intimidation by dogs took place, as dozens of witnesses have placed Glacé and Lum in the cafeteria.

nothing, she told him, as colored sugar fell from her pale lips to the bed-sheet which was her only raiment. She could give no concrete details regarding the Graveyard Riot or the fire at Powell's, no explanation of how the Muse had orchestrated these catastrophes nor where she had passed the time in between. Glacé had only vague sensations, recollections of a purely emotional nature, nothing of use to investigators. From a discreet distance, students and faculty gaped at the strange pair: the well-dressed agent and one of the nine most infamous women in America.

"Let's back up, ma'am," said a skeptical Lum, drumming fingers on the tabletop. "Can you tell me what day it is? Do you know how long you've been away?"

"Is . . . Christmas . . . over?" the professor whispered, as though each syllable cost her dearly, paid from a desperately dwindling account. "I remember . . . shopping . . . I deplore . . . exploitation of religion . . . for commercial purposes." She looked up for the first time. "The reinforcement of class divisions by deployment of . . . a sense of inadequacy: I feel shame because I can't buy a Lexus, and yet it is the fact that I can't buy a Lexus which makes me deserving . . . of this shame."

"Ms. Glacé," said Lum, taking off his jacket.

"*Dr.* Glacé."

He leaned back in the chair, shoulder holster on clear display. "You were photographed at the scene of several incidents of domestic terrorism. You say you don't know how long you've been gone, but admit to having spent that time in the company of the Poet Formerly Known as Calliope Bird Morath. I want you to think about what the penalties might be. Maybe that will stir up some information I'd find useful."

Glacé closed her eyes. "I have . . . no words."

Agent Lum picked his teeth with a business card. "Find them," he said.

She rested her hands in her lap, a brief flash of life in her dull eyes. "So . . . logocentric," she said. "So like a privileged Western male." Her blond hair, normally pulled back in a scalp-ripping bun, cascaded over bare shoulders in the manner of Greek sculpture. "There were never words. We did not speak. We were just . . . alive. Light and color, darkness, silence: This was our language. Heat. Awareness. Unity, participation . . . all subsumed into the Muse. A living poem.

"Words are . . . unrelated," she said. "Words are the opposite of poetry."

Lum stared over the rims of his sunglasses, then leaned back and sucked his teeth. Of course he was familiar with the Blindness Letter, with the apocalyptic origins of the New Poetry, but abstruse theory and aesthetic fashion were neither his strong point nor his immediate concern.

He tried another tack. "What is the meaning of the poem?" he asked, hoping to divine, and thus prevent, a future catastrophe. "What's the poem trying to say?"

At this, she broke into wheezes of laughter. Reaching across the table, she pressed her palm to the side of Lum's face, lips pursed in something like compassion.

"No comment."

In this she would be echoed by Cassandra Beers, discovered the following week shivering in a storeroom in Manhattan's famed bookstore, the Strand; by Tyra Banks, who regained consciousness in the shrubbery behind the Los Angeles home of actress Margot Kidder; and by the other members of the Muse, who turned up in equally unexpected locations around the country.* Each infuriated investigators by claiming to have no memory of the past several months—though when confronted by images of themselves in photos and videotape, they evinced little surprise, smiling as though carried away by sweet memories. Neither polygraph tests, nor home arrests, nor hypnosis would succeed in extracting from the women any concrete information about ♀; in the end, though clearly accessory to the terrible events, there was nothing to prove they had done anything other than stand and watch. No charges would be brought against them; all would return, at least superficially, mechanically, to normal life.

What statements they gave, rich in sensuality and impressionism, rife with synesthesia and metaphor, with references to a "language outside of language,"† would become a minor genre of their own, imitated in chapbooks and poetry slams, exhaustively studied in journals and dissertations

---

*With the exception of the unnamed, ninth woman, whose reappearance, if it happened, went unnoted; and Lubinski Management receptionist Leigh Mulgrew, still missing as of this writing.
†From Banks's monologue opening her talk show, *Tyra!*, on September 17, 200_.

and one incomprehensible item in *Playboy*.* Though still trafficking in the mundane medium of words, *"La parole féminine,"* as it was termed by French critic Hélène Cixous, delighted many in academia for the opportunity it seemed to afford to study the New Poetry, something previously thought impossible, for its confirmation that "there are other god(esse)s than Logos."† Graduate students and professors, authors and critics produced collaborative articles which sought not so much to analyze or criticize as to "riff off" or "mash up" the statements of the former members of the Muse, to expand the new body of work rather than classify it, with more than one English department thrown into disarray by the resulting disruption of traditional hierarchies. And it goes without saying that neither the original statements nor the body of work to which they gave rise provided the authorities with any information to bring them closer to their goal: Calliope.‡

To those who paid close attention, however, Dr. Glacé's return provided tremendous insight into the phenomenon of the Muse and the powerful, hidden structures and motivations that drove Calliope—in other words, into the very nature of the Death Artist. Take, for example, the following excerpt from a post to the Suicide Girls Web site by a user named "Doctor You See I":

> What was the center, the beating heart of us? We sensed it, knew it to be there, never looked directly at it. Dark star, dark star, something hot and hard, something lethal. Petals of a flower, ribbons on the maypole, we spun and spun, our consciousness the spokes leading, led, to the hub, our identity a moving ring of which we were each a part. Only in motion does I exist. To touch the center, to know

---

*The rumor that publisher Hugh Hefner offered the six known, surviving members of the Muse $2 million apiece to model for a special "Girls of the New Poetry" issue could not be confirmed by this author.

†Cixous, *"La Méduse ne rit plus,"* from *Continental Drift*, Winter 200_.

‡*La parole féminine* predictably inspired a backlash from the "word-based poetry community": "What are we to do with such babble and babytalk from women who insist that we take them seriously? This is merely another attempt to seduce and beguile the potent masculine poet, the master of the very words these women claim to despise—no different from other strategies of mystification and exoticization, a linguistic variation on the quote-unquote *lap dance*."—L. Moreno, *International Herald Tribune*, October 1, 200_.

it—O pleasure, O fate worse than death: *Je l'aime, la autre*. Of course it was her.

Readers will note the radical change in rhetoric from the militarism of *Karl. Ché. Kalliope*. Gone are the references to ideology and "poexploitation," the ruthless, if somewhat dry, logical proofs—what emerges instead is something that resembles Lacan's formulation of the "Real." Indeed, readers will recall the startling final passage of Žižek's *Looking Awry*, which reads, in retrospect, like the very blueprint of the Muse:

> [B]y "circulating around itself," as its own sun, this autonomous subject encounters in itself something "more than itself," a strange body in its very center[. . .] It is because of this Thing that at a certain point, love for the neighbor necessarily turns into destructive hatred, in accordance with the Lacanian motto *I love you, but there is in you something more than you*[. . .] *which is why I mutilate you*.*

Chilling.

And though Žižek is loath to name it, what else could this "Thing" be but the Truth?

In fact, this was an idea the author had been working on for some time, even prior to the premiere of *The Hanged Man* and the months of mayhem that followed: the idea that Truth is embodied in each of us—buried, as it were—but repeatedly papered over, palimpsested, packaged and padded and eventually obscured entirely. That beneath the illusory solidity of the self lies something more than self, more than sense and concept, desire and loss, something physically elusive, indescribable, and yet permanent, absolute. Something unspeakable. This Truth awaited only the devoted explorer, singleminded of purpose, to enact its excavation.

This faith, in any case, was what sustained him through that chaotic period—this, and the certainty that the present project might well serve not only as chronicle and document of the emergence of Truth, a latter-day gospel, if you will, but as its very vehicle. Though still not settled on a

---

*Slavoj Žižek, *Looking Awry: An Introduction to Lacan through Popular Culture* (MIT Press, 1992), p. 169. [Itals. in the original.]

title—having discarded *Because She Did Not Stop at Death* and *Once More to Bedlam* and currently working with the unsatisfying ♀: *A Life*—the author was nevertheless consumed with the composition, the Calliope Corner having long since overflowed into the living room, the kitchen, and the recently vacated third bedroom. Late winter evenings, twelve hours of writing behind him, a long night of half-sleep and poetry ahead, the author often wandered these rooms, dim repositories of art and memory, reviewing the day's work or planning the next day's literary adventures. Cold, damp air shuddered his windows, the leonine shiverings of San Diego's wet March; the only sounds were of the occasional passing car, the heart-stricken squeals of seagulls lamenting the sun's disappearance. As he stood watching a night sky sloppy with moonlit mother-of-pearl, the ocean not so much visible as undeniably present, a fundament whose dark gravity both anchored and gave rise to the world, the author could not fend off a feeling of imminence, the sense that something would soon happen. And yet a world beyond the last page, a world in which the biography did not consume him, was as yet inconceivable.

The issue of authorization was still pending, suspended in unbearable limbo due to Rhoda Lubinski's ill-timed decision to take, in the words of Denise Pling, a twenty-year-old communications major from UCLA left in charge of Lubinski Management, "a long, like, needed time away because of like how things can get sort of really stressful and all with former client types hanging around in the newspapers and really kind of immaturely getting revenge on people instead of just, you know, talking about their issues and like processing whatever's bothering her."

The author inquired as to the possibility of getting a message to Ms. Pling's employer regarding precisely that "client-type." "I assure you, she wants to hear what I have to say." He made reference to a recent conversation with a certain federal agent in which that agent had alluded to "some interesting turns" in the investigation.

"I'd totally like to help," said Ms. Pling, "but it's like, I can't even find her? To like, ask her about what to do about all these bills that are piling up? Maybe if she, you know, if you want to give me a number where—"

"Denise, you want to do a good job, do you not?" Denise indicated that she did. "Well," said the author, adopting the tone of parental empathy mixed with experience he had often found effective in dealing with the younger generation—"I'll let you in on a little secret you're probably too young to have discovered yourself. Are you ready? Sometimes we must break the rules. We must disobey. Not willy-nilly, not merely to gratify our own desires, confused as they still might be by the chemistry of adolescence—but enlisting all of our judgment, our understanding of the goals of the grown-up world, sometimes it is clear that only by operating outside normal procedures, by resorting to extraordinary means, can certain ends be achieved. In a sense, Denise, this discernment is precisely the definition of adulthood. *Comprendo?*"

The young receptionist considered this.

"Let's say the following," the author continued. "Let's say someone were to call the office with crucial information about one of Rhoda's clients. Let's say this information, gathered through his wide-ranging network of contacts, were not only of immediate interest—say, that client's whereabouts—but that, and this is all hypothetical, mind you, that coupled with the caller's acknowledged expertise in the matter would unravel some long-standing mysteries about the client regarding, for example, her father . . . or *fathers,* as the case may be. In other words, information the entire world wanted, and which the caller was offering to place within Rhoda's purview in exchange for something it was within her power to give and which—and here's the crucial part—which had *no intrinsic value to Rhoda herself, only to the caller.*

"Denise," he said, "wouldn't that be a situation in which your employer would want you to bend the rules?"

"Umm, I guess?"

"Good. Then here is what I propose."

Authorization thus squarely in his sights, the author embarked upon a frantic period of research, revision, and reorganization, suddenly overcome by the sheer volume of information—paper, photo, floppy disk, DVD—which cluttered his home, the maze of stacked books, piles of photocopies, which confronted him each time he left his desk, analog to the pandemonium of thought and analysis and theme that awaited whenever he closed his eyes. It would not do, this disorder, in the pit of his stomach rankled the hard certainty that only chaos could come of chaos, that from such squalor could never be born the clean, impervious form of Truth. For several days he did not leave the premises, caught up in a frenzy of rearranging, re-classifying, renovating; the living-room furniture, the kitchen stools, a knickknack shelf once filled with Jonestown paraphernalia, indeed all nonessential furnishings were moved to the garage, leaving only the desk and daybed in the office, the larger bed in the master suite. Cartons of books and board games, a small heap of musical equipment from the third bedroom's closet, were left on the sidewalk for passersby to pick over. The empty living room was then converted into what the author thought of as a "living archive," piles of various research materials organized by type and subtype—articles (newspaper, magazine, journal, tabloid), photos (press, publicity, private), poetry, supporting texts, music, video footage, etc.—arranged on the carpet in a design it would be impossible to describe here. Along the kitchen counter were placed, in sequence, clean copies of the thanatography's chapters thus far, title pages turned hopefully toward the ceiling. A complicated network of color-coded thread (and, in one case, dental floss) connected certain pages in these chapters to certain docu-ments or artifacts on the living-room floor, reminders of unresolved ques-tions, distant antecedents, issues requiring further research. The Calliope Corner itself was cleared out, steam-cleaned, and repainted; only the au-thor's computer and telephone remained atop the desk, next to a small framed photograph from an earlier time. Standing in the doorway at the end of this frantic period, the author could look out upon the living room and kitchen and the extensive, still-evolving fruit of his long labors, and for blissful moments feel he comprehended it in all its multifaceted, self-contradictory complexity, that he knew it intimately, its ins and outs and modulations—that he *got it*. Behind him was the stripped office, its bare-ness at last fit to serve as the receptacle, the point of arrival, the *manger*, if you will, for the Truth.

Nevertheless, he could not help but long for a time when, the work finished, even the last items could be discarded, could not help, sitting in the cool dark of the third bedroom's empty closet, but imagine the day those rooms would be emptied entirely.

From the refrigerator door, outside of the living archive he had cre-ated, the two articles he had received anonymously in the mail continued to taunt him. As certain as ever that they contained a vital message—not individually, neither story valuable in and of itself, but in the combination or sequence, the *syntax,* as it were—the author leaned against the counter and willed that message to make itself known. Brandt and Connor, Penny and Connor, the box set, *The Fisher King*—how to incorporate these stories into the system? What was the cipher, in what phrase or quotation, what offhanded comment, lay the Truth?

The passage of time, he thought, death and survival and the petty feuds with which we waste our days on Earth. A fifteen-year span endpointed by the two articles, a span beginning in conflict, ending in conflict—perhaps only amid conflict could art be made. Was this the message? But this was contradicted—or counterbalanced—by the photos, each radiating cama-raderie: Brandt and Connor, arm in arm; Penelope and Connor, older and sadder but still holding hands as Penny kissed the giant Buddha. It was the eyes of the Buddha that held the author now—their blank perfection, their eerie, unseeing permanence. What was it *he* was not seeing?

Scripps Memorial Hospital sits on a high bluff to the east of downtown La Jolla and the I-5 freeway. From the fifth-floor Psychiatric Trauma Unit, pa-tients can gaze out over the Torrey Pines State Reserve to the north, and the long arc of well-maintained beaches that make up the San Diego coast-line, sweeping languorously toward the North County and distant Los Angeles. The ocean—from that distance an undulating expanse of sun-spangles and harmless whitecaps—provides the manic, the schizophrenic, the lobotomized, and the demented with a peaceful panorama upon which to gaze, calming their inner beasts as it has done since time immemorial.

It took some time to convince the charge nurse to permit the author a visit. Though she was admirably protective of her patient, Beulah Marie St. Jean's pugnacity softened when the author explained that he was, in fact, the family's authorized biographer, granted unlimited access to all members, and would happily have Rhoda Lubinski confirm such if St. Jean wished to interrupt her Canyon Ranch Reinvigoration Weekend with a phone call. The promise of a signed first-edition copy of the forthcoming thanatography overcame the nurse's remaining reservations.

"You just can't imagine all them reporters and lawyers and poets, them ratty kids and such, comin' in here and upsettin' my girl day in day out, not to mention them Jesus people always comin' to pray,"* said St. Jean, a heavyset though not-unattractive black woman whose accent, when the author inquired, turned out to be Martiniquais. "No, sir, and every time someone's botherin' her, her vitals just goin' *right* on up through the roof, and pretty soon she be starin' at the mirror again, droolin' and repeatin' them three words over and over, and next thing she be back on the Haldol."

She paused at the door of room 516-D. "Some people take things from the room," she said quietly. "Little things, like a barrette or some letters. After the photo of her daughter disappeared, she be weepin' two whole days and her GI tube backin' up . . . You're not lookin' to take anything from my girl?"

The author rested a hand on Beulah's shoulder. "On the contrary," he said. The nurse stared hard into his eyes and, finding reassurance, walked off.

The author must admit that he was not fully prepared for what he found in room 516-D. The lioness, the savage flaring heart of punk rock, the founder and shattered soul of Fuck Finn—Penelope Morath, née Klein, aka Penny Power, lay curled on a blanketless hospital bed in a white gown printed with blue cornflowers, amid a squid's embrace of tubes and wires. The distant beeping of a heart monitor was the only sound, the barely perceptible rise of her chest the only movement. Late-afternoon sun sheeted through the windows, lending her fetal form an almost angelic glow; her cheek was pressed to the mattress, her eyes open and fixed in such a way that she seemed to be watching the author from the moment he opened the door, as though she had, in fact, been awaiting his visit.

He pulled a chair to the side of her bed, ignoring the reek of bleach that pervaded the room. In her frozen features, the graying but well-brushed mass of her long hair, it was still possible to discern her fearsome beauty, still possible to imagine the face of lovely devastation the author had seen on a terrible April morning almost two decades earlier.

---

*Referring to the representatives of Southwesterners United in Christ, who in the early months of 200_ regularly demonstrated in support of the proposed "Penny's Law," which sought to prevent hospitals from removing feeding tubes from vegetative patients if the patients were females of childbearing age.

"Hello, Penelope." He found his throat dry. "I've come—I'm here to—" He stammered, cleared his throat, glanced at the monitors and the table crowded with potted violets, a jet trail written high across the sky though no jet was visible. "I suppose I wanted to talk to you," he said to the unblinking form. "Silly of me, isn't it?"

Of course there was no answer. He stared at her, wondered if she was aware of his stare. Her career had owed so much to the gaze of her fans, to the ocular strafings of publicity; through it all she had stood defiant and powerful as a Hindu avatar, bolts of emotion radiating from her form as though to meet and repel those anonymous stares. Now she was shrunken and vulnerable as a child's doll, a faint white crust outlining her mouth.

"I suppose I thought," he said, confused by the huskiness in his voice, "I wondered . . . I suppose I had the idea that you might speak to me. I had the idea that there might be something you . . . that you were waiting . . ." He stood then, eyes on the horizon, the ocean. "For someone who could understand."

As he crossed to the window, hands clasped behind his back, Penelope did not stir. The beeping of the monitor did not change tempo.

"I've tried very hard. This . . . well, the book, it's meant as . . . I think you would appreciate it. You'd find it interesting. It's . . . yes, I know, why after all this time would you want more to be written, more to be said? But it's not like all the rest of the claptrap, really." The author touched his fingertips to the glass, still aware of the lifeless figure behind him the way one is aware of a bandaged wound to one's body. "It's a tribute, really. That's what I want, is to do honor. Do you under—"

He stopped, shook his head at his folly. Turning to her, he was mortified to discover the back of her hospital gown untied, the pale, atrophied flesh of her backside peering at him in the bright quarters. He hurried back to the chair.

"There are things . . . you don't know how hard I've tried—to put it all together, to work it through, and yet there are things I can't possibly . . . that perhaps I'll never . . ." He heard a footstep in the hall: Nurse St. Jean patrolling. Short of breath, he reached between two plastic tubes and took Penelope's hand—surprisingly warm, surprisingly vital—to find that his own was shaking. "I want to do this correctly, you see, to do it in such a way that it would please you, that you would . . . approve. Can you help me to understand? I'm on my own, working without a net, as it were—how can you expect . . ."

He squeezed the hand, concentrated on the feel of her skin—and was there, even imperceptibly, a return squeeze? "If you would only . . . instead of withdrawal, instead of silence, if you only trusted me, allowed me to understand, to feel—"

Again the heavy tread outside: listening, satisfying herself that nothing was amiss.

"No one can know, experience—from the *outside,* how can I . . . without your telling me, for heaven's sake? I cannot feel it as you are feeling it, it's beyond my . . . beyond anyone's . . . Don't you understand this?" He was whispering, leaning close to that stricken face. "But I am here. I am trying. I want to know, to feel it myself. Isn't that enough? Don't I deserve some—"

He heard the door open behind him. "It's cruelty. Who has the power to see through another's eyes, to really feel what they feel? No one!" There was a hand on his shoulder; he felt its warmth even as he understood its demand. "You can't believe it's so easy, that one can . . . just by wishing it . . . why can't you just . . ."

He closed her hand between his two, touched his forehead to his thumbs. "Please." The hand on his shoulder tightened. "Just one word." But there was—could be—no response.

It was a largely unsuccessful visit. On the drive home, slowed by a wrong turn through one of the city's least-welcoming neighborhoods, a stop at a convenience store, and a cigarette enjoyed at length in the parking lot, the author's thoughts were as distant and curious to him as small, silvery fish darting in an aquarium. All he knew for sure, all he could name, was the pressure—building somewhere not quite inside him, nor outside him, as though the world itself were struggling to break its form, to give birth to something of a shape not yet foreseen, nor foreseeable.

In the house, he once again took up his post before the refrigerator, staring at the articles, willing himself inside the language, resisting the urge to shred them between his fingers for their intransigence. How long he stood there, the incoherent hash of his work behind him, the maddening puzzle before, is unknown. Toward midnight, the telephone rang, echoing shrilly through an empty house; the author could not bring himself to answer, wondered, in fact, whether anything that could be communicated would yield even the most minuscule relic of the Truth.

"Dad, are you home?" said a voice when the answering machine engaged. "Dad? Where are you?" The voice waited, behind it a jumble of music, high laughter, what sounded like a blender. "I don't even know why I'm calling," the voice whispered. "Why I bother. You probably won't even get this. You're probably standing there, screening . . . Whatever. I don't care. I don't care if you're there but I just—" Someone called out from the background, and the voice, muffled, shouted something in return. "The concert's tomorrow, Dad. I just thought I'd remind you. It's gonna be huge. You've still got those passes, unless you lost them. It's not like I even care if you come, I just didn't—I thought maybe you'd forget and then . . . well, whatever. So I'm reminding you and so at least you can't say you forgot. Do whatever you want to do.

"*Dad?*" The voice took on a quieter aspect. "Whatever. I don't know what I'm saying." A sniff, a guttural noise. "Don't you even care about me anymore? Don't you give a shit? I even called that fucking fat-ass at school, and he said you're trying to find a replacement, like you're looking for something to replace her. That's not true, is it? I mean . . . you know you . . ." He trailed off. The answering machine broadcast static. Then: "Fuck this. Just . . . fuck. You do what you have to do, Dad. You know what? Don't even come to the show. I don't want you there. Good-bye."

The machine disengaged; the house returned to silence. Shadows slid across the living-room walls, projected by a car passing on the street—the patterns different now, the shapes of darkness unfamiliar, though the author had lived there nearly twenty years. He found his hands were gripping the kitchen counter, his fingertips numb. The articles mocked him from the refrigerator, but he could no longer read the words, nor distinguish one gray line from the next, only stare at the two pictures, linked by their similarity, by their setting, only separated by time: Brandt and Penelope, the impervious Buddha.

Trying to replace her. The phrase reverberated in his mind, growing louder until it pushed out all other sensations. He found that he had not drawn breath for many long seconds. He took the photos down, examined them again, a soft explosion detonating in the pit of his throat. His fingertips burned; his toes tingled. He may have let out a cry, it may have rung against the walls, carried through the empty rooms—but the author did not hear it, for he was already rummaging through boxes in the garage, already filling a duffel with a spade and a small shovel, an empty tin box, a hunting knife in a leather sheath, already struggling out of his slacks and into black jeans, pulling a dark sweater over his head. There was no time, not one single second, to lose. The sky was inscrutable, a spiteful new moon withholding light from the world, as the author pulled the car into the street once again and set out, obeying local speed limits, for Malibu.

"I'm very sorry to hear that."

"Yes, well. All good things, and so forth."

"It seems to me we were beginning to make progress. These last few sessions—"

"Let's not make a scene about it. Just a handshake, my sincere thanks. I hope you won't take it personally."

"Why would I take it personally?"

"Well, no. You wouldn't."

"Did you want to finish out the hour? You've paid for it, after all. Why don't you sit down."

"I really must . . ."

"Andrew. Sit down. Do you mind if I dim the lights? My eyes, you know, they've grown a bit sensitive. Is that all right?"

"Windows of the soul."

"Pardon?"

"No. Nothing."

"Well. You seem distracted today. Out of sorts."

"I'm fine, thank you. Perhaps a bit distracted."

"How is everything? Feel free to lie down, stretch out . . ."

"Everything is fine. Status quo."

"Good."

"Every day is much as the last. Writing, researching, striving for understanding. The human condition, is it not?"

"The biography is coming—"

"And yet the intensity of it—quite exhausting, really. I can hardly convey it, this . . . momentum, like a hand in the small of your back. The urgency, as though there were some imminent deadline, as though time were running out."

"Do you feel your time is running out?"

"It's visceral. Literally physical. Exhilarating. Draining. You hardly sleep, meals are a nuisance, when you do drift off you wake with sore muscles, as though you'd gone ten rounds with a heavyweight. I suppose this is what they call inspiration."

"They have other names for it—"

"And yet it comes around again and again to a few insoluble questions, a few Gordian knots. At times it feels as though the Truth were mocking you: Knowing itself, it nevertheless does not want to be known. As though you'd been exiled from it, forbidden entrance without speaking some shibboleth—"

"A few weeks ago we were speaking of empathy."

"The temptation to simply dispense with it. The voice which says all narratives are incomplete, self-contradictory. Urges a more casual approach to the Truth—as though it were something that could be approximated! The perfect is the enemy of the good, it says, seducing you. Why sweat the small facts, the absolute understanding—there is the 'emotional truth,' the language of the heart and so forth . . ."

"You said empathy had 'desired results.' Would you like to talk about that some more? While we have a little time?"

"What?"

"You mentioned empathy as, how did you say it, the concept of empathy as central to your interactions with the world."

"Is that not true of everyone?"

"Is it?"

"Doctor, let me ask you something. It may be beyond your ken, but I've been wondering about this question of Truth, of language, the relationship between the two—"

"Do you believe empathy is as important to others as it is to you, Andrew?"

"—perhaps this is a question for the philosophers, but psychoanalysts must have thoughts on the matter: What makes us real?"

"Andrew."

"If we are constituted by language, defined by the symbolic order as you've said, if our selves are entirely dependent upon that order—if we are mutable 'subject positions' rather than true selves, then how are we to, how can I . . ."

"Andrew."

"If we cannot even locate ourselves then how can we locate another, how can we possibly hope to know anything . . ."

"Andrew."

"What? What, Doctor?"

"What about empathy?"

"I am talking about empathy! I am trying to understand its nature, its mechanism. I am trying to understand what happens when one human being looks at another, examines another, tries to see into their . . . reality, if the term has any meaning. I am trying to understand what makes us human, and what if anything keeps us from living our allotted time in isolation, separate from all others, even those who might in some way be feeling the same . . . with the same . . ."

"Go on. Andrew? I apologize for interrupting. Go on, please."

"This is important, Doctor. It is absolutely crucial to the work. And, I might add, it seems central to any responsible psychology."

"Please continue."

"Really, I would think you, of all—"

"Yes, I understand. Please go on."

"I'm thinking of our discussion, some time ago, about the birthmark."

"The birth—"

"The 'bloodstain,' as she called it, but which now comes into question, dependent as it is on her account of that morning. Or not dependent, but . . . well, anyway, you said it was a 'guarantee,' that it linked the . . . I can't recall how you put it, but that it somehow built a bridge between the symbolic and the real."

"In a manner of speaking."

"That without it, the symbolic was a mere word game, one thing standing for another, referring to another, *symbolizing*, as it were. Everything has a metonym, everything has multiple meanings, people say one thing and mean another, or mean one thing but someone *hears* another. How do we know any communication is successful? If I say, 'It's a lovely day outside,' how can I ever be sure that you hear precisely that and not the equivalent of, say, 'The world is flat,' or 'You are ruining my life,' or something completely nonsensical?"

"Yes, Lacan—"

"And even if you hear 'It's a nice day,' how to be sure you grasp whatever undertones, overtones, I might intend, whatever irony or reference to a previous conversation or even . . . meanings I don't, myself, know I intend, unconscious . . . and then the wild card of memory, recovered or otherwise—"

"It's the central question of linguistics, Andrew. What I would rather focus on is precisely your own understanding of—"

"Except for the bloodstain. The guarantee. You said it yourself: an excess. Something outside language. Real. To stop all the movement. A destination. Irreducible. Isn't this the very definition of Truth? But what if the Truth is false?"

"You've lost me, I'm afraid."

"It isn't real, the guarantee. It was never . . . you said it was a recovered memory, so how can we, or she for that matter—what I'm saying is it turns out that even the guarantee needs a guarantee! Right? Even the guaran— It's a house of mirrors, Doctor, an infinite regress, and now it's gone . . ."

"Slow down, Andrew. Wait just a moment—"

"It's gone!" The author stood up from the divan, sat down again, aware of the pale form above growing closer, receding. "Fraudulent to begin with, now the bloodstain, too, is gone. *There is no guarantee.*"

"Now, wait. Let's . . . I think perhaps you have a somewhat different—"

"I have to leave, Doctor. I have an appointment to keep."

"Let's try it this way: What does the word mean to you? 'Guarantee.'"

"Does it matter? How do you know I'm even hearing the same word?

Perhaps you say 'guarantee' and what I hear, in my mind, means 'artichoke.'"

"Does it?"

"There's no communication possible without the real. Isn't that what you said? So what are we doing right now?"

"We are communicating anyway."

He lay back rigid on the settee, arms crossed over his chest. "But that's so . . . pathetic."

"Lacan might say that pathos is a lack. The origin of desire."

"It's chaos. Nothing can mean anything. What is needed is a *new guarantee.*"

"You insist on turning abstraction into concrete object, on reifying what is meant to remain rhetorical. I think this is something peculiar to men, always needing to touch—"

"That's what she's looking for! *Truth*—she has announced it to all the world. It's not a war cry—it's a plea, a prayer! She's *looking* for the Truth, for a new guarantee."

"And of course this is why you want to discontinue our meetings, to find something that cannot be found, to gallop toward some theoretical glory . . ."

"She will stop at nothing to find it. She will let nothing stand in her—"

"Andrew, this idea of the truth—"

"What could it *be*, Doctor? What can take the place—"

"The guarantee is not something that can be given, not something that can be found. It is a byproduct of the Big Other; it has no fixed meaning. It is *meaningless,* the precise opposite of—"

"And who can provide it? Who can deliver the Truth?"

"No one! This is what you must see. No one can 'deliver' it."

"This, perhaps, is where we must part company. I cannot subscribe to the proposition that Truth is inaccessible or arbitrary. I cannot give in to nihilism."

"You're misinter—"

"Perhaps we cannot speak the Truth, Doctor. Or at least not with absolute certainty. But if not . . . if not, then it must be the case that *the Truth speaks through us.*"

At last she put down the notepad.

"That we are messengers. Conduits. Servants of the Truth."

"Go on."

"The Truth chooses us, speaks through us. Uses us to its own purpose."

"Do you feel you are, have been . . . chosen in this way? Andrew?"

The author felt a strange ease, a dissolution, as though the pressure that had been his very ether had ceased. Like a water droplet relieved of its surface tension, it seemed now, in that spectral chamber, as though the boundaries of his body had given way. He floated in the space between divan and mirror, looking now at the image above, now at the form below, and somewhere in his disembodied heart he felt dread.

"Andrew, you said before that time was running out. Could you say more about that?"

"It's . . . I . . ."

"Are you all right? You look pale."

"Yes, how else can I . . . what else is there to . . ."

"When you said time was running out, were you referring to the biography, or to personal matters? You haven't mentioned your son today—is he—"

"What's the use? I don't . . . all day long I . . . No, it's . . ."

"Yes? Please go on."

"All day. I do nothing but prostrate myself to her. I worship at her altar, pay tribute . . . For hours, day upon thankless day I chip away at it, I slice and grind, push and wheedle, lurch and leap and bang—yes, bang my head against the high adamantine wall of her character, but this . . . this . . ."

"Yes? This what?"

"This *bitch* won't let me in! I feel her—do you understand? I feel her. Through the door I . . . and she won't . . ."

"How does it feel to say—"

"As though she has locked herself in there for spite, locked herself in with her misery and her fear—and for all the world I want to understand it, to *empathize*—and this is precisely what frightens her, what she doesn't want: to be known. To be understood. As though she found herself, her reality, too ugly, too terrible to share with another and so has determined not to share it no matter how sincere, no matter how strenuous his efforts to help shoulder . . . What terrible . . . Doctor? I can see her in there . . ."

"Would you like to take a moment? Can I have Jerome bring you some water?"

"No . . . That won't . . . I have to be going."

"What are you feeling right now?"

"Alone."

"And?"

"It's out of spite. Huddling amid her unhappiness, not allowing . . . and then blaming me, *me* whom she has locked out, blaming me for not finding a way inside."

"You feel she is blaming you?"

"'You don't get it.' As though she has . . . as though I had any opportunity to *get it*. As though she'd extended even a rudimentary . . ."

"Who? Who accuses you of not getting it?"

"Sneering at me. Mocking. No matter how I try to enter that space, to be at her side, to absorb even the tiniest . . . and what *difference* if I don't get it? What fucking *difference,* if I'm willing to bear it nonetheless? Why this insistence on anatomizing it, classifying it, labeling its constituent elements? This is not a science class, goddammit, it's not a dissertation, it's someone's *life!*"

"Whose life? You must give this anger a name."

"And here I am, kneeling outside the door, expending every last . . . and nothing. Nothing at all. And in the end she . . . I can feel it, she'll be gone and I won't . . . I'll know nothing. Time is running out and I don't . . ."

"Why is time running out? What do you think will happen? Andrew? This is crucial, this phantasm or nameless fear. This, too, is a symptom, a signifier. Remember? You must try to name it."

"I don't know." He opened his eyes, found the image of himself: hovering, suspended precariously in midair but ill-defined, shapeless, a mere distortion in the fabric of space, impermanent.

"I don't know," he repeated. He sat up. On the table the face of her antique clock glowed, minute hand ascending in its unswervable arc. "I have to go."

He turned to her then, the small woman in the armchair. He both recognized and did not recognize her. What would it mean, in either case?

"There are still a few minutes," she said, resting a hand atop the clock. He could hear it ticking. Her thin lips were set in an expression that seemed like disappointment, disapproval. "In fact, I don't have anyone coming, if you'd like to keep—"

"I don't think so." He stared down into the lights set into the floor. "Perhaps . . ."

"Yes? Yes? Perhaps?"

"Perhaps you're right. Perhaps she . . ."

"Andrew," she said, "please tell me." He could sense her leaning toward him, extending an arm that was much too short to bridge the distance.

"I don't get it," he said. She froze. The room was still but for whispers of air. "I don't get it, Doctor," said the author, lost in the hot lights. "I just don't . . . get it."

In his influential review dated March 22, 200_, Marky "Mark" Lipschitz declared Bratworst heirs not only to the throne vacated, seventeen years earlier, by Brandt Morath and Terrible Children, but to the entire kingdom of rock music and, by extension, of art itself. More coronation than reasoned analysis, Lipschitz goes on to discuss their EP, *The Hung Man* (Nihon4EVR, 200_)—a note-for-note remake of Terrible Children's first record: every howl of feedback, every snapped string and cymbal flourish and break in the singer's voice faithful to the original, the production values indistinguishable despite changes in recording technology—as well as their Japanese concert tour, whose U.S. leg had just been announced, in which each date was likewise a precise reproduction of a classic Terrible Children concert.

You don't know what to expect. You've heard these guys are good. Real good. You've heard it's just like being at a Kids show, that Drew is a dead ringer, a second coming. You don't know if you want that to be true because what would it mean if it were? How would you react? [. . .] But then the music starts and you don't think about that anymore. You just listen, feel it, surrender. You never thought anything could be as good as "Dirtnap," but Bratworst's version is different, more subtle somehow, even though its exactly the same [sic]. It's more ambiguous, open ended, infinitely richer. You don't know what to make of that.*

Even leaving aside the inexcusably poor writing, it was immediately apparent to most readers that Lipschitz's story—indeed, the entire issue—was more than just puerile hero worship, was in fact a cog in the vast publicity machine that had been ramped up to promote the band and jump-start the music industry's flagging sales. And what are we to make of the claim that the meaning of certain lyrics—though not the words—had changed with time, that intervening events had altered the very nature of the language, a development Lipschitz labels, rather pretentiously, "exegetic mutation"?†

Nevertheless, by April 1, Lipschitz's article was a mere flagship in the armada of adoration Bratworst had garnered in the national press, the wave of critical admiration that began in Ocean Beach swelling to a riptide, gaining force and depth as it traveled, churning filthy, oil-slicked waters and breaking finally as a tsunami over unsuspecting shores—this phenomenon, too, harkening back to an earlier time, as though the flow of history were a series of fractal images reproducing themselves endlessly, only the minuscule variations of chaos to distinguish one instantiation from another. SLAM's glib, charming editor was vaulted into prominence, with appearances on MTV and The Daily Show, job offers from European papers; his words were immortalized on Bratworst T-shirts, posters, concert tickets, and CD packaging, all of which proudly quoted the last line of his review, which declared the new group to be "more real than the original."

---

*"Letter from the Editor," from SLAM, March 22, 200_, an issue devoted entirely to Bratworst.
†Ibid. Take for example his analysis of "Kill the Surfers" and its crucial lyric, "Going out with the tide, absolution is mine." I defy the reader to identify a single word whose meaning has changed. A tide is still a tide, absolution still murderously hard to come by. To accept Lipschitz's claim that "the sense of the words changes faster than we can read them" would make his article—and all texts—unreadable.

It was thus against two backdrops—the band's meteoric rise and the ongoing panic provoked by the Muse—that the Graveyard Gala, originally conceived as a springtime showcase for a handful of Southern California bands, mushroomed into a major event with substantial corporate sponsorship from Seattle-based VerSI-FI and international press coverage, with bands from all points on the spectrum of success clamoring for a slot on the bill and cable networks conducting a fierce bidding war for the rights to simulcast the show. As attendance estimates grew, so, too, did concerns about public safety; California governor Gavin Newsom issued a statement on March 28 asking the organizers to postpone, and for a few tense days it appeared that the Department of Homeland Security might cancel the concert entirely, concerned with both inadequate policing and the venue's proximity to the Mexican border. The gala seemed thus to be in jeopardy, until lobbyists for the Kumeyaay Nation—on whose land the Graveyard sat and who stood to make an estimated $20 million from the event—managed to smooth bureaucratic opposition and save the day.* Despite lack of sufficient infrastructure, despite the overcrowding that all but shut down nearby Inyokern and Borrego Valley regional airfields and created five- to six-hour delays on Highway 86, despite a short-lived "sit-in" held by Earth First!, the show went on—transformed from entertainment into extravaganza, from showcase into spectacle and, finally, disaster.

Although her name did not appear on the bill, no one holding a coveted ticket could claim not to have thought of the Muse—and yet no one could say when or how she would arrive, what new expression of wrath she might yet devise.† By the morning of April 1, then, what drew the thousands stuck in traffic, suspended in landing patterns, lined up at the gates, or waking up on the hard ground of the twenty-eight-acre Michael Hutchence Campground, could no longer be properly considered

---

*Cf. *United States v. Janacek* for a detailed account of the lavish Acapulco vacation the Kumeyaays provided for U.S. Representative Cheri Janacek, allegedly in return for her support.

†That the Muse's appearance was not only expected by the organizers but actually *desired* was obvious from the print ad, which played off the well-known optical illusion in which a woman sitting at a dressing table morphs, depending on one's focus, into a skull—the ad appeared to depict a stage with a rock band, but when viewed differently changed to the bald, expressionless visage of ♀.

a musical event or even, in the words of Governor Newsom, "an orgy of irresponsibility and debauchery": It was a deathwatch.

For the author, however, it was a matter of scholarship, of dedication to the thanatography—*My Shroud, These Words: The Lives of Calliope Bird Morath*—and of allegiance to a Truth that had not yet been fully excavated. Like the fossilized skeleton of some prehistoric behemoth, he had unearthed some of its salient features—a mandible here, a metatarsal there— brought out enough to discern its overall shape, its structure. And yet he could not quite see it, could not bring the entirety of its purpose into his range of vision. Standing knee-deep in the dusty trench of his devotion, scorched by the impassive sun, he was as yet unsatisfied. What he needed was to get above it, to soar high enough that it might shrink to manageable proportions. What he needed was to fly.

"What the fuck do you think you're doing?" The voice—shrill and yet husky, almost comically inflected—interrupted the author's thoughts as he sat in a holding area just below, and to one side of, the stage. Perched atop a speaker cabinet, leaning his head against a steel wall which thrummed with the concert's submarine emanations, he held his eyes shut another second, breathing to himself an imprecation for strength and serenity.

"I've been looking all over for you," came the voice, now directly before him. "Who the fuck do you think you are, beating up on my employees, leaving messages on my home phone which I don't even know how the fuck you got a hold of that—and was that you who called my *sister* last week? I oughtta kick you in the balls right now, mister. You think you're gonna get authorization out of this deal? You'll be lucky if you don't get a fucking restraining order."

Now he opened his eyes, tightening his grip on the bookbag at his side; his gaze first ranged out over the complex anatomy of the giant edifice, the beams and struts and ramps and risers, the thick bundles of wire and cable that ran like a muscular, varicolored root system along the armature of steel that surrounded them. Beyond this man-made labyrinth, beyond the trailer village and its bustle, stretched the dusking desert, its mauve emanations and pockets of shadow, the five foreboding sentinels in the distance and the vivid, startling sunset: pink and orange and pale blue and violet stretched across the firmament, twisted into arcane forms like a divine calligraphy of flame, its letters imprecise, smeared over as by a hand dissatisfied with what it had written.

"Hey, asshole! I'm talking to you," came the voice, and the author looked down to find its source: Rhoda Lubinski. Though he had seen hundreds of photos of the vivacious young publicist, though they had crossed paths once or twice, he had never before been so close to her. Of course he recognized her fashionable helmet of platinum-blond hair, her elfin features. But as he clambered down off the speaker, pulling the bookbag onto one shoulder, what struck him was her aura of glamour and raw sexuality. Dressed in white slacks and a light blue shirt, tails tied coquettishly at her navel, Rhoda looked every inch the playful seductress—except for her brown eyes, slightly and endearingly crossed, which all but lacerated the author with their intelligence and command.

"Let me tell you something," she said, pointing a dangerous index finger. "This isn't how we do things. This isn't the bush leagues, pal, and if—"

"I'm sorry."

"—about to turn over the keys to the kingdom to some phone-happy douchebag, you've got a . . . What did you say?"

"I apologize, Rhoda. I've been out of line."

She crossed her arms and considered this, the tip of her tongue moving visibly inside one cheek. Around them eddied a sea of personnel—cameramen and reporters, BlackBerry-punching scribes, roadies and soundtechs and moon-eyed girls in tank tops and cutoff shorts, the motley entourages of the day's many performers. This current rushed up the metal ramps and stairs that led from the trailers, surged into the staging area, and churned for long enough for the pressure to build and spit them farther up toward the stage wings. Rumbles and blasts of music, filtered and distorted by the giant structure, mingled with the muffled shrieks of the crowd's adulation, such that the author had the sense of being in the hold of a great ship as it tossed in the fury of an ocean tempest.

"Well." Rhoda cocked a hip. "Good, then. What's this crap about the FBI?"

The author peered up the ramp. The music was reaching a crescendo, the final number to be played by Glad Hand, a ska-dancehall outfit he vaguely remembered from his SLAM days, the latest atrocity in the string of atrocities that had passed for opening acts. The day's heat had depleted like air from a balloon; in the growing chill the Graveyard pulsed with frantic energy, all ambient heat now of human origin.

"It doesn't matter," he said.

"Doesn't matter?" The diminutive publicist stepped close to the author, jutting her chin toward his face. "You harass me for months, drag me out here to this fucking *frat party* . . . and now you say it doesn't matter? Do you think I'm just going to *give* you the authorization?"

"It doesn't matter anymore." He waved a hand, trying to step back only to find the speaker cabinet in his path. She came forward, her impressive bosom almost touching his abdomen. "Authorization or no, it's immaterial. It's nearly over. This whole thing, it's almost—" The crowd erupted, ringing and resounding through the structure, followed by a reflux of humanity coming down the ramp: The sweat-soaked members of Glad Hand, wearing only loincloths and foam rooster-combs on their heads, raced past, trailed by a mad gaggle of handlers, fans, security personnel, and hangers-on.

"There's a difference between authorization and authority," he said quietly, pinned by the rush of the crowd between speaker and publicist, the bookbag crushed uncomfortably to his side.

"Yeah," she quipped. "Authority doesn't sell books. Authority's cheap."

"*Au contraire,*" he said. "It has no price. It cannot be purchased at all."

Another bolus of legs and shoulders squeezed her closer. "Look, you wanna stand here and talk metaphysics, or you wanna get down to business?" she said, her lips close to his Adam's apple. "You said you have information. I'm all ears."

He did not answer, watching the dregs of band and crew disappear down the ramp, a dark puddle spreading on the desert floor, flowing back toward whatever wanton depravity awaited in the trailer village. What if the original *could* be improved upon? he thought. What if Mark Lipschitz were right, and with the proper application of love and loyalty we could change that which has already gone by, that which has been written in the stone of history? If emptiness were only the sign of possibility, then might not absence be read as the precursor to presence, impermanence as a kind of transcendence?

He touched his nose to the crown of Rhoda's head as the noise and chaos subsided. "Aren't you frightened?" he said.

"Of you?" She shoved him playfully against the speaker, stepped back to tighten the knot in her shirttails.

"Of her."

Rhoda shook her head. She turned to watch the last roseate feathers vanish from the sky. "I'm tired," she sighed. Five dark fingers of stone stood out against a blue night that was almost fluorescent. A muffled voice made announcements, to the roar of thousands. "What's she gonna do? She's already taken my whole life. She's already ruined me."

"Ruined?"

She leaned against the speaker with an expression of great fatigue. "What's left for me? I made her, and she turned around and made me. Scambiguity—once you start, there's no end."

"Surely you could pursue other . . . your dreams, there must be—" He broke off, troubled by her downcast gaze. He lifted a finger beneath her chin until her eyes met his.

"You know what I dream about?" she said. "Clay. I dream of living in some cabin in the woods making pots and vases. Bird feeders. Selling them in some farmers market. Having lots of cats. Walking around with dried clay under my fingernails, caked to my eyelashes." She laughed, turned her face away. "But no one would believe it. They'd take it as some kind of ironic statement. I'd probably make a fucking killing off those pots."

"I would buy one," said the author.

Rhoda peered at him; in her off-kilter gaze lurked a tentative smile. She fiddled again with the shirttails and glanced up the ramp to the stage. There was nothing left, no other performers but Bratworst; the anticipation was a stiff and powerful wave through air and sand and metal. It tingled when the author touched the speaker, settled in the pit of his stomach like a thorn.

"So, no, I'm not afraid of her," said Rhoda. "This new thing, it's got nothing to do with me. It's outside my area of expertise." She turned back to the author and shrugged. "It's too real."

The author shifted the weight of the bookbag. "Not yet," he said.

That Bratworst's set would begin several hours late was preordained, understood by all present to be a necessary part of the performance itself. A facsimile of Terrible Children's last concert—their triumphant return to the Casbah after the 199_ World Tour—the 97,330* visitors to the Graveyard knew precisely what to expect, knew in advance the set list, the musicians' clothing, the timing of the lead singer's stage dives, of botched solos and broken strings. The band knew down to the second how long to wait between each song, which numbers to perform energetically and which to flub, how to best play, as it were, the instrument of the audience's desire. As many critics have noted, this mutual knowledge was the crucial component of Bratworst's appeal, a collaboration between performer and audience that changed the performance at a fundamental level, altered the very nature of the phenomenon to which each was an indispensable party. One might charitably assume it was to this that Buzz Matapan, the group's drummer, referred when he enthused to MSNBC's Rita Cosby, "We wouldn't be anything without our fans, man. It's like, we don't even exist without them. But the fans love us, so we get to be who we are. And we get crazy play from the ladies—it's all good!"

Unlike the legendary "Kids in the Kasbah" concert, however, this show had begun almost nine hours earlier, under the bright brutality of the Mojave's afternoon sun. The Graveyard's three gates at last open, the slow trickle as the lucky thousands made their way through metal detectors and retina scanners, pat-downs and bag checks, and flowed out over the cracked landscape, merging with streams of prescreened overnighters from the Michael Hutchence Campground and the Richie Valens RV Park, covering the venue's acreage with the kinetic and irregular motions—sprints, leaps, jostles—of human excitement, converging and fragmenting and coming together again like the digestive convulsions of the intestinal tract, finally bunching in quivering restraint along the perimeter of the Yamantaka Mandala. All was curiously silent, the air still but for the occasional lonely gust of desert wind, the growl and release of the first skateboarders to try

---

*The figure is according to the Riverside County Sheriff's Department, adjusted for the 116 arrests made before Bratworst's set and the 380 victims of sunstroke, dehydration, minor injuries, and methamphetamine overdose transported from the site earlier in the day.

out the half-pipe, lilts of hymn wafting from the makeshift Graceland Chapel. Into this strange serenity washed the eerie, compelling sounds of the Mountaintop monks, who stood in a long rank across the stage, dressed in black robes and hats, their mouths hardly seeming to move as their chants crackled across the mighty sound system. The massive video screens flickered and the monks' faces resolved above the crowd: magnified, pixilated, washed out by sun, the cameras scanning down the row, panning in and out, now and again turning to the crowd for a long shot of its flailing, million-limbed appreciation. Over the crowd itself moved the long, insectile arms of the cranes, cameramen hunched in metal baskets as an unseen operator floated them from angle to angle, telescoping toward and away from the stage, toward and away in a strangely graceful tentacular ballet. The effect was disorienting, almost surreal: as though the enormous faces on the screens, one replacing another with cinematic regularity, had nothing to do with the actual human forms on the stage, some essential bond between them having been broken. The crowd, seeing an image of itself, waved fervently, as though greeting an equally enthusiastic Other.

Above all this presided the roshi, elevated like an orchestra conductor to lead his disciples in thirty minutes of the unnerving chants. For perhaps a majority of the audience,* it was their first encounter with the art of "throat singing"—an exotic, multiphonic vocalization in which the singer produces one or more overtones to the base note, such that several voices seem to come from one mouth. One could see it on their flushed and begrimed faces: delight mixed with disorientation, the ear not sure what to hear, the inevitable anxiety provoked by the Buddhist dictum of liberation: "It is neither one nor two." For half an hour the monks produced the grumbling baritones and warbling tenors, tone multiplying upon tone until the Graveyard seemed covered by a dome of sound, the roshi gesturing to sky and earth, to shadow and cloud and the festival's many structures, and the foreboding, distant shapes of the Tombstones, consecrating the exquisite mandala which sat untouched on the desert floor.

---

*But not for the author, who had done considerable research on the subject.

When the presentation came to an end—the last note fading like breath on a cold window—a mutter of excitement began in the crowd and grew to a deafening cheer as the invisible barrier fell and thousands rushed heedlessly into the circle, achieving, in a matter of minutes, the total destruction of the beautiful mandala.

"Such a shame, really," the author commented to the roshi some moments later. They stood just to the side of the stage, shaded from the sun, as the frantic audience writhed in a cloud of dust and oil and colored sand. "All that work and care, all that precision . . . for nothing."

"Why does Mr. Andrew say this?" replied the roshi, slightly breathless, popping the top on a can of Mountain Dew, which he proceeded to consume in one gulp. He turned to the author, his round face glowing from exertion. Behind them, a team of agents and German shepherds led by Carlton Lum was conducting a last sweep of the backstage area and control booths, in a final attempt to uncover and thwart the Muse's plan.

"Well, I . . . it just was so marvelous, the mandala. The 'Opponent of Death,' as you called it. To build such a thing, to put one's sweat and love . . . rushing to complete it, only to see it ruined by those who have no true appreciation . . ."

"But it was not complete." The roshi crushed the aluminum can in his fist and tossed it into a nearby bin with impressive accuracy. He took the author's elbow and led him to the very edge of the stage. "Only now is Yamantaka Mandala complete."

The author looked into the writhing, greased multitudes below, the fans covered head to toe in a variety of colors, faces smeared as in some bizarre aboriginal rite more appropriate to Easter Island than this bleak desert. "This?" he said. "This is chaos. It's mindless destruction. The very death against which the mandala stood."

"It is fulfillment."

"No, Roshi. I beg to—"

"The work embodies its destruction, Mr. Andrew; the image exists in harmony with its absence. It cannot be understood otherwise. Monks of Zen Center cannot complete Yamantaka Mandala. Only with assistance of audience can we say work is finished, and sit back to enjoy cool, refreshing beer and reggae set from Sticky Green. Mr. Andrew will accompany Roshi Bob to Janis Joplin 21+ Texas Teahouse?"

"But something must remain," he insisted. "So that there is a record. So we remember. Isn't the very purpose of art to leave a record? To endure?"

The roshi removed his hat and wiped sweat from his head. "Art is not different from life," he said. "Always seeking completion. Always aspiring to its own negation. Does Mr. Andrew not yet see? The ultimate destination of art is the blank canvas."

Squinting a moment longer at the colorful melee, the roshi replaced his hat and strode off. The author stayed behind to watch the last oily clumps trampled by the crowd, smeared into clothing and hair and body cavities, the labor of so many erased by the carelessness of so many more. He clutched the bookbag, certain that the roshi was wrong. Though the scene before his eyes belied the notion, he felt in his very bones that something must always remain. The alternative was inconceivable.

Standing in the same spot many hours later, what had been an explosion of joy had become a nervous, muttering swarm, thousands of haunted faces staring at the empty stage, the vacant microphone and drumkit, the blank video screens: mud-caked and hideous, disheveled, the whites of their eyes standing out against the dark sand on their cheeks, their hair slicked with oil. Others wore the Poet's Death Mask, its white visage speckled through the crowd, the many repetitions making the mask seem even more sinister. Around the perimeter of the Graveyard, occasional jets of sparks shot into the night, deepening the darkness rather than banishing it. The desert sky had grown heavy, discolored by cloud and by the lights of the concert and the searching beams of the many news helicopters overhead—a textured pinkish canopy which absorbed the jets of flame and sat heavily above as if to engulf them all. Torches weaved through the crowd—the hooded, scythe-wielding minions of Southwesterners United in Christ on patrol, having issued from the Graceland Chapel sometime earlier at the bidding of their leader, Edward J. Labello.

"Go forth now and comfort the lonely souls who do not know Christ. Protect them from the sin of their own hearts which has given rise to ☿," he said from the pulpit. "As long as untruth roams the earth, she will know no peace. Bring peace to the departed, and show the living the meaning of truth."*

More than two and a half hours past Bratworst's scheduled stage time, the crowd's anticipation could no longer be stanched. Cheers of enthusiasm—*We want the Worst!*—had given way to obscenities and fistfights, innocent roadies who had the bad luck to walk across the stage were pelted with all manner of food and filth, the unlucky proprietors of the Billie Holiday Crystal Shoppe were assaulted, their wares defiled, and one intrepid fan had scaled a crane, overpowered the cameraman, and was regaling the crowd with close-up shots of his backside.

The author, too, was nearly prostrate with apprehension. He looked out at the Graveyard's giant muddle, the fires spurting at the periphery, the mottled world beyond, then descended the covered ramp toward the holding area where he had earlier taken refuge. He felt the weight of other footsteps on the ramp, vibrations broadcast throughout the skeletal structure; in a moment three of the four members of Bratworst clamored past, their eyes watery and red-rimmed with excitement, mouths clamped shut and jaw muscles bulging. The last of the three slowed in passing and jabbed an elbow into the author's gut—"Hey, Mr. A! How's it hanging?" said Buzz, his voice echoing off metal.

"Well it's—"

"You ready to mosh?" he said, already moving past. "You ready to fuckin' rock? Don't forget to come to the trailer afterward—number 12. The Charger Girls are coming, dude, it's gonna be hella cool!" The drummer did not wait for the author's reply, hurrying up the ramp into a thunder of adulation, squeals of feedback, all the crowd's pent-up energy sensing its imminent release. Something inaudible came over the speakers, followed by an ovation of bacchanalian proportion. The author waited,

---

*At trial, Labello would insist that SUC had been hired as a "private, supplemental security detail" by VerSI-FI, claiming Dennis Adams had offered the group $5 million for the capture of the poet. Adams denied the allegation vigorously, saying the only time he'd met Labello was at the UCI athletic center, "where I used to wipe up the basketball court with his skinny ass." Justifying the light sentence, Judge Anthony Bright noted that SUC "did play an ameliorative role in keeping order and minimizing delinquency, at least in the hours before the riot began."

surrounded by sound, peered down the tunnel toward a dark figure that ascended slowly, barefoot and heavy of step, as though to its own execution.

"Drew," he said, as his son came near.

The figure stopped, bent forward in the half-light. He looked older, more tired than the author remembered him. Though his eyelids drooped with the same perpetual wariness, the set of his mouth was in some way more vulnerable than it had been, more trusting. Even in the dimness the author could see how pale his son was, his forehead slicked with the acne he'd left behind at fifteen. His hair looked as though it had been cut by a lower primate.

"You're here," said the author's son.

"I'm here," said the author. "I wouldn't miss it for the world."

His son nodded. "No, I guess you wouldn't." Above them came the first concatenations of the drums, Buzz testing each head in turn, flaring the various cymbals and then starting the pounding introduction to "Terrorist Methodist," each impact shuddering the girders above and around them.

"Are you well? Have you been eating enough?" the author said.

"What's in the bag?"

"Oh, that. Nothing. Just some extra clothes."

They regarded each other, standing closer than they'd been in months, perhaps longer. The bass had now begun, the guitar soon to follow, sound rising all around them, crawling over their skin.

"I want you to know I'm here for you," said the author, leaning closer to be heard. "If you need me."

His son snorted. "I don't." He glanced up the tunnel, to the flashing of lights playing across the sky.

"I know." The author rested a hand on his son's shoulder. "But I'm here anyway. I always will be, you know." His son drew back and searched the author's eyes. "I know I haven't been . . . I know that you . . . we both . . ." He held his son's elbow, struggling to form the thought. A roadie was beckoning from the top of the ramp. "I miss her tremendously," he finally sputtered. "Perhaps you never thought of that. Or never . . . I tried to put it aside . . . for you . . . to be all things . . ." His son tried to pull his arm away, but the author held it. "Sometimes I failed. I know that. I do. But I wanted . . . I tried to . . ."

"Dad." His son motioned with his eyes toward the stage, his band, the hot cacophony of love that the Graveyard had become. "I have to go."

The author dropped his arm. "Of course you do." He grinned, attempted a fatherly punch on the shoulder. "Break a leg."

His son hesitated, began to turn away.

"Drew," his father called. "Are you quite sure? What she said to you . . . in the Arizona Café. Do you remember what you told me?"

"Yeah." He turned back with furrowed brow. "That's fucked . . . I mean, that's messed up. That guy from the FBI was just asking me the same thing."

"Did you tell him? Did you tell him anything?"

The author's son grinned, the carefree child he'd once been showing briefly upon his features. "Nah. That dude was an idiot." He looked away, almost physically drawn now to the performance that awaited.

"Indeed," the author said.

"What does it mean, Dad? 'Solve et coagulum.' Do you have any idea?"

The author watched him a moment longer, overwhelmed by the moment, understanding only now the bond he and the child shared—deeper than any mere verbalization, more meaningful than a word could contain. He raised a hand to smooth the hair from his son's eyes.

"It means have a good show," he said. "It means, I am very proud of you."

Of what happened in the next fifteen minutes, much has been written, and much has still to be explained. There are likely as many versions as there were souls in the Graveyard that night, and all this author can do— all any author could do!—is to lay out with absolute frankness what he saw, what he knows from personal experience to have transpired, what he believes with all his heart to be the Truth.

The band's first number was a shattering success, the difficult, dueling guitar solos brought off without a hitch, the lead singer's voice achieving Olympian heights of pathos and agony, now moaning the lyrics in a low, sardonic tenor, now scaling into shrieks of such pain that fans in the front rows doubled over in sympathy. The musicians writhed over their instruments as though wrestling powerful serpents. Watching from the wing, the author could not help but return to that night at the Casbah, so many years earlier, could not help but envision that younger man flushed with ambition and optimism, scribbling furiously at the side of the stage— recently married and become a father, recently named editor of a magazine, the last fetters of adolescence having fallen away, the adult life for which he had long felt ready opening its promising embrace. Now, as the identical melody squealed under the desert sky, he closed his eyes and felt a moment's compassion for that young man. How could he have known what the coming months and years would bring? Certainly he was not the first to ascribe, in his exuberance, insufficient seriousness to events around him. He was not the first to miss the signs, nor would he be the first to wish he could relive certain moments, to indulge in the fantasy of repetition. There must be many like him—perhaps thousands in that very crowd—who closed their eyes and allowed themselves, briefly, to believe it.

When he opened his eyes, the song had ended. Furious joy rippled seismically through the Graveyard, spotlights from above the stage played irrationally through the masses, sparks ejaculating at the venue's perimeter. Buzz rolled his drums, a manic grin on his wide face, while the lead guitarist and bassist fumbled with their instruments. On the video screens was the image of the author's son, who stood before the microphone bathed in sweat, hands at his side, guitar dangling from his neck like some heavy totem of penance. Flowers and plastic bottles and brassieres and marijuana cigarettes and keys to Palm Springs hotel rooms rained upon the stage, but he did not move, his eyes focused beyond the crowd, beyond the gates and vendors, upon some distant point in the vast, insensate desert. The author was trembling, his hand clutched white and slippery around the strap of the bookbag. Time had folded upon itself. It was an endless loop in which they were all forever trapped, forever suffering, condemned to speak their lines again and again with each spin of an unstoppable wheel.

"Drew!" shouted the drummer, struggling to hit the proper note of frustration. When the lead singer did not react, he flung his drumsticks into the darkness behind him. "Fuck!" he shouted, a cry taken up powerfully by ninety thousand throats.

"Drew! Fuck! Drew! Fuck!"

The guitarist played the first discordant notes of "Fishing Pier Frenzy," to no avail.

"Drew! Fuck! Drew! Fuck!" each syllable with enough force to shake the floorboards, to travel up through the author's body and clutch the air from his throat.

And then it stopped.

All noise stopped, a sucking explosion followed by silence. The cameras locked on the singer's face, the crowd gesticulating with its million limbs, the drummer caught in a half-crouch behind his kit. For the space of a breath they all waited, a cold wind sweeping through the Graveyard. Then, like a distant note that finally clarifies into song, she was there.

Pregnant and two-fathered, a living impossibility, the Muse stood alone at the opposite stagewing, her awful gaze fixed on the lead singer. She was dressed in baggy blue jeans, a filthy and shapeless black sweater; her unblemished skin all but shone beneath the lights, her thin nose and dimpled chin unmistakable. Her eyes blinked slowly; her shoulders rose and fell. The singer straightened behind the microphone but made no move. Even the helicopters seemed frozen, hovering inaudibly beneath the belly of clouds. A million rapt faces looked on, pale masks illuminated by torches and the sky's swollen red.

When she took a step toward him, the singer closed his eyes, an enigmatic smile passing across his features. The giant video screens flickered, then flashed to the pale visage of the Muse: her thin lips parted slightly, bald head gleaming, in her eyes an expression not of anger or pain, not even of emptiness, but of absence. It was then that the author recalled what his son had said many months ago, something the author had dismissed as whimsy. But dimly now, like skywriting already faded, it occurred to him that his son had been right, that ♀ did faintly resemble his wife—though a very young version, from a time before his son would have known her, a time before trouble had overtaken her life.

It was this thought that detonated the silence and brought the author back to himself. He gasped, shook his head violently to clear it—once, again—fumbled with the zipper of the bookbag even as the rest of the world remained in thrall. The Muse took another step toward the singer, reaching out as though to draw him into an embrace. In his peripheral vision, the author was aware of the flames, the cannonades of sparks thrusting into the sky, the sea of masked and robed and sand-spattered figures below. His throat was hot and constricted, his skin tingling with passion, as the Muse came within arm's length of his son and opened her arms the author wrestled the tin box from inside the bookbag, flipped the latch, and stepped onto the stage.

"Calliope!" he shouted, his voice tiny in the enormity of that space, but loud enough to startle her. He swallowed hard, took another step. "Don't," he said.

"Dad!" groaned the lead singer.

"I have something for you," said the author, as those cold eyes turned to him. Though she looked right at him, he had the sense that there was no one there, no presence behind those blue irises, that the body standing only yards away may have housed bone and blood, but it did not contain a soul.

"I found him." The author held the box before him, the first nagging whistle of feedback leaking from the dozens of amplifiers on the stage. "It's for you, Calliope. It's what you've always wanted."

"Dad, don't . . ."

"You can stop now." He inched forward, taking advantage of her hesitation. "You can spare him."

The Muse narrowed her eyes as though to take the author's measure. He held out the box, commanded his feet to keep advancing.

"He was there all along," the author said. "Under the Buddha. How many times you must have . . . Please—" he coughed out the word as she turned away. "Please take it!" he said. But she was no longer listening, had returned her attention to the lead singer, his only child, and as she brought a palm to the boy's cheek the author broke into a run, hurtled toward the terrifying figure, all the amplifiers rising into a howl and his son crying a warning—and in the last instant the Muse turned to the author, raised an arm and extended her forefinger like a gun, and fired.

"*Bang!*" she said, and a wire of pain bored into the center of his forehead.

"*Bang!*" she said, breaking her long silence, "*Bang!*" and the world spun and somersaulted over the author and came up to slam him hot and violent along the length of his back.

He looked up through a haze, a flutter and drift of ash, a shower of earth in the cold spotlights. The tin box clattered to the floorboards. The feedback had grown to a deafening screech, everyone but the Muse clutching their ears in pain. He had failed. He writhed empty-handed, gasping at what he saw on his son's face. Something hot streamed down the side of his throbbing head. He tried to reach out an arm but found it would not move, the cry strangled in his throat, as she turned back to his son and thousands held their breath in mute terror.

A terrible rumble filled the air, a flicker of light across the sky. The Muse bowed gracefully, swept her arms around the singer's legs and tenderly, lovingly kissed his bare feet.

Sound and voice and music rushed back. Released from paralysis, the musicians took up their instruments and the first, immortal chords of "Dirtnap" rang from the speakers, rang out over the exhausted and bewildered and energized crowd, rang into a red sky that pulsed with light. The author rolled onto one side, incomparable relief bathing him as the Muse rose to face the crowd, moved away from his son and took one step and then another, gathering her strength and then launching herself from the edge of the stage, the music accelerating like a supersonic jet as she flew, fully extended, the crowd opening their mouths as one, their hungry howls blending with the melody, desperate arms reaching up to receive her. The stunned singer stepped to the microphone and the author closed his eyes and breathed, feeling hands beneath him, lifting, raising him higher—and with the familiar touch of those hands came a sense of absolute peace, of absolute contentment, he rose higher and higher until the hands themselves could no longer reach him, opened his eyes to find himself looking down at the stage, at the figures moving there, the ocean of unrestrained humanity that seemed to spread forever and in all directions; and though the reports that would be written in the days and weeks to come were unanimous on many points, the author did not see any of the gruesome details they related: the fires that spread from torches and over bodies still soaked with oil, scythes swiftly striking, the stage buckling and eventually collapsing under the weight of the stampede, the Muse torn limb from limb as she flew from the stage, her flesh devoured, blood and sinew and viscera smeared over the faces of those who had claimed to love her. He did not see any of this, for it had all become too small.

What he saw in that last moment, not knowing whether his eyes were opened or closed, was a vision of the roshi: robed in white, standing at the center of what had once been the sand mandala. The roshi looked up into the sky as the tumult raged all around him, and with a child's expression of glee began to laugh, a pure and resounding laugh, the heavy clouds released a volley of flat lightning that illumined the desert and its grim topography, lit up the Graveyard and all of the people therein, and the author believed—and believes to this day—that the roshi was looking right at him, staring straight into his tired eyes as the burdened sky split open to deliver a torrent of sharp, cold rain, as though at last to pass judgment on this sad creation of man and, in a cataclysm of steam and dust, scour it clean.

AFTERWORD
IN GIRUM IMUS NOCTE ET CONSUMIMUR IGNI

*Mountaintop, November 200_*

What is a story? What defines it and gives it shape? A causally related sequence of events, a beginning, middle, and end—is story merely this Aris-
totelian movement from point A to point B, encompassing some significant
action, some irreversible change? Yet the distance between A and B is infinite, arbitrary, the incidents innumerable—and what of that which gave
rise to A, that which may come as a result of B? How to determine which
few stones to pluck from that rushing river, to dry off and polish and display as representative of the whole. There is always a remainder, always
too much to be said—who can say that another story does not lurk in the
interstices, that the truth does not lie curled, like wood shavings, on the
cutting-room floor?

And yet it is the contention of every story that it could not be told in
any other way. Indeed, this claim is the very precondition of a story. The
aura of certainty and self-completeness that proclaims *This is what you must
understand! This is what it all* means!

Stories do not create themselves. They do not simply spring, full-
grown and dressed for battle, from the miasma of everyday life. For that
there requires an outside hand—to select, to shape, to say to the world:
Here is a story. There requires a storyteller: he for whom there is no suitable place in the story and whose fate is thus to remain forever in some
undefined space outside—less a god than a shadow, a ghost, whispering to
those inside. And in the end—the story complete, the stage strewn with
bodies—he is sundered from it, condemned to watch it grow distant and

strange until he can no longer recall its origins, until his own creation does not recognize him. For this sacrifice, he is given only a name: Author.

There are many lingering questions about the life of Calliope Bird Morath and the entity known as the Muse. These questions will be asked for decades, keeping scholars and critics busy and providing bottomless inspiration for future poets hungry for new myths to inhabit, to rehabilitate, to cannibalize. In this way art perpetuates itself. In this way the artist achieves immortality.

It was to ponder such questions that the author, in the summer of 200_, retired to the Mountaintop Zen Center, there to take the robes and a vow of silence and submit to the roshi's kindhearted teachings. Away from the pressures and distractions of the world, with only his notes and his memories and the unlimited swell of time, he hoped finally to complete the definitive Life of the Poet, one that would obviate the need for future lives, to weave all the threads into one tapestry, to "shore up the fragments," as Eliot famously put it. To get it right.

It is also true that his home in San Diego had recently been commandeered—emptied and renovated, rendered unrecognizable—for the production of *Bend Over, You're in the Band!*, a "reality TV" show to focus on the remaining members of Bratworst and their efforts to replace drummer Buzz Matapan.* Though the show's creator and producer, Wally Weeks, had offered the author a workspace in the garage (and an occasional role in the show's wandering narrative), it seemed to the author that immersion in that world—the world of art, of spectacle—was no longer advisable, that what the biography needed now was a certain quiet and simplicity, that it might be "recollected in tranquillity," as Wordsworth urged. The world of youth and passion, in which the author had once moved effortlessly, had passed him by—and rather than disappointment or nostalgia what he felt was relief.

And so to the woods, where he spent mornings in *zazen*, arising before dawn to trudge silently with the others and just sit. While the hours

---

*Matapan, who was pulled from the wreckage of the Graveyard stage by three members of the San Diego Chargers cheerleading squad, left the band soon after to apply, successfully, to California Western School of Law.

after breakfast were taken up with sweeping, cutting wood, clearing gutters, and grooming Sonia—who had, it must be said, grown quite fond of him—he had a dispensation to spend afternoons in the business center, evenings in the monastery's small library, pounding away at the keyboard, creeping line by line, word by precious, elusive word, toward his goal. Not until that prey had been captured would he break his silence. Not until the biography was complete would he rejoin the hostile and horrifying cacophony outside.

Will the poet come again? Will the Muse arise from the ashes of adoration, shriek into the sky and hold us accountable to the Truth? Or will Calliope return in some new and gentler guise to inspire the works of men? These are the questions that preoccupy him now. He will leave it to others to solve the more quotidian mysteries: the death of Danny Grier in Twentynine Palms, now ruled a murder by the Imperial County Sheriff's Office; the insider-trading case brought against VerSI-FI and Snow Lion Press. Other puzzles may take longer to solve: the absence of the other members of the Muse from the catastrophe at the Graveyard; the empty envelope found in a Hotel Gansevoort bathroom, addressed in a hand some believe to be Brandt's; the apparent suicide of Leigh Mulgrew, the last known member of the Muse, found in July in a beach cottage north of San Francisco, the pilot lights blown out, Baudelaire's *Les Fleurs du Mal* in her lap. And perhaps no one will ever be able to explain the disappearance of Penelope Morath, who walked away from her hospital bed the night of the Graveyard Riot, though her most recent EEG had showed no brain activity.*

What is the Truth of such collateral tragedies? What rational explanation could bring back the departed?

Some hope glimmers from the discovery of the tapes. Over twenty hours of digital recordings came into the possession of Antonio "Skip" Cárdenas on the morning of September 2, arriving in a padded envelope

---

*Then, too, there are the recent revelations of fraud in the world of Morath Studies, accusations that articles by Edwin Decker and Debi Dennison may have been fabricated or plagiarized, and in the case of Jacqueline Rose, that the writer never existed, was only a pseudonym, her work part of the many-tentacled PR campaign. How shall we ever unravel it all? As Yeats wrote, "How can we know the dancer from the dance?" Will we ever find our way out of this maze?

with no postage, no return address, their contents an unsettling mix of words spoken over eerie, ambient music. By noon the tapes were in the custody of the local U.S. Attorney; the proliferation of injunctions and investigations means it will be some time before they are heard publicly, if ever. Of Cárdenas's insistence that the voice on the tapes is Calliope's, the author can say only that the prizewinning reporter would know as well as anyone. And of the chance that what she says on those tapes might contradict or even invalidate the present work, the author will say only this: No one is an authority on their own life. No one can know the permanence of its shape, the entirety of its consequence, until the last line has been written. The author leaves it to some future editor, infinitely more skilled in such affairs, to determine how best to integrate his narrative with the confessions found on the tapes.

It was, by any measure, a happy autumn. The author slept well, quit smoking, adopted an ovo-lacto vegetarian diet. Manual outdoor labor developed his muscles and brought color to his skin. In late October, as leaves carpeted the monastery paths, he undertook a visit to San Diego, to gather some belongings from storage and attend to personal errands. As he drove down from the San Jacintos, navigated the interstate and at last came in view of the city spread at the edge of the ocean, he felt an old anxiety rising—but he was able to keep it at bay, to detach from it and observe it from a distance, courtesy of his Zen training. Before long he had regained his ease, rolled down the windows to feel the balmy air, to smell the faint tang of the sea. By the time he pulled past the gates of the Colina Seca Memorial Cemetery, rolling slowly past rows of marble and granite markers, he was pleasantly, thoroughly detached, watching his hands steer the car from memory, shift into Park, watching himself walk across soft, manicured grass as though he were not performing these actions so much as watching a scene from a movie; as though he, the observer, were someone entirely other than the observed.

The afternoon was silent but for the chirping of birds, the murmur of the highway beyond the brick wall. He sat for a time next to the headstone, occasionally stroking its smooth, cool surface. It was the anniversary of his wife's death, a day he had for many years commemorated in precisely this fashion, though recently his observance had grown lax. Whereas in the past he might have spent the afternoon talking to her, bringing her up to date on his life, on their son's development and achievements and all the goings-on in the world that she might have found interesting, at which she might have wrinkled her nose or flashed her wry and beautiful smile, today he simply sat with her, trusting her to understand without his saying a word.

When the afternoon grew breezy, the sun spangling low through the branches, he spent a few minutes tidying the grave, pulling weeds and removing dead flowers, scraping grit from the furrows of the stone. He took from his pocket the gift he had brought, a few lines written on parchment, which he had transcribed himself from the Diamond Sutra. He left them under a small rock, that she might read them at her leisure:

> Thus shall ye think of all this fleeting world:
> A star at dawn, a bubble in a stream;
> A flash of lightning in a summer cloud,
> A flickering lamp, a phantom, and a dream.

Back on the highway, he hurried north, hoping to arrive at his destination before it closed. The streets of Rancho Santa Fe were crowded, the quaint village and two-lane country roads clogged with luxury sedans and SUVs, businessmen on their way home, families returning from taking the kids for a Halloween treat. Leaving his car several blocks away, the author walked the remaining distance until he found himself standing at the curb, facing a house he had not laid eyes upon in nearly twenty years.

According to the provisions of Penelope's living will, the house on Azalea Path had fallen into the hands of her estranged parents, David and Marion Klein of Teaneck, New Jersey. Overwhelmed by the costs of upkeep and security, as well as by Penelope's medical bills and mountainous debt, the Kleins had leased the house to The Entertunement Factory, a Hollywood-based carnival/festival/special-events coordinator, which had, after two months of alterations, opened the Spooky Terrible Children Haunted House a week earlier.

The author stood at the edge of the driveway and stared at the house. It had been repainted in black and orange, cobwebs strewn generously across its facade, mechanical bats circling the gables. Bolts of blue lightning flashed between the roof and transformers hidden in the trees, accompanied by peals of thunder. Gawkers milled about on the front lawn, squealing and pointing at the hooded corpse that hung from the lowest branch of the fire-blackened jacaranda. Around the side he could just see the Spooky Beergarden, which had been set up on the tennis court. As he waited on line, it occurred to him that the house seemed smaller than it once had, than it had loomed in memory. Whereas it had once dominated the block, relegated to backdrop the surrounding homes, the very sky above, the house now sat beneath an onslaught of amusement seekers, stoically bearing the humiliation of its new paint job, as though its very heart had shrunk, beating now too feebly to be heard.

He paid the exorbitant entry fee and walked with the many others through the foyer and into the dark living room, the rafters spattered with glowing blood, shadows slithering underfoot, canned screams and moans emanating from every corner, mixing with the blare of punk rock. Children huddled to their parents' legs; a gang of teenagers draped themselves across the couches and lit a joint, only to be hustled off by guards in Frankenstein masks. More than one person, upon seeing his robes and shaven head, mistook the author for one of the house's denizens, obliging their role by shrieking terror in his face before letting him pass. He did his best to fulfill their expectations, screwing his face into a frightening expression and hurrying to the stairs.

On the second floor, he wandered from bedroom to bedroom, each presenting its own set piece of suicidal mannequins, Brandt lookalikes rising gore-splattered from bathtubs, holographic murder scenarios, etc. In one room, a body huddled beneath the bedcovers, responding to poking fingers with a dismissive sweep of the arm such that it was unclear whether this was part of the presentation or merely an exhausted employee. The author pulled aside a heavy curtain for a glimpse of the street: the silent suburbs, remarkably separate from the macabre world in which he stood. He waited, ears ringing from the blaring music, immune to the frights which leapt out at him with mechanical regularity; and when the lights began to flash, a deep voice announcing that the haunted house was closing for the night, he slipped into a walk-in closet and pulled boxes and old blankets around him, until all the footsteps receded, the music stopped, cars pulled away on the street, and the last security guard shut and bolted the front door.

When he was sure he was alone, the author crept from his hiding place and down the stairs, through the dark and silent rooms of Calliope's childhood. He found his way to the kitchen, which glowed with an otherworldly, sepulchral light, the silver of an actual full moon streaming through the windows. The floor was sticky with fake blood, the creaks and groans of a large, empty house only adding to the scene's strangeness. In the vestibule, three long gouges slanted across the wall, as though left by the claws of a crazed animal. At the top of the narrow stairway, the author closed his eyes and practiced a breathing exercise, listening for the sound of other humans, before starting down to the basement.

The studio was no longer accessible; the soundproof door had been replaced by a thick sheet of glass. The author pressed his nose to this surface and squinted into the darkness, seeing only the faintest outlines of unidentifiable shapes. Noticing a switch on the wall next to him, he flipped it on, and the scene came to life.

It would be as she had found it that morning: the stacks of musical equipment, the elaborate drumkit, the red vocal booth at the rear, the wide, gleaming array of guitars which stood in the center of the room as though guarding the honor of the scene over which they presided. Before them sat Brandt Morath, in a flannel shirt and jeans, cross-legged and barefoot, the fleece-lined hunter's hat upon his head. Hunched over, his back to the door, he appeared to be writing something; occasional whimpers floated through the room, the scratch of a pen, a muttered oath. Every detail faithful, everything in its right place, it seemed for all the world as though not a day had passed, as though the intervening years, with all their trouble, had never been.

As the author stood watching, the girl came into the room, a lovely and innocent child in a nightgown, her freckled face blank with curiosity, her eyes shining with love. "Daddy!" she cried, upon which the seated figure raised an arm, there was a muffled explosion, the glass was spattered with red and gray, and the lights in the studio went out.

The author found himself clinging to the banister, found he had bitten his tongue. After an interval of a few seconds the lights came back up to reveal the same scene: the amplifiers and drums, the shining guitars, the seated figure writing his last words. The child wandered in—*Daddy! Boom!*—and the lights went down once more.

For how many repetitions did he stand there, how many times watch the glass mist over and go dark?

Daddy! Boom!

He was alone now, there was no one to tear him away. Above him the house and its history weighed, the outside world and its daily tragedies pressed upon him. He sat on the bottom step, face just inches from the glass.

Daddy! Boom!

Daddy! Boom!

Through the night he watched, waiting for the slightest variation. There was none. He did not sleep; his breathing was slow and steady. Through the hours he waited, bore witness to this perfection—a human being at the end of hope, the tearful child marked by grief—at last and forever in the presence of something larger than himself.

ATTRIBUTIONS

CHAPTER 1: EARLY INFLUENCES
7: The Auden quote is from "Musée des Beaux Arts."

CHAPTER 2: DAWN'S HIGHWAY
The title is shared with Jim Morrison's poem from the Doors' album *An American Prayer*.
11: First sentence is paraphrased from J. D. Salinger, *The Catcher in the Rye*.
12: "A dangerous girl . . . the bolts and the nuts" takes its rhythm and syntax from Sylvia Plath's poem "Daddy."
14: "I am the ghost of a famous suicide . . ." paraphrases Plath's poem "Electra on Azalea Path."
14: "Once, if I remember well . . ." is quoted here, and everywhere else in the novel, from Arthur Rimbaud's *A Season in Hell* (Louise Varèse's 1945 translation).
15: *"bang, smash on the mouth"* is quoted from *The Journals of Sylvia Plath,* and the account of Brandt's meeting Penelope bears resemblance to the account, from same, of Plath's meeting Ted Hughes, her future husband.
20: "lingering in the seaweed" and accompanying imagery is from T. S. Eliot, "The Love Song of J. Alfred Prufrock."
21: "back, back, back to him" takes after Plath's poem "Daddy."
21–22: *"O mon semblable, hypocrite lecteur!"* draws on Charles Baudelaire's poem "To the Reader"; "Blue I love you blue . . ." takes after Federico García Lorca's "Sleepwalking Ballad."
26: "his tired, conquered, soul slipped into mine" echoes "Dawn's Highway."

CHAPTER 3: MILESTONES, MILLSTONES, AND MAELSTROMS
32: The inscription on the headstone is from Baudelaire's "The Balcony."
43: A. Alvarez, in an annotation to a 1963 BBC interview, compared the late Plath to Keats, and *Ariel* to *Hyperion*: "Having written the poems," Alvarez said, "there was

nothing left for him to do except die." (Quoted from Charles Newman, ed., *The Art of Sylvia Plath: A Symposium*.)

46(fn): "Earthenware Head in the Oven" is a (bad) play on Plath's poem "The Lady and the Earthenware Head."

47–48: The letter from Vaughn takes after John Holmes's letter to Anne Sexton, as quoted in Diane Middlebrook's biography *Anne Sexton* (and probably Rilke's *Letters to a Young Poet*, though I can't find a precise citation). Calliope's poem to Vaughn takes after Sexton's response, "For John, Who Begs Me Not to Inquire Further," in *To Bedlam and Part Way Back*.

51: Calliope's dialogue with the Beekeeper quotes (and misquotes) from Virgil, *Georgic 4*.

52(fn): The title of the *Seventeen* article plays on Robert Frost's poem, "Stopping by Woods on a Snowy Evening."

CHAPTER 4: HIDEOUS PAGES

58–60: The chapter title, and the quotes from Brandt's note, are from *A Season in Hell*, as are Calliope's phrases "bad blood" (**p. 60**) and "contemplating undazed the extent of his innocence" (**p. 60**)

59: "We did not speak of it, we passed over it in silence" paraphrases Wittgenstein's *Tractatus Logico-Philosophicus*.

65: "widening gyre" is from William Butler Yeats's poem "The Second Coming."

68–73: Portions of Calliope's recovered memory are painted over Sylvia Plath's essay "Ocean 1212-W"; "forsaken merman" is the title of a poem by Matthew Arnold; "I am he as you are he as you are me . . ." and other lyrics from the Beatles' "I Am the Walrus."

73: Calliope's imagery of a "kelp-covered Goliath" recalls—but does not quote—Plath's poem "The Colossus."

74: "not at home with the living nor the dead" is from Sophocles's *Antigone*.

80–82: Calliope's workshop rant takes ideas and images from T. S. Eliot's poem "The Love Song of J. Alfred Prufrock"; Lawrence Ferlinghetti's poem "Constantly Risking Absurdity"; the Rolling Stones's "2000 Light-Years from Home"; Andrew Marvell's poem "To His Coy Mistress"; and *Star Trek*.

87: "I, too, would never get this colossus put together at all" comes closer to Plath's "The Colossus" (but still does not quote).

102: Brandt's suicide note takes several phrases from *A Season in Hell* and one ("wine-dark sea") from *The Iliad*.

CHAPTER 5: THE HARD KERNEL OF THE REAL

111: "The winter of her discontent" comes from Shakespeare's *Richard III*, as does the imagery from the final paragraph of that section, on p. 113.

116: The biographer's plea to Brandt, and Brandt's reply, recall a similar incident recounted in *The Autobiography of Malcolm X.*

146: "All my pretty ones" and "Hell-kite" come from Shakespeare's *Macbeth,* via Anne Sexton.

CHAPTER 6:

157: Calliope's poem "Villanelle" owes something to Dylan Thomas's poem "Do Not Go Gentle into That Good Night," including the phrase "sad heights."

159: "Do I contradict myself . . . ? I am full of contradictions" is from Walt Whitman's "Song of Myself."

CHAPTER 7: *JE EST UNE AUTRE*

The title, also quoted on **p. 213,** is from the Seer Letter sent by Arthur Rimbaud to Paul Demeny, dated May 15, 1871.

165: Brandt is singing from P. F. Sloan's song "Eve of Destruction" (these lyrics turn up again on p. 187 and p. 209); "last of a royal line" is from *Antigone;* "A voice" is adapted from *Richard III.*

166: "alien people . . . alien god" and "I should be glad of another death" are from T. S. Eliot's poem "Journey of the Magi."

182: Mahmoud read from Mahmud Shabistari's *The Secret Garden.*

183: "kaleidoscope eyes" are also a feature of the Beatles' "Lucy in the Sky with Diamonds."

191: "a far, far better . . ." and Madame Defarge are from Charles Dickens's novel *A Tale of Two Cities.*

203: The poem is William Blake's "To Nobodaddy."

204: "flying suicidal" is from Plath's poem "Ariel."

206: The poem that begins, "After great pain, a formal feeling comes—" is poem #341 from *The Complete Poems of Emily Dickinson.*

CHAPTER 8: THE SILVER CORD

The title, also quoted on **p. 228,** is from Byron.

216: Moreno's introduction alludes vaguely to Robert Lowell's introduction to Sylvia Plath's collection, *Ariel.*

230: The three quotes during the Electra skit are from Sophocles's play *Electra.*

231: Cassandra's speech ("Human destiny sucks . . .") is paraphrased, liberally, from Aeschylus's play *Agamemnon.*

237: The *fatwa* is paraphrased from the *fatwa* issued against Salman Rushdie by Ayatollah Khomeini on February 14, 1989.

241–42: The "Blindness Letter" paraphrases and argues with the Seer Letter.

244: "In Clover" owes a great deal to Plath's poem "Edge."

252: The graffito on Brandt's guitar quotes Billy Roberts's song "Hey Joe" (as performed by Jimi Hendrix).

263–68: The poems recited by the members of the audience are as follows: Walt Whitman, "O Captain, My Captain!" (Terrence "TT-Fly" Marker), via the film *Dead Poets Society;* Edna St. Vincent Millay, "Sonnet XLIII, What Lips My Lips Have Kissed" (Gary North); John Keats, "When I Have Fears That I May Cease to Be" (Connor Feingold); Wallace Stevens, "The Emperor of Ice Cream" (Taryn Glacé); Pablo Neruda, *"Cuerpo de Mujer"* (Talia Z); T. S. Eliot, "The Love Song of J. Alfred Prufrock" (Billy Martinez); Robert Burns, "To a Mouse" (Darlene Cream); Rainer Maria Rilke, "First Duino Elegy" (Esperanza Medina Blumstein); Alfred, Lord Tennyson, "Break, Break, Break" (Skip Cárdenas); William Wordsworth, "Lines Composed a Few Miles Above Tintern Abbey" (Rhoda Lubinski); Matthew Arnold, "Dover Beach" (Joe McAdderly).

273–74: The scene imagined by the biographer owes images and language to Percy Bysshe Shelley's poem "Adonais," including the lament, "weep for Calliope—she is dead!"

THE GREAT GIG IN THE SKY
The title is taken from the song of the same name by Pink Floyd.

CHAPTER 9: THE HANGED MAN
304(fn): The biographer's admonition to Harminder Singh is paraphrased from Ted Hughes's introduction to Plath's posthumous prose collection, *Johnny Panic and the Bible of Dreams.*

337–38: The voice-over in the film's opening scene paraphrases Hole's song "Violet," and quotes from *A Season in Hell.*

CHAPTER 10: SONG OF MYSELF
The title is from Walt Whitman's *Leaves of Grass.*

344: "Let's just say I was testing the bounds of Calliope . . ." and "let's just say I was curious" (**p. 345**) play with lines attributed to Jim Morrison in Oliver Stone's film, *The Doors;* the phrases "pure gold baby" and "dying shout . . . that knocks [you] out" are from Plath's poem, "Lady Lazarus"; "I'm melting!" was first cried by the Wicked Witch of the West in *The Wizard of Oz.*

345: "Abandon hope" is from Dante's *Inferno.*

347: "Suicide right on the stage" is from the Rolling Stones song "It's Only Rock 'n' Roll."

352: "He won't neglect his vengeance" is from *Agamemnon.*

355: The phrase "species of fit" and the general drift of the paragraph in which it appears draw upon Charlotte Brontë's novel *Jane Eyre.*

360: "It was a beautiful night to drown in" refers to Plath's poem "Lorelei."

361: "I [was] large . . . multitudes . . . contradictions . . ." are from Whitman's "Song of Myself."

381–82: "Now I had entered my own wordless year" and other language in that paragraph recall Anne Sexton's poem "For the Year of the Insane."

CHAPTER 11: $\mathcal{Y}$, OR THE MURDER OF THE THING

393: "Lay her i' the earth!" is from Shakespeare's *Hamlet*.

401: Dr. Breve's discussion of the phallus and the veil were inspired by "The Intimate Alterity of the Real: A Response to Reader Commentary on 'History and the Real,'" an essay by Charles Shepherdson of the University at Albany.

414–15: The Beekeeper's monologue bears resemblance to Jonathan Franzen's "Mr. Difficult," an essay in the *New Yorker*, September 30, 2002.

419: William Logan's poem takes its title and vocabulary from *Antigone*.

CHAPTER 12: *TU VATES ERIS*

The title recalls Rimbaud's dream, in which Apollo wrote on his head, "You will be a poet."

449: Jacobo is attempting to sing the Beatles' "She Said She Said."

459: "foe" and "friend" distantly recall Edna St. Vincent Millay's poem "First Fig."

460: "sweeping out the heart's corners . . ." is another reference to *The Secret Garden*.

467–69: The descriptions of the crow are inspired by various poems from *Crow* by Ted Hughes.

474: The shaman's lyrics are adapted from an ancient invocation to Maria Prophetissa by the alchemist Hermes Trismegistus.

475–76: The shaman's quotations are from *A Season in Hell* (the French passage translates: "At first it was an experiment. I wrote silences. I wrote the night. I recorded the inexpressible. I fixed frenzies in their flight") and the "Seer Letter."

488: "I am the ghost . . ." monologue quotes "Electra on Azalea Path," and references *Hamlet*, T. S. Eliot's poem "The Waste Land," and James Joyce's story "The Dead."

491: The city's magnificence is a nod to *A Season in Hell*.

493: "I shall be free to possess truth . . ." is from *A Season in Hell*.

CHAPTER 13: MORE TERRIBLE THAN SHE EVER WAS

The title is from Sylvia Plath's poem "Stings."

529–30: Lipschitz's review owes a debt to Jorge Luis Borges's story "Pierre Menard, Author of the *Quixote*."

AFTERWORD: *IN GIRUM IMUS NOCTE ET CONSUMIMUR IGNI*

549: The Eliot quote is from "The Waste Land"; Wordsworth's injunction is from *Preface to Lyrical Ballads.*

550(fn): The quote is from William Butler Yeats's poem "Among School Children."

IMPORTANT SOURCES

These books served as valuable references for this novel. I have not quoted directly from them, but it's possible that certain images or arguments bear some resemblance to passages found here. In all cases, I am indebted to the authors.

—*The Arts of the Alchemists,* by C. A. Burland (Macmillan, 1968).

—*Shoes Outside the Door: Desire, Devotion, and Excess at San Francisco Zen Center,* by Michael Downing (Counterpoint, 2001).

—*A Book of Bees,* by Sue Hubbell (Houghton Mifflin, 1988).

—*Lipstick Traces: A Secret History of the 20th Century,* by Greil Marcus (Harvard University Press, 1989).

—*The Training of the Buddhist Monk,* by Daisetz Teitaro Suzuki (Eastern Buddhist Society, 1934).

—*Enjoy Your Symptom!: Jacques Lacan in Hollywood and Out* (Routledge, 1992) and *Looking Awry* (MIT Press, 1991), by Slavoj Žižek.

ACKNOWLEDGMENTS

I would like to thank Bronwyn Lea, Geoffrey Wolff, and Ronald Bosco, each of whom played a crucial (if, in some cases, unwitting) role in the genesis of this material. None could have known what a monster they were helping to create.

I am forever grateful for the extraordinary generosity of the Stanford Creative Writing Program. Thank you to John L'Heureux and Tobias Wolff for their wisdom and guidance; to Eavan Boland for her fearless leadership; to Mary Popek and Ryan Jacobs for keeping us all (relatively) sane; and to Elizabeth Tallent, whose insight and encouragement have truly been a gift.

My sincere thanks to Thomas McNeely, Stephen Elliott, Sally Brodeur, Eric Puchner, Kaui Hart Hemmings, Jeff Lytle, Tim and Valerie Brelinski, Rebecca Black, Scott Hutchins, and Tom Kealey, for their time and valuable suggestions. To P. F. Sloan, for an immortal song. To Ellen Gould of Softreturn.net, for my glyph. And to my indomitable agent, Irene Skolnick, and my brilliant editor, Tina Pohlman, who were willing to wait.

PERMISSIONS ACKNOWLEDGMENTS

PERMISSIONS ACKNOWLEDGMENTS